The Convenient Groom

**Center Point
Large Print**

**This Large Print Book carries the
Seal of Approval of N.A.V.H.**

The Convenient Groom

A Nantucket Love Story

Denise Hunter

CENTER POINT PUBLISHING
THORNDIKE, MAINE

This Center Point Large Print edition
is published in the year 2008 by arrangement with
Thomas Nelson Publishers.

The text of this Large Print edition is unabridged. In other
aspects, this book may vary from the original edition.
Printed in the United States of America.
Set in 16-point Times New Roman type.

ISBN: 978-1-60285-244-0

Library of Congress Cataloging-in-Publication Data

Hunter, Denise, 1968-
    The convenient groom : a Nantucket love story / Denise Hunter.--Center Point large print ed.
        p. cm.
    ISBN: 978-1-60285-244-0 (lib. bdg. : alk. paper)
    1. Women authors--Fiction. 2. Marriage counselors--Fiction. 3. Radio personalities--Fiction.
4. Advice columnists--Fiction. 5. Weddings--Fiction. 6. Temporary marriage--Fiction.
7. Nantucket Island (Mass.)--Fiction. 8. Large type books. I. Title.

PS3608.U5925C66 2008b
813'.6--dc22

2008009805

*For Jesus, my tower of strength,
my shelter in the storm*

"The LORD your God is with you,
he is mighty to save.
He will take great delight in you,
he will quiet you with his love,
he will rejoice over you with singing."

Zephaniah 3:17

Let your face shine on your servant;
save me in your unfailing love.

Psalm 31:16

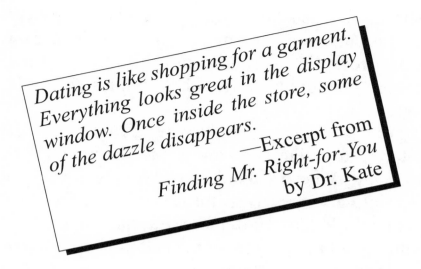

Dating is like shopping for a garment. Everything looks great in the display window. Once inside the store, some of the dazzle disappears.

—Excerpt from Finding Mr. Right-for-You by Dr. Kate

Chapter One

The red light on Kate Lawrence's cell phone blinked a staccato warning. But before she could retrieve the message, her maid of honor, Anna Doherty, waved her pale arms from the beach, stealing her attention.

Anna's smooth voice sounded in her headset. "Kate, can you come here? We've got a few glitches."

"Be right there." Kate tucked her clipboard in the crook of her elbow, took the steps down Jetty Pavilion's porch, and crossed the heel-sinking sand of the Nantucket shoreline. In six hours, thirty-four guests would be seated there in the rows of white chairs, watching Kate pledge her life to Bryan Montgomery under a beautiful hand-carved gazebo.

Where was the gazebo anyway? She checked her watch, then glanced toward the Pavilion, where workers scurried in white uniforms. No sign of Lucas.

She approached Anna, who wore worry lines as naturally as she wore her Anne Klein pantsuit. Anna was the best receptionist Kate could ask for. Her capable presence reassured the troubled couples she ushered through Kate's office.

Right now, Anna's long brown hair whipped across her face like a flag gone awry, and she batted it from her eyes with her freckled hand. "Soiree's just called. Their delivery truck is in for service, and the flowers will be a little late. Half an hour at the most."

Kate jotted the note on her schedule. "That's okay." She'd factored in cushion time.

"Murray's called, and the tuxes haven't been picked up except for your dad's."

Bryan and his best man had been due at Murray's at nine thirty. An hour ago. "I'll check on that. What else?"

Anna's frown lines deepened, and her eyes blinked against the wind. "The carriage driver is sick, but they're trying to find a replacement. The Weatherbys called and asked if they could attend last minute— they were supposed to go out of town, but their plans changed."

Kate nodded. "Fine, fine. Call and tell her they're welcome. I'll notify the caterer."

"Your publicist—Pam?—has been trying to reach you. Did you check your cell? She said she got voice mail. Anyway, your book copies did arrive this morning. She dropped this off." Anna pulled a hardback book from under her clipboard. "Ta-da!"

"My book!" Kate stared at the cover, where the title, *Finding Mr. Right-for-You,* floated above a cartoon couple. The man was on his knee, proposing. Below them, a colorful box housed the bold letters of Kate's name. She ran her fingers over the glossy book jacket, feeling the raised bumps of the letters, savoring the moment.

"Pam wants a quick photo shoot before the guests arrive. You holding the book, that kind of thing. You should probably call her."

Kate jotted the note. While it was on her mind, she reached down and turned on her cell.

"Ready for more great news?" Anna asked. Her blue eyes glittered like diamonds. The news had to be good.

"What?"

"The *New York Times* is sending a reporter and a photographer. They want to do a feature story on your wedding and your book."

Fresh air caught and held in Kate's lungs. Rosewood Press was probably turning cartwheels. "That's fabulous. They'll want an interview." She scanned her schedule, looking for an open slot. After the reception? She hated to do it, but Bryan would understand. The *New York Times*. It would give Kate's initial sales the boost it needed. Maybe enough to make the bestseller list.

"Here's the number." Anna handed her a yellow Post-It. "That tabloid guy has been hanging around all morning, trying to figure out who the groom is. I told him he'd find out in six hours like everyone else. The rest of the media is scheduled to arrive an hour before the wedding, and Pam's having an area set up over there for them." Anna gestured behind the rows of chairs to a square blocked off with white ribbon.

"Good. I want them to be as inconspicuous as possible. This is my wedding, and a girl only gets married once, after all."

"One would hope." Anna said. "Is there anything else I can do?"

Kate gave her a sideways hug, as close to an embrace as she'd ever given her assistant, her fingers pressing into Anna's fleshy shoulder. "You're a godsend. I don't know what I'd do without you."

"Oh! I know what I forgot to tell you. The gazebo. It should have been here by now. I tried to call Lucas, but I got the machine, and I don't have his cell number."

"His shop's closed today, and he doesn't have a cell." The man didn't wear a watch, much less carry a phone. She should've known better than to put something this crucial in his hands. Kate checked her watch. "I'll run over and check on it."

The drive to town was quick and effortless, but Kate's mind swam with a hundred details. She jotted reminders on her clipboard when she stopped for pedestrians, occasionally admiring the cover of her book. She called Pam for a quick recap about the *New York Times* reporter, and by the time she hung up, she was pulling into a parallel slot on Main Street, in front of Lucas's storefront.

The sign above the picture window read "Cottage House Furniture." On the second floor of the Shaker building, the wooden shingle for her own business dangled from a metal pole: "Kate Lawrence, Marriage Counseling Services." She needed to remind Lucas to remove it; otherwise he'd leave it hanging for another year or until someone else rented the space.

Kate exited her car and slid her key into the rusty lock of the shop's door. Once inside, she passed the stairs leading to her office and walked through the darkened maze of furniture to the back, where she hoped to find Lucas. She bumped an end table with her shin. *Ow!* That would leave a mark.

The high-pitched buzz of a power tool pierced the darkness, a good sign. "Lucas?" She rapped loudly on the metal door with her knuckles. The noise stopped.

"Come in."

She opened the door. Lucas Wright looked up from his spot on the cement floor at the base of the gazebo, his too-long hair hanging over one eye. He looked her over, then turned back to the spindle and ran his thick hand over it as if testing the curves.

"Aren't you supposed to be at the beach?" he asked.

Kate crossed her arms. "I could ask you the same thing."

He stood, agile for his size, and backed away from the gazebo. Sawdust from the floor clung to his faded jeans and black T-shirt. "I was just finishing."

"You were supposed to be there an hour ago. The gazebo needs to be put in place before the sound system, and the florist has to decorate it, and there are people waiting to do their jobs."

He faced her, looking into her in that way of his that made her feel like he could see clean through her. "Today's the big day, huh?" Putting his tool on his workhorse, he dusted off his hands, moving in slow motion as though he'd decided tonight wouldn't arrive until next week.

Kate checked her watch. "Do you think you can get this down to the beach sometime today?"

Walking around the piece, he studied it, hands on his hips, head cocked. "You like it?"

For the first time since the week before, Kate looked at the gazebo—the white lattice top, the hand-carved spindles, the gentle arch of the entry. At the top of the arch, a piece of wood curved gracefully, etched with clusters of daisies. The gazebo's simple lines were characteristic of Lucas's work, but she'd never known him to use such exquisite detail. The piece had an elegance that surpassed her expectations. He did beautiful work; she'd give him that.

"I do. I love the etching." She sighed. Just when he irritated the snot out of her, he did something like this, caught her off guard. She always felt like she was tripping down the stairs when she was with him.

Focus! "It needs to find its way to the beach. Pronto."

"Yes ma'am." His salute was unhurried.

Before she could offer a retort, her cell phone pealed and buzzed simultaneously, and she pulled it from her capri pocket.

"Hello?"

"Kate?"

"Bryan." Turning away from Lucas and toward the door, she eyed a crude desk with a metal folding chair that bore countless rusty scratches. "Good morning." A smile crept into her voice. It was their wedding day. The day they'd planned for nearly two years. "Did you sleep well?" She hadn't. She'd rumpled the sheets until nearly two o'clock, but that was to be expected.

The silence on the other end, however, was not. "Bryan?" Had she lost the signal?

"Um, Kate, did you get my message?"

There'd been a blinking red light this morning. She'd assumed it was Pam's voice mail and hadn't checked. Suddenly, she wished she had.

"No. What's wrong?"

"Are you sitting down?"

"No, I'm not sitting down. Just tell me." An ugly dread snaked down her spine and settled there, coiled and waiting.

"I'm on my way back to Boston," he said. "I left a message this morning. You must've had your phone off."

Kate's stomach stirred. She stared at the wall in front of her—a pegboard with a zillion holes, metal prongs poking from it, tools and cords everywhere. "What happened?" Some emergency, maybe?

What emergency could trump our wedding?

"I can't marry you, Kate."

The words dropped, each one crumbling under its own weight. The stirring in her stomach intensified. "That's not funny, Bryan." It was a terrible joke. He'd never been good with jokes. His punch lines left you leaning forward, waiting for the rest.

"I'm in love with someone else."

Pain. A huge wooden spoon, tossing the contents of her stomach. Her legs wobbled, trembling on the wedge heels of her sandals, and she clutched the cold metal of the folding chair. "What?" Was that her voice, weak and thready? Someone had vacuumed all the moisture from her mouth, sucked the air from her lungs.

"I'm so sorry," Bryan was saying. "I know this is awful. You don't deserve this, but I can't marry you. It happened slowly, and I didn't realize what was going on until recently. I tried to put it out of my mind, but I just can't. And I can't marry you knowing how I feel. I'm so sorry, Kate."

"What?" It was the only word her mind could form at the moment.

"I know there's no excuse. I should have told you before now, but I thought it would go away. I thought I was just having cold feet or something, but it's more than that."

"We've been together for two years, Bryan."

It was a stupid thing to say, but it was all she could think of. Memories played across the screen of her mind in fast-forward. The day they'd met in line at Starbucks in downtown Boston when Kate had gone there for a conference. Their first date at the Colonial Theatre. The long-distance courting and weekend visits. The e-mails, the phone calls, the engagement, the book. It all whizzed by, coming to a screeching halt here, at this moment. Here, in Lucas's dusty workshop. Here, in front of the special gazebo they were to be married in.

"I've already called my family and told them. I know there's a lot to do, and I'll help any way you want me to. And then there's your book . . . I'm so sorry."

Sorry. You're sorry? She pictured the precise rows of white chairs, the tent being erected as they spoke, the photographers.

The *New York Times*.

She closed her burning eyes. Everything would have to be cancelled.

At that thought, humiliation arrived on the scene, sinking in past the pain of betrayal. The weight of it pushed at her shoulders, and she grabbed the hair at her nape. *Think, Kate! This is no time to lose it.*

"Stop, Bryan. Just stop and think about what you're doing. Maybe you're letting your issues with your parents' divorce affect your decisions. This kind of fear is perfectly natural before a wedding, and maybe—"

"No, it's not that—"

"How do you know?" She forced reason into her

tone. Used her soothing voice—the one she put on when things got heated between one of her couples. "We love each other. We're perfect for each other. You've said it a hundred times."

"There's something missing, Kate."

She wobbled again and steadied herself with a hand on the chair. "Something missing"? What was that supposed to mean?

As her mind grappled with that seemingly unanswerable question, she felt a hand at her back, leading her into the chair. She was sitting, her head as fuzzy as a cotton-candy machine, her emerald-cut engagement ring blurring before her eyes.

"What do you mean there's something missing? The only thing missing is the groom. For our wedding that starts in five hours. Five hours, Bryan." Now she felt the hysteria building and took a full breath, nearly choking on the way the oxygen stretched her lungs.

"I'll help in any way I can."

"You can help by showing up for our wedding!"

Her mind ran through the list of people she'd have to call. Her dad, the guests, her publisher. She thought of the money Rosewood Press had spent on this elaborate beach wedding. They'd flown in friends and family from all over the country, paid for the photographer, flowers, caterer, the wedding attire. Kate had only wanted a simple wedding, but with the release of the book, the marketing department had other ideas. "An elegant wedding and a surprise groom just as the book releases. Think of the publicity, Kate!"

A knot started in her throat and burned its way to her heart.

"I'll always care about you," Bryan said.

The words fell, as empty as a discarded soda bottle on a deserted beach.

Enough.

The adrenaline coursing through her veins drained suddenly, leaving her once again weak and shaky. She couldn't talk to him anymore. She wasn't going to break down on the phone, wasn't going to beg him to come back. It wouldn't accomplish a thing anyway. She'd heard this tone of Bryan's voice before. He was a man who knew what he wanted. And what he didn't want.

And he didn't want Kate. She suddenly knew that fact as surely as she knew tomorrow would be more impossible to face than today.

She cleared her throat. "I have to go."

"Kate, tell me what I can do. My family will pitch in too. I want to help fix things."

She wanted to tell him there was no fixing this. There was no fixing her heart or the impending collision of her life and her career. Instead, numb, she closed the phone, staring straight ahead at the holes on the pegboard until they blended together in a blurry haze.

He was leaving her. The man she loved was walking away. This wasn't supposed to be happening. Not to her. She'd been so careful, and for what? A hollow spot opened up in her stomach, wide and gaping.

Instead of the headlines reading "Marriage Expert Finds Her Mr. Right," they would read "Marriage Expert Jilted at the Altar."

Kate had never considered herself prideful, but the thought of facing the next twenty-four hours made cyanide seem reasonable. How could this be happening? To her, of all people? She'd written a book on the subject of finding the right mate and had managed to find the wrong one instead. By tomorrow the whole world would know.

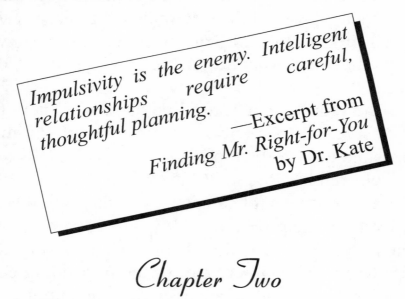

Impulsivity is the enemy. Intelligent relationships require careful, thoughtful planning.

—Excerpt from *Finding Mr. Right-for-You* by Dr. Kate

Chapter Two

Lucas watched Kate snap her phone shut. Maybe he should've left when he heard the gravity in her voice, but he couldn't. Like a pedestrian gawking at a car accident, he'd watched Kate receive the news. When he realized what Bryan was saying, he'd wanted to hunt the man down and pummel him until he felt the same pain as Kate. Instead he'd ushered Kate to the chair, wishing he could pull her into his arms and tell her it was going to be okay.

But that was the last thing she wanted.

Now she faced the wall, unmoving. Her glossy black hair hung straight, almost to her wilted shoulders. He'd never seen her so motionless. She was always on the go, steady as a clock; he'd been mesmerized by that the first time they'd met. Now, her stillness seemed unnatural.

He took a step toward her. "Kate?"

She must have forgotten about him, because she jumped slightly, then ran her hand across her face before turning partway. Her hair, always tucked behind her ears, had come loose. Her eyes only made it to his knees.

"Lucas." She studied the floor as if the paint and varnish stains were one of those abstract paintings to be interpreted. "I guess you heard."

Her voice was small. But he watched her straighten her back and turn to look fully at him. A scared little girl in a woman's body. Her eyes went past him to the gazebo for a second before flittering back.

"I . . . I guess I won't be needing that. I'll pay you for it, though. It's really beautiful." Her voice choked on the last word.

"I'm not worried about that."

He half expected her to cave in then, but instead she shot to her feet and began to pace, her heels clicking across the floor. "I have to think," she muttered. "I have to think."

Ka-clack, *ka-clack*, *ka-clack*, spin. *Ka-clack*, *ka-clack*, *ka-clack*, spin.

Lucas wasn't sure what she meant. Was she trying to figure out how to win Bryan back? Or giving up—making a mental list of everyone to be notified. He couldn't imagine the mess.

But if anyone could wrap her hands around the task, Kate could. He'd watched her patch up marriages that were dangling by a thread, juggle her syndicated column with her counseling service, and write a book in her spare time. Kate was an incredible woman. Bryan was an idiot if he couldn't see what he had.

Kate jerked to a stop and pressed her fingertips to her forehead. "He left me. I have no groom. The newspapers, the media, my publisher. My career. It's over."

She looked fragile and out of place in his expansive and dusty workshop, her short pants and white blouse immaculate, her black belt encircling her tiny waist. But then Kate always looked as if she'd been snapped straight from an ironing board.

"I thought he loved me," she whispered, her words wavering.

Lucas took a step toward her, then stopped, anchoring his hands in his pockets. "It's going to be okay." It felt lame but it was what he always told his baby sister, and it made Jamie feel better. Kate, however, was not Jamie.

"It is not going to be okay." She leveled a look at him. "I've been dumped five hours before my wedding. Everything is riding on this wedding, both personally and professionally. My Mr. Right left me. Do you not understand the irony?"

Maybe he wasn't your Mr. Right. It was on the tip of his tongue, but he caught it in time. He watched Kate's hand tremble against the side of her face. He hadn't known Kate was capable of trembling.

"I'm supposed to be an expert. Not just in relationships, but in finding the right mate. People write me for advice and trust me to give them answers. I wrote a book to help people make good matches, and I can't even make one myself." She looked away and dragged in a shaky breath. "I'm a failure."

"You're not a failure. Your fiancé made an idiot decision; that's not your fault."

The metal chair creaked as she sank into it, the sound echoing in the quietness of the room. "That's not how everyone's going to see it."

He reckoned she might be right about that. People could be judgmental, especially if the media put a nasty spin on it.

"I've got to do something," she mumbled through her fingers. "How can I fix this?"

Lucas didn't think it was possible. She had guests, a slew of media, and all the wedding fixings. Everything but the groom, and that was most important.

Everything but the groom.

The words ricocheted around his head until, one by one, they fell into place like tiles in a Scrabble game.

Everything . . . but . . . the groom . . .

He rubbed the back of his neck, walking toward his

work station. It was crazy. Crazier than crazy. It was insane. She'd laugh if he said it out loud. That thought tightened his gut.

Her phone clattered, vibrating on the metal desk. He watched it do the jitterbug.

"I can't answer," she said. "I can't deal with it right now. I don't know what to say." She crossed her arms, and her shoulders scrunched up as though she wished she could cover her ears with them.

Together they watched the phone. *Ring-bzzzzzzzz . . . Ringb-zzzzzz . . .* When the noise stopped, there was a palpable relief.

Kate drummed her fingers on her lips, quickly at first, then slowing. Her lips loosened, turned down. Her stubborn chin softened. "It's hopeless."

The phone rang again, chittering across the desktop. Kate glared at it, looking as though she might throw it across the room.

"I'll answer." He reached for it.

Kate stopped him with a hand on his arm. Her grip was surprisingly strong. "What'll you say?"

He met her gaze: wide, olive-brown eyes too vulnerable for words. "I'll just take a message."

After a moment, she released his arm, and he picked up the phone, snapping it open.

"Hello?"

A pause. "Is Kate there?" A woman's voice, out of breath.

"She can't come to the phone right now. Can I take a message?"

"Is this Bryan? Don't tell me she's letting you see her before the wedding."

"No. This is a—a friend." That was stretching it. He turned and leaned against the desk.

"Okay, well, tell her to call Pam. No, wait, she won't be able to reach me for a while. Tell her I have good news. This is really important, so be sure and tell her right away. The *Dr. Phil* show called, and they want her to make a guest appearance next month."

Great. Lucas met Kate's eyes, glanced away. Just what she needed.

"Did you get that?" Pam asked.

"Got it. I'll let her know." He closed the phone and set it on the desk. He could feel Kate watching him. Maybe he didn't have to tell her just now.

"Who was it?" Was that hope lilting her voice? Did she think Bryan had changed his mind?

"It was Pam."

She stared at her manicured fingers, clenched in her lap. "Oh."

She'd actually gotten on the *Dr. Phil* show. He'd known her popularity had grown nationwide with the column and book and all. But *Dr. Phil*. That was a whole new ball game.

"What did she want?"

Her knee brushed his leg as she shifted. He crossed his feet at the ankles and gripped the ledge of the desk. "It's nothing that can't wait. She wants you to call her back."

Her upturned face and searching eyes melted him. Have mercy, she was beautiful. He looked away.

"She said something, didn't she? Something you don't want me to know."

Restless energy pushed him away from the desk. He should've known she wouldn't let it go. He shouldn't have answered the phone. Her type A personality required her to know, even when she already had more than she could handle.

"Excuse me, but my life is hanging in the balance right now. Could you please just spit it out?"

Kate had straightened in the chair, her hand grasping the rounded edge of the back. Her left hand. Lucas watched the diamond engagement ring twinkle under the work lights. "She just wanted to let you know about an interview she set up, is all. You can call her later when you—"

"Who's it with?" Her tone demanded an answer.

He exhaled deeply. She was like a ravenous dog with his last meaty bone.

"I know it must be big. She wouldn't have called me today if it wasn't. And stop looking at me like that."

"Like what?"

"Like you feel sorry for me. Who's it with?"

Fine, Kate, fine. You win. "Dr. Phil."

He watched her mouth slacken, watched her blink and swallow, watched her eyes change, deaden. He hated it. Hated he'd had any part in bringing that look to her face.

She was still again, and he hated that too. Maybe it

wasn't too late to chase Bryan down and knock him flat on his face. He should be here picking up the pieces, making things right. But he wasn't. Lucas was there, and what could he do?

Everything but the groom.

The words flashed in his mind like a lighthouse beacon, teasing him. *It's crazy.* And even if it wasn't, it was self-serving.

You could save Kate's wedding. Her reputation. Her career. It's an honorable thing.

But I would also be getting what I wanted. Is that selfish?

You were willing to let her go, because you thought that was right. Was that selfish? She needs you now. And you're in a position to help her.

"What am I going to do?" Kate asked.

She turned her doe eyes on him, looking at him, needing him. It was heady. He wanted to protect her, to gather her close, the way a hen gathers her chicks under her wings.

"How am I going to face everyone? What am I going to tell the media? My publisher?" For the first time, her lip trembled, and she caught it between her teeth. "They paid for everything; did you know that?"

Should he say it? Should he offer himself? Could it even work? "Maybe it could."

"What?"

He didn't know he'd said it aloud until he heard Kate's response. Well, he was in just deep enough, he figured he might as well dive in headfirst. "I have an idea. It's a little crazy."

Surprisingly, she breathed a wry chuckle. "My whole life's a little crazy at the moment."

He studied her. She was actually looking at him with something like hope in her eyes. "Way I see it, the only thing missing is a groom."

Her laugh was sharp. "A necessary ingredient, I think you'll agree."

He nodded once, hoping she'd put two and two together so he wouldn't have to say it. "What if there was a different groom?"

Now she reared back slightly, blinking. *Great. She thinks I'm nuts.*

"I don't exactly have a waiting list, Lucas."

He shuffled his feet, then leaned against the work-horse, not sure if he was ready for what came next. *Just say it. The worst she can do is laugh in my face.* "What if I stood in for Bryan?"

He scuffed at the white paint on the tip of his right tennis shoe as silence closed in around him. A long silence. An uncomfortable silence. If he could've caught the words and pulled them back, he would've. Instead, he glanced at Kate. The expression on her face reinforced his wish.

"Why would—" She cleared her throat. "Why would you do that?"

Why would I do it? Because I love you. But he couldn't say that. Why hadn't he thought this out before he'd opened his big mouth?

He lifted his shoulder. "To help you," he said.

Her brows pulled together. "We're talking marriage here, not some little favor."

Favor. What if he made a bargain with her? What if she could do something for him in return? "I'd want something in return." *What? What do I want in return?*

At that, her eyebrows slackened as her lips took up the tension, pressing together. Her glare was direct and meaningful, and he immediately knew what she was thinking.

"Don't flatter yourself," he said.

She shook her head as if dislodging a distasteful picture. "It doesn't matter. It wouldn't work. Even if the rest of the world doesn't know who I was marrying, my dad does. And so does Chloe, my editor, and Pam and Anna. Not to mention Bryan's family."

A definite glitch, but was there a way around it? Now that the idea had settled a bit, it was growing on him. He shrugged. "Would they keep quiet?"

She gave him a double take. "Keep quiet?" Her fingers found the high collar of her blouse. "You're actually serious."

His heart was a jackhammer gone wild under his rib cage. He scratched at the dried paint on his thumbnail. "Would they?"

She turned away, her black hair swinging saucily. "You can't—you can't just marry me. Marriage is permanent. At least to me it is. You don't just make a willy-nilly decision to marry someone. People don't do that." She faced him again. "I don't do that."

No, Kate didn't do that. She planned every step days in advance, every detail in order, everything in its place.

At least she hadn't laughed at him. He straightened and shrugged as casually as he could, given that he felt like a man whose date had turned her head when he tried to kiss her. "Suit yourself."

He began wrapping the cord around the sander. It was a stupid idea anyway. He could only imagine his mom's reaction if his parents returned from their trip to find their son not only married, but married to Kate Lawrence. He'd never hear the end of it. And neither would his dad.

Nonetheless, it didn't do much for his ego to know Kate would rather see the death of her career than marry him. He stuffed the ache further down and set the sander on the shelf next to his favorite drill, waiting to hear the click of her heels as she left the shop.

Instead, Kate's voice broke the silence. "The people who know Bryan was the groom . . . what if one of them leaked it? Besides, there's the marriage license and the tuxes. Something could go wrong, and if everyone found out, it would be a bigger disaster than what I have now—if that's possible."

Okay, already, I get it. "It was a stupid idea." She'd made that plain enough. "You should get out your little notepad and make a list of things to cancel."

"Wait. Just wait a minute; I have to think." Apparently she did her best thinking while pacing.

Whatever. He turned back to his tools. He didn't see what there was to think about. At this point it was just a matter of facing the music. He didn't envy her that. But if Bryan was loser enough to jilt her at the altar, he wasn't good enough for her.

He kept silent while she pondered her situation. By the time she spoke again, every tool was put away—something that hadn't happened since he'd installed the shelving unit.

"I think I could arrange to keep everyone quiet. My editor and Pam certainly wouldn't say anything. I can trust Anna and my dad implicitly. I have a couple of distant relatives here, but they'd keep it to themselves."

She was thinking out loud, not even looking at Lucas. "Bryan's family is small, and they're mostly from the Boston area. There were eight relatives here, plus his best man. He could surely convince them to keep quiet. He owes me that at least." Her eyes softened for a moment as if the thought of him made her ache.

Kate was actually considering it. He'd never known her to do a spontaneous thing, and here she was, thinking about marrying him at the last minute. *She must be desperate.*

Kate looked Lucas over from head to toe; he squirmed, feeling he'd somehow failed the examination. "The tux won't fit. You're taller; your shoulders are broader. We'd have to get you fitted quickly. Mr. Lavitz is a good friend of yours, isn't he?"

"Well, yeah . . ."

"The marriage license might be a problem." She tapped her foot and chewed on the side of her lip, her eyes searching the buzzing fluorescent fixtures for answers. "And we'd need an exit strategy. Maybe a year? Give my book time to succeed and give me time to get another book going. We could get a quiet divorce . . ."

Her eyes closed. "I can't believe I'm talking about marriage like this. Like it's a cheap business arrangement."

Lucas watched her face as she wrestled with her principles. "He backed you into a corner. It's not like you have so many appealing options."

She looked at him suddenly, her brows pulling together. "Why are you doing this again?"

Why? Why? How could she help him? She was a marriage counselor, but he wasn't married—yet. His parents' marriage was solid enough, though they loved to fuss at each other. Everyone knew it was just who they were, but an outsider might think . . .

"Lucas? I'm running out of time here."

"My parents' marriage. If you could help them."

Her eyes brightened. Ah, he'd hit the bull's-eye.

"It's in jeopardy?" she asked.

He cleared his throat. Stuffed his hands in his jeans pockets. "They fight a lot lately." He needed more, but he didn't want to lie. "My mom left for a few days last month." On a girls' weekend trip, but Kate didn't have to know that. "Jamie—she's my little sister—said Dad

enjoyed her absence." He'd actually said he enjoyed having Jamie all to himself. But that was close enough, wasn't it?

"And you want me to counsel them?"

"No." The word came out a little sharp. "They're both leery of all that psychobabble stuff." Her eyebrows rose, and he rephrased. "You'd have to be sly about it. Get to know them. Get them to open up. You can handle it."

"That's it? That's all you want?"

He wanted much more, but it was a start. "It's my parents' marriage."

"Of course. I didn't mean to make it sound trite." Kate steepled her fingers and tapped the tips together. "I don't even know if this is possible. I think there's a waiting period on the marriage license."

He hadn't thought of that. Maybe the plan was dead in the water. But hadn't his friend Ethan gotten married at the last minute? "I think it can be waived. Nancy Rallings is the town clerk, and I furnished her house. I'll see what I can find out."

He couldn't believe she was considering it. He could be marrying Kate in a matter of hours. In front of friends, family, and media. His legs suddenly quaked as he remembered the article in the paper spelling out the details. The wedding was going to be a media circus. They might want to interview him.

His mouth felt like it was stuffed with sawdust. "No interviews," he said.

It took Kate a moment to hear him, lost in thought as she probably was. "What?"

"I'll let the media snap all the photos they want, but I won't give interviews."

She shrugged, eyeing him. "I agree—we don't need to complicate things. What about your family? How are they going to feel?"

That gave him pause. His mom had been urging him to move on since Emily died five years ago. Kate, however, was the last person his mom would want him moving on with. If he told his mom the marriage was temporary, she would be rude, scare Kate off for good. But if she knew he loved Kate, she'd have to make an effort, wouldn't she?

"My parents are out of town right now, but my brother and sister are here. I'll call my parents afterward and tell them we got married. And I don't want them to know the particulars. As far as they're concerned, it's the real thing." Besides, if it worked the way he hoped, there'd be no exit strategy needed. He held out his hand. "Deal?"

His breath caught and hung below the mass in his throat.

Kate stared at him, her eyes a mixture of fear and resolve. Then she put her hand in his. "Deal."

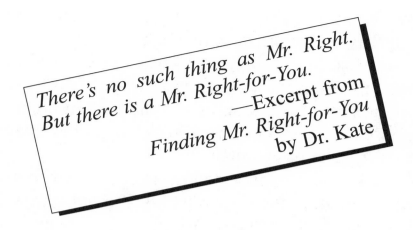

There's no such thing as Mr. Right.
But there is a Mr. Right-for-You.
—Excerpt from
Finding Mr. Right-for-You
by Dr. Kate

Chapter Three

If Kate had to explain the change one more time, she was going to pull every last hair from her head. The horror etched into the eyes of Anna, Chloe, and Pam had been enough to start the second-guessing. They'd run over the pros and cons, quickly, more for their benefit than anyone's. Kate had covered that ground a dozen times already.

Her dad had listened silently, with shoulders squared and back straight, his only parental concession the lone worry line stretching across his squeaky-clean forehead.

It'll be okay, Dad. I know what I'm doing.

He'd taught Kate to think independently, and he never questioned her decisions. Even now, the most he'd said was, "Kate . . ."

When she'd called Bryan with her announcement and demands, she'd been met with a long silence. She'd almost enjoyed his obvious shock and unspoken, *You're what?* Just when she thought he might have gone unconscious behind the wheel of his car, he asked her to repeat what she'd said. She'd ended up going through it three times, until he eventually assured her his family would keep it quiet. She supposed he wasn't eager for word to get out that he'd jilted Dr. Kate at the altar.

At least one group hadn't needed explanations. Lucas had introduced her to his brother and sister, Brody and Jamie. Brody, a lanky, curly-headed version of Lucas, was home from college on summer break, and Jamie was a teenager with dark hair and braces. They accepted the news of their brother's impending matrimony with friendly smiles before exchanging a silent glance Kate didn't have time to decipher.

Now, four hours, one wedding license, and countless moments of stark terror later, Kate stood in her white gown, feet poised at the foot of the aisle. The media cameras clicked in machine-gun fashion, capturing a three-quarter view. She curved her lips upward and forced a twinkle into her eyes.

Thirty feet down the aisle, waiting in the gazebo, was Anna; Lucas's best man, Ethan; the justice of the peace; and Lucas.

Lucas. Is this really happening?

The musicians started the wedding march. Kate curled her arm around the stiff material on her dad's arm and took the first step. A gentle breeze blew off the ocean, ruffling her hair and veil and feathering her strapless A-line gown against her legs. She'd finally found the satin dress at a boutique in Boston after scouring numerous magazines and shops. Now what did it matter that the gown was perfect or that the hem hit the floor precisely?

How had it come to this? Bryan was supposed to be waiting at the end of the aisle. They matched. They were a fit according to everything she knew about personalities and relationships. They had so much in common—their love of exercise . . . organization . . . punctuality . . . loyalty . . .

Well. She supposed she'd have to rethink the loyalty part.

She passed her Aunt Virginia in the second row, wearing her trademark cherry-red lipstick. Her brown hair coiled above her puffy white face like thick chocolate shavings on a pile of whipped cream.

The groom's side was half-empty, but what did she expect with last-minute invitations? Jamie sat on the first row beside Brody, her brown hair caught up in barrette. Two part-time employees from Lucas's shop sat on the next row, straining to see around a tall, spindly man she recognized from someplace.

She imagined how upset Lucas's parents would be at missing the ceremony. And at finding out about the wedding after it was over . . . But it was what Lucas wanted, and it was his decision. They'd have to smooth things over later.

They . . .

She was going to be joining another family. The

thought struck her hard and quick. She didn't even know these people—she barely knew the groom!

What am I doing?

She didn't meet Lucas's eyes until she nearly reached the gazebo and then realized her mistake. A bride would be gazing adoringly at her groom. Was she smiling widely enough? Her dry lips stuck to her teeth.

Lucas had cleaned up well, even shaved his perpetual five o'clock shadow. His long hair was combed back from his face. The hairstyle, combined with the formal suit, gave him the look of a nineteenth-century nobleman. His eyes met hers, pulling her in—a solid lifeline in what felt like a turbulent storm.

They reached the foot of the gazebo, and her dad stopped and kissed her cheek, then took a seat on the first row.

She was on her own now.

What am I doing? . . . What am I doing? . . .

She stepped into the gazebo as the last strains of the wedding march rang out and drew to a halt between Anna and Lucas. Her bare arm brushed his. In the distance, whirring clicks of cameras captured every second of the event, and she knew the best photos would grace the pages of tomorrow's newspapers. But as the justice began talking, all Kate could think about was the way the heat from Lucas's arm seeped clean through his tux and settled against her skin like a thick fog.

"Marriage is commended to be honorable among all

men," the justice began. "And therefore is not by any to be entered into unadvisedly or lightly—but reverently, discreetly, advisedly, and solemnly." He emphasized each word, his bushy gray eyebrows inching upward disapprovingly. When Kate had told him Lucas was taking Bryan's place, she'd been half-afraid he'd refuse to perform the ceremony. But he'd only pressed his lips together and nodded formally.

Now he continued. "Into this holy estate these two persons present now come to be joined for life."

Joined for life. She turned her head a fraction of an inch toward Lucas as the ugly scent of fear filled her nostrils, mingling with the tangy, salt-laden air. Life? She hardly knew him!

What am I doing?

She dragged in a breath and slowly released it, careful to keep her expression neutral. *There's no going back now. Focus. Just get through the ceremony.*

Was Lucas afraid too? Was he asking himself what he'd gotten into, wishing he were back in his shop, sitting in a thin layer of sawdust? Was that his arm trembling against hers? He had every right to panic. He was giving up a year of his life. He was being thrust into the public eye.

What if he backs out? Right here in front of everybody? Jilted twice in one day. Had it ever happened before? She imagined the headline. *"Dr. Kate Jilted at Altar by Two Grooms."*

The justice stopped talking, and the moment's

silence sent alarm scuttling through Kate. Instinctively, she slid her right hand from her bouquet and reached out, searching for an anchor. When her fingers touched Lucas's hand, his encircled hers. It was warm and strong, and—oddly—confident. *It's going to be okay,* his grip said.

Mrs. Petrie began her solo, her warbly, butterfly soprano wafting on the breeze, and Kate's mind wandered. The song had seemed perfect for her and Bryan. How could she have been so wrong? Who was it who had stolen his heart? Just the night before, he'd held her close and kissed her good night at her apartment door. What was it he'd said? *"I guess I'll see you soon."*

Had there been something in his tone? In his expression? Some warning she'd missed? She'd been too flushed with excitement to notice. And just like that he was gone.

And now she was marrying Lucas. Committing a year of her life to a man she didn't love. Good grief, most of the time she didn't even like him. Not that he was a bad person. He was just so . . . irritating sometimes. Vexing. The way he was late and careless and so laid-back she wished she had a remote control so she could push the fast-forward button.

She couldn't think of a man less suited for her.

Mrs. Petrie finished the song and returned to her seat. The justice began talking about the seriousness of the vows they were about to take. Kate wanted to plug her ears. She was a proponent of lifelong marriages. It was her life's work to help couples stay married. And now she was making a mockery of the process.

I'm a hypocrite. A fraud. What would my readers think if they knew?

The justice turned toward her, and Kate focused her attention on him as he announced the reading of the vows. She was supposed to face Lucas. She handed her bouquet to Anna and turned toward Lucas. She wasn't sure if she was capable of breathing, much less speaking.

Then she saw the corner of Lucas's lip tilt up ever so slightly, his eyes soften. Instinctively, she relaxed.

I can do this.

The justice read the vows, and Kate repeated them. "I, Kate Lawrence, take you, Lucas Wright, to be my husband, to have and to hold from this day forward, for better or for worse, for richer, for poorer, in sickness and in health, to love and to cherish, from this day forward." Kate swallowed hard. "Until death do us part."

The last words were rushed, but she'd done it. Now the justice prompted Lucas.

He repeated the vows, and he did it well. His eyes said as much as his voice. The way he looked at her . . . It was the way every bride yearned to be looked at. Like she was precious. Like she was his chosen one. His voice was low, as if rumbling up from the deepest part of the ocean. It was more than credible. It was convincing.

The justice said a prayer and ended it with an amen. "It is tradition to exchange rings as a symbol of the love between a man and a wife."

Rings! Kate felt something akin to a tidal wave inside her. Bryan's best man had her ring. Lucas wouldn't have a ring to put on her finger. She turned a desperate look toward the justice, but he was looking at Lucas as he spoke. ". . . representing the unending love of your union." He cleared his throat as if the words had left a foul taste.

Kate stared hard at the justice, hoping mental telepathy would work just this once. *There are no rings!*

But then Lucas turned to Ethan. When he faced Kate again, he held a ring in the hollow of his palm. He'd taken care of it. Relief washed over her, and she smiled her gratitude.

He took her left hand in his and slid the ring onto her finger until it rested beside the glittering diamond. "With this ring, I thee wed." The look in his eyes burned the words into her heart.

The band was white gold, elegant in its simplicity. When had he had time to buy a ring? And how had he known her size?

The justice was prompting her to get Lucas's ring. She turned to take the ring from Anna. There was no way Bryan's ring would fit Lucas. She hoped it would at least slide over his knuckle. Maybe no one would notice.

She took the ring from Anna's palm . . . but it wasn't

Bryan's white-gold band with diamond-shaped cuts. This one matched the one Lucas had put on her finger. She turned toward him and took his hand in hers. The ring slid easily onto his wide, tapered finger and looked bright against the darkness of his skin. "With this ring, I thee wed," she said.

Lucas caught hold of her hands, and the justice gave his closing thoughts. Kate was aware of nothing except Lucas's hands holding hers, his fingers rough and calloused against hers. She noticed that he was almost a head taller than her five-foot-five frame. One strand of his hair had come loose and fallen over his forehead, rogue-style. Her gaze fell to his eyes. He looked straight at her, into her, anchoring her.

The justice was making his closing statements. "By the power vested in me by the State of Massachusetts, I now pronounce you husband and wife."

The relief she felt brought a smile to her face. *It's done. I made it through.*

"You may now kiss the bride."

Her eyes flew back to Lucas. In all the commotion of last-minute changes, she hadn't even thought about the kiss. Had he?

One of his eyebrows quirked as if challenging her.

She leaned toward him and felt his hands go to her waist. She brought her fingers to his jaw just as their lips met. His mouth was soft against hers. His lips moved slowly, deliberately, as he pulled her closer until their bodies nearly met . . .

Oh my . . . goodness . . .

It was over in seconds, but it left her rattled. Good grief, he was a great kisser. Who would have thought?

He was watching her, most likely noting her newly flushed cheeks. His eyes twinkled as if he could tell the kiss had left her shaken. She drew her shoulders back and tilted her chin as the justice said his final words.

"I now present to you Mr. and Mrs. Lucas Wright."

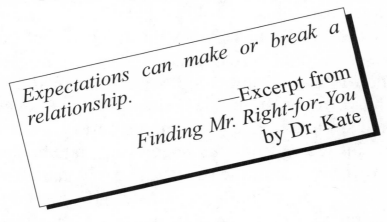

Expectations can make or break a relationship.

—Excerpt from *Finding Mr. Right-for-You* by Dr. Kate

Chapter Four

"In honor of the first man in her life," the DJ announced from the makeshift stage, "The bride would like to have the first dance of the evening with her father."

Kate disengaged herself from Lucas's friends and wound her way through the circular tables to the parquet dance floor, where her dad waited with extended hand. She went into his arms with the first notes of "Unforgettable" playing behind her. It was the only part of the day going according to plan. Everything else had been turned on end, but sharing this dance with her dad was exactly the way it was supposed to be. Kate closed her eyes and relished the normality of it, unwilling—unable—to think past this moment.

"You're holding up well."

She looked up at her father. His face had aged the last couple years, and Kate realized she hadn't visited him in Maryland enough. Phone calls and letters didn't allow the same connection, and she'd spent most of her spare weekends with Bryan in Boston. And for what?

"Really?" She felt as transparent as Saran Wrap and just as fragile. Making rounds with Lucas had been hard. Everyone wanted to know how they'd met and how they'd kept it a secret. Lucas's eyes had said it all. *We didn't.* The two of them had a million details to work out. She didn't know how they'd remember everything they'd come up with on the fly tonight.

"What do you know about this guy?" Her dad shuffled stiffly, leading more like a boot-camp drill sergeant than a dancer. His hair—what was left of it—was combed neatly to the side in a part not quite deep enough to be a comb-over.

What did she know about Lucas? Not even enough to fill a pen cap. "He makes furniture, and his shop is right below my place on Main Street. In fact, he owns the building. I was renting my office space and apartment from him. He did the renovations."

She'd let Lucas know months ago that she was moving out this month. Little had she known she'd be

43

moving into his home. She realized she didn't know where he lived.

"What else?" A benign smile hid his concern.

"He's a nice man, Daddy. Harmless."

She glanced over her dad's shoulder at Lucas. He stood with Ethan, hands resting in his vest pockets, his jacket long since discarded. His white shirt was crisp and fitted, tapering from broad shoulders down to narrow hips. Maybe "harmless" was overstating it.

"I'm not leaving until morning, so if you need any-thing tonight, call me."

Kate laughed. "Not the words most fathers say to their daughters on their wedding night."

"This isn't most wedding nights."

Kate sobered. No, it wasn't. She didn't know how she was going to survive the honeymoon at the White Elephant, much less the next year.

"If anyone can do this, you can." Her father squeezed her hand in a rare gesture of affection. Behind him, the vocalists belted out the chorus, the lead singer's face reddened from the strain.

"Thanks, Dad."

They danced quietly for a few moments before her dad broke the silence. "I know your mom and I had our disagreements, but I wish she could be here tonight."

Kate didn't want to think about her mom, tonight of all nights. "You're here. That's all that matters." They took one last turn as the band wound down the song and the crowd applauded.

Lucas approached as her dad stepped away. "May I cut in, sir?"

Kate knew he'd scored brownie points for the honorific title. Her dad smiled cordially, but the look in his eyes warned that the points wouldn't carry far.

The band struck up the song she'd selected for the bride and groom's "first dance," and her heart stuttered. "When a Man Loves a Woman" had been their song. It had played on the radio the first time Bryan kissed her. A constricting knot lodged in her throat as Lucas's hands came to her waist. She felt his eyes on her, and she worked to steady her smile. There were people watching. Always people watching. She had to hold it together.

As if sensing her need to hide, he pulled her close. She laid her cheek against his chest, away from all the faces. Above the swelling music and chatter, she could hear the waves swooshing the shoreline with rhythmic certainty. The consistency of the sound soothed her.

"It's gonna be okay, Kate," Lucas's voice rumbled next to her ear. "You'll see."

Her eyes burned, threatening to spill, and she blinked. *Breathe, just breathe.* She needed to think about something else, anything else, but the thoughts wouldn't budge: *"I'm in love with someone else."* Were harsher words ever spoken?

"I'm glad we have a minute alone," Lucas said. "Because I have a question for you."

She swallowed. "What's that?"

"Are we going on a honeymoon?"

Her laugh was feeble. "I'm sorry." She pulled back enough to look at him. "We have reservations at the White Elephant for the week. Is that okay?" He had his work, after all. But if they didn't take a honeymoon, people would wonder.

"I have a couple jobs to finish up this week, but I'll get them pushed back." He pulled her closer. "The White Elephant, huh? Your publisher went all out."

She moved her hand down his shoulder. "The hotel offered an unbelievable rate. They'll get a lot of publicity."

"Surprised you didn't want to go to Hawaii or something."

She shrugged. "Nantucket's done so much for me. I wanted to do something to help the community. The publicity is good for the island." She smoothed the stiff lapels of his jacket. He'd put it back on for the dance. For the photos that were being snapped.

He'd been a perfect gentleman all evening. She was beginning to wonder why he'd gotten on her nerves before. "Thanks for not shoving the cake in my face," she said.

His lips tilted. "Wouldn't dream of it."

The singer crooned the chorus, but Kate kept her eyes on Lucas. They were supposed to be the "happy couple." It was harder than she'd imagined; the pretending was wearing her out.

"So when does this shindig end?"

Not soon enough. "The band has to stop at nine thirty."

Lucas started to look at Kate's watch, but she grabbed his hand and kissed it. The hairs on the back of his hand tickled her lips. "You're dancing with your bride. Time is meaningless."

His eyes clouded, and he settled his hand at her waist, looking away.

"When the band winds down, we'll make our exit," she said. "There's a carriage scheduled to take us to the White Elephant."

It hit her how deceiving appearances could be. For all that this looked like a fairy-tale wedding, a true marriage, it was a farce. Empty and fake, it was an elaborate mansion, gutted on the inside.

"I haven't packed." He spun them around, surprisingly graceful.

"That's taken care of."

The flash of a bulb flared just off the dance floor. She gave Lucas her "adoring bride" smile, letting her eyes rove lovingly over the planes of his face even though she was seeing black spots, as the photographer snapped half a dozen more photos. When he stepped away, she continued. "Anna is going to grab some things for you tonight. That is, if you don't mind her riffling through your stuff. You can pick up the rest of your things tomorrow."

"Not sure how I feel about a stranger riffling through my underwear drawer."

She could tell by his tone that there'd been a shift in Lucas's mood, though she had no idea what had caused it. Of all the things to fuss about. He'd married her at the last moment, but the underwear drawer stopped him cold? What else could they do? They couldn't send his family after his things and have them knowing he hadn't planned for his honeymoon. Even Lucas wasn't that disorganized.

"Do you have a better idea?" she asked.

He looked over her head now, wearing an insipid smile. "Fine. Just send Anna."

Kate opened her mouth to respond, then changed her mind. The last thing she needed was an argument on the dance floor.

Kate faced the mirror in the bathroom of the White Elephant's Shoreline suite. Her dark hair, caught up on the sides, disappeared beneath the triple-layered veil. Her makeup still looked fresh, her dress stunning. Her shoulders, carefully tanned over the past month, looked every bit as lovely as she'd hoped.

Only none of it mattered now. Bryan loved someone else, and she was married to a man she barely tolerated.

Ah, but my career is salvaged. At least I have that.

She set her heavy bag on the marble counter and opened it, resting the floppy lid against the beveled mirror. The zipper clanged against the glass.

The carriage ride to the hotel had seemed to take forever even though it couldn't have been more than ten minutes. She was tired of pretending. Which didn't bode well—the entire next year would consist of nothing but pretense, and just one night of it had worn her to the bone. Her feet hurt, her head ached, and all she wanted was to slide between the sheets and pull them over her head.

Maybe it wouldn't feel so awful in the morning. The sun would come up, it would glitter off the harbor, and the fresh air would remind her it was a new day.

At least she wouldn't have to move from Nantucket. It had been the one thing she'd dreaded. She pictured Bryan's apartment in downtown Boston and sighed at the thought. She'd never go there again. Never sit on his couch and eat popcorn while they watched CNN.

She turned her attention to her suitcase. Her clothing, carefully rolled to avoid creases, was packed in colorful bins all lined up in rows. She scanned the pieces and realized the satin and lace article she'd planned for tonight would hardly suffice. Instead, she pulled out a shirt with a mock turtleneck and a pair of knee-length shorts. It would have to do.

She looked in the mirror, noting her drawn expression, and willed herself not to cry. Then, with a sigh, she began the tug-of-war of releasing herself from her gown.

Lucas was sitting in the armchair when she reentered the room, his elbows braced on his knees. His gaze flickered over her, and she realized he must be eager to change.

"Anna should be here soon with your things."

He nodded.

"Sorry she couldn't get them over sooner."

He nodded again.

Well, don't go getting all chatty on me.

Giving up, Kate began hanging up her clothing, one item at a time, trying to ignore the fact Lucas was probably staring at her backside. They steadfastly held on to their silence until a few minutes later when a tap sounded on the door. Kate practically leapt across the room to let Anna in.

"Is everything okay?" Anna whispered with a hug.

"Sure." Kate summoned up one last smile. She would've offered more, but Lucas was hovering, obviously wanting to change.

"Here you go," Anna said to him.

He took a paper bag and a noisy cluster of keys from her.

"I couldn't find a suitcase or duffel bag."

"That's okay. Thanks for going to the trouble."

Anna looked at Kate. "Well . . ."

"Well . . ." Kate's brain raced, trying to think of a reason for Anna to stay. *Perhaps she'll notice the slightly manic look in my eyes and take pity.* But with a wave and a quirk of her eyebrows, Anna was gone.

Traitor.

Rather than run screaming after her assistant, Kate continued unpacking, stashing her socks and underclothes in one of the armoire drawers while Lucas disappeared into the bathroom. He returned in record time.

Wearing only a pair of shorts.

Oh . . . Kate's gaze skittered away. As if things weren't awkward enough already.

She was acutely aware of his appraisal as he sat in the armchair. What was he thinking? More specifically, what did he expect from this marriage? If it were Bryan, she'd ask—or likely, she'd already know. How many conversations she and Bryan had had about their expectations. They'd been as prepared as an engaged couple could be.

Feeling him watching her, knowing she was procrastinating, Kate placed her alarm clock and Day-Timer on the nightstand, then stowed her suitcase in the closet. When she could delay no longer, she returned to the bed and pulled the covers down, glancing at the pillow on the other side.

Just what does Lucas expect tonight?
Does he think . . . ?

She sat on the edge of the bed, facing the wall and a framed print of a lighthouse, back rigid, heart racing. She wasn't naive. Men expected sex on the honeymoon.

She and Lucas were married now, and, technically, it was his right to expect it. But . . . it seemed wrong. Theirs wasn't the typical marriage. There was nothing typical about this honeymoon. And there was no way she was offering her body like some . . . some ancient temple priestess.

Still, this was a conversation they should've had before the wedding.

She didn't want to fret over it all night either. She glanced at him, still sitting in the chair. He was leaning back, his head turned toward her. The room was big, and he seemed far away. A good, safe distance. But she could hardly yell across the room.

Kate forced her tired legs to support her weight and walked toward him.

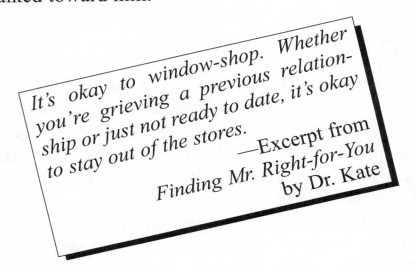

It's okay to window-shop. Whether you're grieving a previous relationship or just not ready to date, it's okay to stay out of the stores.
—Excerpt from *Finding Mr. Right-for-You* by Dr. Kate

Chapter Five

Lucas watched Kate sit on the edge of the couch, perching like a robin on the rim of its nest, alert for the first sign of danger. He wanted to put her at ease, let her know she was safe with him. He wanted to protect her. He would never hurt her. *You are so precious to me, Kate.*

My bride. He savored the word on his tongue.

Kate wrapped her arms around her stomach. "It occurs to me there are some issues we haven't addressed. Perhaps we can discuss the most imminent one now."

So formal. He half-expected her to produce a

twenty-page document, spelling out the lay of the land for the next 365 days, and insist he sign it.

"What's on your mind?" He folded his hands on his bare stomach.

She licked her lips, her eyes flashing down to his bare chest for the briefest of moments before she stared at her tanned knees.

"Sleeping arrangements." She cleared her throat. "I appreciate what you did today by stepping in for Bryan. I don't know what you expected from me tonight, but——"

Her cheeks bloomed with color.

"I don't know what you expected from me tonight, but I have no desire to sleep—or do anything else—in that bed with you." He imagined the words she didn't say. Was that what was worrying her? Making her clutch at the nun-high collar of her shirt, making her face turn a dozen shades of pink?

What kind of jerk did she think he was, expecting to be compensated after she'd just been jilted at the altar by the man she loved? As if he'd want her like that—still pining for someone else. After the tenderness of his previous thoughts, the idea sickened him.

"Believe it or not, Kate, sleeping with you is the last thing on my mind." It came out sharper than he'd intended, but blast it all if it didn't tick him off that she thought so lowly of him.

"I was planning to take the couch," he said. "The bed's all yours."

Her gaze bounced off him, and she stood, nodding

once. He watched her go without a reply, long legs extending from knee-length beige shorts. She flicked out the bedside lamp before slipping into bed.

He turned out the other lights and settled on the sofa. Grabbing one of the puffy throw pillows, he turned on his side and drew up his knees so he'd fit.

Does she really think so little of me?

His thoughts returned to the first time he'd met her, when he'd shown her the space above the shop. She'd worn white slacks, a blazer, and fancy heels that made him wonder how she climbed the stairs without falling flat on her face.

"It's a large space," she'd said. "I didn't realize it would be wide open."

He looked around at the scuffed white walls and wood floor, dulled by a layer of dust. Except for the small office and restroom at the back of the building, it was an open space. "Used to be a photographer's gallery. You said something on the phone about making it a living space and an office of some kind?"

She walked the room, her skinny heels clacking on the floor. "I'm a marriage counselor. I'd need a small lobby area and a private room for counseling. I was hoping to make my living space up here too. It's big enough, I think."

With rent so high on Nantucket, it made sense to combine the two. She moved toward the back of the building, jotting something on a clipboard, and he walked to the front of the room, giving her time to look around undisturbed. Outside the front windows, dead leaves sailed on a gust of wind. A handful of tourists walked the brick sidewalks.

"What's your policy on renovations?" Kate was making her way toward him, her silky black hair swinging. She was all business, straight to the point. He wondered if she was good at what she did. She didn't seem warm enough to be a therapist. Then again, what did he know about it? Or about her?

"How long were you planning to stay?" He didn't mind renovations so long as she'd be there a while.

"It depends on the terms of the contract."

The space had been empty for two months. The summer people were gone for the season, and with winter coming he'd have a hard time renting it to a merchant. "If you cover cost of materials, I'll see to it the renovations are done."

She nodded, glancing around at the space as if she was trying to envision it completed.

Now that the season was over, he'd have extra time. Too bad Brody was back at college or he'd ask his brother to help.

"How soon would you need it done?" he asked.

Kate wrote something on her paper while he noted that she had a tiny mole on one side of her pointed chin and lips full enough to beg a man's attention. "I'd like to get my business up and running as soon as possible. The living portion is less urgent. I can sleep in the office back there or even in my new office until it's finished."

It was an awkward time of year to open a business.

She seemed a little citified, and he wondered if she'd ever wintered on the island before. Oh, well. Wasn't any of his business.

"Give me a day or so to think it over, and I'll get back with you," she said, extending her hand and shaking his.

The next day she signed the contract and moved her luggage into the old office at the back of the building. They agreed to meet that afternoon to go over renovation plans. She was waiting for him when he arrived, and he realized he was probably a tad late. She checked her watch before sitting at a padded card table she must've brought.

"The builder's coming, isn't he?" She set a manila file on the table and folded her long, slender fingers on top of it.

Did she think he was hiring a crew or something? "I'm the builder." He took a seat opposite her.

Her eyes widened, and she blinked twice, her black lashes fluttering. "But—but I thought you built furniture."

Her eyes were a bewitching mix of green and brown. He wondered what color her driver's license said they were. "I do build furniture. But I've done plenty of carpentry and plumbing and wiring. I built my house, and I've done room additions."

"Do you—Are you a *licensed* builder?"

He found her tight little smile amusing. Did she think his walls were going to collapse or his wiring was going to burn the building down? "I'm licensed.

If you want to check out my work, I did all the renovations downstairs. It was an open space like this when I bought it."

"Oh. Well, your shop is very nicely done. I just didn't realize you'd be doing the work, that's all."

Ever since that first meeting, ruffling her feathers had served as a cheap form of entertainment. He knew she'd been pleased with his work, though his pace seemed to aggravate her. She even tried to put him on a schedule at one point, telling him when he should have the drywall completed, when he should have the bathroom and kitchen plumbed. The woman lived and breathed by the agenda she had with her at all times.

Still, there was something about her.

Now, as he lay staring toward the shadowed fireplace in the darkened room, he realized all her plans had blown up in her face. He wondered what she would've thought if he told her that first day that she'd marry him three years later. She probably would've laughed in his face.

And yet here they were, on their honeymoon.

Yeah, I'm on the couch. She made it real clear she wants nothing to do with me.

And he'd made it just as clear he wasn't interested. Too clear, maybe. He hadn't exactly been the picture of loving-kindness.

He heard a sound coming from the general direction of the bed and lifted his head. A sniff, muffled by a pillow or the bedspread. A quiet hiccup, then another sniffle.

With a sigh, he lay his head back down and closed his eyes. He was a dog. Why had he snapped at her like that? She was grieving. She hadn't had time to recover from the shock of being dumped before she'd found herself married to another man for the next twelve months.

His hands fisted, clenching the pillow until his fingers ached. He wished he could put his arms around her and tell her it was going to be okay.

He wished it was him she loved so much.

Kate felt another sob rising and muffled it with the pillow. Two years with Bryan. Two years spent getting to know him, investing in the relationship, coming to love him. How could he leave her so suddenly, so cruelly? The betrayal was almost too much to bear.

Had his lack of commitment been present all along? Is that why he'd never come to the island, except once, early on in their relationship? She'd made the trip to Boston out of respect for his job. Her hours were more flexible than his, and they were able to spend more time together when she traveled to see him. If it had been up to him, maybe he wouldn't have made the long trips.

Their weekends together had been special to her. They holed themselves up in his apartment, talking and just being together. Bryan turned down invitations to events and get-togethers so they could have time to reconnect. He'd seemed committed.

She was so confused! Kate reached out into the

vacant space of the bed where Bryan was supposed to be, her fingers sliding across the cool, empty sheets. Her heart felt as empty.

She pulled the other pillow into her stomach and remembered all the grieving women she'd counseled. Women who'd poured their life into a relationship only to have it jerked from under them at a moment's notice. She hadn't known it felt like this. Seeing others endure it and suffering through it yourself were two different things.

A memory flashed in her mind. It had been shortly after her mom kicked her dad from the house. Her mom's reddened eyes and baggy clothing had become part of her identity, and Kate couldn't remember the last time she'd seen her smile, much less laugh.

Kate entered the tiny living room where her mom sat curled on the couch, staring at the TV, though Kate didn't think she was watching. Kate picked up the remote and flipped through channels. If only she could find something to cheer her mom up. Something to make her forget. Something to make her smile again.

When Kate flipped to *Roseanne*, she turned up the volume. Her mom always laughed at that show. Sitting beside her, she pulled her knees to her chest and yanked her nightgown over them, stretching the thin pink material to its limits.

The show's audience laughed at something Dan said, but a glance at her mom dampened Kate's spirits. Her face was blank, the light from the TV glazing her deadened eyes. Why was she so sad? If she missed Daddy, why didn't she ask him to come back?

Kate felt her own eyes burning, watched Roseanne's living room blur. She missed her dad, and her mom obviously missed him too. Why wouldn't she let him come back?

Her mom popped to her feet. "I'm going to bed, pumpkin." Her words sounded squeezed from her throat, as if a scarf was wrapped too tightly around her neck.

"Good night," Kate answered, but her mom was already down the hall, closing her door. The light in the room flickered as the scenes on TV changed. Kate watched the room glow white, then blue, then white again.

From down the hall the sound of her mom's muffled weeping reached her ears. Kate had grown to hate the sound that escorted her to sleep each night. She turned up the volume and lay on the itchy tweed couch, then pulled a pillow to her ear . . .

Now, Kate turned over and dried her face with the sheet. She hadn't thought about that night in years. Not until now, when her own life seemed to have taken over exactly where her mother's had left off.

A sound reached her ears, and she lifted her head from the pillow, listening. A second later, she heard it again—a long, loud snort coming from the direction of the couch. *Great. Just my luck.*

Her new husband snored.

Chapter Six

A distant clattering woke Kate. She stirred, stretching her limbs, before opening her eyes. The room was dark, and she tried to get her bearings as the events of the day before emerged, rising like a tsunami out of a still sea.

She'd married Lucas.

She was on her honeymoon.

Kate closed her eyes, wishing for the oblivion of slumber again. Maybe she could fall back asleep. For a year.

Another noise, a quiet clinking, disrupted her efforts. Apparently Lucas woke before the break of dawn. She rolled over and tugged the duvet over her head, but moments later the rich aroma of brewing coffee beckoned her. *Aaahhh* . . . She pushed the cover down and sat up against the heap of pillows, untangling her legs from the sheets.

"Sorry," Lucas whispered from the wet bar. "Didn't mean to wake you."

Kate rubbed her eyes. Her lids felt heavy and swollen. "You're forgiven. Especially if you made enough for me." She needed it right now just to keep her eyes open.

He turned on a light over the bar. "How do you take yours?"

"Cream and sugar." What she'd really like was some good espresso, but the coffee should be decent in a fancy hotel like this. "Do you always rise so early?"

She heard the splash of coffee into the cup. "Yep."

Great. She hoped he didn't expect her to talk in the morning.

Before she could make her legs work, he brought her a mug. "Thanks."

He'd apparently already showered and dressed. His wet hair hung in strings beside his face. The five o'clock shadow was back.

She took a sip. It was good for regular coffee. Strong enough to wake her at least. For the rest, they had cappuccino and lattes at the restaurant. She'd made certain of that before she'd made the reservation.

As she sipped the brew, her mind kicked into gear. She thought about the wedding and Lucas's family. She thought about the media and the articles coming out in today's papers. What would they say?

Then she thought about Bryan. Was he planning to

marry this other woman? Why hadn't she asked who it was? Maybe he'd realize he made a mistake and break up with the mystery woman. Why hadn't Kate told him this marriage with Lucas was temporary? Maybe she and Bryan could still be together someday.

"What's on the agenda today?" Lucas's voice startled her.

She sipped her coffee. "What makes you think there's an agenda?"

He gave her that lazy half smile. "Because you're Kate Lawrence." The smile faltered. "Well. Guess you're not anymore."

She was supposed to be Kate Montgomery. She remembered the way she used to jot her name with her boyfriends' last names when she was a teenager. She'd say the name out loud, testing it on her tongue. She hadn't even thought of her married name with Lucas until the justice pronounced them man and wife. *Kate Wright.* It sounded strange.

Lucas studied her from across the room, and she remembered he'd asked a question. The itinerary. She had it memorized. "We were supposed to go to the beach today, surfside. Bryan wanted to—" Why was she rambling about Bryan? "Anyway, it would give us time to make plans, if you're up for it." He didn't seem like a beach person, but she could be wrong.

He shrugged. "Sure. I'll need to swing by my house and pick up my things first."

He'd need to know what she had planned in order to

pack accordingly. She rattled off the agenda, noting the whaling museum, the day trip to Martha's Vineyard, and the other points of interest she'd planned to take Bryan to.

The more things she listed, the higher Lucas's brows went.

"What?" Kate asked.

"There any room for spontaneity on that list?"

"Spontan—what in the world for?"

His crooked smile was slow. "Tell you what. I'll do everything on your agenda if you'll allow one day of spontaneity."

Kate frowned. What was the point? She'd included everything a person could want from one week on Nantucket. She studied Lucas skeptically. "What would we do?"

His head cocked. "Planning kind of ruins the point."

She sighed. She supposed it was his vacation too. "Oh, all right. One day." Her hollow stomach let out a growl. "I'm starving." She hadn't taken more than two bites at the reception.

"Room service?"

She was ready to sit down to a big, hot breakfast. "I was thinking the restaurant."

He leaned against the back of the sofa, hands in his shorts pockets. "Won't that seem odd?"

Odd? Oh. Newlyweds would still be in bed at this hour. For several more hours, at least. She felt her cheeks grow warm. "Maybe you're right. Will you order something while I grab a shower?"

He gave a mock bow. "Your wish is my command."
Kate refrained from rolling her eyes.

While Kate showered, Lucas called room service and placed their order, then puttered around the room awhile, procrastinating.

He couldn't put it off any longer. The last thing he wanted was for his parents to read about the wedding in the paper before he told them. As it was, it wasn't going to be much fun.

He picked up the phone and dialed his mom's cell. "Hi, honey," his mom greeted him. "Hang on a second. I need to plug in the phone."

A moment later she returned. "Ah, there we go. My battery was about to go, and I didn't want to lose you. Everything okay there?"

"Everything's fine. I just called with some news." He gulped, ambled across the room, and leaned on the armoire. "It might be a little, uh, surprising. Are you sitting down?" It didn't matter if she was. When she heard the news, all the miles between them wouldn't seem like enough.

"I'm in the car, Lucas. What's wrong?"

"Well, you won't believe it, but I—" *Just say it.* "I got married last night."

The silence betrayed her shock. Three seconds dragged by. He heard the clock on the wall ticking them off. Then . . .

"Mar-ried!" His dad said something in the background before his mom spoke again. "Who in the world to? I didn't even know you were dating."

Neither had he. "Well. We kind of kept it under wraps. Low-key." Nonexistent key. *I have to tell her; there's no way to soften the blow.* "It's Kate, Mom. Kate Lawrence."

It sounded like his mom sucked the air from the hotel room through the phone line. But he didn't have to wait long for her to recover. "Kate Lawrence. Kate Lawrence?" She jabbed each syllable at him. "Lucas, how could you?"

"I know. I know, Mom. I knew you'd be upset. That's why I didn't tell you until now."

"You mean until it was too late to do anything about it!"

"There's nothing you could've done about it anyway. I'm a grown man, and I make my own decisions. Especially about whom I marry."

"You didn't even invite us to the wedding." She sucked in another breath. "The wedding! She was supposed to have some big production with the media!" His dad mumbled in the background again. "For heaven's sakes, how did it look that we weren't there? The whole country is going to know we missed our son's wedding!"

"It was actually a small, intimate affair, Mom, and I'm sure—"

"This is awful!"

"I know you're shocked, and I don't expect you to be happy about Kate. But I want you to remember one thing." He waited until she stopped huffing. Then waited two beats beyond that. He needed her to hear what he said, take it to heart.

"I love her, Mom. Regardless of the past—which, incidentally, she's not responsible for—Kate makes me happy."

He could almost hear his mom's frustration, her emotions torn between her unresolved anger and her son's happiness.

The shower in the bathroom kicked off. He wanted to be off the phone before Kate returned.

"Were Brody and Jamie there, at least?" His mom's words sounded as though they'd been squeezed from a lemon.

"They were there. My identity was kept a secret from the media, you know. Nobody knew it was me until last night."

"Well, you could have told us."

His dad's words were muffled. "Let it go, Susan. What's done is done."

Sage advice, but easier said than done, and probably not welcome coming from the man she blamed.

Kate left the foggy bathroom, feeling somewhat refreshed, though still sleepy. She should have asked Lucas to order a latte. She walked into the room, where the breakfast food was set out on the coffee table. Lucas sat in the armchair, waiting to dig into his home fries, over-easy eggs, toast, and stack of crispy bacon. In front of Kate's seat was a plate of fresh melon, granola, and yogurt. Her stomach protested.

She put her dirty clothes in a plastic laundry bag, settled on the couch, and stabbed a berry with her fork, sliding it into her mouth.

"What's wrong?" Lucas loaded his fork with potatoes and took a bite of bacon.

"Nothing." The berries were good. Sweet and juicy. Healthy.

"I didn't know what you liked."

Of course he didn't. It wasn't like they'd dated. He didn't even know how she took her coffee or that she liked to sleep in. "This is fine. It's good." She took a bite of granola to prove it. It was homemade, crunchy and sweet. Just not what she'd been in the mood for.

"Here." Lucas scraped an egg and half his potatoes and bacon onto the plate his toast had been on.

Her mouth watered. "I'm fine, Lucas."

He slid the fruit to the side and pushed the plate in front of her. "Eat up."

They ate quietly, and by the time Kate set her fork down, she'd made up for the meal she'd skipped the day before.

"I went out and got the paper while you were getting ready."

"Which one?"

"The *Mirror* and the *New York Times*." He produced sections of the papers from the coffee table's shelf.

Her insides were an ocean buoy in the wake of a speedboat. "Did you read them? What did they say?"

Oh, please, please.

She grabbed the *Times* first. There they were, her

and Lucas, on the cover of the "Style" section. A photo of them dancing. They were looking into each other's eyes, and the photographer had captured Lucas's smile.

"See for yourself," he said.

Her eyes flitted to the article. Its heading read *"Dr. Kate Marries Mr. Wright."* She smiled. "Clever."

"Thought you'd like that," Lucas said.

She read aloud. " 'Syndicated columnist Kate Lawrence, known to audiences as Dr. Kate, married Nantucket native Lucas Wright in a ceremony last evening on Jetties Beach in Nantucket. The wedding was scheduled to coincide with the release of Dr. Kate's book *Finding Mr. Right-for-You*.

" 'The identity of the groom was kept secret until the ceremony—part of the publicity campaign surrounding the book's release.

" 'Lawrence said she met her Mr. Wright when she rented the space above his furniture shop in Nantucket Town. "He renovated my apartment and my office. Then I guess he renovated my heart." ' "

Kate glanced at Lucas, her face warming.

His lip quirked. "I had no idea," he said.

"Dream on." Kate went back to the article.

" 'Lucas Wright is a furniture maker, known locally by wealthy vacationers who summer on the island. When asked about their future plans, Lawrence said, "We plan to stay in Nantucket, of course. It's our home."

" '*Finding Mr. Right-for-You* is Dr. Kate's first book.

She will appear on the *Dr. Phil* show later this summer, and she plans to continue her column while she works on her second book.' "

Kate put the paper down. "It's all good," she said in wonder. *We did it.* They'd pulled it off—at least, if the *Times* was any indication. "What does the *Mirror* say?" She picked up the next section. The photograph was a close-up of them in the carriage, waving good-bye, the tulle of her veil blowing to the side. It had much of the same information as the *Times*, though presented with a more local approach.

When she was finished, she picked up the *Times* again, noticing the way the paper trembled in her fingers. "Rosewood will be thrilled. I can't believe how relieved I am." Relieved wasn't the word. If she'd gone through with the wedding only to be found out, it would've done more damage than being jilted.

"Did we cover all our bases?" she asked. "We have to be sure those who know aren't going to say anything."

"I told Mr. Lavitz when he fitted me for the tux about the need for discretion. He's an old friend—I know he won't say anything. And you know Nancy and the justice will keep quiet. They're town officers. They know how to be discreet."

"Pam and Chloe and Anna won't say anything. My dad's a given. Who else knows?"

"Bryan's family," he said.

It was the biggest risk of a leak. Had Bryan told them? Kate chewed on her lip. What if one of them read an article and told a friend or two the wedding was a farce? What if they contacted the media?

"Maybe you should call him and make sure." Lucas leaned forward, planting his elbows on his knees, bracing his coffee cup between his palms.

Kate had been thinking it herself, but dreading it all at the same time. It hurt to think about Bryan. She'd been up half the night thinking about him, about how he was supposed to be in bed beside her. *This was supposed to be the beginning of our life together.*

Suck it up, Kate, and move on. You've done it before, and you can do it again. She'd made a lot of sacrifices along the way, and she wasn't giving up now.

"You're right." Her watch said it was just after eight. Late enough to call. *What, am I worried about waking the man?* She should have called him in the middle of the night. He'd kept her awake, after all. It would've served him right.

"Why don't I go home and get my things while you make the call?"

Kate nodded, wondering what to say to Bryan. "What about your parents? You need to call them before they see the papers."

Lucas folded the paper and stood. "Already did, while you were in the shower."

"What did they say?"

Lucas shrugged. "They were shocked, naturally. I told them we'd kept it low-key because of the media."

"Weren't they angry they weren't here for the wedding?"

"Disappointed. They were glad Brody and Jamie were there."

Kate tucked her damp hair behind her ears. "Oh, good. Well, I guess we'll have to make it up to them when they return."

Lucas left, and Kate retrieved her cell phone. She dialed Bryan's number, her heart drumming a syncopated beat.

The phone rang twice before a woman answered. "Hello?"

Kate's words clogged her throat. She was there? In his apartment? In the apartment that was supposed to be *theirs*?

"Hello?" the woman repeated.

Kate took the phone from her ear and started to hang up.

But she had to talk to Bryan, had to make sure he'd spoken with his family. She put the phone back to her ear and heard shuffling sounds, then Bryan's voice.

"Hello?" His voice was morning scratched.

Kate clamped her teeth together. Were they in bed together? What had happened to their agreement to save themselves for marriage? Apparently it had only been Kate's conviction.

"Kate?"

"Yes, it's Kate. I can't believe she's there with you. For heaven's sake, Bryan, we were supposed to get married yesterday."

She heard a rustling noise—sheets? "Excuse me if

I'm wrong, but didn't you just spend the night with your new husband?"

His comment made her skin tingle, made the flesh under her arms go hot. "After you deserted me on our wedding day!"

"What do you even know about him, Kate?"

"What do you care?" She stood and paced the length of the room. What was she doing? She had to settle down. It would accomplish nothing to have Bryan angry at her. "I didn't call to argue. I called to make sure you'd talked to your family. Did you make them understand how important it is that they keep their mouths shut?" She could've worded it more nicely, but he wasn't exactly on her favorite-people list right now.

"I talked to them. I told you I would." His voice was tight.

What did he have to be angry about when he had another woman there in bed with him? While she'd been crying over him in their honeymoon bed, he'd been—She closed her eyes and shook her head to dislodge the image. She couldn't bear the thought of it right now.

"My career is riding on this, you know," she said. "Do they understand the magnitude of—"

"Yes, yes, they understand. Do you think I want to be in the spotlight as the jerk who jilted Dr. Kate at the altar?"

"Well said."

The silence was deafening. She should hold her

tongue; she really should. She was a counselor, for crying out loud. Where was her control?

"I'll let you go." Perhaps he'd get the double meaning. "I just wanted to be sure things were taken care of."

She hung up before she said something she'd regret later. When she set the phone on the coffee table, she realized her hand was shaking.

Bryan was in bed with her. Kate's Mr. Right in bed with someone else on what was supposed to have been their wedding night. Could life be more unfair?

At least he'd made his family understand the importance of keeping quiet. That was the main thing. And the articles were positive. *Look on the bright side. I'm going to live through this and come out stronger.* The year with Lucas would pass quickly, and then she could get on with her life and career.

She realized she hadn't told Bryan the marriage was temporary, but given the situation, she didn't want to give him the satisfaction. Let him think she would be bound to Lucas for the rest of her life. Maybe it would make him squirm just a little.

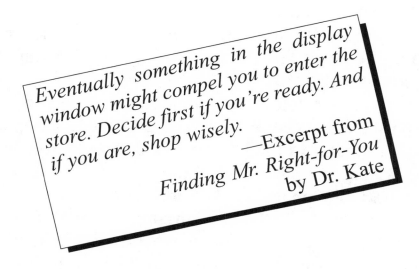

Chapter Seven

Kate shrugged off her cover-up, took her list from the tote, and lay belly down on the beach towel beside Lucas. She squinted against the sun's reflection on the bright white paper.

"Okay, we need a story. We already told people how we met, but I think we need more details to make it realistic. Your family will probably want to know what we do together. They'll expect us to know things about each other."

"I know you take your coffee with cream and sugar." Lucas leaned back on his elbows a foot away from her. The wind blew his hair away from his face.

"But you don't know that I drink a triple-shot latte every day before work. Or that I prefer showers to baths. Or that I'm allergic to cats."

"Hope you're not allergic to dogs."

"Do you have one?"

He lay back against the towel, folding his arms behind his head, his eyes closed against the sun. "A sheepdog named Bo. You'll love him."

She wasn't much of an animal person, but she supposed she could deal with one dog. Wasn't a sheepdog like a miniature Lassie? She could deal with a little dog as long as he was well trained.

"Found him alongside Milestone Road when he was a pup," Lucas said. "He was missing a bunch of fur on his neck, and I couldn't find his owner, so I kept him."

She jotted down the information. *Sheepdog, Bo.*

"What else should I know about you?" she asked.

She watched his chest rise and fall, glistening under the glare of the sun. His skin was dark, his chest well defined. She wondered if he worked out or if the muscles came from his work.

Stop staring! She sneaked a glance at his face to be sure she hadn't been caught looking. He'd probably think she was checking him out. Which she hadn't been.

Well, not too much.

"I like to sail, watch documentaries on TV, and fix anything broken."

Kate scribbled more notes. "Anything else?"

A muscle twitched in his jaw. "I was married before. I guess you need to know that."

How had she not known? "What happened?"

His eyelids fluttered, and he swallowed, then shifted, clasping his hands together on his flat abdomen.

"Sorry if I'm prying, but—" His family would expect her to know. She wondered if his ex-wife lived on the island. Maybe Kate knew her.

"Her name was Emily. She died five years ago."

Oh.

She studied him. His tone was so soft, it obviously still affected him. Did he still love her? Maybe that's why she hadn't seen him with another woman.

"I'm sorry," she said.

"Her family used to summer here. I met her when she came to the shop for a rocking chair. The business was getting off the ground, and we started dating. The rest was history."

Kate waited for him to finish. The only sounds were that of the waves crashing the shoreline and the laughter of children playing in the shallows. "Is that when you built your house?"

He crossed his ankles. His legs were long and thick, covered in wiry black hair. "No. We lived in a cottage in Cisco after we married. I didn't build my house until . . . until after."

She didn't have to ask "After what?" It was still painful for him to talk about. Kate wondered why he'd married her. Given the way he obviously still felt about Emily, he had to care a great deal about his parents to be willing to sacrifice a year of his life to save their marriage.

She hated to grill him, but she'd be expected to know. She set the pen on the towel and propped her head on her palm. "How did she . . . die?"

She didn't think he was going to answer. She wasn't even sure he'd heard her softly spoken question over the seagulls' cries. But after a moment he sighed.

"It was my fault. Guess that's why it's still hard to talk about."

What did he mean? She wanted to ask, wanted to know the details. Even though Lucas irritated her, he wasn't the type to harm anyone. In fact, he was always helping people. In his own time, but helping them nonetheless.

"She had allergies—lots of them. The environmental ones like pollens were easily controlled with medication, so it wasn't a big deal." He shifted. "She'd tested allergic to peanuts as a teenager, but she'd never had a reaction. She avoided them, though, because her doctor told her to."

Two teenagers behind them tossed a Frisbee, and it sailed over them and landed a few feet away, flicking up the sand. Lucas waited while they retrieved it.

"The week she died, I'd done the grocery shopping. I bought a bag of chips that were fried in peanut oil." He shook his head. "Didn't even think about checking the ingredients. I used to tease her about being overly cautious."

Kate's heart went out to him. Couldn't he see it was an accident?

"I'd been at the shop working on an order I was running behind on, and when I came home . . . it was too late."

She watched his face, the way his jaw clenched, the

way his lips tightened. She wished she could console him somehow. "I'm so sorry."

His chest rose and fell. "It was a long time ago."

Five years wasn't that long. He'd been married to the love of his life and now he was sitting on the beach with his counterfeit bride. She wondered how he felt about that.

He turned and opened his eyes, squinting against the glare of the sun. "So that's my story. What's yours?"

She appreciated his desire to change the subject. "What do you want to know?"

Lucas watched Kate turn her head until her cheek rested in her hand. She looked like a little girl, her sun-flushed cheeks bunched up against her palm. He already knew more about her than she was aware. She was twenty-eight, her favorite flowers were daisies, her birthday was November 26, and she color-coded her Day-Timer.

He went for the unknown. "How did you become an advice columnist?"

She smiled. "Friends in high school always came to me for advice, and I was good at giving it." Kate shrugged. "I started on my life plan my junior year in high—"

"Life plan?"

"A plan detailing my short- and long-term goals." She said it as if everyone had one. "Anyway, I realized I had a knack for helping people with relationship decisions. Then I took a fabulous writing class in high school and started my first manuscript." She cocked her head. "It was bad, but I didn't know it at the time. However, I realized I wanted to combine my love for helping people with my love of writing."

"You had all this planned out before high school graduation?"

She flipped onto her side. "Sure. I knew I wanted to get a psych degree from Cornell and go into counseling so I could support myself and gain experience while getting my writing career started."

"You were born on Nantucket, right? Is that why you're here now?"

"My parents grew up here, and, yes, I was born here. We moved to Maryland when I was five because my dad got relocated. Then, when I was in college, a friend invited me here for a week to stay in her parents' cottage in 'Sconset. What can I say? It felt like coming back home."

"So you added Nantucket to your life plan?"

"Are you making fun of me?"

How could he criticize when she'd met all her goals? Except he was sure marrying him hadn't been on that list of hers. "What about the column?"

She stuck her knee out to the side, and he worked to keep his eyes away from the smooth curve of her hips. "I started it at Cornell for the school newspaper. At first I wrote my own questions; then students began writing me, and it all took off from there."

Apparently she set her mind to something and made it happen by sheer will. "Ambitious one, aren't you?"

A wind tousled her fringed bangs. "I like helping

people. Initially in my practice I focused on couples with marriage problems."

"You seemed to build up a decent clientele." He was in his shop enough to see clients passing up and down the stairs on the hour.

"The more I counseled married people, the more I began to see that people were making poor choices in the spouses they selected. They'd come to me, polar opposites, wanting different things out of life, and wonder why they couldn't get along. I started putting together a plan to help people make better choices about who they marry."

She made it sound like it could be boiled down to cold, hard facts. "What about love?"

"Well, of course, there has to be love. But by choosing to date the right people, you limit yourself to those who are best suited to you."

He turned on his side, mirroring her position. "How do you know if they're suited to you until you know them? And once you know them that well, aren't you likely to have fallen in love with them already?"

Her breath huffed out. "What is this, an inquisition?" She rolled onto her back, propping her head on her bag, and closed her eyes. "My plan is detailed and well thought out. If you want to know more, read the stinking book."

She'd gotten snippy in a hurry. Maybe she felt defensive since her fail-proof plan hadn't turned out to be so fail proof.

Which reminded him of her ex-fiancé. Lucas wanted

to ask if she'd called him, but judging by her set little chin, maybe now wasn't the time.

Something at the corner of his vision caught his attention. A man in dress clothes sat on the sand down the shore, holding a camera with a zoom lens. He looked as out of place as a diamond in a toolbox.

Lucas looked at Kate. "I think we have company."

She didn't bother opening her eyes. "Who?"

"One of the photographers from the wedding. Down the shore a ways."

She opened her eyes.

"Don't look."

Kate looked at Lucas instead. "Is he looking this way? Does he have a camera?"

"Yes and yes."

"Which one is he?"

"I don't remember. He was at the wedding, though. The one with spiky hair and artsy glasses."

She sighed. "He's from *Cosmo*. I guess they wanted some honeymoon shots for the article."

"They could've asked instead of sneaking around like the paparazzi."

"They can't. I made it clear to my agent the honeymoon was off limits. Did he see you looking?"

"No. But he has a zoom lens that can probably see the amber flecks in your eyes from a hundred feet."

She tucked her hair behind her ears. "Great. I guess we haven't exactly looked like newlyweds, have we?"

He rolled on his stomach next to her, their sides brushing. Her skin was warm, and the feel of her smooth skin against his leg stoked a fire in his belly. "We could consider that our first fight."

"Wasn't much of one." She smiled.

She was probably thinking they made a much better photo now, lying so close and gazing into each other's eyes. But all Lucas could think about was what her sun-warmed lips would taste like. The wedding kiss seemed like a distant memory and Kate had been shell-shocked. What would a slow, lingering kiss feel like here on the beach, under the sun with the salted breeze stroking their skin?

"Why are you looking at me like that?"

Because I want to pull you in my arms and give that man a lensful. "We're honeymooners, remember?"

She pulled her lip between her teeth. "Oh. Right. And we just had our first tiff. Maybe we should kiss and make up."

With the sun shining into her face, her eyes ran more toward rich brown than olive. Like melted caramel. "It's a thought," he said.

"Okay, go ahead." She tilted toward him. Her eyes skimmed his face and fell on his lips.

He grinned, leaning over her until his shadow blocked the sun from her face. "I have permission now, huh?"

She touched his jaw. "What?"

"Are you sure it's on the list for today?" he teased.

She twitched her eyebrow. "You sure know how to ruin the mood." Was her voice a little breathy?

"There was a mood?" Before she could answer, he

closed the space between them and kissed her slowly, reveling in the way she reciprocated. His hand settled on her side where her silky bathing suit clung to the curve of her waist.

For a moment he let himself forget she was only responding for the camera. He remembered every time he'd seen her leaving her office, every time he watched her walk down the sidewalk, hair swishing with each step. Every time she knocked on his shop door late at night to complain about the noise.

All those times I wanted to grab her and kiss the living daylights out of her.

Kate pulled away from him, breaking his thoughts. "There. He should've gotten plenty of good photos."

The cold wave of her words doused the mood. Trying for nonchalance, he turned onto his back and closed his eyes, hoping she couldn't see his heart thundering against his chest wall. He'd wanted the kiss to be more than show. He wanted it to be real.

You got yourself into this, man.

"Is he still there?" she asked.

They'd only started playing the game, and already he'd tired of it. "I don't know." And he wasn't going to look.

"I guess we shouldn't look."

He felt her hand, delicate against his own.

She's just pretending. Don't forget that.

"Let's talk about your parents. I need to know any-thing that will help me understand their problems."

Lucas was tired of the whole thing. Right now he

wanted to blurt out that his parents didn't have a problem, that he'd married her because he loved her. But that would only scare her away.

He swallowed. "I'm not sure what's wrong between them. They just fuss a lot."

"You said your mom left for a while. Did they have a fight?"

This was going to be harder than he thought. "I don't know. I really don't know what the problem is. That's why I need your help."

Her fingers intertwined with his, and he felt the wedding band.

"Don't you feel you can talk openly with your parents?"

He cringed. He was getting himself in deeper and deeper. "I'm not a talker—you know that much about me." The seagulls cried out, and another wave hit the shore. "I'm just not good with words, and I don't think they'd want me interfering anyway."

He needed to make sure Kate was subtle with his mom. Otherwise Kate would find out it was all a ruse. "You'll need to get to know my mom before expecting her to open up." *Good luck with that.* He couldn't imagine anyone his mom would be less likely open up to.

An instant later panic struck. What if his mom confronted Kate about her mom? No. As soon as the panic hit, it evaporated. His mom didn't confront people. She killed silently with subtle digs and innuendos, God love her.

"That goes without saying."

"And leave Jamie and Brody out of it. I don't want them stressing about our parents." Or setting Kate straight about their fussing.

"If they live with your parents, they know what's going on. Even young children pick up on conflict. It affects them more deeply than you realize."

Her voice held a tone of sadness. He looked at her, but she turned onto her back, withdrawing her hand, and closed her own eyes. Lucas had a feeling there was a load of hurt backing up that statement, and he wondered if Kate would ever trust him enough to share it.

Lucas took Kate's hand as they climbed the steps of the White Elephant. The week had passed quickly. It was hard to believe tomorrow it would be over. His Spontaneity Day with Kate had proved to be a challenge. She seemed unacquainted with the idea of letting things happen and had spent most of the day trying to figure out what they were doing next.

Now, she looked tired and sun drained, her cheeks reddened from their walk through 'Sconset. Maybe he'd order room service so she wouldn't have to go back out for dinner.

They entered the lobby floor and passed the registration desk. Kate stopped suddenly by a woman at the desk, withdrawing her hand from his.

"Mrs. Hornsby?" Kate touched the woman on the shoulder, and she turned. The woman might have been attractive if not for her puffy eyes and tight, bronzed lips.

"Dr. Kate." Mrs. Hornsby straightened and turned her lips into a semblance of a smile.

"Are you okay?" Kate asked.

Lucas stepped away to give them privacy, inspecting some literature on the desk. He couldn't help but hear their conversation.

"I'm fine." The woman said, but her words crumbled like a soggy cookie.

Kate took her arm and pulled her away from the desk. "What are you doing here? Did something happen?"

Lucas heard the woman restrain a sob. "Earl is having an affair. I have proof this time. I just—just couldn't stay there."

"I'm so sorry." Kate's tone softened. She rubbed the woman's arm. "Do you want to talk?"

Mrs. Hornsby laughed feebly, wiping her eyes. "Oh, honey, no. It's your honeymoon. Besides, you're not even counseling anymore." She withdrew a tissue from her beige purse and dabbed her eyes. "I'll be fine."

"Don't be silly," Kate said. "Are you finished checking in?"

The other woman held up a key card. "Yes."

Kate squeezed her rounded shoulder. "I'll be right back."

She approached Lucas, and he put the brochure for a whaling tour back into the holder.

"Would you mind having dinner alone?" Kate asked, then lowered her tone. "She's a former client, and she could use someone to talk to."

"Of course not," Lucas said. "Want me to order you something from room service?"

"Thanks, but I'm not sure how long I'll be."

A moment later, Lucas was alone.

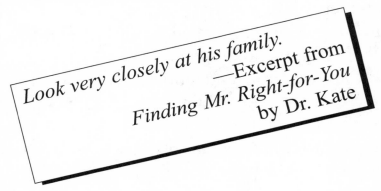

Look very closely at his family.
—Excerpt from
Finding Mr. Right-for-You
by Dr. Kate

Chapter Eight

"Start slowing down," Lucas said. "That's it. The one with the truck out front."

Kate navigated her car down the street. It ran parallel to the shore and was lined on both sides by cottages, generously separated by wide grassy lots.

Kate braked and eased into the drive, the tires slurping through the thick layer of gravel. Lucas's house sat off the road about a hundred yards, and behind it, the ocean provided a deep blue backdrop. The nearest house on his side of the street was a couple hundred yards away, the second story barely visible above a rise in the ground.

Kate stopped behind a beater Ford in the drive. *I married a pickup man.*

That thought was barely out before she surveyed the cottage. Instinctively she liked its character. Gray, weathered shingles covered the small cottage. The trim and porch railing sported bright white paint, and orange flowers of some kind lined the front beds.

She put her car into Park and slid out. "It's nice." Small, but new. There appeared to be a main part of the house and a small addition of some sort.

She popped the trunk and had just grabbed a bag when she heard a shout.

"Welcome home!"

Four people scampered down the hill from the house next door. She recognized Brody and Jamie. The other two must be Lucas's parents. A huge, hairy dog led the pack, and Mrs. Wright trailed the others by several yards, her slender body stiff, her arms stagnant at her sides.

Kate waved and smiled for their benefit. "What is your family doing here?" She wanted to get settled in the house. She was tired of being on public display. The photographer had left them alone after that first day at the beach, but even eating out they'd encountered stares and whispers.

"They live next door," Lucas said. "Didn't I tell you?"

Next door? Maintaining her smile was no easy feat. "You neglected to mention that detail." He was going to get an earful later.

"Hey, guys," Lucas called as his family approached. The dog leaped on Lucas. It was the size of a bear.

"Hey, Bo." He ruffled the animal's floppy ears.

That is not Bo. She considered the size of the house and the size of the dog. What was he thinking? She nearly expressed her thoughts, then remembered his family would find it odd she hadn't seen Bo before. They probably wondered how they hadn't seen her there before, living right next door like they did.

Roy Wright approached first, wearing jeans, a Nantucket polo, and a genuine smile. "Welcome, welcome." He hugged Kate first, patting her shoulder as if to burp her. He had a thick head of gray hair and a tan that leathered his skin. His clear green eyes angled downward at the sides.

"Thank you," Kate said. Her eyes met Susan Wright's as the woman came to a stop at the edge of the gravel driveway. "Hello."

Susan nodded, her rose-colored lips pulled back into what didn't quite pass as a smile. "Kate." Her mushroom-shaped hairstyle framed her narrow face and high cheekbones.

"I wanted to get some pictures." Jamie held up the camera that was around her neck. Her smile revealed braces with purple and pink bands. "Did you have a wonderful week?"

Kate felt like she was trapped in a *Raymond* episode. In real life the situation wasn't so amusing.

"It was perfect," she said as Lucas embraced his

mom. Brody shook her hand, an apology in his eyes, if not on his lips.

What kind of man built a house next door to his parents? Apparently she'd not only married a pickup man, but a momma's boy as well.

Lucas and his parents caught up briefly before Lucas asked them inside.

"No, we're not staying," Susan said pointedly. "Are we, Roy?" She set a fine-boned hand on her husband's arm.

"Of course not; we just wanted to welcome you home, welcome Kate to the family."

"And take a picture of Lucas carrying Kate over the threshold," Jamie said.

Kate had forgotten about the tradition. A stupid tradition. She didn't want to be cast into the helpless maiden role. "How thoughtful." She was tired of smiling. She didn't want to smile for the next week.

"Don't pressure them, Jamie." Susan eyed Kate up and down. "Besides, Lucas might not be up to it."

Score one for the mother-in-law. Kate smiled through clenched teeth.

"No doubt," Brody whispered to Lucas, wearing a sly smile. "Bet you're exhausted."

Lucas elbowed his brother. "Far be it from me to deny tradition."

"Pick her up, Lucas!" Jamie said. "This is so romantic." She clapped her hands.

"Scrubbing the floor would be romantic to you," Brody said.

"Shut up." Jamie whacked him in the gut with the back of her hand while Bo barked loudly and circled around them as if sensing the excitement.

"I'll get your bags," Brody said, walking toward the trunk.

Before Kate could move, Lucas swept her off her feet. She grabbed him around the neck, latching onto his shoulders as he walked toward the cottage and up the three steps. The camera clicked several times.

"You could have warned me," Kate whispered in his ear. First the next-door in-laws, then the big hairy dog, and now another photo op? Who'd started this dumb tradition anyway? She felt like a worthless sack of beans in his arms.

"Just sit back and enjoy, Mrs. Wright." His breath hit her cheek.

Another photo snapped. "Don't call me that."

He shifted her and pulled open the screen door, then twisted the knob on the wooden door. She should probably help, but wasn't in the mood. She heard yet another click as Bo brushed by, squeezing his enormous mass past them.

Kate clenched her jaw. *Please let this end!*

"That's enough, Jamie," Susan said. "For heaven's sake."

Once inside, Lucas set Kate down and she stepped away, relieved to be on her own feet again. Brody had followed and now handed Lucas their luggage. They stood awkwardly for a moment, Brody looking from one to the other with a grin.

"Well, guess you two love birds want to be alone."

Lucas looked at Kate. "Guess so." Kate refrained from responding.

Brody hugged Lucas exuberantly and, after a slight hesitation, did the same for Kate. He clattered down the steps to his waiting family.

" 'Bye, kids!" Roy waved.

"I'll print these out soon and bring them by," Jamie said, holding up the camera.

Susan merely nodded and turned back toward her house.

"Thanks," Kate called.

She stood watching her new in-laws through the screen door as they made their way back up the hill, Brody and Jamie arguing the whole time. Then she turned and narrowed her eyes at Lucas. "You are so dead."

Before he could respond something caught her eye. Her gaze left him to scan the room. "What in the world . . . is all this . . . stuff!"

She stared in horrified amazement at piles and stacks and layers of stuff. Clothes, boxes, magazines . . . The phrase "Early-American Junkyard" came to mind. Was that a shovel leaning against the TV? And what was that smell?

And through it all, Bo wove in and out, his enormous backside wagging. The dog hit a leaning tower of newspapers, and it toppled.

Lucas is a messie. She'd married a messie.

"Sorry about that." Lucas kicked a sack aside and

closed the front door. "Didn't have time to clean up before the ceremony."

There had been clues on the honeymoon. Socks balled up and left lying on the floor, toiletries spread across the marble counter, wet towels left on the couch.

But this . . .

She felt trapped, and she wasn't even a claustrophobic. What was the floor even made of? She could hardly see it through the stuff. Anna could have warned her, for heaven's sake.

Bo bumped up against her, knocking her sideways. Lucas steadied her. "No, Bo. Come here." He rubbed the dog's head and Bo sat. "Settle down, boy."

Kate picked up her bag. Maybe the whole house wasn't like this. "Where can I put my things?"

Lucas grabbed a few articles of clothing from the back of the sofa and draped them over his shoulder. "Let me show you around."

Bo was up again, circling them, panting happily. Kate glared at him and then at Lucas. Lucas appeared to get the idea.

"Come on, buddy." He let Bo out the front door, where the dog sat facing the screen and barking. "He's just a little excited."

Scooping up a Pepsi can and an empty bowl with a sticky-looking spoon, Lucas led the way down a short hall.

"This is the bedroom."

Bed unmade, clothes heaped on the dresser.

"Yours?"

He opened a dresser drawer, shoved the clothes from the living room inside, and pushed it closed. "Uh, yeah. You can put your bag here." He pushed the heap of clothes to the other side of the dresser, having the grace to look sheepish. "I'll make room in the drawers and closet for your things."

"I was planning on taking another bedroom." *Hopefully a cleaner one.*

He set down the can and bowl and took her suitcase, setting it on the dresser. "I'm afraid this is it."

Kate let this sink in as she watched him attempt to make the bed. He pulled the blue quilt up over the pillows, leaving the sheets in a wad underneath. " 'This is it'? What do you mean?"

He pocketed his hands. "There is no other bedroom."

This was getting worse by the minute. "You built a house with one bedroom?"

He lifted his shoulders. "There's only one of me."

How could he be so casual? So indifferent? Wasn't he at all concerned about his space? "Well, now there's two of us, in case you haven't noticed."

One side of his mouth turned up. "I noticed."

"Who builds a home with one bedroom?" And who was going to sleep on the couch? For a whole year.

"I was planning to add on later."

Well, there you go. The answer to their dilemma. How long could it take to build a bedroom? He could add a room on the other side of the house by the living room.

"Uh-uh," he said, watching her face. "Do you know what my family will think if I add another bedroom?"

That they were sleeping separately? Or no—that they were planning to start a family. Why else would they need another bedroom? Jamie would probably start knitting baby blankets and booties. Strike that idea.

"Look. We're grown adults," Lucas said. "The bed's a double, plenty big enough for both of us."

She looked him over. He was easily six feet, maybe an inch or two more, and he was broad. He'd make the bed feel like a twin. The thought of sleeping so close to him left her feeling hot and itchy.

She cleared her throat. "I'll just take the couch." She took the handle of her luggage.

He set his palm flat on the suitcase. "Don't be ridiculous. You can't sleep on the couch for twelve months."

"Sure I can." Especially if he wasn't going to offer. She pulled at the suitcase, but it went nowhere under his grip. "Let go."

"What'll my family think?"

"They won't think anything. They won't even know." She would put her blanket and pillow away first thing every morning. She supposed she'd have to keep her clothing in the bedroom, though.

"You turn in early, Kate. I'm a night owl."

She hadn't thought of that. How could she fall asleep on the sofa if he was watching TV until midnight? She checked the bed out, wavering.

Lucas leaned against the dresser and crossed his arms over his chest, looking smug. "You afraid or something?"

Kate crossed her own arms. "Don't be ridiculous."

"I'm not the one getting all hot and bothered about sharing a bed."

"I'm not—" She ground her teeth and smothered a growl. Why did he have to say things like that? It was like he took pleasure in getting under her skin.

It's just a sleeping arrangement, nothing more. What am I so afraid of? It'll be like sharing a bed with a friend on a girls' outing. Her eyes swept over Lucas's solid frame, down to his hairy legs and sandal-clad feet. She swallowed hard. *Okay, not quite like that.*

I don't have to . . . do anything in that bed except sleep. In fact, I'll be asleep by the time he comes to bed anyway. And he rises before me. I'll hardly notice he's there.

Resolved, she met his eyes square on. "Fine. We'll share the room."

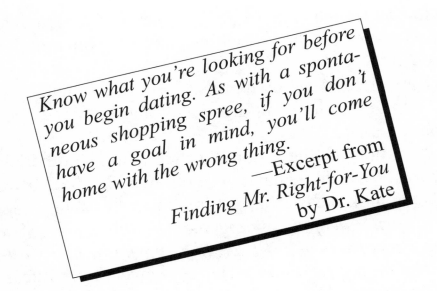

Chapter Nine

It was dark by the time they unloaded Kate's belongings in the cottage. She plugged in her treadmill, which they'd squeezed into a corner of the living room. From here she had a good view out the front window and could watch the news too.

As she contemplated her surroundings, Bo brushed against Kate's legs as if trying to guide her toward the sofa.

"He wants you to sit down and pet him," Lucas said.

"Why is his fur discolored under his mouth?"

Lucas rubbed Bo behind the ears. "Drool yellows the fur." He disappeared into the kitchen, Bo plodding behind him.

Kate grimaced. *I had to ask.*

She turned on the treadmill, making sure it worked,

then straightened the square pillows on the couch. She'd tried to tidy up a bit, and now that the floor was clutter free, she saw the nice rug that covered the oak floors. Too bad it was covered in dog hair.

Bo ambled back and plopped down by the fireplace, watching her, his huge, shaggy head cocked. His white hair hung like a dirty mop over his eyes. At least he didn't smell.

"You didn't tell me Bo was so big," Kate called.

"He's a sheepdog," Lucas called from the kitchen, as if that explained it.

"I thought that was like a miniature Lassie. I wasn't expecting a"—there was no call to be rude—"a large dog." Kate stepped past Bo and surveyed the room. Even clean, it felt tiny. The treadmill looked mammoth against the sand-colored wall.

"That's a Shetland sheepdog. He's an Old English sheepdog." Lucas was in the kitchen doorway, two steps away. He extended a cut-glass vase filled with white daisies. "These are for you."

Kate didn't know what to say. "What for?"

He rubbed the back of his neck. "Our one-week anniversary." Was that a flush climbing his cheeks? "It's silly."

The gesture took her aback. "No, it's very . . . sweet." The petals were satin smooth, the stems and leaves clean and groomed. She wondered where he'd gotten them. And when; they'd been together most of the day. "Daisies are my favorite."

"I know."

Kate was sure she hadn't mentioned it on their honeymoon. Even Bryan had always sent orchids for special occasions just because they were most expensive.

Lucas gestured toward the flowers. "You always have them on your desk at work."

She stopped at Flowers on Chestnut for a fresh bouquet every Monday morning after getting her latte. Having fresh daisies perked up the office and inspired her. Strange that he'd noticed. She remembered the daisies he'd etched on the gazebo. She'd thought it a coincidence.

"Well, thank you," she said. "I'll set them on the kitchen table between the salt and pepper shakers."

"I'll do it."

As he returned, Kate yawned. It was getting late, and there was no delaying bedtime. Besides, if she hoped to be asleep when Lucas retired, she needed an early start.

"I think I'll turn in now," she said.

Lucas sank into the recliner and flipped on the TV. Bo curled up at his feet. " 'Night. Let me know if you need anything."

Kate stood awkwardly for a moment, but it looked as if Lucas was engrossed in what he was watching. *Well, okay then.*

After completing her beauty regimen and brushing and flossing, Kate changed into her pajamas. She surveyed the bed and felt something cold wedge between her ribs.

I can do this. I can. No big deal. She snorted at the

thought. *Yeah, right. I'm about to climb into the bed of a man I barely know. And he's going to climb in later.*

Her eyes fell on a worn quilt crumpled between the bed and wall. She retrieved it, spread it across the bed, then rolled it like a giant burrito. Next, she laid it down the center of the bed as a barrier between the two sides. *There, that should do it.*

Kate clicked off Lucas's lamp and rounded the bed, settling on her side. The sheets were soft and cool against her skin, the mattress giving slightly to her weight.

She turned her face into the pillow and immediately regretted it. It smelled faintly of Lucas, all musk and woodsy. Even here, she couldn't escape him.

She thought of the daisies and chided herself for thinking ill of him. He was trying. It wasn't his fault they were so different. Or even that they were stuck together for a year. In fact, he'd saved her life, and she should be grateful. He'd salvaged her book and her career.

She'd called Pam twice from the White Elephant, and Rosewood was thrilled with the wedding publicity. Several cable network shows wanted Kate to make an appearance. Rosewood was talking about a possible book tour, and Pam had scheduled numerous phone interviews with radio shows and newspapers. Kate wondered how she'd keep up with her articles and find time to write another book.

No matter, though. If the publicity sold book one, it would be worth it. And at least she would still have her office space to work in since Lucas hadn't rented it out yet.

She thought of Lucas's family and wondered how she was going to find time to help his parents' marriage. She'd sensed the tension between Susan and Roy. Maybe she could find an activity to do with Susan. It would give them time to talk.

Kate turned and pulled the quilt over her chilled shoulder. It was quieter here than in town. If she listened closely, she could hear the water hitting the shore, and a clock ticking somewhere. The TV program Lucas was watching barely filtered into the room, and a slit of light from the living room underlined the door.

What time would he retire? She hoped he kept to his own side of the bed. Judging by the rumpled sheets she'd found upon her arrival, she had her doubts. He was used to having the whole bed.

Kate was too, but she planned on hugging the edge all night.

If I ever fall asleep. She rolled over again and resituated the pillow. She'd already made a to-do list for tomorrow, which usually freed her mind to sleep. She was tired, so that wasn't the issue.

As it had all week during quiet moments, her thoughts turned to Bryan. Kate hadn't called him again, nor had he called. She supposed there was no reason to expect him to. She shouldn't even want him to.

But feelings didn't flip off like a light switch. She

wondered if he'd seen the photo and article in the *New York Times*. Part of her regretted not telling him her marriage was temporary. The other part hoped it sowed seeds of jealousy.

He's not jealous; he's with another woman. I'm the one who's jealous.

She didn't want to dwell on it anymore. The sound of the woman's voice when she'd answered the phone, the rustling of covers before Bryan spoke. It was torturous.

Think about something else.

Kate turned her thoughts to her book and upcoming *Dr. Phil* appearance. Ten seconds later, she was thinking of the daisies on the kitchen table. *Ah, we've come full circle.*

And I'm still awake.

Kate was about to shift when the door opened. She lay still, not daring to open her eyes. She heard the whoosh of something dropping to the floor. Then another whoosh.

He was *not* undressing!

Seconds later, the mattress sagged under his weight. The force of it nearly pulled her to the center, but she braced herself on the edge. The bed shimmied, and the covers shifted as he slid under them. His foot brushed hers, and she fought the urge to pull away. How had it gotten past the barrier?

Breathe deeply. I'm asleep.

When he finally stilled, the only sound was the ticking clock and the waves. And her own breath. She could even hear her heart. Her arm, pushed under her pillow, ached, but she didn't move. How awkward would it be if he realized she was awake and started a conversation? What was he wearing over there, anyway? She was afraid to know.

Kate opened her eyes and stared at the big lump beside her. He was facing the other way, and already his breathing had evened out. Not fair. How long would she lie awake? Why couldn't she go to sleep?

She tried to think about her book, about next week's article, about anything other than the very male body inches away. Her skin prickled with heat, and she wished she could throw off the covers.

A few minutes later, a quick snort pierced the silence. Three seconds later a long grating snore sounded.

And he's off to the races.

Kate closed her eyes on a sigh.

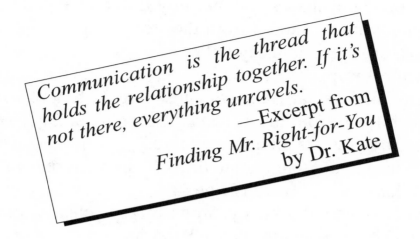

Communication is the thread that holds the relationship together. If it's not there, everything unravels.

—Excerpt from *Finding Mr. Right-for-You* by Dr. Kate

Chapter Ten

Lucas pushed open his parents' door, and Kate entered the bright two-story cottage. She could only hope his family didn't enter his house as freely. They were seventeen minutes late—a fact that didn't seem to bother Lucas at all. How a man could be late when he'd done nothing but piddle around all morning, Kate had no clue.

Inside the door, an oval braided rug covered aged wooden planks, and daylight poured in from the transom over the door. Voices and clattering pans sounded from the back of the house, and the smell of fried chicken beckoned.

"We're here," Lucas called, shutting the door.

Jamie scurried into the cozy foyer and hugged Kate first. "Hi, Kate. Hi, Lucas."

They followed Jamie into the cheery yellow kitchen where Roy drained skinless potatoes in a strainer over the porcelain sink. Susan, her tiny frame wrapped in a lavender apron, turned from the stove long enough to give a brisk nod and say hello.

Jamie disappeared, and for the next few minutes Lucas made small talk with his parents before Roy shooed them from the kitchen. "Go on up and get settled. The kids are already up there."

"What should I get you to drink?" Susan asked Kate.

"Whatever you have is fine . . ."

Susan's penciled-in eyebrows hiked, clearly indicating she was waiting for a better answer.

"She likes tea, Mom, sweetened." Lucas stared pointedly at his mom, giving Kate a moment's gratification. He was actually taking up for her. Strangely, the notion lifted her spirits.

He took her hand, and Kate followed him through the foyer and up the stairs. The banister was thick and swirled at the end. "Why are we going upstairs?" Kate asked halfway up the flight.

He made the turn at the landing and continued. "We eat on the widow's walk."

A mental picture of the two-story house formed. Kate vaguely remembered a large widow's walk on the top, an historical feature of many Nantucket homes dating back to the whaling days.

Her legs wobbled, not from exertion, and her fingers tightened on the banister. "You eat on the roof?"

They reached the second floor and he took another flight of stairs, this one narrow and steep. Their feet thudded on the hollow wooden steps.

"It's tradition."

Tradition. That explained it all. He could have mentioned that little detail earlier. Didn't he know she was—

The dark stairwell opened to bright blue sky. And vast views of the island. High, vast views. Kate stepped to the side, keeping to the brick chimney chase.

Jamie and Brody greeted them from a round table, set for six, and centered on the square wooden platform. A spindled railing encompassed the perch. Lucas pulled out a chair for her on the other side of the table.

"I think I'll sit over here if you don't mind." Kate smiled at Lucas's sister. "By Jamie." As if that was her sole reason.

Lucas sat beside her. "Good idea. This is where the view's at."

For the first time, Kate looked outward. Her only thought had been keeping the solid brick of the chimney at her back, but now that she looked up, all she saw was open sky and the ocean spread out far below, disappearing into the horizon. She put her hands on the table and twisted the rings on her finger.

"Can I see?" Jamie asked, gesturing toward her wedding set. Okay, not a set exactly since Bryan had purchased one and Lucas the other. Luckily they were both white gold.

Jamie touched the emerald-cut diamond with her index finger. "Pretty. I didn't know Luc had such good taste."

"Or that he would part with that kind of cash," Brody said.

Kate and Lucas traded a look. "She's worth it," Lucas said.

"I read all your columns," Jamie said. "I can't believe you married Luc."

Lucas's chair creaked as he shifted. "Thanks a heap, sis." He tugged at his sister's high ponytail.

"You know what I mean," Jamie said.

Kate leaned back until her hair snagged on the brick behind her. "Shouldn't we help your parents? I feel bad just sitting here." Actually she felt bad about sitting up here period, and helping downstairs would get her off this bird perch. *And put you in the ring with your new mother-in-law.*

"Mom likes to wait on everyone," Jamie said.

"If you go down, Dad'll just shoo you away." Brody shook his curls out of his eyes.

"How did school finish up this year?" Lucas asked.

"He's thinking of switching majors again." Jamie snickered.

"Shut up, squirt." Brody elbowed her. "Mom and Dad don't know yet," he warned them.

The wind blew across the roof, ruffling the red plastic tablecloth, and Kate grasped the arms of the lawn chair. What kind of family ate on the roof?

"What do you want to switch to?" Lucas asked.

Brody planted his elbows on the table. "Architecture."

The sound of approaching footsteps halted the conversation. Susan entered, balancing a tray that held a pitcher of iced tea and six glasses. Lucas took the tray and set it down for Susan to pour the drinks. The ice cubes crackled as the tea splashed over them.

Susan set Kate's glass down. "Thanks." Kate let go of the wooden arm long enough to take a sip.

When Roy brought up the food, everyone passed the dishes, helping themselves. Kate couldn't believe the trouble they'd gone to. Fried chicken, mashed potatoes and gravy, buttered noodles, and coleslaw that looked homemade.

She picked up a drumstick and bit into the crispy breading. *Heaven.* "This is delicious."

"Thanks," Roy said.

"I wish you wouldn't fry it." Across from Kate, Susan picked the breading from a wing with a fork. "I keep telling him to bake it skinless. I swear when you get to be our age, the very smell of food causes weight gain."

Kate didn't see a spare ounce on Susan's petite frame.

"You'll walk it off this week." Roy spooned a heap of mashed potatoes onto his plate and covered them with a ladling of gravy.

"Your arteries are clogging as we speak," Susan said. She took a tiny portion of potatoes and set the bowl on the side table.

"I'll die a happy man." The look Roy sent Susan didn't seem happy.

"Suit yourself," Susan said. "But for heaven's sake,

could you at least wipe the grease off your chin so we don't have to look at it?"

Lucas gave Kate a pointed look. Yes, there was tension between the Wrights.

"Would you like the pepper, Kate?" Roy asked.

Kate slid her fork into the slaw. "No, thank you. Everything is perfect. You're a walker, Susan?" She hoped to ease the tension between them.

"I have to be if I want to stay slender. You should try it."

Kate felt her temperature soar as heat singed her cheeks. Maybe she wasn't as small-boned as Susan, but she kept her weight well under control.

"She does," Lucas said. He looked at Kate. "Mom walks every day too. Maybe you could walk together."

Kate's eyes narrowed, but she refrained from outright glaring at the man. Besides, she had to spend time with Susan if she was going to keep her end of the bargain. She just wasn't sure every day was necessary.

Lucas scooted his chair closer to the table and Kate could have sworn the whole platform shook. Her hand tightened on the metal fork.

"Actually, I use a treadmill," she said.

Susan poured Brody a second glass of tea. "Well, that's certainly easier."

Kate chewed a bite of food, then swallowed the dry lump. "On second thought, walking outdoors might be a nice change of pace from my incline training."

She wasn't willing to give up her treadmill time, but

walking with Susan would give Kate time to figure out how to help their marriage. If she could stand being with the woman that long.

"It's settled, then," Susan said.

"Look, the Porters have their boat out."

Kate followed the line of Jamie's finger and saw a bright yellow sail on the water. The view made her dizzy and she focused on her slaw.

Roy was addressing her. "What did you and Luc do on your honeymoon?"

"Roy, for heaven's sake." Susan took a bite of white chicken meat.

"Well, I'm not asking for juicy details. I'm just making conversation."

Kate wanted to crawl under the table.

"We went to the beach." Lucas smoothed things over. "And to the whaling museum. Kate had never actually gone."

"We took a boat to the Vineyard and went shopping," Kate added.

"*You* went shopping?" Jamie asked Lucas.

Roy set his chicken thigh down and wiped the grease from his fingers with a paper napkin. "It's amazing the things a man in love will do."

He said it as if to get a dig in on Susan, though Kate wasn't sure what it meant.

"Well, I wasn't surprised Lucas was in love with you," Jamie said. "The way he spent all that time renovating your apartment and refurbishing your floors. I knew he was falling for you."

Kate tried to catch Lucas's eyes, but he seemed intent on his food.

"And all the time he spent on the gazebo," Jamie continued. "We should have known there was more to it. He worked on it forever."

Kate wondered about the mottled blush that climbed Lucas's cheeks. She hadn't known he was so easily embarrassed. Well, Jamie could think whatever she wanted so long as she bought their story.

Tourists and locals alike clogged the cobblestone surface of Main Street. Lucas took Kate's hand and led her through the Fourth of July throng. They'd watched the watermelon- and pie-eating contests and gotten soaked during the water fight between the fire departments. Now it was time to find a spot on the beach for the fireworks.

When they neared Jetties Beach, Lucas adjusted the blanket and picnic basket in his arms and ushered Kate through the Pavilion. The place looked different than the night of their wedding. Had it only been two weeks? He wondered if she was remembering too.

All day they'd run into friends and acquaintances. Kate had constantly had her hand in his or her arm wrapped around his waist. Having her at his side made him stand taller. At one point, they found themselves standing by Selma Bennett, an editor at the *Mirror*. Lucas had leaned down and pecked Kate on the lips. Her eyes widened before she leaned into him for the briefest moment.

Now they exited through the back of the building and crossed the sand where people were spread out across the beach, lounging on blankets and beach chairs. When they found an empty spot, Lucas shook out the piecework quilt, and they ate their turkey sandwiches and Doritos, then snacked on fresh strawberries.

Lucas popped one in his mouth and leaned back on his hands, his legs stretched out to the edge of the quilt. Smoke from firecrackers and salt from the ocean blended together in a unique concoction that reminded him of Independence Days long past. Laughter and chatter filled the darkness, punctuated by the sharp pop of firecrackers, as the crowd waited for the public display to begin.

"Nantucket knows how put on a Fourth of July shindig," Kate said.

"Can't believe you've been here three years and haven't come."

She shrugged. "I've always been out of town." She didn't have to say she'd been visiting Bryan.

Two blankets over, Bryce Webber, who ran an online community and discussion forum, saw them and waved. They returned the greeting, Kate leaning into Lucas's side as if suddenly realizing they were still on display. He sat up, draping his arm across her shoulders. He could get used to this.

When Kate plucked a strawberry from the Rubbermaid container and looked into his eyes, he wanted to claim her mouth then and there. But she touched the strawberry to his lips instead. Lucas opened his mouth, accepting the offer, and her fingertips brushed his lips. *Have mercy.* The tang of the fruit didn't compare to the sweet taste of her lips.

The first firework exploded, drawing Kate's attention to the sky over the barge where the fireworks were shot from. A red glow, a reflection of the firework, blossomed over her face. Lucas already had fireworks going off inside. The big booms were only an echo of his heart.

With Kate nestled into his side, they watched the display. He could've lain there the rest of the night, her fingers tucked inside his. But all too soon, the fireworks ended, and they were packing their things and heading to his truck.

Lucas felt a disconnect between them as soon as they left the traffic and turned toward home. The ride was quiet. Kate sighed deeply and crossed her arms against the coolness of the night as the truck bumped along the street, jangling his keys. He itched to reach across the expanse and warm her hands in his.

"Quite a day, huh?" he asked.

Kate leaned her head against the passenger window. "Mmm."

Lucas turned off the air and adjusted the temperature. "What'd you think of the fireworks?" They might not compare to Boston's, but he'd always thought Nantucket put on a pretty good display.

"They were good."

Lucas felt his spirits deflating like a punctured inner

tube. They'd been close all day. Kate seemed to enjoy his company, even his touch. Her eyes lit when she laughed at the things he'd said. Somehow he'd let himself believe it was real.

But it wasn't real. Her affection was for appearances. And now, feeling Kate disengage from him was . . . hurtful. He wanted it back, the way they'd interacted, the way she'd looked at him, touched him. How could she turn it off like a spigot?

How had he not realized how difficult this was going to be?

Lucas shut the door hard behind Kate. She set her purse on the sofa table as he brushed by her and disappeared into the bathroom. Ten seconds later, the shower kicked on.

Was it her imagination, or was something bothering him? Kate took the picnic basket into the kitchen and tossed the trash. It had been a good day, but tiring. She'd seen everyone she knew, it seemed, at some point. With everyone congratulating them, she felt obligated to play the happy honeymooners, and it had worn on her.

Not that Lucas was hard to be affectionate with; he'd played along beautifully. But she was tired of being on display. By the time the fireworks ended, she was ready to hole up at the house where she didn't have to pretend.

As Kate finished putting away the picnic supplies, the shower went off. Good. She could use a rinsing herself. Though the weather had cooled after dusk, the sun had been hot and bright overhead all day. Besides, she wanted to wash the sand out of her hair.

Kate gathered her things from the bedroom and headed for the bathroom, her mind on her plans for the next day. When Lucas rounded the corner, she nearly smacked into his bare chest. He wore a blue towel that barely closed around his waist.

Kate stepped aside, averting her eyes. "Do you mind?" She pulled her own bundle of clothing into her chest as she passed.

"Nope." His tone was uncharacteristically sharp.

Kate stopped, ready to return and ask him what was wrong. But when she heard the unmistakable whoosh of the towel dropping to the rug, she darted into the bathroom and shut the door behind her.

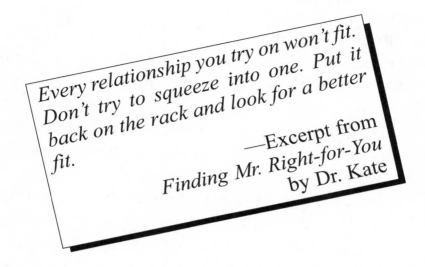

Every relationship you try on won't fit. Don't try to squeeze into one. Put it back on the rack and look for a better fit.

—Excerpt from
Finding Mr. Right-for-You
by Dr. Kate

Chapter Eleven

Lucas watched his mom and Kate cut across the beach, their bare feet kicking up sand, their evening shadows stretching behind them. He hoped his mom behaved herself.

The warm breeze ruffled the corners of the newspaper in his lap as he thought over the past two weeks. He'd enjoyed having Kate around, grown used to it. It felt good seeing evidence of her presence in his house. Her robe on a hook behind the door. Her toiletries a neat row in the medicine cabinet. Her shoes lined up by color inside the closet. He didn't see the point in that one, but whatever.

There'd been a learning curve too. Earlier that week, she'd exited the bathroom, a look of strained patience lining her lips. "I appreciate that you shaved, but would you mind rinsing out the sink since we only have the one?"

He shrugged. "Sure."

She hadn't mentioned the wet towels until the third morning and by then they were a knee-high blue pile in the corner.

What was it with Kate and order? It was like a god she worshipped. Why did everything have to be perfect?

Lucas opened the *Mirror* and shook his head. It did tickle him to watch confusion shadow her face when he cooked. He'd thought everyone dumped the whole package of bacon into the frying pan until he'd seen the way she'd done it, one tedious strip at a time, all neat and tidy.

The woman kept a record of her workouts, for crying out loud. He'd looked at the clipboard one day after she'd exercised, made notes, and disappeared into the shower. She marked the miles, the speed, the incline, and the time she'd walked, down to the minute.

But as much as her librarian ways amused him, he wondered what had her so tightly wound. She lived as if life could be boiled down to one big list. As if by keeping everything in order, somehow she could control things.

You'd think she'd have learned by now that some things were beyond control. If Lucas hadn't known that before Emily's death, he knew it now.

"Hey, Luc." Jamie stepped onto the covered deck and sat in the Adirondack chair beside him. Her lanky legs, already summer brown, extended from a frayed pair of denim shorts.

"Hey, sis. How's summer going?" He gave up on the paper, folding it and dropping it onto the deck.

"Okay, I guess." Jamie twirled a purple flower in her fingers. "Mom and Kate went for a walk?"

He closed his eyes and let his weight sag into the chair. "Yep."

"The gazebo looks good there," Jamie said.

Ethan had helped Lucas move the piece to his backyard overlooking the beach. It was as though it had been built for the spot.

For a while they sat in silence, listening to the sound of the water licking the shoreline. Lucas wondered what Kate was saying to his mom. More important, he wondered what his mom was saying to Kate. What if Kate figured out his parents were fine? He felt bad she was spending so much time on a fictional problem, but he'd had to use some excuse. He could hardly have told her the real reason he'd married her.

"How do you know when you're in love?" Jamie's voice cut through his thoughts.

Lucas looked at his sister, only fourteen, still in braces, and wanted to tell her she shouldn't be thinking about love at her age. But he'd been fourteen once, although it seemed a lifetime ago. Emotions had felt bigger than life then.

"Who is he?"

Jamie wrapped the flower's threadlike stem around her index finger. "His name is Aaron Brinkley, and he goes to my school. I've liked him forever, but he was going out with a girl named Liz." She rolled her eyes.

"Don't like her much?"

"She's a snot. I don't know what he saw in her. But he's been at the beach all week, and Meredith said he broke up with Liz. He asked me to play volleyball today."

Lucas propped his ankle on his knee and clasped his hands on his stomach. "Did you?"

Jamie flicked sand off her shorts. "Yeah, but I beat him."

Lucas laughed. Jamie was a starter on her team and the best player, if he did say so.

Jamie slugged his arm, and the flower went flying. "It's not funny. I think he's mad at me."

Lucas stifled the laugh. "What makes you say that?"

"He didn't talk to me after that." She wrinkled her little nose.

"Were his friends around?"

Jamie's face fell. "I should have let him win." She crossed her arms and chewed on her lip.

"He'll get over it. Trust me."

"What do I say when I see him tomorrow? I really like him."

"*You're* worried about finding something to say?"

She shrugged. "I get tongue-tied with him. I'm afraid I'll say something dumb."

"Be yourself. If he likes you, he'll like you for who you are."

She rolled her eyes. "You sound like Mom."

Maybe he wasn't helping. But given his own love life, he wasn't sure he was qualified to give advice. "What are his interests? People like to talk about themselves. Especially teenage boys."

Her face brightened. "He likes the Red Sox, and I know he's into sailing, so we can talk about that. What else?"

"What do you mean?"

"Duh. I mean, do you have any other advice?"

If only he could condense everything he'd learned about relationships and pass it like a baton. Unfortunately, life didn't work that way. "Just don't be afraid to let him know you like him. He asked you to play volleyball, so it sounds like he's interested. Guys have a lot of pressure to initiate things. It'll make it easier if he knows he's not going to get rejected."

"You think he's nervous too?"

Lucas clasped his hands behind his head. "Trust me, the nerves go both ways."

Jamie was gone by the time Kate returned. The back door fell closed with a smack, and she cornered him in the living room.

"*What* is the deal with your mom?" Her damp bangs clung to her forehead, and her ponytail swung like a pendulum.

Lucas folded the paper again and set it on the table. "What do you mean?"

"I mean she can't talk to me for two minutes without getting in a dig. There's all this subtext going on, and

I think it's more than that she missed our wedding. You want to fill me in?"

It was only fair. He should have already. "It's not you. There's some history you don't know about." Maybe her mom had told her the story, and she didn't realize who Susan was. "Your mom was my mom's best friend years ago. They went to high school together. Did your mom ever talk about that?"

Kate shook her head. "What happened?"

It was all ancient history, but to his mom it was the unpardonable sin. A woman scorned, and all that, he supposed. "When my mom and dad were engaged, your mom was supposed to be her maid of honor, only—" How to put it delicately?

"What?"

He sighed. "I guess your mom had a thing for my dad. Something happened the week before the wedding. I don't know the details, but your mom slept with my dad. My mom cut her out of the wedding and refused to talk to her again."

Kate's eyes widened slowly, her jaw following suit. Then she pressed her lips together and jabbed her hands onto her hips. "Why didn't you tell me?"

"I didn't think it mattered."

"It matters to your mom." Kate walked to the window and turned. "How am I supposed to help your parents when your mom hates me?"

"She doesn't hate you. She doesn't even know you."

"She'll never trust me now."

He supposed Kate was right, but he'd been hoping his mom would come around. It wasn't Kate's fault, and it had been more than thirty years ago. "I'm sorry. I should have told you, but I was hoping she'd get to know you and realize you're not to blame."

That seemed to quench the fire in her eyes. "She probably thinks I'm just like my mom. Not only am I guilty by association, she's probably worried I'll betray you just like my mom did her. She's worried I'll hurt her son."

Funny, he was worried about the same thing. But he hadn't considered his mom might be worried for him. "Being a therapist must come in handy."

Kate gave him a wry smile. "I have a feeling I'm going to need all the expertise I can get."

Two days later, Lucas was remembering his conversation with Kate when a knock sounded on his shop door.

Ethan, his friend and his best salesperson, opened the door. Lucas turned off the sander.

"There's a lady here who's interested in a few custom pieces." Ethan pushed up his wire glasses with his middle finger.

Lucas set the sander on the plywood table. "Be right there."

He removed his goggles and brushed the sawdust from his skin and clothing before entering the showroom. He found Ethan and the customer by his collection of Shaker-style bedroom furniture. The woman had auburn hair that fell in waves past bare, slender shoulders.

"Miss Delaney, this is the owner, Lucas Wright. Lucas, this is Sydney Delaney. She recently purchased a home on Madaket Harbor."

Lucas shook her hand. "Pleased to meet you. That's a nice area."

Though she was tall enough to intimidate most men, her movements were fluid. "I love your work." Her fingers caressed the footboard of a queen-sized sleigh bed made of maple and finished with a caramel stain.

"Thanks. Ethan said you're interested in some custom work."

Another couple entered the store, and Ethan excused himself.

"I love the Shaker style. It's simple but elegant."

It was Lucas's favorite as well. There was something about the old-fashioned simplicity of the lines that drew attention to the beauty of the wood.

"I see a lot of things I like." Sydney gave Lucas a coy look. "But I have some specific pieces in mind for the living room that would need to be custom-made."

"I'd be happy to come and take a look at the space. You could show me what you have in mind."

She cocked her head and smiled slowly.

Lucas realized she'd read too much into his words. He crossed his arms, making sure his left hand showed. "I'll need to take measurements; then I can give you an estimate, and we'll go from there. How does tomorrow at ten a.m. sound?"

"Perfect." She gave him her address and phone number, then hitched her tiny purse on her shoulder. "I can't wait to see what you come up with."

He walked her to the door, but she stopped on the threshold.

"Oh, I hate to be a bother, but I'm looking for a fudge shop I've heard about. Aunt something . . . I have a terrible sweet tooth." Her smile flirted.

"Aunt Leah's Fudge—down on Straight Wharf." He followed her out the door and pointed east. "If you follow Main Street, you'll find yourself on the wharf. It's on the left. You can't miss it."

His brother entered his line of vision, walking up Main Street, his stride slow and loose.

"Hey, Lucas."

Lucas was about to introduce Sydney, but Brody stepped around him and opened the door. "Is Kate upstairs?"

The question caught Lucas off guard. "Sure." He wondered what Brody wanted with Kate.

Lucas watched his brother until Sydney placed a hand on his arm.

The sound of feet thudding up the wood steps of her office pulled Kate's attention from the letter. A glance at her watch told her it was too early for Lucas. They'd begun eating lunch together on Mondays, Wednesdays, and Fridays. Strictly for appearances' sake.

Sun-blond curls appeared first, followed by the lean

frame of her new brother-in-law. He wore a pair of bright orange and blue Hawaiian-print trunks and a white T-shirt.

"Brody." Kate folded the "Dear Dr. Kate" letter and set it on the desk next to the other letters she'd waded through. "This is a pleasant surprise."

He stopped at the top of the stairs and stuffed his hands in his pockets, a move that reminded her of Lucas. "I should've called."

"No, come in. Have a seat. I'm just reading through some letters."

Brody surveyed her desk. "That's a lot of letters." He glanced around the room—what used to be the lobby of her practice. She'd moved her desk to the front so she could take advantage of the natural daylight that streamed though the windows.

"I haven't been up here since Lucas renovated," Brody said.

Kate appraised the room with fresh eyes. The shiny wood floor, the soothing green walls that set off the maple color of the wood trim. She'd found an area rug in shades of green, navy, and beige that tied the colors of the room together.

"He did a nice job," she said. "He's quite the carpenter, your brother." Never mind that it had taken forever to get it done.

Brody sank into the waiting-room chair with a sigh. "I know."

Kate wondered what had brought him here. She set her elbows on the swivel chair's wooden arms and leaned back against the plush leather. Brody crossed his legs, propping his right ankle on his hairy knee. Gravity pulled at the heel of his worn flip-flop.

"So, to what do I owe the pleasure of your visit?" Kate teased.

"I was wondering if you'd help me with something." His eyes darted around the room, settling nowhere.

"I'd be happy to help in any way I can." Kate felt sorry for him in his awkwardness. "Is it a girl problem?" That she was accustomed to. People often sought her advice—not just in letters, but on the street sometimes.

"No, not girls. I got a handle on that." His cocky smile lasted a short second. "It's . . . school." The word dropped like a fifty-pound bag of sand.

"Ah," Kate said. "The switch in majors?"

"Yeah." He shook the bangs from his eyes. "I can't decide what I want to do. I mean, I'm three years into college and I still don't know what I want to be when I grow up." He tucked in the corner of his mouth at his joke.

He was still young at twenty-one, but Kate understood his frustration. "What was your major when you entered college? University of Massachusetts, right?"

"Yeah. I started as an education major. That lasted for a year and a semester."

"What made you decide on education?"

"I thought I could come back here and teach high school. Maybe middle school. I don't know. I did well in school and I thought it would be fun to teach."

"What did you change to?"

"Art." He rolled his eyes. "I know—it's like, what am I going to do with a career in art?"

"Are you good at it?" Kate watched his face, looking for some sign of passion.

"Sure, I guess. My professors thought I was."

Outside the front window a truck braked, the squeal piercing the wall. "What made you change?"

"Does the term 'starving artist' mean anything to you? After a couple semesters, I realized how hard it would be to support a family with an art degree. Megan—she was my girlfriend at the time—thought I should switch to computer science."

"Is that what your major is now?"

"Yeah. I like computers and everything. I get good grades, and I know it would be a good career, but . . ." He punctuated the sentence with a sigh.

Kate waited. She had yet to see him talk about anything that ignited a fire in his eyes.

"So now you're thinking of architecture?"

Brody looked out the window. "It's kind of in the art field, but I could make a decent living."

"Let's talk about things you like to do. Lucas said you play baseball for UMass?"

"I'm shortstop. But I'm not pro material, if that's what you're thinking."

"I'm just trying to get a feel for the things you enjoy. What else? What do you do in your spare time?"

"I spend a lot of spare time at the beach. I surf a little. I wait tables at the Even Keel in the summer to supplement the money my parents give toward college. I've helped Lucas with construction, but I don't have a knack for it like he does."

Kate's legs ached from sitting. She stood and crossed the room. "Any other jobs you've held or volunteer positions you've enjoyed?"

"I enjoy working, so I've liked all my jobs. I was a lifeguard at Cisco beach for a couple summers. When school is in session, I tutor a couple local middle schoolers for extra money. That's rewarding. One of my students is a boy with a learning disability. His parents were really frazzled about his schoolwork. I tutored him last year starting after Christmas break, and his grades went from, like, Ds and Fs to Bs and Cs."

"You must be quite the tutor."

"Nah, Jared just needed some encouragement and help getting organized. He's a bright kid—he just had trouble remembering his homework and focusing." Brody lifted a shoulder. "He's a huge Giants fan and I found ways of relating that to his schoolwork."

"Have you considered changing back to education?"

Brody tucked his chin, and his eyebrows hiked up. "Not really."

"Why not?"

He looked away. "I don't know."

"You seem to like kids and know how to motivate them."

"There's not much money involved in teaching."

"You get summers off . . ."

Brody grinned. His even white teeth reminded her of Lucas's. "Good point."

The bright sunlight from the window beckoned Kate. "Well, it's something to consider. I wouldn't fret about changing gears with your major. This is the rest of your life you're talking about, so it's important to follow your passion. The main thing is finding out where your passions lie."

"Too bad I can't major in girls."

Kate looked out over the street where tourists meandered down the brick sidewalks. A movement below caught her eye. Lucas stood in front of the shop with an auburn-haired woman. She wore a sleeveless ivory sweater and ivory slacks. The woman placed her hand on Lucas's arm, letting it linger. Her head tilted toward Lucas like she would live or die by his next words.

". . . give it some thought," Brody was saying.

Kate peered though the old, wavy pane. "Who's the woman outside? The one talking to Lucas?"

She heard Brody stand. "The leggy redhead? I don't know her. They were talking when I got here."

Kate felt a twinge of something unpleasant. It struck her as odd at first. She tried to rationalize it as common sense. After all, Lucas was wearing a wedding band, and the way Red was hanging on his arm was hardly appropriate. She glared down at the woman. *Boundaries, lady. Have you heard of them?*

Before she could help herself, Kate took a step toward the stairs with the thought of putting the woman in her place. Then she stopped. She imagined Lucas's amused brow, quirking upward, his crooked smile as Kate staked her claim. She wouldn't give him the pleasure. Besides, what did it matter if Red flirted with Lucas? It wasn't as if Kate had feelings for him.

She was *not* jealous, and there was no way on earth she was going to let Lucas think she was.

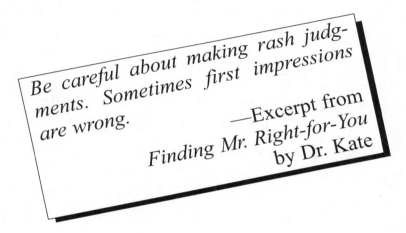

Be careful about making rash judgments. Sometimes first impressions are wrong.

—Excerpt from
Finding Mr. Right-for-You
by Dr. Kate

Chapter Twelve

Kate slipped from the bed shortly after four o'clock and felt her way across the floor. From the floor on Lucas's side of the bed, Bo shifted. As she pulled her thin robe from the hook and tiptoed from the room, she heard his toenails clicking across the wood floor. Kate saw no way of making him return without disturbing Lucas.

The house was dark and quiet, except for the living room clock ticking off time. In the darkness she made her way to the back door and opened it quietly, keeping Bo inside. A warm breeze tugged at her cotton robe, and she gathered the belt, tightening it around her waist before sitting.

The dream that had awakened her surrounded her like a thick wet fog. In it, Bryan had come to her office, climbing the stairs with purposeful steps like Brody had. But Bryan wasn't there for advice. He took her in his arms and proposed to her. When they left the building, they weren't on Main Street, but at Jetties Beach for their wedding. As Kate approached the altar, he turned. But it wasn't Bryan. It was Lucas.

Now, Kate watched the moonlight flickering on the surface of the shadowed water. She closed her eyes and leaned against the wooden back. The oscillating sound of the waves washing the shoreline didn't soothe her. Inside she felt as jolted as she had in the dream when she realized Lucas had replaced Bryan.

It happened for real too. Kate sighed. She wished she could fast-forward through the year and get her life back on track. How had she gotten so far off course? What was she doing in this house with a man she barely knew and hardly liked?

That's not true, her conscience corrected. *He might grate on the nerves sometimes, but Lucas has his good qualities.* And the last few weeks had been better than she expected in terms of getting along with him. It was just that her life was careening out of control like it hadn't since she was a child. She felt shaken and vulnerable.

A vision of her mom surfaced from the dusty corridors of her mind. Kate had been eleven and had just returned from her best friend's house. She often went to Mackenzie's house just to escape her own. But Mackenzie was mad because Kate never invited her over, and Kate had run out of excuses.

Kate closed and locked the front door before removing her snow boots and wiggling her numb toes. "Mom?" she called, not knowing whether or not to expect an answer. Sometimes she found her mom doing laundry and humming game-show tunes, and other times Kate wished she hadn't returned at all. It was the uncertainty she hated most. Even at eleven she knew it was true.

There was no answer on this night, so Kate set her heavy book bag on the rocking chair, flipped off the lights, and climbed the creaky stairs. Maybe her mom was asleep. She crossed her fingers on the banister as she ascended.

The bathroom light glowed in the darkness. She opened the door and found her mom on the green shag carpet next to a mystery stain they'd inherited with the house. One of her mom's sweater-clad arms draped over the tub ledge, and the other hugged a clear bottle of alcohol. The room smelled sour, and Kate turned on the fan.

"Mom," Kate whispered. She shoved aside the fuzzy pink slippers her dad had sent for her birthday and knelt on the carpet. "Mom."

Her mother stirred as Kate slipped the empty bottle, still warm from her mother's hand, out of her grasp.

"Katie, baby." She licked cracked lips and opened her eyes to glassy slits, reaching toward Kate with her delicate white hand. It didn't quite make it and instead thumped on the carpet beside her leg.

"Come on, Mom. Let's get you to bed." Kate helped her mom stand, wrapped an arm around her gaunt waist. Propping her mom's arm around her own shoulders, Kate led her next door to the bedroom. Her mom wobbled and staggered, bumping her bony hip into Kate's and stepping on her cold toes.

When they reached the bed, Kate helped her mom out of her sweater and black slacks. She tugged a nightgown over her head, turned back the covers, and guided her mom into the bed, then pulled the woolly blanket over her. Her breath reeked of vodka.

"Katie . . ." If her mom wanted to say more, it was swallowed by oblivion.

"'Night, Momma," Kate whispered before extinguishing the bedside lamp and leaving the room.

It hadn't been the first time Kate put her mom to bed and it wasn't the last. If her dad had known how bad things had gotten for her mother, he would've gotten custody of Kate. But Kate couldn't stand the thought of leaving her mother all alone, so she kept their secret and spent her childhood feeling anxious and ashamed.

Now, as Kate curled her leg under her, she realized life felt as out of control as it had during those days. And just like then, there was nothing she could do but wait and hope things improved.

Only they never had. Her mother had died an alcoholic.

She tried a pep talk. *You made a better life for yourself. Look how far you've come from that cold house on Stinton Street. You have a successful career, a promising book, and you get to help people for a living. Help people that otherwise might be swallowed whole by their problems, like your mom.*

But regardless of all my planning, I lost Bryan to another woman, and I'm married to a man I don't love.

Only for a year, Kate. Bryan will come to his senses when he realizes his mistake. This other woman is just an outlet for his fear of commitment. Once he realizes that, he'll be back.

What am I saying? I can't believe I still want him back after what he did.

Beside her, the door clicked open, and Bo barreled through, with Lucas following. In the dark, his silhouette revealed tousled hair and a shirt that hung open at the front. Kate looked away.

"You okay?" Lucas whispered.

Bo licked the back of her hand, leaving a warm, wet film on her skin. Kate wiped her hand on her robe and crossed her arms.

"I'm fine. I didn't mean to wake you."

Lucas sank into the chair next to hers and silence settled around them. His presence changed the atmosphere. The masculine scent, the warmth of his large frame only inches away, the sound of his quiet breaths. Before it had felt empty. Now it felt . . . alive.

Kate shifted in her chair. Why had he come out here? He was an early riser, but not this early. Even the birds still slept and there was no light yet on the horizon.

"My family treating you all right? My mom didn't say something to hurt your feelings?"

"Your family's fine." Strange but fine. She hadn't gotten far with Susan, but it was early. First Susan had to like and trust Kate. Then maybe she would open up. And given the history between Susan and Kate's mom, that was going to take time.

"Mom can be tactless sometimes."

Tactless she could handle. It was the crazy that unnerved her. Lucas was probably wondering when Kate was going to keep her end of the bargain. Maybe he didn't understand that subtlety took time. "We're getting to know each other. I'm hoping in the next month or so I can introduce the subject of marriage. I'll let you know how it goes and keep you up-to-date on any progress."

The chair creaked as Lucas shifted. A cricket chirped from someplace under the deck. "Not worried about that."

Kate wondered why he brought it up. Oh, well. She was too tired to figure Lucas out.

She wondered if Bryan was still in bed. She wondered if he was alone. There were things she missed about him—mannerisms. Did Bryan set his hand in the small of the woman's back when he escorted her to the car? Did he hold her pinky on the console as he drove?

A yawn started, and she stifled it. The dream that had chased her from bed kept her from returning for fear that it would resume. Her only hope of escaping it was to stay awake. And even that wasn't working.

Lucas felt Kate move in the darkness. The smell of her hair, a blend of sunshine and citrus, wafted over on a breeze. Did she know how maddening it was to be so close, so *married*, and yet have none of the normal privileges?

No, of course she didn't. From her perspective this was a business deal. Lucas's presence was a means to a goal. She had no idea how much he craved her. How he loved her slightly pointed chin and her almond-shaped eyes, loved the way she brushed her hair behind her ears when she was intent on something.

His advice to Jamie replayed in his mind: *"Don't be afraid to let him know you like him."* What a hypocrite he was.

Bo rubbed against his leg, and Lucas set a hand on his furry head. His situation was different from Jamie's. Kate didn't have feelings for him. She was still in love with Bryan. Was probably thinking about him right now. Maybe that's why she wasn't sleeping.

He remembered the nights after Emily had died. Lying awake until his eyes ached. Turning a dozen different ways on the bed. Feeling for her empty pillow and pulling it to his chest. If Kate was going through anything close to that, he needed to give her space. And time to get to know him.

"Go for a walk?" he asked. Bo perked up at the word, but Kate only looked his way.

"I'm in my robe."

He scooted to the edge of his seat. "Come on. We'll be back before light."

"But what about—"

"Who cares?" he said. "It'll clear your head." He extended his hand, wondering if she could see it in the moonlight.

She was going to say no anyway. What was he thinking? Kate wouldn't go for a walk unless she'd penciled it in a week ago.

"I guess I can go. I'll have to change first, though." She was inside before he could reply.

When she returned, they stepped off the deck and into the grass. Somewhere in the distance a dog barked, and Bo stopped to listen, his bulk a shadow in the dim light. Then, satisfied the other was of no importance, he led the way down the path toward the water.

When they reached the beach, they turned away from town. The wet, packed sand was cool and spongy under his feet. Lucas wondered what Kate was thinking. He remembered his advice to Jamie and started there.

"How's your column going?"

A wave washed up under their feet. Kate sucked in her breath at the coldness of the foamy water and scampered a few feet up the beach. "I've decided on the letter for my column. The woman wrote a four-page saga, so tomorrow I'll boil it all down to a one-hundred-word question."

He had no idea what went into an advice column, and he started to ask how she'd become syndicated, then thought again. Maybe she didn't want to talk about work at four thirty in the morning.

Bo ran ahead of them, trotting through the intermittent waves that washed ashore, then turned toward them, a still, shaggy silhouette. The moonlight offered enough light to see by. It washed gently over Kate's features, highlighting the bridge of her nose, the bow of her lip. Lucas looked away.

A wind blew across the water, and Kate shivered. "I didn't expect it to be so cool."

Lucas shrugged out of his shirt and placed it over her shoulders.

"Thanks." She put her arms through the sleeves, and he thought her eyes lingered on his bare chest for a moment.

Kate pulled Lucas's shirt tight, overlapping it like a robe. The material was still warm from his skin and smelled like him. The gesture had surprised her, but he'd done many small things that surprised her. Pulling out her chair at dinner, pouring her coffee every morning . . . And she had to admit he was trying to mend his messy ways. He'd even been hanging up his wet towels.

She wondered how Emily had coped with his disorganization. But maybe Emily had been like Lucas. Or maybe she'd considered Lucas's homemade meals and good manners a fair trade-off. Kate wanted to ask, but he never mentioned Emily. Bringing up his late wife would feel as if she was trespassing on sacred ground.

She wondered how Lucas felt about their pretend marriage after having had the real thing. It must feel hollow. Kate could hardly believe even now that he'd done it. That he'd stepped in at the last moment and rescued her.

Then again, he was getting something in return.

"Tell me about your dad," Kate said. Susan was guarded, but maybe Kate could get a fuller picture by learning about Roy.

They caught up with Bo, and he ran ahead of them down the shore, a giant lumbering fur ball.

"He's a man's man. Always liked to work with his hands. His dad was a criminal lawyer, and from what I understand, was disappointed when Dad didn't follow in his footsteps."

"Your dad held his ground?"

"Yep. Dad got a job working for a builder on the island. He framed houses and eventually started his own company."

"Is that how you got involved with wood?" Another wave washed over Kate's feet, tickling her with foam.

"Dad had me using tools by the time I was four."

"But you didn't want to build houses?"

He shook his head. "I like the detailed work. Knew

it the first time I made a mantel for a house we built."

"When did your dad retire? And what happened to his business?"

Lucas picked up a shell, examined it, then tossed it into the water before answering. "A few years ago he started having some trembling in his hands. A while later he was diagnosed with Parkinson's disease."

Kate's stomach knotted. How come she hadn't known this before? Neither Lucas nor Susan had mentioned it, and she hadn't noticed any trembling. "I didn't know."

"He decided to sell the business. He was set for retirement anyway, and the work wasn't good for him in the long run.

"What's his prognosis?" She knew a little about Parkinson's, but how quickly did it progress?

"It's a degenerative disease, but its rate of progression varies. Eventually he'll be completely incapacitated, but he's only stage one. There are five stages, and he's progressing slowly."

"Do you think the diagnosis played a role in their marriage problems? It must cause a lot of stress." Why would Lucas worry about them divorcing when his father was ill? Surely Susan wouldn't leave him now. But then, how well did she know Susan?

"They were devastated when they found out. We all were."

No wonder she hadn't known about the disease. Maybe the family was in denial. How would they cope as his condition worsened? "It's lucky you live so close. Your mom will need help." Eventually Roy would be bedridden, and Susan wouldn't be able to handle his weight.

"That's why I built next door."

Kate met Lucas's gaze in the darkness. A glimmer of moonlight shone in his shadowed eyes. "Oh. I thought—" Kate looked away, embarrassed. She'd thought he was a momma's boy. There was no kind way to say it. It hadn't been kind to think it. Especially when his real reason was so unselfish.

"After Emily died, I couldn't live in that house anymore." He seemed about to say more, but stopped.

Kate wanted to know more, but what right did she have to pry? After finding Emily dead in the house, Lucas probably couldn't put the image from his mind. Who could blame him for moving on, starting over? But instead of choosing his own place to live, he'd built beside his parents, to be available for them, and instead of starting over with a new love, he'd stepped in and rescued her. The more she learned about Lucas, the more she realized she hadn't known him at all.

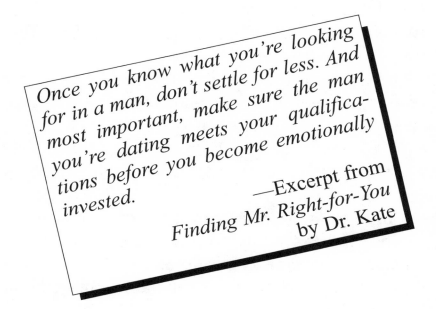

Chapter Thirteen

"Let's go sailing," Lucas said as Kate stepped off the treadmill the following Saturday, toweling the sweat from her forehead.

He'd just returned from walking Bo, and the dog trotted over to Kate and nudged her toward the bathroom as if to escort her to the shower. Like she needed help deciding where she was going. She stopped at the doorway and pushed Bo with her knee, glaring at the dog.

"I can't," she said. "I need to clean and catch up on laundry and prepare for a phone interview. Plus we need groceries, and I need to run to the bank."

"I saw your list." Lucas filled a glass with tap water. "We can do those things tomorrow. I'll help." He gulped down the water.

"The bank is closed tomorrow."

"We can run by the bank on our way to the harbor."

"My phone interview—"

"Can wait until tomorrow." He set the glass on the countertop. At her look, he opened the dishwasher and set it inside. "Any more excuses?"

They weren't excuses. Well, not exactly. She just wanted to get her list done. But she'd never seen Lucas's eyes lit like they were now, and he'd done so much for her lately in return for so little.

"Come on. It's seventy-five degrees, the sky is clear blue, and there's a good steady breeze."

"I've never been sailing," she said lamely, hoping he'd rescind the offer.

"Doesn't matter." His Colgate smile illuminated his face. "Get your shower, and I'll gather supplies."

Two hours later, Kate watched Lucas from a bench seat on the boat. He hadn't stopped since they'd left the harbor, pulling on this line and that, tying them off on their cleats.

"Can I do anything?" She tightened the strap on her bulky orange life vest.

He pulled up a sail, his muscles straining under his red tank. "Nope," he called over the wind. As he turned the boat with the tiller, the sails fluttered like gulls' wings, and he adjusted them with one hand. He continued doing what seemed like three things at a time, handling the jobs with the ease and dexterity of a man who'd done it a thousand times.

Soon, he turned the boat slightly into the wind and pulled the white sails tight. Kate dug in her satchel for sunglasses and joined Lucas where he steered the vessel. The deck felt unsteady under her feet, and she grappled for a hold.

"Having fun yet?" he asked. His eyes hid behind his own sunglasses, and she saw herself reflected in them.

"I had no idea there was so much involved in sailing."

He smiled, clearly in his element. "It's a blast. I sail a couple times a month at least. More, if I have time."

"Who taught you?" Kate thought it'd take her years to learn everything he'd just done, but then she wasn't a mechanical person. And she could tell already sailing wasn't going to become her favorite pastime. Being at the mercy of the wind was unsettling. What happened when it changed directions? How did you go back where you came from if the wind was blowing the other way?

"Mom. Dad knows how, too, but Mom's the expert. Want to take a stab at it?" He moved to the side, offering her steering privileges.

Her legs shook at the thought. "No, you go ahead."

He shrugged. "Suit yourself. There's soda in the cabin if you get thirsty. Otherwise, just relax and enjoy."

Kate took the bench nearby and grabbed the railing. The hot sun beat down on her face, and she was glad she'd applied sunscreen before they left. Lucas hadn't applied any and she wondered if he'd burn. His sandal-clad feet were braced a shoulder width apart, and his dark hair and T-shirt fluttered behind. He seemed unconcerned about the lack of sunscreen and life vest.

In the distance, other sailboats dotted the ocean. She looked down at the water rushing by and wondered how deep it was. Just then the boat tilted. She gasped and gripped the metal rail. A glance at Lucas hinted nothing was awry, but her nerves jangled just the same. What if they tipped over? The idea of floating in the middle of the ocean made her palms clammy. Maybe she'd feel better below deck, where she didn't have to see the wide expanse of water.

She stood, steadying herself with whatever she could grab. "I think I'll get a soda," she said.

Lucas nodded, lost in apparent nirvana, oblivious to her discomfort.

"Okay, then."

Rolling her eyes, she took the steps down to the galley. Below, the room was dark and cool after the brightness of the sun. Sliding her glasses up, she noted the tiny galley and a booth; beyond that a bed consumed an entire room. The cabin was pleasantly tidy, but she supposed it had to be; otherwise things would bump around.

As if reading her thoughts, the boat turned, and Kate sank onto the soft blue cushions of the booth. A fake plant was anchored to ivory Formica, and Kate smoothed her hands over the surface, appreciating the solid coolness against her palms.

She hadn't known sailing would disconcert her. She

hoped she didn't get motion sickness. *Just my luck I'll be hurling over the side of this thing while Lucas laughs at me. Gee, how fun.*

Was her stomach feeling unsettled now, or was she imagining it? She swallowed compulsively as the boat turned again. Was he zigzagging? *For heaven's sake, can't he just point the thing in one direction?*

She remembered the soda Lucas had mentioned and walked carefully across the galley, grabbing a Sprite from the fridge before falling onto the bench as the boat heeled once again.

How long would Lucas want to be on the water? Was this an all-day thing, or would a couple of hours suffice? She checked her watch and wondered if she'd have time to finish her list once they got home. She didn't want to spoil his fun, but there was nothing to do down here, and she hadn't brought a book to read or writing materials to work. What did people do on boats? She didn't see anything in the small cabin to occupy herself, but the thought of going up on deck was enough to weaken her legs.

Suddenly, the boat slowed, its change in momentum bottoming out her stomach. Had something gone wrong? She wanted to go see but couldn't make herself leave the booth's security. Instead she sipped her Sprite, then realized her stomach felt worse. *Please don't let me puke!*

Footsteps sounded, and Lucas entered the cabin, ducking under the header.

"Is something wrong?" Kate asked.

He grabbed a soda from the fridge, then a brown bag, which he dangled in front of her. "Thought you might be getting hungry."

"You packed food?" He intended to be out here awhile. Her spirits sank.

"Just sandwiches. You hungry?"

Kate's stomach protested, but the sooner they ate, the sooner they could return. "Sure."

He put the food on paper plates with sides of potato salad and chips and headed up the steps. "Coming?"

She wanted to eat there in the enclosed cabin where she could almost pretend she was on dry land. But Lucas was already on deck. The last thing she needed was to give him one more reason to tease her. She stood and followed. The next time he suggested sailing, the answer would be a flat no.

Outside the sun was too bright. Kate pulled down her sunglasses and followed Lucas to the bench she'd vacated earlier. The wind drove the boat, and it rocked gently in the waves.

Lucas handed her a plate. "Beautiful day," he said around a bite of sandwich.

The heat of the sun made her skin prickle, and its glare on the water hurt her eyes. "That it is."

She started on the turkey and bacon sandwich. Would they head back after they ate? She could only hope. She scanned the horizon. Land was nowhere to be seen. With that knowledge, a sudden dizziness overtook her, and she focused on her plate. Did Lucas know where they were, how to get back?

"Love the sounds out here, don't you?"

The water splashed against the boat's side, and the wind billowed the sails. A seagull, on its way somewhere, called out. Maybe she was just a city girl, but she liked the sound of people, vehicles splashing through puddles, and the scrape of sandals on the sidewalk.

Ugh. Her stomach stirred uncomfortably. Maybe she shouldn't eat. The boat dipped. *Be still!* she thought, as if she could stop it. She set her sandwich on her plate and sipped her Sprite.

"You okay?" Lucas cocked his head, but she couldn't see his eyes past the sunglasses.

"I'm fine." She smiled to prove it and bit into a salty chip.

When the wind gusted and the boat dipped again, she steadied herself with the first thing she could reach: Lucas's leg. "Sorry." She removed her hand as quickly as she'd placed it.

The second chip went down. On the third, she stopped. There was no getting around it: her stomach was definitely threatening to expel her lunch. Kate couldn't take another bite. Her head spun, exacerbated by the boat's movement, and she grasped her plate with both hands.

"Kate." Lucas took her plate, tugging it from her tightened grasp. He set it on his other side. "What's wrong?"

She closed her eyes, but that made her head and stomach feel worse. "I'm not—feeling so well." She swallowed, reminding her stomach that things were supposed to go down, not up.

"Oh, honey, why didn't you say something?" He helped her up. "Come over here."

She pulled toward the cabin. "I just want to lie down. I'm sure I'll be fine." *If I don't die first.* She hadn't felt this bad since she had the stomach flu in the seventh grade and vomited all over Miss Heinschneider's white leather Reeboks in gym.

"Lying down is the worst thing you can do." He guided her to the center of the boat and turned her toward the ocean. She didn't want to look at the water. And there was no place to sit. She was willing to sink to the floor, but there wasn't room. Instead she grabbed the railing and leaned over it. She was beyond pretending she was fine. Pride had fled, leaving desperation it its wake.

Lucas put an arm around her middle and pulled her against him. "Look at the horizon. It'll help."

Kate had read something about that, but given the condition of her stomach, she was skeptical. She followed his directions anyway.

"I don't think we have any medications aboard," Lucas said.

Her head fell against his chest, and she smothered a moan. How had she lived this long and not known the body could feel so bad? At this point, she wished she could just get it over with, Lucas's presence notwithstanding.

"Are you watching the horizon?"

His stubbly chin rubbed against her temple, a welcome distraction. She nodded. The horizon was a fuzzy line against the blue sky. She focused on that line like her life depended on it.

"I'm sorry, Katie." His hand moved up and down against her side. His stomach was like a solid wall against her back. "I should point us toward shore. The sooner you're on dry land, the better you'll feel." His arms loosened, but she clutched them, fearing dizziness would overtake her.

"Wait," she said. If only she could sit down.

He tightened his arms, supporting her, and she stared at the horizon. Was the dizziness improving?

"I shouldn't have let you go down to the cabin earlier. You probably would've been fine."

She hadn't been feeling right before she'd gone down, but she didn't have the strength to say so.

"There are saltines and Coke in the cabin. Will you be all right for a minute if I get them?"

Kate wasn't sure she'd ever feel all right again. She wanted to say no, hesitant to stand without the strength of his support, but she nodded anyway and realized she must have a shred of pride left. She leaned forward on the railing, wishing she'd vomit while he was gone and get it over with.

No such luck. He returned a quick minute later and handed her a cracker. "This'll help."

Kate bit into it and followed the cracker with a sip of the Coke he'd brought while he rubbed her shoulders. It seemed her infirmity had granted him touching rights, but it was a welcome distraction. So welcome, she leaned against him moments later and his arms came around her again.

The saltines were working a little magic, and for the first time since she'd eaten, Kate began to believe lunch might stay put. Relief flowed through her and she relaxed against Lucas's chest. She became aware of his breath at her temple, the heat of his arms against hers. Gradually, relief morphed into self-consciousness. She felt silly and vulnerable. She wanted her strength, her dignity back. Yet, the security of his embrace comforted her.

"Feeling better?" The closeness of his voice startled her.

"I am, actually." Her stomach still rebelled; her head still swam. *But at least I'm not wishing I was dead.* It was an improvement.

"Good." He squeezed her and let go. "I'll get us back to shore as quick as I can."

He left, and the wind brushed the heat of her back where he'd been, chilling her skin. She watched him walk away, his long, steady legs navigating the deck. The wind tousled his hair as he adjusted one of the sails.

For some reason it was harder than she expected to look away. She rested her forearms on the railing and turned toward the horizon.

Later that night, Kate lay in bed alone, grateful to feel human again. Dry land was a wonderful thing. She didn't plan on leaving it anytime soon. After they'd docked, Lucas had brought her straight home, even though she felt better. He'd left with her grocery list and returned with a half dozen bags of food, then scolded her for cleaning while he'd been gone.

She smiled against the feather pillow. She hadn't figured on him being a mother hen. Then she remembered the feel of his solid arms around her and the roughness of his jaw at her temple, and something inside her stirred. Had he called her "honey" earlier?

What is wrong with me? I love Bryan. This isn't a real marriage, but a business arrangement.

And good thing. You couldn't find a more polar-opposite husband. Lucas is everything you need to avoid in a permanent relationship.

If she were to receive a Dear Dr. Kate letter spelling out her own circumstances, her advice would be to run. *"Don't get involved with someone ill suited to you; it's an invitation for disaster,"* she'd write.

But moments later, when the bed sank behind her with Lucas's weight, she couldn't stop her heart from speeding or her breath from catching. The covers shifted, and she felt the mattress dip down, felt his body almost touching hers.

Then she felt something else. A kiss pressed to the crown of her head.

Everything stilled for a moment as she waited . . . hopeful? Fearful? She wasn't sure what emotion made her heart stutter.

The bed quivered again as Lucas settled on his side, and her heart's pace slowly returned to normal as her eyes searched the darkness.

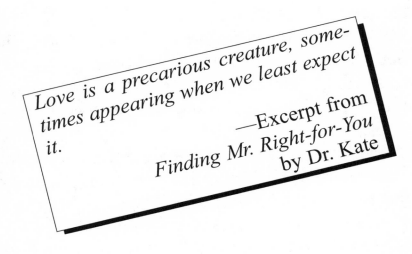

Love is a precarious creature, sometimes appearing when we least expect
it.
—Excerpt from
Finding Mr. Right-for-You
by Dr. Kate

Chapter Fourteen

Kate's feet pounded the pavement beside Susan's as they turned the corner and headed toward their homes. She'd decided she would bring up Susan and Roy's marriage today, but if she didn't hurry, Susan would be giving her a curt good-bye and striding up the grassy hill to her house.

Kate checked her watch. She had a scheduled meeting with Mr. and Mrs. Hornsby in an hour. Mr. Hornsby had broken it off with the other woman and they were trying to put their marriage back together. Even though Kate wasn't officially counseling them, she knew they were counting on her help.

She would need a shower before the meeting, so there was no extending the walk.

Their breaths slowed as their strides shortened. Kate tried to find the words. She had to be subtle so she didn't come across like a know-it-all counselor interfering in her in-laws' relationship.

Silence had settled between them; now would be the perfect opportunity to say something.

"Susan, can I ask you something?"

Her mother-in-law stepped over a crack in the pavement. "All right."

"Well," Kate took a few breaths. "I've been thinking lately about conflict in marriage. Well, really, conflict resolution. When you and Roy have a disagreement, how do you handle it? How do you resolve it?"

She stopped, afraid she'd put her foot in her mouth if she continued. Truthfully she wondered if the couple even employed conflict resolution the way they picked at one another.

Susan quirked a brow. "I'm surprised you're asking."

Kate stiffened. "Why do you say that?"

Susan flipped her hair from her face. "Well. You're the expert."

Why did the woman have to rub her the wrong way? "I know. It's just—" *Just what? Tell her I'm taking a poll or something?*

"I suppose studying relationships and actually being in one are two different things," Susan said.

Kate wasn't sure where Susan was going, but she nodded. "Marriage isn't easy. Conflict is a normal part of it, though. You're lucky Lucas is so easygoing."

Susan must think—Oh, great. She thought Kate and Lucas were having problems. She'd probably made the woman's day.

A yappy little dog scurried down a gravel driveway but stopped short of reaching them.

"Roy used to give me the silent treatment for days when he was upset. Sometimes I didn't even know why he was mad and by the time we talked about it, he'd blown it all out of proportion." Susan shook her head. "I used to get so mad when we argued that I'd storm out of the room or even take off in the car."

"Really?"

Susan launched into a story, and Kate realized she'd hit pay dirt: Susan thought Kate needed advice, and she certainly had no trouble offering it. Finally, Kate had a way to get Susan to open up. Of course, Susan was coming at it from the wrong angle, but still . . . Maybe now Kate could finally get some real insights into Susan and Roy's marriage. And finally begin fulfilling her promise to help Lucas.

That evening Lucas was fixing a broken lamp when a knock sounded at the back door. Kate, who was in the kitchen loading the dishwasher, opened the door. Lucas heard his sister's voice. "Is Lucas home?"

"Of course," Kate said.

Jamie entered the living room, and Lucas saw tears sparkling in her eyes. He set the lamp on the table. "Hey, what's wrong, sis?"

Jamie plopped beside him and crossed her arms over her T-shirt. "I just got back from Meredith's house and she said—" Jamie sniffed as a tear escaped. "She said Aaron said I was a loser."

"Now why would she say that?"

Jamie flicked the tear off her cheek. "When we were at the beach last week, you know, after I talked to you, I went up to Aaron and sat with him. We talked and I tried to, like, show him I was interested like you said."

Lucas's stomach sank. He hoped he hadn't given her bad advice. The last thing he'd do was hurt her.

"I thought things went pretty well, but he didn't come to the beach anymore that week, and I haven't seen him since."

"And then you went to Meredith's today?"

"Yeah. We were having a good time and everything, and then she just brings up Aaron and says that he called her a few days ago after I sat with him on the beach, and that he called me a loser!" Jamie wept into her hands. "I made such a fool of myself!"

"Oh, honey, come here." Lucas wrapped his arm around Jamie, and she turned in to his shirt.

"I flirted with him and everything." Her hands muffled her voice. "I practically threw myself at him."

Lucas rubbed Jamie's shoulder. Across the room, Kate loaded a plate in the dishwasher and met his glance, a sympathetic smile on her face.

Lucas returned his attention to Jamie. "Now, hang on. Why did Aaron call Meredith?"

"What?"

"You said Aaron called Meredith and he said you were a loser. Why was he calling her?"

She uncovered her mottled face. "I don't know."

"How do you know she's telling the truth?"

Jamie sniffled. "Why would she lie?" Her eyes widened.

"Well," Lucas said. "Relationships can be complicated. For instance, what if Meredith likes Aaron? What if she's jealous?"

Jamie straightened a bit and wiped her face with the back of her hand. "I guess that could happen. But if Aaron called her, he might like her and not me."

"That's possible too. I'm just saying you should think it through and not necessarily believe everything you're told."

Jamie tilted her head and stared at the stone fireplace. "He did seem interested at the beach." Jamie ran her finger along the couch's trim. "He even said I have pretty hair."

Lucas smiled. "That doesn't sound like a boy who thinks you're a loser."

"I know. I thought he'd call, but it's been almost a week, and he hasn't been at the beach either."

Lucas squeezed her shoulder. "Give it time. Maybe he doesn't want to appear too anxious."

"I guess."

Jamie and Lucas talked until she felt better, and when his sister left, she hugged him before sliding out the back door.

Kate changed into pajamas and opened the closet door, peeking at the suit she'd bought for her appearance with Dr. Phil. It was a dove-gray Ann Taylor with a structured jacket and streamlined pants. The classic white oxford under the jacket was a good contrast for her skin tone and black hair.

She ran her fingers down the soft material of the suit coat, feeling anxiety work into her fingers. She'd been invited on the show to advise an engaged couple who was having difficulty merging their personalities. What if she said the wrong thing? Worse, what if Dr. Phil disagreed with her advice?

Relax. You're trained for this. You're an expert.

Except in my own relationships, where I'm the epitome of disaster.

Nobody knows that. As far as they're concerned, you married your Mr. Right.

But what if the media attention from this appearance invited scrutiny of her marriage? What if someone figured it out? What if one of Bryan's relatives saw the show and leaked the truth?

Kate closed the closet door. She could only hope for the best. She'd already taken preventative measures. Maybe one more call to Bryan, asking him to check in with his family, wouldn't hurt.

But maybe that was just her wanting to talk to Bryan. She was suddenly tired, though it was only nine o'clock. She approached the nightstand, ready to set her alarm, when she noticed a box on the new nightstand Lucas had brought home.

The box was wrapped in pale pink paper with a white bow. She picked it up. "To Kate," it said on the tiny gift tag in Lucas's left-handed scrawl. She pried open the piece of tape, unwrapped the package, and pulled out a navy-blue velvet box.

The hinge creaked as she opened the lid. Inside, a delicate pair of earrings were nestled side by side. Elegant in their simplicity, they were the same silvery tone as her wedding band.

"Hope you don't mind." Lucas's voice startled her from the doorway. He looked boyishly shy, and she couldn't keep from smiling.

"What kind of woman minds getting jewelry?"

He shrugged, walking toward her. "You don't wear much jewelry. I just thought . . . Well, it's been a month today."

Their anniversary, such as it was. Lucas stopped at the foot of the bed. She watched a blush creep into his cheeks.

"It was very thoughtful. Actually, they're perfect for the *Dr. Phil* show."

What did the gift mean? Flowers was one thing, jewelry another. Was Lucas trying to make their relationship appear real? Or was there more to the gesture? Her insides fluttered at the thought. She remembered the way he'd laid a kiss on her head. It had been sweet. It made her feel . . . protected.

She glanced at the box in her hand. "I'm sorry. I didn't—"

Lucas waved her off. "I didn't expect you to. I saw those in the window at Pageo's and thought of you."

He was making nothing of it. Maybe it didn't mean anything, but it had been a thoughtful gesture. Lucas had some irritating qualities, but he could be awfully sweet when he wanted to be. Carried away by the moment, Kate reached up and kissed him on the cheek. Her lips tingled against the roughness of his jaw.

When she pulled back, she saw something in Lucas's eyes and wondered if she'd crossed some invisible line. But then he rubbed the back of his neck and turned away. "You heading to bed?"

She closed the lid of the box, watching him go. "Yeah, I'm beat."

He turned as he pulled the door. " 'Night."

"Oh, I forgot to tell you I talked with your mom this morning. The subject of conflict came up and I asked her about her and your dad."

Lucas stilled, his hand on the knob. "What did she say?"

Kate sighed and rolled her eyes. "She thought I was asking her because we were having trouble. Like I wanted her advice on how to handle conflict."

Lucas chuckled. "That's rich."

Kate frowned at him. "It's not funny. She must think I'm a lousy counselor." *She's wondering what kind of idiot her son married.*

"Relax. She's just doing what moms do."

Well, then. How would Kate know that? In her experience moms didn't give advice and nurture. They went out and came back unexpectedly and left you wondering what would happen next.

"Anyway," she said. "I wanted to tell you I'd gotten

the ball rolling, that's all." She sat on the bed. "Good night."

After Lucas pulled the door shut, Kate threw the wrapping paper in the trash and tucked the jewelry box inside the top nightstand drawer. She flipped off the lamp and crawled under the covers, but it was a long time before she drifted to sleep.

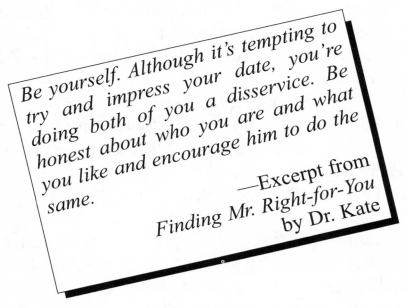

Be yourself. Although it's tempting to try and impress your date, you're doing both of you a disservice. Be honest about who you are and what you like and encourage him to do the same.

—Excerpt from Finding Mr. Right-for-You by Dr. Kate

Chapter Fifteen

Kate stepped from the fog of the bathroom and toweled off her wet hair. She could smell bacon frying and hear it sizzling on the griddle. She'd come to expect Lucas's big breakfasts on Saturday and had decided it was a nice start to a weekend. As long as she stayed out of the kitchen while Lucas cooked and she didn't have to see the counters splotched with pancake batter or the cracked eggshells in a pile near the sink. If she faced the wall as she ate and didn't have to see the mess, she could almost put it from her mind.

Kate was shoving her towel into the bedroom hamper she'd bought when the phone rang. By the time she entered the kitchen, Lucas had answered.

"Who's calling?" he asked, setting the greasy spatula on the counter. "Just a minute." He handed her the phone, wearing an inscrutable expression.

"Who is it?" she mouthed.

"Bryan." Lucas turned and stirred the pancake batter.

Kate's adrenaline spiked like she'd had three shots of espresso. Why was Bryan calling? She walked toward the back door and put the phone to her ear.

"Hello?" Her tone was cool and collected.

"Hi, it's me."

It rankled that he could still say that. *It's me.* Like they were still so close he needn't identify himself. Had he forgotten he'd dumped her for someone else? Kate stepped out the back door and closed it behind her, keeping Bo inside.

"Bryan. How are you?" There was nothing in her voice to make him think she actually cared to hear the answer.

"I'm good. Better than I've been in weeks."

"Wonderful. Is there something I can help you with?" Polite. Friendly, but not too friendly. It unnerved her that it was such a strain. Was it just barely over a month ago that he'd kissed her good night on the eve of their wedding day?

"Kate, I'm so sorry. It's killing me to hear you like this. Like we're strangers or business acquaintances."

Did he have any right to tell her about his pain?

"I called to say I was wrong," he said. "I know that now."

Kate stared toward the horizon and leaned against the square column that supported the roof.

"Things are over with Stephanie." He said it like he expected her to shoot off fireworks in celebration.

Stephanie. So that was her name. It was no one Kate knew. She was glad for that.

The pause was deafening. Emotions twisted in her like vines around a tree. She wasn't sure which was strongest.

"Kate, did you hear me?"

What did he want from her? Now that he'd dropped his other woman, was Kate supposed to fall in his arms again? "What am I supposed to say?"

"I know. I know," he said. "I—" Kate could hear the frustration in his voice. She imagined him running his hand through his blunt cut.

"I was a fool," he continued. "It was just like you said. It was nothing more than a fear of commitment. I was afraid and looking for an outlet, and Stephanie was convenient."

"Your outlet was costly."

Costly wasn't the word. It had changed her life, changed their future. It was a little late to realize he'd made a mistake. Did he think he could fix it so easily?

A seagull cried out overhead and swooped over the

beach, soaring with wide wings. Kate wished she could leave all this behind her and soar over the land-scape of her life as the bird did.

"I miss you, Kate."

The words, spoken softly, pried at the door of her heart. Kate closed her eyes. *I will not tell him I miss him.* He didn't deserve to hear it, and she wasn't even sure it was true. Her feelings for him were muddled, blurry, like the line between the ocean and sky. How could that be when she'd been so certain of her feel-ings for him only five weeks ago?

"I'm married, Bryan." It gave her no pleasure to say it. She'd heard the pain in Bryan's voice, and even though he'd hurt her terribly, she didn't wish to hurt him.

"I know." He swore. It was the first time Kate had heard him swear. Why had he called? He didn't know her marriage was temporary, though he must realize genuine feelings weren't involved. Did Bryan think she'd divorce Lucas the moment he returned?

"Who is he, Kate? Do you know what it's doing to me, imagining the two of you together?"

"Yeah, actually, I do," she snapped.

"I'm sorry. Of course you do." He sighed. "I don't know what I'm saying. I'm just—I'm just going crazy over here. My whole life has been so planned, all my ducks in a row, and now I just feel like it's all exploded in my face."

Have you forgotten you're the one who lit the fuse? She wanted to say it out loud, but what good would it do? What was done was done. She had to stay married. The media would have a heyday if she divorced Lucas and married Bryan. She shook the thought from her head. It was ludicrous to even entertain the idea.

"You don't love him, do you?"

Kate grabbed the hair at her nape and squeezed. To tell him yes would be a lie, but to tell him no felt like a betrayal to Lucas. She let the silence grow. She wanted to ask if he'd loved Stephanie, but what did it matter now? The other woman's journey with Bryan was over, and she had nothing but a foiled wedding as a souvenir.

A bolt of fear struck her thoughts. *What if Stephanie leaks the information to the media? What if she told them Bryan was supposed to be my husband and that I'm nothing but a fraud?*

"Bryan, how did things end with you and Stephanie?"

The pause seemed to last a lifetime. "What do you mean?"

"How did things end?" she asked sharply. "Did you break it off? Was she upset?" She grasped the phone tightly, wanting to wring the answer from it.

"I broke it off," Bryan said. "She was upset. Why, Kate?"

Kate descended the deck steps and crossed the sandy grass toward the shoreline. "What if she goes to the media and tells them everything?" She felt like swearing herself. She didn't know what kind of a person Stephanie was. Was she the vindictive sort?

"She wouldn't do that," Bryan said.

"How do you know?" She wanted proof. Or better yet, a reason Stephanie wouldn't want the news out that she'd broken up Dr. Kate's marriage. Maybe she detested being in the spotlight or had a career that would be damaged by the gossip.

"She's not like that. There would be no reason for her to do it."

"You said she was upset."

"Well, she was, but I think she'd—"

"You *think* or you know?" Kate kicked a hill of sand and took a breath.

"I'll call her if it'll make you feel better. I'll do whatever I have to do to protect you, I promise."

His tone was sincere, but the last promise Bryan had made ended with her at the altar saying "I do" to another man.

Lucas turned off the griddle and scooped the bacon onto a plate. It clanked as he set it too hard on the table. He opened the oven and removed the warming pancakes.

He had no idea how long Kate would be on the phone, but he was going to eat while it was hot. He scooted his chair back and sank into it. Bo, knowing better than to beg for food, settled on the rug beside him.

When Bryan had identified himself, Lucas had wanted to ask what business he had calling *his* home on a Saturday morning and asking to speak to his wife.

He might have done it, if Kate hadn't been standing there with her wide eyes and tousled wet hair.

She'd gone outside for privacy, but he'd heard every word through the open window.

Lucas grabbed a piece of bacon and took a bite. He'd been relieved at Kate's cool tone even though he knew she was only guarding her heart.

When he heard her say, "I'm married, Bryan," he wondered what had prompted those words. Did Bryan want her back? Is that why he'd called?

The back door opened, and Kate entered. She set the phone in the cradle and joined him at the table. Her face revealed nothing. Was she wishing she'd never married him? Was she wishing it was Bryan at the breakfast table now?

Well, Bryan had left her for another woman. It was Lucas who'd cared enough to follow through. Lucas who'd stuck by her though all those publicity photos. Lucas who got up at the crack of dawn and fixed her eggs over easy, the way she liked them.

Kate picked up her fork, and the diamond on her finger glittered under the kitchen lights. Bryan's diamond. Lucas wanted to slide it off her finger and toss it into the ocean.

He took a drink of coffee and set the mug down hard. It clattered against the saucer and splattered on the table. Without a word he stood and retrieved a towel, wiping up the mess before settling in his chair.

"What's wrong?" Kate asked.

"Nothing." *My wife's ex-fiancé called my home and*

probably declared his love for her. What could be wrong? He bit into his eggs.

"Well, something's wrong."

Lucas swallowed hard, trying to suppress words he shouldn't say. "I don't appreciate your ex-fiancé calling here, is all." He applauded his calm tone. Across from him, he felt Kate still.

"I didn't think—I mean—" She cleared her throat. "It's not like this is a real—"

He looked at her, daring her to say it. Yeah, maybe it wasn't a real marriage in theory, but there were feelings involved. His. And he'd been hoping hers were a little involved. Had he been wrong?

"I just meant—"

"I know what you meant, Kate." Lucas stood and took his plate to the trash, dumping a half slice of bacon and the remainder of his sticky pancakes.

"Bryan was supposed to be my husband. Things ended very quickly and there was no time for closure—"

"I was there, remember?" He rinsed his plate in the sink, washing the yellowed yolk with the scrub brush.

"Of course you were."

She said it so quietly, he almost didn't hear over the running water.

"If you hadn't married me, I'd—I don't know what I would've done. I appreciate what you did. I hope you know that."

Did her voice shake on those last words?

Lucas had too many emotions storming through him.

He was still angry, and yet, from her point of view, it wasn't justified. It couldn't be unless she knew how he felt, and it was too soon for Kate to learn that.

"What did he want, if you don't mind my asking?" He shut off the water and leaned on the sink ledge, keeping his back to her. His thumbs curled around the sink's corners.

"Of course not."

He heard her pick up her coffee cup and take a sip. It settled into the saucer with a quiet click.

"He had some unsettling news about the woman he was with. Apparently he broke it off with her and she's somewhat upset."

Lucas steeled himself at her words. What was to keep Kate from going back to him? Her career? Her book? Would she let those things stand in the way if she still loved Bryan?

"I'm concerned that she's going to leak the news to the media," Kate said. "If she's angry enough, it would be a one heck of a way to retaliate."

Lucas heard a scuffle on the deck. Bo? Then he remembered Bo was lying on the rug under the table. That meant . . .

Oh, shoot! He leaned forward and peered out the window far enough to see Jamie running from the house.

"Jamie," he called out the window, but she didn't stop. He rushed after her, opening the door and taking the steps in one leap. Had she heard everything they'd said? "Jamie, wait!"

He caught up with her on the grassy knoll and took hold of her arm.

She jerked her arm from his grip. "Let go of me!" Her chest heaved.

"What were you doing snooping outside my house?"

"I wasn't snooping. I came to talk to Kate and I heard you fighting." She crossed her arms.

"We weren't fighting."

"It's not my fault the window was open."

Lucas stuffed his hands in his shorts pockets and thought back to what Jamie might have heard. They'd said enough. "It's complicated, Jamie."

His sister glared at him. "You lied to us."

Lucas swallowed around the lump of pancakes that seemed to have congealed in his throat. He looked back at the house to where Kate stood on the deck, one foot in front of the other, as if torn about whether to stay or come. He waved her back. It would be better to handle Jamie alone.

"I don't know how much you heard but—"

"I heard enough to know it's all a big lie."

"That's enough. It's not a lie. Kate was in a fix. Her career was on the line, and I stepped in to help her."

"How could you just pretend to love each other? We all thought she was part of our family, and now you're telling me it's fake."

Lucas turned toward the ocean. He remembered being out there with Kate the week before, remembered the feel of her in his arms when she'd been sick. There'd been nothing fake about that.

"I'm telling Mom and Dad the truth." Jamie turned to go.

Lucas grabbed her wrist. "Don't, Jamie." If their mom knew the marriage wasn't real, there would be no holding back the resentment. She'd scare Kate away for good.

His sister whirled around. "Why shouldn't I? You should've been honest to begin with instead of making us think your marriage was real."

"It *is* real."

"I'm not a baby, Lucas. I know your marriage is real on paper, but it's not real in here." She tapped her heart. "And that's the only thing that counts."

All those romance novels had gone to his sister's head. Sometimes reality couldn't live up to the happily-ever-afters in her books.

"Can you keep a secret?" Lucas asked.

Jamie stared at him, her green eyes squinting against the glare of the sun. She crossed her arms. "You know I don't like secrets."

She was growing up. He remembered a time when she'd collected secrets like seashells.

"This is personal. Like your feelings for Aaron. I'd never tell anyone about that."

He could see her acquiescence in the way she tucked in the corners of her mouth. "What is it?"

Lucas glanced over his shoulder toward the house. Kate had gone inside. "Kate loved Bryan." He rubbed the back of his neck. "She probably still loves him, for all I know. She married me because she was backed into a corner and I was her only way out."

Jamie's eyes softened, and her squared shoulders relaxed.

Lucas turned his face into the wind and let the salty breeze push his hair off his face. "But I had different reasons." Lucas met Jamie's gaze, then took his hand from his pocket and touched his heart. His eyes clung to Jamie's, and he saw hers glaze over.

"It's not a fake marriage." His voice deepened with emotion. "I love her. I'd lay down my life for her if necessary. Do you know how rare that kind of love is?"

Jamie blinked rapidly. "But she doesn't love you?"

Lucas gave her a half smile. "I chose to love her. Whatever she does with that is her decision."

Jamie sniffed. "That's so sad."

Great, now she pities me. "Hey, she's got to come around eventually, right?" He tapped her nose and struck a ridiculous pose. "I mean, what's not to like about this?"

Jamie pushed him, but she smiled around her tears.

"Are we okay now?" Lucas asked. He couldn't stand to have Jamie mad at him.

Jamie nodded.

"I can count on you to keep my secret?"

Jamie kicked his ankle with her flip-flop. "You know you can."

Lucas pulled her toward him and held her there, his hand on her head. He realized it felt good to admit how he felt about Kate. A relief to release it.

Then he heard Jamie's muffled voice. "And to think I was coming to *you* for love advice."

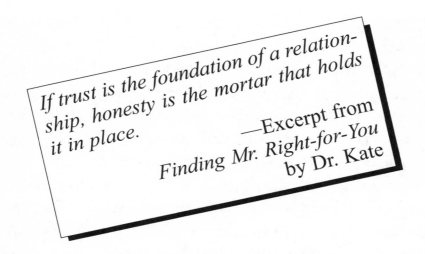

If trust is the foundation of a relationship, honesty is the mortar that holds it in place.

—Excerpt from Finding Mr. Right-for-You by Dr. Kate

Chapter Sixteen

Kate clutched her hands in her lap, feeling her palms grow hot and sweaty. Dr. Phil's set looked exactly as it did on TV. She'd already been coached by Pam and Chloe, her publicist and her editor. Her agent, Ronald, had also met her at the studio for emotional support. But now she was on her own. When she'd left the green room, Dr. Phil had welcomed her graciously and congratulated her on her new book.

But now, as the cameras were ready to roll, Kate felt as if her nervous system was on overload. The newlyweds she was to advise sat on stage with Dr. Phil. The crew was placing mikes on their lapels and giving them last-minute instructions. Hope was a cute blonde with a pixie face and good taste in shoes. Ryan had dark hair, well trimmed, and repeatedly pushed his glasses up the bridge of his nose with his finger.

Kate was grateful to be on the first row of the audience rather than under the bright lights of the stage. Beside her was a child psychologist who was there to advise a family in crisis. She'd brought her husband, and they whispered back and forth. On Kate's other side were the parents of the couple Kate was to advise.

Kate straightened her suit coat, making sure the mike was well placed, then twisted the earrings Lucas had gotten her.

Be still, Kate. It's not live, only tape. And they can edit if anything goes wrong.

Oh, please, don't let anything go wrong!

She wished she had someone beside her to tell her everything was going to be okay. At that thought, Lucas's image flared in her mind like a Fourth of July firework. And just as quickly she reared back in surprise. *What is with me? I'm an independent woman.* She was accustomed to being on her own, and no one needed to tell her she didn't need a man to be happy. She'd been dispensing that advice for years.

But her thoughts returned to her last few moments with Lucas at the airport the day before. He'd managed to get her there on time and had insisted on walking her to the counter where she checked in. Then he walked her to security. Among the people being herded through security, Kate recognized Dahlia Stevens from the Chamber of Commerce, setting her bag and laptop in a gray tub. She waved at Kate and Lucas.

"Our first night apart," Lucas teased, setting her bag down.

"I'm not sure I'll be able to sleep without your snoring."

"I don't snore."

"Hah!" she said, and he grinned.

There was an awkward moment when they realized it was time to say good-bye. Kate was about to leave Lucas for the first time since their wedding. She was excited about the show, but also nervous. She wasn't used to hiding personal secrets and certainly not from the country at large. Now she would be on national TV, and what if something went wrong?

"You'll do great." Lucas seemed to read her thoughts. "Dr. Phil will probably make you a regular if you're not careful."

"I don't think I'm ready to move to Hollywood."

Lucas smiled. "Good."

Kate glanced at her watch. "I should get to my gate." She pulled her boarding pass and driver's license from her suit pocket.

"Have a safe flight." Lucas looked over her shoulder, and Kate knew he was conscious of Dahlia. He leaned forward and gave her a kiss. The gentleness of his touch tugged at her, even with the brevity of it. Would she ever get used to him kissing her? Wasn't it supposed to become old hat after a while?

Now, as Kate waited for the cameras to roll, she touched her lips, remembering the way they had tingled after the kiss.

Do I have feelings for Lucas? Feelings that go beyond friendship?

176

Before she could chase the thought, one of the crew gave the signal for taping to begin, and the show was underway. Her couple was up first, thankfully.

Dr Phil started. "Today we have Hope and Ryan. They've been married for eight months and are wondering if they're just too different to make it work. Come on, guys, you're supposed to be in the deliriously happy newlywed stage, so what gives?"

Hope twined her fingers with Ryan's. "The delirious stage lasted about two days for us."

"It was a whirlwind kind of courtship," Ryan said. "I guess we didn't know each other very well, didn't realize how different we were."

"How long did you all date?" Dr. Phil asked.

They looked at each other; then Hope cringed. "Five weeks."

The audience groaned.

"Five weeks!" Dr. Phil's voice rose. "You barely know how he takes his coffee in five weeks."

"I know, I know," Hope said. "It was impetuous, and we regret that we didn't wait longer. I guess I let the whole 'falling in love' thing go to my head. I mean, we are in love, and we want to make it work. But we're so different—we just aren't sure how to find a middle ground."

"Well, they say opposites attract," Dr. Phil said. "Tell us what your hot buttons are. What are the differences that drive you crazy?"

Hope and Ryan eyed each other again. "I guess our spending habits are one of the biggest issues," Hope admitted. "It's not like I go on spending sprees or anything, but I like to dress nicely, and Ryan was raised to be more tightfisted—"

"Frugal," Ryan corrected. "I believe in a budget."

"And I think 'What's money for if you can't spend a little?'" Hope wrinkled her nose.

They went on to discuss their differing views on household duties, their differing social needs, and their differing recreational preferences.

"Well," Dr. Phil said. "We brought in reinforcements on this one. Dr. Kate, syndicated columnist and author of the newly released *Finding Mr. Right-for-You* is here to see if we can't help you two make this thing work out."

Kate smiled as the camera focused on her, and the audience applauded. She could feel prickles of heat singeing the skin under her arms.

"Dr. Kate has something else in common with you two—she's also a newlywed, so congratulations on that."

"Thank you." Kate smiled.

"Now, Dr. Kate," Dr. Phil said, "We know you advocate investing the time and energy to make a solid match, but what about situations like this? Are they too different to make it work?"

Kate felt a bolt of energy at the opportunity to help Hope and Ryan. How many times had she advised similar couples in her office? At least this couple hadn't waited until they had years of animosity between them.

"First of all," Kate began, "Congratulations on your marriage and on your willingness to seek help from the beginning. Every marriage is a merging of two personalities—sometimes more if there are children involved. When you're blending two sets of ideals and expectations, there's bound to be conflict. And when you're opposites, there's a greater amount of conflict." *Boy, can I relate to that.*

"The key," she continued, "is to determine which areas need changing and find the middle ground. Pick your battles. Does it really matter that he balls up his socks before he throws them in the hamper? Probably not. Does it matter that you disagree on how much of your income is expendable? Definitely."

Kate swallowed, hoping nobody could tell how dry her mouth was. "Relationships are constantly negotiated," she added. "Opposites can make it work if they're both willing to find the middle ground. And both of you seem willing to make this work."

"We are," Hope said. "But every time we have discussions about our differences, we end up arguing."

Kate jumped in. "It's important to choose the right timing when you discuss your differing opinions. For instance, the arrival of the Visa bill isn't a good time to discuss Hope's spending habits. It's too late, and that leaves Ryan feeling stressed and out of control."

"Exactly," Ryan said. "I'm already angry that she's spent the money without regard for my budget."

Dr. Phil spoke up. "And, Hope, did you sit down

with Ryan and work out this budget, or was it foisted upon you?"

Hope nodded. "Ryan did the budget on his own. There is no room for good shoes in that budget."

The audience laughed.

"A woman's got to have good shoes, Ryan," Dr. Phil said. "Rule number one."

He turned toward the camera. "You can read more about how to find a suitable mate in Dr. Kate's book *Finding Mr. Right-for-You*." There was a close-up of her book cover, then Dr. Phil continued. "All right, next we have a blended family who can't seem to blend." He looked at Hope and Ryan. "And you thought blending two was tough! We'll be right back."

After the show, Kate slid into the black limo for her trip to the airport. In the back of the car, her nerves still jangled. It had been an exciting experience, and she felt giddy with energy. She'd already celebrated with Pam, Chloe, and Ronald in the green room, but now that she was away from the moment, she wanted to share it with a friend. Before she would have called Bryan, but who did she call now?

Anna? No, her former assistant was out of town with her new job.

Her dad? She considered it a moment, then took out her cell and dialed. It rang and rang before going over to voice mail, and she hung up.

She had to tell somebody. What good was exciting news if she had no one to share it with?

Well, I know exactly who I could call.

Well, then, Kate, just do it.

She dialed Lucas's shop, and when Ethan answered, she asked for Lucas. As she waited, she second-guessed herself. Would he find it odd that she'd phoned him when she'd see him at the airport in several hours? Why should he even care how the show had gone? It was her career, her book. In a matter of months, she'd be nothing to him but a name on the divorce papers.

Shoot, why did I call him? Maybe I should hang up. Kate pulled the phone from her ear.

"Hello?"

She put the phone back. "Hi, it's Kate."

"Hey!" He sounded happy to hear from her. "How'd it go?"

Kate relaxed a bit. He didn't seem confused by her call. "It went very well. Quick, but good."

"All your worries were for nothing. I knew you'd do great."

"Easy for you to say. You weren't the one on national TV."

He chuckled, and she realized she missed the warmth of his laugh. "That's why I make furniture and you give interviews."

She sighed, the excitement of the morning giving way to something calmer.

"Where are you now?"

"In the back of a limousine." The driver turned onto the freeway and accelerated.

"Aren't you special. How was the hotel?"

"Gorgeous, accommodating, and pristine. You could have eaten off the floors."

"Hope you didn't get too accustomed to that."

"Don't worry—I'm already anticipating the condition of the house."

He chuckled again, and Kate let a comfortable silence fall as she settled back into the leather seats.

"My flight's running on time. The question is, will you be?" she joked.

"Only time will tell," he retorted.

"Is that supposed to be a pun? It might help if you wore a watch, you know."

"What fun would that be?"

Kate chuckled. He was hopeless. "I guess I'll meet you outside baggage claim. Do you have my flight number?"

"Uh, let's see." She heard crackling, like he was holding the phone between his ear and shoulder. He was probably riffling through his cluttered wallet.

Some things never changed. "Here, let me give it to you again." Kate consulted her ticket and rattled off the flight number and arrival time.

When they hung up, Kate tucked the ticket into her suit coat and looked out the window, watching palm trees and tall buildings go by. In two weeks, the show would be broadcast, and the sales of her book, already good, from what Rosewood told her, might just sky-rocket. Would it hit the *New York Times* bestseller list? She could only keep her fingers crossed. It couldn't hurt to have Dr. Phil announcing her title on the air.

But she couldn't quell the niggling fear that national attention would expose her to personal scrutiny. And now that she'd gone so public, what was to stop someone from digging around and finding out the truth? The answer was as close as Bryan and his family. Or, more likely, Stephanie.

Now that she was in the public eye, reporters would jump at the chance to smear her reputation. And, for the first time, she realized it wouldn't only be her reputation that got ruined. What would the exposure do to Lucas and his family? Jamie might already know the truth, but the rest of his family would feel betrayed, and Lucas would suffer the scrutiny and distrust of his own hometown.

What am I doing?

It felt as though she'd been asking herself that question every day for the past month. And she still didn't know the answer.

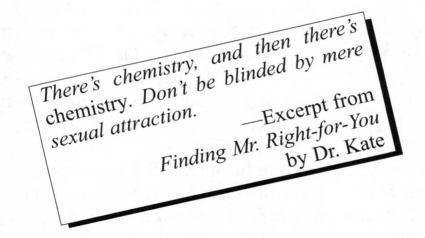

There's chemistry, and then there's chemistry. Don't be blinded by mere sexual attraction.

—Excerpt from *Finding Mr. Right-for-You* by Dr. Kate

Chapter Seventeen

"Ready?" Kate heard Lucas call from the shop downstairs.

She saved her article and grabbed her purse. When she reached the bottom of the stairs, Lucas was waiting, keys in hand.

"What are you doing?" she asked.

"Taking you home to watch the show."

"Oh." The realization that he wanted to see it sent warmth through Kate. She avoided his gaze as she slid past. "Well, come on, then. It starts in fifteen."

After a quick trip home, Kate flipped on the TV, and Lucas made a pot of coffee. Kate's fingers fluttered like a ship's sails as she waited.

A tap sounded at the front door. Roy peeked around the edge.

"Hello! We're not late, are we?" He entered, followed by Susan, Brody, and Jamie.

"Oh, my goodness, you all came." Kate hadn't expected it to be a family affair.

"We wouldn't miss this for the world, would we, dear?" Roy said. "It's your national debut."

The group of them congregated on and around the sofa.

"Are you nervous?" Jamie asked.

"A little," Kate said. "Which is silly since it's taped."

"I'm sure you did fabulously," Roy said. "I'll bet your book is going to make that bestseller list yet. We have a real celebrity in the family!"

Kate glanced at Jamie, feeling awkward at the mention of family. Jamie withdrew a romance novel from her bag and propped it open on the arm of the couch.

"Coffee, anyone?" Lucas asked from the kitchen.

"Sure." Roy grabbed the remote and turned up the volume.

"Turn it down, Roy; that's too loud," Susan said.

Brody checked his watch. "You better hurry. Two minutes and counting."

Kate sank into the armchair.

"When is your segment on?" Brody asked.

"It's first—if they air it in the order they taped it."

Moments later, Lucas handed Kate and Roy their mugs, then retrieved his own cup and sat on the arm of Kate's chair. Bo settled on the rug beside Jamie and she scratched behind his ears.

"Hey, his icky yellow beard is gone."

Kate had donned rubber gloves the day before and

185

scrubbed the mutt's chin. "I cleaned him up and put cornstarch in the fur under his mouth."

The corner of Lucas's lips twitched. "Cornstarch?"

"It's amazing what you can learn when you Google something."

The *Dr. Phil* theme song began. "Be quiet; it's on." Roy increased the volume until Susan glared at him.

Jamie closed her book and leaned forward.

As they watched the opening, Kate's hands grew cold. Lucas's family's attention was rapt on the TV. She was the only reason they'd come. How easily they'd accepted her into their family, counting her as one of their own. Even Susan seemed to be giving her a chance. They couldn't be more supportive if it were Lucas on the show.

I'm a horrible, horrible person.

Dr. Phil introduced Kate, and her face appeared on screen.

"There you are," Jamie said.

"Shhhh!" Brody said.

The room got quiet as Dr. Phil mentioned her newlywed status. Kate felt her face heat, and Lucas set his hand on her shoulder. Kate sipped her coffee.

The segment continued, going exactly as Kate remembered. Her makeup, which had seemed too heavy on the day of the show, looked natural under the lights, and the stylist had done a nice job with her hair.

When Dr. Phil announced the title of her book and showed the cover, Lucas squeezed her shoulder. She'd hoped they wouldn't edit that out.

The segment ended and they broke for a commercial.

"Well done, Kate." Roy said.

"You did great," Jamie said. "How did you stay so calm? I wouldn't know what to say."

Brody elbowed her. "That'll be the day."

Jamie jostled him back.

"It's second nature by now," Kate said. "Though I was nervous since it was national TV."

"I couldn't tell," Roy said.

The phone rang, and Kate jumped up. "It's probably my publicist." She dashed to the kitchen and picked up. "Hello?"

"Hi, it's me."

Her stomach flopped. "Bryan," she said quietly, peering into the living room where Lucas's family continued their conversation. Lucas met her gaze, and she turned away, walking to the kitchen window.

"You were amazing, Kate," Bryan said. "I was so proud of you."

What right did he have to be proud? He didn't deserve to say those words. He hadn't coached her on what to say or driven her to the airport. *He didn't even show up for our wedding.*

Kate hadn't even thought of Bryan watching the show. She didn't think he'd even known it was airing today. Plus it was during work hours, and it wasn't like they were together anymore.

"You weren't even nervous," Bryan said. "And the way he plugged your book. I bet it'll take off now." He gave a familiar whistle. She'd forgotten that about Bryan—that little whistle he did to punctuate his excitement.

"That's the hope."

A long silence followed her words. Kate heard a ruckus in the living room and knew Lucas's family was leaving. Outside the window, the sea oats on the hill bowed against the breeze. Why had Bryan called again? Didn't he realize it was awkward for her?

"I miss you, Kate."

She gritted her teeth. "Stop it, Bryan."

"It's true. I miss the way you leave everything in tidy stacks, and the way you squint your eyes at me when I say something foolish. I miss the way you—"

"Stop it." He was getting to her, and she hated that. She rubbed her eyes. "You have to stop calling me here."

"Your cell was off."

"That's not what I mean. You can't just call me whenever you want now."

Kate heard footsteps behind her, heard the clatter of something being put in the sink. She turned and met Lucas's eyes. He knew it was Bryan; she could see that much in his expression. There was something in his eyes that tugged at her heartstrings. Hurt? Lucas looked away before she could pursue the thought.

". . . where we can talk in person," Bryan was saying.

What had she missed? He wanted to meet?

Lucas leaned against the sink, facing her, his palms

braced on the ledge behind him. His stance said, *Talk all you want. I'm not going anywhere.* What did he expect her to do? Hang up on Bryan? *It's not my fault he called. I didn't ask him to.*

"What about it, Kate?"

What about what? She couldn't think straight.

"Or I could come there if that's easier. Whatever you want to do, but I want to see you. I need to be with you. Please." He grated out the word.

Lucas cocked a brow.

Kate's heart beat like a frightened bird's, and she wasn't sure why. She felt cornered. By both of them. She had to get out of here. Away from Lucas's strange looks, away from Bryan's hurt pleas.

"I can't talk right now."

"I'll call you back," he managed to get out before Kate hung up. She set the phone in the cradle. A step away, she could feel Lucas's tension.

"I'm going for a walk." Kate grabbed the doorknob leading to the beach.

"I want him to stop calling here." Lucas crossed his arms over his chest, his right bicep bulging over his left fist. He looked away.

"I'm a little tired of everyone telling me what they want right now." Kate pulled at the door.

Lucas put his hand against it. "He has no right calling my house."

"*Your* house? I thought I lived here too." Kate turned and was surprised to find Lucas so close, his arm extending past her.

"You know what I mean."

Did she really? Was he being possessive of the house or of her? Why did he care if Bryan called? Sometimes she thought she saw something in Lucas's eyes, but right now she thought it had nothing to do with her. It was about possession. Bryan and Lucas were like two wolves fighting over an animal carcass.

And I'm tired of being caught in the middle.

She jerked on the door, but he held it fast.

What was it with men and control? "Let me go." She pulled at the knob again. It didn't budge. "Lucas! Let me—"

"What if I don't want to?"

And just like that, time slowed.

Almost against her will she looked at him. And was caught by his eyes. They pulled her in, held her hostage. She stilled, her anger fading, replaced by something . . . more complicated . . . less welcome . . .

"What if I don't want to?" What did he mean? Suddenly desperate to understand, she searched his face and watched as his eyes darkened into shadowed whirlpools.

She forgot how to breathe.

"What if I want you to stay?" His gaze traveled the planes of her face and stopped at her lips.

"What . . ." He was so close she couldn't think. His thumb grazed her cheekbone, barely a touch, and yet it heated her skin. She shuddered and closed her eyes against the riptide tugging inside her. What was happening? This was Lucas, not Bryan. Lucas, who frustrated her with his lack of organization. Lucas, who annoyed her with his sluggishness.

Lucas, who held you in his arms when you were seasick. Lucas, who stepped in and saved you when you were desperate.

"Open your eyes, honey."

Her stomach tightened at the endearment. She was powerless against the emotion raging inside her. It felt wonderful and terrible and scary.

"Lucas." Nothing more than a whisper.

"Open your eyes," he said. "See what's right in front of you."

She obeyed his request. What was this spell he'd cast? She wanted to fall into the depths of his eyes and get lost. She wanted to touch his jaw and feel the roughness against her fingers.

But before she could follow the impulse, he closed the distance between them. And his lips touched hers, gentle and slow.

Without thought, Kate laid her palm against his face and heard his intake of breath before he deepened the kiss, pulling her closer, making her head spin. His movements were sure and slow, like everything else he did.

It wasn't even their first kiss. But the others hadn't been like this. There was no photographer snapping pictures, no public judging the validity of their vows, no family to convince.

It was just Lucas and Kate. All alone. Exploring feelings she hadn't known existed.

No. That's not true.

Maybe she had known, or maybe she'd been in denial. Maybe she'd been blinded by Bryan's rejection. But she was seeing things now. And feeling them. Things that she'd never felt before, not even with Bryan. The way Lucas made her forget everything except the feel of his lips. Made her want more. Made her need more.

More. She slid her hand into his hair, cupping his head, and arched closer. He was warm and strong. He smelled like cedar and musk. All man.

"Katie . . ." Lucas whispered against her lips.

She didn't think, just felt. The urgency pushed her on. *It's okay, Kate. You're married. Lucas is your husband.* She submitted to the thought, letting her emotions guide her.

But . . . what happens when it ends?

Against her will, the question rose from a deep and distant well of reason. Kate ignored it, let the feel of Lucas's body against hers drown everything out.

But the voice grew louder, more insistent.

What'll happen when the year ends? Why are you becoming emotionally invested in a temporary relationship?

And it had to be temporary. Muddled as her thoughts were, she hadn't lost all sense of reason. She and Lucas were too different—more dissimilar than her mom and dad had been, and look how that had ended. She of all people knew the odds against opposites making a marriage work.

You have to stop. Now!

Somehow mustering the strength, she pushed at Lucas's chest, separating them. Her chest heaved. She was beyond her target heart rate and she hadn't moved. Judging from Lucas's expression, he felt the same. A pink flush mottled his face. His eyes were glazed, his lips swollen. She was tempted to soothe them with her thumb.

Stop it! You have to stop before this gets out of hand. You're too different.

They might be different, but heavens to Betsy, the chemistry was there in spades. She had to escape before she lost her resolve.

She reached for the doorknob and pulled.

"Running, Kate?" The dare emerged, raspy and breathless.

She ignored it, pulling the door shut behind her and dashing toward the shoreline. Yes, she was running. And too afraid to say anything for fear it might reveal too much.

As if her actions hadn't already revealed far too much.

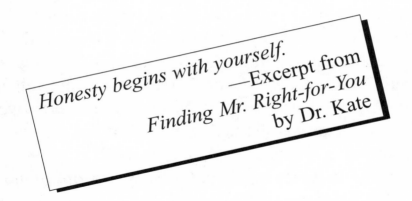

Honesty begins with yourself.
—Excerpt from
Finding Mr. Right-for-You
by Dr. Kate

Chapter Eighteen

Lucas slammed his fist on the counter. He hadn't succeeded in opening Kate's eyes; he'd only succeeded in pushing her away. As he watched her scramble across the sandy grass toward the beach, he feared he'd scared her away for good.

He punched the counter again, then shook his throbbing hand. Bo nudged his leg with his wet nose. "Not now, boy."

Why had he moved so fast? He'd only meant to kiss her gently, to show her how he felt. But then her hand had wound into his hair, and she'd pressed herself against him.

His own hand now raked his hair. His timing couldn't have been worse. Fresh from a phone call from Bryan, she was probably thinking of him. She wasn't over Bryan; that much he knew.

It's too soon to tell her how you feel.

But her response was so—

She was thinking about Bryan. Wishing it was him she'd married.

Lucas left the kitchen and paced the length of the living room as if he could distance himself from the thought. But she wasn't Bryan's wife.

She's my wife . . . Yeah. Temporarily. In name only.

You agreed to those terms, Luc, so stop your whining.

Only he hadn't known it would be so hard. Hadn't known it would make him long for her more. Hadn't known it would hurt so much.

He sank into the recliner and let his head fall against the cushion. What was Kate thinking right now? Would she expect an apology when she returned?

Well, she wouldn't get it. He wasn't sorry, even if she had been thinking about her idiot ex-fiancé while he kissed her.

All I did was lay my feelings out. Nothing to be ashamed of.

So why was his gut strung tighter than a bowline knot?

By the time Kate returned, the house was empty. Lucas's truck was gone, which meant he must've gone back to his shop. Relieved, but dreading the inevitable confrontation, Kate started dinner.

Her walk had helped clear her head. Obviously Lucas had feelings for her, and Kate admitted she'd grown fond of him as well.

Fond? You were all over him, girl.

She emptied a package of ground beef into the skillet, threw away the Styrofoam platter, and washed her hands. Okay, so maybe she had feelings for him. She had to remember the advice she dispensed in her book. "Once you realize a man is not well suited to you, it's imperative to end the relationship before you become emotionally invested."

Well, she couldn't end the marriage, but she could put the relationship back on track. They were friends. No—roommates. That was all. The sooner Lucas realized it, the sooner they could put this awkwardness behind them.

Bo sat by the back door and turned his big head toward her. She let him out and kept an eye on him through the window while she cooked. The smell of dinner soon drew him back.

The taco filling was hot and bubbly by the time she heard the front door open and click closed. Kate lowered the heat to a simmer and stirred the beef mixture as it sizzled. Would Lucas join her or would he grab a shower? She hated this indecision, this awkwardness. She didn't like walking on eggshells in her own home. She wanted to return to the way things were before.

When Lucas entered the kitchen, Kate gave the beef one last stir and turned. They might as well put this behind them.

Lucas removed a can of Coke from the fridge and popped the tab. He wouldn't even look at her. She wondered what he was thinking, what he was feeling. His expression revealed nothing.

"About earlier," Kate started, then wondered what to say next. Why hadn't she planned something? *Think!*

Lucas took a drink, then shook his head, a barely perceptible movement. "Not necessary."

He moved closer, and Kate pressed her back against the oven. The metal handle dug into her back. But Lucas reached into the cabinet instead. Shaken, Kate turned.

Lucas removed two plates and shut the cabinet door. "It was a mistake," he said as he stepped away.

Kate heard him setting the plates on the table. *A mistake?*

Well, what did you expect him to say?

She wasn't sure, but it wasn't this. Maybe she thought he'd confess he had feelings for her. But maybe he only missed Emily. Maybe he missed the intimacy of their marriage.

"Let's just forget it happened." His voice penetrated her thoughts.

Let's just forget it happened? Forget the way you took my mouth, forget the way you touched me, forget the way you felt against me? She wondered if that were possible. "Right."

Dinner consisted of tacos, avoided eye contact, and stilted conversation. When Susan dropped by and invited Kate on a walk, Kate readily agreed. Because despite her agreement with Lucas, she couldn't seem to eradicate the memory of the kiss.

Kate felt warm and cocooned as she stirred from sleep, only half-conscious. She kept her eyes closed, hoping to fall back asleep. The covers twisted around her legs in a snug knot, but a big pillow, snuggled into her stomach, warmed her.

She wondered about that because her pillow was under her head. Coming more fully awake, Kate opened her eyes. She could barely see by the soft morning light that filtered through the curtains. More important, her arms and face felt the softness of flesh against them and she knew it was no pillow she cuddled with. Her arm curved around Lucas's side and her body spooned into him, her face against his back. Her thighs pressed into the backs of his.

She started to jump away then stopped herself. Maybe he was asleep—completely unaware that she clung to him like a barnacle on a boat. A sudden move would wake him. If she disengaged slowly, he'd be none the wiser. *Oh, please, let him be asleep.*

She lay quietly listening to the sound of his breathing. He wasn't snoring, but that didn't mean he wasn't asleep. His respirations were deep, a good sign.

How had she ended up on his side anyway? Had she had some weird dream about their kiss? Where was her rolled-up quilt barrier? The way the covers tangled around her legs, she or Lucas must've had a fitful sleep.

Okay, time to disengage.

She carefully removed her hand from his stomach. Inch by inch, she lifted her arm until it had no contact with Lucas. Next she lifted her head, moving her face away from the heated hardness of his back.

So far, so good.

The only thing against him now was . . . well, the rest of her body. Her legs tingled with awareness.

Stop that! Good grief, what has gotten into me?

She eased her weight onto her elbow and held her breath as she moved away from him.

Lucas stirred and turned, settling on his back. Kate froze above him. His side pressed into her now and his face was inches away. Thankfully, his eyes remained closed. She lay still, hardly daring to breathe. Was her heartbeat shaking the entire bed?

She glanced at his clock. It was later than she'd thought. The alarm would sound in three minutes. She had to break away.

Kate scooted back, easing away from him. She'd moved only a few inches when she felt resistance. Her pajama top was caught. Lucas had rolled on top of it.

Gritting her teeth, she grasped the material and tugged slowly, watching Lucas's face for any sign of awareness. But it freed without incident, and she sighed quietly. Being careful to steady the bed, she used her feet and right elbow to support her weight and scooted her hips away.

When she reached her own side of the bed, she rolled to her back and let out a shaky breath. Her heart, beating more rapidly than could be accounted for, really was shaking the bed. Thank goodness Lucas had slept through it. There was no telling what he'd think if he knew she'd snuggled up to him like that.

"Next time you want to cuddle, just say so."

The voice from beside Kate startled her. Then the meaning of his words penetrated her mind. He still lay perfectly still, his breathing deep and even. *That jerk!* He'd been awake the whole time and let her suffer.

She yanked the pillow from under her head and swung it at him. But the only response she got was his insufferable laughter.

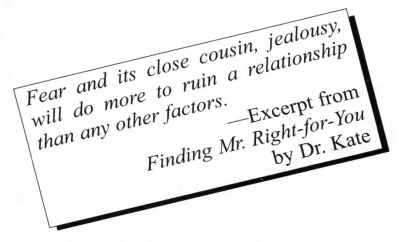

Fear and its close cousin, jealousy, will do more to ruin a relationship than any other factors.

—Excerpt from *Finding Mr. Right-for-You* by Dr. Kate

Chapter Nineteen

The Wright house was buzzing with activity when Kate and Lucas arrived the next Saturday.

"Come in, kids!" Roy called from where he emptied ice cubes into glasses. He was about to say something else, but Susan turned on a noisy mixer and began running it through a pot of steaming potatoes. In the next room, the TV blared, but Jamie was curled into a fat armchair with a book.

Lucas and Kate greeted them; then Roy took Lucas into the garage to show him the new mower he'd bought. When Susan turned off the mixer, silence settled on the kitchen.

"Can I help with something?" Kate asked.

"No, thank you."

Kate searched for something to say. It was easier when they were walking; she didn't feel the need to fill the silence. For the hundredth time, she thought about addressing the issue of Susan and Kate's mom. Would it clear the air between them if she apologized on behalf of her mom? Would it open the door for Susan to confide in Kate about her marriage problems? Or would it just anger Susan that Lucas had told her?

She was formulating her thoughts on the matter when Lucas and his dad reentered. "You can borrow it anytime," Roy was saying to Lucas as he took a pitcher of tea from the fridge.

Oh well, it would have to wait for another time. "Is Brody around?" Kate asked.

"He's upstairs already," Roy said.

"I think I'll join him, if you don't need any help," Kate said.

Roy shooed her on, and Kate climbed the two flights, dreading the rooftop experience but wanting to catch up with Brody. They hadn't had an opportunity to discuss his majors since he dropped by her office.

She found Brody leaning on the widow's-walk railing, high above the landscape. He greeted her as she slipped into her chair against the chimney chase.

"Great day, huh?" he asked.

Kate forced her eyes from him. The blue of the sky melted into the expanse of ocean, its unending vastness interrupted only by the colorful dots of sails. The sun burned hot, and the breeze chopped at the water's surface. Kate's fists tightened around the chair's arm, its edges cutting into her palm.

"Beautiful." She tucked her feet under the chair. Why wasn't it getting easier to face her fear of heights? She'd thought she could overcome it if she only forced herself up here every week.

Her mind went back to the first time she'd felt the fear. Ironically, it hadn't been her own life she'd feared for at the time. Her mom, belly filled with alcohol, had climbed out her bedroom window and onto the sloped roof of the porch. Kate had come home from a friend's house to find her teetering on the edge.

"Mom, don't move!" Kate ran upstairs, down the short, narrow hall, and into her mom's bedroom. The wooden sash was thrown open and the curtains fluttered in the night breeze.

"Mom, come here." Kate climbed out the window and took slow steps down the slope. Her mom's blouse rippled in the wind, and for a moment, Kate thought it would be enough to blow her right over the edge. She grabbed her mom's hand. "Come on, Momma."

Kate didn't know how frightened she'd been until they were safely inside the house. Only then did she realize her heart felt as though it was going to burst through her ribs.

Now, her heart pounded in remembrance. Ever since that day, heights had frightened her.

This is not helping. I need to focus on something else.

Brody shifted, drawing Kate's attention, and she remembered her purpose in coming. "I've been wondering about your career path. Have you given it more thought?"

Brody leaned his weight against the railing. Didn't he realize it could give way? If it did, he'd hurtle three floors to his death. Okay, maybe just a broken leg, but still. Kate's palms grew clammy; she felt dizzy at just the thought.

"It's all I think about," Brody said. "Other than girls, that is." He flashed a smile, revealing a dimple she hadn't noticed before.

Kate remembered the passion in his voice when he'd talked about tutoring his little friend. She had a suspicion education was his main interest. The question was, why had he changed majors? What was holding him back?

"When I look into the future," he said, "I can see myself teaching middle school. Maybe art or computers or even science. But—"

Kate waited for him to finish, although she had to look away; the mental image of the rail breaking loose was too much. She watched her oval thumbnail follow the square edge of the chair's arm.

"I don't know. I changed majors for a reason. I keep trying to remember why."

"You switched to art next, right?"

The wind tousled his hair, and he shook it from his eyes. "Yeah. Dumb move."

Kate shook her head. "We make decisions for a reason. Sometimes you just have to dig deep to find them."

She was beginning to think she understood Brody's reasons.

She leaned back, and her chair, its legs not quite even, rocked an inch. She stiffened, clutching the table's edge. Her breath caught in her throat, and prickles of adrenaline flared under her skin.

When she looked up, Brody was studying her. "What's wrong?"

Kate forced her fingers to loosen and crossed her legs. "The chair rocked back and I lost my balance."

Brody's head cocked. "You always sit with your back against the wall, and you never walk around up here." He pointed his finger at her. "You're afraid of heights, aren't you?"

Kate gave a wry laugh. "I'm not afraid of heights so much as I'm afraid of falling."

Brody sat at the table. "You should have said something. We could eat downstairs."

She shrugged. "I don't want to break tradition. Besides, I don't like letting fear rule my life. This little once-a-week trek is my way of telling my fear to take a hike."

Brody laughed, and as he did, a thought struck Kate. There was nothing like fear to change your course.

How many people had she counseled whose fear of intimacy kept them from experiencing the very thing they desired?

She leaned back. "Maybe you're a little like me."

"What, me? Afraid of heights? No way. I've been parasailing lots of times and even hang gliding a couple times. Don't tell Mom and Dad. They'd freak."

Kate shook her head, sure she was onto something. "No. Afraid of falling." She watched him, waiting for him to connect the dots.

His head tipped back, his eyes narrowing. "You think I'm afraid of failing."

He was obviously offended, and Kate wondered if she'd overstepped her boundaries. "Only you know the answer to that." She smiled to soften the words. "I'm just putting it out there."

It made sense. Maybe he'd only changed majors because he excelled at many things and couldn't make up his mind. But in light of his passion for teaching, fear of failure made sense. He wouldn't be the first.

The sound of feet thumping up the stairs warned them they had company coming, and the topic was tabled for the day.

Kate was eating alone at the Even Keel when her agent, Ronald, called with great news. *Glamour* magazine wanted to feature her in a monthly "Dear Dr. Kate" column. They'd seen her appearance on *Dr. Phil* and had been tracking her career. It had been between her and another syndicated columnist, and she was their first pick.

Kate paid her bill and rushed back to the shop, hoping Lucas was there, wanting to share her good news. She would have been eating with him except he'd canceled because of an appointment.

But what Kate saw when she neared the shop pushed her good news from her mind and stopped her feet midstride. Someone behind her bumped her, treading on her good heels.

"Sorry," Kate mumbled as the tourist passed her with a glare, pulling a golden retriever on a leash. She shifted over, moving closer to the gift shop, out of the stream of traffic, her eyes returning to the scene that had stopped her.

Lucas helped a woman from a silver car. The woman unfolded herself from the compact vehicle, and Kate saw her long red, hair. Lucas shut the door and followed the woman into his shop.

It was the same woman Kate had seen him with the day Brody stopped by her office a month or so ago. Was she the reason Lucas had cancelled their lunch plans? Had he and Red had lunch together?

Something tightened deep in her stomach like a dishrag wrung hard.

Don't be ridiculous. She's probably just a friend. Or a business acquaintance.

From a distance, Kate watched Lucas hold the store's door for the woman. She turned and laughed at something he said, cocking her head.

Kate's lips pursed in reaction. She disliked the way the woman looked at Lucas. She disliked her own reaction to it more.

It's not jealousy. She looked away and watched the tourists and locals walking past her. What would people think if they saw Lucas and Red eating together? Especially if the woman was hanging on him like she had the first time Kate saw them together? He was married to her, Dr. Kate, and she couldn't have people thinking he was wining and dining another woman. As careful as they'd been to make the marriage appear legitimate, she couldn't believe he'd be so careless.

A passing dog bumped her thigh, and Kate straightened. She'd have to say something to him tonight.

He'll think I'm jealous.

Not if you handle it carefully.

Kate hitched her bag on her shoulder and set her feet in motion, her ire rising with each step. Didn't Lucas know she had a reputation to protect? Hadn't he given any thought to how it would appear, him gallivanting all over the island with another woman?

She composed her features as she entered the shop, the bell jangling against the glass door. Soft music greeted her, and the air-conditioning was welcome against her heated skin. But there was no sign of Lucas or the woman on the floor.

"Nice lunch, Kate?" Ethan called from behind the mahogany desk. He adjusted his wire-rimmed glasses.

"Sure." She hesitated on the first step. "Is Lucas around?"

"He's in the back." Ethan leaned over his papers.

Behind her, a customer entered the store, and Ethan stood.

Kate started up the stairs. "Thanks, I'll just . . . talk to him later."

Why would he take Red to the back of the store? There was nothing there but the pieces he was working on and a bunch of tools.

Her heels clicked up the wood steps. When she reached the top, she hung her bag on the coatrack and sat at her desk. Ethan hadn't acted as if anything was amiss. He would know if something was going on between Lucas and Red. Kate was letting her imagination run wild.

Come on, Kate; get back to work. She moved the computer mouse, stopping the screen saver, and the article she'd been working on before lunch appeared. She'd already condensed the letter and needed to formulate an answer for Never a Bride in Albany, whose letter smacked of desperation.

Kate wrote a reply then reread it, editing as she went. The second letter she'd chosen was already succinct, but she edited it down and typed it into the document as well, then formulated her answer. When she was finished with the article, she stood and stretched. Of their own volition, her feet carried her to the street window.

Below, in the parking slot in front of the store, was the silver car. Her heart sank. She checked her watch. It had been an hour. What were Lucas and that woman doing downstairs? What if . . . ?

What if Lucas had been dating Red before they got married? Was it possible he was seeing someone on the side? Was it possible he was in love with the woman?

A space inside her hollowed out.

What do I care? Our marriage isn't real. We'll be divorced in less than ten months.

But the memory of their kiss kicked to the surface of her thoughts.

There is more than a contractual agreement between us.

The confession filled the pit of her stomach with something both pleasant and disturbing. She was relieved to finally admit actual feelings for Lucas were growing like tenacious weeds in a carefully cultivated garden. But like those weeds, the feelings were undesired. They didn't belong; their presence was a hindrance.

Kate's gaze centered on the silver car, and she bit the tender flesh inside her mouth. What possible reason could the woman have for being down there so long? Were they still in the back? Maybe Kate could go down under some pretense.

But what reason could she have? Her mind was a blank screen. She could almost see a skinny cursor blinking on the white space, taunting her.

It would be suspicious if she went down. She never interrupted Lucas while he worked, and the last thing she wanted was to give him the pleasure of thinking she was curious about Red. Or worse, jealous.

If only she could hear what they were saying. Then she would know if anything—

She remembered something. The vents. Kate walked across the room to her old apartment, the sound of her heels muffled by the rug. The noise from the workshop carried through the heating ducts into her old living room. She remembered all the nights listening to Lucas's sander through the vents. She'd contemplated throttling him some evenings when she wanted peace after a day of listening to people's problems.

She walked to the vent against the back wall, where she kicked off her heels and squatted down, listening. Were they still in the workshop or had they gone back into the store? On the balls of her stocking feet, she balanced with a hand on the wall and stilled.

There were voices, barely audible. She heard the deep tones of Lucas's voice, but couldn't make out the words. Was that a woman's voice she heard now? She couldn't be sure. Kate set her knees on the floor by the register and leaned down further, pressing her palms to the dusty floor. There was nothing now, just silence.

No, there it was, a woman's voice, too quiet to make out.

She needed to get closer. Maybe then she could hear what they were saying.

Kate glanced down at her suit, weighing the dirty wood floor against the notion of letting her curiosity go unsatisfied. Then, with a sigh, she lowered herself to the floor, lying flat on her stomach. The suit was bound for the cleaners now.

As she bent her head, her thick metal earring clanged on the vent's louvered cover and she rose up enough to remove it, then set her ear against the cool metal surface.

There was a screech, like the sound of a chair against the concrete floor. Lucas was saying something. She stilled.

". . . that's what I thought."

Red spoke again, but Kate couldn't make it out. *Speak up, woman!*

It was quiet again, and Kate didn't even dare to swallow in case she missed something.

"What do you . . ." The rest of Lucas's words were muffled, like he'd turned away. Kate heard a creak and knew he'd leaned against his old metal desk.

". . . like the way . . . very nice . . . ." Kate didn't like her tone, even muffled through the ductwork.

The sound of heels clicking on the floor reached Kate's ears. Was the woman walking toward Lucas? Away from him? She didn't hear his footsteps, though his sandals were soft soled.

Then there was nothing but quiet from below. The silence unnerved her. What were they doing down there? Her imagination filled the gap. She imagined Red approaching Lucas, placing her long, slender fingers along the side of his neck. Was he wrapping his arms around the woman even now? Was he kissing her the way he'd kissed Kate the week before?

Heat prickled the back of her neck.

That's silly. If he were seeing someone else before he married me, he wouldn't have married me.

But that doesn't mean he isn't interested in the woman now.

Maybe he'd met her after they married and was pursuing the relationship. Did Kate really have any rights to him? Any say in what he did in the privacy of his own workshop?

He's married to me. Even if it is in name only, he owes me the respect of keeping his vows.

She had kept hers, after all. It wasn't her fault that Bryan called sometimes.

She sighed. Though now that the cramped stiletto was on the other foot, she realized it was unfair to take Bryan's calls. Lucas had been angry last time Bryan called. *"He has no right to call my house,"* he'd said. Maybe it was just caveman tactics that inspired the words, but followed so closely by those other words— the ones she'd repeated in her mind ever since—his anger took on a different meaning.

"What if I want you to stay?"

Had he meant it the way she thought? Did Lucas want their marriage to be real?

That's crazy. Although the notion held more appeal than was healthy for two individuals so incompatible, Lucas had never given any other indication he considered the marriage binding. Except, well, the fact that he'd kissed her. And boy, had he kissed her. Her stomach fluttered now just thinking about it. Maybe he did want more.

Yeah, Kate, that's why he's alone downstairs with that beautiful, leggy redhead.

And why is it so quiet down there? Kate pressed her ear on the vent and listened.

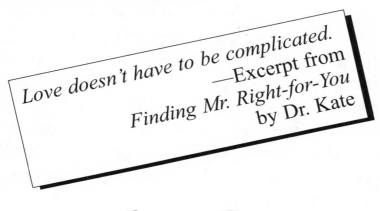

Love doesn't have to be complicated.
—Excerpt from
Finding Mr. Right-for-You
by Dr. Kate

Chapter Twenty

"It shouldn't be too long." Lucas opened the door for Sydney. "I'll call you when it's finished."

"Feel free to call before then if you have any questions." Sydney's smile indicated a call would be welcome, questions or not.

With nothing more than a polite nod, Lucas let the door close and wiped his hands on his jeans. He appreciated the business—she was giving him plenty—but the woman had the subtlety of a shark in a fish pool. He had little respect for a woman who ignored a man's wedding band. Did she even care that he belonged to someone else?

You're only a name on a wedding certificate, man.

His eyes wandered up the staircase to Kate's office. Would she mind if he interrupted her work? He hated to admit it, but he'd missed having lunch with her. Missed the way she wiped her lips after every bite. Missed the way she separated the food on her plate so nothing touched.

Mostly, he missed listening to her talk about her work. At first glance, some might think Kate's career was self-serving. But if they heard her talk about people—heard the excitement in her voice when she helped someone—they'd know differently.

It was quiet upstairs, not even the clacking of her computer keys. Maybe she was taking a break. Lucas took the stairs, glad for the opportunity to shake the cloying cloud of Sydney's perfume.

When he reached the second floor, her office chair was empty. A colorful screensaver danced on the computer, indicating she hadn't been typing for some time. Strange—he knew she was there; her car was out front.

He was about to call for her when he saw movement at the back of the building, through her old apartment doorway. He walked the length of the rug—and stopped. Beyond the coffee table, Kate lay flat as a mat on the floor. Her head faced the wall, ear to the floor—or was that the vent? One hand clutched the hair at her nape, pulling her cream-colored suit coat up at the waist. Her pants hugged the curve of her derrière, and the tops of her feet skimmed the floor.

What in the world? Why would she be lying over the—

Unless . . .

His lips curved into a smile as the wonder of it washed over him, cool and refreshing.

Oh yeah. This was going to be good.

Lucas leaned against the door frame, crossing his arms, biding his time. Finally, when she didn't budge, he cleared his throat.

Kate jumped, turned toward him, letting loose of her hair. The air must have kicked on because a blast blew a strand across her face.

"Looking for something?" He almost felt sorry for her as she scrambled into a sitting position. But the look on her face was too comical, and the feelings her jealousy inspired, too heartening.

"Lucas. I was just—" She dusted her suit coat, working her flattened fingers down the length of her arm in short swipes. "My earring." She held out a circular piece of jewelry lying in her palm. "I was getting my earring."

Who was she kidding? She'd been lying flat on the floor, her ear against the register. She was caught. Nailed. Busted.

"Did it fall down the vent?" He held back a smile, barely.

Her cheeks bloomed with color as she attempted to put the earring in. Even across the room he could see her hand shaking. "Of course not. It just—" Kate tried again to poke the earring through the hole and failed. She gave up and looked at him like a butterfly caught in a net.

He raised his brows, waiting.

At that, her shoulders drew back, her chin tipped. "All right, all right," she snapped. "You made your point."

Lucas approached her, feeling sorry for her now that she knew she was caught. Still, there was that whole jealousy thing that tugged the corners of his mouth.

Kate set her earring on the coffee table and struggled to stand. When he extended his hand, she smacked it away, her eyes narrowing as she straightened. Her crisp white shirt had come loose from her waistband, and her hair was tousled like she'd just awakened. She smoothed it and tucked it behind her ears with quick hands.

"I saw you after lunch with that . . . woman," Kate said. "I was worried about how it might look to other people." She crossed her arms over her chest. "We have an image to maintain, and it's not proper for you to be gallivanting all over the island with someone else."

Her words were so ridiculous he didn't know where to begin. *"Gallivanting?"*

She looked him in the eye. "You know what I mean. People will notice when you're eating with another woman. It's a small island—"

"I didn't eat with Sydney." Was that really what was bugging Kate? What everyone else thought? The notion sucked some of the air from his sails.

"Well, whatever. It's not proper for you to be seen with someone like that." Her lips, free of artificial color, pressed together.

Was she only concerned about her reputation, or was she hiding her jealousy behind its mask? "Someone like what?" he asked, curious to hear her answer.

"Someone like—You know what I mean. She isn't exactly unattractive, and she's . . . clingy."

"Clingy?"

"Like socks out of the dryer," she retorted. She tilted her head. "You know exactly what I mean."

Lucas lost the tug-of-war with his smile. "You're jealous," he said.

Kate turned away, tucking in her shirt before grabbing the earring off the table and walking toward a mirror that hung over the armchair. "I'm concerned about my reputation." She took the back off the earring and put it in.

"And that's why you were spying through the vent?" It didn't wash. If she were concerned about gossip, she would confront him, not eavesdrop.

Her eyes met his in the mirror. "I'm just trying to protect my career."

He walked closer until he was behind her. "Is that what you're telling yourself?"

Her hands fell slowly to her sides. In the light of the window to the side of the mirror, her eyes brightened to a caramel color. He wanted to get lost in there. Better yet, he wanted to climb behind those eyes and see what was holding her back.

Did she love Bryan still? He reviewed their kiss for the hundredth time and felt his confidence climb. A woman didn't kiss a man like that when she was in love with someone else. Maybe she'd never been in love with Bryan.

All Lucas knew was she had some kind of feelings for him.

"Why are you so afraid to be honest with yourself?" he asked.

Kate stared back. "I'm not afraid."

Her bravado seemed to have shrunk two sizes. He wanted to reach out and wrap his arms around her, pull her against him as he had on the sailboat. But he had a feeling he didn't dare move or she'd run.

"Why can't you admit you're jealous? It's not a crime." He found the courage to open up. Someone had to. "When Bryan called last week, I was jealous."

Something in her face softened. Her lips parted to speak. Then, as if she thought better of it, they sealed again.

Why was it so hard to admit something was happening between them? They had almost ten more months together. Would it hurt to explore the feelings?

"There's something here, and you know it," he said.

She blinked, her eyes fastened on his for just a split second before she walked away. "Stop it, Lucas. Leave things as they are." She stopped behind the barrier of the sofa.

Heaven forbid she let her guard down. "All neat and tidy, you mean?"

"What's wrong with neat and tidy? Neat and tidy is simple and clear-cut, and nobody gets hurt."

"Is that what's got you worried?" Was she still nursing wounds Bryan had inflicted? Couldn't she see he'd never forsake her as Bryan had? He always wanted to be there for her. To protect her. To cherish her. To love her.

"Nobody likes to get hurt."

He held the image of her on their wedding night. Remembered the sound of her sobbing in that big empty bed. "I'm not the one who left you at the altar," he said gently.

Kate wrapped her arms around her stomach. "Look, it just—It just won't work between us. We're too different. *Completely* incompatible, for heaven's sake. I've seen what happens too many times."

Did she think feelings were planned? Scheduled and carried out like entries on her color-coded calendar? "There's never been another you and me. You can't compare us to some couple you counseled in your office."

"I don't have to look any further than my parents to strike a comparison."

Something in her tone alerted him. "What about your parents?"

"They argued constantly. Good grief, they were like hot and cold, hard and soft, and whatever other opposites you can think of. I can still close my eyes at night and hear their bickering."

It was starting to make sense now. Her passion for helping others find a compatible mate. Her parents had divorced, possibly damaging her greatly, and now she was out to save the world. "Is that why you do it?"

"Do what?"

"Counsel others. Help people find their soul mate."

She rolled her eyes. "Huh. I don't believe in soul mates. I believe in helping women find a compatible mate whose values and personality line up with hers."

"All neat and tidy."

"We can't all live a messy, jumbled life."

Is that the way she saw his life? Like a chaotic heap of garbage?

"It might not be pretty to look at, but I found love nonetheless."

It was out before he could stop it. His heart skipped a beat.

The look on Kate's face made him glad he'd risked it. The way her eyes widened ever so slightly before she looked down at her fingers curled around the sofa's cushion. Was it awe or joy he'd seen before she looked away?

"I didn't mean to disregard what you had with Emily. I'm sorry."

Emily. She thought he was talking about Emily. The disappointment was keen. Hadn't he shown her his feelings these weeks they'd had together? Even if he hadn't said them. Apparently, he'd been too subtle. Or she just didn't want to see the truth.

She was waiting for his response. "Don't worry about it," he said, feeling like a fool. She didn't want anything between them; she'd made that clear. Maybe he wasn't the kind of man she wanted. Maybe she was waiting to be with Bryan.

For the first time he wondered if he'd ever be able to change her mind.

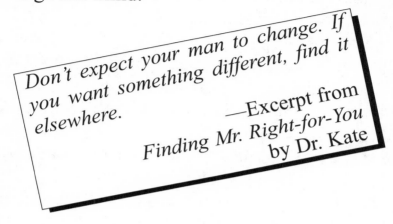

Don't expect your man to change. If you want something different, find it elsewhere.

—Excerpt from Finding Mr. Right-for-You by Dr. Kate

Chapter Twenty-One

The phone on Kate's desk rang. She saved her column before answering.

"How's my favorite author?" Pam, Kate's publicist, greeted her.

"Pam! How are you?"

"Good, good. I wanted to update you on a few interviews I've scheduled. I e-mailed them to you a minute ago, but I have a last-minute opportunity, so I wanted to see if you were available. My contact from *Live with Lisa* called a few minutes ago, and they want to interview you tomorrow morning. They probably had a cancellation, and it's a fabulous opportunity for exposure on cable TV."

An interview on the popular program would be a

boon. "That's great. Let me check my schedule." Kate pulled out her calendar. There were a couple appointments, but nothing that couldn't be rescheduled. She was almost finished with her column and her *Glamour* piece.

"I can do it."

"They intimated that Lucas would be welcome if he'd like to take part," Pam said.

Kate doubted he would but said she'd mention it to him and get back to Pam.

The discussion turned to the other radio interviews scheduled for several weeks out.

"Is *Mr. Right* doing okay saleswise?" Kate asked. Rosewood had hoped it would make the *New York Times* list, but so far it had only appeared deep on the *USA Today* list. She was afraid they were disappointed with sales, and this far out from the release, it wasn't likely to improve much, although an appearance on *Live with Lisa* wouldn't hurt.

"The book's fine. I know Chloe is eager for a new proposal."

"I'm working on an idea. Once I have it nailed down, I'll send it."

After Kate hung up, she closed her document and gathered her things. She had to get home and pack because her flight would leave that evening. Unless Lucas agreed to participate, they'd be apart another night, but what would it matter? It seemed as if they were on two different planets since their confrontation in her office nearly a month earlier.

• • •

"You didn't have to take me, you know." She almost wished he hadn't, since he'd dawdled around for fifteen minutes—after she'd rushed to pack and stowed her suitcase in the car. Now she was arriving later than she'd planned.

Kate grabbed for her suitcase handle, but Lucas reached it first. They walked toward the airport.

"I don't mind."

Her heels clicked against the pavement. After hurrying with the packing, Kate felt as if she'd forgotten something. She mentally checked off the necessary items to assure herself.

After she'd gotten off the phone with Pam, she'd gone to Lucas's shop and told him about the interview.

"They'd like to have us both on, if you'd like to participate," Kate said.

He'd lowered a tool, his eyes widening. The cliché of deer in headlights came to mind.

"Don't think so," he said before picking up a rag and wiping down a chest of drawers with a honey-colored stain.

"Why not? It might be fun." And good for the public to see them together.

He gave the bureau one last swipe and stood back, looking it over. "Talking's not my thing." He set the cloth on the plywood table. "Words don't come easy to me, like they do you."

The more she thought about it, the more she wanted him there with her. Maybe getting off the island, away from the grind of life, would break the stalemate they'd had between them the past month. Ironically, she'd thought she'd wanted distance between them. But now that she had it, she was lonely.

"I'll fill in the gaps," Kate said. "You wouldn't have a thing to worry about."

"I can't."

Did he have work that couldn't be put off? Or maybe he just wanted a break from her.

"Look, something happened when I was a kid. I was supposed to give a speech in front of my school. In a school assembly." He picked up the rag and twisted it in his stained fingers. "I froze. Forgot everything I was going to say." He wiped the top of the bureau again. "I haven't talked in front of an audience since."

Now, as he walked her to security, she imagined Lucas as a frightened little boy, paralyzed in front of his peers. He seemed so far removed from that little boy, so strong and capable. But she remembered his one request when he agreed to marry her: *"No interviews."* It must've been hard enough for him to be in the spotlight as he had. But he'd done it for her.

And his parents, she reminded herself.

As they approached the security officer, Kate remembered the first time he'd brought her here. Dahlia Stevens had been in line, and he'd kissed her good-bye. Today no one waited in security, and Kate noted the edge of disappointment that pricked her heart.

What is wrong with you, Kate?

What's wrong? I want him to go with me. Want him to kiss me. That's what's wrong.

Lucas handed Kate the overnight case before they reached the balding security officer. "Kate . . ."

She checked her watch before meeting his gaze.

He shifted his weight. "When you get back, we need to talk."

Something hardened in her stomach, gelling into a thick lump. She hated when people did that. Now, the whole time she was gone, she'd wonder what he wanted. The sudden fear that he wanted to end their arrangement left her speechless. What if he was tired of pretending? Tired of the awkward silence between them these last few weeks? She wanted to say she was sorry, but sorry for what?

"Is something wrong?" she asked instead.

Lucas waved her off. "Nothing to worry about." He looked at her as if studying her features. She'd only be gone one night. *What's going on?*

He reached out and rubbed her chin with his thumb.

Kate stilled at his touch, feeling the roughness of his thumb all the way to her toes.

"You had a little something right there," he said.

She remembered the globby grape jelly on toast she'd scarfed down on the way out the door and ran her finger over the spot, rubbing away the feeling his touch had left behind.

He scanned the area around them. Was he remembering Dahlia and wishing for an audience? The airport was quiet as a sepulchre tonight. *Where's the media when you need them?*

Kate wanted to run her fingers along the rough surface of his stubbly jaw. What would he think of that? Would he kiss her then, if she took the first step?

Lucas caught her staring. She was loath to leave him for a night. How had she gotten so accustomed to his company? She remembered how he'd irritated her when he was just her superintendent. How had he found a way through the cracks in her heart? How had she come to expect his presence, depend on it?

He cleared his throat and pocketed his hands. "Well. Have a safe trip."

Kate blinked and looked away, hiking the weighty bag on her shoulder. "Thanks."

When he walked away, Kate realized her feelings for Lucas were rising dangerously high, like floodwaters on the banks of an unprotected shore.

Three cups of coffee and Kate was finally awake. She sat opposite the interviewer, Lisa Evans. A mike had been placed inconspicuously on the collar of her red Donna Karan blazer. The makeup people had done a good job, but the foundation was heavy and felt like it was melting under the hot lights.

The producer gave last-minute instructions, but Kate had heard most of it before. She settled back in the chair and waited while they opened the show with news on the other side of the studio. A copy of *Mr. Right* was propped on the glass cube between them.

Lisa, in a robin's-egg blue suit, reviewed her notes, making no conversation. That was typical. Interviewers liked to save it for the show.

When it was time for their segment, they were cued, and Lisa straightened, smiling toward the camera.

"This morning we have syndicated dating-advice columnist and noted author Dr. Kate. Welcome."

Kate smiled. "Thank you for having me."

"I have to say I read your recent release, *Finding Mr. Right-for-You* and was riveted." Lisa's eyebrows inched up into her blonde bangs.

"Thanks, Lisa. There's a lot of interest lately in compatibility in dating and marriage."

"Which begs the question," Lisa said. "There are numerous Web sites and books on the subject. What makes yours different?"

"Good question. In my counseling with couples, I've found the key ingredient to a lasting relationship to be compatibility. So many times we women get our hearts way ahead of the game. In the book, I teach women to put their hearts on hold long enough to establish compatibility."

"Is that what you did with your Mr. Right?" Lisa tilted her head.

The personal question caught Kate off guard. "Of course. You really can't make a rational decision about someone's suitability when your emotions are clouding your judgment."

Lisa nodded. "We know how emotions can affect good judgment."

Lisa asked several more questions about the book; then they opened the line for callers.

"Stephanie from Boston, you're on the air." Lisa said.

"I have a question for Dr. Kate," the caller said.

"Go ahead." Lisa smiled, her berry lip gloss shimmering under the lights.

"I'd like to know why she married someone else when her real fiancé dumped her on their wedding day."

What? The malicious tone, the ugly words, sent a wave of fear through Kate. She smiled through it. *What was the caller's name?* Had Lisa said Stephanie?

"Dr. Kate?" Lisa asked, clearly confused. "I'm not sure what the caller's referring to."

"I'm not sure either . . ." *Hang up. Disconnect the caller.* Her eyes pleaded with Lisa.

"Her real fiancé was Bryan Montgomery," the voice on the line continued. "And he dumped her the morning of the wedding. I'm not sure where Dr. Kate found her fake groom, but the wedding was phony, and so is she."

This isn't happening. Kate's thoughts seized in a paralyzing spasm. She fought to control her expression. The camera was on her. What could she say? Her mind was a numb void. *Say something. Anything.*

"Dr. Kate?"

Her head buzzed with electrical activity, all of it sparking nothing. No clever turn of phrase. No smooth transition of subject. The seconds stretched out like a long empty runway.

"My marriage is not fake." She forced a calm tone.

"It's legal in every way." *Change the subject!* "The advice in my book comes from years of extensive counseling and research. I have a passion for helping women find suitable partners, and that's what this book is about."

The producer was cuing a commercial. Sure, just as soon as Kate had found her tongue.

But Lisa was ending the segment. When they were off the air, she reached over and placed her hand on Kate's. "I'm so sorry about that, Kate. I assure you it was as unexpected for me as it was for you."

Kate stood on shaking legs as someone disengaged her mike and battery pack. She had to get out of there. She wanted to run someplace far away and hide.

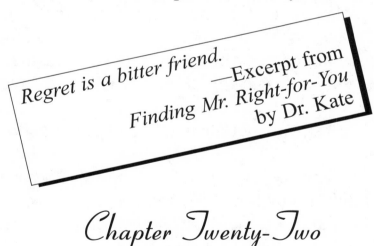

Regret is a bitter friend.
—Excerpt from
Finding Mr. Right-for-You
by Dr. Kate

Chapter Twenty-Two

The same plump woman who'd escorted Kate around the studio since her arrival accompanied her to the green room, where Kate collected her things. Her mind spun, but she feigned a smile and followed the woman to the car that waited at the curb.

Once in the luxury vehicle, she told the driver she was going to the airport. He pulled away.

What now? What should I do? Everyone knows.

Rosewood was going to be turned on its head! She reached for her cell phone and turned it on. She'd missed three calls. Kate didn't stop to listen to the messages. She had to call Pam. They needed damage control. But how could they control damage that was already done? It was live TV, and every viewer watching this morning had heard she was a fraud.

She punched in Pam's cell number. The driver had a talk radio program on in front, so she could talk quietly without being overheard.

Pam picked up on the first ring. "Kate! That was just awful."

"It was Stephanie. The woman Bryan left me for." The shock was wearing thin, revealing a layer of anger beneath.

"I know. I saw the whole thing. This is not good. Not good at all."

"What are we going to do? Did Chloe see it?" Kate's editor might know about her marriage, but she would have to explain it to her boss, who didn't know. *Have I jeopardized Chloe's and Pam's jobs?*

"She called me after the segment. She's pretty upset," Pam said. "Listen, we need to figure out how to handle this. There's going to be a lot of media wanting an interview with you now."

"Sure, there will, but I can't do that, Pam." The idea

of exposing herself to that kind of spectacle was unthinkable. *How can I defend myself when it's true?*

"You need to do whatever Paul says." Pam's tone chided, reminding Kate that Chloe's boss was in for a rude awakening. "It's the least you can do at this point."

Of course Pam was angry with her. Chloe would be too, and Kate didn't blame either of them. Rosewood would come off like frauds, same as Kate. Everyone who'd known the truth would pay a price.

Lucas. She closed her eyes and let her head fall against the firm leather headrest. He'd watched the interview; she was certain of that. What was he thinking now? Thank goodness he hadn't come along for the interview. But how would this affect him? How would it affect his family?

What have I done?

"This is bad, Kate. The media will make this into a huge scandal, and we'll have to fight our way through it."

It was a career-busting scandal. Who would want her advice now that she'd proven herself a hypocrite by marrying her complete opposite, a virtual stranger? It would kill sales on her book. And she could probably kiss the *Glamour* and syndicated columns good-bye. How could she face Rosewood after disappointing them so? How could she face her faithful readers?

"I suggest you call Chloe and offer to break the news to Paul. She probably won't let you, but—"

"I will. I'll do that. What else can I do?"

"Don't talk to anybody. You might be getting calls, or worse. Let us get a game plan together before you say anything publicly."

No need to worry about that. All she wanted to do was crawl into a hole and have someone fill it with dirt. "All right. Calling Chloe now."

"Good luck." The sarcastic tone wasn't lost on Kate.

She punched in her editor's cell number, seeing the calls she'd missed on the screen and thinking about Lucas again.

Chloe answered immediately. Her tone was basted in stress. "Kate." She swore. "I guess you know the spot this puts me in."

"I'm so sorry, Chloe. I'll take complete responsibility." And she should, as it was entirely her fault. "Let me call Paul and tell him. He needn't know you were involved."

Chloe raised her voice. "You don't think he's going to ask me if I knew? I'm not going to lie, Kate."

Kate rubbed her forehead. *Why did I do it? If I could only go back and do the day over.* She should have done the honest thing and admitted to the media that the engagement was broken. But how could she have done that at the release of her book? Rosewood would have paid the cost for her personal crisis.

They were paying now anyway. A higher price than before.

"I know. I know, Chloe. Tell me what I can do." She waited, sure Chloe was doing her deep yoga breaths.

There weren't enough yoga classes in the world to help ease this kind of stress.

"Just give me time to think. I'll tell Paul when we get off the phone and get back with you. Just—just go home and hole up until you hear from me." She huffed. "You know this is going to be all over the news by tonight. The papers, the news—it's going to be everywhere."

Kate had been hoping it might quietly blow over, but she knew that kind of optimism was unjustified.

Chloe ended the call, and Kate thought again about calling Lucas. She decided to listen to the voice mails first.

The first two were Pam and Chloe. Lucas's was the third. She listened to the familiar deep tone, closing her eyes and wishing he were beside her in the car.

"Kate? Are you all right? I saw the interview." A long pause followed. "I'm just—Call me, okay?" There was another long pause, like he wanted to say something else, before the click came.

Kate exited voice mail. It wasn't lost on her that Lucas was the only one of her messages that sounded remotely sympathetic. He, who had more personally at stake than anyone.

She still had a while before they reached the airport. She checked her watch and punched in their home number. Lucas answered quickly.

"It's me," she said.

"Kate." He breathed her name like he'd been holding his breath waiting for her call. "Are you okay?"

"I'm fine." *So much for honesty.* "Well. Fine as I can be given that my whole career came crashing down around my feet this morning. On national television." Her throat stopped up and her eyes burned. *Not now. Buck up until you're home at least. You still have to face a two-hour wait at the airport, and it won't help matters if you're seen crying in public.*

"It's gonna be okay." He was only trying to help—she knew that—but they were trite words. Trite and untrue.

"It's not going to be okay, Lucas. The jobs of my editor and publicist are in jeopardy because of me, Rosewood is going to drop me like a rotten apple, and my readers are going to turn on me. What's okay about that?"

Kate rubbed her temple, frustration choking further words.

"I'm sorry, honey."

Now she felt like a slug. It wasn't his fault. He was a victim in this nutty escapade—her short trip down Insanity Boulevard. He wasn't guilty of anything but trying to help her.

She sighed. "It's not your fault. It's all mine." She beat the back of her head against the seat. "How could I have done something so stupid? I don't do foolish, impetuous things, like marry a man last minute."

"You were backed into a corner. Give yourself a break, Katie. We'll get through this."

His soft tone broke her. Kate felt tears welling, and she blinked them away. She had to get off the phone before she lost it. She had a feeling once she did, she wasn't going to come up for air for a while. "I have to go. I'll talk to you when I get home, okay?"

By the time she hung up, they were nearly to the airport. She'd have to call her agent, Ronald, while she waited for her flight. And her dad.

Lucas's words echoed in her head. *"We'll get through this."* But there was no "we" now. No need for them to remain together. No reason for their marriage. Because come tonight, everyone would know their marriage—and Kate herself—was nothing but a fraud.

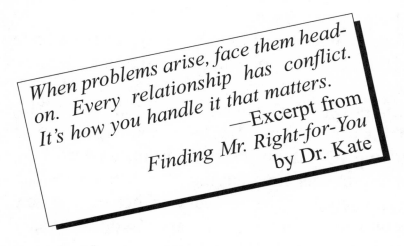

When problems arise, face them head-on. Every relationship has conflict. It's how you handle it that matters.
—Excerpt from
Finding Mr. Right-for-You
by Dr. Kate

Chapter Twenty-Three

Lucas arrived at the airport, not merely on time, but early. He waited for Kate in a sling-back chair, his elbows propped on his knees. Their phone conversation haunted him. Her tone, so lost and broken, begged him to fix the mess. But there was no easy fix this time. The problem was too big, too overwhelming.

Guilt clung to him like grains of sand on wet skin. The marriage had been his idea. He'd practically talked her into it. He'd only been trying to help. He'd done it out of love, but look what happened. He'd hurt her instead.

When the time came for her flight's arrival, he watched for her. How would she react to him? How did this change their relationship? And he had no doubt it would change their relationship. Lucas regretted wasting the past month. He should have been winning Kate over, showing her his love. Instead he'd given her space.

Well, he was out of time now. Pretense had been the glue that held their marriage together and there was no need for it now.

Kate has feelings for me. I know she does. Maybe it was wishful thinking, but he was sure he'd caught her watching him lately with a certain look in her eyes. And there was no denying the passion of the kiss they'd shared or the jealousy in her eyes when he'd caught her spying on him and Sydney. Was it too much to hope that she might open her heart to him?

Kate appeared down the corridor, and he stood. She walked with her chin up, shoulders back. To anyone else she was the picture of a composed business-woman in her stylish gray pantsuit. Her hair swung saucily with each step, and her eyes focused on a point straight ahead.

It was only then that he noticed another man

walking toward Kate with a pad and pencil in hand. Lucas recognized him as Herb Owens, a reporter for the *Mirror*, and he made a beeline for Kate.

"Dr. Kate, I'm Herbert Owens from the *Mirror*. Would you like to make a comment concerning the allegations—"

"No comment." Kate's mouth pressed together as she looked away, quickening her steps.

Herb began walking toward her, then met Lucas's glare and slowed his steps.

Lucas knew when Kate saw him because her rigid features relaxed the slightest bit, her mouth decompressing, her eyes softening. The fact that his presence had that effect on her buoyed Lucas. He grabbed onto the notion, blew it up like an inflatable raft and took a ride on it.

Get a grip, he told himself. *She's probably just relieved to see a friendly face.* Who knew what she'd faced on the way home.

How should he greet her? They had an audience, but would she want him to keep up the charade? Was it a charade anymore? But as she neared, Lucas forgot about pretense. Kate's eyes looked weary, her face strained. He wanted to ease her worry, soothe it away with a touch. Lucas took her bag, then set his palm alongside her face, making eye contact. He leaned close and pressed a kiss to her lips. His only thought was to comfort her.

She gripped his arm like it was a life preserver, returning the brief kiss.

When he pulled back, he draped his arm over her shoulder. "Let's get you home." He looked over her shoulder where Herb stood against the wall, watching.

By the time they reached the car, Kate had grown distant, remote. Did she think his kiss was for show? The ride to the house was quiet. Kate, her hands clutched together in her lap, her feet crossed at the ankles, seemed lost in thought. She stared out the window instead of facing him. Lucas felt her slipping away more each second.

"What can I do?" He asked, desperate to help, desperate to keep her.

There was a long pause, and he wondered if she'd heard him through the chaos of her own thoughts.

He braked at a stop sign, then accelerated. Was she shutting him out already? Hadn't they become more than just business partners? They'd shared a life these past three months. A life that meant everything to him.

"There's nothing we can do but wait," she said, still looking out the window where the glaring sun cut harsh shadows across the ground. "And hope the rest of the media won't hop on board and make it into the scandal of the year."

Even so, the news was out. Lucas didn't know much about publishing, only the little bit he'd gleaned from Kate, but it seemed her publisher wouldn't be interested in promoting her career after a scandal. Her readers wouldn't be too keen on her either. It didn't seem fair to crucify her for one decision. Bryan was the one who'd dumped this mess in her lap. Where was he now, when the chips were falling?

Lucas pulled into the drive and turned off the truck. When Kate didn't make a move to exit, he faced her, propping his knee on the cracked vinyl seat between them.

"We have to tell your family." Kate looked over the hill to where his parent's rooftop peeked above the sea oats.

"I already did." His dad had watched the segment. Lucas had gone over and told the rest of them in person.

Kate faced him. "I'm sorry I wasn't here. How did they respond?" Her forehead wrinkled, her eyes puppy-dog sad.

His mom had been angry at first, then seemed to realize she'd proven herself right. *"Kate's just like her mom, Lucas,"* she'd said. *"You're better off without her."* Of course, it was no surprise to Jamie, but Brody was hurt. His dad tried to be understanding, but Lucas could tell by the way he avoided Lucas's eyes that he was disappointed.

"My family will be fine," he said. "Don't worry about them."

A few quiet moments later, she exited the truck. Lucas followed her inside and set the bag in the bed-room. Bo, excited to see Kate, rubbed against her leg and shepherded her into the kitchen, where she started a pot of coffee.

"I feel like I've been run over by a city bus," Kate said.

Lucas pulled two mugs from the cabinet and the creamer from the fridge. "No wonder. What did the people at Rosewood say?"

Kate scooped grinds into the filter. "Right now they just want me to sit tight. I think a lot depends on how widespread this becomes."

Could they go on as if nothing happened? Would the readers who saw the interview conclude that it was an unfounded rumor? Apparently there was nothing they could do but wait and see. It had been so easy to step in and save Kate when her wedding plans had fallen apart. Now, all he could do was wait with her, and that was a notion that didn't set well.

Kate pulled her knees close, letting her toes dig through the hot surface of the sand to the cooler layer beneath. In the distance, the ferry horn sounded, announcing its arrival to the island. After stalling as long as she could, she'd called her dad and told him about the interview. She could hear his shock in the silence that drew out over the lines. It pulled her spirits even lower.

"Oh boy, Kate," he'd said when he'd found words.

She'd never done anything so careless and never planned to again. How could someone who planned every facet of her life have taken this reckless road?

Once her dad had a moment to think, he begged her to come for a visit. *"Come to Maryland, just to get away for a while. You'll have time to think here. Time to plan your future. Maybe you can open an office in the city."* It was a tempting offer and one she'd give some thought to once she heard from Chloe.

After they'd returned from the airport, Lucas seemed to sense her need for space and had gone back to his shop. But now, as the sun seemed to still in the sky, Kate wished for a distraction.

She'd already finished her column and didn't want to be near the TV after watching it half the afternoon. Two cable news shows had mentioned the scandal, saying they were looking into the allegations. With a scorned woman like Stephanie on the loose, they wouldn't have to look far.

Her cell phone rang incessantly, but she didn't answer the calls. Two reporters had had the nerve to show up on their doorstep, but she hadn't answered, and eventually they'd gone away.

She'd wait and see if the afternoon papers picked up the story. She imagined that's what Chloe was waiting for. Would the *Mirror* pick up the story? The thought of the locals knowing the truth was enough to put a lump in her throat. They knew her here not as Dr. Kate, but as a friend and neighbor. She ate and shopped and worked among these people. They would feel betrayed when they found out. And Lucas's family, natives of the island, would be center stage.

My life is spinning out of control, and I'm helpless to stop it. It was the same feeling she'd had as a child. Never knowing what to expect or what to feel because she had no control over it.

She pulled her legs closer, set her chin on her knees, and rocked in the sand.

Kate waited to hear from Chloe the rest of the day, but no call came. What was her editor waiting for? The morning papers? She slept restlessly that night. Beside her, Lucas seemed to sleep peacefully, his breaths deep and even in the darkened room.

She hadn't heard a peep from his family. Maybe Lucas had asked them to give her space. Maybe they were relieved she wasn't really part of the family. His mom was probably thrilled.

How were they treating Lucas? Were his dad and Brody angry at him for the deception?

Just when Kate thought it couldn't get any worse, she remembered his parents' marriage. She sighed, regret filling the hole in her gut. *I didn't do a thing to help—haven't kept my end of the bargain at all. Lucas married me for nothing—except all the grief he's getting.*

It's not like Susan wanted your help.

Maybe not, but Lucas kept his part of the deal, and I let him down.

You didn't exactly have the twelve months you expected. You're not a miracle worker.

If only I'd had more time.

Kate faced the wall, turning quietly so as not to disturb Lucas.

Why didn't Chloe call back? Were she and Paul and Pam deciding how to handle things, or was she so angry, she was making Kate suffer? Because that's exactly what Kate was doing: suffering. The waiting was killing her. She couldn't plan her next move until someone told her what to do.

Kate felt the bed shift as Lucas moved. Then she felt his arm settle around the curve of her waist, felt the warmth of his stomach against her back.

He pressed a kiss on the top of her head. Kate's heart sped. In his arms she felt safe and loved—cherished. Like her world wasn't a whirling top, spinning toward the edge of a table. She wanted to sink into his weight and let him be her shelter from the storm. But she was unaccustomed to counting on anyone other than herself. The very thought of sharing her burden made her anxious. *How do I know I can count on him? What if he fails me?*

And why was he holding her? *What is it he wants from me?*

She lay still, tense, waiting. He'd played his part of the game, met his end of the bargain. If anything, he should be angry with her too. Angry, like everyone else.

As moments passed and Lucas made no further move, Kate felt her body slowly sink into the hardness of his stomach. *Just for tonight. It doesn't mean I'm turning over control.* She closed her eyes again. Kate knew she shouldn't let herself find comfort in his arms, but she was too tired to fight the urge.

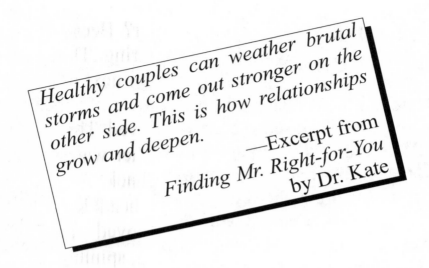

Healthy couples can weather brutal storms and come out stronger on the other side. This is how relationships grow and deepen.

—Excerpt from
Finding Mr. Right-for-You
by Dr. Kate

Chapter Twenty-Four

The shrill of the phone pulled Kate from slumber. She stirred, orienting herself, then crawled across Lucas's empty side of the bed. The events of the day before crashed in on her like a tidal wave. *It must be Chloe.* She cleared her throat before answering.

A male voice greeted her. "Hi, kiddo. How are you holding up?" It was her agent.

She sat up in bed and looked at the clock. Seven forty-two. "Ronald. I'm doing as well as can be expected." Given that her career was on the line. She'd fallen asleep somewhere around three o'clock, when the rain had started, and had slept fitfully. Thunder cracked outside.

"I haven't heard from Chloe yet." Kate had told Ronald she'd call when she heard something. He must've thought she'd forgotten.

"Actually, Chloe called me this morning," he said.

If Chloe was using her agent as a go-between, her editor was distancing herself from Kate. Not a good sign. "You have bad news."

"I'm afraid so, Kate. It hit the papers this morning."

Her throat constricted. She rubbed the sleep from her eyes and braced herself for the news. "Which ones?"

"*New York Times, Washington Post, Chicago Tribune, LA Times*. The Associated Press picked it up. I'm afraid it's everywhere. Mainly in the entertainment section, from what I can see."

Entertainment. Like her life was a circus meant for the public's amusement. The worst had happened. *I'm a laughingstock. A fraud.* The letters from her disappointed readers would pour in. She'd disappointed so many people. The weight of it dragged her under the choppy water, and she fought for breath.

"Paul and Chloe scheduled a conference call with us at noon to discuss how to handle the media. They'll want your story in detail to determine if there's any way to spin this in a positive light."

"Of course." She didn't see how. For the life of her, Kate couldn't see how they could control the damage. It was all true. She was an expert on finding Mr. Right, and she'd impulsively entered a loveless marriage. A marriage with no real feelings.

That's not true, Kate, and you know it.

All right, maybe she did have feelings for Lucas now, but she didn't have them when they'd married.

"They'll call you on your home phone, and I'll be there too," Ronald said.

"What about my column? What about *Glamour*? Do you think—" She was afraid to pose the question, but she had to know. She pulled at a loose thread on the quilt and balled the string between her fingers.

"I wasn't going to say anything; you've got enough on your plate right now. But *Glamour* has asked you to step down for the time being. Maybe when this blows over . . ."

But even when it blew over, Kate knew the damage left behind would be irreparable. "I'm guessing the syndicated column is in jeopardy too?"

The silence on the other end spoke for itself.

Kate felt her throat closing, her eyes burning. *I can't believe this is happening. How have I fallen so far? So hard?* She was on the verge of losing control of her emotions. She cleared her throat again, hoping for a space to open up. "Listen, I've got to go. I'll talk to you at noon."

After they hung up, she set the phone on the night-stand. In the other room, she heard her cell phone ringing. She'd forgotten to turn it off. She couldn't talk to anyone. She wanted to pull the covers over her head and pretend none of this had happened.

But what good would that do?

Come on, Kate. Buck up. Get out of bed and figure a way out of this hole you're in.

That's what she would do. She had four and half

hours to find a way to spin this to the good for Rosewood. Four and half hours to develop a plan.

Kate jumped out of bed, took a quick shower, then dressed. Realizing she detected the robust aroma of brewed coffee, she entered the kitchen, Bo on her heels. A note, scribbled on the back of the utilities bill sat beside the coffeepot.

KATE,
WENT OUT FOR A WHILE.
BE BACK SOON.
L

Where had he gone so early in the morning? It was pouring buckets outside. Maybe he really was having an affair with Red. Maybe he'd gone out to meet her. Maybe he realized the marriage was over now.

She'd no sooner finished the thought when she heard the door open. By the time Lucas appeared, she'd poured herself a mug of hot coffee and added cream.

"Morning." His voice was deep and groggy, a welcome sound. Even the stubble on his jawbone had grown on her.

"Morning," she replied. His navy T-shirt was plastered to his shoulders, and his hair was spiky-wet and tousled from the rain. Or maybe someone had run her hands through it.

She wasn't going to ask where he'd been. It really wasn't her business anyway.

"Don't suppose you heard from your editor," he said.

"My agent called. We have a conference call with the people from Rosewood at noon. The news has hit the press in a big way."

Kate realized this was bad for Lucas. It was his life they were talking about too. Everyone would wonder why he'd stepped in last minute, and he could hardly admit it was because of his parents' souring relationship. She'd put him in a tight spot.

"I saw the papers." He poured himself a cup of coffee and let Bo out the back door.

"Is that why you went out?" She didn't mean to ask.

"I was hoping to bring back good news." He tucked his hands in his pockets.

Kate pulled her laptop from her case and flipped it open. She still had—she checked her watch—almost four hours to come up with an idea. Something that would make the media back off or at least soften the blow.

"Do you have any of the papers?" Kate asked. "I need to see what I'm up against." She pushed the On button and tapped her fingers, waiting for it to boot.

"I left them in the truck." He shifted his weight. "What's the plan?"

Kate plugged her laptop into the outlet under the table. "My plan is to come up with a plan. I need some ideas for my publisher, some way of spinning this so they, at least, don't come off smelling like a pig."

Kate opened the word processor, and a blank document appeared on the screen.

"I'll be right back." Lucas left the room.

There wasn't much Kate could do until she knew what the media was saying. Maybe it was only hearsay, her word against Stephanie's. Though Kate hadn't exactly defended herself on TV. She'd only tried to change the subject. People would see right through that.

When Lucas returned, he carried a thick stack of damp newspapers. He set them beside the laptop and sat across from her. "Sure you want to do this?" His was the look of someone who'd already read the articles.

"Everyone else is going to know what they say; *I* may as well."

The kitchen light was off and the storm outside darkened the room, but there was enough light to read by. She'd start with the Nantucket paper. The *Inquirer* and *Mirror* had tried to call the day before, but she hadn't answered. The paper was already opened to the article. Kate unfolded it and read.

"Famous Local Advice
Columnist Jilted at Altar"

In a TV interview on *Live with Lisa*, local resident and famous author Dr. Kate was accused by a call-in listener of marrying a stand-in groom. The caller, who identified herself as Stephanie from Boston, claimed Dr. Kate's original fiancé, Bryan Montgomery, broke the engagement on the morning of their wedding. A marriage license bearing the names of Montgomery and Dr. Kate was found on record, substantiating the woman's claim. Neither Montgomery nor Dr. Kate could be reached for a comment.

Dr. Kate and local furniture maker Lucas Wright were wed on June 21, the same day as the release of Dr. Kate's first book *Finding Mr. Right-for-You*. It is unclear how Wright came to be the stand-in groom.

"I should have tried to eradicate the evidence," Kate said. "I didn't think about the marriage license." Kate set the paper down and sighed. "I'm sorry they mentioned your name. I was hoping at least the local papers . . ." *Who am I kidding? It's not like everyone on the island doesn't already know Lucas is married to me. Now they just know it's a sham.*

"Which one has the Associated Press article?" She riffled through the papers.

Lucas pulled one from the stack and laid it open to the article.

Kate read the headline. "Dr. Kate's Mr. Wright is Mr. Wrong."

"Clever," Kate said, sarcasm oozing from a deeply wounded spot. The article read much like the local one; only the journalist had scored an interview with Stephanie. They cited the marriage certificate as well.

"This isn't good," Kate said, setting the paper down.

"I didn't realize they'd find proof so quickly. I hope Pam hadn't planned to deny it, because there's no way I can do that now."

Kate glanced at her watch. She had to think. There must be a way to make this better. She shoved the papers to the other side of the table.

"Let's think this through," Lucas said. "Maybe we can come up with something if we put our heads together." He leaned on the tabletop, his bulky forearms planted squarely in front of him.

Kate didn't want to hurt his feelings, but she was done with depending on someone else for help. She worked better alone. "If you don't mind, I think I need to do this on my own. I need to focus, because I have less than four hours."

He shrugged and gave that half smile that charmed her. "We pulled off a wedding in barely under that."

She smiled wryly. "Seems to me that's what got us into this mess to begin with."

By the time the phone rang at noon, Kate had all her notes on the screen. Lucas was somewhere else in the house. She'd been lost in her own thoughts since he'd left the table four hours earlier, and she hadn't seen him since.

Kate answered the phone.

"Hello, Kate. It's Chloe. Pam, Paul, and Ronald are already on the line."

"Hi, everyone," Kate said.

Their greetings were less than enthusiastic. Hopefully, they'd agree to what Kate had come up with as the best approach.

Lucas entered the room and leaned against the doorway as she opened the conversation.

"Can I just say something first? I want to tell you how sincerely sorry I am for the trouble this is causing. It was never my intention to damage your businesses or careers, and I'm deeply sorry." Kate hoped her tone expressed the depth of her regret. "I'll do anything I can to help rectify this."

"Fair enough," Paul said. "The damage is done now, and we need to figure out how to proceed. Kate, if we could hear what happened, in your words, that might help."

Kate took a deep breath and told the story of her wedding morning: Bryan's phone call, Pam's news of the *Dr. Phil* show invitation, Lucas's offer.

Chloe stopped her there. "You said Lucas was only an acquaintance. Why did he offer to take Bryan's place?"

Kate stopped pacing, her eyes fastened on Lucas's. Could she tell them about Lucas's parents? She wasn't going to hang him out to dry again.

"I agreed to help him on a personal project. That part of the story really has no bearing on this."

"Tell us the rest of the story," Paul said.

Kate finished, explaining the temporary nature of the agreement. "I've done a lot of thinking this morning, and I think our best bet is for me to face up to what I've done publicly. I'm genuinely sorry, and I think once my readers see I was jilted at the altar and made a poor quick judgment, they'll be generous with their grace."

"Let's not overlook the fact," Ronald said, "that any publicity is good publicity. It's quite possible the scandal could increase Kate's sales. It's happened before with other books."

Kate stopped at the back window. Now that was the best news she'd heard in a while. Was it possible this might turn out well for her publisher?

"Keep in mind," Pam said, "that Kate's book is a self-help book, not a novel or a memoir. Her readers are willing to plunk down their money because they trust her advice. That trust has been broken. She might be seen as hypocritical since she advised her readers one direction and took an entirely different direction herself."

Kate jumped in. "That's why I should apologize, offer an explanation. I think my readers would sympathize with the fact that I was jilted at the altar. What woman wouldn't be confused and prone to bad judgment at that point?"

"The fact is, though," Paul said, "you aren't every woman. You are Dr. Kate, expert in love relationships. Your whole book is about finding a marriage partner for a lifelong relationship, and you've entered a loveless marriage on a one-year lease. I'm not going to sugarcoat it, Kate. The media sure isn't."

Kate felt heat flush her neck and cheeks. That was as close to a dressing down as she'd received since her dad scolded her for loaning out her Nikes when she was in fourth grade.

"We need time to digest this," Paul continued. "We'll get hold of you later today and let you know what we've decided. Until then, don't answer your phone."

By the time they disconnected, Kate felt wrung out. More waiting. *I'm tired of waiting. I want to do something.* She leaned against the windowsill. Outside, the landscape looked gray through the blanket of rain.

"How'd it go?" Lucas asked.

Kate shrugged. "They're going to decide how they want to handle it. They'll call back later today. I don't think they were too keen on my honesty plan."

Kate didn't think they were too keen on her either, and she didn't blame them.

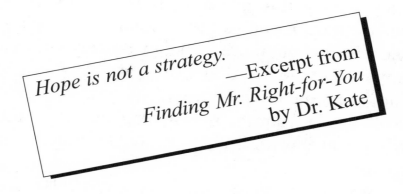

Hope is not a strategy.
—Excerpt from
Finding Mr. Right-for-You
by Dr. Kate

Chapter Twenty-Five

Kate searched for ways to stay occupied as she awaited Paul's call. She filled the sink with soapy water and washed dishes. She wiped down the counters and table. When she was finished, she decided the linoleum needed a good scrubbing. Lucas worked on a design for an armoire while she cleaned.

Later, they had a quiet lunch of soup and sandwiches, then resumed working. The phone rang often, but the numbers were unfamiliar. She wished their number was unlisted. At least no one had shown up at the door today.

The storm raged on, rain tapping on the windows like a stranger with bad news. The sea oats bent in submission to the wind, and gulls floated high in the air, riding the gusts wherever it took them.

Lucas was stirring a pot of boiling pasta when the call came. Kate picked up.

"Kate," Ronald said. "I just heard from Paul."

"What did they decide?"

"They want you to avoid the press, kiddo. They're afraid you'll open yourself to all kinds of speculation. People will find out more than they already know, and from what they've heard, it's not good."

"They want me to do nothing?"

Lucas turned from the pot of spaghetti and studied her. As his eyebrows lifted, long lines formed across his forehead.

"Unfortunately, I agree, Kate. As much as I'd like to think this publicity will be advantageous, I think it's going to cause damage. And the more details the media gets, the longer this is going to brew. The best we can hope is that it'll blow over soon and be forgotten."

The thought of doing nothing was demoralizing. It wasn't in Kate to sit back and let things happen. She was a planner, a doer. She wanted to work this out; she wanted to fix it.

"If you're confronted by the press, Paul suggested you say, 'No comment' and keep moving. It would be prudent to tell your family and anyone who has details to avoid the press also."

Thunder cracked in the distance, and the rain pummeled the roof over the kitchen. "Paul asked about Bryan. I didn't see him quoted in any of the articles. They're hoping that's an indication he won't submit to an interview. They want you to confirm that."

"I'll call him," Kate said. Her voice sounded choked. The burden of her mistake weighted her. Her body felt heavy—too heavy for her trembling legs.

As she ended the phone call, her legs buckled, and she dropped on the wooden window ledge. "I have to call Bryan." She wasn't up for it, but that didn't matter. She dialed his home phone. It rang four times before the voice mail kicked on.

"Bryan, it's Kate." She ran her fingers through her hair. *What should I say?* "Can you call me when you get this? Listen, it's very important that you not talk to the press." *Unlike your skanky girlfriend.* Kate gritted her teeth. She needed Bryan to cooperate, and a snarky attitude wouldn't help. "Just call me."

She hung up. Lucas was looking at her with an expression she couldn't read and didn't have the brainpower to decipher. She dialed Bryan's cell and got voice mail again. She left a similar message and hung up.

"What did your agent say?" Lucas asked.

"They want me to stay quiet. Do nothing. Hope it blows over."

"You're not happy."

"I see where they're coming from. They might even be right; they've got more experience than I. It just makes me feel so—"

Helpless. Useless. Like a sitting duck. Like a twelve-year-old girl waiting to see if her mom is Jekyll or Hyde that day.

She walked away from the thought, into the bedroom, but it followed her there, like a persistent shadow. She didn't bother to flip on the lamp, though only remnants of daylight seeped through the curtains.

Instead, in the darkness, she paced the short length of the room while rain pounded the roof, a surge of the storm's temper.

Lucas appeared in the doorway. He leaned against the doorjamb, watching her.

"I just—I hate this doing nothing." She whipped around, her hair slapping her on the cheek, and sank on the edge of the mattress. Would this be the way her career went down? With her forfeiting the match; not even putting up a fight?

Lucas approached Kate, aching to comfort her. "Maybe they're right," he said. "Maybe it'll blow over."

And what will happen to us? He wanted to know but couldn't ask. Not now, when she'd been bombarded by everyone else. Heavy clouds seemed to roll in, darkening the room.

"What if they're wrong? What if my readers think I'm a hypocrite?" Her eyes glazed over and she blinked rapidly. "Maybe I am a hypocrite."

He'd never seen her look so fragile, so vulnerable, not even on her wedding day. She looked broken, her always neat hair a disheveled mess, hanging in her face.

"Hey . . ." he said, smoothing the sides of her hair with both hands. He tucked it behind her ears the way she liked it. "Stop talking like that. It's going to be okay." He cupped her face between his palms. "We'll get through this."

A tear escaped, and he brushed it away with his thumb.

"Why did we ever plan my wedding around my book's release? It was stupid. I thought it was a brilliant idea, but it was just stupid. Look where all my planning has gotten me. My career is over, Lucas." Her voice wobbled. The tears chased each other rapid fire.

"Shhhh." He pulled her to him and caressed her hair, letting her cry. Her arms wrapped around his waist, her fingers clutching his T-shirt. She was falling apart, his composed Kate. He hadn't thought it possible.

A bucket of guilt poured down on him like the rain that deluged the ground outside. This was all his fault. He was the one who'd offered to stand in for Bryan. If not for him, Kate would have told the truth. Sure, it would have been hard. It may have ruined her book sales, but it wouldn't have wrecked her career.

"I'm sorry, Kate," he whispered into her hair. He'd thought he was saving her, but he'd ruined her instead. "It's my fault."

She sniveled. "No, it isn't." She shook her head against his chest. "It was my decision."

"It was *my idea*." His arms tightened around her as his thoughts went back to that morning when he'd seen her so shaken, seen her eyes deaden to the reality of her situation.

"I was just trying to—" *Save you. Love you.* His gut tightened.

She pulled away, looking up at him. "Stop it." One

last tear trailed down her cheek. "You were only trying to help."

He brushed the tear away, dried her face with his thumbs. Her eyes were sad pools of regret, her lashes spiked with moisture. If only he could clean up the mess he'd made so easily. He had been trying to help that day, trying to wipe that look of despair from her face. He would have done anything to accomplish that.

And yet here was despair again, sevenfold.

"I would never hurt you," he whispered. Did she believe him? It was important that she did.

"I know." Her lips barely moved on the words. A tear trembled in the corner of her mouth. He swept it away, his thumb lingering over the plump curve of her lower lip.

Mercy, did she know how much he cared for her? How much he wanted her to be completely his? Did she know he'd do anything to protect her?

Did she know he loved her? The words hovered on the tip of his tongue, wavering, eager to escape, yet afraid of the consequences. What would she do if she knew? What would she say if she knew he'd loved her from the beginning?

Kate wanted to lose herself in Lucas's eyes, in those fathomless green depths. Something stirred in her. His words replayed in her head. *"I would never hurt you."*

She knew it was true. He would never have deserted her on her wedding day, like Bryan had. Lucas would stand by and defend her, protect her no matter what. Kate had never considered herself the kind of woman who yearned for a knight in shining armor, but just now the notion was appealing. And the look in his eyes was irresistible.

He was so close. She felt the warmth of him through his T-shirt. Kate turned her face into his hand and pressed a kiss against his calloused palm. He was a man's man, a hard worker. Loyal to the death. So many good things. She wanted all of them.

She kissed the curve of his jaw, feeling the coarseness of his stubble against her lips and relishing him for the man he was.

She heard his breath catch, and it emboldened her. With a hand against his face, she turned him toward her. Their lips met gently, and Kate soaked up his response. Her fingers tightened on the cotton material of his shirt.

Lucas pulled her closer, into the strength of his embrace. His stomach was hard against hers, his shoulders like solid rock. He was a sure foundation in a raging storm.

"Katie," he whispered.

The taste of her name on his lips, so desperate and devoted, was sweet and heady.

I want him.

No, I need him.

He deepened the kiss, and she responded in kind, drawing her fingers through his hair. Lucas leaned into her, pressing her back against the bed, the weight of him more welcome than a cool breeze on sun-scorched skin.

What am I doing? The thought had no more than formed than she pushed it down.

But it resurfaced with force. *Is this right? Do I love him?*

He's your husband. You have every right.

She latched onto the thought, clinging with everything in her. *He* is *my husband. He's mine.*

With the thought came complete surrender. She ran her hands along the plane of his back and returned his kiss with fervor.

"Katie," he said, his breath ragged. He pulled back, putting space she didn't want between them. His eyes were deep shadows of longing, a mirror of her own. "Are you sure, honey?"

Kate pulled him close, kissing his jaw and the corner of his lips before he claimed her mouth.

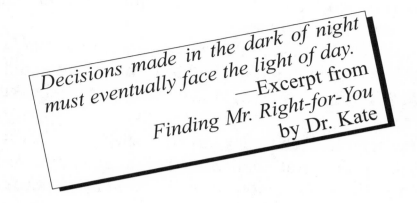

Chapter Twenty-Six

Morning light flooded through the windows, piercing Kate's aching eyes. She checked the clock and realized she'd slept late. Yesterday's shirt hung from the cone-shaped lamp shade.

The memory of the night before struck her like a rogue wave. She swiveled her head on her pillow and met Lucas's gaze.

" 'Morning," he said. He lay on top of the covers in jeans and a T-shirt.

How long has he been watching me? Her own nakedness under the covers made her squirm. Kate clutched the quilt, pulling it to her shoulders, reality slamming into her hard. *What have I done? We didn't even use protection. What was I thinking?*

She was unaccustomed to waking with him in bed. Unaccustomed to what they'd done the night before. The two realities clashed, ushering in an awkward moment.

"You're still here."

He propped his elbow on the pillow, head in hand. "Just watching you sleep."

She could get lost in those eyes again if she let herself. But she shouldn't. Couldn't. What sense did it make? She looked away under the guise of checking the time.

Daylight had chased away the shadow of desire, exposing the irrationality of her actions the night before. She'd let herself become swept up in her feelings for Lucas.

And yes, she admitted she did have feelings. Strong ones.

But he's all wrong for me. How could I forget that? Me, who wrote an entire book on the subject? Maybe I am a hypocrite.

"Look at me, honey."

Her stomach tightened at the endearment, the same one he'd used just before they'd—

Kate turned her head. Lucas's cheek was pillow creased. She'd kissed that cheek the night before. Kissed those lips, run her hands over the sharp curve of his jaw. *Stop it!*

"What's going on behind those big brown eyes?" He brushed her hair from her cheek.

She flinched at his touch, wary of being swept into the tide pool of longing, and Lucas withdrew his hand, a frown pulling his mouth.

Kate needed time to think. Time to sort through her feelings. Time to get dressed, for heaven's sake. She pulled the quilt to her chin.

"I just need . . . a little time, Lucas. Everything's changing so quickly, I can't wrap my brain around it. I need time to figure things out."

The sparkle left his eyes. She wanted to say something that would light them again, but it wouldn't be fair to offer false hope.

"Right," he said.

She should say something. Something to soothe the hurt on his face, but nothing came to mind. Nothing honest. Not when her mind was a riot of confusion.

Lucas got up, the bed shaking in his wake. He cleared his throat. "I have errands to run anyway." At the foot of the bed, he slid on his sandals.

"I didn't mean for you to leave."

He walked toward the door without looking back. "It's okay."

Moments later she heard the door open and shut. His truck roared to life outside, and Bo entered the room, his paws clicking to a stop beside her.

What had she done? As if life needed to get more complicated. *What was I thinking last night?*

She'd been thinking with her heart, that's what. The way he'd touched her, like she was the most precious object in the world. Even now, she shivered in remembrance. She'd never felt so cherished, so . . .

Loved.

Lucas doesn't love you. He was a man, wanting what a man wants.

But it hadn't felt that way. Hadn't felt that way when she'd awakened and caught him watching her.

Stop it, Kate. You need to think with your head, not your heart. Be smart. Listen to your own advice.

Forcing herself to move, Kate got up and showered, dressing in her favorite jeans and her royal blue shirt. It was Sunday and she wondered if Lucas's family would welcome her to their family meal. Maybe she shouldn't go. But she had to face them eventually, even if only to apologize.

As she poured her coffee, she heard a car pull into the driveway. Her nerves immediately clanged, like the wind chimes on the back porch on a windy day. She didn't know what to say to Lucas yet. What they'd shared had been so intimate, and yet now, in the light of day, she knew it was a mistake. How could she tell him that?

Maybe he's thinking the same thing.

The thought disturbed her. Hurt her feelings—which was ludicrous considering she felt the same way. She couldn't even agree with herself.

Maybe a walk on the beach would clear her head. Through the kitchen window she saw the weather had calmed. It was no longer storming, just overcast and gloomy. The ocean was gray and choppy, its waves striking the shore with white foam fingers.

One thing she knew: she had to escape the island. There was no reason to prolong the marriage, and staying was too difficult emotionally. Obviously her feelings for Lucas had grown into something beyond her control. *If only we weren't so different. If only we weren't completely incompatible, we could make it.*

Her heart ached for the chance to try.

But the memories of her parents' arguments, their vicious battles over every little thing, stopped her, even if her experience as a counselor didn't. She wasn't going to waste her life forcing a round peg into a square hole. She'd watched too many people try and fail. She'd watched her parents try and fail. That wasn't the life she wished on anyone.

A knock sounded at the front door.

Kate set down her mug and walked into the living room, peering through the window in the door. She prayed it wasn't another reporter coming to get the scoop on her private—

No.

Through the glass, the top of a head was visible, but she would've recognized that neatly clipped brown hair anywhere. She paused, gathering her thoughts a moment before she pulled open the door.

"Bryan." She hadn't seen him since the eve of their wedding day. He looked older. Tired. Wrinkles and creases covered his dress shirt and slacks, like he'd slept in them. "What are you doing here?"

"Kate." He heaved a sigh. Relief? "I've been trying to reach you."

She leaned against the door, keeping it partway closed. She'd expected to feel something if she saw him again. Longing, regret, anger. Something. The lack of emotion was a welcome surprise.

"I turned off my phone," she said. "But I guess you can understand why."

"I'm sorry I missed your call. So many reporters were trying to reach me that I turned mine off too. I just got your message when I got off the plane."

"What are you doing here?" Had he come thinking he could comfort her? Help her? Maybe he had a plan to make this disaster go away. He'd always been clever. And her own plan had failed.

"We need to talk," he said. "Can I come in?"

Kate looked across the street where two houses were visible from the front porch. It would be better than having Bryan seen on her doorstep. She opened the door wide and stepped back against the wall, giving him a wide berth.

Inside, she gestured him toward the sofa. She scanned the tiny, simple living room, seeing it through his eyes. It was a far cry from his contemporary city apartment. Bo appeared at his side, and Bryan inched away, but the dog only sniffed Bryan's shoe before following Kate to the recliner across the room.

"I'm sorry it got leaked." Bryan planted his elbows on his knees. "I'm sorry about the interview on TV. It must've been very uncomfortable for you."

Uncomfortable is hardly the word. "Your girlfriend must be having a field day."

"She's not my girlfriend. It was a big mistake. *She* was a big mistake."

Kate felt weary suddenly, like her bones might melt into the chair. "Let's not go through this again, Bryan. What's done is done. The main thing is that you can't talk to the press. You haven't, have you?"

"Of course not. I wouldn't do that to you."

He had some nerve acting as if he'd never hurt her. Kate stared him down until he looked away. "If anyone questions you, just say 'No comment,' okay?"

"Of course. I'll do whatever you want. I owe you that. I owe you so much more than that." His baby blue eyes shone under the lamplight. She'd once thought them beautiful, too pretty to be wasted on a man. Now they were a thin, cool sheet of ice, ready to crack under pressure.

"I know this is bad," Bryan said, "Our personal business all over the news, your career—jeopardized. I can't tell you how sorry I am, Kate."

His apology was sincere, his regret legitimate. Unfortunately it changed nothing.

But anger was futile. And even though he'd backed out of their wedding, it had been her decision to marry Lucas.

"What are you going to do now?" Bryan asked. "Can I help in any way?"

Kate shook her head. "I'm just going to hole up somewhere. My dad invited me to stay with him awhile, so I might do that. I need time for this to blow over, and time to rethink my career, if need be."

Two notches formed between Bryan's brows, and he shook his head as if to clear the cobwebs. "But what about—"

Kate realized her mistake too late. The public—and Bryan—didn't know the particulars of her and Lucas's arrangement. She'd never told Bryan the marriage wasn't a real one.

"Your marriage," he said. "It was just temporary? You're leaving him?" The hope in his voice was a warning siren.

A sick feeling worked its way into her middle, churning her stomach the way the wind churned the waves outside. "I'm going to visit my dad for a while, that's all."

His eyes narrowed. "It was temporary from the beginning, wasn't it? You never had feelings for him, never planned to stay married. It was just . . . a way out of the mess I put you in."

There was a certainty in his tone, and Kate knew she wasn't going to erase that. *He won't alert the media, so what harm is there if he knows?*

"Yes, it was temporary, all right?" she said. "But that's between you and me, and if you say one word to the press—"

Bryan extended his hands palm out. "I swear, I won't." He stood and crossed the rug, closing the space between them, dropping to his knees at her feet.

"Kate, do you know what this means to me?" He took her hands, pressing them between his own. The coolness of his palms, the shape of his fingers felt foreign against hers.

She pulled away. "It doesn't mean anything. It doesn't change anything."

"You need to get away. Come with me. We can stay

at my place in Aspen. I'll take a leave of absence. You can figure out where to go from there."

Kate pressed her back into the cushion. "No, Bryan. It's over between us." She knew as the words left her mouth that she meant them now as she never had. There was nothing left, no feelings for him.

Because they've been replaced by feelings for Lucas. Kate shrugged the thought away.

"You don't mean that. Just think. We could move anywhere you want. You could open a counseling service like you did here. We could have a fresh start."

The thought of starting over was tempting compared to the months of uncertainty she faced, but she knew it was implausible. She was about to say so when the front door opened.

Somehow she'd missed the rattle of Lucas's truck arriving. He stopped on the threshold, his hand on the doorknob. His gaze darted between Kate and Bryan. She imagined the scene from Lucas's perspective and cringed.

Lucas's heart stuttered at the sight of Kate and Bryan. He'd thought the unfamiliar car might belong to some nosy reporter and charged up the porch steps ready to confront the jerk who'd had the nerve to show up on their doorstep.

But it wasn't some reporter who knelt on the floor at his wife's feet. It was her ex-fiancé. The look of shock on Kate's face at his entry would have been comical if it weren't plain hurtful.

His hands balls into fists. "What are you doing here, Montgomery?"

Bryan stood slowly, blocking Lucas's view of Kate as if to guard her. What a joke. It was Bryan she needed protection from.

"Knock off the doting husband charade. I know the truth."

Kate stood, and Lucas's eyes went to hers. He saw guilt there. And something else, before her gaze dropped to the floor. It was enough to shake his confidence.

Lucas took a step closer to Bryan, wanting to beat the smug expression off his face. "Get out of my house."

"Not without Kate."

"Stop it, Bryan," Kate said. "You should go." She grabbed his arm, but Bryan didn't budge. Kate's hand trembled.

"You heard her," Lucas said. "Get lost."

Bryan turned to Kate and touched her arm. Lucas wanted to grab him by the collar and haul him out the door. He ground his teeth together instead. Did Kate want to go with Bryan? Is that why she regretted the night before? She'd apparently told Bryan their marriage was a sham. *Why would she have done that unless—*

"Come with me, Kate," Bryan said. He added something else, too softly for Lucas to hear.

Kate shook his hand loose. "No."

Bryan whispered something. He took Kate's face in his hands.

Something red and hot spread through Lucas. He surged forward. "Get your hands off my wife." He grabbed Bryan's fancy shirt and shoved him toward the door. Lucas had five inches and forty pounds on him, and Bryan knew it.

Bryan caught his balance in front of the doorway, smoothing his sleeves, regaining his composure. He nailed Lucas with a glare. "She's not your wife, *friend*. She's just playing house with you."

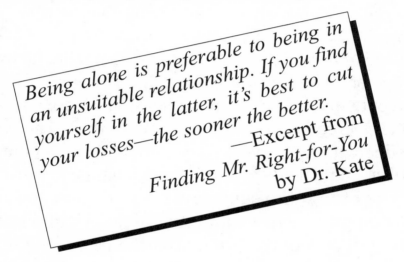

Being alone is preferable to being in an unsuitable relationship. If you find yourself in the latter, it's best to cut your losses—the sooner the better.
—Excerpt from *Finding Mr. Right-for-You* by Dr. Kate

Chapter Twenty-Seven

If Bryan hadn't left on his own, Kate would have shoved him out the door after the way he'd spoken to Lucas. She wanted to soothe the hurt from Lucas's face with a well-placed kiss, but the anger lining his stubborn jaw stopped the thought as it materialized.

Lucas exited the room, leaving her to wonder what he was thinking. She heard him open a cabinet, remove something. The cabinet door slammed shut. Then she heard the pouring of coffee and the sound of the pot clanking back into its cubby.

Kate didn't know whether to follow him or not. Clearly they had a lot to discuss. He must be wondering what Bryan was doing there. He must be wondering what she was going to do.

Kate checked her watch. They were due at his parents' in an hour. *How will I face them? How can I tell these people who've become my family that I'm leaving?*

How can I tell Lucas I'm leaving? But then, he must know there was nothing holding her here now.

Except what had happened the night before.

Kate peered out the living room window. The wind wrestled with the leaves. They were already beginning to turn. Fall had arrived, and changes were in progress. The warm summer days were gone, and the cooler autumn days would usher in the frigid winter.

She'd never enjoyed winter on the island. With the winds blowing in off the ocean, it was impossible to keep a warm house. She mentally put another check in the pro column for visiting her dad in Maryland. There were many checks in the column already. Increasingly, she felt the need to escape. And soon.

Lucas's sandals shuffled to a stop somewhere behind her. His presence pulled her shoulder muscles tight, pushed the air from her lungs.

"Did you ask him to come?" Lucas said.

Kate pivoted. "No." She hated that he thought it.

Did he think last night meant nothing? She wouldn't have slept with him if she were in love with Bryan. *Surely he knows that.*

Lucas took a sip of his coffee from the oversized Nantucket mug. It looked small in his hands.

Kate had to tell him what she'd decided, but getting the words out was harder than she imagined. *Strange, when I planned to leave him all along.* When he'd planned for her to leave all along. It shouldn't come as any surprise now that there was no point in her staying.

Except for your feelings.

She brushed the thought away, zooming in on the logical reasons that had added checks to her pro column.

"We need to talk," she said. It was a start. A slow one, maybe, but easing into it seemed kinder.

"Go ahead." He held the mug in front of him, a fragile barrier between them. His feet were braced as if for a blow.

She hated that she would deliver it. "I'm leaving the island." She measured his reaction and came away with nothing. "Now that the word is out about . . . our marriage, there's no reason for me to stay."

Kate chest pounded with the force of her heartbeats, walloping her ribs like a prizefighter. She waited for his response—and got nothing but silence.

"I need to get away." She filled the gap. "I'm too accessible here, anyway, to the press. I think if I go away somewhere, this will die down more quickly."

It occurred to her that she was leaving Lucas to deal with the press, with all the locals and their questioning glances. She was sorry for that, but staying wouldn't make it easier. People would talk even if she stayed.

She wished she could interpret his expression, but the light from the kitchen silhouetted him. She kept talking. "If there's nothing left of my career when this is over, maybe I can open another counseling service." She tried to sound upbeat, but the words fell flat. She imagined driving away, leaving Lucas behind. Never seeing him again. Her throat closed off.

"Are you going back to him?"

It took Kate a moment to realize what Lucas was asking. "No." She shook her head emphatically. "Bryan is—It's over between us." Hadn't Lucas heard her telling Bryan to leave?

"He doesn't seem to think so."

"I don't have feelings for him anymore. I wouldn't have—" *Slept with you if I did.* If she finished the thought, it would raise the subject she wanted to avoid.

"Wouldn't have . . . ?"

Her mind went back to the night before, returning like a dehydrated woman to a spring of fresh water. Kate knew she'd never wipe the moments from the slate of her memory. She crossed her arms, hugging her waist.

"I'm going to stay with my dad awhile," she said, avoiding his question. "In Maryland. Hopefully the scandal will fade quickly."

He walked toward her, and she tensed with each step. But he stopped an arm's length away. She could see his face now, lit by the light seeping through the window behind her.

"You could stay here . . ."

Did he know how tempting it was, with him looking at her that way? His eyes burning a path straight to her heart? It was the first time either of them had hinted at making the marriage permanent. It took courage for him to verbalize the idea that had floated between them for days. The night before, they'd silently brought the idea to life, but now that he said it aloud, it had a pull stronger than a riptide.

Kate tore her eyes away. *Be strong. Think with your head, not your heart. Think of your parents. Think of what you've learned from all your experience.*

"You know it wouldn't work, Lucas," She said. "And even if you don't know it, I do." She felt him watching her and wanted to run now, far away.

"What was last night?"

The edge of hurt in his voice broke her. No matter what, no matter that she was leaving, no matter that it was over, she wouldn't leave him thinking it meant nothing. She wouldn't cheapen something so special.

She was touching his face before she knew what she was doing. "Oh, Lucas. Last night was—it meant so much." The words jammed her throat. Her eyes burned.

He turned away, leaving her hand to fall on empty space.

Lucas walked away, putting space between them. Kate's touch had too much power. He would be lost if she touched him again. How could she leave if she felt anywhere near what he did? The thought of being without her ripped him in half, worse in some ways than Emily's death. That loss had been no one's choice, something that just happened. If Kate left him, it would be of her own choosing.

But maybe she didn't feel the way he did. He knew she had feelings, but maybe the depth of his love was . . . unrequited. Such a proper term for such a painful feeling.

"Lucas?" His name on her lips reminded him of the night before. She'd said his name over and over. Would he ever forget the sound of it? The heady way it made him feel to have her as his own?

He needed to change her mind. *If she would only give me a chance.* He faced her again, and now that he saw her watery eyes, he wanted to be close to her again, holding her. But he couldn't think with her in his arms.

"Stay here, Kate. There's something between us; won't you stay long enough to figure out what it is?"

She wet her lips and swallowed. "I told you about my parents—about their differences and how miserable they were. What I didn't tell you was how it ripped my mom apart when they divorced."

She looked out the window, and the daylight lit half her face. "Even though it was her choice, she couldn't be without him. She started drinking." Kate gave a wry smile. "Of course, I didn't understand it at the time. But I know now she was using the alcohol to escape reality. And the reality was, she couldn't live with my dad and she couldn't live without him. She was miserable either way. What kind of hope is there in that?"

"We're not your parents, Kate."

"We're *just like* my parents. Opposites in every way. I don't think I could've found someone less compatible. I should've followed my own advice and distanced myself before there were—feelings."

She made it sound so rational. Like you could tuck unwanted emotions in a box and toss them. "That's crazy," Lucas said. "Love isn't some item on a checklist."

Her fingers clutched the curtain, and she wouldn't look at him. He'd expected an argument. He'd expected her to rationalize why her way was best. He would find a counterargument to everything she said.

"I'll make reservations on the ferry as soon as I can," she said. "Possibly today. I'll have to send for my things."

Lucas felt like she'd punched him in the gut. She wasn't going to defend her decision? Wasn't going to give him a chance to convince her? He couldn't believe it was happening so quickly. Not after the night before, when he'd felt like a surfer riding the crest of a dream wave. Now he'd crashed headfirst into the rocks.

She checked her watch. "I want to talk to your family before I go. I owe them an apology."

It was his heart she'd broken, not his family's. *Say something. Say something to stop her before her plans set in her mind.* "You're in the middle of a crisis. Wait until things settle down. Don't make a rash decision." It was something she would say, something she could relate to.

Her eyes darkened with her frown. "It's not rash, Lucas. I planned to leave from the beginning, remember?"

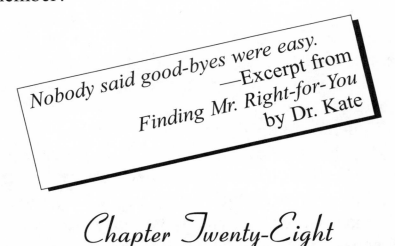

Nobody said good-byes were easy.
—Excerpt from
Finding Mr. Right-for-You
by Dr. Kate

Chapter Twenty-Eight

Kate knocked on the Wrights' door, then clasped her shaking hands behind her back. Lucas had offered to accompany her, but she needed to face his family on her own. This was her fault, not his.

The door opened, and Susan's welcoming smile drooped. Kate watched the woman rise to her full height, watched her narrow chin notch upward. Regardless of how the woman responded, Kate was going to apologize to the family. Then she was going to have a heart-to-heart with Susan.

"Kate." Her name was a sour ball on the woman's tongue. "What are you doing here?"

"I came to talk to your family. Can I come in?"

Susan waffled in the doorway, clearly torn between opening the door wider and slamming it in Kate's face. Finally, she stepped back.

Kate followed Susan through the foyer and into the kitchen where Roy was putting a pan of dinner rolls into the oven. The smell of pot roast and garlic filled the air, and Kate's stomach growled in response. Jamie was on a stool at the kitchen island, a book propped open on the Formica counter. They both turned at her entry.

"Hi, Kate," Jamie said, a genuine smile on her face, and maybe a touch of pity in her eyes.

Roy shut the oven door and turned, offering her a nod and a reserved smile. Kate noticed his hands trembling for the first time and recognized it as a Parkinson's symptom. Guilt pricked her hard. As if the Wrights didn't have enough grief, she had made things worse.

"Is Brody around?" Kate asked. He was back from college for the weekend, and she hoped he hadn't left already.

"He went for a walk," Roy said. "Have a seat, Kate."

"No, thanks," Kate said. "I won't stay. I just wanted to tell you how sorry I am."

"I should think so," Susan said.

"Give her a chance." Roy pinned his wife with a look. "Go ahead, Kate."

Where should I start? There had been so much deception, and now the entire family was being publicly embarrassed. "I'm sure you're aware that my original fiancé backed out of the wedding on our wedding day. I can't begin to tell you how devastated I was. When Lucas offered to stand in, I thought it was crazy at first."

Kate tucked her hair behind her ears. "And then it began to seem like the only sane solution. With my book releasing the same day, I realized it would sink like an anchor if my wedding didn't go off as planned, and with all the media there to cover it—well, I guess I took the coward's way out."

Susan crossed her arms. Roy leaned his elbows on the island beside Jamie and studied Kate, the leathery lines around his eyes deepening.

"I never expected the truth to get leaked to the press. Lucas and I were going to divorce quietly after a year—we had it all planned. Obviously, everything's changed now."

Kate's throat was dry as desert sand. She wet her lips. "I take full responsibility, and I'm sorry for the embarrassment I've caused. I'm leaving the island this afternoon, but I wanted to let you know that you've become very special to me."

Jamie's eyes turned glassy and she blinked rapidly. Roy's face had softened, and Kate's own eyes burned. Even Susan seemed to lose some of her starch. That might change by the time Kate was finished.

Memories of the past few months flew through Kate's head at digital speed. The first time she'd met the Wrights, when she and Lucas had returned from their honeymoon. The time they'd come to watch her on *Dr. Phil*. All the walks with Susan. They were the family Kate never had, and she'd miss them. Even Susan.

Her throat thickened. "Thanks for opening your home to me. It was truly an honor to become part of your family, even if only for a little while."

Jamie jumped up and hugged her. "I'll miss you, Kate."

Kate returned the embrace. "Me too, Jamie. You're the sister I never had."

When they parted, Roy embraced her. "I wish you didn't have to go."

Kate wrapped her arms around his broad shoulders and spoke around her closed throat. "It's for the best. Thanks for all those home-cooked meals."

There was a moment of awkwardness as she faced Susan. "Can I have a word with you in private, Susan?" Kate asked.

Susan gave a short nod, her styled hair bouncing, and Kate followed her into the foyer. The woman turned to her and crossed her arms over her chest. The overhead light was harsh on the woman's face, making her appear older than her years.

Kate tempered her words with grace. "I wanted to talk to you about my mom."

Susan's jaw went slack; then she pressed her rosy

lips together and looked away. "Lucas shouldn't have told you."

Kate shrugged. "I asked him why you didn't like me, and he felt he owed me an explanation."

"I don't want to talk about this with—"

"You don't have to say a word; just let me say my piece. Please." It was the last time Kate would see her anyway. The woman needed to hear the truth from someone, and if her own family wouldn't say it, Kate would.

"What my mom did was wrong. I don't know if she ever apologized, but it's too late for her to say it now, so I'll say it for her." Kate waited until Susan met her gaze. "I'm sorry. It was a terrible thing for a friend to do."

Kate wondered if it would help for Susan to know the misery her mom had gone on to endure. A failed marriage and a battle with alcoholism. Not to mention a premature death. Kate had dreamed of the kind of childhood Susan had provided her kids.

Kate could've sworn she saw a filmy glaze on Susan's eyes.

"I'm sure Roy regrets it as well," Kate continued. "And I hope somewhere along the way, he's found the words to tell you that."

"Saying you're sorry doesn't erase the pain," Susan choked out.

Boy, can I relate to that. How many times had Bryan apologized? "I know." She hoped Susan was remembering that Kate had her own heart broken not long ago. "But at some point you have to forgive the other person. It doesn't mean what he did was okay. It just means you're going to stop punishing him for it."

Susan stood to her full height, her jaws hollowing as she sucked in her pale cheeks.

Kate was treading where she was unwelcome, but the woman had held the mistake over her husband's head for over thirty years. Kate didn't know how Roy had endured it.

"Well, that's all I wanted to say," Kate said. She knew Susan hadn't wanted to hear it, especially not from her, but she hoped the woman took it to heart anyway.

Kate reached out and put her arms around Susan, feeling the stiffness of her shoulders, but embracing her regardless. "Thanks for all the walks, Susan. And for your hospitality."

She felt Susan's arms unfurl, felt her hands land on Kate's arms. It was enough.

Kate pulled back and smiled. "I'll try and catch Brody later. Will you let him know I'm looking for him?"

"Of course," Susan said.

Kate said good-bye one final time and left the house. Her feet took the uneven porch steps before she cut through the yard to the grassy knoll that separated their houses.

This is the last time you'll see them. You'll never sit down to a meal on that insanely high rooftop or listen to Jamie and Brody tease one another again. It's over.

Somehow, in a few short months, the Wrights had wiggled their way into her heart. And now she was leaving.

The crisp autumn air washed across her face, tugging at the short strands of her hair. She crossed her arms against the coolness and looked toward the ocean, the direction she'd soon go. A movement on the beach below caught her eye.

Brody threw something into the water, walking backwards, then turned toward his house. Kate changed directions, aiming her feet toward him.

When she reached the place where the long grass gave way to the sandy shore, Brody saw her. He stopped at the steps leading up from the beach, waiting for her approach. The wind pulled at his white T-shirt and tousled his blond curls.

"Hi," Kate said over the sound of the waves lapping the shoreline. "I was just at your house."

Brody nodded, his guarded smile reminding her of Roy's.

"I came to say I'm sorry," she said. "Sorry about deceiving your family. I never meant to hurt anyone, but I realize I have."

Brody dug his bare feet into the sand. "It wasn't right."

"I know," Kate said. "I'm not going to offer excuses." A seagull soared above the water and cried out—a lonely, high-pitched squeal. "I also came to tell your family good-bye."

Brody met her gaze, his eyes flinching for just a

second. She watched the emotions dancing across his face. He'd never been good at hiding his feelings. "I didn't think you'd leave."

She shrugged, turning her face into the wind, letting her hair blow off her face. "Everyone knows the truth now. There's no reason for me to stay."

Brody studied her, his head cocked to the side. "Isn't there?"

His tone held a challenge, but she wouldn't take it. *There are things he doesn't know, doesn't understand. How can he?*

"How are things going this semester?" she said. "If you don't mind my asking."

The pause was so long, Kate thought he wasn't going to answer. When he finally did, she was relieved.

"You were right," he said. "About my being afraid to fail." He smiled and she saw a glimpse of the old Brody. "If you tell anyone that I'll have to come after you."

Kate held up her right hand, palm out. "I promise."

Brody sank onto the sandy wooden step, and Kate eased down beside him.

"Teaching is what I want to do," he said. "I think switching from major to major was a stall tactic because I was afraid I'd get out in the real world and fail. If you hadn't shown me that, I would have been a college student the rest of my life."

Kate breathed a laugh. "Nah, you would've figured it out."

"Yeah, when I was thirty and on my tenth major."

Kate was glad something positive had come from her time here, because everything else was a disaster.

Silence fell again. The seagull flapped its wings, flying away, growing smaller on the horizon.

"I'm still afraid," Brody said. "I guess that makes me a total wuss."

Kate traced a dry crevice in the step with her index finger. "It's fear that makes an act courageous, you know."

Brody drew in the sand with his big toe. "Huh. Never thought of it like that."

"You'll make a great teacher, Brody. I hope we can stay in contact." Kate huddled against the cool wind, tucking her knees close to her.

"Sure. There's always e-mail." He looked at Kate. "What about Lucas?"

Her heart wobbled at the mention of Lucas's name. "I suppose e-mail is out for him, huh? I guess we can keep in touch by phone."

"That's not what I mean."

He wasn't playing the part of Kate's brother-in-law now; he was a little brother watching out for big brother. She envied Lucas having a sibling that looked out for him.

"Lucas will be fine," Kate said. "It—it wasn't like that between us."

The words felt soiled coming out. It may have been true at one time, but not after the night before.

It hasn't been true for weeks.

"It's best that I leave." What would happen to her heart if she stayed? She'd already lost it to Lucas, and what hope did they have for a future together?

Brody nodded thoughtfully.

Kate let silence fill the space between them, let the sound of the surf rushing the shoreline fill the gap.

"Well," he said, "at least you won't have to fight your fear of heights anymore."

Kate smiled, remembering all the rooftop meals they'd shared. She elbowed Brody. "Fear of *falling*," she corrected.

Brody's expression changed, growing serious. "You know, a wise person once told me it's fear that makes an act courageous."

Kate's breath caught in her lungs as Brody held her captive with his pointed look. He knew. He knew she cared for Lucas. Thought she was a coward for running.

But sometimes, running was the courageous thing to do. At least, that's what she told herself.

Lucas was gone by the time Kate returned home. She realized he must've gone to his parents' house while she was on the beach with Brody. Kate made reservations on that evening's car ferry and packed her belongings. Everything would fit in the car except her treadmill. She'd have to send for it and her things from the apartment when she found a place in Maryland.

For tonight, she'd take the ferry to Hyannis then

drive as far as Wareham or New Bedford, then find a hotel. She called her dad and told him she was coming.

By late afternoon, she was wondering if she was going to have to track Lucas down. She had to leave soon if she wanted to make the ferry, but she owed him a good-bye at least.

Kate was packing her laptop and cord when she heard Lucas return. He opened the door, and his eyes landed on her suitcases. He paused for a moment before shutting the door.

Kate wrapped the recharging cord around the battery pack and stowed it in her bag with the laptop, then zipped it shut.

Lucas pocketed his keys and leaned against the sofa back. Rather than focus on him, she looked at the sofa itself. How many nights had they sat on that couch, disagreeing about what program they should watch? Kate had learned it was easier to read in the evenings because they could never settle on a show.

"When do you leave?" he asked.

Bo nudged Lucas's leg, but when he got no response, he crossed the room and settled on the rug with a loud sigh.

Kate checked her watch. She had to leave soon or take the risk of missing the ferry. "Now."

He was wearing the black T-shirt that stretched across his broad shoulders, and the faded jeans that made his legs look long and solid. *I'll miss him.* Kate didn't want to consider how much. She just needed to get out of there. She could deal with the feelings of loss later, when she was a safe distance away.

Lucas watched Kate hitch the leather strap on her shoulder and turn to him. The moment seemed surreal. It was happening so fast. Last night they'd been closer than ever, and tonight she was leaving.

He wanted to beg her to stay. He swallowed his pride and opened his mouth to do just that. Maybe he could find the words that would change her mind.

But what good would it do to beg? She had to want to stay. She had to want him. He could love her all he wanted, but it had to be her choice.

He closed his mouth, clamping his lips over the words.

"I'm not sure how to say good-bye," Kate said.

Then don't. Stay. Stay with me forever.

Kate tucked her silky hair behind her ears. He would miss that simple action.

"Regardless of how this turned out," she said, "I'm grateful for what you did. I've never had anyone go to so much trouble to save my skin." She tried to smile, but it wobbled on her lips.

It was no trouble. It had been his pleasure. He wished he could save her now, save her career from spiraling out of control. Save their marriage from falling apart.

"I'm sorry I wasn't able to help your parents," Kate said. "I hope they'll work things out."

Tell her now. Tell her your parents are fine, that it

was all a ruse to conceal the fact that you loved her from the beginning. Tell her you love her now and that if she stays, you'll spend every day proving it.

But he had shown his love every day for the past three months. And still she was leaving.

"Say something." Her brown eyes, warm as melted chocolate, pleaded.

He tried to imagine sleeping in an empty bed, waking to a quiet house, making coffee for one again. The thought hollowed his stomach.

"Is there anything I can say to change your mind?" He would say it, whatever it was. *Do you know how much I love you? I'd give anything to call you my own.*

Kate looked away, clutching her purse strap. "It's for the best, Lucas. You'll see. It's hard right now, but later . . . later we'll know it was the right thing."

"Are you trying to convince me or yourself?"

She checked the time. Her eyes seemed to catch on her fingers. He watched her touch the wedding band he'd bought her, watched her slide it down her finger with the engagement ring. She closed the distance between them, pocketing the engagement ring, and held out the wedding band.

"Keep it," he said.

She shook her head. "I can't."

When he refused to take it, she sighed softly and set the band on the end table. Lucas wanted to snatch it up and force it back on her finger. She was his wife, even if only for a short while longer.

But what good would it do? He couldn't force her to

wear his ring any more than he could force her to stay. *Any more than I can force her to love me.*

"I have to go."

Lucas straightened. *Have it your way, Kate.* "I'll drive you."

"You won't have any way back."

He opened the door and picked up her bags. "I'll take a cab." He carried her suitcases to her car.

"There'll be too many people there," she said, her voice sounding like it was being pushed through a sieve.

Lucas loaded her bags in the backseat, then faced Kate. Her eyes glistened like the surface of the ocean on a sunny day. She didn't want to say good-bye in front of an audience.

Neither did he. "All right." He opened the driver's side door for her.

"I'll file papers for the . . . divorce. And cover all the costs." A breeze blew, and dead leaves scuttled past their feet. There was a nip in the air that warned of winter's approach. "And I'll send for my treadmill," she said. "I think I got everything else."

Including my heart. Did she think she could run from these feelings? Did she think mere miles would separate her from his love?

Lucas studied her face, memorizing the way her eyes looked when she squinted against sun, the way her brows puckered when she frowned. He reached out and smoothed the hair the wind had ruffled, wanting to remember the feel of it between his fingers.

She closed her eyes on a sigh. "I hate good-byes."

He thought of Emily and how sudden her death had been. He'd always regretted that he hadn't kissed her that morning when he left for work. He was running late and only called good-bye on his way out the door.

Lucas took Kate's face in his palm, waiting for her to look at him. If she was going to leave him, she was going to do it with her eyes wide open.

He closed the space between them, pressing a soft kiss to her lips. Her hair smelled of lilacs, and her lips tasted like honey. He wanted to remember everything about her. He wanted to close his eyes at night and be able to summon the feel of her lips on his, the sound of her voice.

Kate pulled away. "Good-bye."

She refused to meet his gaze as she lowered herself into the car and put her keys in the ignition. Refused to look at him as she put the car in Reverse and backed out of the drive. He watched until her car disappeared over the slope in the road, knowing that all that awaited him was a house that would feel empty without her.

His feet felt heavy as he entered the house. Bo, seeming to sense his sadness, nudged his leg, tried to shepherd Lucas toward the couch. But Lucas didn't want to sit and think. Think about Kate leaving—getting further away by the minute.

The room seemed big. Kate had decluttered every corner of the house, leaving it spick-and-span, but now it felt bare. The treadmill was the only token of her existence, and it stood in the corner like a memorial.

He walked to the bedroom and stopped in the doorway. The spaces where her alarm clock and jewelry box had been were empty. He saw something on her nightstand and went closer. A small blue-velvet box. He opened it and looked at the earrings he'd given her for their first-month anniversary. It was as if she'd wanted to leave everything behind, to have no reminder of her time with him.

A scrap of paper on the clean hardwood floor caught his eye, and he retrieved it. It was a list of things she'd done in her preparation to leave. A laugh caught in his throat. Kate and her lists. Someday she would learn that life is what happens when you're busy making plans.

He threw the paper in the wastebasket and left the room. It felt as if the walls of the house were closing in on him. He realized for the first time that the house smelled like Kate. He wanted to get away from this place, occupy his mind with something else. If it weren't so late, he'd go sailing.

Bo barked from the back of the house. Lucas followed the sound to where the dog sat by the back door. Bo craned his massive head around, looking at him with inquisitive brown eyes.

"Wanna go for a walk, boy?"

Bo wagged his tail.

At least it would get Lucas out of the house.

They walked westward down the beach, Lucas occasionally tossing a piece of driftwood for Bo to fetch. The sun lowered in the sky, casting a pinkish hue over the beach. Bo trotted beside him, sometimes wading into the incoming surf or chasing a seagull that landed nearby. The dog had just returned from such a chase when Lucas heard it: the haunting sound of the ferry's horn in the distance.

He stopped, a catch in his breath, a stutter in his heart. The sound was the period at the end of a sentence, the whisper of goodbye from a lover, the clock striking midnight for Cinderella.

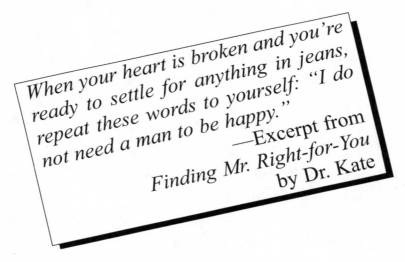

When your heart is broken and you're ready to settle for anything in jeans, repeat these words to yourself: "I do not need a man to be happy."
—Excerpt from *Finding Mr. Right-for-You* by Dr. Kate

Chapter Twenty-Nine

Kate opened the *Columbia Flier* on the picnic table and perused the apartment rentals section. The savory smell of grilled sirloin wafted by on the breeze. Her dad, draped in a red canvas apron, checked the meat, then closed the grill lid.

Kate noticed a new apartment listing and marked the ad with a yellow highlighter.

"See anything interesting?" Her dad sat across from her and brushed a red leaf from the wooden table with the side of his hand.

"There are a couple new ones I'll check on tomorrow. I'm still considering the one on Green Meadow Drive." Kate didn't want to overstay her welcome. She'd planned on staying at a hotel, but her dad had insisted she take his spare room. And she had to admit it had been a relief to hide away the past three weeks.

"How much longer on the steaks?" she asked.

"Oh, seven or eight minutes," he said.

"I'll put the salad together." Kate entered the house through the sliding door, careful not to fingerprint the glass. She found the head of lettuce and chopped it, then sliced a ripe tomato and placed the knife in the dishwasher.

Her cell rang as she was getting the dressing. Every time it rang, her thoughts turned to mush. She hadn't heard from Lucas since she left, but Jamie had e-mailed her twice.

It's not Lucas, Kate. For heaven's sake. Get on with your life.

Bryan had called the day she arrived in Columbia. She'd told him not to call again, and so far, he'd respected her wishes.

She pulled her cell from her purse's side pocket and answered.

"Kate. How are you?" Her agent's voice greeted her.

Kate squelched the inevitable disappointment. "Hi, Ronald. I'm okay. Getting settled in, looking for an apartment, avoiding the media. You know, the usual." It had been easier than she'd hoped to avoid the press since only a few people knew her whereabouts.

"Yeah, I've noticed," Ronald said. "It looks like they've run out of things to say about you."

"That's what we were hoping." A flurry of papers had covered the story initially, and several tabloids had joined the fray, but the scandal seemed to have died down already.

"That part's working for us." The caution in his tone warned of a negative flip side.

"What's wrong? Have you heard from Chloe or Paul?" Her editor had been quiet. In fact, Kate hadn't heard from Chloe since their conference call over three weeks earlier.

"I called her this morning just to check in," Ronald said. "I'm afraid sales have dropped off quite dramatically. She mentioned the ugly 'R' word."

"Returns?" It was every author's worst fear—that the stores would be unable to sell their stock of books and would return them to the publisher, unsold.

Kate set the plastic tongs in the salad bowl and faced the sliding door. "I don't understand. I've done what they asked. I've avoided the spotlight, and everything has died down. I thought that's what they wanted."

"Yeah, I know. I called Pam after I talked to Chloe to get her take. The public is impossible to predict.

They'd been hoping that with no new information, the story would die and the public would forget it."

"But that hasn't happened?"

"Pam said it's too early to say for sure. But the numbers aren't looking good."

Kate ran her hand through her hair. All this for nothing? The public apparently believed the reports and had decided she was a fraud. They were voting with their dollars, and she'd lost.

"Is it too late to fix it?"

"If you mean going to the press with your side of the story, Pam didn't recommend it. She thinks coming this late, it would feel phony. The public would be suspicious of all the time you were quiet."

Kate slapped the counter. "I was quiet because they told me to be."

"I know, kiddo, I know."

Kate dragged her hand down her hair and anchored the ends in her fist, pulling until her scalp stung.

"I'm afraid there's more bad news."

Kate braced herself. "My column?" If she lost her syndicated column, what would she have left?

"I'm afraid so," Ronald said. "I'm sorry."

Not my column. She'd already lost *Glamour*, but the column had been her baby forever. It was how she'd become Dr. Kate. She'd helped thousands of readers, and now it was gone. She remembered all the hours she'd spent reading letters and formulating answers. She remembered all the letters she'd answered privately because column space prevented her from answering all of them, and some of the letters seemed too desperate to ignore.

"We'll get through this, kiddo. Let's give it more time. Maybe your book sales will pick up again."

Kate grasped onto hope. "Is that what Pam said?"

If anyone would know, it would be Pam. Her publicity experience allowed her to read the public better than anyone.

"No, she didn't say that. But you're too good at giving advice to be holed up in some office. It's your calling, your gift, and we can't give up just yet."

It felt like it was over. She could write all the articles and books she wanted, but if readers didn't trust her anymore, what did it matter?

Kate hung up and put the salad on the table as her dad entered with a plate of sizzling steaks. They served themselves and began to eat. Kate hardly tasted the food.

They were halfway through the meal before her dad spoke. "You're quiet." He speared a chunk of meat and put it in his mouth.

Kate told him about Ronald's phone call and the apparent effect the scandal had on her career. "It's not looking good, Dad." That was an understatement.

He set his knife and fork down. "Look, Kate. I realize it must be devastating and maybe even humiliating for your wedding fiasco to be public knowledge. But your goal has always been to help troubled relationships. Ever since you were a little girl, you were helping people solve problems. You don't need fame or notoriety or even a book contract to achieve that."

Kate swallowed the bite of salad. He was right. She had enjoyed helping couples in counseling. However, it was more logical to prevent the impossible relationships than it was to fix them. And no one sought counseling until there was a problem. That's why writing relationship books made sense.

But lately, Kate wondered if she knew anything about relationships at all. Everything that made sense in theory was more complicated in real-life application. Case in point: Lucas.

Her stomach clamped down on the food she'd eaten, and she pushed her plate away, the sirloin half-eaten. A week ago, she'd realized her night with Lucas hadn't resulted in a pregnancy. She'd expected profound relief. Instead she'd gone to her room and closed the door before having a good cry. What was wrong with her?

"What's really wrong, Kate?" Her dad's brown eyes were an antique reflection of her own.

"My career is falling apart. Isn't that reason enough to be depressed?"

Her dad sliced the steak with the serrated knife and placed it beside his plate. "Is that why you don't eat? Why you stare off into space for minutes at a time? Why your eyes are so sad all the time?"

Kate's head throbbed. She'd had a constant headache since she'd left Nantucket. Like her body was having withdrawal from the island.

Or from Lucas. She stifled the thought.

She stood and carried her plate to the sink. "I'd rather not talk about it." She didn't even want to think about it, but her mind never cooperated. She tried to put it behind her, but her thoughts returned to the island, to Lucas, like waves to a shoreline.

"It's that Lucas, isn't it?"

Kate gave him a warning look. He'd never been one to pry, and she hoped he didn't start now.

"Don't look at me like that. You've been moping around here for—"

"I am not moping."

"—three weeks, and I may be a man, but I know lovesick when I see it."

Kate gave a wry laugh. "Lovesick?" She pulled the sprayer from the sink and ran water over her plate. "It was an arrangement, Daddy, remember? You were there. You read the papers."

Her dad's chair scraped the ceramic tile as he stood. "And I saw the look in that boy's eyes on your wedding day." He held out his plate.

Kate pulled it from his hands. "That's ridiculous."

"Is it?"

She sprayed the salad dressing and A1 Sauce off the plate while her father cleared the table. Her father had imagined what he'd seen on Lucas's face.

"Anyway," Kate said. "It could never have worked. We were different as day and night."

"Opposites attract, you know." He leaned around her to wet a dishrag and went to wipe down the oak table.

"It's not like that. We have nothing in common, Daddy, and I'm not going to spend the rest my life arguing like—" She stopped, realizing she was crossing a line. Who was she to criticize her parents' marriage?

"Like your mom and me?" Her dad finished the thought.

Kate loaded the two plates back to back in the dishwasher and shut the door. The crestfallen look on her dad's face exacerbated her regret. "I'm sorry. I shouldn't have said that."

He nodded slowly. "No, that's fair." He leaned against the kitchen counter across from her, bracing his hands against the ledge, reminding her of the way Lucas had stood so many times.

"I've always wondered how much you remembered," he said.

She remembered more than the yelling. She remembered the time her dad had dumped sacks of her mom's new clothes out the front door. She could still see the new dresses, tags still attached, strewn across the spring green lawn. "When two people are so different, conflict is inevitable," Kate said.

Her dad shook his head. "Your mother and I weren't so different."

"Oh, come on, Daddy. She was a spender; you were a saver. She was messy and disorganized; you were a neat freak. She wanted to go places; you wanted to stay home."

"Is that what you think? That our marriage fell apart

because we were too different?" Her dad drew in a deep breath, exhaled, then straightened and walked toward the living room. "Come sit, Kate."

She followed her dad into the room and sat on the center of the sofa, opposite his recliner.

"Your mother and I had a good marriage in the beginning," he said. "But soon, we began to disagree about a lot of things. At the time, I thought I was right about everything. I thought it was smart to control the money the way I did. I told myself I was looking out for our best interests. And I thought the house had to be kept a certain way. Your mom liked things neat too, but my standards were high. Unfeasibly high."

"Mom was a clutter bug."

"Not initially. The things I did drove her crazy. The way the labels on food packages had to be turned facing front, the way the towels had to be folded in thirds and hung in the center of the towel rack, the way our lives had to run by the clock, down to the second. It all became too much for her."

"You weren't the problem, Daddy. It was her. I remember. She was a spendaholic. She used to go out and shop and buy new furniture, new clothes, when we didn't have the money—"

Her dad tilted his head and gave a sad smile. "Your mom never liked to shop. She didn't care about new clothes or new furniture. She did it because she was angry with me."

"Why?" Kate shook her head, trying to make sense of it. "Why would she be angry with you?"

"You know what OCD is?"

"Of course. Obsessive-compulsive disorder. I've counseled a couple clients who—" Kate stopped, letting it soak in. *OCD*. "You, Daddy?"

"I didn't know it at the time. Your mom was after me for years to go and get checked. She insisted something was wrong, but I thought she was being critical. As the years went by, she got angrier and angrier. I wanted the house impossibly neat, so she made sure it wasn't. I wanted to control the money, so she spent it. I wanted to be punctual, so she dawdled."

Her dad pinched the crease in his pants, mechanically, following it down the thigh. "I didn't see any of it at the time. Of course, her actions made me furious, and we had terrible arguments. Unfortunately, you heard a lot of them. It was a vicious cycle that would've been broken if I'd just been able to see that I had a problem."

How could all of Kate's assumptions about her parents' marriage have been wrong? So much of what she advised stemmed from what she thought she'd learned from her childhood.

"One day, when you were eight or nine," he said. "I walked by your bedroom and heard you playing. I stopped and listened. Barbie was screaming at Ken, and Ken was yelling at Barbie. You were holding them face-to-face, and as you were talking in your angry little-girl voice, your mouth was all screwed up, your brows drawn together. I realized you thought that's the way families behaved. You thought that was normal."

Kate had spent a lot of time playing with her Barbies. When you were an only child, you learned to make believe. "I don't remember that."

Her dad folded his hands across his stomach. "It was then that I began to wonder if your mother and I would be better off apart."

Kate had thought it was her mom's decision. She'd been angry with her mom for months. But even though she'd blamed her mom—the woman was her caretaker, the one who fixed her French toast in the morning and made sure her favorite jeans were washed—Kate couldn't conceive of leaving her home. Even when her mom started drinking.

"When did you find out about the OCD?" Kate asked.

"Not until years later. You were nearly in college by then. None of the women I had dated could tolerate my behavior for long, and I finally opened my mind to the possibility that it was me."

Kate wasn't naive. She knew it took two people to nurture a relationship and two people to ruin it. But how had she gotten things so twisted around? Her mom had never set her straight, had never said a bad thing to Kate about her dad, even after they divorced. Instead, her mother drowned her sorrow in alcohol.

"I'm sorry about how I handled my marriage to your mom, Kate. I'm sorry you didn't have a better childhood."

Kate's eyes stung. "I appreciate that, Daddy. I know it's hard to make a marriage work under the best circumstances."

"I did love your mom. You know that."

"I know." *Does he know Mom went to her grave loving him? Mourning him?* Sometimes it was better not to know.

"I'm not very good at this stuff," he said. "But I love you, too, you know." He squeezed his hands together so tight, the tips of his fingers whitened.

Kate didn't remember ever hearing those words from her father. She'd known he loved her, but hearing them was a balm to her aching heart.

"I love you too, Daddy."

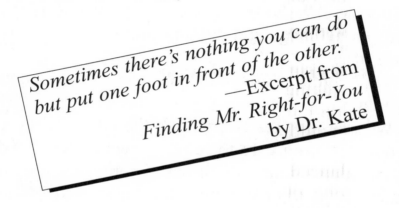

Sometimes there's nothing you can do but put one foot in front of the other.
—Excerpt from
Finding Mr. Right-for-You
by Dr. Kate

Chapter Thirty

Lucas dipped the tack cloth in mineral spirits and wiped the sawdust from the oak pie safe. One more coat of polyurethane and it would be ready for Sydney. He was eager to be done with that job. The day before she'd come into the shop to check on his work, even though he'd told her it wouldn't be ready for two more days. She'd closed the distance between them and caressed the unfinished piece with her slender fingers as if it were a man's arm instead of a hunk of wood.

"Very nice, Lucas. You have a certain touch." She smiled slowly.

He put space between them, wiping his hands on the rag. He'd done everything he could to make it clear he wasn't interested. He tried to show professional courtesy without stepping one inch past that line. For the life of him, he couldn't see why she continued to pursue him when there were probably a dozen men who'd be willing to buy whatever she was selling.

The phone rang, and Ethan called him. "If you'll excuse me . . ."

"Well," Sydney said, "I'll check back in a couple days then."

Now Lucas ran the cloth along the edges of the cabinet doors, taking care to remove every speck of dust so it wouldn't mar the finish. There was only one woman he couldn't get from his mind, and it wasn't Sydney.

Lucas glanced at the calendar hanging cockeyed from a prong on the pegboard. October 21. Today would have been their four-month anniversary. If Kate were here, he might've bought her a bouquet of daisies and taken her to Cioppino's for lobster. Afterward, they would've gone home, and he'd have put on her favorite classical CD and kissed her on the corner of her lip, right where—

Cut it out, Luc. You have got to move on. How many

times had he relived moments of their time together? Especially the last night.

He'd tried to stay busy. He worked well into the night until he was too tired to do anything but shower and fall into bed. It was easier that way. He was tired of pitying glances from friends and neighbors. He could imagine what they were thinking. *Poor Lucas. First he lost Emily; now he's lost Kate. Tsk, tsk, tsk.* But no one brought up Kate, as if the very mention of her name would shatter him.

Everyone wondered where she was, though, including the media, some of whom had come to the island, hoping for an interview. Was it any wonder he spent his days holed up in his shop? Even here, he hadn't escaped the phone calls. Ethan intercepted them, and at least now the calls were coming farther apart.

The story had quieted down the past couple weeks—a blessing for Kate, he was sure. He supposed her career would rebound since the scandal died so quickly. She'd probably have her next book on the shelves next year sometime, and her life would continue as it had before he'd entered it.

But Lucas couldn't imagine his life returning to normal. Even though the story had fizzled out, he still found himself avoiding people. Even his family—a fact that hadn't gone unnoticed.

"We missed you at lunch Sunday," his mother had said when she dropped by the shop the previous week. Lucas noticed right away there was something dif-

ferent about her. She seemed less on edge. Happier, despite Lucas's withdrawal. Was his mom that happy to have Kate out of their lives?

Lucas didn't think she'd bought his excuse about being late on an order. His dad had come by later that week under the premise of borrowing his jigsaw, but Lucas had seen through that.

"You're putting in a lot of hours lately," his dad said.

"Business is good." He wasn't fooling anyone, and he knew it.

"You know, that Kate was something special."

Lucas clamped down hard on his jaw. Was his dad trying to rub it in? Didn't he know Lucas knew it better than anyone?

"She had a talk with your mom before she left," his dad said.

When had Kate had a chance to do that? Whatever she'd said must've worked a miracle. His dad said he was seeing a side of Susan he'd hadn't seen in years. She'd finally forgiven him for the mistake he'd made all those years ago. Lucas was happy for them.

Jamie visited him at the shop at least once a week and filled him in on her love life with Aaron. Brody kept bugging him to get an e-mail address so they could communicate more.

Lucas dipped the cloth in mineral spirits again and smoothed it over the drawer face a second time. He was nearly ready to apply the final coat of polyurethane when his shop door opened. Jamie entered, shutting the door. She turned and held up a copy of the *New York Times*.

"Did you see this?" Her chin jutted forward.

"See what?"

"The article about Kate." She extended the paper.

Lucas wiped the side panel of the pie safe, wiped the rim along the top, taking care to get into the crevices.

"Luc." Jamie approached, her flip-flops shuffling on the cement floor.

"I'm not interested."

The newspaper smacked against her jeans-encased leg. "You are, too, and you know it."

He moved around the pie case and wiped down the other panel.

"She lost her syndicated column," Jamie said.

Lucas's hand paused over the rim, then continued. Why had Kate lost her column? The story had died down just as her publisher hoped it would. Had the scandal done irreparable damage? *How could they cancel her column when she'd worked so hard? She's Dr. Kate, for pity's sake.*

"You have to do something, Luc."

He shook his head. "Maybe Kate decided to focus on books instead of the column."

"That's not what the article says."

Lucas looked at the paper, torn between grabbing it and reading every detail he could find about her life without him, and burning the paper so he could spare himself the agony.

"I'm sure she's fine. The story faded quickly enough."

"Her book sales are in the toilet."

Lucas arched his brow. "Did the article say that too?"

Jamie hitched her pointed little chin up a notch. "I've been keeping track of her numbers on Amazon."

"What's that?" He wished he hadn't asked. His sister was drawing him in, and he only wanted to put it behind him. He wiped the top of the pie case even though it was already clean.

"Amazon—where people buy books online?" Her look said, *Duh.* "She used to be ranked, like, below two hundred, and now her book is nearly at two hundred thousand!"

Lucas gave up on the pie case and threw his rag on the bench. He hoped it wasn't true. Kate was too good at what she did to let it all go to waste. "I take it that's a bad thing."

"Terrible. I'm telling you, her career is falling apart. You have to do something."

"Me . . . What am I supposed to do?"

Jamie dropped the paper on the bench and crossed her arms, eyeing him. She tapped her foot, her glittery pink toenails rising and falling.

"You didn't tell her, did you." It wasn't a question so much as an accusation.

"Tell her what?"

"That you love her."

Lucas turned and wrapped the cord around the sander, then hung it on a prong. His sister had gotten too good at reading his thoughts. Maybe it was all those romances she devoured.

"Well," Jamie said, "I guess that answers my question."

Lucas pocketed his hands. "That's between me and Kate, munchkin."

"How can it be between you and Kate if she doesn't even know?"

Little squirt. She was getting too smart for her own britches.

"It might've made a difference if she'd known," Jamie said. "I know it's none of my business . . . but I want you to be happy. Besides, if you hadn't helped me with Aaron, we probably never would've gotten together."

"How's that going, anyway?"

"We're still going out, but stop trying to change the subject. Are you going to help Kate or not?"

Later that night Lucas lay wide eyed in bed. Jamie's question rang through his head. *"Are you going to help Kate or not?"* But what could he do when she was gone? He couldn't turn back time or make that Stephanie chick rescind the story.

The headline that had appeared in *USA Today* snagged in his mind. *"Dr. Kate in Loveless Marriage."* Two of the tabloids he'd picked up had an article that focused on their loveless marriage arrangement.

When he'd read it, he'd almost laughed. Little did they know, there had been plenty of love in the marriage. Unfortunately it was all his.

Was it? Would she have given herself to me that last night if she didn't love me? His chest tightened, aching at the thought. Maybe it was only wishful thinking.

But what if it's true? What if Kate loves me? What if she only left because she's afraid?

He remembered the articles about their loveless marriage and wondered if it would accomplish anything if her readers knew he'd loved her. *Still love her,* he corrected himself. Would it somehow redeem her in the public's eyes?

Even if it did, there was no way he could trust the media. They were sharks, out for their scoop and willing to trample anything that stood between them and their prey. Even if Lucas could somehow convey his feelings to the media, they would twist it and warp it and use it to hurt Kate.

Maybe he should call that publicity woman Kate worked with—Pam? Maybe he could bounce the idea off her without letting Kate know. Maybe then, if he did everything in his power to help her, he'd finally have peace.

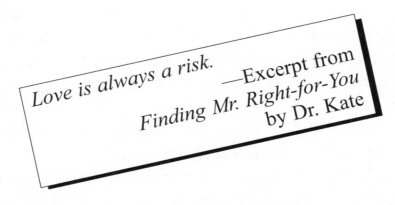

Love is always a risk. —Excerpt from *Finding Mr. Right-for-You* by Dr. Kate

Chapter Thirty-One

"I'm going to the grocery, Dad." Kate shut the dishwasher, latched it closed, and pushed the button to start it. It whirred into action.

In the living room, her dad turned on the TV to a Taco Bell commercial. He reached for his wallet. "Here, let me pay this time."

Kate waved him off. "I got it." She picked up her purse. It was the least she could do when he was letting her stay there until she found a place. She had a nice nest egg in her savings account. "I might run by that apartment on—"

"Kate." Her dad turned up the TV's volume.

Kate followed his widened eyes to the screen. *Lucas.* Lucas was on TV. He wore a suit and tie. Her breath caught.

"—happened between Dr. Kate and her Mr. Right?"

The screen changed to show *NewsWire* correspondent Nancy Lopez. "Can you tell us how you came to be married to Dr. Kate?"

There was a quick clip of Lucas shrugging, a mischievous look on his face; then the camera cut to Nancy.

"Dr. Kate has been ridiculed for entering a marriage as if it were a business arrangement. Was it really a loveless marriage?"

The camera cut to Lucas. "Funny you should ask that." He gave his charming half grin.

The *NewsWire* logo appeared on the screen and a voiceover sounded. "Everyone wants to know why renowned columnist Dr. Kate married Mr. Wright, and *NewsWire* has the exclusive. Tune in tomorrow night at ten o'clock Eastern Standard Time."

Another commercial started and her dad turned down the volume. Kate sank onto the couch, numb. *I don't understand. Why did Lucas do it? Just when the scandal died down, he went and brought it to the surface again.*

"I can't believe it." She stood again and paced the room as anger fired through her veins, her heart beating double time. She was furious—and hurt. *Why is he doing this?*

"You should call him," her dad said. "Maybe there's a—"

Her cell rang. She pulled it from her purse, hoping it was Lucas, because she had a few things to say to him. Her hand shook as she answered.

"Kate, what's going on?" her friend Anna asked. "I just saw a promo for *NewsWire*—"

"I know. I saw it too."

"You didn't know about it?" She'd kept Anna up-to-date on everything through e-mail.

"No, I didn't know. I can't believe he's done this." Kate ran her hand through her hair.

"Just when everything was starting to die down," Anna said. "Why would he do it?"

"I don't know, but I'm going to find out. I'll call you back after I talk to him."

They hung up, and Kate looked at her dad. Her throat was tight, her head ached behind her eyes, and she wanted to hit something.

"Maybe there's an explanation," her dad said.

"Sure there is. About two hundred thousand of them." They'd probably paid him at least that for an exclusive. Did Lucas hope to expand his shop with the money? She'd never thought him ambitious, yet what other reason could he have?

She remembered how he'd turned down the opportunity to be interviewed on *Live with Lisa* alongside her. What had he said? *"Talking's not my thing. Words don't come easy to me, like they do you."* She remembered the sob story he'd told her about being paralyzed with fright in front of a school assembly. Apparently he could keep his composure if enough money was involved.

The betrayal hurt.

Kate dialed Lucas's number. He should be home by now, probably making a mess in the kitchen. *I hope he chokes on his dinner.*

"Maybe you should wait until you've calmed down." Her dad flipped off the TV.

The phone rang over to voice mail. The beep sounded. Kate tried to swallow the lump in her throat, but it was firmly lodged. "What are you doing, Lucas? I just saw the *NewsWire* promo. I can't believe—" Her voice wobbled, and she took a steadying breath. *I am not going to let him know he has me in tears.*

"I can't believe you'd do this. Call me." She disconnected the call.

She paced the room. She was a traveling earthquake, and Lucas was the epicenter.

"So, this is the guy you've been mooning over for weeks," her dad said. "He doesn't deserve you."

"He doesn't have me, Dad." Not now. Not after this. She couldn't stand the thought of him anymore.

Come on, Kate. Feelings don't evaporate simply because you've been betrayed. She knew it was true. All she had to do was remember Mrs. Hornsby and all the other victims of unfaithful spouses she'd counseled. But couldn't she just be mad without her internal therapist kicking in?

"Well, I suppose your career can't be damaged any more than it already was."

No, but Kate had hoped the public humiliation was over. She'd hoped to fade from the public eye and return to private counseling. The last thing she needed was to have the scandal revived. She'd thought if anyone would betray her to the media, it would've been Bryan.

She'd never thought for a minute Lucas would cave to the pressure.

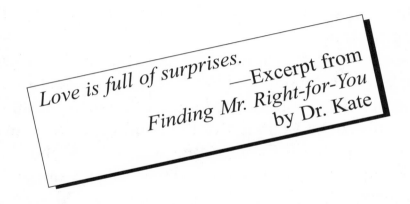

Love is full of surprises.
—Excerpt from
Finding Mr. Right-for-You
by Dr. Kate

Chapter Thirty-Two

Kate tidied the kitchen, then straightened the seasonings on the wooden rack. Two more minutes. Each one passed like a turtle on Valium.

All day she'd tried to reach Lucas. When she called the shop, Ethan said he was out, yet he didn't answer at home. No one picked up at his parents' house, and her e-mails went unanswered. They were probably embarrassed by Lucas's betrayal. But maybe they'd been interviewed too. Maybe they were splitting the bounty and taking a trip to Europe to celebrate.

A dish towel fell to the floor and Kate kicked it, leaving it crumpled between the fridge and cabinet. No one from Rosewood had returned her calls either. She'd phoned Ronald first thing that morning, but he hadn't been able to reach Paul or Chloe. It seemed she had become persona non grata. They had to know about the exclusive. They were probably angry with her for letting it happen. *As if I had a choice.*

"Kate, it's coming on," her dad called from the living room.

Kate entered the room where her dad perched on the edge of the brown sofa, his elbows on his knees.

Kate sat beside him and hugged the chenille pillow to her stomach. A barrier for the coming sucker punch.

The *NewsWire* theme song played as the logo appeared. They showed previews of the upcoming segments, including the same preview she'd seen the night before. The first segment began, but it wasn't Lucas's.

When they cut to a commercial. Kate released her breath. "I hope it's not last."

Her dad crossed his legs at the knee. "It might be."

She'd waited all day, a nervous ball of energy. Why hadn't Lucas returned her calls? Why hadn't anyone returned them? Was he too ashamed to face her? *He should be.*

"Want some coffee?" Her dad asked. "I can put on a pot."

Kate shook her head. "I feel like I could run across water as it is."

When the show returned, they focused on the TV, but it was a segment about trans fats in restaurant food.

Kate wondered what questions they would ask Lucas. Would he tell them she'd cried herself to sleep on their honeymoon? Would he tell them his mom disliked her from the beginning because of whose daughter she was? Would he tell them about the special moments—the ones when they forgot their marriage was an arrangement?

Fear sucked the moisture from her mouth. Kate felt as if she stood on the gallows, with a thick rope at her neck, waiting for the floor to open. And there was nothing she could do but wait.

The segment ended and another commercial break ensued. It was half past the hour.

"Hang in there, Kate. Whatever comes, I'll be here for you." Her dad reached over and squeezed her cold hand.

"Thanks, Daddy." She couldn't sit anymore. She stood and walked to the patio door. Outside, darkness swallowed the yard and a sliver of moon peeked from behind a curtain of clouds. She kept remembering the last days with Lucas, the way he'd held her that night, pressing kisses to her forehead and chin, smoothing her hair from her face. She'd never felt more cared for, more cherished.

And now he's airing our dirty laundry on national TV. It doesn't make sense.

"It's back on," her dad said.

Kate returned to the living room, stopping behind the recliner. Evan Greggory began a segment about the sole survivor of a ferry accident overseas. They were saving Lucas's segment for last, which showed they viewed it as important. *They must've gotten some juicy material from Lucas.*

The ferry segment seemed to last forever. A long commercial break followed. Kate's heart rate tripled as she waited for the commercials to end. This was it. There was only twelve minutes remaining—only enough time for Lucas's story.

When the program returned, her dad cranked up the volume. The camera panned in on Nancy Lopez. "Welcome back to *NewsWire*." She turned to a different camera. "She is the queen of relationships and the author of recent self-help book *Finding Mr. Right-for-You*."

Nancy held up a copy of the book. "Dr. Kate's book was released with much media attention on her wedding day this summer, and it soared to the bestseller's list."

Kate nearly rolled her eyes. The book had barely made it to the bottom of the bestseller's list, achieving less than Rosewood had hoped.

Nancy continued. "But Dr. Kate's career recently turned upside down when it was revealed that her real fiancé, Bryan Montgomery, left her at the altar, and that Dr. Kate impulsively entered a loveless marriage arrangement with Nantucket native Lucas Wright as a last-ditch effort to save her book from certain death.

"Little is known about the terms of the arrangement or Dr. Kate's feelings on the matter, but *NewsWire* has gained an exclusive interview with the man who found himself at the altar with marriage expert Dr. Kate." Nancy smiled and turned as the camera cut to Lucas. "Welcome to the show, Mr. Wright."

Kate honed in on Lucas. He'd shaved, and his hair was combed neatly off his face as it had been at their wedding. He wore a dress shirt and tie she'd never seen. He thanked Nancy.

"Can you tell us how you knew Dr. Kate and for how long before the wedding?"

Lucas shifted subtly. He was uncomfortable. *Good.*

"Kate had been on the island for three years," Lucas began. "She was born there, but her family left when she was young. I didn't know her then. When she moved back, she wanted to open an office in town. She rented the space over my shop."

"Can you tell us what happened on the day of her wedding?"

He nodded slowly. "I was working in my shop that morning. Actually I was putting the finishing touches on the gazebo she'd asked me to make."

"For her wedding with Bryan Montgomery?"

"Yes. She'd hired me to build it months earlier. Kate came to the shop to check on it because I was supposed to have delivered it already. When she was there, she got a call from her fiancé."

"Mr. Montgomery?"

"Yes. I only heard her end of the conversation, but it was enough to tell me he wasn't going through with the wedding."

"What was Kate's state of mind after the phone call?"

Lucas tilted back, and he shook his head. "She was devastated. She was trembling." He gave a sad smile. "You'd have to know Kate to know how unlike herself she was after that phone call. She's the most calm, capable individual I've ever met. She's the kind of person you want during a crisis because she—She just takes care of things. But it was five hours before her wedding, and her groom just left her at the altar, and with the publicity surrounding the release of the book . . . who wouldn't panic?"

"How did you come to be part of the solution?" Nancy asked.

"It was my idea. I don't know where it came from. It was impulsive, and it seemed like the only solution at the time. She needed a groom, and I wanted to help her."

"That's some help. Why would you agree to step in and save her wedding?"

Lucas looked down at his lap and paused a moment. "The reason I gave Kate was that I needed her help on a personal project."

"But that wasn't the real reason, I take it," Nancy said.

"No."

"What?" Kate whispered, staring at the screen.

"We'll get back to that in a moment," Nancy continued. "What were the terms of the arrangement?"

Lucas's mouth tilted in a smile as if remembering the moment. "There had to be an escape clause. We agreed to remain married for a year."

"Was there a contract between you? Financial arrangements?"

"It wasn't like that. We knew each other well enough to trust one another. We kept our finances separate."

"And no money exchanged hands?"

A pink flushed climbed Lucas's neck. He looked like a bashful schoolboy. "She didn't pay me for the honor of being her husband, if that's what you mean."

Nancy's smile made it clear she was captivated by Lucas's charm.

"Can you define your relationship with Dr. Kate prior to the wedding? Were you lovers, friends . . ?"

Lucas ran his fingers between his neck and collar. "No, we weren't lovers. I guess you could say we were friends. We spent quite a bit of time together when I renovated her space into an office and apartment. She lived and worked above my shop, so we saw each other frequently." His smile tilted. "Kate probably would've said we were acquaintances. I think I got on her nerves a bit."

"You say that like you enjoyed it."

Lucas smiled. "Little bit."

Kate squeezed the cushion on the back of the recliner, unable to take her eyes off Lucas.

Nancy continued. "You've denied being paid to marry Dr. Kate, and you've hinted that the reason you gave her was false." The camera cut to Lucas's face while Nancy stated the question. "Why *did* you stand in as her groom?"

Lucas looked down at his lap, his smile faltering. He swallowed.

Kate wondered for a long moment if he was going to freeze as he had so long ago on a school gym stage.

She found herself pulling for him, wanting to help him formulate an answer.

But then he spoke. "I wanted to help her. If you'd seen her after that phone call—she was panicked. Afraid. Hurt." Lucas shrugged. "I wanted to help."

"Why?" Nancy asked.

Kate leaned forward, her breath on hope's threshold.

He gave a sad little smile. As his head tilted down, his hair fell forward, partially covering his eyes. Then he looked back at Nancy. "I love her," he said in a throaty voice.

Kate sucked in her breath. She stared into his familiar face and felt an ache behind her eyes. *He loves me? He married me . . . because he loves me? But his parents' marriage—*

The camera stayed on Lucas even though he stopped talking. He was clearly uncomfortable, like he wanted to squirm right out of the starchy suit.

He filled the silence. "When I saw how upset she was, I wanted to fix it for her." He lifted one shoulder. "Maybe I was a little selfish too. Maybe I thought if she was mine for a year, she'd somehow fall in love with me too." He shifted, looking away. "I was trying to save her wedding. I guess it was wrong of me to take advantage. She was vulnerable. I came up with the idea and convinced her it was the only solution. If anyone's to blame, it's me."

He went blurry as Kate's eyes filled. She blinked, not wanting anything blocking her view of Lucas's face.

The camera cut to Nancy. "In reality, you were only married three months. What was it like?"

"Being married to Kate?" He smiled. "Great. Fun. Challenging."

"Challenging because . . . ?"

Lucas tugged at his suit coat. "Because I love her. Because I wanted the marriage to be real, and it wasn't." He paused, looking down again. "In three months she solved problems that have been in place for years. She's got this deep well of wisdom . . . I don't know where it comes from. If something's broken, she fixes it."

"Except your heart?"

The camera slowly closed in on Lucas's face. His jaw clenched, then loosened. "I'm not sure she knows she broke it."

Nancy smiled. "She does now. It's fairly common knowledge that Kate left the island shortly after the scandal erupted. Can you give us your thoughts on that?"

Lucas sucked in a breath and blew it out. He shifted.

Kate wanted to brush the hair out of his face, run her palm down his tense jawline and kiss away the frown on his lips.

"I didn't want her leave. I asked her to stay."

"But she didn't."

"No."

"Was she still in love with her former fiancé?" Nancy asked.

"I asked her that. She said she wasn't, and I believed her."

The camera cut to Nancy as she studied Lucas, a thoughtful expression on her face. "Why are you here today? What do you hope to accomplish?"

"I wanted to tell Kate's side of the story. I wanted to take responsibility for my part in it . . ." Lucas pulled at his tie.

The camera cut to Nancy. "Anything else?"

Lucas looked down, then met Nancy's eyes again. "I wanted to tell her what I was afraid to say before she left."

He swallowed, then looked at the camera, his eyes burning into Kate's. She locked onto his face, feeling as if he were right in front of her, right now.

Lucas's chin came up.

Kate watched his lips, waiting.

"I want to tell her I love her," he said.

Kate put her hand against her chest, squeezed the stiff material of her shirt.

Nancy paused for a full three seconds, letting the words sink in. "On national TV?"

He gave his crooked smile. "I guess I'm laying it all on the line. I love her. I have for a long time, and I always will." He looked down again.

"That's a lot of pressure for a girl," Nancy said.

Lucas shook his head. "Hope not. That wasn't my intention. Kate's entitled to make her own choices, to choose her own life. I just want her to have all the facts before she does."

Nancy said something that tied the story into a neat bow, then signed off. Kate's dad flipped off the TV.

Without the light and noise of the TV, the room fell into darkness and silence. Her mind whirled faster than a carnival ride.

"Well." Her dad flipped on the lamp.

Kate's legs felt wooden as she rounded the recliner and sank into it. She was shaking, her hands and legs trembling uncontrollably. *He loves me. He's loved me from the beginning.*

She felt a sudden, inexorable need to talk to him. To see him.

"Do you love him, Kate?" Her dad's voice broke through her thoughts.

Do I love him? She remembered the way he held her on the sailboat when she was sick. Remembered the way he held her when the scandal broke. Remembered how treasured she felt when he looked at her, touched her.

"Yes," she whispered.

But they were so different. It was why she'd left. She didn't want to wind up like—

My parents? Well, I've already discovered how wrong I was on that one. It wasn't their differences that broke them apart but her dad's disorder.

But even with that understanding, her heart faltered in fear. *What am I afraid of? That I'm going to wind up alone and desperate like Mom?*

But I can't control the future. I can't even control the present. I just have to make reasonable decisions and hope for the best. Look how meticulously I planned my engagement and wedding. And still, it all fell apart.

Did her obsessive need to plan stem from a desperate desire for control?

Kate remembered the conversation she'd had with Brody that day on the widow's walk. *"I'm not afraid of heights so much as I'm afraid of falling,"* she'd said. Was that her problem? Why she'd nearly married a man she didn't love? Why she'd been in such a hurry to leave the man she did love? She was afraid of becoming her mom. Afraid of becoming like the hundreds of women she'd counseled.

Kate gave a wry laugh. Some psychotherapist she was. She was only now figuring out that she was avoiding love.

"You think you should call him?" her dad asked.

What should she do? She wanted to tell him she loved him. She wanted to say she was sorry for leaving. A shiver of fear snaked its way up her spine. What if it didn't work? What if he broke her heart?

It's already been broken. Let him heal it. Her advice to Brody came back to her: *"It's fear that makes an act courageous." Do I have the courage to love him back?*

Kate straightened. She did. She was ready to put it all on the line, like he had.

But she wanted to do it face-to-face. She wanted to touch him, feel the strength of his arms around her when she said the words.

"I have to go to him," she said firmly.

Her dad nodded.

She checked her watch. "I can be there by morning if I drive to Hyannis and take the ferry."

"And drive all night? Kate . . ."

"I have to see him." She had to tell him she loved him. She could take a flight, but then her car would be here. No, it was settled. She'd never be able to sleep anyway. She might as well spend the night closing the distance between them.

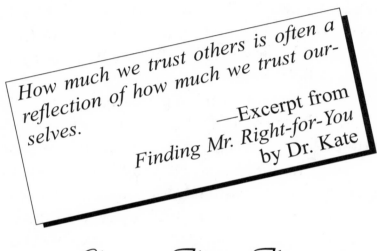

How much we trust others is often a reflection of how much we trust our-selves.

—Excerpt from *Finding Mr. Right-for-You* by Dr. Kate

Chapter Thirty-Three

She didn't call.

It was impossible to soothe the ache in his gut. Lucas rolled over and stared out the window, where dawn stretched, spreading gray across the midnight canvas. He pulled Kate's pillow close, inhaling. The scent of her was nearly gone—that subtle lilac scent that perfumed her hair.

He'd been pleased with the interview, relieved that the words had come when he needed them, relieved that he'd survived the interview without cracking under the pressure. After the show aired the night before, he waited, pacing the floor until Bo tired of his excess energy and curled up at the foot of the sofa.

When the phone had rung, his feet made quick work of the distance to the kitchen, and he answered breathlessly, not caring if Kate knew he was waiting for her call.

But it had been his mom. *"Honey, I'm so sorry. I knew you loved her, but I guess I just didn't realize how much."* She apologized for treating Kate badly and asked if he'd heard from her.

He didn't give up hope until after midnight. And even though he turned off the lights and lay in bed, he still couldn't sleep. His ears strained to hear the phone's ring. He slept restlessly, awake as much as he was asleep, and now that morning had arrived, his hopes washed away like a sand castle at high tide.

He forced himself from bed, showered, and put on a pot of coffee, draining the first cup like it was medicine for his wounded spirit. When Bo picked up his tennis ball and carried it to the back door, he stood.

"Go for a walk, boy?"

He followed the dog outside, past the gazebo—a constant reminder of Kate and their wedding day. He crossed the beach and turned eastward, tossed the tennis ball into the surf, and watched Bo lumber after it.

Had Kate even watched the show? He knew from her voice mail that she'd been angry when she'd seen the preview. What if she hadn't watched it?

Worse, what if she had? What if she heard his

proclamation of love and didn't feel the same way? What if he'd accomplished nothing other than publicly humiliating himself?

I've done all I can. She knows how I feel now. The rest is up to her.

Bo returned the ball, dropping it in the wet sand at Lucas's feet. Lucas picked it up and heaved it into the waves before stuffing his hands into his pockets. His fingers wrapped around cool metal. Kate's wedding band. He ran his thumb around the smooth surface. Its presence comforted him, like he carried a piece of her with him.

Bo turned in a circle, the tennis ball between his teeth, his paws dancing in the foamy sand. The sun glittered off the surface of the water like a million diamonds. When Lucas reached Bo, he tugged the wet ball from his jaws and threw it as far as he could down the shoreline, then followed Bo's footprints.

Kate stepped off the ferry, her overnight case clutched in her hand. She'd left her car in Hyannis since there was no room on the ferry. Now as the crowd dissipated on the concrete dock, she wondered if she'd be able to get a cab.

She tugged the baseball cap low on her head to avoid recognition and pulled her sweater tighter against the nip in the air. The trees had fully turned, washing Nantucket down in vibrant hues of yellow and red.

Her phone pealed, and she moved to the side of the

dock as she pulled her cell from her bag and checked the caller ID. It was Pam. Kate didn't want to talk business; she wanted to get to Lucas. She was so close.

But her publicity gal wouldn't call on a Saturday for nothing. Kate answered. "Hi, Pam. How are you?"

"Good. Great. Have you seen the papers?"

Kate had seen nothing all night but the yellow lines on the road. And she'd given little thought to her career or what others would be saying. "No, why?" Kate was almost afraid to know, but Pam didn't sound dismayed.

"It worked! Listen to this. 'Dr. Kate's counterfeit groom broke his silence on TV newsmagazine show *NewsWire* when he proclaimed his love for the well-known author and syndicated relationship columnist.' Blah, blah, blah—backstory and quotes from the interview. Ah, here we go. 'It seems, even in the case of unpredictable disasters, Dr. Kate's own brand of relationship magic works like a charm. Even for herself.'"

Kate sank to the cement ledge overlooking the harbor. Through the phone, she heard the rattling of newspaper pages. "There are a dozen more just like it. And I caught it on several cable news programs this morning too. They keep running the portion of the interview where Lucas says"—she lowered her voice—"'I guess I'm laying it all on the line. I love her. I have for a long time, and I always will.' Oh, man, he has every woman in America fanning her face, Kate. I'll bet your book is flying off the shelves as we speak."

I can't believe it. How have I gone from—

Something Pam had said earlier popped into her mind. *"It worked."* The words had been buried beneath the good news, but now they surfaced like a piece of driftwood through the sand, uncovered by the relentless wind.

Kate interrupted Pam. "Wait. You said 'It worked.' What did you mean?"

The rustling of paper stopped. A seagull swooped down and landed in the harbor, bobbing on the waves beside a fat buoy.

"You haven't called him?" Pam's tone revealed shock.

Dread filled Kate, numbing her to the fingertips. "What's going on, Pam?" Her thoughts spun. Terrible thoughts that tortured her. "Was this just a ploy to fix my book sales?" She could choke on the acid that rose in her throat. Had Lucas only been pretending?

"No, sweetie, it's not like that."

"Then what is it like?" Her voice quavered.

Pam sighed loudly. "You should hear this from Lucas. Why didn't you call him?"

Kate suddenly felt like a fool for driving all night like this was some 911 emergency. "I wanted to talk to him in person." Her answer was feeble. Kate swallowed the acid and her pride. "I'm here now, on Nantucket."

"Oh, I am such a dolt!" Kate imagined Pam

335

smacking her own forehead. "I've ruined everything. Go. Go talk to him. I'm hanging up now."

"No, wait. Pam!" A click, then a dial tone buzzed in Kate's ear. She jabbed the Off button and gulped three breaths of air, laden with salt and exhaust fumes. What was going on? Had Pam called Lucas and devised some scheme to get her book sales back on track? What if Lucas hadn't meant any of it? But why would he have put himself through it if he didn't love her?

Uh, the money?

She felt like a sailboat, pushed at the whimsy of the wind, and she'd just suffered a gust from an unexpected direction.

But this was the new Kate. The one who didn't have to plan every action. She was going to go with the flow. And right now, she needed to find Lucas, find out if he meant what he said.

Kate stood, hitching the bag on her shoulder, and turned toward town.

When she reached Main Street, she hailed a cab and gave him the address. Though she hadn't slept, the phone call and nervous energy at seeing Lucas again kept her alert.

What will I say to him? Do I have the courage to face him? To put up my sails and let the wind take me where it may?

Her muscles tightened until they cramped. She relaxed her hold on the leather handle of the overnight bag as Lucas's words returned to her: *"Love isn't some item on a checklist."*

Maybe sometimes you had to loosen your grip. But it was scary. It required trust and faith. Two things she ran short on.

If there's anyone I can trust, it's Lucas. Kate allowed herself that. Reminded herself it was true. He'd never given her any reason to distrust him.

"I love her. I have for a long time, and I always will." She'd played his words over and over on the drive, drinking them up, soothing her troubled spirit with the promise. But now she wondered if he meant them.

A picture of her mom flashed in her mind. She was hunched over the kitchen table in her terry bathrobe, a bottle of scotch in her bony hand. A photo album was open on the table in front of her, and her hand smoothed over the glossy page as if she stroked the face in the photo. How many times had she seen her mother like that, dying one memory at a time?

Kate shook the thought. She wasn't her mother. And Lucas wasn't her father. It was like he'd said all along. She needed to stop analyzing and let herself love him. Let herself be loved, if he was willing. She couldn't think of anyone more trustworthy.

When the cab pulled in the drive, Kate withdrew some cash and paid the driver, then gathered her bag and exited the car. Lucas's old truck was in the drive. He'd surely heard the cab on the gravel, yet even after it pulled away, the front door remained closed.

Kate walked toward the house and up the steps, hesitating on the porch. Lifting her hand, she rapped on the wooden door, anticipating Bo's loud, gruff bark. But the only reply was the sound of the wind swishing through the trees. The small window in the door revealed only darkness. She knocked again. Maybe he was in the shower. It was still early for a Saturday, though Lucas was normally out and about by now.

She bit her lip, wondering if she should enter. Before she could dissuade herself, she twisted the knob and stepped inside.

"Lucas?" The rich aroma of brewed coffee permeated the house. The bedroom was empty, the blankets a tangled heap at the foot of the bed. The bathroom was dark, and several crumpled towels littered the floor. She smiled.

"Lucas?" In the kitchen, his empty Nantucket mug sat on the table. The coffeemaker was still plugged in. He must've taken Bo for a walk.

Kate exited through the back, passing the gazebo, tracing the numerous footprints down the sandy path. The beach was empty except for a few gulls, plucking through the wet sand. Kate looked down the shoreline toward the Wrights' house. The beach was deserted as far as she could see.

She looked the other direction, and her eyes paused on two figures: a man and a dog.

Lucas.

Her feet carried her down the shoreline, her heart pumping in rhythm with her quick steps. Halfway there, Bo spotted her and lumbered toward her, but

Lucas stared out across the ocean, oblivious to her appearance. Bo reached her side and barreled into her leg, tail wagging.

"Hi, boy." At least Bo was happy to see her again. It was Lucas she was unsure of.

Kate looked at Lucas in time to see him turn. He stilled, watching her approach. She closed the distance between them with long, eager strides. As she neared, she tried to read his expression, but the sun glinted over his shoulder, making it impossible to decipher.

She stopped a car's length away, suddenly uncertain. Would he welcome her home after she'd left so suddenly? He'd asked her to stay, but would he forgive her for leaving?

Fear left her mouth dry, sucked the words from her lips. It clawed at her throat and churned her thoughts like sand in the surf. Her limbs felt as stiff as a ship's mast. Tears glazed her eyes, and she told herself it was the biting wind.

Then he moved, walking toward her, stopping just a touch away. "You came back," he said.

His eyes were just the way she remembered, warm and soft. Welcoming.

"I had to see you," she said.

"Why?"

All the words she'd planned in the car scattered like startled gulls. Pam's call had changed everything. She was no longer sure of anything, least of all, Lucas's feelings.

"I saw the interview." *Was it all a ruse, or did you mean it?*

"I was hoping you'd watch." He tilted his head. "Are you angry?"

He was remembering the voice mail she'd left. Her anger had drained away with his proclamation of love. "No." The wind kicked up, and she pulled her sweater tighter. She had to settle this before her heart jumped through her rib cage. "Pam called."

He tucked his hands in his pockets. "She told you, then?"

Suddenly, Kate realized it didn't matter why Lucas had done the interview or what plan Pam had been talking about. She'd come to tell Lucas how she felt, and she was going to do it.

"She didn't tell me anything." Kate gathered her courage and drew a shaky breath. "I realized something last night while I watched you on TV." *"I love her. I have for a long time, and I always will."* His words were a pedestal for her courage.

"What's that?"

Kate swallowed the fear and took a step closer. The wind ruffled his hair, and she smoothed it from his face, then trailed her fingertips down the rough plane of his jaw. "I love you."

She ignored the burning in her eyes and plunged forward, a sailboat into the wind. "I don't know when it started or how it happened. I only know that you captured my heart, and I don't want it back. I want to stay here forever. I want to wake up to your stubbly, scratchy face and lie next to you in bed, even if you snore loudly enough to peel the paint off the walls. I want to—

Lucas broke off her words with his kiss. Kate felt his fingers sliding into her hair, knocking her cap to the ground. She relished the tenderness in his touch, and as he claimed her, she gave herself fully to him.

When she finally pulled away, it was only to look him in the eyes. "Did you really—love me from the beginning?" She had to know if it was true. Had to see him face-to-face when he said it.

One corner of his lip drew up. "Yeah."

let it soak in. "And that's why you took me as your bride?"

He cupped her chin. "The only reason."

Kate released her pent-up breath. It was true, then. Everything he'd said, everything that mattered, was true.

Lucas reached into his pocket and withdrew something. He took her hand and opened his palm.

"My wedding band," Kate said.

He looked her in the eye, pausing with the ring at the tip of her finger. "I love you, Kate Wright. There aren't enough miles on the earth to separate you from it. I want you to be mine." He squeezed her hand. "Fully mine." He looked at her, looked into her.

"I want that too." Kate said.

Lucas slid it in place. It was right where it belonged. *I'm right where I belong.*

He placed a kiss on her mouth and wrapped his strong arms around her. She felt safe in his arms. Loved. Cherished.

"Forever this time?" he asked.

She snuggled into his chest, inhaling the familiar scent of him, all musky and woodsy. *Man, I missed that.* "Forever." She smiled at the taste of the word on her tongue. No temporary arrangement this time. No twelve-month escape clause. She wanted in, and she never wanted out again.

She fingered the wedding band with her thumb. "My finger has felt naked since I took it off."

Lucas lifted her hand and kissed it. "Too bad I didn't accept the money for the interview. Could've bought you one heck of a diamond."

Kate squeezed his hand. "I could put the other one back on."

"Don't you dare." Lucas gave her a mock glare before pulling her back in his arms. "Did Pam tell you I called her?" He asked against her hair.

"You called *her*?" Kate couldn't imagine why he'd do that.

"I told her I loved you and asked what I could do to save your career and—" Lucas swept Kate off her feet, as a wave rushed under their feet. He set her down up shore on the dry sand. "Didn't think you'd want your shoes wet."

Bo bumped Lucas's thigh, a slobbery tennis ball in his jaws. Lucas tossed the ball a long ways down the beach.

"What did Pam say?" Kate slipped her hands into Lucas's, savoring the security of his warm grip.

"She said women love a fairy-tale romance."

Kate laughed, joy bubbling inside for the first time in a long time. "And you love being the knight in shining armor."

His shoulders rose in a shrug and he gave her his crooked grin. "If the armored boot fits . . ."

Kate elbowed Lucas then fell in step beside him as they walked toward home.

Home.

The word had a nice ring to it, and she felt a smile lift her lips. It wouldn't matter where she was or what she was doing, home would always be wherever Lucas was.

Dear Reader,

I hope you enjoyed reading about the special love between Lucas and Kate. I so appreciate you and the time you spent going on this journey with me.

In *The Convenient Groom*, Lucas's love for Kate represents in many ways Christ's love for us. Lucas is a hero in every sense of the word. If reading about such a man leaves you frustrated or disappointed with your own mate (Where's my knight in shining armor?), or lack thereof, know that there is only One who will never fail or forsake you. It is human nature for us to build our lives and rest our hopes on what is tangible. But substitutes—whether they are material or human in nature—are pale substitutes. Worse yet, they are a weak foundation that's bound to fail us when tested by life's storms.

I hope you have discovered that Christ is the creator of love (and everything else!) and that you are receiving the full benefit of His grace and mercy. I wish you the very best!

In His grace,
Denise

Acknowledgments

My deepest thanks go to all the people who had a hand in the making of this book. Thanks to my editor, Amanda Bostic, and the amazing team of creative, talented people in Thomas Nelson's fiction department. I'm truly honored and blessed to work with you. Thanks to Leslie Peterson for helping me polish the story. Thanks to my wonderful agent, Karen Solem, and my critique partner, Colleen Coble, who squeezed in my chapters while on her own tight deadline. Thanks to my writing buds, Kristin Billerbeck, Colleen Coble, and Diann Hunt: you bless my life in immeasurable ways!

A special thanks to my readers—you make it all worthwhile! I'd love to hear from you. E-mail me at denise@denisehunterbooks.com, or visit my Web site at www.DeniseHunterBooks.com.

Reading Group Guide

1. Lucas's love for Kate is an allegory for Christ's love for us. In what ways are the timing and qualities of Lucas's love symbolic of Christ's love?

2. What are some of the ways Lucas saved Kate in the story? What was Kate's reaction to his saving her? How has Christ saved you? Have you ever responded in some of the ways that Kate did?

3. One thing Kate was apt to do is fix things on her own. In our culture, that's a popular reaction. Do you respond to crises in a similar way? Is that the best way to deal with problems?

4. One of the hardest things to do when trouble comes is wait. Kate had difficulty waiting when her publisher was trying to find a solution to the problem. Is it hard for you to wait on God? Psalm 46:10 says, "Be still, and know that I am God." How can that be applied to trying times? Psalm 27:14 says, "Wait for the LORD; be strong and take heart and wait for the LORD." What can we learn about patience from this verse?

5. When Kate made the choice to leave Lucas, he knew it was a decision Kate had to make for herself. How has God been patient in waiting for you to come to Him?

6. When Kate left Lucas, he said that a thousand miles couldn't separate her from his love. How is Christ's love like that?

7. Lucas laid it all on the line when he faced his biggest fear and publicly proclaimed his love for Kate. How has Christ proclaimed His love for you?

8. Even though Kate broke Lucas's heart by leaving and by fighting her relationship with him, he gladly welcomed her back. Have you ever pushed Christ away or run from His love? What does it feel like to know that no matter what you do, He will always welcome you home?

HEALTH

An Economic

POLICY

Perspective

ISSUES

Paul J. Feldstein

HEALTH

An Economic

POLICY

Perspective

ISSUES

Paul J. Feldstein

AUPHA

Chicago, IL

Your board, staff, or clients may also benefit from this book's insight. For more information on quantity discounts, contact the Health Administration Press Marketing Manager at (312) 424–9470.

Reprinted April 2014

Library of Congress Cataloging-in-Publication Data
Feldstein, Paul J.
    Health policy issues : an economic perspective/Paul Feldstein.—5th ed.
        p.; cm.
    Includes bibliographical references and index.
    ISBN 978-1-56793-418-2 (alk. paper)
    1. Medical economics—United States. 2. Medical policy—Economic aspects—United States. 3. Medical care—United States—Cost control. 4. Medical care, Cost of—United States. I. Title.
    [DNLM: 1. Economics, Medical—United States. 2. Cost Control—United States. 3. Health Care Costs—United States. 4. Insurance, Health—United States. W 74 AA1]
        RA410.53F455 2011
        338.4'73621—dc23   201101461

The paper used in this publication meets the minimum requirements of American National Standard for Information Sciences—Permanence of Paper for Printed Library Materials, ANSI Z39.48-1984. ⊚ ™

Acquisitions editor: Janet Davis; Project managers: Eduard Avis and Joyce Dunne; Cover design: Marisa Jackson; Layout: Putman Productions

Found an error or a typo? We want to know! Please e-mail it to hap1@ache.org, and put "Book Error" in the subject line.

For photocopying and copyright information, please contact Copyright Clearance Center at www.copyright.com or at (978) 750–8400.

Health Administration Press
A division of the Foundation of the American
    College of Healthcare Executives
One North Franklin Street, Suite 1700
Chicago, IL 60606–3529
(312) 424–2800

Association of University Programs
    in Health Administration
2000 North 14th Street
Suite 780
Arlington, VA 22201
(703) 894–0940

To Colette, Lauren, Kip, and Poppy.

CONTENTS IN BRIEF

List of Exhibits. xv

Preface. xxi

1   The Rise of Medical Expenditures. 1

2   How Much Should We Spend on Medical Care? 15

3   Do More Medical Expenditures Produce Better Health? 27

4   In Whose Interest Does the Physician Act?. 39

5   Rationing Medical Services 49

6   How Much Health Insurance Should Everyone Have? 59

7   Why Are Those Who Most Need Health Insurance Least Able
to Buy It? 71

8   Medicare. 85

9   Medicaid. 105

10 How Does Medicare Pay Physicians? 121

11 Is There an Impending Shortage of Physicians? 135

12 The Changing Practice of Medicine 151

13 Recurrent Malpractice Crises 167

14 Do Nonprofit Hospitals Behave Differently than For-Profit Hospitals?. . . . 183

15 Competition Among Hospitals: Does It Raise or Lower Costs?. 195

16 The Future Role of Hospitals 207

17 Cost Shifting. 225

18 Can Price Controls Limit Medical Expenditure Increases?. 239

19 The Evolution of Managed Care. 249

20 Has Competition Been Tried—and Has It Failed—to Improve the
    US Healthcare System?. 269

21 Comparative Effectiveness Research 285

22 US Competitiveness and Rising Health Costs 297

23 Why Is Getting into Medical School So Difficult? 307

24 The Shortage of Nurses 317

25 The High Price of Prescription Drugs. 331

26 Ensuring Safety and Efficacy of New Drugs: Too Much of a
    Good Thing? 347

27 Why Are Prescription Drugs Less Expensive Overseas? 363

28 The Pharmaceutical Industry: A Public Policy Dilemma 377

29 Should Kidneys and Other Organs Be Bought and Sold?. 393

30 The Role of Government in Medical Care. 403

31 Medical Research, Medical Education, Alcohol Consumption,
    and Pollution: Who Should Pay?. 415

32 The Canadian Healthcare System 425

33 Employer-Mandated National Health Insurance 443

34 National Health Insurance: Which Approach and Why? 455

35 Financing Long-Term Care. 471

36 The Politics of Healthcare Reform 487

Appendix   A Brief Summary of the Patient Protection
           and Affordable Care Act (PPACA) of 2010 509

Glossary 517

References. 527

Index 543

About the Author 561

CONTENTS IN DETAIL

List of Exhibits xv

Preface. xxi

1 The Rise of Medical Expenditures. 1

    Before Medicare and Medicaid 1
    The Increasing Role of Government 1
    Changing Patient and Provider Incentives 4
    Government Response to Rising Costs 7
    A Look Ahead 12

2 How Much Should We Spend on Medical Care? 15

    Consumer Sovereignty 15
    Economic Efficiency. 17
    Government and Employer Concerns over Rising Medical Expenditures. . 19
    Approaches to Limiting Increases in Medical Expenditures 22

3 Do More Medical Expenditures Produce Better Health? 27

    Medical Services Versus Health. 27
    Health Production Function. 28
    Improving Health Status Cost Effectively 30
    Relationship of Medical Care to Health over Time 33

4 In Whose Interest Does the Physician Act? 39

    The Physician as a Perfect Agent for the Patient 39
    Supplier-Induced Demand 40
    Increase in Physician Supply 43
    Insurers' Response to Demand Inducement 43
    HMOs 44
    Informed Purchasers. 45

5 Rationing Medical Services 49

    Government Rationing. 49
    Rationing by Ability to Pay. 50

Decision Making by Consumers of Medical Services 51
Marginal Benefit Curve 52
Price Sensitivity 54

6   How Much Health Insurance Should Everyone Have? 59
Definitions of Insurance Terms 59
Insurance-Purchase Decision Making 61
Tax-Free, Employer-Paid Health Insurance 62

7   Why Are Those Who Most Need Health Insurance Least Able
to Buy It? 71
Medical Loss Ratios 73
How Health Insurance Markets Work 75
Additional Legislative Changes Affecting the Health Insurance Market . . . 80

8   Medicare 85
The Current State of Medicare 85
Part A (HI) 85
Part B (SMI) 87
Part C: Medicare Advantage Plans 88
Part D: Outpatient Prescription Drugs 88
Medigap Supplementary Insurance 90
Concerns About the Current Medicare System 90
The Impending Bankruptcy of Medicare 95
Proposals for Medicare Reform 99
Politics of Medicare Reform 102

9   Medicaid 105
An Illustration of Medicaid Eligibility 106
State Children's Health Insurance Program (SCHIP) 107
Medicaid Beneficiaries and Medicaid Expenditures 108
The Patient Protection and Affordable Care Act (PPACA) 111
Medicaid Policy Issues 112
Medicaid Managed Care 114
Reforming Medicaid 115

10 How Does Medicare Pay Physicians? 121
Previous Medicare Physician Payment System 121
Reasons for Adopting the New Payment System 122
Components of the New Payment System 123
Effects of Medicare's Payment System 128

11 Is There an Impending Shortage of Physicians? 135
Definitions of a Physician Shortage or Surplus 136
Consequences of an Imbalance in the Supply and Demand for Physicians . . . 138
Economic Evidence on Trends in Physician Demand and Supply 141
Longer-Term Outlook for Physicians 147

12 The Changing Practice of Medicine 151

    Types of Medical Groups 151
    Changes in the Size of Medical Groups. 152
    Reversal of Fortunes of Large Multispecialty Groups. 157
    Outlook for Medical Group Practices 159

13 Recurrent Malpractice Crises 167

    Explanations for the Rise in Malpractice Premiums 167
    Objectives of the Malpractice System .171
    Proposed Changes to the Malpractice System 175
    Enterprise Liability 178
    The Effects of Various Tort Reforms. .179

14 Do Nonprofit Hospitals Behave Differently than For-Profit
Hospitals? 183

    Why Are Hospitals Predominately Nonprofit? 185
    Performance of Nonprofit and For-Profit Hospitals 186
    The Question of Tax-Exempt Status 190

15 Competition Among Hospitals: Does It Raise or Lower Costs? . . . 195

    Origins of Non-price Competition 195
    Transition to Price Competition 199
    Price Competition in Theory 200
    Price Competition in Practice 201

16 The Future Role of Hospitals 207

    From Medicare to the Present 207
    The Hospital Outlook 212
    Hospital Revenues 213
    Potential Hospital Threats 217
    Alternative Hospital Scenarios. 220

17 Cost Shifting 225

    Setting Prices to Maximize Profits. 226
    Origins of Claims of Cost Shifting 231
    Price Discrimination 232
    Conditions Under Which Cost Shifting Can Occur. 233
    The Direction of Causality 234

18 Can Price Controls Limit Medical Expenditure Increases? 239

    Effect of Price Controls in Theory 239
    Effect of Price Controls in Practice .242
    Global Budgets. 245

19 The Evolution of Managed Care. 249

    Why Managed Care Came About 249
    What Is Managed Care? 250

Types of Managed Care Plans 251
How Has Managed Care Performed? 254
One-Time Versus Continual Cost Savings 256
The Change in Managed Care 260
Recent Developments in Managed Care 262
Consumer-Driven Health Care 264
Accountable Care Organizations 265

**20 Has Competition Been Tried—and Has It Failed—to Improve
the US Healthcare System?** 269

Criteria for Judging Performance of a Country's Medical Sector 269
How Medical Markets Differ from Competitive Markets 271
Demand-Side Market Failures 274
Supply-Side Market Failures 277
How Can Medical Markets Be More Competitive? 279
What Might Competitive Medical Markets Look Like? 280
Are the Poor Disadvantaged in a Competitive Market? 281

21 Comparative Effectiveness Research 285

CER and the Role of Government 285
Concerns over How CER Will Be Used 287
Cost-Effectiveness Analysis 290
Quality-Adjusted Life Years 291
The National Institute for Health and Clinical Excellence 294

22 US Competitiveness and Rising Health Costs 297

Who Pays for Higher Employee Medical Costs? 297
Who Pays for Retiree Medical Costs? 301
Possible Adverse Effects of Rising Medical Costs on the US Economy . . 303

23 Why Is Getting into Medical School So Difficult? 307

The Market for Medical Education in Theory 309
The Market for Medical Education in Practice 309
Accreditation for Medical Schools 310
Recommended Changes 311

24 The Shortage of Nurses 317

Measuring Nursing Shortages 317
Nursing Shortages in Theory 317
Nursing Shortages in Practice 319
Federal Subsidies to Nursing Schools and Students 326

25 The High Price of Prescription Drugs 331

Reasons for the Increase in Pharmaceutical Expenditures 331
Pricing Practices of US Pharmaceutical Companies 339

26 Ensuring Safety and Efficacy of New Drugs: Too Much of a
Good Thing? 347

History of Regulation of Prescription Drugs. 347
FDA's Stringent Guidelines for Safety and Efficacy 351

27 Why Are Prescription Drugs Less Expensive Overseas? 363

Accuracy of Studies on International Variations in Drug Prices 363
Why Prescription Drugs Are Expected to Be Priced Lower Overseas. . . .366
Public Policy Issues. 369

28 The Pharmaceutical Industry: A Public Policy Dilemma 377

Public Policy Dilemma 378
Structure of the Pharmaceutical Industry 378
Development of New Drugs by the US Pharmaceutical Industry 381
The Political Attractiveness of Price Controls on Prescription Drugs. . . .382
Consequences of Price Controls on Prescription Drugs. 385

29 Should Kidneys and Other Organs Be Bought and Sold?. 393

Sources of Organs for Transplant 393
Donor Compensation Proposals. 396
Opposition to Financial Incentives to Organ Donation 398
Additional Considerations 400

30 The Role of Government in Medical Care. 403

Public-Interest View of Government. .404
Economic Theory of Regulation. 406

31 Medical Research, Medical Education, Alcohol Consumption,
and Pollution: Who Should Pay?. 415

External Costs and Benefits 416
Government Policies When Externalities Exist 419
Divergence between Theoretical and Actual Government Policy 421

32 The Canadian Healthcare System 425

Higher Life Expectancy and Lower Infant Mortality Rate 425
Universal Coverage. 427
Controlling Healthcare Costs in Canada. 427
Consequences of Strict Limits on Per Capita Costs 432
Is Canada Abandoning its Single-Payer System? 438
Should the United States Adopt the Canadian System? 439

33 Employer-Mandated National Health Insurance 443

The Uninsured. 443
Why the Uninsured Do Not Have Health Insurance. 447
Consequences of Employer-Mandated Health Insurance. 447

Political Consequences of Employer-Mandated Health Insurance 451

34 National Health Insurance: Which Approach and Why? 455

Criteria for National Health Insurance 456
National Health Insurance Proposals 458
Refundable Tax Credits: An Income-Related Proposal 461

35 Financing Long-Term Care. 471

The Nature of Long-Term Care 471
Current State of Long-Term Care Financing. 473
Why Do So Few Aged Buy Long-Term Care Insurance? 476
Approaches to Financing Long-Term Care 480

36 The Politics of Healthcare Reform 487

Differing Goals of Healthcare Reform. 487
The Need for Visible Benefits to the Middle Class and Aged 489
Groups with a Concentrated Interest in Healthcare Reform 492
The Legislative Process. 498
The Administration's Objective for Healthcare Reform: A Hypothesis . . 503
The Years Ahead. 506

Appendix   A Brief Summary of the Patient Protection
and Affordable Care Act (PPACA) of 2010. 509

Glossary 517

References 527

Index 543

About the Author 561

LIST OF EXHIBITS

Exhibit 1.1   Personal Health Services Expenditures by Source
of Funds, 1965 and 2008 2

Exhibit 1.2   National Health Services Expenditures, Selected
Calendar Years, 1965–2009 (in Billions of Dollars) 3

Exhibit 1.3   The Nation's Health Services Dollar, 2009 5

Exhibit 2.1   Federal Spending on Health, Fiscal Years 1965–2016
(in Billions of Dollars) 20

Exhibit 2.2   Annual Percentage Changes in National Health
Expenditures and the Consumer Price Index,
1965–2009 23

Exhibit 3.1   Effect of Increased Medical Expenditures on Health 29

Exhibit 3.2   Neonatal Mortality Rates, by Race, 1950–2008 32

Exhibit 3.3   Cost per Life Saved Among Three Programs
to Reduce Neonatal Mortality (Whites) 33

Exhibit 3.4   Leading Causes of Death, by Age Group, 2008 34

Exhibit 3.5   Relationship Between Medical Care and Health 35

Exhibit 4.1   Number of Active Physicians and Physician-to-
Population Ratio, 1950–2008 41

Exhibit 5.1   Health Spending and Personal Income in Different
Countries, 2008 51

Exhibit 5.2   Relationship Among Prices, Visits, and Marginal Benefit
of an Additional Visit........................... 53

Exhibit 6.1   Deductibles, Coinsurance, and Catastrophic Expenses ... 61

Exhibit 6.2   Value of Tax Exclusion for Employer-Paid Health
Insurance, by Income Level, 2008.................. 66

Exhibit 6.3   Distribution of Employer-Paid Health Insurance Tax
Exclusion, by Income, 2010 67

Exhibit 7.1   Determinants of Health Insurance Premiums.......... 72

Exhibit 7.2   Distribution of Health Expenditures for the US
Population, by Magnitude of Expenditures, Selected
Years, 1928–2007 79

Exhibit 8.1 Number of Medicare Beneficiaries, Fiscal Years 1970–2030 86

Exhibit 8.2 Estimated Medicare Benefit Payments, by Type of Service, Fiscal Year 2009 87

Exhibit 8.3 Medicare Prescription Drug Benefit. 89

Exhibit 8.4 Growth in Real Medicare Expenditures per Enrollee, Part A, Part B, and Part D, 1966–2009 94

Exhibit 8.5 Population Pyramid, United States, 1960, 2010, and 2040. . .97

Exhibit 8.6 Cash Deficit of the Medicare HI Trust Fund, 2008–2018 . . .99

Exhibit 9.1 Percentage Distribution of Medicaid Enrollees and Benefit Payments, by Eligibility Status, Fiscal Year 2008 . .109

Exhibit 9.2 Number of Medicaid Beneficiaries and Total Medicaid Expenditures, Actual and Projected, 1975–2019 110

Exhibit 9.3 Medicaid Expenditures, by Service, 2009. 111

Exhibit 10.1 Calculations of Physician Payment Rate Under RBRVS Office Visits (Level 3), New York City (Manhattan), 2010. 124

Exhibit 10.2 Medicare Physician Fee Schedule Effect on Fees by Specialty, 1992 125

Exhibit 10.3 Recent and Projected Payment Updates for Physician Services 127

Exhibit 11.1 Annual Percentage Changes in the Consumer Price Index and in Physicians' Fees, 1965–2010. 142

Exhibit 11.2 Annual Percentage Changes in Median Physician Net Income, After Expenses and Before Taxes, 1982–2000 . .143

Exhibit 11.3 Average Annual Percentage Change in Net Income from Medical Practice, by Specialty, 2003–2008 144

Exhibit 11.4 Annual Ordinary Incomes, Before Taxes, for Various Professions and Educational Attainment Levels, Ages 22–65. 146

Exhibit 11.5 Percentage Distribution of Physician Expenditures, by Source of Funds, Selected Years, 1965–2009. 148

Exhibit 12.1 Physicians by Subspecialty and Practice Setting, 1996–97 and 2008 153

Exhibit 12.2 Physicians by Practice Setting, 1996–2001, 2004–05, and 2008. 154

Exhibit 13.1 Jury Awards for Medical Malpractice Cases,
1975–2007 169

Exhibit 13.2 Malpractice Insurers' Financial Ratios, 1997–2006 171

Exhibit 13.3 Evidence and Probable Effects of Malpractice Reform . . .180

Exhibit 14.1 Selected Hospital Data, 2009 184

Exhibit 15.1 Trends in Hospital Expenditures, 1966–2009 197

Exhibit 15.2 Annual Percentage Changes in the Consumer Price
Index and the Hospital Room Price Index, 1965–2010 . .198

Exhibit 15.3 The Number of Hospitals in Metropolitan Statistical
Areas, 2009 203

Exhibit 15.4 Hospital Cost Growth in the United States, by Level
of Managed Care Penetration and Hospital Market
Competitiveness, 1986–1993 .204

Exhibit 16.1 US Community Hospital Capacity and Utilization,
1975–2009 208

Exhibit 16.2 Aggregate Total Margins and Operating Margins
for US Hospitals, 1980–2008 .210

Exhibit 16.3 Annual Rate of Increase in Hospital Expenditures,
Actual and Trend, GDP Price Deflated, 1961–2009 211

Exhibit 16.4 Sources of Hospital Revenues, by Payer, Selected
Years, 1965–2009 214

Exhibit 17.1 Aggregate Hospital Payment-to-Cost Ratios for
Private Payers, Medicare, and Medicaid, 1980–2008 . . .226

Exhibit 17.2 Determining the Profit-Maximizing Price 227

Exhibit 17.3 Profit-Maximizing Price With and Without a Change
in Variable Cost 227

Exhibit 17.4 Effect on Total Revenue of a Change in Price 229

Exhibit 19.1 The Trend Toward Managed Care 253

Exhibit 19.2 How an HMO Allocates the Premium Dollar 254

Exhibit 19.3 Annual Percentage Increase in Health Insurance
Premiums for the United States, California, and the
CPI, 1988–2010 257

Exhibit 19.4 Trends in Hospital Utilization per 1,000 Population:
United States, California, and New York, 1977–2009 . . .258

Exhibit 20.1 Trends in Payment for Medical Services, 1960–2009 273

Exhibit 21.1 Medicare Spending per Decedent During the Last Two Years of Life (Deaths Occurring 2001–05), Selected Academic Medical Centers 286

Exhibit 21.2 Use of Acute Interventions (Pharmaceuticals) for Myocardial Infarction 290

Exhibit 21.3 Selected Cost-Effectiveness Ratios for Pharmaceuticals, with a Focus on the Medicare Population 293

Exhibit 22.1 Inflation-Adjusted Compensation and Wages per Full-Time Employee, 1965–2009 301

Exhibit 23.1 Medical School Applicants and Enrollments, 1960–2009 308

Exhibit 24.1 RN Vacancy Rates, Annual Percentage Changes in Real RN Wages, and the National Unemployment Rate, 1979–2009 318

Exhibit 24.2 Nursing School Enrollment, 1962–2008 321

Exhibit 25.1 Annual Percentage Changes in the Prescription Drug Price Index and Prescription Drug Expenditures, 1980–2009 332

Exhibit 25.2 Total Prescriptions Dispensed and Prescriptions per Capita, 1992–2009 333

Exhibit 25.3 Average Number of Prescription Drug Purchases, by Age, 2006 334

Exhibit 25.4 Distribution of Total National Prescription Drug Expenditures, by Type of Payer, 1990–2009 335

Exhibit 25.5 Share of Prescription Drug Spending, by Source of Funds, Selected Years, 1960–2009 337

Exhibit 25.6 Prescription Sales by Outlet, US Market, 2009 339

Exhibit 26.1 Number of and Mean Approval Times for New Molecular Entities in the United States, 1984–2009 352

Exhibit 26.2 The FDA and Type I and Type II Errors 355

Exhibit 26.3 Domestic R&D Expenditures as a Percentage of US Domestic Sales, Pharmaceutical Companies, 1970–2009 357

Exhibit 26.4 Decile Distribution of Present Values of Postlaunch Returns for the Sample of 1990–94 New Chemical Entities 358

Exhibit 27.1 Prices for Prilosec, Selected Countries, 2001 364

Exhibit 27.2 World Pharmaceutical Market, 2009 368

Exhibit 27.3 Pharmaceutical Expenditures as a Percentage of Total Health Expenditures, Selected Countries, 2008 . . .369

Exhibit 28.1 Country-Level Output of NCEs by Category and Time Period, 1982–92 and 1993–2003 383

Exhibit 28.2 Life Cycle of a New Drug 386

Exhibit 28.3 Effect of Price Controls on Drug Returns 387

Exhibit 28.4 Annual Percentage Change, US R&D, Pharmaceutical Companies, 1971–2009 389

Exhibit 29.1 Demand for Organs and Total Number of Organs Donated, 1995–2010 394

Exhibit 29.2 Number of Organ Transplants, Selected Years, 1981–2010 395

Exhibit 30.1 Health Policy Objectives and Interventions 405

Exhibit 30.2 Determining the Redistributive Effects of Government Programs 405

Exhibit 30.3 Health Policy Objectives Under Different Theories of Government 413

Exhibit 31.1 Optimal Rate of Output 416

Exhibit 32.1 Five-Year Relative Survival Rates for Cancer in the United States and Canada, 1999 427

Exhibit 32.2 Annual Percentage Growth in Real per Capita Health Expenditures in Canada and the United States, 1980–2008 430

Exhibit 32.3 Average Length of Hospital Stay in Canada and the United States, 1980–2008 431

Exhibit 32.4 Indicators of Medical Technology per Million People, 2004, 2006, and 2007 435

Exhibit 32.5 Canadian Hospital Waiting Lists: Total Expected Waiting Time from Referral by General Practitioner to Treatment, by Specialty, 2009 437

Exhibit 33.1 Uninsured Workers, by Age Group, 2008 444

Exhibit 33.2 Uninsured Workers, by Size of Firm, 2008 445

Exhibit 33.3 Percentage Distribution of Uninsured Workers, by Wage Rate and Hours Worked, 2008 446

Exhibit 34.1 A Comparison of Three National Health Insurance Proposals 467

Exhibit 35.1 Percentage of US Population Aged 65 Years and Older,
1980–2050 472

Exhibit 35.2 Percentage of People Aged 65 Years and Older, by Age
and Disability Level, 2004/2005 472

Exhibit 35.3 Estimated Spending on Long-Term Care Services, by
Type of Service and Payment Source, 2009 475

Exhibit 36.1 Voting Participation Rates in Presidential Elections,
by Age, 1984–2008 491

PREFACE

Being an economist, I believe an economic approach is very useful, not only for understanding the forces pressing for change in healthcare but also for explaining why the health system has evolved to its current state. Even the political issues surrounding the financing and delivery of health services can be better understood when viewed through an economic perspective, that is, the economic self-interest of participants.

For these reasons, I believe an issue-oriented book containing short discussions on each subject and using an economic perspective is needed. The economic perspective used throughout is that of a "market" economist, namely one who believes markets—in which suppliers compete for customers on the basis of price and quality—are the most effective mechanisms for allocating resources. Of course, at times markets fail or lead to outcomes that are undesirable in terms of equity. Market economists generally believe government economic interventions, no matter how well-intentioned or carefully thought out, can neither replicate the efficiency with which markets allocate resources nor fully anticipate the behavioral responses of the economic agents affected by the intervention. In cases of market failure, market economists prefer solutions that fix the underlying problem while retaining basic market incentives rather than replacing the market altogether with government planning or provision.

Healthcare reform has been an ongoing process for decades. At times, legislation and regulation have brought about major changes in the financing and delivery of medical services. At other times, competitive forces have restructured the delivery system. Both legislative and market forces will continue to influence how the public pays for and receives its medical services. Any subject affecting the lives of so many and requiring such a large portion of our country's resources will continue to be a topic of debate, legislative change, and market restructuring. I hope this book will help clarify some of the more significant issues underlying the politics and economics of healthcare.

For this fifth edition, in addition to revising and updating each of the chapters and exhibits, a new chapter has been added on one of the more topical issues in healthcare, "Comparative Effectiveness Research." The last chapter in the book, "The Politics of Healthcare Reform" has been completely rewritten to discuss the new Patient Protection and Affordable Care Act of 2010. An appendix has also been included that provides a summary of the Patient Protection and Affordable Care Act. A previous chapter on the Internet and healthcare has been omitted.

Given the large number of chapters and topics covered, and given that not all chapters will be assigned to students, some overlap naturally occurs in subject matter.

To help the reader focus on important points related to each issue, a list of discussion questions appears at the end of each chapter. A glossary is also included.

For instructors, an instructor's manual and PowerPoint slides are available. The instructor's manual includes a brief overview of each chapter and a list of the key topics covered. Also included are discussion points related to the discussion questions that appear at the end of each chapter. Additional questions and answers have been provided for instructor use. The instructor's manual and PowerPoint slides reside in a secure area on the Health Administration Press (HAP) website and are available only to adopters of this book. For access information, e-mail hap1@ache.org.

I thank Glenn Melnick, Thomas Wickizer, Jerry German, Jeff Hoch, and several anonymous reviewers for their comments. For this fifth edition I also thank Elzbieta Kozlowski and Mary Alice Pike for the collection of data, construction of the exhibits, and preparation of the manuscript.

Paul J. Feldstein
Irvine, California

THE RISE OF MEDICAL EXPENDITURES

The rapid growth of medical expenditures since 1965 is as familiar as the increasing percentage of US gross domestic product (GDP) devoted to medical care. Less known are the reasons for this continual increase. The purpose of this introductory chapter is twofold: to provide a historical perspective on the medical sector and explain the rise of medical expenditures in an economic context.

Before Medicare and Medicaid

Until 1965, spending in the medical sector was predominantly private—80 percent of all expenditures were paid by individuals out of pocket or by private health insurance on their behalf. The remaining expenditures (20 percent) were paid by the federal government (8 percent) and the states (12 percent) (see Exhibit 1.1). Personal medical expenditures totaled $35 billion and accounted for approximately 6 percent of GDP—that is, six cents of every dollar spent went to medical services.

The Increasing Role of Government

Medicare and Medicaid were enacted in 1965, dramatically increasing the role of government in financing medical care. Medicare, which covers the aged, initially consisted of two of its current four parts, Part A and Part B. Part A is for hospital care and is financed by a separate (Medicare) payroll tax on the working population. Part B covers physicians' services and is financed by federal taxes (currently 75 percent) and by a premium paid by the aged (25 percent). Medicare Parts C and D have since been added. Part C is a managed care option, and Part D is a prescription drug benefit, financed 75 percent by the federal government and 25 percent by the aged. Medicare Parts B, C, and D are all voluntary programs. Medicaid is for the categorically or medically needy, including the indigent aged and families with dependent children who receive cash assistance. Each state administers its own program, and the federal government pays, on average, more than half of the costs.

EXHIBIT 1.1

Personal Health
Services
Expenditures
by Source of
Funds, 1965
and 2009

Source of Funds	1965		2009	
	In Billions	%	In Billions	%
Total	34.7	100.0	2,089.9	100.0
Private	27.6	79.5	1,099.8	52.6
Out-of-pocket	18.2	52.4	299.3	14.3
Insurance benefits	8.7	25.1	712.2	34.1
All other	0.7	2.0	88.3	4.2
Public	7.1	20.5	990.1	47.4
Federal	2.8	8.1	798.9	38.2
State and local	4.3	12.4	191.2	9.1

SOURCE: CMS (2010b).

Two important trends are the increasing role of government in financing medical services and the declining portion of expenditures paid out of pocket by the public. As shown in Exhibit 1.1, 47.4 percent of total medical expenditures in 2009 were paid by the government; the federal share was 38.3 percent and the states contributed 9.1 percent. The private share declined to 52.6 percent; of that amount, 14.3 percent was paid out of pocket (compared to 52.4 percent out of pocket in 1965).

The rapid increase of total healthcare expenditures is illustrated in Exhibit 1.2, which shows expenditures on the different components of medical services over time. Since 1990, per capita healthcare expenditures have risen from $2,853 to $8,086. The two largest components of medical expenditures, hospital services and physician and clinical services, have increased 303 percent and 318 percent, respectively, during this time frame.

In the United States, $2.486 trillion, or 17.6 percent of GDP, was spent on medical care in 2009. From 2000 to 2009, these expenditures increased by about 8.9 percent per year. Since peaking in the early part of the decade, the annual rate of increase in healthcare expenditures has been declining, although it remains above the rate of inflation. Health expenditures continue to increase as a percentage of GDP.

Exhibit 1.2 National Health Services Expenditures, Selected Calendar Years, 1965–2009 (in Billions of Dollars)

	1965	1970	1980	1990	2000	2009
Total national health expenditures	$41.9	$74.8	$255.7	$724.0	$1,378.0	$2,486.3
Health services and supplies	37.2	67.0	235.6	675.3	1,288.5	2,330.1
Personal healthcare	34.7	63.1	217.1	616.6	1,164.4	2,089.9
Hospital care	13.5	27.2	100.5	250.4	415.5	759.1
Physician and clinical services	8.6	14.3	47.7	158.9	290.0	505.9
Dental services	2.8	4.7	13.3	31.5	62.0	102.2
Other professional care	0.5	0.7	3.5	17.4	37.0	66.8
Home healthcare	0.1	0.2	2.4	12.6	32.4	68.3
Nursing home care	1.4	4.0	15.3	44.9	85.1	137.0
Drugs, medical nondurables	5.9	8.8	21.8	62.7	152.5	293.2
Durable medical equipment	1.1	1.7	4.1	13.8	25.1	34.9
Other personal healthcare	0.7	1.3	8.5	24.3	64.7	122.6
Program administration and net cost of private health insurance	1.8	2.6	12.0	38.7	81.1	163.0
Government public health activities	0.6	1.4	6.4	20.0	43.0	77.2
Research and construction	4.9	8.1	20.9	50.7	94.0	157.5
Research	1.5	2.0	5.4	12.7	25.5	45.3
Construction	3.2	5.8	14.7	36.0	64.1	110.9
National health expenditures per capita	$210	$356	$1,110	$2,853	$4,878	$8,086

SOURCE: CMS (2010c).

In the mid-1990s, medical expenditures increased at a slower rate because of the growth of managed care, which emphasized utilization management, and price competition among providers participating in managed care provider networks. By the end of the 1990s, managed care's cost-containment approaches lost support as a result of public dissatisfaction with managed care, lawsuits against managed care organizations (MCOs) for denial of care, government legislation, and a tight labor market that led employers to offer their employees more health plan choices. As a result, medical expenditures rose at a more rapid rate. The recent decline in the annual rate of increase in expenditures can be attributed to the financial crisis in the United States, the recession, growing unemployment, a larger number of uninsured, and the decline in the number of employers paying for employee health insurance.

National health expenditures are likely to rise at a faster rate this decade as the first of the baby boomers become eligible for Medicare; as new technology that improves quality, but at a higher cost, continues to be introduced; and when President Obama's 2010 health legislation, with its expansion of Medicaid eligibility and subsidies for low-income employees, becomes effective in 2014. By 2019, national health expenditures are expected to double to $4.5 trillion and consume an even greater portion of GDP.

Exhibit 1.3 shows where healthcare dollars come from and how they are distributed among the different types of healthcare providers.

Changing Patient and Provider Incentives

Medical expenditures equal the prices of services provided multiplied by the quantity of services provided. The rise of medical expenditures can be explained by looking at the factors that prompt medical prices and quantities to change. In a market system, the prices and output of goods and services are determined by the interaction of buyers (the demand side) and sellers (the supply side). We can analyze price and output changes by examining how various interventions change the behavior of buyers and sellers. One such intervention was Medicare, which lowered the out-of-pocket price the aged had to pay for medical care. The demand for hospital and physician services by the aged increased dramatically after Medicare was enacted, spurring rapid price increases. Similarly, government payments to the poor under Medicaid stimulated demand for medical services among this demographic. Greater demand for services multiplied by higher prices for those services equals greater total expenditures.

Prices also increase when the costs of providing services increase. For example, to attract more nurses to care for the increased number of aged patients, hospitals raised nurses' wages and then passed this increase to payers in

Exhibit 1.3 The Nation's Health Services Dollar, 2009

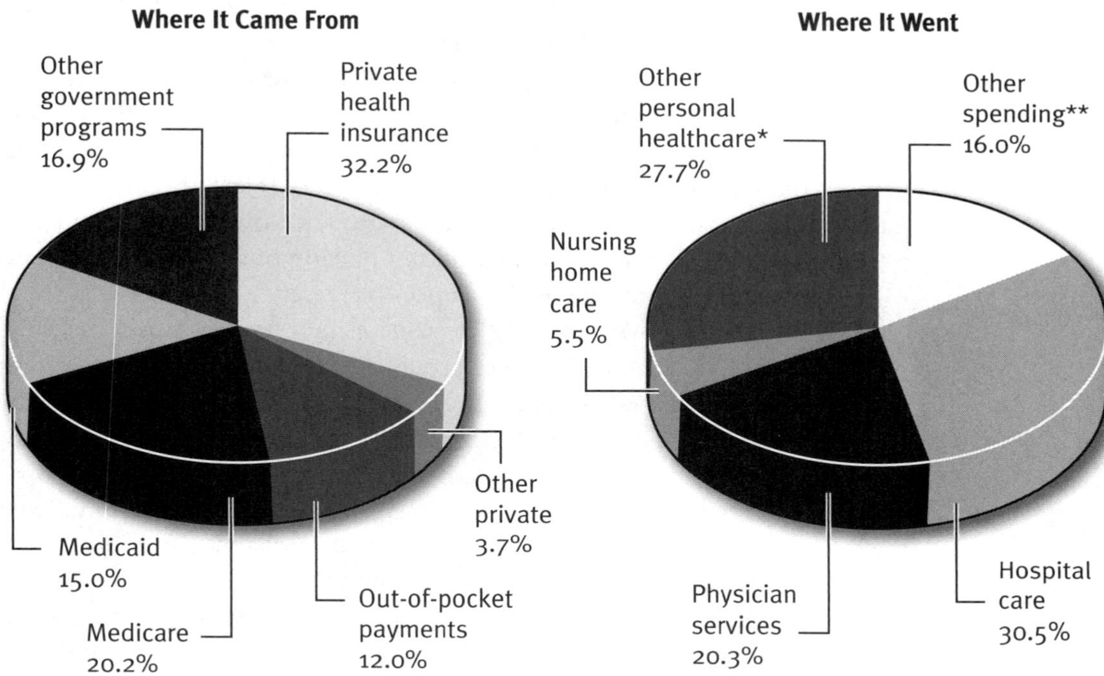

Where It Came From

Other government programs 16.9%

Private health insurance 32.2%

Medicaid 15.0%

Medicare 20.2%

Out-of-pocket payments 12.0%

Other private 3.7%

Where It Went

Other personal healthcare* 27.7%

Other spending** 16.0%

Nursing home care 5.5%

Physician services 20.3%

Hospital care 30.5%

*"Other personal healthcare" includes dental care, vision care, home healthcare, drugs, medical products, and other professional services.

**"Other spending" includes program administration, net cost of private health insurance, government public health, and research and construction.

SOURCE: Data from CMS (2010a).

the form of higher prices for services. Increased demand for care multiplied by higher costs of care equals greater expenditures.

At the same time the government was subsidizing the demands of the aged and poor, the demand for medical services by the employed population also was increasing. The growth of private health insurance during the late 1960s and 1970s was stimulated by income growth, high marginal (federal) income tax rates (up to 70 percent), and the high inflation rate in the economy. The high inflation rate threatened to push many people into higher marginal tax brackets. If an employee were pushed into a 50 percent marginal income tax bracket, half of his salary in that bracket would go to taxes. Instead of having that additional income taxed at 50 percent, employees often chose to have the employer spend those same dollars, before tax, to buy more comprehensive health insurance. Thus, employees could receive the full value of their raise, albeit in healthcare benefits. This tax subsidy for employer-paid health insurance stimulated the demand for medical services in the private sector and further boosted medical prices.

Demand increased most rapidly for medical services covered by government and private health insurance. As of 2009, only 3.2 percent of hospital care and 9.5 percent of physician services were paid out of pocket by the patient; the remainder was paid by some third party (CMS 2010d). Patients had little incentive to be concerned about the price of a service when they were not responsible for paying a significant portion of the price. As the out-of-pocket price declined, the use of services increased.

The aged, who represent 13 percent of the population and use more medical services than any other age group, filled approximately 40 percent of hospital beds as of 2007 (Hall et al. 2010). Use of physician services by the aged (Medicare), the poor (Medicaid), and those covered by tax-exempt employer-paid insurance also increased.

Advances in medical technology were yet another factor stimulating the demand for medical treatment. New methods of diagnosis and treatment were developed; those with previously untreatable diseases gained access to technology that offered hope of recovery. New medical devices, such as imaging equipment, were introduced, and new treatments, such as organ transplants, became available. New diseases, such as acquired immune deficiency syndrome (AIDS), also increased demand on the medical system. Reduced out-of-pocket costs and increased third-party payments (both public and private), on top of an aging population, new technologies, and new diseases, drove up both the prices and quantity of medical services provided.

Providers (hospitals and physicians) responded to the increased demand for care, but the way they responded unnecessarily increased the cost of providing medical services. After Medicare was enacted, hospitals had few incentives to be efficient because the program reimbursed hospitals their costs plus 2 percent for serving Medicare patients. Hospitals, predominantly not for profit, consequently expanded their capacity, invested in the latest technology, and duplicated facilities and services offered in nearby hospitals. Hospital prices rose faster than the prices of any other medical service. Similarly, physicians had little cause for concern over hospital costs. Physicians, who were paid fee-for-service, wanted their hospitals to have the latest equipment so that they would not have to refer their patients elsewhere (and possibly lose them). They would hospitalize patients for diagnostic workups and keep them in the hospital longer because it was less costly for patients covered by hospital insurance and physicians would be sure to receive reimbursement; outpatient services, which were less costly than hospital care, initially were not covered by third-party payers.

In addition to the lack of incentives for patients to be concerned with the cost of their care and the similar lack of incentives for providers to supply that care efficiently, the government imposed restrictions on the delivery of services that increased enrollees' medical costs. Under Medicare and Medicaid, the government ruled that insurers must give enrollees free choice of provider. Insurers such as health maintenance organizations (HMOs) that preclude their enrollees from choosing any physician in the community were violating the free-choice-of-provider rule and were thus ineligible to receive capitation payments from the government; HMOs were instead paid fee-for-service, reducing their incentive to reduce the total costs of treating a patient. Numerous state restrictions on HMOs, such as prohibiting HMOs from advertising, requiring HMOs to be not for profit (thereby limiting their access to capital), and requiring HMOs to be controlled by physicians, further inhibited their development. By imposing these restrictions on alternative delivery systems, however, the government reduced competition for Medicare and Medicaid patients, forgoing an opportunity to reduce government payments for Medicare and Medicaid.

The effects of increased demand, limited patient and provider incentives to search for lower-cost approaches, and restrictions on the delivery of medical services were escalating prices, increased use of services, and, consequently, greater medical expenditures.

Government Response to Rising Costs

As expenditures under Medicare and Medicaid increased, the federal government faced limited options. It could (1) raise the Medicare payroll tax and income taxes on the nonaged to continue funding these programs, (2) require the aged to pay higher premiums for Medicare and increase their deductibles and copayments, or (3) reduce payments to hospitals and physicians. Each of these approaches would cost the administration and Congress political support from some constituency (e.g., employees, the aged, healthcare providers). The least politically costly options appeared to be to increase taxes on the nonaged and to pay hospitals and physicians less.

Federal and state governments used additional regulatory approaches to control these rapidly rising expenditures. Medicare utilization review programs were instituted, and controls were placed on hospital investment in new facilities and equipment. These government controls proved ineffective as hospital expenditures continued to escalate through the 1970s. The government then limited physician fee increases under Medicare and Medicaid; as a consequence, many physicians refused to participate in these programs, reducing access to care for the aged and the poor. As a result of their refusal to participate in Medicare, many Medicare patients had to pay higher out-of-pocket fees to be seen by physicians.

In 1979, President Carter's highest domestic priority was to enact expenditure limits on Medicare hospital cost increases; a Congress controlled by his own political party defeated him.

The 1980s

By the beginning of the 1980s, political consensus on what should be done to control Medicare hospital and physician expenditures was lacking, and private health expenditures continued to increase rapidly. By the mid-1980s, however, legislative changes and other events imposed heavy cost-containment pressures on Medicare, Medicaid, and the private sector.

Legislative and Government Changes

Several events in the early 1980s brought major changes to the medical sector. The HMO legislation enacted in 1974 began to have an effect in this decade. In 1974, President Nixon wanted a health program that would not increase federal expenditures. The result was the HMO Act of 1974, which legitimized HMOs and removed restrictive state laws impeding the development of federally approved HMOs. However, many HMOs decided not to seek federal qualification because imposed restrictions, such as having to offer more costly benefits, would have caused their premiums to be too high to be price competitive with traditional health insurers' premiums. These restrictions were removed by the late 1970s, and the growth of HMOs began in the early 1980s.

To achieve savings in Medicaid, in 1981 the Reagan administration removed the free choice of provider rule, enabling states to enroll their Medicaid populations in closed provider panels. As a result, states were permitted to negotiate capitation payments with HMOs for care of their Medicaid patients. The free-choice rule continued for the aged; however, in the mid-1980s they were permitted to voluntarily join HMOs. The federal government agreed to pay HMOs a capitated amount for enrolling Medicare patients, but less than 10 percent of the aged voluntarily participated (CBO 1995). (As of 2009, of the 40 million aged, 18.4 percent were enrolled in Medicare HMOs, referred to as Medicare Advantage plans [US Census Bureau 2011b; CMS 2011b].)

Federal subsidies were provided to medical schools in 1964 to increase the number of students they could accommodate, and the supply of physicians increased. The number of active physicians increased from 146 per 100,000 civilian population in 1965 to 195 per 100,000 in 1980; it reached 229 per 100,000 in 1990 and 283 per 100,000 in 2008 (AMA Division of Survey and Data Resources 1991, 2010). The increased supply of physicians created excess capacity among physicians, dampened their fee increases, made it easier for HMOs to attract physicians, and, therefore, made it easier for the HMOs to expand.

A new Medicare hospital payment system was phased in during 1983. Hospitals were no longer to be paid according to their costs; fixed prices were established for each diagnostic admission (referred to as diagnosis-related groups [DRGs]), and each year Congress set an annual limit on the amount by which these fixed prices per admission could increase. DRG prices changed hospitals' incentives. Because hospitals could keep the difference if the costs they incurred from an admission were less than the fixed DRG payment they received for that admission, they were motivated to reduce the cost of caring for Medicare patients and to discharge them earlier. Length of stay per admission fell, and occupancy rates declined. Hospitals also became concerned with inefficient physician practice behaviors that increased the hospitals' costs of care.

In 1992, the federal government also changed its method of paying physicians under Medicare. A national fee schedule (resource-based relative value system [RBRVS]) was implemented, and volume expenditure limits were established to limit the total rate of increase in physician Medicare payments. The imposition of price controls and expenditure limits on payments to hospitals and physicians for services provided to Medicare patients continues to be the approach the federal government takes to contain Medicare expenditures today.

The RBRVS also prohibited physicians from charging their higher-income patients a higher fee and accepting the Medicare fee only for lower-income patients; they had to accept the fee for all their Medicare patients or none. Medicare patients represent such a significant portion of a physician's practice that few physicians decided not to participate; consequently, they accepted Medicare fees for all patients.

Private-Sector Changes

In addition to the government policy changes of the early 1980s, important events were occurring in the private sector. The new decade started with a recession. To survive the recession and remain competitive internationally, the business sector looked to reduce labor costs. Because employer-paid health insurance was the fastest-growing labor expense, businesses pressured health insurers to better control the use and cost of medical services. Competitive pressures forced insurers to increase the efficiency of their benefit packages by including lower-cost substitutes for inpatient care, such as outpatient surgery. They increased deductibles and copayments, intensifying patients' price sensitivity. Further, patients had to receive prior authorization from their insurer before being admitted to a hospital, and insurers reviewed patients' length of stay while patients were in the hospital. These actions greatly reduced hospital admission rates and lengths of stay. The number of admissions in community hospitals in 1975 was 155 per 1,000 population. By 1990 it had fallen to 125 per 1,000, and it continued to decline, dropping to

116 in 2009. The number of inpatient days per 1,000 population fell even more dramatically, from 1,302 in 1977 to 982 in 1990 to 628 in 2009 (AHA 2011; US Census Bureau 2011b).

Due to the implementation of the federal DRG payment system, the changes to private programs, and a shift to the outpatient sector facilitated by technological change (both anesthetic and surgical techniques), hospital occupancy rates declined from 76 percent in 1980 to 65.5 percent in 2009 (AHA 2010).

Antitrust Laws   The preconditions for price competition were in place: Hospitals and physicians had excess capacity, and employers wanted to pay less for employee health insurance. The last necessary condition for price competition was set in 1982, when the US Supreme Court upheld the applicability of the antitrust laws to the medical sector. Successful antitrust cases were brought against the American Medical Association for its restrictions on advertising, against a medical society that threatened to boycott an insurer over physician fee increases, against a dental organization that boycotted an insurer's cost-containment program, against medical staffs that denied hospital privileges to physicians because they belonged to an HMO, and against hospitals whose mergers threatened to reduce price competition in their communities.

The applicability of the antitrust laws, excess capacity among providers, and employer and insurer interest in lowering medical costs brought about profound changes in the medical marketplace. Traditional insurance plans lost market share as managed care plans, which controlled utilization and limited access to hospitals and physicians, grew. Preferred provider organizations (PPOs) were formed and included only physicians and hospitals that were willing to discount their prices. Employees and their families were offered price incentives in the form of lower out-of-pocket payments to use these less expensive providers. Large employers and health insurers began to select PPOs on the basis of their prices, use of services, and outcomes of their treatment.

Consequences of the 1980s Changes   The 1980s disrupted the traditional physician–patient relationship. Insurers and HMOs used utilization review to control patient demand, emphasize outcomes and appropriateness of care, and limit patients' access to higher-priced physicians and hospitals by not including them in their provider networks; they also used case management for catastrophic illnesses, substituted less expensive settings for more costly inpatient care, and affected patients' choice of drugs through the use of formularies.

The use of cost-containment programs and the shift to outpatient care lowered hospital occupancy rates. The increasing supply of physicians, particularly specialists, created excess capacity. Hospitals in financial trouble closed, and others merged. Hospital consolidation increased. Hospitals' excess capacity was not reduced until years later, when the demand for care began to exceed the available supply of hospitals and physicians. Until then, hospitals and physicians continued to be subject to intense competitive pressures.

Employees' incentive to reduce their insurance premiums also stimulated competition among HMOs and insurers. Employers required employees to pay the additional cost of more expensive health plans, so many employees chose the lowest-priced plan. Health plans competed for enrollees primarily by offering lower premiums and provider networks with better reputations.

The 1990s

As managed care spread throughout the United States during the 1990s, the rate of increase of medical expenditures declined. Hospital use decreased dramatically, and hospitals and physicians agreed to large price discounts to be included in an insurer's provider panel. These cost-containment approaches contributed to the lower annual rate of increase. However, although price competition reduced medical costs, patients were dissatisfied. The public wanted greater access to care, particularly less restriction on referrals to specialists. There was also public backlash against HMOs; HMOs lost several lawsuits for denying access to experimental treatments, and Congress and the states imposed restrictions on MCOs, such as mandating minimum lengths of stay in the hospital for normal deliveries. Cost-containment restrictions weakened as a result of these events, and increases in prices, use of services, and medical expenditures reaccelerated.

The Decade 2000–2010

The excess capacity that weakened hospitals in their negotiations with insurers dried up. Financially weak hospitals closed. Because hospital consolidation reduces the number of competing hospitals in an area, thereby increasing a hospital's bargaining power, the number of hospital mergers increased. As hospital prices increased, so did insurance premiums. It was no longer possible to use past approaches—decreased hospital use and price discounts—to achieve large cost reductions. Instead, insurers tried to develop more innovative, less costly ways of managing patient care.

Several of the newer approaches to cost containment included high-deductible health plans, evidence-based medicine, and disease management programs. Insurers' method of shifting a larger share of medical costs to consumers is referred to as *consumer-driven healthcare* (CDHC). In return for lower health insurance premiums, consumers pay higher deductibles and co-payments. Consumers are then presumed to evaluate the costs and benefits of spending their own funds on healthcare. Instead of relying on consumer incentives to reduce medical costs, other health insurers use evidence-based medicine, which relies on the analysis of large data sets to determine the effect of different physician practice patterns on costs and medical outcomes.

To the same end, insurers are using disease management programs to provide chronically ill patients with preventive and continuous care, which not only improves the quality of care but also reduces costly hospitalizations.

Another development was pay-for-performance (P4P) programs. Insurers pay physicians and other healthcare providers more if they provide high-quality care, which is usually defined on the basis of process measures developed by medical experts. Insurers also made report cards available to their enrollees. Report cards evaluate hospitals and medical groups in the insurer's provider network according to medical outcomes, preventive services, and patient satisfaction scores to enable enrollees to make more informed choices about the providers they use.

In the latter half of the decade, rising premiums and increased unemployment prompted people to drop their insurance or switch to new types of insurance that charge lower premiums, such as high-deductible plans. Many Americans are concerned that premiums will continue increasing and that insurance will become ever less affordable.

A Look Ahead

The forces increasing demand and the costs of providing care have not changed. If anything, these factors promise to increase medical expenditures and insurance premiums more rapidly in coming years. The population is aging (the first of the baby boomers retire in 2011), technological advances enable early diagnosis, and new methods of treatment are emerging, all of which stimulate increased demand for medical services. Of these three developments, new technology is believed to be the most important force behind rising expenditures. For example, the number of people receiving organ transplants has increased dramatically, as have the diffusion of new equipment and the use of imaging tests. The cost of providing medical services is also increasing as more highly trained medical personnel are needed to handle the increased technology and as wage rates increase to attract more nurses and technicians to the medical sector.

There are also increasing concerns that a shortage of physicians is developing. The demand for physician services is increasing faster than the number of physicians is increasing, and physician payment under Medicare and Medicaid has not kept pace with these market changes.

The enactment of President Obama's new health legislation in 2010 (to take effect in 2014) will further increase the demand for care. More people will become eligible for Medicaid, including more privately insured individuals; as a result, the private insurance market will become smaller. Everyone will be required to have insurance under the legislation's individual mandate, and under the employer mandate, employers will be required to provide insurance for their employees or pay a fine. On the basis of financial need, some uninsured individuals will receive new subsidies to buy insurance. Insurance exchanges will become available in each state, promoting greater competition among insurers. In anticipation of the forecasted increase in demand, the legislation includes a few demonstration projects that may over time become potential cost-containment programs. However, the legislation makes no changes to patient or provider incentives to encourage them to be more efficient in their use of medical services. Medical expenditures and premiums will likely increase more rapidly than they are today.

As the cost of financing these expansions of Medicaid eligibility and new subsidies increase, the already large federal deficit will grow even faster than it is growing today. The federal government will be under great pressure to reduce the rising deficit and the burden of increasing premiums faced by the middle class. Will the government rely more on regulatory or competitive approaches to reduce medical expenditures and premium increases?

Innovative approaches to reducing healthcare costs are more likely to be taken in a system that has price incentives to do so (e.g., health insurers compete for enrollees) than in a regulated system. Any regulatory approach that arbitrarily seeks to reduce the rate of increase in medical expenditures will result in reduced access to both medical care and new technology.

Summary

Although the United States spends more on healthcare than any other country spends, a scarcity of funds to provide for all of our medical needs and population groups, such as the uninsured and those on Medicaid, still exists. Therefore, choices must be made. The first choice we as a society must make is to determine how much we should spend on medical care. What approach should we use to make this choice? Should individuals decide how much they want to spend on healthcare, or should the government decide the percentage of GDP that goes to healthcare?

The second choice is to identify the best way to provide medical services. Would competition among health plans or government regulation and price controls bring about greater efficiency in providing medical services?

Third, how rapidly should medical innovation be introduced? Should regulatory agencies evaluate each medical advance and determine whether its benefits exceed its costs, or should the evaluation of those costs and benefits be left to the separate health plans competing for enrollees?

Fourth, how much should be spent on those who are medically indigent, and how should their care be provided? Should the medically indigent be enrolled in a separate medical system, such as Medicaid, or should they be provided with vouchers to enroll in competing health plans?

These choices can be better understood when we are more aware of the consequences of each approach (e.g., which groups benefit and which groups bear the costs). Economics clarifies the implications of different approaches to these decisions.

Discussion Questions

1. What are some of the reasons for the increased demand for medical services since 1965?
2. Why has employer-paid health insurance been an important stimulant of demand for health insurance?
3. How did hospital payment methods in the 1960s and 1970s affect hospitals' investment policies and incentives to improve efficiency?
4. Why were HMOs and managed care not more prevalent in the 1960s and 1970s?
5. What choices has the federal government had to reduce greater-than-projected Medicare expenditures?
6. What events during the 1980s in both the public and private sectors made the delivery of medical services price competitive?

HOW MUCH SHOULD WE SPEND ON MEDICAL CARE?

The United States spends more on medical care than any other country—17.6 percent of its GDP—and this percentage is expected to continue to increase. Can we afford to spend that much of our resources on medical care? Why do we view growth of expenditures in other areas, such as automobiles, more favorably than growth of expenditures on medical services? Increased medical expenditures create new healthcare jobs, do not pollute the air, save rather than destroy lives, and alleviate pain and suffering. Why should society not be pleased that more resources are flowing into a sector that cares for the aged and the sick? Spending on medical care would seem to be a more appropriate use of a society's resources than spending on faster cars, alcohol, or other consumer products, yet increased expenditures on these other industries do not cause the concern that increased medical expenditures cause.

Are we concerned about rising medical costs because we believe we are not receiving value for our money—namely that the additional medical services and technologies are not worth what they cost compared to other potential uses of those resources—or is there a more fundamental difference of opinion regarding the rate at which medical expenditures should increase?

To answer these questions, we must define what we consider an appropriate or "right" amount of expenditure. Only then can we evaluate whether we are spending too much on medical care. If we determine that we are spending too much, how does public policy have to change to achieve the right expenditure level?

Consumer Sovereignty

The appropriate amount of health expenditure is based on a set of values and on the concept of economic efficiency. Resources are limited, so they should be used for what consumers value most. Consumers decide how much to purchase on the basis of their perception of the value they expect to receive and how much they have to pay for it, knowing that an expenditure on one good or service means forgoing other goods and services. Consumers differ greatly with regard to the value they place on medical care and what they are willing to forgo to spend more on healthcare. In a competitive market, consumers receive the full benefits of their purchases and in turn pay the full costs of receiving those benefits. When the benefits received from the last unit consumed (e.g., the last visit to the doctor) equal the cost of consuming that last unit, the quantity consumed is said to be optimal. If more or fewer services were consumed, the benefits received would be either less or greater than the cost of that service.

Consumer sovereignty is most easily achieved in a competitive market system. Consumers differ with regard to the medical services they value and their willingness to pay for a given service. Through their expenditures, consumers communicate what goods and services they value. In response, producers use their resources to produce the goods consumers desire. If producers are to survive and profit in competitive markets, they must use their resources efficiently and produce the goods consumers are willing to pay for; otherwise, they will be replaced by more efficient producers in tune with what consumers want.

Some people believe that consumer sovereignty should not determine how much we spend on medical care. More than in other areas, patients lack information and have limited ability to judge needs for medical treatment. Other concerns are the quality of care patients receive and how much care is appropriate.

Consumer sovereignty may be imperfect, but alternatives are equally imperfect. If medical care were free to all and physicians (paid on a fee-for-service basis or salaried) decided the quantity of medical care to provide, the result would be provision of "too much" care. Physicians are likely to prescribe services as long as they perceive the services will benefit the patient, even if only slightly, because the physician is not responsible for the cost of that care.

The inevitable consequence of a free medical system is a government-imposed expenditure limit to halt the provision of too much care. Although physicians would still be responsible for determining who would receive care and for which diagnoses, "too little" care would likely be provided, as is sometimes the case in government-controlled health systems such as those in Canada and Great Britain. Queues are established to ration available medical care, and waiting times and age become criteria for allocating medical resources.

No government that funds healthcare spends sufficient resources to provide all the care demanded at the going price. As does an individual making purchases, the government makes trade-offs between the benefits received from additional health expenditures and the cost of those expenditures. However, the benefits and costs to the government are different from those consumers consider in their decision-making processes. To the government, *benefit* means the political support it gains by increasing health expenditures; *cost* means the political support it loses when it raises taxes or shifts resources from politically popular programs to fund those additional expenditures.

Let us therefore assume that consumer sovereignty will continue to guide the amount we spend on medical care. Having consumer sovereignty as a guide, however, does not mean that this country is spending the right amount on medical services. This judgment is influenced by another factor: economic efficiency.

Economic Efficiency

Efficiency in Providing Medical Services

If medical services were produced in an inefficient manner, medical expenditures would be excessive. For example, rather than treating a patient for ten days in the hospital, a physician might be able to achieve the same outcome and same level of patient satisfaction by treating the patient in the hospital over a fewer number of days, sending the patient home, and having a visiting nurse finish the treatment. Similarly, the patient might be able to be treated in an outpatient setting rather than in the hospital. Physicians' practice patterns vary greatly across the country, causing medical expenditures to vary widely with no apparent difference in outcomes. Unless providers have appropriate incentives to be efficient, economic efficiency in providing medical services is unlikely to be achieved.

When hospitals were paid on a cost-plus basis, they had an incentive to increase their costs. Subsequent events changed those incentives, and since the early 1980s, both the government and the private sector have been pressing for increased efficiency of the delivery system. Cost-based payment to hospitals under Medicare gave way to fixed payment based on diagnosis-related groups (DRGs). Price competition has increased not just among hospitals and physicians; it has increased among insurance companies, as they are themselves competing on the basis of premiums in the sale of group health insurance. PPOs, HMOs, and managed care systems have increased their market share at the expense of traditional insurers. Hospitalization rates have declined as utilization review mechanisms have increased, and the trend toward implementing case management for catastrophic illness and monitoring providers for appropriateness of care and medical outcomes is also increasing.

Few would contend that the provision of medical services is as efficient as it could be; waste exists in the health system. *Waste* is difficult to define. Is it any medical intervention that provides no medical benefit, or is it a medical intervention in which the potential for a negative outcome exceeds the potential for the patient to benefit (Fuchs 2009)? *Economic waste* occurs when the expected benefits of an intervention are less than the expected costs. It is important to remember that waste is also a provider's income.

However difficult it is to define and reduce waste, the emphasis on cost containment and the growth of managed care are efforts to decrease inefficient use and delivery of medical services. Even if administrative costs for private health insurance were reduced by 50 percent (which would have saved $80 billion in 2009), the profits of the pharmaceutical drug companies were reduced by 50 percent (saving $40 billion), and all physician incomes were reduced by 25 percent (saving $50 billion), the combined savings of $170 billion represent less than two years' annual percentage increase in total medical expenditures. Inefficiency, although important, is not the main cause for concern over the rise of medical expenditures.

Efficiency in the Use of Medical Services

Inefficiencies in the use of medical services result when individuals do not have to pay the full cost of their choices; they consume too much medical care because their use of services is based on the out-of-pocket price they pay, and that price is less than the cost of providing the service. Consequently, the cost of providing the service exceeds the benefit the patient receives from consuming additional units of the service. The resources devoted to providing these additional services could be better used for other services, such as education, that would provide greater benefits.

The effect of paying less than the full price of a service is easy to understand when the concept is applied to some other consumer product, such as automobiles. If the price of automobiles were greatly reduced for consumers, they would purchase more automobiles (and more costly ones). To produce these additional automobiles, manufacturers would use resources that could have been used to produce other goods. Similarly, when the price people have to pay for medical services decreases, they use more services. Studies have shown that patients who pay less out of pocket have more hospital admissions, visit physicians more often, and use more outpatient services than patients who pay higher prices (Feldstein 2011). This relationship between price and use of medical services also holds for patients classified by health status.

Inefficient use is an important concept in healthcare because the price of medical services has been artificially lowered for many consumers. The government subsidizes medical care for the poor and the aged under Medicaid and Medicare. Those eligible for these programs use more services than they would if they had to pay the full price. Although the purpose of these programs is to increase the use of medical services by the poor and the aged, the artificially low prices also promote inefficient use, for example, when a patient uses the more expensive emergency department rather than a physician's office in a non-emergent situation.

A greater concern is that the working population contributes to use inefficiency. Employer-purchased health insurance is not considered taxable income for employees. If an employer gave the same amount of funds to an employee in the form of higher wages, the employee would have to pay federal and state income tax as well as Social Security tax on that additional income. Because employer-purchased health insurance is not subject to these taxes, the government in effect subsidizes the purchase of health insurance and, when the employee uses the insurance, the purchase of medical services. Employees do not pay the full cost of health insurance; it is bought with before-tax dollars, as opposed to all other purchases by consumers, which are made with after-tax dollars.

The greatest beneficiaries of this tax subsidy are employees in higher income tax brackets. As discussed in Chapter 1, rather than receive additional income as cash, which is then subject to high taxes (in the 1970s, the highest federal income tax bracket was 70 percent), these employees choose to receive more of their additional wages in the form of increased health insurance coverage. Instead of spending after-tax dollars on vision and dental services, they can purchase these services more cheaply with before-tax dollars. The price of insurance is reduced by employees' tax bracket; as a result, they purchase more health insurance than they otherwise would because they did not have to pay the full cost of that coverage, and the additional insurance coverage is worth less to the employee than its full cost.

With the purchase of additional health insurance, the out-of-pocket price consumers paid for medical services declined, prompting increased use of all medical services covered by health insurance. As employees and their families became less concerned with the real cost of medical services, few constraints limited the rise in medical expenditures. Had the inefficient use of medical services (resulting from the tax subsidy for the purchase of health insurance) been less prevalent, medical expenditures would have risen more slowly.

Inefficiencies in the use and provision of medical services are legitimate reasons for concern over how much is spent on medical care. Public policy should attempt to eliminate these government-caused inefficiencies. However, there are other, less valid reasons for concern over the rise in medical expenditures.

Government and Employer Concerns over Rising Medical Expenditures

As payers of medical expenditures, the federal and state governments and employers are concerned about rising medical costs. State governments pay half the costs of caring for the medically indigent in their state; the federal government pays the remaining half. Medicaid expenditures have risen more rapidly than any other state expenditure and have caused states to reduce funding for other politically popular programs so they do not have to increase taxes. At the federal level, the government is also responsible for Medicare

EXHIBIT 2.1 Federal Spending on Health, Fiscal Years 1965–2016 (in Billions of Dollars)

	1965	1975	1985	1995	2010	2016*
Total federal spending	118.2	332.3	946.3	1,515.7	3,456.2	4,467.8
Federal health spending	3.1	29.5	117.1	307.1	916.2	1,355.5
Medicare	N/A	12.9	65.8	159.9	451.7	638.4
Medicaid	0.3	6.8	22.7	89.1	272.8	427.0
Veterans Administration	1.3	3.7	9.5	16.4	45.7	58.7
Other	1.5	6.1	19.1	41.7	146.2	231.3
Federal health spending as a percentage of total federal spending	2.6%	8.9%	12.4%	20.3%	26.5%	30.3%

*Projected data
Note: N/A = not applicable.

SOURCE: Office of Management and Budget (2010).

(acute medical services for the aged). The hospital portion of this program is financed by a specific Medicare payroll tax that has been increased numerous times, and the physician and prescription drug portions of the program (Parts B and D) are financed with general income taxes. Medicare expenditures have also risen rapidly. As a result of President Obama's healthcare legislation, government subsidies to pay for expanded Medicaid eligibility and for employees in small firms will greatly increase starting in 2014.

As shown in Exhibit 2.1, federal health spending as a proportion of total federal spending is increasing rapidly, from 12.4 percent of total federal expenditures in 1985 to 20.3 percent in 1995, 26.5 percent in 2010, and a projected 30.3 percent in 2016. As baby boomers begin to retire and become eligible for Medicare in 2011, Medicare expenditures are expected to increase dramatically. Unless the federal government can reform Medicare and reduce its growth rate, the Medicare payroll tax on the working population will be sharply increased to prevent the Medicare trust fund from going bankrupt. To fund Medicare Part B, the prescription drug benefit (Medicare Part D), and subsidies under the new health legislation will require increasing income taxes, increasing an already large federal deficit, or reducing funding for other federal programs.

Thus, even if inefficiencies did not exist in the use or provision of medical services, large increases in Medicare and Medicaid expenditures, together with the additional expenditures to finance the subsidies included in the new health legislation, will lead to federal expenditures that exceed what the government is able to finance. The consumer products comparison presented earlier can be applied here as well: If the government were the purchaser of 50 percent of all automobiles, it would become concerned with the price and use of automobiles and expenditures on them. The pressure to continue funding Medicaid, Medicare, and the new healthcare entitlements through increased taxes or larger budget deficits is driving government to seek ways to limit medical expenditure increases.

Similarly, unions and employers are concerned with the rise in employee medical expenditures for reasons other than inefficiencies in the provision or use of services. The business sector's spending on health insurance premiums has risen rapidly over time, both as a percentage of total employee compensation and as a percentage of business profits. Health insurance, when offered, is part of an employee's total compensation. Employers are interested only in the total cost (income) of an employee, not in the form in which the employee takes it (i.e., wages or health benefits). Thus, the employee bears the cost of rising health insurance premiums because a rise in premiums means lower cash wages. Large unions, whose members receive generous health benefits, want to reduce the rate at which medical expenditures are increasing because they have seen more of their gains in compensation spent to finance health insurance payments than paid out to their members as increased wages.

Large employers were also seriously affected by the Financial Accounting Standards Board ruling stating that, starting in 1993, employers that promised medical benefits to their retirees are required to list this unfunded liability on their balance sheets. Employers previously paid their retiree medical expenses only as they occurred and did not set aside funds, as is done with pensions. By having to acknowledge these liabilities on their balance sheets, many large corporations, such as the automobile companies, have seen their net worth decline by billions of dollars. Furthermore, because these companies have to expense a portion of these future liabilities each year (not only for their present retirees but also for their future retirees), they have to report lower earnings per share. If the government were to reduce the rate of increase in medical expenditures, the net worth of companies with large unfunded retiree liabilities would increase, as would their earnings per share.

These differing reasons for concern over rising medical expenditures are important to recognize. Which concern should drive public policy—the government's desire not to raise revenues to fund its share of medical services, unions' and employers' interest in lowering employee and retiree medical expenses, or society's desire to achieve the appropriate rate of increase in medical expenditures? The interests of government, unions, and large employers have little to do with achieving an appropriate rate of growth in medical expenditures. Instead, their particular political and economic burdens drive their proposals for limiting increases in medical expenditures.

Approaches to Limiting Increases in Medical Expenditures

The United States should strive to reduce inefficiencies in both the provision and the use of medical services. Inefficiencies in the provision of services, however, are decreasing as managed care plans are forced to compete on price for enrollees. Vigilant application of the antitrust laws is needed to ensure that healthcare markets remain competitive and that providers, such as hospitals, do not monopolize their markets. Inefficiencies in the use of services are also declining as managed care plans control use of services through utilization management and patient cost sharing. As these inefficiencies are reduced, the growth rate in medical expenditures will approximate the "correct" rate of increase.

The public would naturally like to pay lower insurance premiums and out-of-pocket costs for their medical care and still have unlimited access to healthcare and to the latest medical technology. As in other sectors of the economy, however, choices must be made.

Medical expenditures have consistently increased faster than the rate of inflation, sometimes several times faster and sometimes by just several percentage points. Exhibit 2.2 shows the annual percentage change in health expenditures and inflation since 1965. During the mid-1990s, expenditure increases moderated as managed care enrollment increased. By the late 1990s, however, expenditures increased more rapidly as a result of the backlash against managed care and the consequent relaxation of managed care's cost-containment methods. In the past decade, medical care prices have moderated as the economy experienced problems, such as the financial crisis, and unemployment and the number of uninsured increased. Over time, medical expenditures are expected to continue rising faster than the inflation rate, driven by rising incomes, medical advances, and a growing aged population.

Some politicians believe they will receive the public's political support by proposing arbitrary limits on the amount by which medical expenditures and premiums may increase, discounts on drug prices for the aged, and managed care regulations that give enrollees freer access to specialists and other healthcare providers. What would be the consequences of limiting expenditure and premium increases to a rate lower than what we would otherwise see in an efficient but aging and technologically advanced medical system?

The United States is undergoing important demographic changes. The population is aging, and as it does, it will require more medical services, both to relieve suffering and to cure illnesses. Furthermore, the most important

EXHIBIT 2.2 Annual Percentage Changes in National Health Expenditures and the Consumer Price Index, 1965–2009

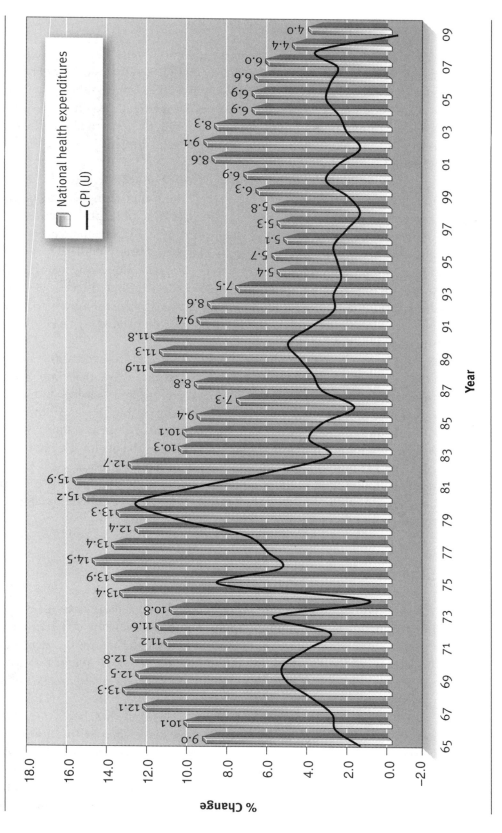

NOTE: CPI (U) = Consumer Price Index for all urban consumers.

SOURCE: BLS (2011); CMS (2011c).

reason for the rapid rise in medical expenditures has been the tremendous advances in medical science. Previously incurable diseases can now be cured, and other diseases can be diagnosed at an earlier stage. Although no cure is available for some diseases, life can be prolonged with expensive drugs, such as those for cancer and AIDS patients. Limiting the growth in medical expenditures to an arbitrarily low rate will decrease investment in new technologies and limit the availability of medical services.

Proposed cost-containment methods can achieve some reduction in the rate of increase. Insurers and payers could impose higher out-of-pocket payments; managed care organizations could require physicians to follow evidence-based medicine guidelines and disease management protocols; or plans could restrict enrollees to using only participating physicians, specialists, and hospitals. The middle class, however, appears unwilling to make these trade-offs; it wants both lower expenditures and unlimited access. (Politicians are responding to these concerns by indicating their willingness to regulate broader access to providers and services—without, however, acknowledging the higher premiums that would result.)

Yet, to significantly lower the rate of increase in expenditures and enable us to fund universal access to all will require more than implementing these cost-containment measures. To achieve this end, services and technology will have to be made less available to many people (Fuchs 1993).

Some politicians have led the public to believe these trade-offs are not necessary; they claim that by eliminating waste in the health system, universal coverage can be achieved and everyone can have all the medical care they need at a lower cost. Such rhetoric merely postpones the time when the public realizes it must make the unpleasant choice between spending and access to care.

Summary

Who should decide how much is to be spent on medical care? All countries face this basic question, and different countries have made different choices. In some countries, the government determines the allocation of resources among the medical sectors and controls medical prices. When the government makes these decisions, the trade-offs between cost and access are likely to be different from those that consumers will make.

In the United States, consumer sovereignty has been the guiding principle in allocating resources; consumers determine the amount of their income to be spent on medical services (except for those enrolled in Medicare and Medicaid). Yet, consumers have not always received value for their money. Inefficiencies in the medical sector, inappropriate provider incentives, and certain government regulations have made medical services more costly.

Furthermore, subsidies for the purchase of health insurance (tax-exempt, employer-paid health insurance) have resulted in greater use of services.

Thus, the debate over the appropriate amount to be spent on medical services is likely to be clarified once these two issues—the concept of consumer sovereignty and how to improve the efficiency of the current system—are separated.

Discussion Questions

1. How does a competitive market determine what types of goods and services to be produced, how much it costs to produce those goods and services, and who receives them?
2. Why do economists believe the value of additional employer-paid health insurance is worth less than its full cost?
3. Why do rising medical expenditures cause concern?
4. Why do inefficiencies exist in the use and provision of medical services?
5. Why are large employers and government concerned about rising medical expenditures?

Additional Readings

Aaron, H. 2003. "Should Public Policy Seek to Control the Growth of Health Care Spending?" *Health Affairs* (January 8): W3-29–W3-36. http://content .healthaffairs.org/cgi/reprint/hlthaff.w3.28v1.

Baker, L., H. Birnbaum, J. Geppert, D. Mishol, and E. Moyneur. 2003. "The Relationship Between Technology Availability and Health Care Spending." *Health Affairs* (November 5): W3-537–W3-551. http://content .healthaffairs.org/cgi/reprint/hlthaff.w3.537v1.

Pauly, M. 2003. "Should We Be Worried About High Real Medical Spending Growth in the United States?" *Health Affairs* (January 8): W3-15–W3-27. http://content.healthaffairs.org/cgi/reprint/hlthaff.w3.15v1.

DO MORE MEDICAL EXPENDITURES PRODUCE BETTER HEALTH?

The United States spends more per capita on medical services and devotes a larger percentage of its GDP to medical care than other countries, yet our health status is not proportionately better. In fact, many countries that have lower per capita medical expenditures than the United States also have lower infant mortality rates and higher life expectancies. Is our medical system less efficient at producing good health than these other countries, or are medical expenditures less important than other factors that affect health status?

Medical Services Versus Health

Medical services are often mistakenly considered synonymous with health. When policymakers talk of "health reform," they mean reform of the financing and delivery of medical services. Medical services consist of diagnosis and treatment of illness, which can lead to improved health. But medical services also consist of efforts to ameliorate pain and discomfort, of reassurance to well people who are worried, and of heroic treatments to those who are terminally ill. An indication that the objective of medical expenditures is primarily treatment of illness and not, more broadly, for improving health is that 23 percent of all medical expenditures ($511 billion in 2007) are spent on just 1 percent of the population.[1] Furthermore, almost one-half of those in that top 1 percent are over the age of 65. Increased medical expenditures, therefore, may have relatively little effect on a nation's health status.

The United States is generally acknowledged to have a technically superior medical system for treating acute illness. (For a brief but excellent discussion of criteria used to evaluate a country's health system, see Fuchs [1992].) Financing and payment incentives have all been directed toward this goal, and physician training has emphasized treatment rather than prevention of illness. Public policy debates with regard to medical services have been concerned with two issues: (1) equity, namely whether everyone has access to medical services and how those services should be financed, and (2) efficiency, such as whether medical services are efficiently produced. But knowing how to provide a medical treatment efficiently is not the same as knowing how to produce health efficiently.

In contrast to policy regarding medical services, health policy has been less well defined. The goal of health policy presumably should be to improve the population's health status or increase its life expectancy, in which case we should be concerned with the most efficient ways to improve that status. Assuming policymakers come to recognize this goal, they should understand that devoting more resources to medical care is just one way to improve health and is unlikely to be the most efficient way to do so.

The more accurate the definition of health, the more difficult health is to measure. Health is a state of physical, mental, and social well-being. More simply, health is defined as the absence of disease or injury. Empirically, health is defined by negative measures, such as mortality rates, days lost to sickness, or life expectancy. Measures of health can be broad, such as age-adjusted mortality rates, or they can be disease specific, such as neonatal infant mortality rates (within the first 27 days of birth) and age-adjusted death rates from heart disease. The advantage of using such crude measures is that they are readily available and are probably correlated with more comprehensive definitions of health. Unavailability of morbidity or quality-of-life measures, however, does not mean they are unimportant or should be neglected in analyses.

Health Production Function

To determine the relative importance of medical expenditures in decreasing mortality rates, economists use the concept of *health production function*. Simply stated, a health production function examines the relative contribution of each factor that affects health to determine the most cost-effective way to improve health. For example, mortality rates are affected by the use of medical services, environmental conditions (such as the amount of air and water pollution), education levels (which may indicate knowledge of disease prevention and ability to use the medical system when needed), and lifestyle behaviors (such as smoking, alcohol and substance abuse, diet, and exercise).

Each of these determinants of health has differential effects. For example, medical expenditures may initially cause mortality rates to drop significantly, as when a hospital establishes the first neonatal intensive care unit (NICU) in its community. Beds will be limited, so the first low-birth-weight infants admitted to the NICU will be those who are most critically ill and those most likely to benefit from the medical care provided and from continuous monitoring. As NICUs are added within that community, the neonatal infant mortality rate will decline by a smaller percentage. With a larger number of NICU beds, either the beds may be unused or the infants admitted to

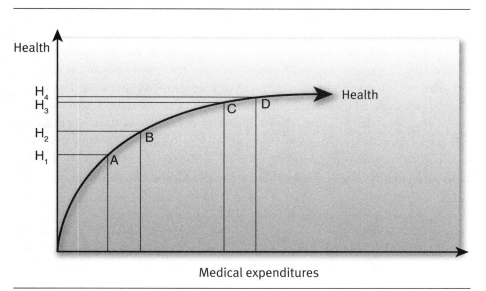

EXHIBIT 3.1
Effect of
Increased
Medical
Expenditures
on Health

those beds will not be as critically ill or high risk. Therefore, investment in additional NICU beds will have less of an effect on infant mortality.

Exhibit 3.1 illustrates the relationship between increased medical expenditures and improvements in health status. Increased expenditures produce a curvilinear rather than a constant effect on improved health. The marginal (additional) improvement becomes smaller as more is spent. As shown in Exhibit 3.1, an initial expenditure to improve health, moving from point A to point B, has a much larger marginal benefit (effect) than subsequent investments have, such as moving from point C to point D. The increase from point H_1 to point H_2 is greater than the increase from H_3 to H_4.

This same curvilinear relationship holds for each determinant of health. Expenditures to decrease air pollution, such as to install smog-control devices on automobiles, would reduce the incidence of respiratory illness. Additional spending by automobile owners, such as to have their smog-control devices tested once a year rather than every three years, would further reduce air pollution. The reduction in respiratory illness, however, would not be as great as that produced by the initial expenditure to install smog-control devices. The reduction in respiratory illness resulting from additional expenditures to control air pollution gradually declines.

Everyone would probably agree that additional lives could be saved if more infants were admitted to NICUs (or respiratory illness further decreased if smog-control inspections were conducted more frequently). More intensive monitoring might save a patient's life. However, those same funds could be spent on prevention programs to decrease the number of low-birth-weight infants, such as prenatal care programs or education programs that reduce teen pregnancy. The true "cost" of any program to decrease mortality is the number of lives that could have been saved if those same funds had been spent on another program.

Physicians, hospitals, dentists, and other health professionals all want increased government expenditures to decrease the unmet needs among their populations. However, the government cannot spend all that would be necessary to eliminate all medical, dental, mental, and other needs. To do so would mean forgoing the opportunity to eliminate other needs, as in welfare and education, because resources are limited. At some point it becomes too costly in terms of forgone opportunities to save all the lives that medical science is capable of saving. Reallocating those same expenditures to apprehend drunk drivers or improve highways might save even more lives.

Deciding which programs should be expanded to improve health status requires a calculation of the cost per life saved for each program that affects mortality rates. Looking at the curve in Exhibit 3.1, assume that an additional medical expenditure of $1 million results in a movement from point H_3 to point H_4, or from point C to point D, saving 20 additional lives. The same $1 million spent on an education program to reduce smoking may result in a movement from H_1 to H_2, or from A to B, saving an additional 40 lives from lung cancer. The expenditure for the smoking reduction program results in a lower cost per life saved ($1 million ÷ 40 = $25,000) than if those same funds were spent on additional medical services ($1 million ÷ 20 = $50,000). Continued expenditures on smoking cessation programs will result in a movement along the curve. At some point, fewer lung cancer deaths will be prevented (and the cost per life saved will increase), and a lower cost per life saved could then be achieved by spending additional funds on other programs such as stronger enforcement of drunk-driving laws.

Crucial to the calculation of cost per life saved is knowing (1) where the program, such as medical treatments or smoking cessation, sits on the curve shown in Exhibit 3.1 (that is, knowing the marginal benefit of that program) and (2) the cost of expanding that program. The costs per life saved by each program can be compared by dividing the cost of expanding each program by its marginal benefit. The enormous and rapidly increasing medical expenditures in the United States have likely placed the return to medical services beyond point D. Further improvements in health status from continued medical expenditures are very small. The cost of expanding medical treatments has also become expensive. Consequently, the cost per life saved through medical services is much higher than that for other programs.

Improving Health Status Cost Effectively

Numerous empirical studies have found that additional expenditures on medical services are not the most cost-effective way to improve health status. Medical programs have a much higher cost per life saved than nonmedical programs. Researchers have concluded that changing lifestyle behavior offers the greatest promise for lowering mortality rates, at a much lower cost per life saved.

The leading contributors to reductions in mortality rates over the past 40 years have been the decline in the neonatal infant mortality rate and the reduction in deaths from heart disease.

Neonatal Infant Mortality Rate

The neonatal mortality rate represents about two-thirds (65 percent in 2008) of the overall infant mortality rate; the decline in the overall mortality rate has been primarily attributed to the decline in the neonatal rate (National Center for Health Statistics 2010). For many years the neonatal infant mortality rate had steadily declined; however, starting in the mid-1960s the rate began declining more rapidly. The neonatal mortality rates for whites declined from 16.1 per 1,000 live births in 1965 to 3.6 in 2008, as shown in Exhibit 3.2. For African Americans the corresponding decline was from 26.5 to 8.2. During that period the availability of NICUs increased, government subsidies were provided for family planning services for low-income women, maternal and infant nutrition programs expanded, Medicaid was initiated and paid for obstetric services for those with low incomes, and abortion was legalized. Corman and Grossman (1985) found that increased education levels and subsidized nutrition programs were the most important factors in reducing the neonatal mortality rate among whites. The availability of abortion, followed by the increased availability of NICUs and higher education levels, was the most important factor among African Americans.

Simply knowing the reasons for the decline in neonatal mortality, however, is insufficient for deciding how to spend money to reduce neonatal mortality; it is important to know which programs are more cost effective. Joyce, Corman, and Grossman (1988) determined that teenage family planning programs, NICUs, and prenatal care saved 0.6, 2.8, and 4.5 lives, respectively, per 1,000 additional participants. The corresponding costs of adding 1,000 participants to each of these programs (in 1984 dollars) were $122,000, $13,616,000, and $176,000. To determine the cost per life saved by expanding each of these programs, the cost of the program was divided by the number of lives saved. As shown in Exhibit 3.3, the cost per life saved was $203,000 ($122,000 ÷ 0.6) for teenage family planning, $4,778,000 for NICUs, and $39,000 for prenatal care, the last being the most cost-effective program for reducing neonatal mortality. Reducing the potential number of women in high-risk pregnancies and the number of unwanted births (e.g., by providing teenage family-planning programs and prenatal care) offers a greater possibility of more favorable birth outcomes than investing in additional NICUs.

EXHIBIT 3.2 Neonatal Mortality Rates, by Race, 1950–2008

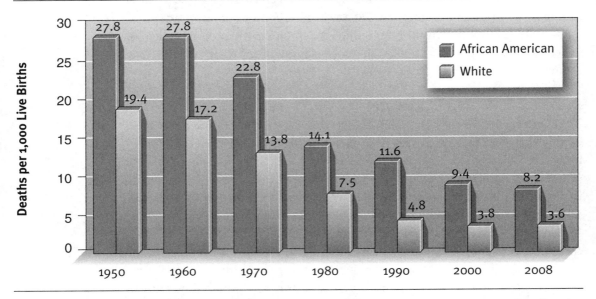

SOURCE: 1950–1970 data from US Census Bureau (2009a); 1980–2000 data from US Census Bureau (2009b); 2008 data from National Center for Health Statistics (2010, table 4).

Heart Disease Mortality Rate

The leading cause of death in the United States is cardiovascular disease. Between 1970 and 2008, the mortality rate from diseases of the heart declined more rapidly than that for any other cause of death, from 362 per 100,000 to 203 per 100,000 (National Center for Health Statistics 2010). Improvements in medical technology (such as coronary bypass surgery, coronary care units, angioplasty, and clot-dissolving drugs) as well as changes in lifestyle (such as the reduction in smoking, increased exercise, and changes in diet that lower cholesterol levels) contributed to this decline in mortality from heart disease. One study estimated that the development of new treatment techniques and their increased use over time decreased cardiovascular disease deaths by about one-third. The remaining two-thirds of the reduction in deaths from heart disease are attributed to a reduction in risk factors through prevention, including new drugs to control hypertension, high cholesterol, and smoking cessation (Cutler and Kadiyala 2003). These lifestyle changes, however, are not seen uniformly across the population; those with more education are more likely to undertake them.

Cutler and Kadiyala (2003) and many others that have examined the reduction in heart disease deaths over time reach a similar conclusion: Lifestyle changes are more important—and much less expensive—than medical interventions (Feldstein 2011) in improving health.

Exhibit 3.3 Cost per Life Saved Among Three Programs to Reduce Neonatal Mortality (Whites)

	Number of Lives Saved per 1,000 Additional Participants	Cost of Each Program per 1,000 Additional Participants ($1,984 in Thousands)	Cost per Life Saved ($1,984 in Thousands)
Teenage family planning	0.6	$122	$203
Neonatal ICUs	2.8	$13,616	$4,778
Prenatal care	4.5	$176	$39

SOURCE: Joyce, Corman, and Grossman (1988). Reprinted with permission.

Causes of Death by Age Group

Perhaps the clearest indication that lifestyle behavior is an important determinant of mortality is the causes of death by age group. As shown in Exhibit 3.4, the main causes of death for young adults (aged 15 to 24 years) are accidents (particularly auto), homicides, and suicides. For those in the middle age groups, accidents, cancer, heart disease, suicides, homicides, and human immunodeficiency virus (HIV) infection are the major causes of death. For those in late middle age, cancer and heart disease are the leading causes of death. After examining data by cause of death, Victor Fuchs (1974, 46) concluded that medical services have a smaller effect on health than the way in which people live: "The greatest potential for reducing coronary disease, cancer, and the other major killers still lies in altering personal behavior."

Relationship of Medical Care to Health over Time

The above studies have shown that the marginal contribution of medical care to improved health is relatively small. Improvements in health status can be achieved in a less costly manner through increased spending on lifestyle factors. Over time, however, major technological advances have been seen in medical care, such as new drugs to lower cholesterol and treat hypertension, diagnostic imaging, less invasive surgery, organ and tissue transplants, and treatment for previously untreatable diseases. Few would deny that these advances have reduced mortality rates and increased life expectancy.

EXHIBIT 3.4
Leading Causes
of Death, by
Age Group,
2008

Age Group	Major Causes of Death	Deaths per 100,000
15–24	All causes	75.7
	Accidents	32.9
	Homicide and legal intervention	12.4
	Suicide	10.1
	Cancer	3.9
	Heart disease	2.5
25–44	All causes	142.3
	Accidents	36.3
	Cancer	19.5
	Heart disease	17.4
	Suicide	14.3
	Homicide and legal intervention	9.0
	HIV infection	4.6
45–64	All causes	618.6
	Cancer	198.2
	Heart disease	133.8
	Accidents	42.0
	Pulmonary disease	23.6
	Diabetes mellitus	21.8
	Chronic liver disease/cirrhosis	21.5
	Cerebrovascular disease	21.3

SOURCE: National Center for Health Statistics (2010).

Cutler and Richardson (1999) reconcile these seemingly conflicting findings by separating medical care's effect *at a point in time* versus its technological contribution *over time*. The authors illustrate the relationship between the total contribution of medical care to health and greater quantities of medical care using the graphic shown in Exhibit 3.5. Comprehensive health insurance and fee-for-service physician payment reduce both the patient's and the physician's incentive to be concerned with the cost of care, resulting in the medical care system moving to point A in Exhibit 3.5, where the marginal

EXHIBIT 3.5
Relationship
Between
Medical Care
and Health

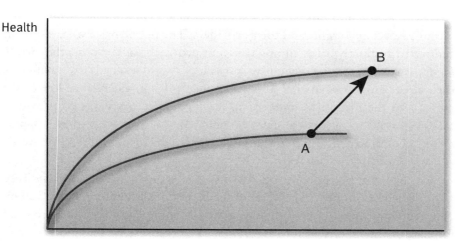

Health

B

A

Medical care

SOURCE: Reprinted from David Cutler and Elizabeth Richardson, "Your Money and Your Life: The Value of Health and What Affects It," in *Frontiers in Health Policy Research*, vol. 2, ed. Alan Garber (Cambridge, Mass.: MIT Press, 1999), pp. 99–132, figure 5-6.

contribution of medical care to health is very small. Additional medical care expenditures increase health, but at a decreasing rate.

Eventually, however, medical advances shift the production function for health upward. The level of health has improved, and the number of patients treated has increased, but the marginal contribution of medical care is still low, at point B. Too many patients whose need for treatment is doubtful are treated with the new technology, or excess capacity occurs as too much of the new technology is made available.

Thus, although the public believes the medical care they receive today is much more valuable than treatments received 30 years ago, the medical care system remains inefficient; the marginal benefit of additional medical expenditures is low (Skinner, Staiger, and Fisher 2006).

Summary

If expenditures on medical services have been shown to be less cost effective in reducing mortality rates than are changes in lifestyle behavior, why does the United States spend an increasing portion of its resources on medical care?

First, health insurance coverage has been so comprehensive, with low deductibles and small copayments, that individuals faced a very low out-of-pocket price when they went to the hospital or a specialist. Thus, patients used more medical services than if they had to pay a greater portion of the cost. The expression "the insurance will cover it" is indicative of the lack of incentives facing patients and their providers. The public has also had little incentive to compare prices among different providers, as the costs they would incur searching for less expensive providers would exceed any savings on their already low copayments. It is also not surprising, given these low copayments and the incentives inherent in fee-for-service payments to providers, that enormous resources are spent on people in their last year of life. Rapidly rising medical expenditures and limited reductions in mortality rates are the consequences of this behavior.

Second, the primary objective of government medical expenditures has not been to improve health and decrease mortality rates. Medicare benefits the elderly, and approximately half of Medicaid expenditures are spent for care of the elderly in nursing homes. The purpose of these government expenditures is to help the aged finance their medical needs. Were the government's objective to improve the nation's health, the types of services financed would be very different, as would the age groups that would most benefit from those expenditures. (One factor to consider is that the aged are perhaps the most politically powerful group in US society.)

Although medical expenditures have a relatively small marginal effect on health, it would be incorrect to conclude that the government should limit all medical expenditure increases. To an individual, additional medical services may be worth the additional cost, even when they are not subsidized. As incomes increase, people are willing to purchase medical services to relieve anxiety and seek relief of pain, which are not life-saving events but are entirely appropriate personal expenditures. From society's perspective, financing medical services for those with low incomes is also appropriate. As society becomes wealthier, individuals and government are willing to make more non-life-saving medical expenditures. These "consumption" versus "investment" types of medical expenditures are appropriate as long as everyone involved recognizes them for what they are.

When government attempts to improve the health of those with low incomes, using the concept of a health production function, expenditures will be directed toward the most cost-effective programs, that is, those that result in the lowest cost per life saved. Allocating funds in this manner will achieve a greater reduction in mortality rates for a given total expenditure than any other allocation method.

The health production function concept is increasingly used by employers and health plans that face financial pressures to reduce their medical costs. Employers' use of health risk appraisal questionnaires recognizes that employees' health can be improved less expensively by changes in lifestyle behavior. Incentives given to employees who stop smoking, reduce their weight, and exercise enable employers to retain a skilled workforce longer while reducing medical expenditures. The emphasis by health plans on reducing per capita medical costs has led them to identify those high-risk groups that can benefit from early preventive measures to reduce costly medical treatments.

The recognition by government, employers, health plans, and individuals that resources are scarce and that their objective is improved health rather than provision of additional medical services will lead to new approaches to improve health. The concept of a health production function should clarify the trade-offs between different programs and improve the allocation of expenditures.

Discussion Questions

1. How can a health production function allocate funds to improve health status?
2. Why does the United States spend an increasing portion of its resources on medical services, although they are less cost effective than other methods for improving health status?
3. How can employers use the health production function to decrease their employees' medical expenditures?
4. Describe a production function for decreasing deaths from coronary heart disease.
5. Describe a production function for decreasing deaths of young adults.

Note

1. Furthermore, in 2007, 50 percent of total medical expenditures were spent on 5 percent of the population. Nearly half (42 percent) of those upon whom a great amount of money was spent were elderly (Yu 2010).

IN WHOSE INTEREST DOES THE PHYSICIAN ACT?

Physicians have always played a crucial role in the delivery of medical services. Although only 24.2 percent of personal medical expenditures are for physician services, physicians control the use of a much larger portion of total medical resources (CMS 2011c). In addition to their own services, physicians determine admission to the hospital, length of stay in the hospital, use of ancillary services and prescription drugs, referrals to specialists, and even the necessity for services in non-hospital settings, such as home care. Any public policies that affect the financing and delivery of medical services must consider physicians' responses to those policies. A physician's knowledge and motivation will affect the efficiency with which medical services are delivered.

The role of the physician has been shaped by two important characteristics of the medical system. The first is the legal system: Only physicians are permitted to provide certain services. Second, both patients and insurers lack the necessary information to make many medically related decisions. The patient depends on the physician for the diagnosis and the recommended treatment and has limited information on the physician's qualifications or on specialists to whom he is referred. This lack of information places patients in a unique relationship with physicians: The physician becomes the patient's agent (McGuire 2000).

The Physician as a Perfect Agent for the Patient

The agency relationship gives rise to a major controversy in the medical economics literature. In whose best interest does the physician act? If the physician were a *perfect agent* for the patient, he would prescribe the mix of institutional settings and the amount of care provided in each based on the patient's medical needs, ability to pay for medical services, and preferences. The physician and the patient would behave as if the patient were as well informed as the physician. Traditional indemnity insurance, once the prevalent form of health insurance, reimbursed the physician on a fee-for-service basis;

neither the physician nor the patient was fiscally responsible or at risk for using the hospital and medical services.

Before the 1980s, Blue Cross predominantly covered hospital care; all inpatient services were covered without any patient cost sharing. Although hospital stays are more costly than outpatient care in terms of resources used, patients paid less to receive a diagnostic workup in the hospital than they would have as outpatients. While this was an inefficient use of resources, the physician acted in the patient's interest and not the insurer's. Similarly, if a woman wanted to stay a few extra days in the hospital after giving birth, the physician would not discharge her before she was ready to return home.

As the patient's agent, the quantity and type of services the physician prescribed would be based on the value to the patient of that additional care and the patient's cost for that care. As long as the value to the patient of that care exceeded the patient's costs for that care, the physician would prescribe it. By considering only the patient's costs and the benefits of additional medical services, the physician neglected the costs to society of those resources and the costs to the insurance company.

Indemnity insurance and the role of the physician as the patient's agent led the physician to practice what Victor Fuchs (1968) referred to as the *technologic imperative*. Regardless of how small the benefit to the patient or how costly to the insurer, the physician would prescribe the best medical care technically possible. As a consequence, heroic measures were provided to patients in the last few months of their lives, and inpatient hospital costs rose rapidly. Prescribing "low-benefit" care was a rational economic decision because it still exceeded the patient's cost, which was virtually zero with comprehensive insurance.

Supplier-Induced Demand

The view of the physician as the patient's agent, however, neglects the economic self-interest of the physician. As shown in Exhibit 4.1, large increases in the total number of physicians and the number of physicians relative to population have occurred since the 1970s. The number of physicians has almost tripled since 1970, and the physician-to-population ratio has almost doubled. The standard economic model, which assumes the physician is a perfect agent for the patient, would predict that an increase in supply, other things (such as increased consumer incomes) being equal, would result in a decline in physicians' fees and, consequently, in physician incomes.

Increases in the physician-to-population ratio, however, did not lead to declines in physician incomes. This observation led to the development of an alternative theory of physician behavior. Physicians are believed to behave differently when their own incomes are adversely affected. In addition to being patients' agents, physicians are suppliers of a service. Their incomes

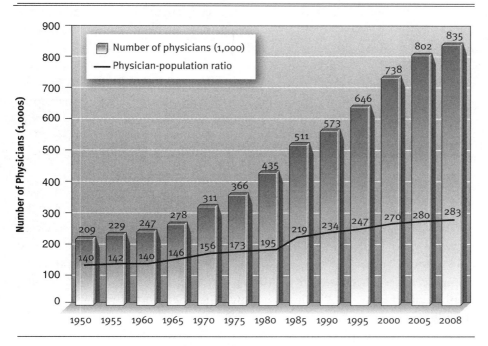

EXHIBIT 4.1

Number of Active Physicians and Physician-to-Population Ratio, 1950–2008

NOTE: Physician-to-population ratio is for active physicians and the noninstitutionalized civilian population.

Active physicians are federal and non-federal physicians who are involved in patient care or non-patient care (teaching, research administration, or other professional activities) for more than 20 hours a week. Active physicians also include unclassified physicians, i.e., physicians whose activity status or present employment setting is not known.

SOURCES: *Physician Characteristics and Distribution in the United States,* 1981, 2010 eds., Division of Survey and Data Resources (Chicago: American Medical Association, 1982, 2010); Bureau of the Census, *Statistical Abstract of the United States,* various editions.

depend on how much of that service they supply. Do physicians use their information advantage over patients and insurers to benefit themselves? This model of physician behavior is referred to as *supplier-induced demand.*

The supplier-induced demand theory assumes that if the physician's income falls, the physician will use her role as the patient's agent to prescribe additional services. The physician provides the patient with misinformation to increase the patient's demand for physician services, thereby increasing the physician's income. In other words, the physician becomes an *imperfect agent.*

Physicians might rationalize some demand inducement by arguing that additional services or tests would be beneficial to the patient. However, as more and more services are recommended, the physician must choose between the additional income received and the psychological cost of knowing that those additional services are not really necessary. At some point, the additional revenue the physician receives is not worth the psychological cost of prescribing such services. The physician must make a trade-off between increased income and the dissatisfaction of knowingly providing too many services.

Thus, one might envisage a spectrum of demand inducement depending on the psychological cost to the physician of greater demand inducement. At one end of the spectrum are those physicians who act solely in their patients' interests; they do not induce demand to increase or even maintain their incomes. At the other end of the spectrum are physicians who attempt to increase their incomes as much as possible by inducing demand; these physicians presumably incur little psychological cost when they induce demand. In the middle are physicians who induce demand to achieve some target level of income. (The idea that physicians induce demand only to the extent that they can maintain or achieve a given level of income is referred to as the *target income theory.*)

The extent to which the physician is willing and able to induce additional demand for medical services is controversial. Few believe that the majority of physicians would induce demand as much as possible solely to increase their incomes. Similarly, few would disagree that physicians are able to induce some additional demand. Thus, the choice is between the idea of physicians as perfect agents for their patients and the target income model of physician behavior. The issue is how much demand physicians are able to induce.

Demand inducement is limited to some extent by the patient's recognition that the additional medical benefits are not worth the time or cost of returning to the physician. The patient's evaluation of the benefits from additional services, however, varies according to the treatment prescribed. Patients may more easily determine that additional office visits are not worth their time and the cost of returning; however, they have more difficulty evaluating the benefits from certain surgical services. Demand inducement presumably is more likely to occur for those services about which the patient knows least; consequently, there is more concern about inducement in such cases.

Many studies have attempted to determine the extent of demand inducement (see, for example, Feldstein 2011), and the issue is still unresolved. Evidence shows that geographic areas (cities and counties) that have a larger supply of physicians (in relation to the population) also have greater per capita use of physician services. This relationship, however, may merely indicate that physicians locate where the population has higher insurance coverage and, consequently, where demand for their services is greater. One study concluded that primary care physicians are limited in the amount of demand they can induce, although how much demand they may already have induced remains unknown (McCarthy 1985). The positive correlation between the number of surgeons and the number of surgeries has been used as empirical support for the supplier-induced demand theory. Furthermore, studies have found that the rates of surgeries for procedures such as tonsillectomies and hysterectomies are higher when physicians are paid fee-for-service than when they have different income incentives, such as those available to physicians in an HMO.

Increase in Physician Supply

The large increase in physician supply since the 1970s illustrates the importance of knowing which model of physician behavior, the perfect agent or supplier-induced demand, is prevalent. As a perfect agent for the patient, the physician would consider only the patient's medical and economic interests when prescribing a treatment, regardless of the fact that his income may decline because the greater supply of physicians may decrease the number of patients he sees.

On the other hand, according to the supplier-induced demand model, an increase in the supply of physicians will cause physicians to induce demand to prevent their incomes from falling. Total physician expenditures would also increase as a larger number of physicians, each with fewer patients, attempt to maintain their incomes. Thus, depending on whether one believes in standard economic models or supplier-induced demand, increases in the supply of physicians lead to opposite predictions of their effect on physician prices and incomes.

Insurers' Response to Demand Inducement

Insurers recognize that under fee-for-service payment, physicians act either as the patient's agent or to maintain their own income. In either case the value of additional benefits a physician prescribes is lower than the insurer's cost for those services. Consequently, the premium for indemnity insurance will be higher in a fee-for-service environment than for managed care plans, which theoretically attempt to relate the value of additional medical treatment to the resource costs of those additional services. As a result of the higher relative premium of indemnity insurance to that of HMOs, more of the insurer's subscribers will presumably switch to HMOs. Since about 2000, therefore, insurers have developed mechanisms to overcome the information advantage that physicians have over both the insurers and the patients.

Insurers have, for example, implemented second-opinion requirements for surgery. Once a physician recommends certain types of surgery of doubtful medical necessity, such as back surgery, a patient may be required to receive a second opinion from a list of physicians approved by the insurer. Another approach insurers use is the creation of preferred provider organizations (PPOs). Physicians are selected who offer lower fees, use fewer medical services, and are considered to be of high quality. A third approach is utilization review. Before a hospital admission or a surgical procedure, a patient must receive the insurer's approval; otherwise, the patient is subject to a financial penalty. The length of stay in the hospital is also subject to the insurer's approval.

These cost-containment approaches by insurers are an attempt to address the imbalances in physician and patient incentives under a fee-for-service system. Furthermore, they ensure that the patient receives appropriate care (when the physician acts to increase her own income) and that the resource costs of a treatment are considered along with its expected benefits.

HMOs

The growth of HMOs and capitation payment provides physicians with incentives to increase their incomes that are opposite those of the traditional indemnity fee-for-service approach. HMOs typically reward their physicians with profit sharing or bonuses if their enrollees' medical costs are lower than their annual capitation payments. What are the likely effects of these differing models of physician behavior—the perfect agent and the imperfect agent—on an HMO's patients?

In an HMO setting, a perfect-agent physician would continue to provide the patient with appropriate medical services. Regardless of the effect of profit sharing on his income or pressures from the HMO to reduce use of services, the perfect-agent physician would be primarily concerned with protecting patients' interests and providing them with the best medical care, so there is little likelihood of underservice. Unlike with indemnity insurance, in an HMO the physician would not need to be concerned over whether the patient's insurance covered the medical cost in different settings. HMO patients are also responsible for fewer deductibles and copayments. Thus, the settings chosen for providing the patient's treatment are likely to be less costly for both the patient and the HMO.

The concern that patients would be underserved in an HMO exists with regard to imperfect-agent physicians, those who attempt to increase their incomes. HMO physicians have an incentive to provide fewer services to their patients and to serve a larger number of patients. Those HMO physicians who are concerned with the size of their income are more likely to respond to profit-sharing incentives. At times, a physician, who may even be salaried, may succumb to an HMO's pressures to reduce use of services and thereby become an imperfect agent. If HMO patients believe they are being denied timely access to the physician, specialist services, or needed technology, they are likely to try to switch HMO physicians or disenroll at the next open enrollment period. Too high a dissatisfaction rate with certain HMO physicians could indicate that their patients are underserved.

An HMO should be concerned with underservice by its physicians. Although the HMO's profitability will increase if its physicians provide too few services, an HMO that limits access to care and fails to satisfy its subscribers risks losing market share to its competitors.

The more knowledgeable subscribers are regarding access to care provided by different HMOs, the greater will be the HMO's financial incentive not to pressure its physicians to underserve its patients. Instead, it will have incentive to monitor physicians to guard against underservice. Gathering information on HMOs and their physicians or on how well their enrollees are served is costly for individuals in terms of time and money. It is less costly for employers to gather this information, make it available to their employees, and even limit the HMOs from which their employees can choose.

Informed Purchasers

Informed purchasers are necessary if the market is to discipline imperfect agents. An HMO's reputation is an expensive asset that can be reduced by imperfect-agent physicians underserving their patients. Performance information and competition among HMOs for informed purchasers should prevent these organizations from underserving their enrollees. The financial, reputation, and legal costs of underservice should mitigate the financial incentives to underprescribe in an HMO.

Both indemnity insurers and HMOs lack information on a patient's diagnosis and appropriate treatment needs. Thus, the insurer's (or HMO's) profitability depends on the physician's knowledge and treatment recommendations. Depending on the type of insurance plan and the incentives physicians face, a potential inefficiency exists in the provision of medical services. Physicians may prescribe too many or too few services. When they prescribe too many services, the value to the patient of those additional services may not be worth the costs of producing them. Too few services are also inefficient in that patients may not realize that the value of the services and technology they did not receive (and for which they were willing to pay) is greater than their physician led them to believe. To decrease the inefficiencies arising from too many services as a result of demand inducement, indemnity insurers who pay physicians on a fee-for-service basis have instituted cost-containment methods.

Medicare, as a fee-for-service insurer for physician services for the aged, has not yet undertaken similar cost-containment methods to limit supplier-induced demand. Until Medicare is able to institute such mechanisms, imperfect-agent physicians will be able to manipulate the information they provide to the aged, change the visit coding to receive higher payment, and decrease the time spent per visit with aged patients.

Monitoring physician behavior within HMOs and other managed care insurers has increased. Physicians who were previously in fee-for-service and who increased their incomes by prescribing too many services are being reviewed to ensure that they understand the change in incentives. Once they are aware of the new incentives, imperfect-agent physicians must be monitored to ensure that they do not underserve their HMO patients.

The market for medical services is changing. Insurers and large employers are attempting to overcome physicians' information advantage by profiling physicians according to their prices, use and appropriateness of services provided, and treatment outcomes. These profiles allow imperfect-agent physicians less opportunity to benefit at the expense of the insurer. Information on physician performance is available on the Internet, and states such as New York publish data on physician and hospital performance, such as risk-adjusted mortality rates for different types of surgery.[1] Demand inducement, to the extent that it exists, will diminish. One hopes that with improved monitoring systems and better measures of patient outcomes, physicians will behave as perfect agents, providing the appropriate quantity and quality of medical services, where the costs of additional treatment are considered as well as the benefits.

Insurers serving millions of enrollees have very large data sets, which information technology allows them to use to analyze different treatment methods and physician practice patterns. These data will enable insurers to determine which physicians deviate from accepted medical norms in their treatment patterns.

Not all insurers or employers, however, are engaged in these informational and cost-containment activities. Those who are not are at an informational disadvantage to the physician and the HMO. Insurers and employers who are less knowledgeable regarding the services provided to their employees pay for overuse of services and demand-inducing behavior by fee-for-service providers and underservice by HMO physicians. Medicare and Medicaid, whose payment methods are primarily fee-for-service, are also limited in cost containment activities to reduce demand inducement. At some point such purchasers will realize that investing in more information will lower their medical expenditures and improve the quality of care provided.

Summary

Under fee-for-service payment, the inability of patients and their insurers to distinguish between imperfect-agent and perfect-agent physicians led to the growth of cost-containment methods. The changes occurring in the private sector and in government physician payment systems must take into account different types of physicians and the fact that, unless physicians are appropriately monitored, the response by imperfect-agent physicians will make achieving the intended objectives difficult.

Discussion Questions

1. Why do physicians play such a crucial role in the delivery of medical services?
2. How might a decrease in physician incomes, possibly as a result of an increase in the number of physicians, affect the physician's role as the patient's agent?
3. What are some ways in which insurers seek to compensate for physicians' information advantage?
4. What forces currently limit supplier-induced demand?
5. How do fee-for-service and capitation payment systems affect the physician's role as the patient's agent?

Additional Readings

McGuire, T. G. 2008. "Physician Fees and Behavior: Implications for Structuring a Fee Schedule." In *Incentives and Choice in Health Care*, edited by F. Sloan and H. Kasper, 263–89. Cambridge, MA: MIT Press.

Mitchell, J. M. 2008. "Do Financial Incentives Linked to Ownership of Specialty Hospitals Affect Physicians' Practice Patterns?" *Medical Care* 46 (7): 732–37.

Note

1. Information on websites and reports on physician and hospital performance come from www.consumerhealthratings.com/index .php?action=showSubCats&cat_id=301. That website includes links to different states' reports, for example:
   - www.massdac.org/sites/default/files/reports/CABG%20FY2007 .pdf
   - www.state.nj.us/health/healthcarequality/cardiacsurgery .shtml#CSR
   - www.nyhealth.gov/statistics/diseases/cardiovascular.

RATIONING MEDICAL SERVICES

No country can afford to provide unlimited medical services to everyone. Although few would disagree that waste exists in the current system, all of America's medical needs could not be fulfilled even if that waste were eliminated and those resources redirected. A large, one-time savings would result from eliminating inefficiencies, but driven by population growth, an aging population, and advances in medical technology, medical expenditures would continue to increase faster than inflation. As new experimental treatments, such as Avastin, a tumor-starving drug therapy used for cancer treatment, are developed—no matter how uncertain or small their effect—making them routinely available to all those who might benefit would be costly. The resources needed to eliminate all our medical needs, including prescription drugs, mental health services, long-term care, dental care, and vision care, as well as for acute, chronic, and preventive services, would be enormous.

The cost of eliminating all medical needs, no matter how small, means forgoing the benefits of spending those resources to meet other needs, such as food, clothing, housing, and education. Forgoing these other needs is the real cost of fulfilling all our medical needs. As no country can afford to spend unlimited resources on medical services, each must choose some mechanism to ration or limit access to medical services.

Government Rationing

Rationing occurs by one of two methods. The first and most frequently used method is government limits on access to goods and services. During World War II, for example, food, gasoline, and other goods were rationed; their prices were kept artificially low, but people could not buy all they wanted at the prevailing price. Similarly, in the 1970s, a gasoline shortage developed when the government kept the price of gasoline below its market price. The available supply was effectively rationed because people had to wait long hours at gasoline stations. Although they were willing to pay higher prices, they were not permitted to do so, because gas prices were set by the government.

This type of rationing is also used to allocate medical services in countries such as Great Britain. The British government sets low prices for medical services and limits expenditures on those services. Because there is a shortage of services at their prevailing prices, these scarce services are explicitly allocated according to a person's age, as when denying kidney transplants to those over a certain age, or by setting a value on a human life to determine whether costly treatments should be provided (Harris 2008). In Canada (Barua, Rovere, and Skinner 2010), rationing is implicit according to a queue, in which a person may wait months or up to a year for certain surgical procedures, such as hip replacements.

In the United States, only Oregon has proposed such an explicit system of rationing medical services. In contrast to other states, which provide unlimited medical services to a small portion of the poor, the Oregon legislature decided to limit Medicaid recipients' access to expensive procedures, such as organ transplants, and in turn to increase Medicaid eligibility for more low-income persons. The state ranked all medical services according to the outcomes that could be expected from treatment (e.g., "prevents death with full recovery") and according to their effect on quality of life. Because the state budget is unlikely to ever be sufficient to fund all medical procedures to all of the poor, those procedures at the lower end of the rankings would not be funded.

Rationing by Ability to Pay

Among the general population in the United States, medical services are not rationed so explicitly. Instead, a different type of rationing is used, essentially to distribute goods and services according to those who can afford to pay for them. There are no shortages of services for those who are willing to pay (either out of pocket or through insurance). People with low incomes and without health insurance receive fewer medical services than those who have higher incomes.

Medical services involve a great deal of discretionary use. Empirical studies show that a 10 percent increase in income leads to an approximate 10 percent increase in medical expenditures (Congressional Budget Office 2008b). As incomes increase, the amount spent on medical services increases proportionately. This relationship between income and medical spending exists not only in this country but across all countries. As shown in Exhibit 5.1, the higher the country's income, the greater its medical expenditures.

This observed relationship between income and medical expenditures suggests that as people become wealthier, they prefer to spend more on medical care to receive more and higher-quality services. They also make greater use of specialists, and they are willing to pay more to avoid waiting to receive those services.

EXHIBIT 5.1 Health Spending and Personal Income in Different Countries, 2008

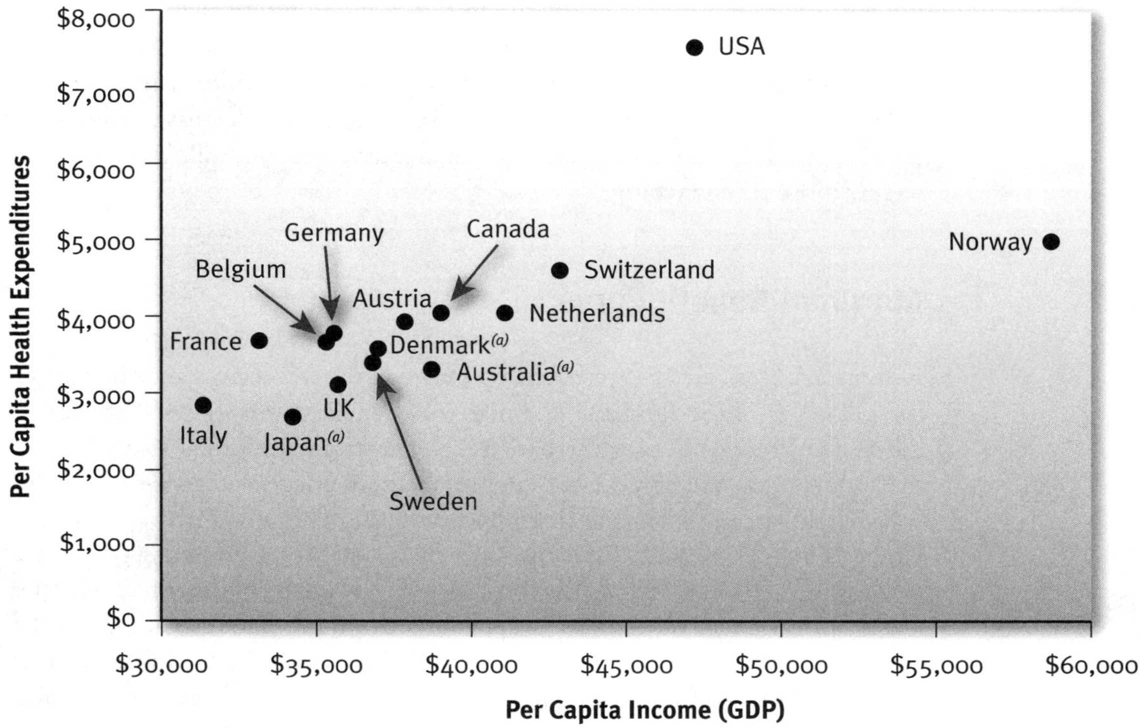

(a)Per Capita Health Expenditures for 2007

NOTE: All values are US dollars measured in GDP purchasing power parities.
SOURCE: Organisation for Economic Co-operation and Development. 2010. *OECD Health Data*. Paris: OECD.

Decision Making by Consumers of Medical Services

Understanding why people use medical services requires more than knowing whether they are ill. Also important are their attitudes toward seeking care, the prices they must pay for such care, and their incomes.

Whether rationing is based on ability to pay or on government expenditure limits on medical services, patients are faced with prices they must pay for medical services. These prices may be artificially low, as in Great Britain or Canada, or they may reflect the cost of providing those medical services, as in a market-oriented system such as the United States has. Regardless of how they are determined, prices are an essential ingredient in consumer decision making.

Consumers spend (allocate) their money based on the value they place on different needs, how much income they have, and the prices of their different choices. Consumers are faced with an array of choices, each offering additional benefits, but each choice has a different price. Consumers choose not just on the basis of the additional benefits they would receive but also on the cost of achieving those benefits. In this manner, prices enable consumers to decide to which services they will allocate their incomes.

Of course, making one choice means forgoing other choices. Similarly, as the prices of some choices increase while others decrease, consumers are likely to reallocate their spending. An increase in income allows consumers to buy more of everything.

Marginal Benefit Curve

Exhibit 5.2 illustrates the relationship between use of services and the cost to the patient of those services. The marginal benefit curve shows that the additional (marginal) benefit the patient receives from additional visits declines as use of services increases. For example, a patient concerned about her health will benefit greatly from the first physician visit. The physician will take the patient's history, perhaps perform some diagnostic tests, and possibly write a prescription. A follow-up visit will enable the physician to determine whether the diagnosis and treatment were appropriate and provide reassurance to the patient. The marginal benefit of that second visit will not be as high as the first visit. Additional return visits without any indication of a continuing health problem will provide further reassurance, but the value to the patient of those additional visits will be much lower than the initial visits.

How rapidly the marginal benefit curve declines depends on the patient's attitude toward seeking care and the value she places on that additional care. Not all patients place the same value on medical services. For some, the marginal benefit curve will decline quickly after the initial treatment; for others, the decline will be more gradual.

The actual number of patient visits is determined by the cost to the patient for each visit. Given the patient's marginal benefit curve and a price per visit of $100, as shown in Exhibit 5.2, the marginal benefit to the patient of the first visit exceeds the cost of $100. The patient will demand a total of two visits because the marginal benefit of that second visit equals the cost of that visit. If the patient makes more than two visits, the value the patient receives from the third visit would be less than its cost.

Thus, the demand for medical services is determined by the value to the patient (either real or imagined) of those visits and the patient's cost for each visit. When the cost is greater than the value of an additional visit, the patient will not make the additional visit; the patient could receive greater value for his money by spending it on other goods and services.

Health insurance reduces the patient's costs for medical care. Although the insurer pays the physician (or hospital) the full price, the patient

EXHIBIT 5.2 Relationship Among Prices, Visits, and Marginal Benefit of an Additional Visit

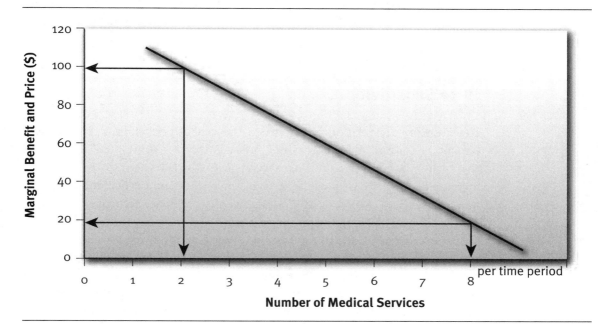

pays a reduced out-of-pocket price. For example, if the charge for a physician's office visit is $100 and health insurance pays 80 percent of the charge,
the "real" price to the patient is only $20. As the patient's cost for an office
visit declines from $100 to $20, the patient will increase the number of visits.
The patient will make additional visits until the value received from the last
visit is worth only $20.

The patient's decision to use medical services is based solely on a
calculation of her own costs (copayment) and the perceived value of those
additional visits. Although the real cost of each visit is $100, the patient's cost
for additional visits is only $20. The consequence is too much medical care;
the value to the patient of additional visits is worth less than the full cost of
those visits.

In using medical services, the patient usually incurs travel and waiting
costs. The importance of these costs differs among patients. Typically, retired
persons have low waiting costs, whereas working mothers have high waiting
costs. To predict use of services, travel and waiting costs, as well as out-of-
pocket payments, must be weighed against the marginal benefit of another
visit. A medical system that has high out-of-pocket payments and low waiting
costs will affect usage patterns differently than a system that relies on low
prices but high waiting costs.

An important empirical question is this: How rapid is the decline in
value of additional services to the patient? If the first visit is worth more than

$100 to the patient and the second visit is only worth $10, little if any overuse of medical services will occur. If, however, a second visit is worth $100 and the value of subsequent visits declines slowly, the patient will make many visits before the value of a visit falls below $20.

Price Sensitivity

Research on the relationship between the out-of-pocket price paid by the patient and use of medical services indicates that for some medical services, the decline in value of additional services is gradual. In general, a 10 percent increase in the price of medical services leads to about a 2 percent reduction in use of services (Morrisey 2005). Price sensitivity varies according to type of medical service. Mental health services are quite price sensitive; a 10 percent reduction in price leads to a 10 percent increase in use of services. Hospital services are the least price sensitive; hospital admissions would increase by about 1.5 percent with a 10 percent decrease in price. Lowering the price of physician services by 10 percent increases use by about 2 percent. Higher-income groups are generally less price sensitive than lower-income groups. Nursing home services are price sensitive; lowering prices by 10 percent leads to about a 10 percent increase in use (Morrisey 2005). This finding suggests that including long-term care as part of national health insurance will result in large increases in nursing home use and expenditures.

The price sensitivity faced by individual physicians, hospitals, and other providers is much greater than the overall market because each provider is a possible substitute for other providers. For example, although a 10 percent overall price decrease leads to a 2 percent increase in overall use of physician services, if an *individual* physician raises (or lowers) his price by 10 percent, and other physicians do not change their prices, the individual physician will lose (or gain) a large number of patients, approximately 30 percent. Similarly, greater price sensitivity exists toward any single health plan than toward health insurance in general. When employees have a choice of health plans and have to pay an out-of-pocket premium (co-premium) for these plans, their choice of health plan is very price sensitive. One study found that a difference in HMO co-premiums of as little as $5 to $10 a month would cause about 25 percent of the HMO's enrollees to switch to the less costly HMO (Strombom, Buchmueller, and Feldstein 2002).

Moral Hazard

When patients use more medical services because their insurance lowers the out-of-pocket cost of those services, the insurance industry refers to this behavior as *moral hazard*. This term means that having insurance changes a person's behavior; the cost of medical services to the insurance company is increased. Those with insurance (or more comprehensive insurance) use more services, see more specialists, and incur higher medical costs than those who do not have insurance (or less comprehensive insurance), and the value patients and their physicians place on many of these additional services is lower than their full costs.

Indemnity insurance also places an annual limit (referred to as a *stop loss*, e.g., $2,500) on a patient's responsibility for out-of-pocket payments. If a patient has a serious illness, that out-of-pocket maximum is reached fairly early in the treatment process. After that point, the patient and her physician (assuming fee-for-service payment) have an incentive to try all types of treatments that may provide some benefit to the patient, no matter how small that benefit. The expression "flat-of-the-curve medicine" came to indicate the use of all medical technology, even when the benefit to the patient is extremely small. The only cost to the patient is nonfinancial—the discomfort and risk associated with the treatment. Not surprisingly, medical expenditures for those who are seriously ill are therefore extraordinarily high. Patients in such circumstances have everything available to them that modern medicine can provide.

The problem of moral hazard has long plagued health insurers, as it results in excessive use, increased cost of medical care, and increased insurance premiums. Until the 1980s, health insurers primarily controlled moral hazard by requiring patients to pay a deductible and part of the cost themselves by use of a copayment. In the 1980s, insurers began to use more aggressive methods to control overuse of medical services, such as prior authorization for hospital admissions, utilization review once the patient was hospitalized, and second surgical opinions. Unless prior authorization was received, the patient would be liable for part of the hospitalization cost (and often the patient's physician had to justify the procedure to the insurer). Requirements to obtain a second surgical opinion were an attempt to provide the patient and the insurer with more information as to the value of the recommended surgical procedure.

These cost-containment or rationing techniques are often referred to as *managed care*. Managed care methods also include case management, which minimizes the medical cost of catastrophic medical cases, and preferred physician panels, which exclude physicians who overuse medical services. These provider panels are marketed to employer groups as less costly, thereby offering enrollees lower out-of-pocket payments and insurance premiums if they restrict their choice of physician to members of the panel.

In addition to changing patient incentives and relying on managed care techniques, moral hazard can also be controlled by changing physicians' incentives. HMOs are paid an annual fee for providing medical services to their enrolled populations. The out-of-pocket price to the enrollee for use of services in an HMO is low; consequently, usage rates would be expected to be high. Because the HMO bears the risk that its enrollees' medical services will exceed their annual payments, the HMO has an incentive not to provide excessive amounts of medical services. An HMO patient must instead be concerned with receiving too little care. HMO physicians ration care based on the physician's perception of the benefits to the patient and the full costs to the HMO of further treatment. Because HMO enrollees have low copayments, the onus (and incentives) for decreasing moral hazard, hence rationing care, is placed on the HMO's physicians.

These insurance company and HMO approaches to decreasing moral hazard attempt to match the additional benefit of medical services to their full cost. Copayments and financial penalties for not receiving prior authorization are incentives to change the patient's behavior. In an HMO, the HMO's physicians are responsible for controlling moral hazard.

Summary

Important differences exist between government rationing of services and the rationing (by price) that occurs in a competitive market. In a price-competitive system, patients differ in the value they place on additional medical services; however, those who place a higher value on those services can always purchase more services. As their incomes increase, patients may prefer to spend more of their additional income on medical care than on other goods and services. If an HMO is too slow to adopt new technology or too restrictive on access to medical services provided to its enrollees, those enrollees could switch to another HMO or to indemnity insurance, pay higher premiums, and receive more services.

Under a system of government rationing, even if a patient places a higher value on additional medical services than does the government and is willing to pay the full cost of those services, the patient will still be unable to purchase them.

Medical services must be rationed because society cannot afford to provide all the medical services that would be demanded at zero price. Which rationing mechanism should be used? Having people pay for additional services and voluntarily joining an HMO or a managed care plan, or allowing the government to decide on the availability of medical resources? The first, or market, approach permits subscribers to match their costs to the value they place on additional services. Only when the government decides on the costs and benefits of medical services, and does not permit individuals to buy services beyond that level, will availability be lower than desired by those who value medical services more highly. Choice of rationing technique, relying on the private sector versus the government, is essential for determining how much medical care will be provided, to whom, and at what cost.

Regardless of which rationing approach is taken, knowledge of price sensitivity is important for public policy and for attaining efficiency. If the government wants to increase the use of preventive services such as prenatal care, mammograms, and dental checkups for underserved populations, would lowering the price (and waiting cost) of such services achieve that goal? If insurers raise the out-of-pocket price for some visits, would that decrease the use of care that is of low value? If stimulating competition among health plans is the goal, how great a difference in premiums would cause large numbers of employees to switch plans? If consumers are to be able to match the benefits and costs of use of medical services, and face the costs of their decisions, they will be more discriminating in their choice of health plan and use of services.

Discussion Questions

1. What determines how many physician services an individual demands?
2. What is moral hazard, and how does its existence increase the cost of medical care?
3. In what ways can moral hazard be limited?
4. Assume that medical services are free to everyone but that the government restricts the supply of services so that physician office visits are rationed by waiting time. Which population groups would fare better?
5. How would you use information on price sensitivity of medical services for policy purposes, for example, to increase the use of mammograms?
6. Discuss: The high price sensitivity of health plan co-premiums indicates that if employees had to pay out of pocket the difference between the lowest-cost health plan and any other health plan, market competition among health plans would be stimulated.

HOW MUCH HEALTH INSURANCE SHOULD EVERYONE HAVE?

Why do some people have health insurance that covers almost all their medical expenditures, including dental and vision care, while others do not? Why does the government subsidize the purchase of private health insurance for those with high incomes? Has health insurance stimulated the growth in medical expenditures, or has it served as protection against the rapid rise in medical expenses? The answers to these questions are important in explaining the rapid increase in medical expenditures and understanding healthcare reform issues.

The purpose of health insurance is to enable people to eliminate uncertainty and the possibility of incurring a large medical expense. Buying health insurance converts the possibility of a large loss into a certain but small loss. Insurance spreads risk among a large number of people; when each person pays a premium the aggregate amount of the premiums covers the large losses of relatively few people.

Definitions of Insurance Terms

Before this discussion continues, a number of terms should be defined. *Indemnity insurance* reimburses either the health provider or the patient a fixed amount (or a percentage of the bill), requiring the patient to pay any balance of the cost for medical treatment. When the insured patient has a *service benefit* policy, he receives all the services needed at no additional cost—regardless of the amount the insurer pays the provider. Current health insurance policies typically contain indemnity and service benefit features. Physician services and out-of-hospital services are usually treated with indemnity insurance features, whereas hospital admissions are usually paid for as a service benefit.

The difference between the provider's charge and the insurance payment is made up by deductibles and copayments. A *deductible* is a given dollar amount that the patient will have to spend before the insurer will pay any medical expenses. Typically, indemnity policies require an insured family to spend between $250 and $500 of their own money before the insurer will start paying part of their medical bills. A deductible lowers the insurance premium because it eliminates the many small medical expenses most families have each year. The insurer is also able to lower its administrative costs by eliminating the claims processing for a large number of small claims.

The effect of a deductible on an insurance premium is illustrated in Exhibit 6.1. As shown, a large percentage of families have relatively small medical expenses, while a small percentage of families have a very large (referred to as *catastrophic*) expense. Eliminating the area designated as a deductible would reduce the overall amount spent on medical care, thereby reducing the insurance premium.

When a patient pays a percentage of the physician's bill—for example, 20 percent—this is referred to as *cost sharing* or *coinsurance*. (The term *copayment* has been used to indicate a specific dollar amount, such as $20, payable by the patient.) Coinsurance provides the patient with an incentive to be sensitive to physicians' charges, perhaps by shopping around, as the patient will have to pay part of the bill. The patient will also have an incentive to use fewer services because he will have to balance the value of an additional visit against its cost (coinsurance). Coinsurance also reduces the insurer's share of medical expenses, as shown in Exhibit 6.1. Indemnity policies are typically 80/20 plans, meaning that the insurer pays 80 percent of the bill and the patient pays 20 percent. These policies also contain a *stop loss*, which places an overall limit on the patient's out-of-pocket expenses. For example, once a patient has paid a deductible and copayments that add up to, say, $2,000, the insurer pays 100 percent of all remaining expenses during that year. Without a stop loss, unlimited coinsurance or copayments could become a financial hardship. Coinsurance typically applies to out-of-hospital services considered discretionary.

Only a small percentage of families incur catastrophic claims (see Exhibit 6.1). The definition of a catastrophic expense depends on the patient's family income, as a $2,000 expense may be catastrophic to some families but not to others; however, few policies define catastrophic expense this way. Insurance policies that cover only catastrophic medical expenses are referred to as high-deductible insurance plans.

The amount of medical expenditures paid out by the insurance company is called the *pure premium*. The pure premium for a group of people with the same risk level (age and sex) represents their expected medical cost, that is, the probability that they will need medical services multiplied by the cost of those services. For example, assuming that the probability of my needing surgery (given my age and sex) is 5 percent and the cost of the surgery, if it were needed, is $50,000, I (and others in my risk group) would have to pay a pure premium of $2,500 a year ($50,000 × 0.05). If I chose not to buy insurance, I would theoretically have to put aside $50,000 to pay for that possible medical expense. However, I may not be able to put aside such a large amount—or even larger amounts, for example, the amount needed for an

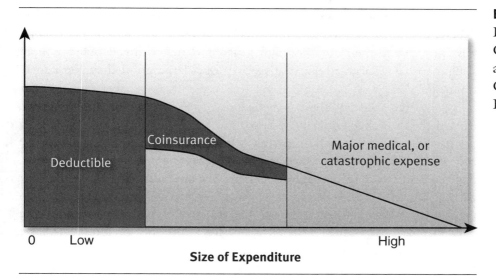

Exhibit 6.1
Deductibles,
Coinsurance,
and
Catastrophic
Expenses

organ transplant—or I may not want to tie up my funds in that way. Insurance offers me an alternative; it permits me to pay a premium that is equivalent to budgeting for an uncertain medical expense. I can eliminate the uncertainty of a large medical expense by paying an annual premium.

When everyone in a particular group has the same chance of becoming ill and incurring a medical expense, each person is considered to be in the same risk class and is charged the same pure premium. The *actual premium* charged, however, is always greater than the pure premium because the insurer has to recover its administrative and marketing costs and earn a profit. This difference between the pure and actual premium is referred to as the *loading charge*. (Another way to indicate the size of the loading charge is to use the *medical loss ratio*, which is the percentage of the collected premiums an insurance company pays out for medical expenses, typically 85 percent. The remaining 15 percent is the loading charge.)

Insurance-Purchase Decision Making

The size of the loading charge often explains why people buy insurance for some medical expenses but not for others. If people could buy insurance at the pure premium, they would buy insurance for almost everything because its price would reflect, on average, what they would likely spend anyway. However, when people are charged more than the pure premium, they must decide whether they want to buy insurance or self-insure, that is, bear the risk themselves. The higher the loading charge relative to the pure premium, the less insurance people will buy. For example, part of the loading charge is related to the administrative cost of processing a claim, which is not too different for small and large claims. Small claims therefore have larger loading costs (relative to their pure premium) than do large claims. People are more willing to pay a large administrative cost for a large claim than for a small claim.

In the above example, in which the pure premium is $2,500 a year, even if the insurance company charged me $2,600 a year ($100 more than the pure premium), I would probably buy the insurance rather than bear the risk myself. However, my decision would be different if I were required to pay the same loading charge with a smaller expected medical expense. For example, let's say I'm considering dental coverage. I know my family will probably need dental care in the coming year, and it will cost me $200. The insurance company offers a dental policy for $200 pure premium, plus the $100 administrative cost. Buying insurance for dental care is like prepaying the same amount I would otherwise spend, plus a 50 percent loading charge. In the second case, I would rather bear the small risk myself than buy insurance.

This discussion suggests that people are more likely to buy insurance for large, unexpected medical expenses than for small medical expenses (for a more complete discussion of the factors affecting the demand for health insurance, see Feldstein [2011]). This is the pattern typically observed in the purchase of health insurance. A hospital admission and the physician expenses connected with it, such as the surgeon's and anesthesiologist's fees, are more completely covered by insurance than are expenses for a physician office visit. Thus, an important characteristic of good insurance is that it covers large catastrophic expenses. People are less able to afford the catastrophic costs of a major illness or accident than they are front-end or first-dollar coverage, which is typically small expenses with relatively high loading charges.

Tax-Free, Employer-Paid Health Insurance

Surprisingly, however, we also observe that many people have insurance against small claims such as dental visits, physician office visits, and vision services. How can we explain this?

Advantages

The predominant source of health insurance coverage for those under 65 years of age is through the workplace, where, as of 2008, 92 percent of all private health insurance is purchased by the employer on behalf of the employee (Health Policy Center 2010). This occurs because the federal tax code does not consider employer-paid health insurance part of the employee's taxable income; it is exempt from federal, state, and Social Security taxes.

Until the early 1980s, marginal tax rates for federal income taxes were as high as 70 percent. Throughout the late 1960s and 1970s, inflation increased, pushing employees into higher marginal tax brackets. Social Security taxes have also risen steadily; as of 2010, the employer and employee each pay 6.2 percent of the employee's wage up to a maximum wage of $106,800 (US Social Security Administration 2010). In addition, the employee and employer each pay a Medicare tax of 1.45 percent on all earned income, for a combined total of 7.65 percent on the employee and employer. (After 2011, the Medicare tax will also apply to unearned income and will be increased for those with higher incomes.) Employees and their employers have a financial incentive for additional compensation in the form of health insurance benefits rather than cash income. The employer saves its share of Social Security taxes, and employees do not have to pay federal, state, or Social Security taxes on additional health insurance benefits.

For example, assume an employee was in a 30 percent tax bracket, had to pay 5 percent state income tax and 7 percent Social Security tax, already had basic hospital and medical coverage, and was due to receive a $1,000 raise. That employee would be left with only $580 (0.30 + 0.05 + 0.07 = 0.42 subtracted from 100 percent = 0.58 × $1,000) after taxes to purchase dental care and other medical services not covered by insurance for her family. Alternatively, the employer could use the entire $1,000 to purchase additional health insurance, and no taxes would be paid on it. This additional insurance would likely cover the employee's dental care and other previously uncovered medical expenses, which could easily add up to more than the $580 she would have received had she simply been given a $1,000 raise.

As employees move into higher tax brackets, the higher loading charge on small claims is more than offset by using before-tax income to buy health insurance for those small claims. Using the example of dental care, the choice is between spending $200 of after-tax income on dental care or buying dental insurance for $300 ($200 dental expense plus $100 loading charge). Spending $200 on my family's dental care would require me to earn $350 in before-tax income (30 percent federal tax, 5 percent state tax, and 7 percent Social Security tax). However, if my employer used that same $350 to purchase dental benefits for me, the premium, including the $100 loading charge, would be more than covered, leaving me $50 to buy even more insurance. Tax-free, employer-purchased health insurance provides a financial incentive to purchase health insurance for small claims.

Another way to view the tax subsidy for health insurance is to consider that if an employee saves 40 percent when the employer buys health insurance, the price of insurance to that employee has been reduced by 40 percent. Studies indicate that the purchase of insurance has an approximate proportional relationship to changes in its price (Cutler and Reber 1998). Thus, a 40 percent price reduction would be expected to increase the quantity of insurance purchased by 40 percent.

The advantages of tax-free, employer-purchased health insurance stimulate the demand for comprehensive health insurance coverage, particularly among higher-income employees. More services not traditionally thought of as insurable, such as a dental visit or an eye exam, all small routine expenditures, have become part of the employee's health insurance.

Consequences

Employer-paid health insurance became tax exempt during World War II, when the government agreed not to consider employer-paid health insurance as an increase in an employee's income. This move came in response to wage and price controls and to prevent a West Coast shipbuilder's union from striking for higher wages. The growth in employer-paid health insurance increased rapidly in the late 1960s when inflation rose and more employees were pushed into higher marginal tax brackets. The greater comprehensiveness of tax-exempt, employer-purchased health insurance has had important consequences. First, too many services were covered by health insurance. Administrative costs increased as insurers had to process many small claims that a deductible would have excluded. A $20 prescription drug claim and a much larger medical expense cost the same to process. Second, as insurance became more comprehensive, patients' concern with the prices charged for medical services decreased. Physicians, hospitals, and other health providers could more easily raise their charges because they would be covered by insurance—someone else was paying. Similarly, as the amount patients had to pay out of pocket for medical expenses declined, they increased their use of those services, sought more referrals to specialists, and underwent more extensive medical imaging and testing.

The growth of health insurance and medical technology was intertwined. Expensive technology, which increases the cost of a medical service, causes people to buy health insurance to protect themselves from those large, unexpected medical expenses. At the same time, the availability of insurance to pay for expensive technology stimulates its development. When comprehensive insurance removes any concern insured persons may have about the cost of their care, they (and physicians acting on their behalf) want access to the latest technology as long as it offers some additional benefit, no matter how small. The benefits of that technology to patients outweigh their out-of-pocket costs for using it. Because insurance was available to pay the costs of expensive technology, such as transplants, financial incentives existed to develop benefit-producing technology. Thus, medical technology was stimulated by, and in turn stimulated, the purchase of health insurance.

Conversely, cost-reducing technology generated little interest because employers could pass on higher insurance costs to employees in the form of reduced wages or to consumers in the form of higher prices. Furthermore, the after-tax value of savings to employees from stringent cost-containment measures was small. If, for example, insurance premiums could be reduced by $300 by limiting employees' choice of physician, the inconvenience to the employee and his family associated with changing physicians would probably not be worth the after-tax savings of $150.

The lack of concern over the price of medical services and increased use of those services caused medical expenditures to sharply increase, which in turn caused health insurance premiums to rapidly rise. Higher insurance premiums meant smaller wage increases, but this was not obvious to employees because the employer was paying the insurance premium.

Hundreds of billions of dollars in tax revenues have been lost because of employer-paid health insurance. The value of this tax subsidy was forecast to be $270 billion in 2010 in forgone federal, Social Security, and state taxes simply because employer-paid health insurance is not considered part of the employee's taxable income (Joint Committee on Taxation 2008). These lost tax revenues primarily benefit high-income employees because they are in higher tax brackets. As shown in Exhibit 6.2, the higher an employee's income, the greater the value of the exclusion from income of employer-purchased health insurance. This $270 billion in lost tax revenues is equivalent to a huge subsidy for the purchase of health insurance to those who can most easily afford it. In comparison, in 2010 the federal government spent $280 billion on Medicaid, a means-tested program for the poor (Congressional Budget Office 2010c).

Exhibit 6.3 shows how the value of the exclusion from income of employer-purchased health insurance is distributed. Families with incomes of $100,000 or greater in 2010 (26 percent of all families) received 40.6 percent of the federal portion of this tax subsidy for the purchase of health insurance.

Finally, tax-free, employer-paid health insurance reduced employees' incentive to choose lower-cost health plans. Many employers paid the entire premium of any plan the employee selected (or contributed more than the premium of the lowest-cost plan offered); as there was no visible cost to the employee, the employee's incentive was to choose the most comprehensive plan with the easiest access to physicians and specialists.

It is likely that the incentive for those with higher incomes to have their employers *increase* their employer-paid health insurance will be greater after 2011. The Patient Protection and Affordable Care Act (PPACA) of 2010 increases the Medicare payroll tax on high-income earners and, for those same people, imposes a 3.8 percent tax on unearned income. The Bush tax cuts for higher-income families were recently extended for an additional two years; however, if those tax cuts were to expire, these families would move into a higher income tax bracket and have more reason to use before-tax income to expand the comprehensiveness of their health insurance.

Exhibit 6.2 Value of Tax Exclusion for Employer-Paid Health Insurance, by Income Level, 2008

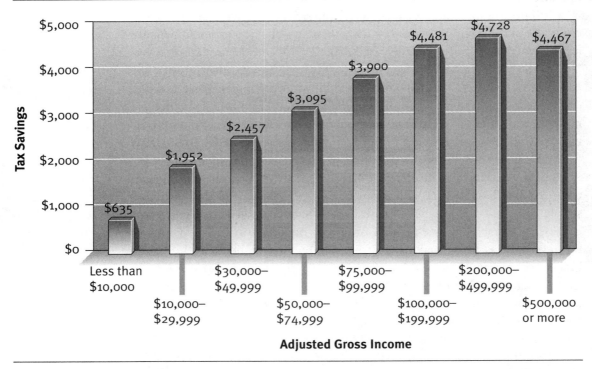

SOURCE: Julie Appleby. "How Congress Might Tax Your Health Benefits." *Kaiser Health News*, June 8, 2009. [Online information.] http://www.kaiserhealthnews.org/Stories/2009/June/08/taxes.aspx based on Joint Committee on Taxation calculations of Medical Expenditure Panel Survey data.

Limitation of Tax-Free Status

To encourage competition among health plans on the basis of access to services, quality, and premiums, employers would have to require that employees pay the additional cost of a more expensive health plan out of pocket. The employee would then evaluate whether the additional benefits of that plan are worth its additional costs. Unless a limit is placed on the tax-free employer contribution, many employees will continue to select health plans based on their benefits without regard to their premiums. Competition among health plans based on premiums, reputation, and access to services will not occur until employees have a greater financial stake in these decisions.

Not surprisingly, economists favor eliminating, or at least setting a maximum on, the tax-exempt status of employer-paid health insurance. Those with higher incomes would no longer receive a subsidy for their purchase of health insurance. Instead, increased tax revenues would come from those who have benefited most, namely those with higher incomes. These

EXHIBIT 6.3
Distribution of
Employer-Paid
Health
Insurance Tax
Exclusion, by
Income, 2010

Income	Tax Exclusion, Billions ($)	Percent of Total
Less than $20,000	8.1	3.0
$20,000 – $29,999	11.3	4.2
$30,000 – $39,999	16.7	6.2
$40,000 – $49,999	21.0	7.8
$50,000 – $74,999	49.3	18.3
$75,000 – $99,999	54.0	20.0
$100,000 – $149,999	60.0	22.3
$150,000 or more	49.2	18.3
Total	269.6	100.0

SOURCE: John Sheils. *Ideas for Financing Health Reform: Revenue Measures That Also Reduce Health Spending.*
Statement for the Senate Committee on Finance, May 12, 2009. Figure 1. [Online information.]
http://finance.senate.gov/imo/media/doc/John%20Sheils.pdf.

funds could then be used to subsidize health insurance for those with lower incomes. Employees using after-tax dollars would be more cost conscious in their use of services and choice of health plans. The Obama administration's healthcare legislation enacted in 2010 (PPACA) included a 40 percent tax on "Cadillac" health insurance (amounts greater than $27,500 a year for a family and $10,200 for an individual are subject to the tax). Unions that had negotiated comprehensive health benefits with their employers, however, opposed this provision of the legislation, and Congress delayed the imposition of the tax until 2018. (Starting in 2020, the value of a Cadillac health plan, set at $27,500 a year for a family, will be adjusted for inflation.)

Increased price sensitivity by employees (or employers acting on their behalf) has two likely outcomes. First, health insurance coverage would become less comprehensive. It would no longer be worthwhile to buy insurance for small claims that have relatively large loading charges. Consequently, dental and vision services would likely be dropped from insurance policies. Deductibles would be increased on out-of-hospital services, and the number of small claims paid by insurers would decrease, thereby decreasing administrative costs and insurance premiums. Copayments would also be common, both as a means of decreasing the insurance premium and for controlling use of services. Patients would also have a greater incentive (lower copayments) to use a restricted provider panel. Second, those employees who prefer to have comprehensive benefits and not pay large copayments would be more likely to join managed care systems, such as HMOs, in which the decision on use of services is made by the provider rather than the patient.

Whether patients become more price sensitive because of copayments or delegate the decision to restrict use of services to their managed care plan, use of services will decline. The basis for making treatment decisions will change. Use of services and choice of health plan will no longer be based solely on a consideration of their benefits. Employees (and physicians in managed care plans) will also have to consider the costs of their choices.

Summary

Health insurers play a valuable role in society. Assume a person is at risk for an operation costing $100,000. How many people would be able to pay that amount? Insurers pool risks; thus, a person can pay an insurance premium and eliminate the uncertainty that arises as to whether he will incur a large expenditure if he becomes ill. Insurance reduces a person's risk of a large financial loss.[1]

However, health insurance also provides protection against relatively small losses, such as physician office visits and dental care. People buy insurance against such small losses because health insurance is subsidized; employer-paid health insurance is tax exempt. Employees purchase more comprehensive health insurance because of this tax subsidy. The primary beneficiaries of this tax subsidy are those with higher incomes, because they are in a higher marginal tax bracket.

Tax-exempt, employer-purchased health insurance has distorted consumers' choices in healthcare and diminished consumer incentives to be concerned with the cost of medical services. Reducing or limiting this tax subsidy may not only provide more funds to assist those with lower incomes, it may also make consumers more price sensitive in their choice of health plans and use of medical services.

Discussion Questions

1. How is a pure premium calculated?
2. What does the loading charge consist of?
3. How does the size of the loading charge affect the type of health insurance purchased?
4. Why does employer-purchased health insurance result in more comprehensive health insurance coverage?

5. What are the arguments in favor of eliminating the tax-exempt status of employer-purchased health insurance?
6. How has health insurance affected the development of medical technology, and how has medical technology affected the growth of health insurance?

Note

1. In addition to pooling risks, insurers can decrease their premiums by performing two additional tasks. First, to decrease the probability of a large loss occurring, insurers can encourage preventive measures among its insured population. Second, if an expensive procedure is needed, insurers can lower the cost of that procedure by selecting physicians and hospitals that are higher quality and less costly.

WHY ARE THOSE WHO MOST NEED HEALTH INSURANCE LEAST ABLE TO BUY IT?

We have all heard stories of individuals who are sick and need, for example, open-heart surgery, but no insurance company will sell them health insurance. Health insurance seems to be available only for those who do not need it. Should health insurance companies be required to sell insurance to those who are sick and need it most? To understand these issues and consider what would be appropriate public policy, one must understand how insurance premiums are determined and how health insurance markets work.

Most private health insurance for nonelderly Americans, 64.2 percent in 2009 (down from 73.4 percent in 2000), is purchased through the workplace. While private non-group coverage has remained relatively stable at about 5 percent, employer coverage has declined from 68.3 percent in 2000 to 59 percent in 2009 (Holahan 2011). The insurance premium paid by an employer on behalf of its employees consists of (1) the loading charge, which represents approximately 15 percent of the premium, and (2) the claims experience of the employee group, which makes up the remaining 85 percent of the premium (see Exhibit 7.1). The loading charge reflects the insurance company's marketing costs, the administrative costs of handling the insurance claims, and profit. The claims experience of an employee group is the number of claims submitted by members of that group multiplied by the average cost per claim; this is also the medical expenditure portion of the premium, referred to as the *medical loss ratio*. Differences in premiums among employee groups, and the difference in annual premium increases, result primarily from differences in claims experience. An *experience-rated* premium is based on the claims experience of the particular group.

When a new group applies for health insurance, the insurer attempts to estimate the likely claims experience of the group. As shown in Exhibit 7.1, the insurer will consider factors that affect the group's medical expenditures, such as

- the types of medical and other benefits provided to the employees and their dependents,
- the types of mandates the state requires to be included in the insurance policy (e.g., hair transplants or coverage for chiropractors),

EXHIBIT 7.1
Determinants
of Health
Insurance
Premiums

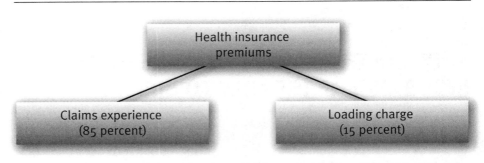

Determinants of Claims Experience

Benefit coverage

State mandates

Demographic characteristics of
    the insured population
    (age, sex, and family status)

Industry

Region

Medical inflation rate

Cost-containment policies

– Copayments

– Deductibles

– Benefit design

– Utilization review

– Case management

– PPOs

Determinants of Loading Charge

Administrative costs

Marketing costs

Reserves

Profits

- the average age of the group (older employees have higher medical expenditures than younger employees),
- the proportion of females (females have higher medical expenditures than males until age 45 and are similar to males beyond that age),
- the industry in which the firm competes (e.g., physicians, nurses, accountants, and lawyers tend to be heavier users of healthcare than, say, bank tellers),
- the region of the country in which the employees are located (hospital costs and physician fees are higher on the West Coast than in the South), and
- an estimate of the growth rate of medical inflation.

    Once an insurer has insured a group long enough to have a history of that group's claims experience, the insurance company will project that claims experience and multiply it by an estimate of the medical inflation rate.

Various approaches can be taken to reduce a group's claims experience. For example, increasing the deductible and the coinsurance rate will decrease employees' use of services; expanding insurance benefits to include lower-cost substitutes to inpatient admissions will lower treatment costs; and requiring utilization review of hospital admissions, case management of catastrophic cases, and use of preferred provider organizations (PPOs) will lower use rates and provider charges. Thus, the claims experience of a group is related to the characteristics of that group, the medical benefits covered, and the cost-containment methods included in the insurance policy.

The insurer bears the risk of incorrectly estimating the group's medical experience. If the premium charged to that group is too low, the insurer will lose money. In the past, Blue Cross and other insurance companies have lost a great deal of money by underestimating claims experience and the medical inflation rate. An insurer cannot merely increase the premiums of the group in the following period to recover its losses because the insurance market is very price competitive. If an insurer says to an employer, "We need to increase our profit this coming year because we lost money on your employees last year," the employer may switch to a competitor or to an HMO.

Even if the claims experience of two employee groups is similar, one group may have a lower insurance premium because it has a lower loading charge. Larger groups have smaller loading charges because administrative and marketing costs, which are generally fixed, are spread over a larger number of employees. Furthermore, insurers earn a lower profit when they insure larger groups because they fear that, if their profit is too high, large groups will decide to self-insure by bearing the risk themselves. Smaller groups, on the other hand, are less likely to be able to bear the risk of self-insurance. If a very large claim were to occur in one year, the financial burden could be too large for a small group to bear. In a larger group, large claims are likely to be offset by premiums from employees making only small or no claims in a given year. In addition to charging small groups a higher rate, an insurer is likely to maintain a higher reserve in case a large claim is made, further increasing the loading charge for small groups. However, the amount of profit the insurer is able to make from a small group still is limited by competition from other insurers and HMOs.

Medical Loss Ratios

Some provider organizations have viewed the medical loss ratio as an indicator of a health plan's efficiency and even the quality of care. The higher the ratio, the more of the premium dollar is paid out for medical services and the lower the administrative expenses. However, the use of the ratio as an evaluative measure is misleading. Higher administrative expenses (hence a lower medical loss ratio) can result from an insurer (1) enrolling a greater mix of small groups, which have higher marketing and administrative costs than large groups; (2) having a smaller enrollment base and therefore having to spread fixed administrative costs over a smaller number of enrollees; and (3) having a larger number of insurance products, which are more costly to administer than a single product. Additional factors are the method used to pay hospitals and physicians (by capitating providers, the administrative and claims processing expense is shifted to the provider, compared with the fee-for-service approach, in which the insurer retains those functions) and the number of cost-containment and quality-review activities the insurer undertakes.

For example, a health plan that merely pays out a large percentage of its premiums (high medical loss ratio) is more likely to be inefficient and lower in quality than a health plan that has a higher administrative expense ratio because it reviews the accuracy of claims submitted by providers, conducts reviews of the quality of care provided, and undertakes patient satisfaction surveys.[1]

In a price-competitive health insurance market, a health plan cannot afford to be inefficient in its administrative functions. If it were, its premiums would be higher and it would lose market share. A health plan must undertake a cost-benefit analysis to determine whether each of the administrative functions it performs either saves money (lower claims cost) or provides increased purchaser satisfaction (as shown by enrollee satisfaction surveys). To do otherwise places the plan at a competitive disadvantage.[2]

Rather than leaving the size of medical loss ratios to be determined through insurer competition, the Patient Protection and Affordable Care Act (PPACA) of 2010 establishes limits on medical loss ratios. Starting in 2011, insurers must have no less than an 80 percent ratio in the individual and small group markets and a minimum ratio of 85 percent in the large group market, otherwise the insurer must refund the difference to their insured. For example, if an insurer has a ratio of 70 percent in the individual market, it is required to provide the difference between 70 and 80 percent back to the insured individual (Kaiser Family Foundation 2011). Currently, medical loss ratios in the individual market are lower than the politically determined 80 percent ratio because of higher enrollment, marketing, and administrative costs. It is likely that many insurers, unable to increase their loss ratios to the higher ratio, will exit these markets, leading to less insurer competition.

Although the regulations have not yet been developed regarding which services should be classified as administrative or medical expenses for determining the medical loss ratio, insurers are concerned that they may have to eliminate cost-containment programs, such as disease management, and quality improvement programs, such as physician profiling and evidence-based medicine, which are included in their administrative costs, to be able to increase their ratios to 80 and 85 percent. The elimination of these programs to achieve the prescribed ratios would be an unintended consequence of the legislation.

How Health Insurance Markets Work

This brief description of how insurance premiums are determined serves as background to examine why those who are ill find buying insurance difficult.

Adverse Selection

Assume that an individual without health insurance requires a heart transplant and tries to purchase health insurance. If the insurer does not know that the person requires expensive medical treatment, the person's premium will be based on the claims experience of persons in a similar age (risk) group. This difference in information about the individual's health status between the individual and the insurer can lead to *adverse selection*, that is, the insurer enrolls people whose risk level is much higher than the risk level on which their premium is based. This occurs because a person in ill health will attempt to conceal that information so the insurer will not know of the higher risk.

For example, if 100 people were in a risk group, each with a 1 percent chance of needing a medical treatment costing $100,000, the pure premium for each (without the loading charge) would be $1,000 (0.01 × $100,000). Each year, one member of the group would require a $100,000 treatment. Now, if a person who needs that particular treatment (whose risk is 100 percent) is permitted to join that group at a premium of $1,000 (based on a mistaken risk level of 0.01), that high-risk person receives a subsidy of $99,000, as her premium should have been $100,000 based on her risk level. Because the $1,000 premium was based on a risk level of 1 percent, the insurer collects insufficient premiums to pay for the second $100,000 expense and loses $99,000.

This example does not differ from one in which a man learns that he has a terminal illness and, without revealing his condition to the insurer, decides to purchase a $10 million life insurance policy to provide for his wife and children, or one in which a woman whose home is on fire quickly decides to buy fire insurance. Insurance enables a person to protect against uncertainty. Once uncertainty no longer exists, however, the person is not insurable for that particular treatment or situation.

If the insurance company knew that the individual wanted health insurance to cover the costs of a heart transplant, it would charge a premium that reflected the person's expected claims experience, that is, the person's premium would be equal to the cost of the heart transplant plus a loading charge.

We all favor subsidizing those who cannot afford but need an expensive treatment. Similarly, we favor subsidies to poor families. However, is it not more appropriate for the government, rather than the insurer, to provide those subsidies? When insurers are made to bear such losses, they will eventually be forced out of business unless they can protect themselves from persons who withhold information and claim to be in lower-risk groups.

To protect themselves against adverse selection (insuring high-risk persons for premiums mistakenly based on those with low risks) the insurer could raise everyone's premiums, but then many low-risk subscribers, who might be willing to pay $1,000 but not $2,000 for a 1 percent risk, would drop their insurance. As more low-risk subscribers drop out, premiums for remaining subscribers would increase further, causing still more low-risk subscribers to drop out. Eventually large numbers of low-risk persons would be uninsured, although they would be willing to pay an actuarially fair premium based on their (low) risk group.

Instead, an insurer will attempt to learn as much as the patient about the patient's health status. Examining and testing the person who wants to buy health insurance is a means of equalizing the information between the two parties. Another way insurers protect themselves against adverse selection—that is, misclassifying high risks into low-risk groups—is by stating that their insurance coverage will not apply to pre-existing conditions, medical conditions known by the patient to exist and to require medical treatment. Similarly, an insurer might use a delay of benefits clause or a waiting period; for example, obstetric benefits may not be covered until a policy has been in effect for ten months. Large deductibles will also discourage high-risk persons because they will realize that they will have to pay a large amount of their expenses themselves.

Insurers are less concerned about adverse selection when selling insurance to large groups with low employee turnover. In such groups, health insurance is provided by the employer as a tax-free benefit (subsidized by the government); the total group includes all the low-risk persons as well. Typically, people join large companies more for other attributes of the job than for health insurance coverage. Once in the employer group, employees cannot just drop the group insurance when well and buy it when ill. Thus, for insurance companies adverse selection is more of a concern when individuals or small groups (with typically higher turnover) want to buy insurance. For example, an insurer might be concerned that the owner of a small firm might hire an ill family member just so she could receive insurance benefits. Thus, employees with pre-existing medical conditions will be denied coverage.

Some state and local governments have attempted to assist people with pre-existing conditions by prohibiting insurers from using tests to determine, for example, whether someone is HIV positive. Rather than subsidize care for such individuals themselves, governments have tried to shift the medical costs to the insurer and its other subscribers. This is an inequitable way of subsidizing care for those with pre-existing conditions. Government use of an income-related tax to provide the subsidy would be fairer. Another consequence of government regulations that shift the cost of those who are ill to insurers and their subscribers is that insurers will rely on other types of restrictions not covered by the regulations, such as delay of benefits and exclusion of certain occupations, industries, or geographic areas to protect themselves.

Healthy people may not have health insurance for several reasons. An insurance premium that is much higher than the expected claims experience of an individual will make that insurance too expensive. For example, if an employee is not part of a large insured group, he will be charged a higher insurance premium because the insurer suspects he will be a higher risk. The loading charge will also be higher for the self-employed and those in small groups because the insurer's administration and marketing costs are spread over fewer employees, leading to a higher premium. Furthermore, state insurance mandates that require expensive benefits or more practitioners to be included in all insurance sold in that state result in higher insurance premiums; consequently, fewer people are willing to buy such insurance. (Large firms that self-insure are exempt from costly state mandates.) Many individuals and members of small groups also lack insurance coverage because premiums are too high relative to their incomes. Such persons would rather rely on Medicaid if they become ill. Others can afford to purchase insurance but choose not to; if they become ill, they become a burden on taxpayers because they cannot be refused treatment in emergency departments or by hospitals.

The best way to eliminate the problem of adverse selection is to require everyone to have health insurance (an "individual mandate"). Subsidies to purchase insurance have to be provided to those with low incomes and to those who are high risk in relation to their incomes. Requiring an individual mandate and removing the pre-existing condition exclusions would eliminate "job lock"; employees could change jobs without fear of losing their health insurance or being denied insurance because of a pre-existing condition.

The Obama administration's healthcare legislation, PPACA, enacted in 2010 to take effect in 2014, requires an individual mandate and the elimination of pre-existing condition exclusions; an insurer would have to sell insurance to a person regardless of how sick he was. Although insurers were not opposed to these proposals, they were strongly opposed to the small penalty a person would pay if he did not buy insurance under the individual mandate. The penalty for not being insured under the PPACA is only $95 per year for an individual in 2014, increasing to $695 in 2016. Compare this to the cost of individual insurance, which could easily be $10,000 per year, and it is easy to imagine that many people will opt for the small penalty until they get sick, buy insurance at that time, and then drop it as soon as they recover. Under these conditions, insurers will suffer adverse selection, and if they raise their rates to cover these costs, more of their insured will also drop their coverage. A private health insurance system cannot survive under these conditions.

Also included in the PPACA, since the removal of pre-existing conditions will not occur until 2014, is a federal high-risk pool (at subsidized premiums) to cover those who are uninsurable because they have pre-existing conditions.

Previously, to prevent adverse selection in Medicare Part B (physician and outpatient services) and Part D (prescription drugs), both of which are subsidized (75 percent) by the government and are voluntary programs, the monthly premiums were increased the longer an eligible beneficiary delayed enrolling in those programs. These penalties help prevent people from waiting until they need the services and then joining the program, which would result in adverse selection to the government.

Preferred-Risk Selection

Because insurers want to protect themselves against bad risks, they clearly prefer to insure individuals who are better-than-average risks. Although their risks vary, as long as different groups and individuals pay the same premium, insurers have an incentive to engage in *preferred-risk selection*, that is, seek out those who have lower-than-average risks.

As shown in Exhibit 7.2, in 2007, 1 percent of the population incurred 23 percent of total health expenditures (39 percent of those in the top 1 percent are aged 65 years or older). In 1963, 1 percent of the population incurred only 17 percent of total expenditures, which demonstrates the effect medical technology has had on increasing medical expenditures. Five percent of the population incurs 50 percent of total expenditures. Given this high concentration of expenditures among a small percentage of the population, an insurer could greatly increase its profits and avoid losses by trying to avoid the most costly patients. An insurer able to select enrollees from among the 50 percent of the population that incurs only 3 percent of total expenditures will greatly profit. The only way to provide insurers with an incentive to take the high-risk, hence costly, patients is to provide insurers with risk-adjusted premiums. For example, premiums for persons in older age groups should be higher than premiums for those in lower age groups. Insurers would then have an incentive to enroll these patients and manage their care to minimize their treatment cost rather than search for low-risk enrollees.

When the premium is the same for all risks, insurers attempt to enroll persons with better-than-average risks in several ways. For example, if everyone enrolling with a particular health insurer pays the same annual premium, the HMO would prefer those who have lower-than-average claims experience, are in low-risk industries, and are younger-than-average employees. To encourage younger subscribers, the HMO might emphasize services used by

Exhibit 7.2 Distribution of Health Expenditures for the US Population, by Magnitude of Expenditures, Selected Years, 1928–2007

Percentage of US Population Ranked by Expenditures	1928	1963	1970	1977	1980	1987	1996	2007
Top 1 percent	–	17%	26%	27%	29%	28%	27%	23%
Top 2 percent	–	–	35	38	39	39	38	33
Top 5 percent	52%	43	50	55	55	56	55	50
Top 10 percent	–	59	66	70	70	70	69	65
Top 30 percent	93	–	88	90	90	90	90	89
Top 50 percent	–	95	96	97	96	97	97	97
Bottom 50 percent	–	5	4	3	4	3	3	3

SOURCES: Adapted with permission from "The Concentration of Health Care Expenditures, Revisited, Exhibit 1," by M. L. Berk and A. C. Monheit, *Health Affairs*, 20(2), 2001, March/April: 12. Copyright © 2001 Project HOPE–the People-to-People Health Foundation, Inc., All rights reserved. 2007 data from Yu, W. W. 2010. Agency for Healthcare Research and Quality. Personal correspondence, August 3.

younger couples, such as prenatal and well-baby care. Emphasizing wellness and sports medicine programs is also likely to draw a healthier population. Similarly, de-emphasizing tertiary care facilities for heart disease and cancer treatment sends a message to those who are older and at higher risk for those illnesses. Locating clinics and physicians in areas where lower-risk populations reside also results in a favorably biased selection of subscribers.

Medicare beneficiaries can voluntarily decide to join an HMO. Previously, if an aged person decided to change her mind, she could leave the HMO with only one month's notice. (This one-month notice, which was permitted to the aged but not to those in Medicaid HMOs, reflected the greater political power of the aged.) When some HMOs determined that a Medicare patient required high-cost treatment, they were able to encourage patients to disenroll by suggesting that they might benefit from more suitable treatment for the condition outside the HMO. By eliminating these high-cost subscribers, an HMO could save a great deal of money. To discourage some HMOs from using this approach to maintain only the most favorable Medicare risks, the one-month notice by the aged was repealed in 2003.[3]

Additional Legislative Changes Affecting the Health Insurance Market

Biased selection, both adverse and preferred risk, is a problem in the health insurance market that occurs because of differences in information on health status, consumer choice of health plans, and similar premiums for subscribers whose expected medical expenses differ from those of the average subscriber. Legislation affecting the health insurance market should consider how proposed changes affect insurer and consumer incentives for adverse and preferred-risk selection.

Several proposals have been made for improving the health insurance market, although not all of them will improve its efficiency.[4] One such example is requiring all insurers to *community rate* their subscribers, that is, charge all subscribers the same premium regardless of health status or other risk factors, such as age. The cost of higher-risk individuals would be spread among all subscribers. Community rating, however, provides insurers with even stronger incentives to select preferred risks (that is, lower-risk persons) while receiving a premium based on the average for all risk groups because it will increase the insurer's profits. Furthermore, with uniform premiums, regardless of risk status, insurers and employers would no longer have an incentive to encourage risk-reducing behavior among their subscribers and employees, for example, by providing smoking cessation and wellness programs. Premiums for employee groups could not be reduced relative to other groups who do not invest in such cost-reducing behavior. Skydivers, motorcyclists, and others who engage in risky behavior are subsidized by those who attempt to lower their risks. Rather than reducing the cost of risky behavior to these groups, higher premiums for those who engage in higher-risk activities would provide them with an incentive to reduce such behavior and bear the full cost of their activities.

Additionally, when there is only one choice of health plan, the higher, community-rated premium results in lower-risk individuals dropping their coverage. The result is an increase in the number of uninsured. When there is a choice of community-rated health plans, those who are low risk will select less costly, but more restrictive, health plans that are less attractive to higher-risk individuals. As low-risk individuals leave these more costly plans and choose plans that are less costly and more restrictive, the more generous plans will include a higher portion of higher-risk individuals. This appears to have happened in New Jersey (Monheit et al. 2004). Consequently, the premiums in these more costly plans will increase, likely leading to their demise.

Community rating also has serious equity effects. A community-rated system benefits those who are at high risk and penalizes those who are at low risk. Those at lower risk pay higher premiums and those at higher risk pay lower premiums than they would under an experience-rated system. Those at higher risk are in effect subsidized by a tax on those who are lower risk. Because these "subsidies" and "taxes" are based on risk rather than income, low-risk individuals who also have low incomes end up subsidizing some higher-risk, higher-income people. (Not all high-risk persons are poor, and not all low-risk persons are wealthy.)

Under *experience rating*, premiums reflect the individual's or group's risk level. No incentive exists for insurers to engage in preferred-risk selection; insurers have an incentive to enroll and manage the care for high-risk groups, and those who are low risk and low income do not subsidize those who are high risk and high income. When subsidies are required, they should be given directly to those with low incomes, not by requiring similar premiums for different risk groups. PPACA requires a modified form of community rating by age; differences in age-related premiums are limited to less than their actual cost differences. The biased selection effects of this provision will take several years to analyze, since it will not take effect until 2014.

State *insurance exchanges* were included in the recent health legislation. Administered by a government agency or nonprofit organization, individuals and small employer groups (up to 100 employees) will be able to choose from among a greater number of insurers within each state. After 2017, businesses with more than 100 employees will also have access to an insurance exchange. These insurance exchanges should provide more insurance options for those in the individual and small group markets.

PPACA also provides states with regulatory authority to limit insurers' premium increases. If a state review board considers an insurer's premium increase to be unjustified, the insurer can be excluded from participating in the state's insurance exchange and, consequently, suffer a large loss in enrollment. Limiting insurers' premium increases is unlikely to be successful in lowering health insurance costs. In a competitive insurance market, insurers must be efficient, negotiate as hard as possible with providers, and undertake cost-effective cost-containment programs, otherwise they would be less competitive against other insurers. Imposing a cap on premiums is unlikely to improve insurers' efficiency.

If an insurer's premiums are capped, how may the insurer respond to reduce its costs? As noted previously, premiums are mainly determined by what the insurer pays providers, which depends on the use of services by its enrollees and the prices charged by the providers. If providers, such as hospitals, have market power and are able to raise their prices, capping insurance premiums will either reduce insurers' profits, possibly resulting in their leaving the market, or force insurers to lower beneficiaries' use of medical services. Access to care will decline. Establishing price controls on insurance premiums does not address the reasons for rising medical costs.

Reducing rising medical costs ultimately requires delaying the introduction of new technology, an important driver of medical use, and limiting access to such treatments. In other countries, governments decide both of these issues. Placing caps on premiums is an indirect approach to having insurers limit payment for and access to new technological advances.

The effects of PPACA will not be known for several years, since many of its provisions do not become effective until 2014. Although several insurance provisions, such as the individual mandate, the elimination of pre-existing conditions, the federal high-risk pool for the uninsurable, and the insurance exchanges, should be beneficial, others, such as the low financial penalty for being uninsured under the individual mandate, minimum medical loss ratios, modified community rating by age, and regulation of insurers' premium rate increases, are likely to have adverse effects on the insurance markets and some of the insured. It remains to be seen how the private health insurance market will evolve as a result of these provisions.

Summary

Adverse and preferred-risk selection occur because the premium an individual is charged does not match the risk group he is in. These selection problems would be minimized if premiums were related to risk group, because insurers would not need to reject high-risk persons or search for low-risk persons. Requiring mandatory insurance and eliminating the pre-existing condition exclusion will enable employees to switch jobs without fear that they will be denied insurance. However, requiring only a small penalty for not buying insurance will only serve to increase adverse selection, consequently increasing premiums, as people will wait until they are sick to buy insurance. Mandating a modified form of community rating is likely to raise premiums for the young and decrease risk-reducing behavior by employers. Establishment of state insurance exchanges will likely increase competition among insurers and offer consumers greater choice of insurers. Minimum loss ratios and regulation of insurer premiums are likely to reduce insurers' profits and result in fewer insurers.

Adverse and preferred-risk selection are constant concerns with regard to the design of insurance products, whether it is private or government insurance. These selection issues affect premiums and access to care by subscribers and behavior by health insurers. Solving these problems will require an understanding of why biased selection occurs. Proposed solutions should be evaluated on the basis of whether they encourage risk-reducing behavior, include incentives for efficient utilization of medical services, and impose a burden on those with low incomes who are also low risk. If health insurers compete on the basis of risk-adjusted premiums, insurers will compete on the basis of how well they can manage care rather than how well they can select better risk groups. Finally, health insurance reform should be directed toward eliminating uncertainty, which is what people want when they buy health insurance. The recently enacted PPACA will affect all aspects of the insurance market. However, its effects will not be known for several years because many provisions do not become effective until 2014.

Discussion Questions

1. What are the different components of a health insurance premium? If an employer wanted to reduce its employees' premiums, which components could be changed?
2. What is adverse selection, and how do insurance companies protect themselves from it? If the government prohibited insurers from protecting themselves against adverse selection, how would it affect insurance premiums?
3. Why do insurers and HMOs have an incentive to engage in preferred-risk selection?
4. What are some methods by which insurers and HMOs try to achieve preferred-risk selection?
5. What is the difference between experience rating and community rating, and what are some consequences of using community rating?

Additional Readings

Feldstein, P. 2011. "The Demand for Health Insurance." In *Health Care Economics*, 7th ed. Albany, NY: Delmar Publishers.
Morrisey, M. 2008. *Health Insurance*. Chicago: Health Administration Press.

Notes

1. Robinson (1997) discusses many of these interpretive problems (and more) with medical loss ratios and demonstrates how medical loss ratios vary greatly within nonprofit and for-profit health plans, as well as the wide variations that exist in these ratios for the same health plan located in different states.

2. Expense ratios for private insurers are much larger than for Medicare. Rather than being an indication of differences in efficiency, some of the reasons for higher expense ratios among private insurers are as follows:
   - Medicare's per capita claim costs are much higher; thus, their administrative expenses are a smaller proportion of total costs.
   - The Centers for Medicare & Medicaid Services (CMS), which performs administrative services for Medicare, is generally excluded from the calculation of Medicare's administrative costs.
   - Additional costs necessary for the operation of Medicare, such as enrollment and billing, are included in the Social Security Administration's costs and not attributed to Medicare.
   - Medicare also has lower costs because it relies on price controls and thus does not negotiate with providers or undertake cost-containment and quality improvement functions, such as medical management, or spends too little to reduce fraud and abuse.
   - Medicare is exempt from paying state premium taxes or incurring regulatory and compliance costs that affect insurance companies.
3. This change was a result of the Balanced Budget Act of 1997, which sought to decrease Medicare expenditures. To compensate for this change, the aged were provided with additional preventive benefits.
4. These proposals are directed toward improving the health insurance market for small employee groups and assume that these small groups can afford to purchase health insurance. Financing healthcare for the poor is discussed in later chapters, as are other aspects of healthcare reform, such as competitive medical systems and malpractice.

MEDICARE

In 1965, Congress enacted two different financing programs to cover two separate population groups: Medicare for the aged and Medicaid for the poor. As a result, the government's (particularly the federal government's) role in financing personal medical services increased dramatically. Federal and state expenditures represent about 52 percent of total medical expenditures.

Medicare and Medicaid have serious problems. Medicare's financial deficits mean that the program will require substantial changes to survive. Medicaid must be improved if it is to serve more than half of those classified as poor, and it faces huge financial liabilities, as an aging population requires long-term care. Medicaid is discussed in Chapter 9.

The Current State of Medicare

Medicare is a federal program that primarily serves the aged. In addition, those younger than age 65 who receive Social Security cash payments because they are disabled become eligible for Medicare after a two-year waiting period. People requiring kidney dialysis and kidney transplants, regardless of age, were added to Medicare in the early 1970s. As shown in Exhibit 8.1, Medicare covers 39.1 million aged and 8.0 million disabled beneficiaries, for a total of 47.1 million beneficiaries as of 2010 (CMS 2011a); the aged population is expected to double over the next three decades.

Medicare has four parts, each of which offers different benefits and uses different financing mechanisms. Part A provides hospital insurance (HI), Part B provides supplemental medical insurance (SMI), Part C offers Medicare beneficiaries a greater variety of health plan choices (Medicare Advantage plans), and Part D is a prescription drug benefit.

Part A (HI)

All the aged are automatically enrolled in Part A when they retire at age 65. Part A covers acute hospital care (up to 90 days for each episode of care), skilled nursing home care after hospitalization (up to 100 days), and hospice care for the terminally ill. If a Medicare patient requires hospitalization, she must pay a deductible that is indexed to increase with health costs each year

EXHIBIT 8.1 Number of Medicare Beneficiaries, Fiscal Years 1970–2030[a]

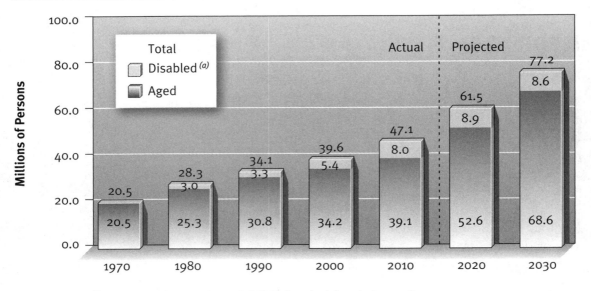

[a]Includes beneficiaries whose eligibility is based solely on end-stage disease.

NOTE: Disabled became eligible for Medicare in 1973; therefore, no values for disabled prior to 1974.

SOURCES: CMS (2011a); "projected data" from Centers for Medicare & Medicaid Services (then the Health Care Financing Administration). 2000. *Medicare 2000: 35 Years of Improving Americans' Health and Security.* Baltimore, MD: CMS.

($1,132 for 1 to 60 days of hospital stay as of 2011) (Kaiser Family Foundation 2011). Part A is financed by an earmarked Medicare HI payroll tax, which is set aside in the Medicare Hospital Trust Fund. In 1966, this tax was a combined 0.35 percent (0.175 percent each on the employer and the employee) on wages up to $6,600. As Medicare expenditures continually exceeded projections, the HI tax and the wage base to which the tax applied were increased. Since 1994, the total HI tax has been a combined 2.9 percent on all earned income (National Bipartisan Commission on the Future of Medicare n.d.).

The Medicare Hospital Trust Fund is a pay-as-you-go fund; current Medicare expenditures are funded by current employee and employer contributions. The HI taxes from current Medicare beneficiaries were never set aside for their own future expenses; instead, they were used to pay for those who were Medicare eligible at the time the funds were collected. This is in contrast to a pension fund, in which a person sets aside funds to pay for his own retirement. When Medicare actuaries have estimated that the Trust Fund will become insolvent, that is, when current HI taxes will be insufficient to pay current Medicare expenditures, Medicare HI taxes on employees and employers have been increased.

Exhibit 8.2 Estimated Medicare Benefit Payments, by Type of Service, Fiscal Year 2009

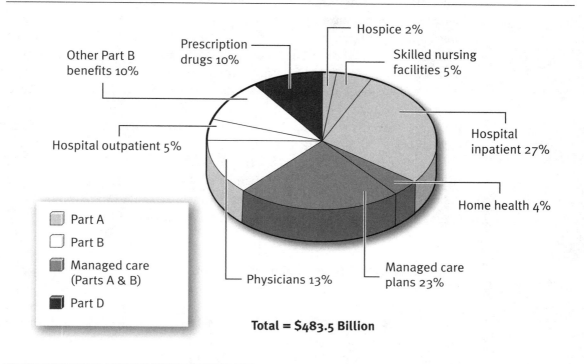

Hospice 2%

Prescription drugs 10%

Other Part B benefits 10%

Skilled nursing facilities 5%

Hospital outpatient 5%

Hospital inpatient 27%

Home health 4%

Part A

Part B

Managed care (Parts A & B)

Part D

Physicians 13%

Managed care plans 23%

Total = $483.5 Billion

SOURCE: Congressional Budget Office, Medicare Baseline, March 2009, www.cbo.gov/budget/factsheets/2009b/medicare.pdf.

In 2009, the federal government spent $243 billion on Part A; this amount is estimated to rise to $380 billion by 2019. Medicare's expenditures by type of service are shown in Exhibit 8.2.

Part B (SMI)

Medicare Part B (SMI) pays for physician services, outpatient diagnostic tests, certain medical supplies and equipment, and (since 1998) home healthcare (previously included in Part A). Medicare beneficiaries are not automatically enrolled in SMI, which is a voluntary, income-related program, but 95 percent of the aged pay the premium. In 2010, new Part B beneficiaries will pay $110.50 a month. Single individuals whose income is greater than $85,000 or married couples with a combined income of greater than $170,000 pay an additional amount. Beneficiary premiums represent only 25 percent of the program's costs. The remaining 75 percent of Part B expenditures are subsidized from federal tax revenues. The aged are also responsible for an annual $162 deductible (in 2010) and a 20 percent copayment for their use of Part B services (US Social Security Administration 2011).

In 2007, against much opposition, the Medicare Part B premium became income related; those aged earning $80,000 to $100,000 receive a 65 percent premium subsidy, and those earning more than $200,000 receive only a 20 percent premium subsidy. At the time the premium became income related, only 3 percent of Part B enrollees were affected by the reduced premium subsidies (US Social Security Administration 2011).

Unlike the Hospital Trust Fund, when Part B expenditures exceed projections there is no concern with insolvency. The federal subsidy simply becomes larger than expected; Part B expenditures increase the size of the federal deficit. In 2010, the federal subsidy for Part B expenditures exceeded $207 billion; this is estimated to rise to $358 billion by 2020. By way of comparison, Medicare's share of the federal budget was 12.1 percent ($451 billion) in 2010 and is expected to rise to 16.8 percent ($957 billion) of all federal expenditures by 2020 (Office of Management and Budget 2011).

Part C: Medicare Advantage Plans

Since the 1980s, the aged have been able to voluntarily enroll in a managed care plan, such as an HMO or a PPO (referred to as Medicare Advantage plans). The managed care plan receives a capitation payment from Medicare based on the total Part A and Part B expenditures for a Medicare beneficiary in that particular geographic area (adjusted for age, sex, and Medicaid and institutional status). In return for this capitation payment, the managed care plan provides more comprehensive benefits, such as lower out-of-pocket payments and additional services not covered under Medicare Part B. The managed care plan, which is at risk for providing all the promised benefits in return for the capitation payment, limits the aged enrollees' choice of physicians and hospitals to those in the managed care plan's provider network. Thus, the managed care plan has a financial incentive to reduce inappropriate care and manage the aged's care in a cost-effective manner.

About 11 million, or more than 20 percent, of the aged are enrolled in Medicare Advantage plans; the remainder are in traditional Medicare, where the hospitals and physicians are paid on a fee-for-service basis and the government regulates prices. Since 2003, the aged have to remain in a given health plan for a minimum of one year, whereas previously they were able to switch health plans with one month's notice.

Part D: Outpatient Prescription Drugs

In 2003 the Medicare Modernization Act was enacted. This legislation provided the aged with a new stand-alone outpatient prescription drug benefit

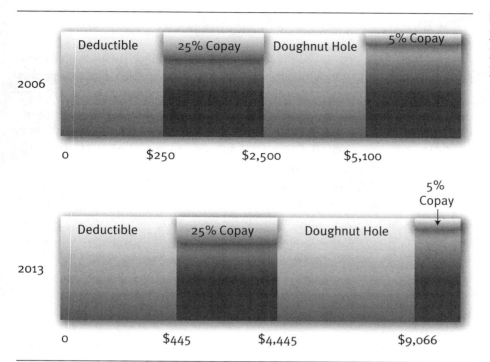

Exhibit 8.3
Medicare
Prescription
Drug Benefit

that started in 2006. The drug benefits are provided by private, risk-bearing plans. The aged use more outpatient prescription drugs than any other age group, and the out-of-pocket financial burden of these drugs was often of greater concern than the costs of hospital and physician services, most of which were covered by Medicare. Although the aged are required to pay a monthly premium of, on average, $38.94 (as of 2010) to private plans for the new, voluntary benefit, the cost of the program is heavily subsidized (75 percent) from federal tax revenues (Weaver 2010).

The design of the new prescription drug benefit was affected by an overall budgetary limit and legislators' desire that all the aged receive some benefit, that it should not be limited to just those aged with very large drug expenses. As shown in Exhibit 8.3, after meeting a $250 deductible, the aged must then pay 25 percent of their drug expenses between $250 and $2,500 (so almost all of the aged would receive some benefit). Then, to remain within the budget limit for this new benefit, the aged must pay 100 percent of their drug expenses between $2,500 and $5,100 before the government picks up 95 percent of their remaining drug expenses. The deductibles increase over time, as shown for 2013 in the bottom part of Exhibit 8.3. (As part of the Patient Protection and Affordable Care Act [PPACA], enacted in 2010, the size of the "doughnut hole" will be reduced.)

Medigap Supplementary Insurance

About 18 percent of the aged (mostly middle- and high-income aged) also purchase private Medigap insurance to cover the HI and SMI out-of-pocket costs not covered by Medicare. (An additional 16 percent are covered by Medicaid, 35 percent have additional coverage through their previous employers, and 19 percent have their out-of-pocket costs covered through their Medicare Advantage plan.) These out-of-pocket expenses—the HI and SMI deductibles and the 20 percent SMI copayment—can be a substantial financial burden, as Medicare does not have any stop-loss limit for out-of-pocket expenses. (When their out-of-pocket expenses become too great a financial burden, the low-income aged must fall back on Medicaid.) Medigap policies provide the aged with nearly first-dollar coverage, eliminating patients' financial incentives to limit their use of services or join managed care plans.

Concerns About the Current Medicare System

Three basic concerns with Medicare are whether its redistributive system is fair, whether it promotes efficiency, and whether it will remain solvent (and how its solvency will affect the federal deficit).

Redistributive Aspects of Medicare

Does Medicare promote equity in terms of who receives and who finances its subsidies? When a person pays the full cost of the benefits she receives, no redistribution occurs. However, when a person pays less than the full costs of his benefits, he receives a subsidy and other population groups must bear the financial burden of that subsidy. Because Medicare is a pay-as-you-go system, its beneficiaries contributed, on average, much less than the benefits they have received.

Redistribution is based on a societal value judgment that subsidies should be provided to particular groups. Typically, subsidies are expected to go to those with lower incomes and be financed by those with higher incomes.

Medicare's redistributive system raises two concerns. First, Medicare benefits have been the same for all the aged regardless of income. Almost all the aged (97 percent) pay the same Part B premium and therefore receive the same subsidy. Medicare has relatively high deductibles and no limit on out-of-pocket expenditures, and nonacute services, such as long-term care, are not covered. Furthermore, those aged requiring home care or nursing home services unrelated to an illness episode must typically rely on their own funds to cover such expenses. Thus, out-of-pocket payments for excluded benefits as a percentage of income are high for the low-income aged, exceeding 20 percent, whereas the corresponding figure for the high-income aged is less than 6 percent, on average. Consequently, many low-income aged find the out-of-pocket expenses a financial hardship, and 16 percent must rely on Medicaid (Kaiser Commission on Key Facts 2011).

How equitable is the financing of Medicare? Medicare beneficiaries do not pay the full costs of the medical services they receive; the aged are subsidized by those who pay state and federal taxes and Medicare HI taxes. The subsidy to Medicaid recipients is acknowledged to be "welfare," as recipients receive benefits in excess of any taxes they may have paid. As a welfare program, Medicaid is appropriately financed through the income tax system, whereby those with higher incomes contribute more in absolute and proportionate payments in relation to their income. This is the fairest way to finance a welfare program.

Thus, the second concern with Medicare's redistributive system is that Medicare enrollees currently receive a very large intergenerational transfer of wealth (subsidy) from those currently in the labor force, which is no different from a conventional form of welfare. Several studies have estimated the difference between the Medicare payroll tax contributions made by the aged and the average value of the benefits they received; the difference between these contributions and benefits is the size of the intergenerational subsidy. For example, those aged who became eligible when Medicare started in 1966 received a 100 percent welfare subsidy. In subsequent years, as more aged became eligible, they made some contributions into the Hospital Trust Fund. Vogel (1988) estimates that 95 percent of Part A expenditures in 1984 should be regarded as subsidies, and Iglehart (1992, 966) states that "for those who retired in 1991, the current average value of a beneficiary's Medicare hospital benefit far exceeds his or her contribution: $5.09 of services has been paid for under Part A for every $1 contributed. The ratio of benefits to contributions is even greater for people who retired earlier."

To these Part A subsidies should be added the 75 percent federal subsidy for Part B (SMI) premiums, which exceeded $207 billion in 2010, and the 75 percent federal subsidy for Part D (prescription drugs), which is estimated to exceed $1.14 trillion over the period from 2011 to 2020. However, because the Part B and Part D subsidies are financed from general income taxes, those with higher incomes provide relatively more of the intergenerational subsidy to the aged. With regard to Part A, on the other hand, the subsidy to the aged is financed by a payroll tax on all employees. Thus, an inequitable situation arises. Lower-income employees are taxed to subsidize the medical expenses of higher-income Medicare beneficiaries.

Payroll taxes are not a desirable method of financing a welfare program. Although the employer and the employee each pay half of the Medicare HI tax, studies confirm that employees end up paying most of the employer's share of the payroll tax as well (Brittain 1971; Gruber 1994b; Blumberg 1999). When an employer decides how many employees to hire and what wage to pay, it considers all of the costs of that employee. Any tax or regulatory cost imposed on the employer based on its number of employees is the same as requiring the employer to pay higher wages to those employees. Whether the cost of that employee is in the form of wages, fringe benefits, or taxes does not matter to the employer; each is considered a cost of labor. An increase in the employer's HI tax increases the cost of labor.

When the cost of an employee is increased such that it exceeds her value to the employer, the employer will discharge the employee unless it can reduce the employee's wage to the point where the cost does not exceed the employee's value. Typically, when payroll taxes are increased, wages are eventually renegotiated. Employees receive less than they would otherwise have received because of higher payroll taxes imposed on the employer. Thus, most of the employer's share of the tax is shifted to the employee in the form of lower wages.

A tax per employee imposed on the employer rarely stays with the employer. Although the employer pays the tax, the part of the tax not shifted back to the employee in the form of lower wages will be shifted forward in the form of higher prices for goods and services. For example, most industries are competitive and do not earn excessive profits; otherwise, new firms would enter the industry and compete away those profits. When the HI tax is increased on the employee and the employer, employment contracts cannot be immediately renegotiated. Rather than being forced to reduce its profits and potentially leave the industry, the employer will shift the tax forward to the consumer by raising prices.

Whether the tax is shifted back to the employee or forward to the consumer, the tax is regressive; those with low incomes pay a greater portion of their income in Social Security taxes than do higher-income people. Only recently has the HI payroll tax become proportional to income. (Under PPACA, interest and dividend income for those whose family income exceeds $250,000 a year will be subject to a Medicare tax; however, these funds will *not* be used to support the Medicare program; they will be used to offset the increased expenditures under PPACA to expand Medicaid and provide subsidies for those under age 65 who become eligible to buy insurance from the new insurance exchanges.) When the tax is passed on to consumers, the higher prices are a greater proportionate burden on low-income consumers.

Why is half of the Medicare tax imposed on the employer? The reason is related more to a tax's visibility than to who ends up paying it. Politicians would prefer to make employees believe their share of the tax is much smaller than it actually is.

If society makes the value judgment that it wants to help those with low incomes by providing them with a welfare benefit, the most equitable way to do so would be to provide the majority of benefits to those with low incomes and finance those benefits by taxing those with higher incomes. The burden of financing Medicare Part A, however, has fallen more heavily on those with lower incomes. Many aged who receive Part A benefits have higher incomes and assets than those who are providing the subsidies. An income tax, which takes proportionately more from those with higher incomes, would be a more equitable way to finance benefits to those with low incomes. Although the investment and retirement incomes of high-income aged are not subject to payroll taxes, they are subject to income taxes.

Efficiency Incentives in Medicare

Traditional Medicare was designed to provide limited efficiency incentives to beneficiaries or providers of medical services. The elderly had no incentives to choose less costly hospitals, as the deductible was the same for all hospitals (and hospitals were precluded from competing for the aged by decreasing the deductible) and there were no copayments for inpatient admissions or lengths of stay. Hospitals were initially paid according to their costs for caring for an aged patient. In 1984, Medicare changed hospital payment to a fixed price per admission, but neither hospitals nor physicians have a financial incentive to manage the overall costs of an episode of care for an aged patient or provide preventive services that lead to lower acute medical costs. Only Medicare Advantage plans, such as HMOs, paid on a capitation basis, have such incentives.

Medicare can best be thought of as a state-of-the-art 1960s health insurance plan. Congress modeled Part A after Blue Cross, which paid for hospitalization, and Part B after Blue Shield, which covered physician services. Cost-containment and utilization management methods used extensively in the private insurance market are virtually nonexistent in Medicare.

The lack of financial incentives for providers to coordinate care and minimize the cost of that care led to rapid increases in the cost of Medicare over time. In 2010, Medicare spent $524 billion, compared with $1.8 billion in 1966. As Medicare expenditures have exceeded government projections, every administration, regardless of political party, has increased the HI payroll tax and reduced the rate of increase in hospital payments for treating Medicare patients.

As shown in Exhibit 8.4, when the Medicare hospital diagnosis-related group (DRG) pricing system was introduced in the mid-1980s and an annual limit was placed on increases in the DRG price, the rate of increase in Medicare hospital expenditures declined. However, since the late 1980s, expenditures for skilled nursing homes, and particularly home healthcare, which were included in Part A, have increased rapidly, causing total Part A expenditures to sharply increase.

In 1997, concerned by the rate of increase in Part A expenditures, Congress enacted several changes intended to keep the Medicare (Part A)

EXHIBIT 8.4 Growth in Real Medicare Expenditures per Enrollee, Part A, Part B, and Part D, 1966–2009

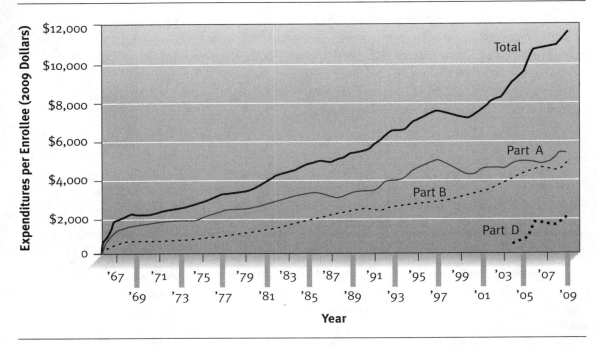

NOTE: Values adjusted for inflation using the Consumer Price Index for all urban consumers. Part A and Part B expenditures exclude patient deductible. In 1997, home healthcare was moved from Part A to Part B. As a result, Part A expenditures per enrollee dropped.

SOURCES: Data from Social Security Administration. 2000. *Social Security Bulletin, Annual Statistical Supplement.* Washington, DC: HHS. 2000–09 data from Centers for Medicare & Medicaid Services, Office of the Actuary, 2010. *Annual Report of the Boards of Trustees of the Federal Hospital Insurance and Federal Supplementary Medical Insurance Trust Funds,* Tables III.A3, III.B4, III.C8, and III.C19. [Online information.] http://www.cms.gov/ReportsTrustFunds/downloads/tr2010.pdf.

HI Hospital Trust Fund solvent. Home healthcare expenditures, which were increasing rapidly, were simply moved from Part A to Part B. This change shifted the financing of home healthcare from the payroll tax to the income tax. Congress also reduced payments to hospitals and to Medicare HMOs, which caused many HMOs to reduce their enrollment of Medicare beneficiaries. (Both changes resulted in a reduction in Medicare Part A expenditures, as shown in Exhibit 8.4.)

To limit the increase in Part B expenditures, in 1997 Congress also changed the method by which physicians' fees would be updated annually. Medicare physician fee increases were to be based in part on the percentage increase in real GDP per capita, which is unrelated to the supply and demand for physician services by Medicare beneficiaries. This is referred to as the sustainable growth rate (SGR). The consequences of the SGR were not to be felt for several years.

At the same time Congress was limiting provider payment increases, the aged received additional benefits through the expansion of Medicare coverage for preventive services such as mammograms, Pap smears, and prostate and colorectal screening tests.

Perhaps the clearest indication of Medicare's inefficient design is the wide variation in Medicare expenditures per beneficiary with chronic illness across states, without any difference in life expectancy or patient satisfaction.[1] For example, in 2005 Medicare spent, on average, $39,810 per beneficiary in New Jersey, compared with an average of $23,697 per beneficiary in other states. Patients with chronic illness in New Jersey had an average of 41.5 physician visits during the last six months of their lives, compared with an average of 17 visits for similar patients in Utah. Hospital days during the last six months of their lives varied from 32.1 per beneficiary at one medical center in New York to 12.9 at another medical center in Minnesota. During the last two years, Medicare spent an average of $79,280 per year at one academic medical center, compared with $37,271 at another academic center (Dartmouth Atlas Project 2006). Medicare pays for quantity, not quality.

Medicare Modernization Act of 2003

The largest and most significant change to Medicare since its inception was the passage of the Medicare Modernization Act, which provided the aged with an outpatient prescription drug benefit. The initial cost of this drug benefit was estimated at $400 billion over ten years. This estimate has since been revised upward to $1 trillion over the period from 2011 to 2020. To receive the political support of hospitals and physician groups, Congress included in the legislation additional payments for hospitals and reversed the 4.5 percent decrease in Medicare physician fees that was to occur based on the SGR. Instead, physicians were provided with a 1.5 percent increase.

The Impending Bankruptcy of Medicare

The current Medicare program, without improvements, is ill suited to serve future generations of seniors and eligible disabled Americans.

Medicare's future includes a series of challenges. The numbers of aged are increasing both in absolute and percentage terms. The aged are living longer. Medical care costs continue to increase, and technology is driving medical costs still higher. To maintain the solvency of Medicare Part A by imposing higher payroll taxes on the working population is politically infeasible and inequitable for those with low incomes. Medicare Part B and Part C expenditures, which are funded from general tax revenues, will eventually consume the entire federal budget and require politically unpopular income tax increases, unless something else is done.

Medicare expenditures for Parts A, B, and D are expected to increase from 3.1 percent of GDP in 2010 to 4.0 percent by 2020. As a percentage of the federal budget, total Medicare expenditures are estimated to increase from 12.1 percent to 16.8 percent by 2020, based on the more likely pessimistic projections (Office of Management and Budget 2011).

In addition, the Medicare Supplementary Medical Insurance Trust Fund, which pays for physician services and the new prescription drug benefit, will require substantial increases over time in both general revenue financing and premium charges. As the reserves in HI are drawn down and SMI general revenue financing requirements continue to grow, the pressure on the federal budget will intensify.

The currently projected long-run growth rates of Medicare are not sustainable under current financing arrangements.

In coming years the aging of the population will place great pressures on the HI Trust Fund. The first of the 77 million baby boomers retire in 2011. In 1960, just 9.2 percent of the population was older than 65 years. In 2010, 13.0 percent of the population was aged 65 or older. Under the demographic pressure of the baby boomers, the number of Medicare recipients will double by 2040 (from 40 million to 81 million), after the last of the baby boomers will have turned 65 (see Exhibit 8.5). At that time, one in five Americans (20 percent) will be older than 65.

People older than 65 years have five times the medical costs of younger Americans. Large numbers of retirees, combined with increased longevity and more expensive and advanced medical technology, will generate huge increases in Medicare spending. The magnitude of this projected shortfall is shown in Exhibit 8.6.

The pressure to reform Medicare will most likely occur as the Medicare Trust Fund approaches insolvency. The HI Trust Fund currently has negative cash flows, and annual cash flow deficits are expected to grow rapidly after 2011, as the baby boomers begin to retire. (The current cash deficit is financed by previous payroll taxes in excess of outlays.) The growing deficits will exhaust the Trust Fund reserves before the end of the current decade.

While Medicare expenditures are projected to sharply increase, the employee base supporting Medicare is eroding. Per aged person, the number of workers paying taxes and financing the program has steadily declined, increasing the tax burden on each employee. In 1960 there were 5.1 workers per beneficiary, in 1970 that declined to 3.7 per beneficiary, and currently it is 3.5 per beneficiary. By 2030, when the last of the baby boomers retire, the number will fall to 2.3 per beneficiary. Intermediate projections indicate that the HI tax will have to be increased from 2.9 percent to 6.21 percent (CBO 2010b). However, as actual experience has been much closer to pessimistic (high-cost) assumptions, the HI tax rate will likely have to be increased to 10.86 percent by 2030.[2] These increased tax rates are only for Part A. The

EXHIBIT 8.5 Population Pyramid, United States, 1960, 2010, and 2040

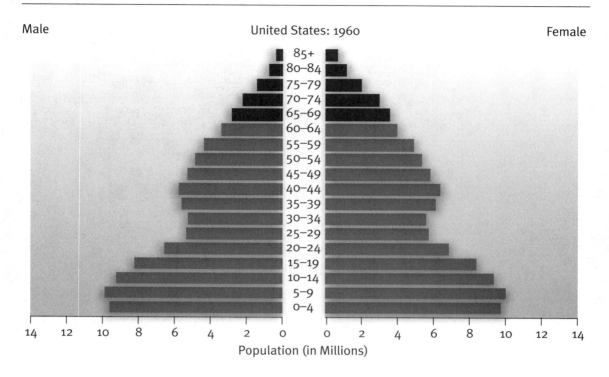

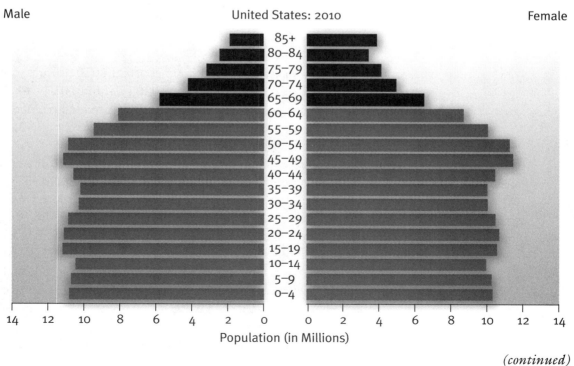

(continued)

Exhibit 8.5 *(continued)*

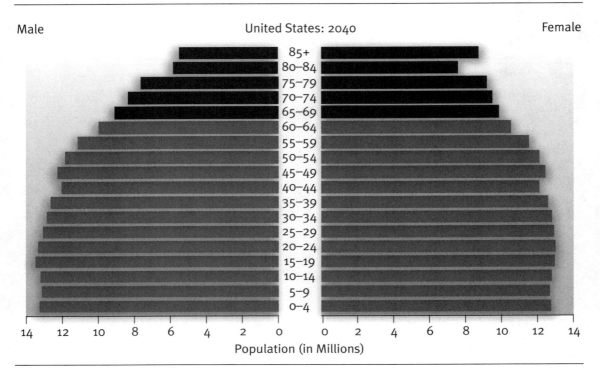

SOURCE: Data from DOC, US Census Bureau. 2010. International Data Base. [Online information.] http://www.census.gov/ipc/www/idb/country.php.

annual subsidy for Medicare Parts A, B, and D (in constant 2010 dollars) will rise from $451 billion (2010) to $957 billion by 2020 (Galston 2010) (total expenditures minus premium income).[3] Unless taxes are increased or Medicare benefits are reduced, these federal expenditures will require reductions in other politically popular federal programs.

Political support for Medicare is likely to decline as the costs to the non-aged increase, with a consequent increase in intergenerational political conflict. Our political system cannot wait until more of the baby boomers retire to resolve an issue that involves such a large redistribution of wealth among different groups in society. The baby boomers who start retiring in the next several years have certain expectations about what they will receive from Medicare. Politicians cannot change Medicare's benefits at the last moment. No presidential candidate will campaign on decreasing Medicare benefits. Any changes will have to be agreed upon in nonelection years and gradually phased in. Yet the longer Congress waits, the higher the payroll tax will be.

Enacting legislation to decrease Medicare benefits or eligibility in a presidential or congressional election year will be difficult, as Medicare has

Exhibit 8.6 Cash Deficit of the Medicare HI Trust Fund, 2008–2018

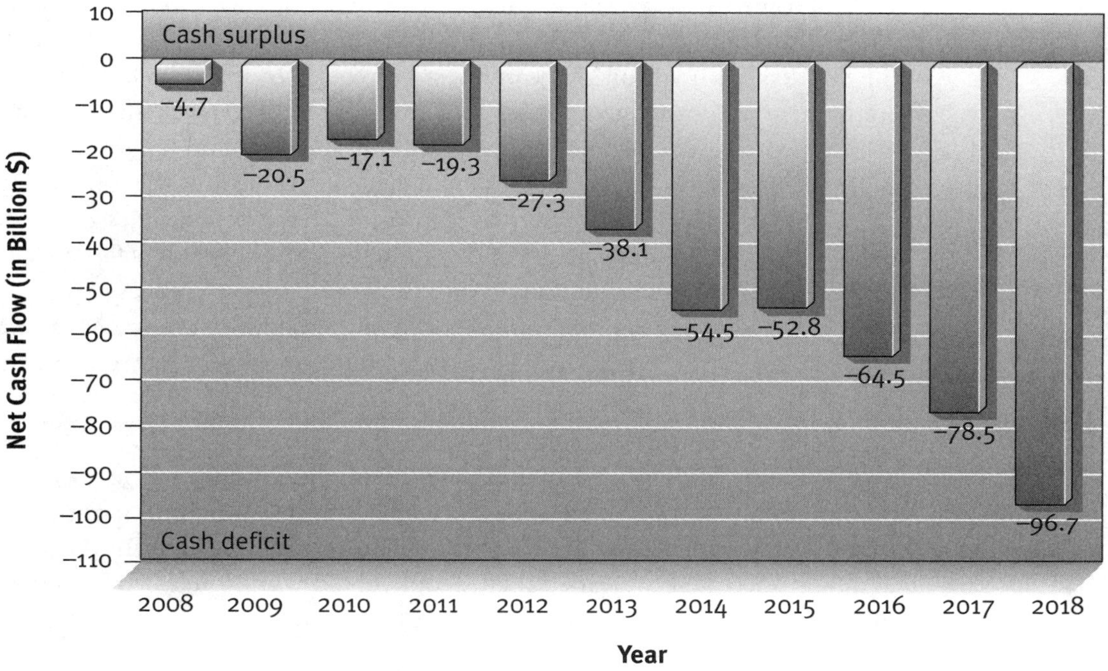

SOURCE: CMS, 2009, *Annual Report of the Board of Trustees of the Federal Hospital Insurance and Federal Supplementary Medical Insurance Trust Funds,* http://www.cms.gov/ReportsTrustFunds/downloads/tr2009.pdf.

such widespread political support among the elderly, the near elderly, and their children, who might be faced with an increased financial burden of paying their parents' medical expenses. Given that a new Medicare system must be phased in and there are few nonelection years in which to enact such controversial legislation, any changes must be enacted within the next few years.

Proposals for Medicare Reform

The financial problems of Medicare cannot be solved by past approaches alone—increasing the HI tax and reducing hospital and physician payments—because the funds required would be too great and the tax base too small. Employees will begin to oppose politicians who vote to increase their payroll taxes. Hospitals and physicians will reduce access to care for the aged, and quality of services will decline as costs exceed government payments. Instead, Medicare will have to be restructured. Furthermore, the financial burden will likely be spread over several constituencies—taxpayers, employees, healthcare providers, and the baby boomers. As in previous attempts to save the Trust Fund, the current aged are least likely to be adversely affected by these changes.

Proposals to restructure Medicare should be based on two criteria: equity and efficiency. To make Medicare an equitable redistribution system, the entitlement myth of Medicare must be recognized, and its large welfare component acknowledged. Either Medicare should become similar to a pension system whereby people save for their own medical (and long-term-care) expenses, or government subsidies should be used to help only the low-income aged, or both. Health plans should also compete for beneficiaries based on price, quality, outcomes, and enrollee satisfaction. Health plans will then have incentives to be efficient and responsive to beneficiary preferences.

The following approaches have been proposed for reforming Medicare. A combination of proposals will likely be used to spread the financial burden.

Increase the Eligibility Age to 67
Similar to one of the solutions used to increase the solvency of the Social Security system, the age of eligibility would be increased by one month each year so that the eligibility age for Social Security and Medicare are the same, 67. With increased life expectancy, people could work longer and maintain their employment-based health insurance.

Reduce the Rate of Increase in Medicare Provider Payments
This approach has been used previously and is likely to be part of any long-term solution. However, decreasing provider payments will ultimately reduce provider participation and access to care by Medicare beneficiaries.

Increase the HI (Part A) Tax
This approach, which has also been used previously, is likely to be part of any proposed solution. An increase in the HI tax would increase the financial burden on low-wage workers.

Increase the Part B Premium
The elderly currently pay a premium that covers only 25 percent of Part B expenditures; a higher percentage will likely be phased in over time. A uniform premium increase for all the aged places a greater financial burden on low-income aged.

Make the Part B and Part D Premiums Income Related
As a result of the Medicare Modernization Act of 2003, the Medicare Part B premium became income related; however, only about 3 percent of the aged receive subsidies smaller than 75 percent. Medicare Part D subsidies should also be made income related, and both should include more of the aged who

can afford to pay a higher percentage of the premiums. As the Part B and Part D premiums are increased, the hardship on the low-income aged would be minimized by a greater use of income-related premiums. Equity would be improved and the deficit reduced if subsidies to higher-income aged were eventually completely phased out.

Change Medicare from a Defined-Benefit to a Defined-Contribution Plan

Medicare currently pays for a defined (and continually expanding) set of benefits regardless of their costs, which is an open-ended government commitment. A defined contribution is a predetermined amount of money (including Parts A, B, and D), similar to a voucher, that the government would pay to a health plan on behalf of the aged. (This capitation payment should be risk adjusted based on age, health status, and geographic location to reflect the expected variation in a beneficiary's health costs.) Older and sicker beneficiaries would receive higher amounts, so that health plans would have an incentive to enroll them. Health plans would compete for the defined contribution, and the aged would have an incentive to shop for the plan that offered the most benefits for their "voucher" but did not exceed the expense covered by the voucher.

In addition to providing greater predictability to the government, the financial risk of caring for the aged is shifted to the health plan. Under a defined-contribution plan the government would pay the premium for the low-cost health plan (an HMO) in an area. The aged would be able to join other, more expensive plans by paying the additional cost of those plans. (This approach is similar to the Federal Employees Health Benefits Plan.)

Change Medicare to an Income-Related Program

The voucher idea described above could also be used to change Medicare to an income-related program. Each recipient would receive a voucher, but its value would be determined by the recipient's income. The value of the voucher would equal the entire premium required to provide a uniform set of benefits for low-income aged, but wealthier aged would receive proportionately smaller vouchers. As a transition to this approach, all the current aged could receive the maximum voucher. The income-related voucher would be phased in for future aged.

In addition to improving equity, the income-related approach would improve efficiency, unlike traditional fee-for-service Medicare, because as more of the aged have to pay part of the premium, they would be more receptive to enrolling in more efficient plans.

An income-related approach would reduce the cost of the program and the huge intergenerational subsidies from low-income workers to high-income aged. Income-related benefits would also help the low-income aged, who are less able to afford the deductibles, cost sharing, and Part B and D premiums than the high-income aged are.

Medical Individual Retirement Account

Medicare could be changed from a pay-as-you-go plan (in which the contributions from current employees pay the expenses of current retirees) to a true pension-type system in which the funds contributed by current employees are invested and available to pay their future retirement medical benefits. Under this scenario, employees would be able to invest their 2.9 percent HI tax in a medical individual retirement account (medical IRA) to be used only when they retire. Obviously, such a plan would have to be phased in over a long transition period, as many workers have already contributed to Medicare. Additional government funds would be required under this approach because the government would lose the HI payroll tax revenues from those employees who choose the medical IRA option. Individuals would have greater control (and incentive) over how their healthcare funds are spent; they could be used to buy a high-deductible plan or join a health plan. These funds could also be used for long-term care.

Politics of Medicare Reform

The popularity of Medicare means that politicians who attempt to change it without the endorsement of both political parties are at great political risk. Previously, imposing financial burdens on providers by paying them less and increasing payroll taxes was easier than increasing the financial burden on the elderly.[4]

Unfortunately, the longer it takes to phase in a system that is more equitable, the greater will be the political problems. Current workers will have to pay higher payroll taxes, intergenerational transfers from low-income workers will increase, beneficiaries will have less access to providers as provider fees are reduced, and the financial hardship on low-income aged who cannot afford high out-of-pocket expenditures and rising Part B and D premiums will increase. The sooner the financial burden is shared among the different groups in a more equitable manner, the smaller future tax increases will be.

Summary

The potential cost of suggesting dramatic solutions to the problems of Medicare is high to any one political party. Whatever the combination of approaches selected, a vast redistribution of wealth will result. A bipartisan commission whose recommendations are adopted by Congress has in the past resolved such highly visible redistributive problems. Although the National Bipartisan Commission on the Future of Medicare (created by Congress as part of the 1997 Balanced Budget Act) was unable to reach agreement (by just one vote) on reforming Medicare in 1999, whether and when a commission approach will again be used for reforming Medicare remains to be seen.

Discussion Questions

1. Which population groups are served by Medicare, what are the different parts of Medicare, and how is Medicare financed?
2. Discuss how Medicare's patient and provider incentives affect efficient use of services.
3. How equitable are the methods used to finance Medicare?
4. How does the Medicare Hospital Trust Fund differ from a pension fund?
5. Why is it necessary to reform Medicare?
6. Evaluate the proposals mentioned to reform Medicare in terms of their equitability and effects on efficiency.

Notes

1. The Dartmouth Atlas Project (2006) online report, *The Care of Patients with Severe Chronic Illness*, examined differences in the management of Medicare patients "with one or more of twelve chronic illnesses that accounts for more than 75% of all U.S. healthcare expenditures. Among people who died between 1999 and 2003, per capita spending varied by a factor of six between hospitals across the country. Spending was not correlated with rates of illness in different parts of the country; rather, it reflected how intensively certain resources—acute care hospital beds, specialist physician visits, tests and other services—were used in the management of people who were very ill but could not be cured. Since other research has demonstrated that, for these chronically ill Americans, receiving more services does not result in improved outcomes, and since most Americans say they prefer to avoid a very 'high-tech' death, the report concludes that Medicare spending for the care of the chronically ill could be reduced by as much as 30%—*while improving quality, patient satisfaction, and outcomes.*"
2. The rate of growth in real wages (because HI is a payroll tax) and life expectancy at retirement are important components of these projections.

Pessimistic projections assume a rate of growth in real wages similar to the growth rate in the past 25 years, which is half as large as that used in the intermediate assumption. Advances in medicine, genetics, and biotechnology are also projected to result in a more rapid increase in life expectancy at retirement than the intermediate projections that assume the same rate as for the past 50 years.

3. In 2010 annual federal expenditures were $250.3 billion for Medicare Part A, $207.6 billion for Part B, and $58.2 billion for Part D—a total of $516.2 billion. Projected federal subsidies (expenditures minus premiums) in 2020 for each part of Medicare, in constant dollars, are $391.5 billion for Part A, $358.6 billion for Part B, and $176.9 billion for Part D—a total of $927 billion (CBO 2010b).

4. The Medicare Catastrophic Act of 1989 illustrates how much difficulty Congress will face in enacting equitable Medicare reform. High-income aged were required to increase their Part B contributions to finance greater benefits to low-income aged. Protests by the high-income aged were so great that Congress repealed the legislation the following year, and this attempt to increase fairness failed.

MEDICAID

Medicaid is a means-tested welfare program for the poor, providing medical and long-term care to more than 21 percent of the population. In 1985, Medicaid covered 22 million people, the federal government spent $23 billion on the program, and it represented 2.4 percent of the federal budget. By 2010, Medicaid covered 71 million people, total federal expenditures reached $275 billion, and the program increased its share of the federal budget to 7.4 percent. Despite these rapidly increasing Medicaid expenditures, which represent a growing financial burden on federal and state budgets, many low-income persons do not qualify for Medicaid.

Medicaid is administered by each state, but policy is shared by the federal government, which pays between 50 and 76 percent matching funds based on each state's financial capacity (per capita income).[1] These federal dollars make Medicaid a less expensive approach for the states to use in expanding access to medical care by those with low incomes, compared with other state programs, such as General Assistance. Each state Medicaid program must cover certain federally mandated population groups to qualify for federal matching funds.

The first and largest federally mandated population group is those receiving cash welfare assistance, which includes single-parent families, who were previously eligible for Aid to Families with Dependent Children (AFDC), and low-income aged, blind, and disabled persons who qualify for Supplemental Security Income. The second mandatory eligibility group is low-income pregnant women and children who do not qualify for cash assistance. Third are those considered to be "medically needy," that is, persons who do not qualify for welfare programs but have high medical or long-term-care expenses. The fourth group consists of low-income Medicare beneficiaries who cannot afford the deductibles, cost sharing, premiums for Medicare Parts B and D, or cost of services not covered by Medicare.

States may expand eligibility and enroll additional groups (and add services beyond those for groups mandated by the federal government). Thus, wide variations in coverage and eligibility exist among the states. Groups typically added at the state's option include medically needy groups beyond those that are federally mandated, such as the elderly and people with disabilities; children and pregnant women at a higher percentage in excess of the federal poverty level (e.g., 200 percent); and all uninsured persons with incomes be-low a certain level. However, the percentage of the Medicaid-covered popu-lation that is poor (less than 100 percent of the poverty level) varies greatly by state—from 28 to 61 percent. Just being poor is insufficient to qualify for Medicaid. On average, only 44 percent of those classified as poor are enrolled in Medicaid. The percentage of near-poor (100 to 199 percent of the poverty level) enrolled by states varies from 13 to 40 percent (with an average of 23.6 percent).

In 1996, Temporary Assistance to Needy Families (TANF) was enact-ed to replace AFDC. TANF retains the same eligibility rules as AFDC. Before welfare reform, many poor children qualified automatically for Medicaid be-cause their families were receiving AFDC, the national cash benefits program for poor children. Welfare reform ended that link by abolishing AFDC. Be-cause Congress did not want anyone to lose Medicaid eligibility as a result of welfare reform, it decreed that states should continue using their old AFDC rules for determining Medicaid eligibility, such as covering pregnant women, the medically needy, and children, if their parents would have qualified for AFDC under the old law. The children of women who leave welfare for work are still eligible for Medicaid if their family income remains low enough.

An Illustration of Medicaid Eligibility

Within federal guidelines, states may set their own income and asset eligibility criteria for Medicaid. Following is an illustration of how those who are medi-cally needy qualify for Medi-Cal (Medicaid in California). A person cannot have more than $2,000 in assets ($3,000 for two people), excluding a house, car, and furniture. One's financial assets can be reduced in many legitimate ways to qualify for Medicaid. Money could be spent fixing up one's house, purchasing a new car, or taking a vacation, or it could be put in a special burial account. Selling one's house and giving the cash to one's children will make one ineligible for Medicaid for months. (The penalty period for doing so is determined by dividing the amount transferred by the average private-pay cost of a nursing home in the state. For example, if a person gave away property to his children worth $100,000 and the monthly cost of nursing home care in California in 2010 was $6,311, the person would be ineligible for Medicaid benefits for 16 months.)

When a couple is involved, special spousal financial protections exist. If a husband enters a nursing home, the wife can remain in their home and is entitled to have about $2,739 a month in income and $109,560 in financial assets (excluding primary residence and a car). If the wife's Social Security pay-ments are below $2,739, the husband's Social Security can be used to bring her monthly income to $2,739. (These data on eligibility apply to Orange County, California.)

Retirement accounts and other assets can be partially shielded from the government by counting the income from those retirement accounts toward the $2,739 monthly income. For example, if a person has $100,000 in an IRA and takes out $500 a month, the $500 counts toward his monthly income, but the $100,000 does not count as an asset. A number of states have begun to crack down on various schemes used by some wealthy aged to shield their assets to become Medicaid eligible, such as setting up annuities, trusts, and life contracts.[2] In general, many middle-class elderly become distraught when they find they must spend down their hard-earned assets for a spouse to become Medicaid eligible.

State Children's Health Insurance Program (SCHIP)

A major expansion of Medicaid eligibility occurred in 1997. As part of the 1997 Balanced Budget Act, Congress enacted the State Children's Health Insurance Program (SCHIP). SCHIP was enacted to provide coverage for low-income children whose family incomes were not low enough to qualify for Medicaid. Politically, children are considered a vulnerable and more deserving group than other uninsured groups; consequently, this program expansion received bipartisan support. (Medical benefits for children are considered relatively inexpensive compared with benefits for uninsured adults.) Furthermore, providing coverage to older children was viewed as an expansion of existing Medicaid policies, which expanded Medicaid coverage to infants, younger children, and pregnant women in the late 1980s. This program provided the states with federal matching funds to initiate and expand healthcare assistance for uninsured low-income children up to age 19 with family incomes as high as 200 percent of the federal poverty level (FPL). Federal matching funds may be as high as 83 percent (Henry J. Kaiser Family Foundation 2010c).

The number of children eligible for public coverage increased dramatically, as did participation rates in SCHIP. The percentage of uninsured children whose family income is between 100 percent and 200 percent of the poverty level (as well as those whose family income is less than 100 percent of the federal poverty level) has declined since 1997. In each of these groups, the percentage of children with public coverage has increased; the percentage of children with private insurance decreased over this same period. This points to the fact that not all of the increase in public coverage for poor and low-income children was the result of uninsured children being enrolled in SCHIP. A significant increase in public coverage also resulted from a shift away from private insurance to free or lower-cost public coverage (referred to as "crowd-out" because public insurance "crowds out" private insurance). It has been estimated that as many as 60 percent of those newly enrolled in public insurance programs, such as SCHIP, were formerly in private insurance plans (Gruber and Simon 2008).

Bipartisan support for SCHIP was also achieved as a result of an ideological compromise on how SCHIP services would be delivered to eligible children. States may either purchase health insurance coverage for eligible children in the private market or they may be included in the state's Medicaid program.

The Children's Health Insurance Program (now referred to as CHIP) was renewed in 2010. A concern with the renewal of CHIP was that it was originally intended for children of low-income families but has now been extended to include more children from middle-income families. CHIP eligibility in some states is as high as $72,275 for a family of four; further, a number of states use CHIP funds to cover adults other than expectant mothers.

Medicaid Beneficiaries and Medicaid Expenditures

Broadened eligibility requirements for Medicaid have caused the number of recipients to sharply increase, from 22 million in 1975 to 71 million in 2010 to an estimated 74 million by 2020, with federal expenditures expected to reach $488 billion. Most of the enrollment growth resulted from federal and state expansions in coverage of low-income children and pregnant women. As of 2008, the major beneficiary groups consist of low-income children (49.5 percent); nondisabled low-income adults (pregnant women and adults in families with children receiving cash assistance, 25.7 percent); the blind and people with disabilities receiving acute medical and long-term care services (16.0 percent); and aged persons receiving Medicare who need Medicaid ("dual eligibles") to pay for their deductibles, cost sharing, premiums for Medicare Parts B and D, and other services not covered by Medicare (8.8 percent).

As shown in Exhibit 9.1, the distribution of Medicaid expenditures does not match the distribution of Medicaid enrollees. Although about 75 percent of Medicaid recipients are low-income parents and children, they account for only about 33 percent of Medicaid expenditures. By comparison, about 67 percent of Medicaid expenditures are for medical services and institutional care for the aged, people with disabilities, and people with mental handicaps (25 percent of Medicaid recipients).

Although the number of Medicaid beneficiaries has increased over time, from about 22 million in the 1970s and 1980s, to about 35 million in the 1990s, to over 70 million in 2010, the distribution of beneficiary groups has stayed roughly constant over this period.

EXHIBIT 9.1
Percentage
Distribution
of Medicaid
Enrollees and
Benefit
Payments,
by Eligibility
Status, Fiscal
Year 2008

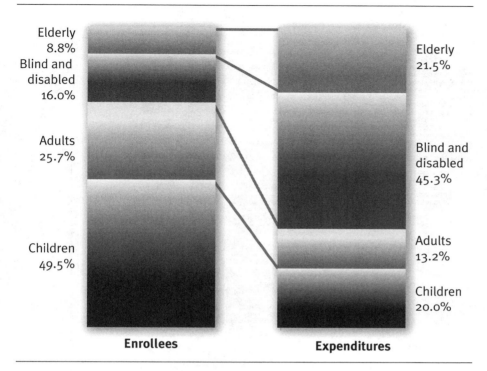

Enrollees	Expenditures
Elderly 8.8%	Elderly 21.5%
Blind and disabled 16.0%	Blind and disabled 45.3%
Adults 25.7%	Adults 13.2%
Children 49.5%	Children 20.0%

Enrollees   **Expenditures**

NOTE: 2007 data for HI and UT.

SOURCE: Centers for Medicare & Medicaid Services, Medicaid Statistical Information System State Summary Datamart, 2010. [Online information.] http://msis.cms.hhs.gov/.

State and federal Medicaid expenditures have rapidly increased and are expected to continue to rise sharply over the next decade. Medicaid represents one of the largest items in state budgets, along with elementary and secondary education expenditures. Federal and state Medicaid expenditures were $55.1 billion in 1988, rose to an estimated $344 billion in 2008, and are expected to reach $794 billion by 2019. The federal share of Medicaid expenditures is expected to increase from $251 billion in 2009 to $427 billion by 2019. The remaining expenditures represent the state's financial burden. During this same period, the number of beneficiaries is expected to increase by 19 percent (see Exhibit 9.2).

Exhibit 9.3 shows the distribution of Medicaid expenditures by type of service. The largest share of Medicaid expenditures is for acute care (63 percent), which is made up of fee-for-service payments (74 percent), managed care (23 percent), and Medicare premiums (3 percent). Long-term care (which includes nursing home care and home healthcare) represents the second-largest category (33 percent). Since Medicaid pays providers relatively low rates, payments to disproportionate-share hospitals (4.8 percent) compensate those hospitals that serve proportionately more Medicaid beneficiaries and low-income people.

Exhibit 9.2 Number of Medicaid Beneficiaries and Total Medicaid Expenditures, Actual and Projected, 1975–2019

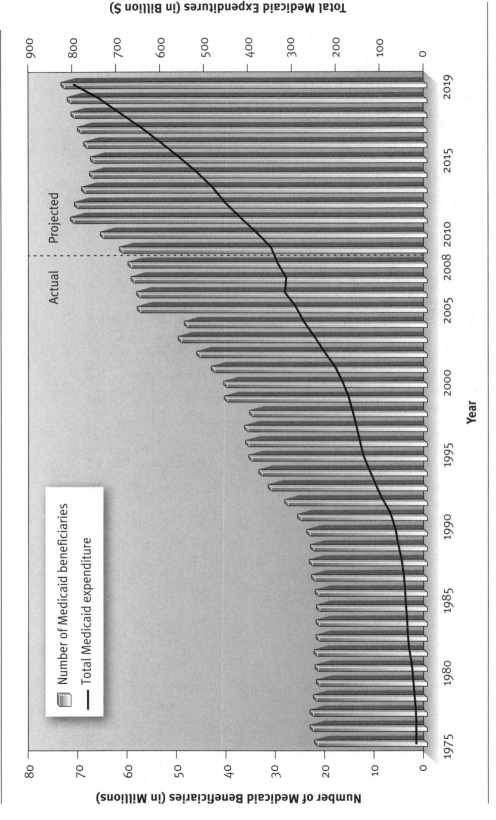

SOURCES: Data on the "Number of Medicaid beneficiaries" from Centers for Medicare & Medicaid Services, CMS Statistics, various editions; Projected data from Congressional Budget Office, *Spending and Enrollment Detail for CBO's March 2010 Baseline: Medicaid. 2010.* [Online information.] http://www.cbo.gov/budget/factsheets/2010b/medicaidBaseline.pdf. Data on the "Total Medicaid expenditures" from Centers for Medicare & Medicaid Services, Office of the Actuary, National Health Statistics Group, 2010. [Online information.] http://www.cms.hhs.gov/.

Exhibit 9.3 Medicaid Expenditures, by Service, 2009

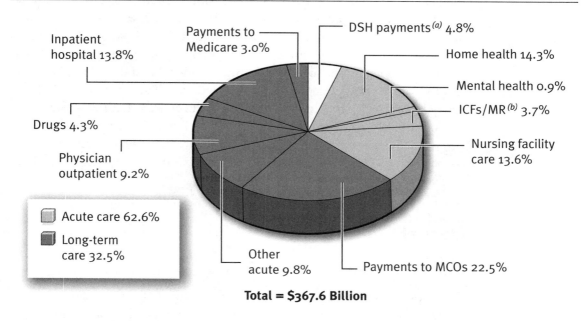

Inpatient hospital 13.8%

Payments to Medicare 3.0%

DSH payments[a] 4.8%

Home health 14.3%

Mental health 0.9%

ICFs/MR[b] 3.7%

Nursing facility care 13.6%

Drugs 4.3%

Physician outpatient 9.2%

Acute care 62.6%

Long-term care 32.5%

Other acute 9.8%

Payments to MCOs 22.5%

Total = $367.6 Billion

[a]DSH = Disproportionate-share hospital payments

[b]ICFs/MR = Intermediate care facilities for the mentally retarded

SOURCE: Centers for Medicare & Medicaid Services, Center for Medicaid and State Operations. 2010. Personal correspondence with Abraham John, April 13, 2010.

The Patient Protection and Affordable Care Act (PPACA)

As part of the PPACA, enacted in 2010, eligibility for Medicaid and federal Medicaid expenditures will be greatly increased. Starting in 2014, all those younger than 65 years of age with incomes up to 133 percent of the FPL will become eligible for Medicaid. (In 2010, 133 percent of the FPL was $14,404 for an individual and $29,327 for a family of four.) These eligibility standards, which will become uniform for all states, will include, for the first time, childless adults. As parents of children in CHIP become eligible for Medicaid, their children will be transferred from CHIP to Medicaid. The federal government will finance the full cost of increasing eligibility levels up to 133 percent of the FPL. In 2017 the federal matching rate will decline from 100 percent for these new eligibles (bringing others up to 133 percent of the FPL) to 90 percent by 2020 (Henry J. Kaiser Family Foundation 2010a). The federal government will spend an estimated additional $434 billion on Medicaid and CHIP coverage increases between 2010 and 2019; states will spend an additional $20 billion. States have expressed concern regarding their additional costs in later years.

These changes in eligibility are expected to increase those eligible for Medicaid by 16 million by 2019. Given the large expected increase in Medicaid by 2014, the government was concerned that the Medicaid population would have limited access to primary care physicians, particularly since Medicaid pays physicians lower fees than any other payer. Thus, just for the years 2013 and 2014, the federal government will pay the additional cost of making Medicaid fees to primary care physicians equal to Medicare fees. After 2014 Medicaid fees will presumably be determined by the states and will return to their previous lower levels, with a consequent sharp drop in physician availability.

As under the current Medicaid rules, states may increase eligibility levels beyond 133 percent of the FPL and receive the same federal matching funds.

Medicaid Policy Issues

Current major Medicaid policy issues include

- providing Medicaid coverage for all those eligible for Medicaid,
- providing full or partial coverage for those with low incomes who are not Medicaid eligible,
- providing high-quality coordinated care to those receiving Medicaid services, and
- reducing the rate of increase in Medicaid expenditures.

Several of these goals are contradictory. Covering all those who are eligible, expanding coverage to low-income persons who are not Medicaid eligible, and providing quality coordinated care cannot be achieved while reducing the rate of increase in Medicaid expenditures. Rising Medicaid expenditures have become an increasing financial burden to the states and the federal government. At the federal level, the administration will finance the expansion of Medicaid starting in 2014. However, the federal government currently faces a huge deficit, which will increase further as a result of its commitment under the PPACA. Unless the federal government is able to reduce current and future Medicaid expenditures, it will be unable to reduce its ever-increasing deficit.

States are limited in the amount of funds they can spend on Medicaid. To continue spending an increasing portion of state budgets on Medicaid would require a reduction of expenditures on politically popular programs, such as education and prisons, or tax increases. Each option is politically costly. Instead, many states have resorted to reducing Medicaid eligibility and setting low provider-payment rates, which reduce provider participation and reduce access to care by those on Medicaid. Further, states are concerned that the increasing federal deficit will cause the federal government to shift more Medicaid expenditures to the states.

Increasing the "take-up" rate, that is, increasing enrollment of those eligible, involves two benefit/cost trade-offs by those who are eligible but not participating in Medicaid. An eligible but not participating person must weigh the additional medical benefits she would receive if she participated in Medicaid versus the stigma "costs" of participating. Second, because income is one criterion for Medicaid eligibility, a person would lose his eligibility if his income increased above a certain level. Thus, another trade-off is between earning a higher income versus losing all Medicaid benefits. (This is referred to as the "notch" effect.) Medicaid eligibility would be increased if, as people's wages increased, they would lose only a portion of their Medicaid benefits. Graduating Medicaid benefits according to income would provide an incentive for those who want to keep their benefits to work more hours and seek higher-paying jobs.

Expanding Medicaid coverage to a greater portion of those with low incomes involves addressing state funding issues and maintaining incentives for working low-income persons who have health insurance to maintain their private insurance. Working low-income people with insurance have an incentive to drop their private insurance and accept the free public insurance. Although Medicaid is considered less valuable than private insurance (because of the stigma cost and more restricted access to physicians due to low Medicaid reimbursement), as the cost of private insurance increases, Medicaid becomes a more desirable substitute. Expanded public coverage in some states has displaced existing private coverage with little additional overall gain in coverage. (Part of the private coverage replaced by public coverage may have had relatively limited benefits.)

To lessen the cost of expanding Medicaid eligibility to the working poor, incentives, such as partial Medicaid subsidies (tax credits), should be developed to lessen employees' incentive for shifting from private coverage to Medicaid.

The remaining two Medicaid policy issues, providing high-quality coordinated care to Medicaid beneficiaries and reducing the rate of increase in Medicaid expenditures, are related. Medicaid has traditionally relied on fee-for-service provider payment. To reduce rising Medicaid expenditures, Medicaid programs reduced the fees paid to healthcare providers. The consequence of fee-for-service payment and reduced provider fees was a lack of coordinated care and low provider participation rates. Physician fees affect not only access to care but also willingness to treat Medicaid patients and time spent with Medicaid patients. Lower physician fees also result in a shift away from physician offices to use of hospital emergency rooms (Decker 2009; Zuckerman, Williams, and Stockley 2009).

Managed care offered Medicaid programs a way to reduce rising Medicaid expenditures and provide coordinated care to its enrollees. By paying managed care plans, such as HMOs, a fixed fee per person per month (i.e., a capitation fee), states were able to shift their risk for higher expenditures to a managed care plan. In addition, states could monitor how well the managed care plan achieved specific goals, such as immunization rates, preventive care, reduced use of hospital emergency departments, and so on. Medicaid managed care has become an important approach to providing Medicaid services.

Medicaid Managed Care

The largest change in the distribution of Medicaid expenditures has been the growth in Medicaid managed care. Almost all states rely on some form of managed care for their Medicaid populations. About 70 percent of Medicaid beneficiaries are enrolled in some form of managed care program. The types of managed care plans states use vary. Initially many states used primary care case management, whereby Medicaid beneficiaries are enrolled with a primary care gatekeeper who does not assume financial risk but receives a monthly fee of about $2 to $3 per enrollee per month and is responsible for coordinating the enrollee's care. Under the primary care case management concept, providers themselves are paid fee-for-service. In the mid-1990s, many states moved toward contracting with HMOs and paying them a capitated amount for each enrolled Medicaid beneficiary. Under full-risk capitation the HMO provides a comprehensive range of required benefits that includes preventive and acute care services.

States contract with managed care plans for two reasons. The first is to reduce the rate of increase in Medicaid expenditures. Managed care produced substantial savings in the private sector. Similar savings have not occurred in fee-for-service Medicaid programs, where providers do not have similar incentives to reduce inpatient utilization, use less costly outpatient settings, and reduce unnecessary use of the emergency department.

Second, contracting with managed care plans increases Medicaid enrollees' access to care. To save money, Medicaid programs have reduced payments to hospitals and physicians (well below rates paid by other insurers) so that many health providers refuse to serve Medicaid patients. Medicaid enrollees have typically had to rely on emergency departments and on clinics that predominantly serve large numbers of Medicaid patients. By contracting with managed care plans, the states expect their Medicaid enrollees to have greater access to primary care providers, receive coordinated care, and spend fewer dollars than previously.

The percentage of Medicaid beneficiaries enrolled in managed care plans has increased rapidly, from 4.5 percent in 1991 to 70 percent in 2008.

Medicaid managed care programs have a great deal of experience caring for relatively young demographic groups, such as children and working-age adults, similar to their commercial businesses. However, these population groups—non-disabled, low-income adults, and children (who make up about 75 percent of Medicaid beneficiaries)—account for a relatively small share of Medicaid spending (about 33 percent of Medicaid expenditures). Managed care plans have had less experience in caring for chronically ill and disabled populations, a more difficult group for which to provide managed care but for whom the potential savings of coordinated care is much greater. The aged, blind, and disabled and those in nursing homes (about 25 percent of beneficiaries) account for most Medicaid expenditures (about 67 percent). Until managed care plans enroll and manage care for the chronically ill, those with severe mental illness, and the institutionalized aged who require long-term care, Medicaid managed care savings will not be very large (CMS 2010e).

If managed care plans are to enroll these more costly Medicaid beneficiaries, states must provide these plans with appropriate financial incentives. State capitation payments should reflect the costs of caring for different types of beneficiaries (risk-adjusted payments). If the payment rate is set too low, managed care plans will be unwilling to enroll these groups. To date, it has been difficult to develop capitation rates that adequately reflect the costs of caring for elderly and chronically ill population groups.

It is also necessary for state Medicaid programs to monitor the care provided and the access to care by beneficiaries in any delivery system, whether it is managed care or traditional fee-for-service. Unfortunately, many states' performance in monitoring the quality of care their Medicaid populations receive has been notoriously inadequate. For budgetary reasons, some states are unwilling to monitor and punish low-performing providers. Nursing home scandals continue to surface, and many Medicaid programs are inadequate in terms of the quality of care and accessibility. Private insurers use various monitoring mechanisms and financial incentives, such as pay for performance, to reward providers who practice high-quality care. It remains to be seen how well state agencies will use the quality information they receive to similarly reward and penalize Medicaid providers.

Reforming Medicaid

Although Medicaid is the main program for providing medical services and long-term care to those with low incomes, it is generally perceived to be inadequate. Currently, Medicaid does not cover a large portion of those with low incomes; only 35 percent of those who are considered poor and near poor (below 200 percent of the FPL) were covered in 2009. (And only 46 percent of people below 100 percent of the FPL are covered. In 2011, 100 percent of the federal poverty level was $22,350 for a family of four, $14,710 for a couple, and $10,890 for a single person [US Census Bureau 2011a].)

Those on Medicaid lose their eligibility once their incomes rise above the Medicaid cutoff level, which could still be below the federal poverty level. As noted before, the potential loss of their medical benefits is a disincentive for Medicaid recipients to accept low-paying jobs.

Medicaid should be reformed to include all those with low incomes through an income-related voucher, and the size of the subsidy should decline as income increases. An income-related voucher would include a uniform set of benefits for all persons with low incomes in a private managed care plan. As incomes increase, the value of the voucher would decline. If those on Medicaid lost only a portion of their vouchers as their incomes rose, they would no longer have a disincentive to accept low-paying jobs. Although in 2014 the PPACA will establish uniform eligibility and benefit standards across the states, the sharp cutoff for Medicaid eligibility will remain. An income-related voucher would eliminate these large differences in the percentage of low-income populations eligible for Medicaid.

This income-related approach, in addition to improving equity, would improve efficiency. An income-related voucher would reinforce the movement to Medicaid managed care, with its emphasis on coordinated care, increased access to primary care physicians, and incentives to provide care in less costly settings.

To be effective in having health plans compete for Medicaid enrollees, the income-related voucher should be risk adjusted; specifically, chronically ill enrollees should receive more valuable vouchers than those who are younger and in better health. Risk-adjusted premiums will result in health plans competing for chronically ill enrollees and developing disease management programs to better care for them.

When contracting with managed care plans, some states allow their Medicaid beneficiaries a choice among such plans. Managed care plans therefore have an incentive to compete for Medicaid patients. States, however, need to provide the Medicaid population with relevant information on their plan choices. To the extent that beneficiaries do not choose and are assigned to a managed care plan, the role of choice in disciplining plan performance is negated.

Several states, including Florida, are trying innovative approaches to serving their Medicaid populations. Previously, to control Florida's rising Medicaid expenditures, provider fees were reduced, medical benefits were limited, Medicaid eligibility was reduced, and access to prescription drugs was limited. In 2006, the state decided instead to rely on patient choice and health plan competition to improve patient care and reduce rapidly rising Medicaid expenditures. Each Medicaid enrollee receives a defined contribution based on her risk level and health status; an enrollee with a disability, for example, receives a larger amount than a healthy child. Medicaid enrollees select among several competing, state-approved health plans, such as HMOs and PPOs, or they can use their defined contribution to join their employers' health plans. With risk-adjusted defined contributions, health plans have an incentive to enroll the chronically ill, as they receive higher premiums for doing so. Under this arrangement, health plans have a financial incentive to develop disease management programs for patients with diabetes, heart disease, and other chronic conditions (Coughlin et al. 2008).

The movement to having health plans compete for Medicaid enrollees and receive premiums reflecting the care needs of the diverse Medicaid population is likely to result in greater patient satisfaction and improved care outcomes.

To reduce Medicaid expenditures, attention must be focused on those groups consuming the largest portion of Medicaid expenditures, namely the chronically ill and people with disabilities. (These groups will also be the fastest-growing segment of the Medicaid population.) The challenge for the states in coming years is to include these vulnerable population groups in managed care, pay managed care plans and PPOs appropriately for their care, and vigorously monitor the care they receive.

Medicaid's movement to managed care has made survival difficult for many traditional safety-net providers, such as public and not-for-profit hospitals and community clinics that have traditionally served large Medicaid and uninsured populations. These providers rely on disproportionate-share hospital payments and need Medicaid patients if they are to survive. As managed care firms seek less expensive hospital settings and reduce inpatient use, these safety-net providers must become part of a provider network that competes for Medicaid capitation contracts. Unless they are able to do so, their financial stability is threatened. The loss of these safety-net providers would be unfortunate, as an income-related voucher will not likely be enacted in the near future. Until then, those without private insurance or Medicaid coverage will need access to medical care, which is likely to be provided primarily by safety-net providers.

Summary

Medicaid is a means-tested program to provide medical services to those with low incomes. Although Medicaid programs are federally required to serve designated population groups, states have discretion to include additional medical services and population groups in their programs. Medicaid does not cover all those with low incomes or all of the uninsured. In contrast to Medicare, Medicaid recipients and their supporters are not able to provide legislators with political support. For these reasons, the generosity of Medicaid programs (eligibility levels and included services) varies across states, and Congress does not mandate the level of funding as it does with Medicare. (Medicare is a defined-benefit program to specific population groups, which requires the federal government to fund those benefits.) In times of budget difficulties, many states attempt to reduce their deficits by cutting Medicaid eligibility and benefits.

Starting in 2014, Medicaid eligibility standards will be increased and become uniform across states. A major problem likely to occur is that the increased number of Medicaid beneficiaries will greatly increase the demand for physician services. Unless Medicaid increases physician fees, Medicaid beneficiaries will not have increased access to coordinated medical services but instead will have to rely on hospital emergency rooms. Providing Medicaid beneficiaries with the option to use managed care plans will increase their access to care, since managed care plans will be able to reduce their costs of caring for Medicaid patients by providing coordinated care and increasing physician productivity. This potentially will lead to higher pay for physicians.

An important challenge facing Medicaid reform, however, concerns the most costly Medicaid beneficiaries, people with disabilities and long-term nursing home patients. The current Medicaid system has not performed adequately in this arena, and managed care plans have to demonstrate their ability to care for such patients.

Discussion Questions

1. Describe the Medicaid program. What are the differences between Medicare and Medicaid?
2. How well does Medicaid achieve its objectives?
3. Why would it be difficult to enroll all of the Medicaid population in HMOs?
4. What are some approaches to reforming Medicaid?
5. What are the arguments for and against having one government program instead of both Medicare and Medicaid?

Notes

1. Many states have used various financing schemes, sometimes using intergovernmental transfers, to make large supplementary payments to government-owned or government-operated healthcare providers, such as nursing homes, to inappropriately increase federal Medicaid payments. These supplementary payments are in excess of the established Medicaid

payment rate and create the illusion that these are valid payments for services delivered to Medicaid beneficiaries. The state payments above the usual payment rate allow states to obtain federal reimbursement, only to have the local government providers, under agreements with the states, transfer the excessive federal and state payments back to the state. Once the states receive the returned funds, they have increased their federal matching rate above the established federal law and can use those funds to substitute for their share of future Medicaid spending or even for non-Medicaid purposes (Allen 2005).

2. As part of deficit-reduction legislation in 2005, Congress included limits on the ability of people with homes and assets to get Medicaid to pay their nursing home costs. The legislation toughens rules that prevent individuals seeking to become Medicaid eligible from transferring assets, usually to their children. Examples of these changes include lengthening the time period states are to examine for inappropriate transfer of assets to five years and excluding from Medicaid coverage persons whose home equity is in excess of $500,000 (previously there was no limit on home equity).

HOW DOES MEDICARE PAY PHYSICIANS?

In 2009, fee-for-service Medicare spent more than $62 billion on physician services (Congressional Budget Office 2010b). Medicare represents, on average, more than 20 percent of total physician revenues, although for many physicians and specialties it represents a sizable portion of revenues. As such, it is important to understand how Medicare pays physicians. In 1992, a new payment system was instituted for physician services under Medicare. Why was it necessary to change the system? How does the new payment system compare with the previous one? What are the effects of this new payment system on access to care by Medicare patients, on physician fees paid by the nonaged working population, and on physicians' incomes?

Previous Medicare Physician Payment System

When Medicare Part A, which pays for hospital care, was enacted in 1965, Part B, which pays for physician and out-of-hospital services, was included. (Part B is a voluntary benefit for which the aged pay a monthly premium that covers only 25 percent of the total cost of that program.) Physicians were paid on a fee-for-service basis and given the choice to be participating physicians (or even participate for some medical claims but not others). When physicians participated, they agreed to accept the Medicare fee for that service, and the patient was responsible for only 20 percent of that fee after she paid the annual deductible.

If a physician was not a participating physician, the patient would have to pay the physician's entire charge, which was higher than the Medicare fee, and apply for reimbursement from Medicare. When the government reimbursed the patient, it would only pay the patient 80 percent of the Medicare-approved fee for that service. Thus, a patient who visited a nonparticipating physician would have to pay 20 percent of the physician's Medicare-approved fee plus the difference between the approved fee and the physician's actual charges. This difference is referred to as *balance billing*. Medicare patients who saw nonparticipating physicians were also burdened by the paperwork involved with sending their bills to Medicare for reimbursement.

Physicians' fees and Medicare expenditures rapidly increased, and in 1972 the government placed a limit, referred to as the Medicare Economic Index, on physicians' Medicare fee increases. Physicians' fees, however, continued to increase sharply in the private sector, and as the difference between private physician fees and the Medicare-approved fees became larger, fewer physicians chose to participate in Medicare. Consequently, more of the aged were balance billed for the difference between their physician's fee and the Medicare-approved fee.

Another consequence of the limits on participating physicians' fee increases was the possibility that physicians would encourage more visits and engage in more testing to increase their Medicare billings (induced demand). Even with limits on physicians' fees, Medicare Part B expenditures continued to increase rapidly, as shown previously in Exhibit 8.4.

Reasons for Adopting the New Payment System

The new Medicare physician payment system was adopted for three reasons. The most important was the federal government's desire to limit the increase in the federal budget deficit, an issue of great political concern in the early 1990s. In 1992, physicians received 75 percent of all Part B payments (this has decreased to 30 percent as of 2009); the remaining expenditures were for other nonhospital services (this portion was increasing rapidly, at approximately 10 percent per year). Part B expenditures increased from $777 million in 1967 to more than $50 billion by 1992 and were expected to continue their rapid rise. (In 2009, Part B expenditures reached $204 billion; they are expected to be $335 billion by 2019 [Congressional Budget Office 2010b].) As Medicare physician payments continued to increase, the government's portion of the cost of the program, 75 percent of the total (again, the aged paid a monthly premium that covered only 25 percent of Part B expenditures), contributed directly to the growing federal budget deficit. Both Republican and Democratic administrations believed that if the government was to reduce the size of the federal deficit, the growth in Part B expenditures had to be slowed.

The government, however, was constrained in the approaches it could take to limit Part B expenditures. Given the political power of the aged, the government was reluctant to ask them to pay higher Part B premiums or to increase their cost sharing. Furthermore, the government could not simply limit Medicare physician fees for fear that physicians would reduce their Medicare participation, which would adversely affect the aged.

Thus, the second reason Part B was changed was that members of Congress were concerned that unless they ensured that the aged had access to physicians, they would lose their political support at election time. As limits were placed on Medicare physician fee increases, fewer physicians were willing to participate (accept Medicare payment) and more aged were either charged additional amounts by nonparticipating physicians (balance billed) or, if they could not afford the additional payments, had decreased access to physician services. Congress wanted to increase physician participation in Medicare.

Third, many physicians and academicians believed the previous Medicare payment system was inequitable and inefficient. A newly graduated physician establishing a fee schedule with Medicare could receive higher fees than could an older physician whose fee increases were limited by the Medicare Economic Index. Physicians who performed procedures such as diagnostic testing and surgery were paid at a much higher rate per unit of physician time than were physicians who performed cognitive services, such as office examinations. Medicare fees for the same procedure varied greatly across geographic areas and were unrelated to differences in practice costs. The fee-for-service payment system encouraged inefficiency by rewarding physicians who performed more services. These inequities and inefficiencies caused differences in physician incomes and affected their choice of specialty and practice location.

Components of the New Payment System

Reducing the federal deficit by limiting Part B expenditures, achieving greater Medicare fee equity among physicians, and limiting the aged's payments led to the three main parts of the physician payment reform package. The inefficiencies inherent in the fee-for-service system were not addressed by the new payment system.

Resource-Based Relative Value Scale Fee Schedule

The first, and most publicized, part of the physician payment reform package was the creation of a resource-based relative value scale (RBRVS) fee schedule. The RBRVS attempted to approximate the cost of performing each physician service. Its premise was that, in the long run, in a competitive market, the price of a service will reflect the cost of producing that service. Thus, the payment for each physician service should reflect his resource costs. However, this cost-based approach to determining relative values was complex, as it required a great deal of data; relied on interviews; was based on certain assumptions, such as the time required to perform certain tasks; and would have to be continually updated because any of the elements of cost and time could change.

Three resource components were used to construct the fee for a particular service. The first, the work component, estimated the cost of providing a particular service, including the time, intensity, skill, mental effort, and stress involved in providing the service.[1] Second were the physician's practice

EXHIBIT 10.1
Calculations of
Physician
Payment Rate
Under RBRVS
Office Visits
(Level 3), New
York City
(Manhattan),
2010

	Relative Value		Geographic Adjustment	Adjusted Relative Value
Physician work	0.97	×	1.06	1.03
Physician expense[a]	0.80	×	1.30	1.04
PLI[b]	0.05	×	1.01	0.05
				2.12
		Conversion factor	×	36.87
		Payment rate		$78.16

[a]Non-facility practice expense

[b]Professional liability insurance

expenses, such as salaries and rent. Third was malpractice insurance, because its cost varies across specialties. Each component was assigned a relative value that was summed to form the total relative value for the service; the greater the costs and time required for a service, the higher the relative value unit (RVU) was. A procedure with a value of 20 was believed to be twice as costly as one with a value of 10.

The actual fee was then determined by multiplying these RVUs by a politically determined conversion factor. For example, "transplantation of the heart" was assigned 44.13 work RVUs, 49.24 practice-expense RVUs, and 9.17 malpractice RVUs for a total of 102.54 RVUs. The 1992 conversion factor was $31, making the fee for this procedure $3,178 ($31 × 102.54). This fee was then adjusted for geographic location. (The initial conversion factor was set so that total payments under the new system would be the same as under the previous one, that is, the system was budget neutral.) A separate conversion factor was used for surgical services, primary care, and other nonsurgical services. (In 1998, a single conversion factor was instituted for all services.) Exhibit 10.1 illustrates how the RBRVS and the conversion factor are used to calculate the fee for an office visit.

RBRVS reduces the variation in fees both within specialties and across geographic regions. New physicians receive 80 percent of the Medicare fee schedule in their first year, and the percentage rises to 100 percent by the fifth year. Medicare fees can still vary geographically by 12 percent less and 18 percent more than the average, but this is greatly reduced from the

EXHIBIT 10.2
Medicare
Physician Fee
Schedule Effect
on Fees by
Specialty, 1992

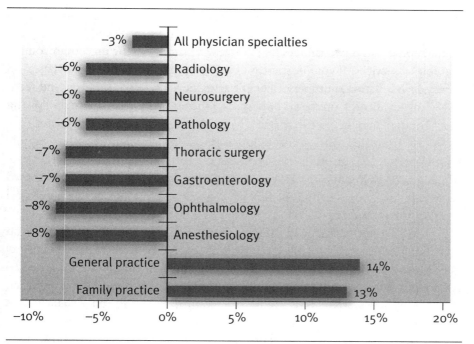

All physician specialties −3%
Radiology −6%
Neurosurgery −6%
Pathology −6%
Thoracic surgery −7%
Gastroenterology −7%
Ophthalmology −8%
Anesthesiology −8%
General practice 14%
Family practice 13%

−10%   −5%   0%   5%   10%   15%   20%

SOURCE: "Medicare Physician Payment Reform Regulations," Hearing before the US Senate Subcommittee on Medicare and Long-Term Care of the Committee on Finance, 19 July 1991.

previous geographic variation. As a result, fees were reduced for physicians in California, whereas fees in Mississippi increased by 11 percent.

The new payment system reflected the cost of performing 7,000 different physician services. When constructing the RBRVS fee structure, Harvard professor William Hsiao and colleagues (1988) found that physician fees were not closely related to the resource costs needed to produce those services. In general, cognitive services, such as patient evaluation, counseling, and management of services, were greatly undervalued compared with procedural services, such as surgery and testing. The RBRVS reduces the profitability of procedures while increasing payment for cognitive services. By changing the relative weights of different types of services, the RBRVS system caused substantial shifts in payments, and consequently incomes, among physicians. In large metropolitan areas, for example, surgeons' fees declined by 25 percent. The "winners" and "losers" among physician specialties after the new system was introduced are shown in Exhibit 10.2.

Medicare Expenditure Limit

The RBRVS approach is still fee-for-service payment, and by itself it does not control volume, mix of services, or total physician expenditures. Because the government was concerned that physicians would induce demand to offset their lower Medicare fees, the second part of the new payment system limited overall physician Medicare expenditures. This limit was achieved by linking the annual update on physician fees (the conversion factor) to the growth in volume and mix of services. If volume increased more rapidly than a target rate based on increases in inflation, number of beneficiaries, newly covered services, and technological advances, Congress would reduce the annual fee update the following year. Too rapid an increase in services would result in a smaller fee update.

As it turned out, volume and mix of services increased less rapidly than expected for surgical services. Consequently, to maintain the target rate of Medicare payments for surgical services, the conversion factor increased more rapidly. These changes in fees were unrelated to any supply or demand changes for such services.

As part of the Balanced Budget Act of 1997, the annual update method was changed. The sustainable growth rate (SGR) in Medicare physician expenditures became the new government objective. The SGR was designed to reduce physician fee updates if physician spending growth exceeded a specified target. This new system holds Medicare spending growth for physician services to that of the general economy (the GDP), adjusting for several factors. (Tying the SGR to GDP per capita represented an affordability criteria: how much the government could afford to subsidize physician Part B expenditures.)

The SGR consists of four elements:

1. The percentage increase in real GDP per capita
2. A medical inflation rate of physician fee increases
3. The annual percentage increase in Part B enrollees (other than Medicare Advantage enrollees)
4. The percentage change in spending for physicians' services resulting from changes in laws and regulations (e.g., expanded Medicare coverage for preventive services)

Under the SGR system, physician fee updates are adjusted up or down depending on whether actual spending has fallen below or exceeded the target. Over time, fees tend to increase at least as fast as the cost of providing physician services as long as volume (number of services provided to each beneficiary) and intensity growth (complexity and costliness of those services) remain below a specified rate, about 1.5 percent per year. If volume and intensity grow faster than the specified rate, the SGR lowers fee increases or causes fees to fall. The SGR formula does not provide any incentives for *individual* physicians to control volume growth.

During the late 1990s and early 2000s, physicians received generous fee increases from Medicare (5.4 percent in 2000 and 4.5 percent in 2001). However, the government then revised upward its estimate of previous years' actual physician expenditures and lowered the spending target based on revised GDP data. Physician fees dropped by 5.4 percent in 2002, a decline that

Exhibit 10.3 Recent and Projected Payment Updates for Physician Services

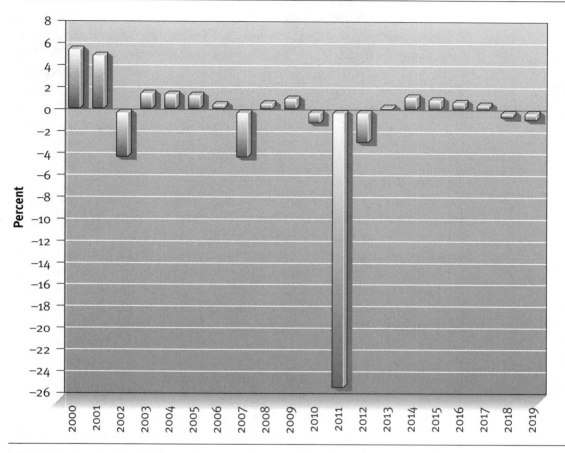

SOURCE: Based on data in the *2010 Annual Report of the Boards of Trustees of the Federal Hospital Insurance and Federal Supplementary Medical Insurance Trust Funds*, Table IV.B1. [Online information.] https://www.cms.gov/ReportsTrustFunds/downloads/tr2010.pdf.

was, in part, a correction for fees that had been set too high in prior years because of errors in forecasting. Physician fees were also to be reduced in subsequent years to recoup excess spending accumulated from averted cuts in previous years and partly because real spending per beneficiary (volume and intensity) on physician services increased faster than allowed under the SGR. Responding to pressure from physicians and concerned about Medicare patients' access to care after the 2002 reduction in physician fees, Congress repealed all scheduled fee reductions, which, if implemented all at once, would total 26 percent in 2011 (MedPAC 2010).

In Exhibit 10.3, the years from 2000 to 2010 describe actual physician updates. The sharp decrease in physician fees for 2011 shows the accumulated required fee decreases according to the SGR formula. However, as in previous years, Congress overrode the 26 percent scheduled fee decrease and pushed them further into the future.

Congress faces a dilemma. Recognizing that rapid expenditure growth in Medicare physician expenditures is not sustainable, Congress can maintain fiscal discipline by relying on an automatic mechanism, such as the SGR. By doing so, however, Congress risks having physicians limit their participation with Medicare, thereby dramatically reducing Medicare beneficiaries' access to physician services.

Tying Medicare physician fees to economic growth completely ignores changes in physician supply and demand.

Balance Billing Limit

The third part of the new payment system limits the amount physicians are able to balance bill Medicare patients. Physicians can no longer participate in Medicare for some patients but not others. Few physicians are able to forgo such a significant source of revenue. Physicians who decide not to participate in Medicare still cannot charge a Medicare patient more than 109 percent of the Medicare-approved fee. Thus, even physicians who decide not to participate in Medicare are restricted in how much they can charge for treating a Medicare patient.

Effects of Medicare's Payment System

Procedure-Oriented Specialists

To analyze the likely effects of Medicare's physician payment system, assume initially that physicians do not induce demand, that is, as specialist fees and incomes are reduced, physicians are not motivated to manipulate patients' demand. It is also important to keep in mind that physicians work in at least two markets: They serve Medicare patients and private or non-Medicare patients. (The private market could also be subdivided into HMO and non-HMO patients.)

RBRVS reduces fees for procedures and increases fees for cognitive services. With lower fees for surgery, for example, surgeons might be expected to perform fewer Medicare surgeries and reallocate their time to performing surgeries for private patients, whose fees were not reduced. However, if surgeons are not as busy as they would prefer, and the Medicare fee still exceeds the value of their time spent doing nonsurgical tasks, surgeons will not reduce their Medicare surgeries. The effect of lower fees for procedures with no change in the number of procedures will result in a decrease in Medicare procedure-type expenditures and lower specialists' incomes.

Would specialists increase their fees to their private patients to make up for lower Medicare fees? Fees for private patients are presumably already at their highest level, consistent with making as much profit as possible from those patients. If specialists do not charge as much as the market will bear, they forgo income they could have earned. If private fees are increased beyond what the market will bear, the loss in revenue from lower volume would exceed the gain in revenue from those higher fees. The specialist would be worse off. (See Chapter 17.) A specialist might be able to increase his volume from private-pay patients by decreasing his fees to health plans to increase the number of private patients. Lowering the fee would be a more profitable strategy than raising it if the gain in revenue from increased volume more than offsets the loss in revenues from decreased fees.

Assume that before Medicare lowered specialist fees, specialists were allocating their time between private and Medicare patients so that the profit from each type of patient was the same. Once Medicare reduces its fees, the profit per hour of the specialist's time becomes greater when serving *private* patients. The specialist should serve fewer Medicare patients and more private patients. However, the only way the specialist can serve more private patients is to reduce her fees (to managed care organizations). Thus, the specialist would not likely want to or be able to cost shift to private patients.

If a specialist has excess capacity and does not attempt to induce demand, the aged would have the same access as before specialist fees were reduced. Specialists would provide the same volume of services, but their incomes would be reduced and overall Medicare expenditures for specialist services would decline.

Physicians who are willing to create demand to offset declines in their incomes would first attempt to induce demand among their private patients. A greater volume of private patients would be more profitable because the private fee has not been reduced. Only after private fees were reduced would the specialist create demand among the Medicare patients, whose fees had already been reduced. If specialists are not busy enough, they have probably already tried to induce as much demand as possible and would be unable to induce much further demand. Instead, they might engage in such fraudulent practices as "code creep" as a way of increasing their Medicare fees.

Medicare expenditures and specialist incomes would still be expected to decline among physicians who are inclined to induce demand, assuming that these specialists previously had excess capacity. To the extent that demand inducers are able to engage in code creep, they will be able to offset some of the decline in their incomes. If specialists are fully busy, the reductions in Medicare specialist fees would result in a reallocation of specialists' time to private patients (whose fees are higher) and, consequently, reduced access by Medicare patients.

Given the excess capacity that existed among specialists, when Medicare introduced the new RBRVS system and reduced Medicare fees to surgical specialties, the new, lower fees likely reduced such specialists' incomes, reduced Medicare expenditures for such services, and did not reduce Medicare patients' access to these services.

Primary Care Physicians

Under RBRVS, Medicare fees for cognitive services increased. Because the higher fees increase the profitability of Medicare patients, primary care physicians were expected to serve more Medicare patients and fewer private patients (assuming the Medicare fees are higher than private insurance fees). As physicians were expected to decrease their available time to private patients, and as demand exceeded the available physician time for private patients, fees for private patients were expected to increase. Total Medicare expenditures for cognitive services, particularly for primary care physicians, increased.

Primary care physicians who may otherwise have been willing to induce demand to increase their incomes might have been less inclined to do so because their incomes increased as a result of their fee increases. Those still inclined to induce demand would have found that it was more profitable to do so for their Medicare patients, whose fees increased, than for their private patients.

What was the RBRVS fee schedule's likely overall effect on expenditures? Assuming specialists were not busy enough, little additional demand inducement occurred, and (adjusting for the increased number of aged) Medicare Part B expenditures for specialists did not increase. Medicare expenditures for primary care physicians were expected to increase because their fees were increased; however, these increases were smaller than the decreases in specialist expenditures. Exhibit 8.4 (in Chapter 8) illustrates these changes in the trend in Part B expenditures after the new physician payment system was introduced in 1992. (Part B expenditures have increased slightly more rapidly in recent years as a result of Congress shifting home healthcare expenditures from Part A to Part B in 1997 to solve an impending bankruptcy in the Part A Trust Fund.)

The expenditure limit that was part of the RBRVS system was meant to control demand inducement. Although specialists had excess capacity, demand inducement, hence volume of surgical services, was less than the government anticipated.

The Present

The SGR formula has for a number of years required decreases in physician fees, since actual expenditure growth has exceeded SGR projected physician expenditures. Congress, concerned that decreasing physician fees will reduce the aged's access to care, has postponed these annual fee decreases. The accumulated amount of these fee decreases will grow to 26 percent (in 2011). Although Congress realizes that Medicare physician fees will not be reduced by such a large amount, they are reluctant to change the SGR formula. To do so would mean that, according to budget rules, Congress would have to acknowledge a $275 billion increase in the federal deficit over the next ten years. Given the political concern over increasing federal deficits, each Congress prefers to make adjustments one year at a time.

The aged's demand for physicians continues to increase because of growth in the aged population (the baby boomers start retiring in 2011), new technologies, and legislated new services. Further increasing demand for physician services is President Obama's 2010 health legislation, which expands Medicaid eligibility. Unless Congress changes the SGR to allow for physician fee increases, shortages of primary care physicians will occur. As demands for care by both Medicare and non-Medicare (Medicaid and private) patients increase, primary care physicians will attempt to increase their fees. To the extent that Medicare fees remain less than those of private patients, physicians will find it more profitable to serve an increased number of private patients. As Congress limits Medicare fee increases to save money, the relative profitability to physicians of Medicare patients will continue to decline.

As Medicare fees fall relative to private fees, only by raising their Medicare fees—by such methods as reducing the time spent per Medicare visit, having the patient return more often, or performing more imaging tests (for which the physician receives payment)—would it be equally profitable for primary care physicians to continue seeing the same number of Medicare patients.

If physicians were able to balance bill their Medicare patients, relative fees between Medicare and private patients would remain the same, and physicians would not reallocate their time away from Medicare patients. The inability of primary care physicians to balance bill is likely to result in shortages of physician services for Medicare patients; the demand for such services will exceed the amount physicians are willing to supply at Medicare's relatively lower fee.

As an alternative to balance billing to equate supply and demand, some primary care physicians have begun charging their Medicare patients a concierge fee of about $2,000. This fee is technically for services not provided under Medicare and provides a concierge patient with greater access to his physician. Since a concierge physician sees fewer patients, the shortage of primary care physicians is exacerbated for those who do not pay such a fee. A concierge fee is an indication that the demand for physicians exceeds the supply at the fees Medicare is willing to pay.

To determine whether Medicare's physician fees are too low, thereby affecting Medicare patients' access to care, the Medicare Payment Advisory Commission (MedPAC) undertakes several types of surveys. The first is a survey of physicians' willingness to serve Medicare patients; the second is a survey of Medicare patients' access to care—both of which take several years to conduct and analyze before the results become available. Because of this delay, MedPAC conducts a telephone interview survey of Medicare beneficiaries and non-Medicare privately insured persons aged 50 to 64 years to compare any differences in their access to physician services. As of 2009, these data indicate that access to care by Medicare patients was generally good, although some new Medicare patients were having difficulty finding a primary care physician. Medicare fees remained at about 78 percent of private insurer fees. Unless the SGR formula is changed, projected reductions in Medicare physician fees for the next several years (under current law) will decrease Medicare patients' access to care, particularly as the baby boomers become eligible for Medicare.

Given the delay in receiving information with which to evaluate the adequacy of Medicare physician fees, MedPAC is unlikely to be able to bring demand and supply for physicians into equilibrium. In a normal market situation, rising doctor fees would indicate demand increasing faster than supply and the need to take corrective action. But since balance billing—which acted as a market-driven indicator—is no longer allowed, there is no automatic mechanism to indicate a current shortage, hence access problems.

Limiting balance billing and establishing a uniform fee schedule among physicians within the same specialty have another unfortunate effect. Previously, differences in fees for the same service may have reflected differences in that service. For example, some physicians are of higher quality or spend more time listening to the patient's concerns. Although the service code may be nominally similar, the content of that service may differ. In the above examples, the costs of providing that service in terms of the physician's time differ. Patients are willing to pay more for certain physician attributes, such as their ability to relate to the patient. A uniform fee schedule prevents a physician treating Medicare patients from charging for these extra attributes. Busy primary care physicians could provide additional visits and earn a higher income instead of spending time cultivating these attributes, which are not rewarded.

Proposed Physician Fee Changes

MedPAC proposes to undertake payment demonstration projects over the next several years that are different from Medicare fee-for-service payment for physician services. One approach being considered is episode-based payment. A single payment would be made to cover all the services provided in caring for an episode of illness. The hospital, specialists, and primary care physicians involved in the patient's treatment would receive a specified amount, which they would have to share, for a patient's episode of care, such as a heart attack. Episode-based payment would require physicians and hospitals to more closely coordinate the patient's care. Each participant would have an incentive to be concerned with the efficiency with which the care is provided, and participants' performance outcome in providing an episode of care will be more easily evaluated in terms of quality compared to the care provided by other organizations for the same episode of illness.

A second change in physician payment being considered is pay for performance (P4P). In this approach, physicians meeting certain quality guidelines will receive increased payments. P4P offers incentives to physicians different from fee-for-service, in which quality is not rewarded (MedPAC 2010).

Summary

The RBRVS national fee schedule, with expenditure controls and limits on balance billing, attempted to limit federal expenditures for Medicare physician services, improve equity among different medical specialties, and limit out-of-pocket payments and Part B premiums by the aged, while increasing the aged's access to care. Medicare expenditures, however, will continue to rise as the number of eligible aged increases along with inflation, legislated new Medicare benefits, and advances in technology.

Under the present Medicare SGR formula for paying physicians, Congress continually faces the decision between limiting Medicare physician fees and expenditures and decreasing the aged's access to care.

Congress is unlikely to be able to accurately forecast the "right" rate of increase in Medicare expenditures (SGR) because it is more likely to be concerned with limiting the rise in Medicare expenditures than with properly adjusting for changes in the number of aged, inflation, and technology. The consequences to the aged of "too slow" an increase in Medicare expenditures will be a shortage of primary care services.

A uniform fee schedule cannot indicate that a shortage is developing in some geographic areas or among certain physician specialties, nor can uniform fees eliminate such shortages. Unless a national fee schedule is flexible and allows fees for some services, physicians, and geographic regions to increase more rapidly than others, shortages will arise and persist. Furthermore, delays in gathering survey data and their analysis to determine whether the aged have physician access problems is likely to result in imbalances between supply and demand for physicians. Permitting physicians to balance bill their Medicare patients would be similar to a market mechanism indicating that an imbalance between demand and supply has occurred. The government could then raise fees in those areas and among those specialties where balance billing is increasing.

Fees provide information; they signal that changes have occurred in the costs of providing care, the demands for that care, or both. If the government does not want to overpay specialties and services that are in oversupply while underpaying those that are in short supply, a flexible payment mechanism is needed. Otherwise, the aged will find that they have reduced access to care, and the government will not be spending its money wisely. Movement toward episode-based payment and P4P offer the possibility of greater care coordination and increased efficiency that is lacking in fee-for-service payment.

Discussion Questions

1. What were the reasons for developing a new Medicare physician payment system?
2. In what ways does the current physician payment system differ from the previous system?
3. What are the likely effects of Medicare's payment system on its patients' out-of-pocket expenses, Part B premiums, and access to physicians (primary care versus specialists)?
4. What, if any, are the likely effects of Medicare's payment system on patients in the non-Medicare (private) sector?
5. What are the likely effects of Medicare's physician payment system on physicians (by specialty)?

Additional Readings

Centers for Medicare & Medicaid Services. 2010. *2010 Annual Report of the Boards of Trustees of the Federal Hospital Insurance and Federal Supplementary Medical Insurance Trust Funds.* [Online document; retrieved 3/7/11.] www.cms.gov/ReportsTrustFunds/downloads/tr2010.pdf.

Frech, H. E., III., ed. 1991. *Regulating Doctors' Fees: Competition, Benefits and Controls Under Medicare.* Washington, DC: AEI Press.

Note

1. Two methods were used to estimate the complexity of a task: personal interviews and a modified Delphi technique in which each physician was able to compare her own estimate to the average of physicians within that specialty. Many assumptions were required; for example, in calculating opportunity cost, it was assumed that the years required for training in a specialty were the minimum necessary. Further assumptions were made regarding the lengths of working careers across specialties, residency salaries, hours worked per week, and an interest rate to discount future earnings.

IS THERE AN IMPENDING SHORTAGE OF PHYSICIANS?

About every 10 to 20 years, concern arises that the United States is producing either too many or too few physicians. The Council on Graduate Medical Education (COGME), which advises the government on the size of the physician workforce and its training, issued a report warning that there is likely to be an overall shortfall of 85,000 to 95,000 physicians by 2020 (COGME 2005).

This represents a shift in COGME's assessment, which, as late as 1992, had warned that by 2000 a surplus of specialists would be seen, as high as 15 to 30 percent of all physicians, as well as a shortage of primary care physicians (COGME 1992).

Evidence for the belief in a large physician surplus was the rapid growth occurring in the number of active physicians, which increased from 435,000 in 1980 to 573,000 in 1990 to 738,000 in 2000 to 835,000 in 2008. When adjusted for population, the number of active physicians per 100,000 population (the physician-to-population ratio) increased from 195 in 1980 to 234 in 1990 to 270 in 2000 to 283 in 2008. (See Exhibit 4.1 in Chapter 4.) Some researchers, assuming that a large portion of the US population would be enrolled in HMOs, compared the relatively low physician ratio within HMOs to the national physician ratio and claimed that an overall surplus of 165,000 physicians, or 30 percent of the total number of patient care physicians, would occur by 2000. A 30 percent surplus in the number of specialists was also projected.

The projected physician surplus was expected to have adverse effects on physician incomes, especially specialist incomes, for many years. To forestall such surpluses, COGME and physician organizations recommended reducing medical school enrollments, reducing the number of specialists and increasing the number of primary care physicians (from 30 percent to 50 percent of all physicians), and limiting the number of foreign medical school graduates entering the United States.

The projected huge surplus of physicians did not materialize.

COGME's more recent (2005) recommendations are the opposite of their prior policy recommendations. More physicians are needed, and medical students should be encouraged to become specialists and not primary care physicians.

What is the basis for these projections of physician surpluses and shortages? Should public policy attempt to manipulate the supply of physicians based on such supply projections? What is an economic definition of a physician surplus or shortage? And what are the consequences and self-correcting mechanisms of a shortage or surplus?

Definitions of a Physician Shortage or Surplus

Physician-to-Population Ratio

Different approaches have been used to determine whether a surplus (or shortage) exists in a profession. One approach often taken in the health field is a physician-to-population ratio. This definition often relies on a value judgment about how much care people should receive or a professional determination of how many physician services are appropriate for the population.

This method generally uses the existing physician-to-population ratio and compares it with the physician-to-population ratio that is likely to occur in some future period. First, the likely physician-to-population *supply ratio* is estimated by projecting the future population and then calculating the likely number of medical graduates that will be added to the stock of physicians, less the expected number of deaths and retirements. Second, *physician requirements* are projected by estimating the extent of disease in the population (usually based on survey data), the physician services necessary to provide care for each illness, and the number of physician hours required to provide preventive and therapeutic services. (Some studies attempt to modify the requirements ratio by basing it on utilization rates of population subgroups, such as age, sex, location, and insurance coverage, and multiplying these utilization rates by the future population in each category.) Third, assuming a 40-hour work week per physician, the number of hours is translated into number of physicians and into a physician-to-population ratio. The same approach is used to determine the number of physicians in each specialty. The difference between the supply ratio and the requirements ratio is the anticipated shortage or surplus.

The Graduate Medical Education Advisory Committee to the government (the predecessor organization to COGME) also used a physician-to-population ratio methodology to determine the appropriate number of physicians.

The ratio technique has served as the basis for much of the health manpower legislation in this country and has resulted in many billions of dollars of subsidies by federal and state governments. Nonphysician health professional associations, such as those for registered nurses, have also used this approach in their quest for government subsidies.

Using a physician-to-population ratio for judging whether a shortage (or surplus) exists has serious shortcomings. First, the use of a ratio, whether based on health professional estimates of the need for services or on the current physician-to-population ratio, as a guideline for determining whether future ratios will be adequate does not consider changes in physician demand. For example, if demand for physicians is increasing faster than the supply because of an aging population, because of new medical advances that increase the public's use of medical care, or because patients' insurance coverage has changed, maintaining a particular ratio is likely to result in too few physicians. Second, the ratio method does not include productivity changes that are likely to occur or could be attained. It is possible to achieve an increase in physician services without increasing the number of physicians. Technology, such as health information systems, and personnel with less training can be used to relieve physicians of many tasks; delegation of some tasks would permit an increase in the number of physician visits. A smaller physician-to-population ratio would be needed if productivity increases were considered. Conversely, if the percentage of female physicians (who work fewer hours on average than male physicians) increases or if physicians prefer an easier lifestyle, will a greater number of physicians be needed?

Third, the ratio technique does not indicate how important a surplus or shortage is, if in fact one exists. Is a shortage or surplus of 10,000 physicians significant, or does the number have to reach 200,000 to warrant concern? What are the consequences in terms of physician fees, incomes, and patients' access to care?

Projections of shortages and surpluses using the ratio technique have been notoriously inaccurate. Many assumptions are used in calculating future ratios, and public policies based on inaccurate projections will take many years to correct, exacerbating future shortages or surpluses.

Rate of Return

Economists prefer a different approach to determining whether a surplus or shortage exists. This approach relies on the concept of a rate of return. Medical education is viewed as an investment. The rate of return is calculated by estimating the costs of that investment and the expected higher financial returns achievable as a result of that investment while discounting that cash flow to the present.

If a person decides to enter medical (or any graduate) school, he is in effect making an investment in an education that offers a higher future income. The cost of that investment includes tuition, books, and other expenses. The largest part of this investment is often the income that could have been earned had the person taken a job, which is known as the "opportunity cost" of a graduate education.

The return earned on this educational investment is the higher income received. Because this income is earned in the future, and future income is valued less than current income, it must be discounted to the present. Does the discounted rate of return on a medical education exceed what the student could have earned had she invested an equivalent amount of money in a savings or bond account? If the rate of return is higher than what could have been earned by investing an equivalent sum of money, there is a shortage of physicians. If the return on a medical education is lower than alternative investments or an investment in education for other professions, a surplus exists.[1]

The rate-of-return approach does not imply that every prospective student makes a rate-of-return calculation before deciding on a medical or other graduate education. Many students would become physicians even if future income prospects were low, simply because they believe medicine is a worthwhile profession. However, some students are at the margin; they may be equally excited about a career in medicine, business, or computer science. Changes in rates of return affect these students. High rates of return in medicine shift more students to medicine (eventually lowering the rate of return), whereas low rates of return shift them into other professions, eventually eliminating the physician surplus.

The rate-of-return approach incorporates into its calculations all the relevant economic factors, such as likely income lost if the person does not become a physician (opportunity cost), the longer time to become a specialist (greater opportunity costs), likely physician incomes by specialty, and educational costs, such as tuition. Changes in any of these factors change the rate of return on a medical education.

Consequences of an Imbalance in the Supply of and Demand for Physicians

What is likely to occur if demand for physicians exceeds supply (or, under a surplus scenario, supply exceeds demand)? Each scenario has a short- and a long-term consequence. And these effects will vary depending on whether the patient is a private-pay patient or a publicly funded patient for whom the government regulates the physician's fee.

Private Market for Physician Services

Short-Term Effects of a Physician Shortage
An increase in the number of patients seeking physician services will initially mean patients will find it more difficult to schedule an appointment with a physician. Waiting times will increase. Physicians' bargaining position with insurers will improve, and they will eventually increase their fees. They will

likely add staff to increase their productivity so they can see more patients. And physician incomes will increase.

Equilibrium will be reestablished, similar to what existed before the increase in demand occurred; however, physician fees and incomes will be higher, patients will pay higher copayments each time they go to the physician, and some patients will not see the physician as often as they did previously.

Over time, as physician incomes increase, the demand for a medical education will increase, as will demand for residency positions in those specialties experiencing the largest increases in demand for services. An important issue is whether medical schools will accommodate the higher demand for a medical education. If medical schools expand and new medical schools start, the supply of US-trained physicians will slowly increase. If not, the applicant-to-acceptance ratio will increase, and more students desiring a medical education will seek education overseas and return to the United States for their residencies. **Long-Term Effects of a Physician Shortage**

In either case the supply of physicians will increase. Eventually this greater supply will moderate physician fee increases, and physicians' incomes will no longer increase more rapidly than those of other professions. The specialties in which demand has increased fastest will have a greater number of physicians.

The response by patients, physicians, college graduates, and medical schools will result in the elimination of a shortage. The response by these different parties will not be immediate, as it takes time for patients and physicians to realize demand for physicians has increased, for some college graduates to decide to enter medicine, and then for those students to graduate, complete their residencies, and enter practice.

A surplus is characterized by patients not having to wait to see a physician, physicians not being as busy as they would like and being more willing to participate with insurers to receive a greater volume of patients, a greater willingness among physicians to discount their fees, and physician incomes not keeping up with inflation. The rate of return on a medical education will decline as incomes rise more slowly than those for other professions. **Short-Term Effects of a Physician Surplus**

Under the physician surplus scenario, a medical profession becomes less desirable. Physicians may decide to retire early, less use will be made of staff to increase physician productivity, and the applicant-to-acceptance ratio for medical schools will decline. Although medicine will always be a desirable profession, some students who might have chosen a career in medicine will choose another profession. The supply of physicians will increase more slowly than it would if the rate of return on a medical education were higher. Over time, as demand for physician services increases more rapidly than physician **Long-Term Effects of a Physician Surplus** supply, the surplus situation will disappear. Physicians will become busier, their fees and incomes will increase, and the rate of return on a medical education will become comparable with the rate of return for other professions.

Public Market for Physician Services

Short-Term Effects of a Physician Shortage

The main difference between the private and public (Medicare and Medicaid) markets is that in public markets the government regulates the price of physician services. Governments are rarely able to accurately determine the price for physician services and for each specialty so that it equilibrates supply and demand for physician services for Medicare and Medicaid patients. Often budget considerations influence how much should be spent on physician services.

If a shortage situation occurs in the private market for physicians, physicians will serve fewer Medicare and Medicaid patients unless the government increases physician fees. They will shift their time to higher-paying private patients. This has previously occurred with Medicare patients and is a continual problem for Medicaid patients.

Long-Term Effects of a Physician Shortage

Unlike in the private market, a shortage may continue indefinitely in the public market if government fees are not sufficiently increased to match those in the private market. Low out-of-pocket payments by Medicare and Medicaid patients result in high demand by those patients, which will continue to exceed the supply of services physicians are willing to devote to these patients. Waiting times will increase and fewer physicians will be willing to serve new public patients. To increase their access to physician services, more publicly funded patients will join HMO-type organizations, which are able to attract physicians by paying them a higher rate of pay. These organizations, paid an annual amount per enrollee (known as a capitation payment), are able to reduce their costs by using more nonphysicians and providing preventive and disease management services to publicly funded patients, which reduces costly hospital care.

Short-Term Effects of a Physician Surplus

Physicians will serve more Medicare and Medicaid patients when they are not as busy as they would prefer. Surpluses result in lower fees from private insurers, which makes government fees more attractive. This compels physicians to shift more of their time to publicly funded patients.

Long-Term Effects of a Physician Surplus

As the physician surplus is resolved in the private market and fees by privately insured patients begin increasing, publicly funded patients may experience some access problems, depending on whether government fees are increased in line with privately determined fees.

The public and private markets are interrelated. Physicians will allocate their time to each market depending on the relative profitability of serving patients in each market. (This is not meant to imply that all physicians behave similarly, but that a sufficient number of physicians are willing to shift their services based on the profitability of serving Medicare, Medicaid, and private patients [Rice et al. 1999].) Consequently, the effects on patients of a physician shortage or surplus depend on the flexibility of fees in each market. Markets that permit greater flexibility in fees and entry of new physicians are more likely to resolve a shortage situation than markets that rely on government-regulated fees, which are slow to recognize and adjust to changes in demand and supply.

A crucial issue regarding long-term shortages in the private market is whether the supply of medical schools and spaces responds to student demands for a medical education.

Economic Evidence on Trends in Physician Demand and Supply

Several measures are used to indicate whether this country has a shortage or a surplus of physicians. If demand for physician services were increasing faster than physician supply, physician fees would be increasing, as would physician incomes, both adjusted for inflation. However, economists prefer to examine the economic rate of return to a medical education, namely whether an investment in a medical education offers higher returns than other professional education opportunities or just going to work after graduating from college. The applicant-to-acceptance ratio for medical schools is indicative of whether prospective medical students believe the returns to a medical career are more favorable than for other professions. Each of these indicators is discussed in the following sections.

Trends in Physician Fees

In the late 1980s, physician fees rose much more rapidly than inflation and more rapidly than in the 1990s, when managed care began having an effect. Exhibit 11.1 indicates that in recent years physician fee increases have barely exceeded inflation. In 2009, however, the economic recession resulted in a sharp drop in inflation; the Consumer Price Index (CPI) fell 0.4 percent while physician fees increased, on average, by 3.0 percent.

Although average private physician fees, adjusted for inflation, remained relatively unchanged from 2003 to 2008, the volume of services has increased, in part from greater productivity and greater use of imaging tests (Hadley et al. 2009). Also, Medicare physician fees have actually declined when adjusted for inflation; however, the volume of Medicare physician services (including imaging tests) has increased.

Exhibit 11.1 Annual Percentage Changes in the Consumer Price Index and in Physicians' Fees, 1965–2010

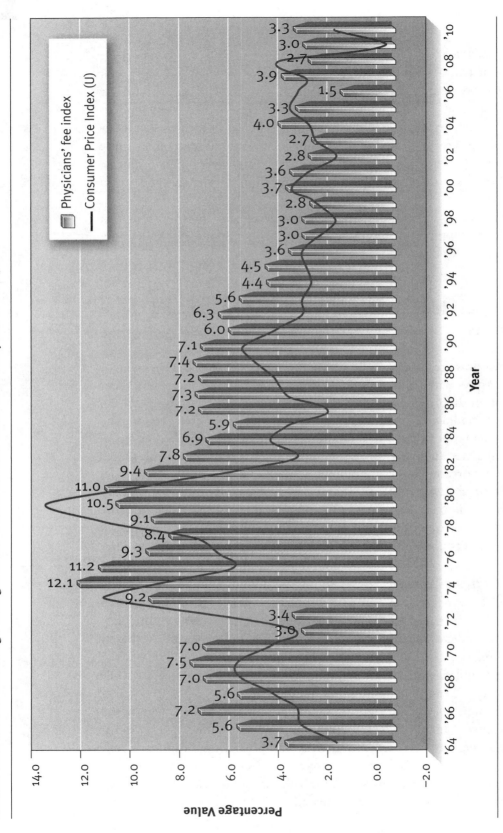

NOTE: CPI (U) = Consumer Price Index for all urban consumers.

SOURCE: Bureau of Labor Statistics (2011).

Exhibit 11.2 Annual Percentage Changes in Median Physician Net Income, After Expenses and Before Taxes, 1982–2000

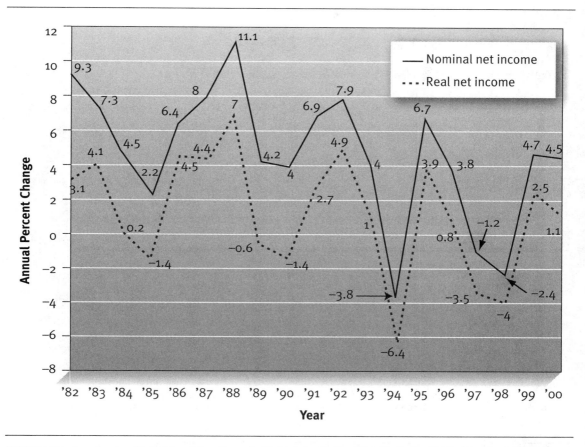

SOURCE: Data from American Medical Association, Center for Health Policy Studies, 2003. *The Profile of Medical Practice, Socioeconomic Characteristics of Medical Practice, and Physician Socioeconomic Statistics,* various editions. Chicago: AMA.

Trends in Physician Incomes

At the beginning of the 1980s a severe recession caused median physician incomes to decline, but they rose during the second half of the decade. During the entire decade of the 1980s, median physician incomes increased on average 2.4 percent per year (adjusted for inflation). Although physician incomes suffered a sharp drop in 1994, they recovered, but after peaking in 1995, they declined for the next three years. In 1997 and 1998, physician incomes not only increased less rapidly than inflation, they fell in absolute dollars. (See Exhibit 11.2.[2])

Managed care and the increased supply of physicians began to negatively affect physician fees and incomes by the mid-1990s. Furthermore, these data indicate that the ability of physicians to increase the demand for their

EXHIBIT 11.3 Average Annual Percentage Change in Net Income from Medical Practice, by Specialty, 2003–2008

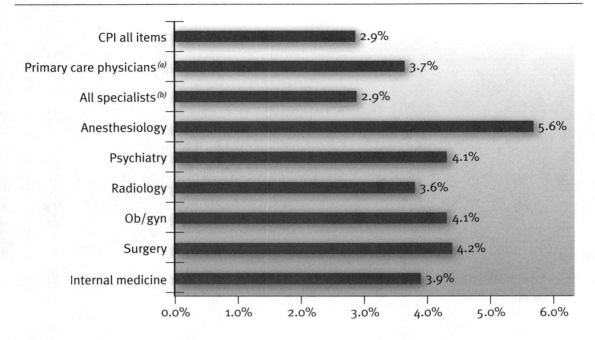

(a) Primary care physicians group includes family practice (without obstetrics), internal medicine, and pediatric/adolescent medicine.

(b) All specialists group includes anesthesiology, cardiology, dermatology, emergency medicine, gastroenterology, hematology/oncology, neurology, obstetrics/gynecology, ophthalmology, orthopedic surgery, otorhinolaryngology, psychiatry, pulmonary medicine, radiology, general surgery, and urology.

SOURCE: Medical Group Management Association. 2008. *Physician Compensation and Production Survey: 2008 Report Based on 2007 Data*. MGMA. 2009. *Physician Compensation and Production Survey: 2009 Report Based on 2008 Data*. Englewood, CO: MGMA.

services appears to be limited; otherwise, physician incomes would not have fallen as much as they have.

Physician income data are not adjusted for changes in the number of hours worked. To the extent that in more recent years there are more female physicians, who work fewer hours on average than male physicians, and more male physicians are deciding to work fewer hours, physician incomes will not rise as rapidly. This change in physicians' lifestyle may have contributed to the downward trend in physician incomes.

Unfortunately, the American Medical Association no longer conducts its annual survey of physician incomes. To understand what has been occurring with physician incomes in the past decade, data from a different source are used; this source also enables comparisons to be made between different physician specialties. As shown in Exhibit 11.3, between 2003 and 2008, physician incomes rose slightly more than the inflation rate, by about 1 to 2 percent per year. Physicians in surgical specialties, hospital-based physicians (anesthesiologists), obstetric/gynecologic physicians, and those in primary care received the largest annual increases in income.

Trends in Rates of Return on a Medical Education

Data on rates of return on a career in medicine are intermittent and only available up to 1997.[3] These studies have been conducted by different researchers, and their methodologies may not be similar. What do they indicate? Throughout the post–World War II period, rates of return on a medical career were sufficiently high to suggest that a shortage existed. In 1962, the rate of return was estimated to be 16.6 percent. By 1970, it had risen to 22 percent. The rate of return declined slightly between 1975 and 1985, when it was estimated to be 16 percent, which still indicates a shortage, not a surplus (Feldstein 2011).

Rates of return have varied greatly among physician specialties. In 1985, some specialties, such as anesthesiology and surgical subspecialties, earned 40 percent and 35 percent returns, whereas pediatrics earned only 1.3 percent (indicative of a surplus). During this period, the rate of return on a physician education was more than 100 percent greater than the rate of return for a college professor. In 1994 the rate of return for primary care physicians was estimated to be 15.9 percent and those of specialists, 20.9 percent. Weeks and Wallace (2002) calculate that in 1997 the rate of return for a primary care physician was about the same (15.8), while for specialists it had declined to 18 percent.

These data indicate that the economic return on a medical career was quite high, indicating a physician shortage.

A recent study provides additional information on the economic value of a medical career. Vaughn and colleagues (2010) calculated the net present value of going to graduate school for an MBA degree, becoming a primary care physician, and becoming a cardiologist, and compared it to the net present value of an undergraduate degree. In contrast to a rate-of-return calculation, in which the discount rate of a future income stream is the rate of return, the calculation of net present value uses a predetermined interest rate to discount future income streams. Since the higher incomes of a graduate education occur over time, and a dollar earned in the future is worth less than a dollar earned today, those income streams are discounted by an interest rate to determine the economic value of the additional educational investment in 2008 dollars.

Exhibit 11.4 shows the income streams for the four career paths and illustrates when the income starts for each career path and its magnitude at different ages. Based on these data, Vaughn and colleagues (2010) calculated that the net present value from college graduation to age 65 was $5,171,407 for cardiologists, $2,475,838 for primary care physicians, $1,725,171 for

EXHIBIT 11.4 Annual Ordinary Incomes, Before Taxes, for Various Professions and Educational Attainment Levels, Ages 22–65

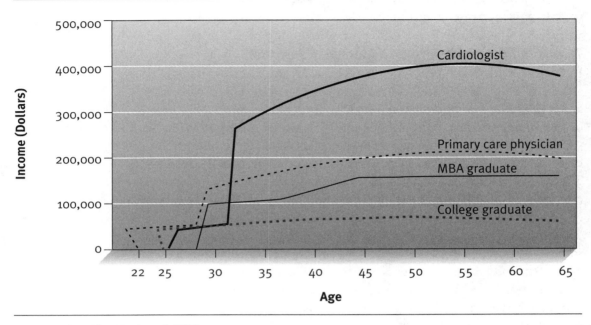

SOURCE: Adapted from Vaughn et al. (2010).

MBA graduates, and $340,628 for college graduates with only bachelor's degrees. Thus, even accounting for the longer years of training, earning income years later and for fewer years, and incurring higher levels of debt, a medical career, particularly one in cardiology, has a great deal of economic value.

The current economic returns of an investment in medicine are sufficiently high to indicate that a shortage, rather than a surplus, exists in the medical profession. If a surplus were indicated, the net present value of a medical career would be less than that of a regular college graduate. Whether or not the investment return to a medical career has fallen in the last several decades, it is still sufficiently high to suggest that there are too few physicians. An increase in physician supply would reduce the current high returns on a medical education.

Applicant-to-Acceptance Ratio in Medical Schools

Another indicator of the economic value of a medical career is the demand for a medical education. The applicant-to-acceptance ratio has always been greater than one. (See Exhibit 23.1 in Chapter 23.) After reaching a high of 2.9:1 in 1973, the applicant-to-acceptance ratio steadily declined to 1.6:1 in 1988, rose again in the mid-1990s, and, after declining again and reaching 1.9:1 in

2002, has increased and is currently 2.2:1. An excess demand for a medical education still exists.

What can one conclude from the data on physician fees, incomes, rates of return, net present value, and the applicant-to-acceptance ratio? A medical career is an attractive investment. Physician incomes are still sufficiently high to offer a higher economic return on a medical career relative to other careers available to prospective medical students. Also indicative of a shortage is the continual excess demand for a medical education; more qualified students seek admission to medical school than are accepted. An increase in the supply of physicians would reduce these high rates of return, making them comparable to the return on other educational investments.

Longer-Term Outlook for Physicians

The physician shortage is unlikely to be resolved for some time. Efforts are currently under way to increase the supply of physicians. New medical schools are starting, and existing schools are expanding their number of spaces. The Association of American Medical Colleges (AAMC) projects that first-year enrollment in medical and osteopathic schools will increase by 36 percent, or 26,550, in 2015 over the year 2002. Even this large projected increase will not provide the number of physicians policy analysts believe are needed. To expand the supply of physicians further, innovations will have to occur in medical education, such as reducing graduation time from the current four years to three years, and in physician productivity, by using lesser-trained personnel to perform certain tasks.

The demand for physicians is expected to increase sharply in coming years, thereby exacerbating the physician shortage. The population is growing by about 1 percent per year. In addition, the population is aging; the first of the baby boomers become eligible for Medicare in 2011. The aged have much higher visit rates than the nonaged, and these use rates have been increasing over time. In addition, laboratory tests and diagnostic imaging services are being used to a greater extent.

Most of the aged purchase private supplementary health insurance (Medigap) policies. This coverage pays for their Medicare deductibles and copayments, reducing the price they must pay for physician services and decreasing their price sensitivity to physician fees. With virtually complete coverage for physician services, a larger number of aged are likely to further increase their demand for physician services.

The role of government in physician payment also is growing, as shown in Exhibit 11.5.

An important factor increasing use of medical services is new medical technology, such as new diagnostic and surgical procedures. Technological

EXHIBIT 11.5 Percentage Distribution of Physician Expenditures, by Source of Funds, Selected Years, 1965–2009

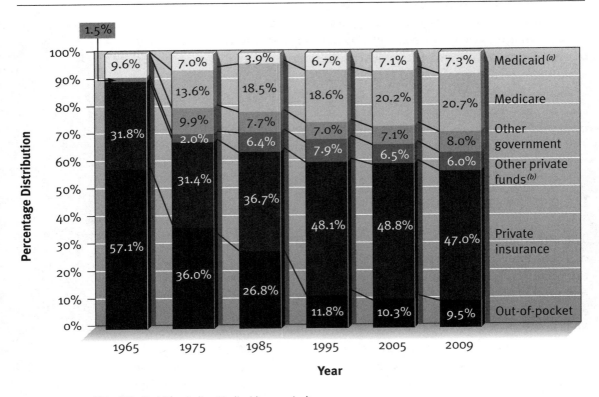

(a) Total Medicaid (excluding Medicaid expansion)

(b) "Other private funds" category includes industrial inplant and other private revenues (including philanthropy). Other private funds in 1965 and 1975 were 1.5% and 2.1%, respectively.

SOURCE: Centers for Medicare & Medicaid Services, Office of the Actuary, National Health Statistics Group, 2011. http://www.cms.hhs .gov/NationalHealthExpendData/downloads/tables.pdf.

advances are likely to continue, further expanding demand for physicians, particularly specialists. (More expensive diagnostic and surgical procedures have raised average fees, resulting in procedure-oriented specialists receiving much higher profit margins than physicians in primary care, who perform few procedures.)

Starting in 2014, the Patient Protection and Affordable Care Act of 2010 will require most US residents to have health insurance. About 32 million additional people are expected to enroll in some type of health plan; one-half of those will become eligible for Medicaid. Given the current shortage of physicians, the smaller than desired projected increases in physician supply, and the expected large growth in public and private insurance by 2014, the demand for physicians should greatly exceed their supply. Unless Medicare and Medicaid increase the fees paid to physicians during this period when demand is increasing faster than supply, those with low incomes (Medicaid) and the aged (Medicare) will suffer significant reductions in access to physician services.

In coming years physicians will have to increase their productivity to be able to serve a greater number of patients. Demands for nurse practitioners, physician assistants, and other personnel who perform some physician-type (particularly primary care) services are likely to increase. The physician shortage will become more severe before it gets better.

Summary

Forecasts of physician shortages or surpluses are subject to a great deal of error. COGME has proven itself a faulty prognosticator of trends in the demand for and supply of physicians. Public policy based on COGME's recommendations has adversely affected the career paths of many students. Projecting the future supply of physicians is more certain than projecting demand.

The economic data indicate that this country is facing a physician shortage. Continual high rates of return on a medical education, rising physician fees and incomes (adjusted for inflation), and an increasing applicant-to-acceptance ratio for medical schools are signals of a physician shortage. An increase in the supply of physicians would reduce these high rates of return, making them comparable to the return on other educational investments.

Shortages and surpluses are resolved over time through the adjustment of rising or falling fees. Market imbalances are not resolved quickly, as it takes many years to train additional physicians (in a shortage situation) and many years before physicians retire (in a surplus case). Information on future trends is important to prospective medical students; they will be able to make better-informed decisions on the attractiveness of a medical career. Students who have to bear the cost of their decisions would prefer to have the freedom to choose their professions rather than have their choices limited by expert panels (which are often wrong) deciding on the need for different types of physicians.

A particular problem with medical education is that it is highly regulated by the medical profession. It is difficult for entrepreneurs to develop new medical schools with innovative curricula, have their students graduate in less time, and achieve the same outcomes as graduates from more traditional medical schools. As long as these restrictions, along with an excess demand for a medical education, continue, medical schools will be unresponsive to increased demands for a medical education and to curriculum innovations.

Whether a shortage or surplus is beneficial often depends on whether one is a patient or a physician. A smaller physician supply increases physician incomes, whereas greater competition among physicians benefits patients by increasing their access to care.

Discussion Questions

1. Evaluate the use of the physician-to-population ratio as a means of determining a surplus or a shortage of physicians.
2. Describe and evaluate how a rate of return on a medical education would determine the existence of a physician surplus or shortage.
3. What demand and supply trends in the physician services market will affect the incomes of surgical specialists and primary care physicians?
4. Prices change in a competitive market for two basic reasons: increased operating costs and changes in physician demand. In what ways do these reasons explain physician fee increases?
5. Based on the evidence presented on physician incomes, physician fees, physician-to-population ratio, and applicant-to-acceptance ratio in medical schools, would you conclude that a physician shortage currently exists?

Notes

1. If physician incomes do not increase as fast as other professions, the rate of return on becoming a physician decreases because the opportunity cost to prospective physicians has increased—their forgone income has increased.
2. Physician incomes are highly skewed; that is, the physician income distribution contains large values at the high end of the income distribution. Therefore, using the average income per physician is a less accurate measure of the "typical" physician's income. For this reason, the middle of the income distribution, the median, is used in Exhibit 11.2.
3. The internal rate of return is the discount rate that, when applied to the future earnings stream, will make its present value equal to the cost of entry into that profession, or the present value of the expected outlay or cost stream. A normal rate of return might be similar to the rate of return on a college education or on the return the individual could have received had he or she invested a sum of money comparable to what was spent on a medical education.

THE CHANGING PRACTICE OF MEDICINE

The practice of medicine has changed dramatically since the mid-1980s. For many years the predominant form of medical practice was solo practice with fee-for-service reimbursement. With the increase in medical knowledge and technological advancements, however, more physicians became specialists. Insurer payment and federal education subsidies also encouraged the growth of specialization. The development of managed care changed the practice of medicine; more physicians joined together in increasingly large medical groups.

What are the reasons for this shift away from solo and small group practice toward larger medical groups? Is the consolidation of medical practices into larger groups likely to continue? And what other changes are occurring that will impact how physicians practice?

Types of Medical Groups

Different types of medical groups have developed to serve the differing needs and preferences of practicing physicians. Following is a description of the two basic types of medical groups.

Single- or Multispecialty Groups

Physicians in these types of groups share facilities, equipment, medical records, and support staff. Physicians may be paid according to one or more methods: salary plus a share in remaining net revenues, discounted fee-for-service with a share in remaining net revenues, or capitation. Leaving a group practice is difficult for physicians, as they cannot take their patients with them. Any contracts the group has with a health plan belong to the group and include the patients covered by those contracts.

Independent Practice Associations

Physicians who want to be associated with other physicians (on a nonexclusive basis) for the purposes of joint contracting with a health plan will form a loose organization, such as an independent practice association (IPA). These physicians continue to practice in their own offices, see their own patients, hire and pay their own staff, and do their own billing.

When the IPA contracts with a health plan, the IPA physicians are paid on a discounted fee-for-service basis. If an IPA receives a capitation contract from a health plan, the physicians may be paid a discounted fee for service with the possibility of receiving additional amounts if total physician billings are less than the total capitation amount at the end of the year. The IPA may also subcapitate some specialists. As IPAs competed for capitated contracts and assumed financial risk, they began to exercise more oversight of their physicians' practice patterns.

Changes in the Size of Medical Groups

Data on physicians' practice settings are based on nationally representative surveys published by the Center for Studying Health System Change of physicians who spend at least 20 hours a week in direct patient care. These surveys were conducted over different periods, starting in 1996 to 1997, with the latest in 2008. Although the survey methods differed for the two periods—the earlier survey was taken via telephone while 2008 data were based on a mail survey and are not directly comparable—they provide an indication of the changes that have occurred over time.

Exhibit 12.1 shows the changing distribution of office-based physicians according to physician subspecialty and size of group for different time periods. Three types of physicians are examined: those in primary care, medical specialists, and surgical specialists. Over the period surveyed, it appears that all three types of physicians have moved toward practicing in larger groups.

Exhibit 12.2 illustrates the changes in physician practice arrangements by type of setting. In 1996 to 1997, 40.7 percent of physicians practiced in solo- or two-physician practices, with only 2.9 percent in groups of greater than 50 physicians. Only 10.7 percent worked in a hospital setting. In 2008, the number of physicians in solo- and two-physician practices declined to 32 percent, the largest physician group increased to 6 percent, and physicians working in hospitals increased to 13 percent. The trend appears to be physicians becoming part of larger groups and working in hospitals.

In a highly competitive managed care market, physicians in individual and small group practices were at a disadvantage. Therein lies an important explanation for the formation of large medical groups.

Medical Groups as a Competitive Response
Before managed care became dominant in the insurance marketplace, physicians were less concerned with being included in an insurer's provider panel or competing for insurance contracts. The growth in private insurance reduced the out-of-pocket price of physician services paid by private patients. As patients' out-of-pocket payments declined, they became less price sensitive

EXHIBIT 12.1 Physicians by Subspecialty and Practice Setting, 1996–2001 and 2008

	Solo–2 Physician Practices		3–5 Physician Practices		6+ Physician Practices		Other[a]	
	1996–97	2008	1996–97	2008	1996–97	2008	1996–97	2008
Primary Care	37.5	34.6	10.3	15.7	15.1	26.0	37.1	23.7
Medical Specialists	38.1	27.3	9.6	10.0	17.3	24.6	35.1	38.2
Surgical Specialists	47.8	34.4	17.9	18.8	15.5	26.0	18.8	20.9

[a] Includes physicians employed by medical schools, HMOs, hospitals (including those in office-based practices), community health centers, freestanding clinics, and other settings, as well as independent contractors.

SOURCES: Adapted from Liebhaber, A., and J. Grossman. 2007. "Physicians Moving to Mid-sized, Single-Specialty Practices." Tracking Report No. 18, Center for Studying Health System Change, Washington, D.C. Based on correspondence with Ellyn Boukus for 2008 data based on HSC Tracking Report No. 18 using data from the 2008 Health Tracking Physician Survey.

to physicians' fees, and their demand increased. Patients had access to all physicians, who were paid according to their established fee schedules. Patients had similar insurance (indemnity) and limited, if any, information on physician qualifications or the fees they charged.

Price competition among managed care plans for an employer's enrollees changed all that. To be price competitive, insurers had to reduce the price they paid for their inputs (physician and hospital services) and reduce the quantity of services used.

The physician services market in the 1980s consisted of a rising supply of physicians, particularly specialists, and a high proportion of them were in solo or small group practices. Physicians were eager to contract with new managed care health plans. Insurers and HMOs were able to form limited provider networks by selecting physicians according to whether they were willing to sharply discount their fees in return for a greater volume of patients. Physicians excluded from such networks lost patients.

The growth of managed care had two main effects on physicians. Patients enrolled in managed care plans were required to use providers who were part of their plan's provider network; otherwise, the patient had to pay the full price charged by a non-network provider. For physicians to have access to

Exhibit 12.2 Physicians by Practice Setting, 1996–2001, 2004–05, and 2008

	1996–97	1998–99	2000–01	2004–05	2008
Solo/2 Physician Practices	40.7%	37.4%	35.2%	32.5%	32.0%
3–5 Physician Practices	12.2	9.6	11.7	9.8	14.5
6–50 Physician Practices	13.1	14.2	15.8	17.6	19.4
>50 Physician Practices	2.9	3.5	2.7	4.2	6.1
Medical School	7.3	7.7	8.4	9.3	7.3
HMO	5.0	4.6	3.8	4.5	3.5
Hospital[a]	10.7	12.6	12.0	12.0	13.1
Other[b]	8.3	10.5	10.4	10.1	4.1

[a] Includes physicians employed in hospitals and office-based practices owned by hospitals. Forty percent of physicians in this category were in office-based practices in 2004–05.

[b] Includes physicians practicing in community health centers, freestanding clinics, and other settings, as well as independent contractors.

SOURCES: Adapted from Liebhaber, A., and J. Grossman. 2007. "Physicians Moving to Mid-sized, Single-Specialty Practices." Tracking Report No. 18, Center for Studying Health System Change, Washington, D.C. Based on correspondence with Ellyn Boukus for 2008 data based on HSC Tracking Report No. 18 using data from the 2008 Health Tracking Physician Survey.

an insurer's enrollees, the physician had to be part of the insurer's provider network. Managed care plans limited the number of physicians in their provider networks and selected physicians based on how much they were willing to discount their fees (and not overutilize medical services). Thus, the first effect of managed care was to force physicians to deeply discount their fees in return for a greater volume of the plan's enrollees.

Managed care's second effect was to reduce enrollee access to specialists. Managed care relied on physician gatekeepers, primary care physicians, to determine whether a patient would receive a referral to a specialist. The growth of managed care increased the demand for primary care physicians while decreasing the demand for specialists.

The growth of medical groups was a competitive response to the greater bargaining power of insurers and HMOs. Being part of a medical group, particularly a large group, provided physicians with a competitive advantage over physicians who were not similarly organized. Large medical groups were able to bid for HMO contracts and serve as preferred provider organizations for employers and insurers. Negotiating and contracting with one large medical group is less costly than carrying out separate, time-consuming negotiations with an equivalent number of individual physicians. Tasks performed by the insurer, such as utilization management, can be delegated to the medical group. Thus, large medical groups were better able than individual physicians and smaller medical groups to compete for patients.

HMOs were also able to shift their insurance risk to a large medical group by paying that group on a capitation basis instead of a fee-for-service basis. Similarly, a large medical group can spread financial risk over a large number of capitated enrollees and physicians.

Capitation also provided medical groups with financial incentives to be innovative in the delivery of medical services and the practice of medicine, because by saving part of the capitation payment, they could increase their profits. These incentives do not exist in small group practices that are paid on a fee-for-service basis. As a consequence, several large medical groups developed expertise in managing care and in developing "best-practice" guidelines.

In the 1990s, medical groups in California, more so than medical groups in other states, sought greater financial risk and rewards by accepting a greater percentage of the HMO premium. These medical groups believed that by being responsible for all of the patient's medical services, they could better manage care; furthermore, by reducing hospital admissions, lengths of stay, and payments to hospitals, they could make greater profits. Unfortunately, many of these medical groups were inexperienced in managing the financial risk associated with capitation and suffered financially. Most medical groups no longer accept capitation payments.

Increased Market Power

An employer or a health plan contracting with a large medical group has less reason to be concerned with physician quality. Large medical groups have more formalized quality control and monitoring mechanisms than do independently practicing physicians. Within a large group, physicians refer to their own specialists; thus, specialists who are not part of a group are less likely to have access to patients. These contracting, quality review, and referral mechanisms provide physicians in large medical groups with a competitive advantage over physicians who are unaffiliated with such groups.

These advantages gave large groups greater bargaining power over health plans compared with independent and small physician practices. As a result, large groups were more likely to be able to negotiate higher payments and increased market share (receiving a greater portion of the health plan's total number of enrollees).

Large medical groups also have greater leverage over hospitals. Because such groups control large numbers of enrollees, the group can determine to which hospitals it will refer its patients. Hospitals in turn were willing to share some of their capitated revenues with these groups. When hospitals were capitated, a "risk-sharing pool" was formed from part of the hospital's capitation payments, whereby the savings from reduced hospitalization were shared between the hospital and the medical group. These risk-sharing pools enabled physicians in medical groups to increase their incomes compared with what they would have earned in independent or small group practices.

Economies of Scale in Group Practice

An obvious reason for moving toward larger medical groups in a price-competitive environment is to take advantage of economies of scale. Larger groups have lower per-unit costs than do smaller groups. Larger groups are also better able to spread certain fixed costs over a larger number of physicians. The administrative costs of running an office (including making appointments; billing patients, government, and insurance companies for services rendered; maintaining computerized information systems to keep track of patients; and staffing aides to assist the physician) do not increase proportionately as the number of physicians increases. Larger group practices are also able to receive volume discounts on supplies and negotiate lower rates on their leases than the same number of physicians practicing separately or in smaller groups.

Informational economies of scale also provide large groups with a competitive advantage over small or independent practices. A distinguishing characteristic of the physician services market is the lack of patient information on physicians, including their quality, their fees, their accessibility, and how they relate to their patients. Physicians are better able than patients to evaluate other physicians. Evaluating and monitoring member physicians is less costly for the medical group than for patients. Being a member of a medical group conveys information regarding quality to patients, giving physicians in that group the equivalent of a brand name.

A new physician entering a market is at a disadvantage compared with established physicians, in that developing a reputation among patients and building a practice take time. Joining a medical group immediately transfers the group's reputation to the new physician. The reputation of the group is more important to the patient for those specialist services that are less frequently used and more difficult for the patient to evaluate. Multispecialty groups offer greater informational economies of scale than do groups made up of family practitioners.

Medical Groups and Quality of Care

Large medical groups are more likely than physicians in solo or small group practices to invest in management and clinical information systems, such as electronic medical records (Burt and Sisk 2005). Large multispecialty medical groups have been found to deliver higher-quality care on average and lower annual costs per patient than physicians who do not work within such large groups (Weeks et al. 2010). Medical groups are also likely to use more recommended care management processes for patients with chronic illnesses. (In a study comparing California medical groups with those in the rest of the country, Gillies and colleagues [2003] found that California medical groups used 35 to 50 percent more care management processes, such as use of hospitalists [who manage the patient's care during a hospital stay], case management, and diabetes, asthma, and depression care management, than physician organizations in other parts of the country.) Large groups are able to hire professional management to deal with an increasingly burdensome regulatory environment and achieve operational efficiencies by taking advantage of economies of scale.

The growing emphasis by insurers, employers, and Medicare on monitoring systems to measure patient outcomes and satisfaction and the growing interest in pay for performance provide large medical groups with a competitive advantage in attracting patients and receiving bonuses for achieving certain quality benchmarks. Pay-for-performance revenue is likely to become a larger share of physician incomes; thus, medical groups that invest in information technology and are able to demonstrate improved patient performance will receive a greater share of physician revenues.

Reversal of Fortunes of Large Multispecialty Groups

The promise of large multispecialty medical groups in managing patient care and being rewarded for accepting greater capitation risk foundered in the late 1990s, particularly in California.

Changing Market Environment

The prosperity created by the economic expansion in the United States in the late 1990s led employees to demand broader provider networks and freer access to specialists from their HMOs. Large medical groups had been using primary care gatekeepers to control specialist referrals and utilization management to control the growth in medical costs. But when the market changed, it was no longer willing to reward large capitated medical groups for strict cost-control measures.

During this time, competition among HMOs led to low premium increases, leaving large capitated groups with low capitation rates. Medical groups found themselves in financial difficulty as their costs increased and state and federal governments enacted patient protection measures. These included 48-hour hospital stays for normal deliveries, requiring HMOs to allow obstetricians/gynecologists to serve as primary care physicians, and prohibiting limited lengths of stay after a mastectomy. These measures further increased the medical groups' costs.

HMOs were wary of being sued for withholding appropriate treatment even when the HMO had delegated such treatment decisions to its large medical groups. As HMOs began to undertake those decisions themselves, some of the advantages of capitation payment to large groups faded.

Difficulty of Developing a Group Culture

A well-functioning medical group cannot be formed overnight; the group may not coalesce even after years. An important difference between group and nongroup physicians is the willingness of group physicians to give up some of their autonomy and abide by group decisions. Physicians may not share values or accept the same assumptions regarding their external environment, mission, and relationships with one another. This cultural difference often determines whether physicians will remain in a group. Many physicians are very independent and do not want other physicians involved with their practice, whether it relates to contracting with certain health plans, reviewing their practice patterns, or determining their compensation.

A large multispecialty group must have various committees, one of which determines physician compensation. Disputes among physicians over their compensation are an important reason such groups have dissolved. For example, when a multispecialty group is capitated for a large number of enrollees, the group must decide how the primary care physicians and each specialist will share in those capitation dollars. Because the primary care physicians control the specialist referrals, some groups pay them more than they would earn under a discounted fee-for-service environment. These funds must come from paying specialists less.

Another issue in medical group compensation is how much of each physician's income should be tied to productivity. Productivity incentives decline when a physician's payment is not directly related to his clinical work. More productive physicians may decide to leave if large differences occur between productivity and compensation.

When physicians in a large group share the use of inputs, that is, personnel and supplies, they are less concerned with those costs than they would be if they were in independent or small group practice, where their costs are more directly related to their earnings. This lack of efficiency incentives offsets some savings from economies of scale.

Lack of Management Expertise

As medical groups increased in size and number, many had inadequate management expertise to handle the clinical and financial responsibilities of the group. The groups did not have adequate information systems for tracking expenses and revenues, they lacked actuarial expertise for underwriting risk when they were receiving capitation payments, and they did not have sufficient management specializing in marketing, finance, and contracting. Unfortunately, many medical groups expanded more rapidly than their management ability to handle the increased risk and patient volume.

Instead of developing such management expertise themselves, many groups joined for-profit (publicly traded) physician practice management (PPM) companies. These PPM companies promised a number of benefits to a participating medical group, such as including it in a larger contracting network with health plans, handling its administration, and improving its efficiency. In return for these services, the PPM company received a percentage of the group's revenues (e.g., 15 percent). However, several publicly traded PPM companies were themselves poorly managed and declared bankruptcy. A further disappointment with PPM companies was that the cost savings they were able to achieve in the medical group and the additional contracting revenue they were able to bring to the group were often lower than the 15 percent management fee they charged.

Lack of Capital

Medical groups typically pay out all of their net revenues to their member physicians. Thus, no funds are available to reinvest in expanding the group, such as by establishing new clinics, purchasing expensive diagnostic services, or buying costly hardware and software for information technology. Their lack of capital is an important reason expanding medical groups seek partners.

Hospitals have generally been willing to provide the capital for medical groups to expand and to develop their infrastructures. In return for such investments, hospitals hope to secure the medical group's inpatient referrals and negotiate joint contracting arrangements with a health plan. The hospital may also manage or become a part owner in a joint management company that contracts with the medical group for medical services.

The main concerns groups have with hospitals as capital partners are that the hospital will somehow gain control of the group and that it may not be the most advantageous facility to which to refer patients. Many hospitals have lost a great deal of money investing in their physician partners because the hoped-for returns have been lower than anticipated, particularly when hospitals purchased physician practices and physician productivity, separated from compensation, declined.

Outlook for Medical Group Practices

The organization of medical practice is based on a number of factors, but one that is increasing in importance is the method of payment for medical services. As a major payer, Medicare is likely to have a strong impact as it considers alternative payment strategies for medical services.

The Movement to Single-Specialty Groups

An important trend is the growth of single-specialty medical groups. In the earlier period of tightly managed care plans, multispecialty groups had market power in negotiating payment with health plans and hospitals and benefited from economies of scale. Tightly managed care, with its use of primary care physicians as gatekeepers and preauthorization for referrals, limited the use of specialist services. As managed care plans loosened their restrictions on patients' use of providers and specialist referrals, the demand for specialist services increased. Rather than being considered cost centers when medical groups were paid a capitation rate, specialist services became profit centers under the fee-for-service system.

Under fee-for-service payment, greater profits accrue to those physicians who can provide profitable procedures and ancillary services, such as imaging and diagnostic services. Single-specialty groups are also able to take advantage of economies of scale.

Medical groups have become more entrepreneurial as they attempt to increase physician revenues. Concerned that growth in physician revenues from providing physician services to Medicare and Medicaid patients is limited, medical groups became more aggressive in expanding the services they offer. Based on a large-scale interview survey, Pham and colleagues (2004) found that physicians' healthcare investments in new services have increased. Medical groups were more likely than physicians in solo practice to invest in equipment to provide ancillary services, such as imaging and laboratory testing, within their existing practices. Patients' use of such services has sharply increased. Some survey respondents stated that if it were not for the ancillary services, some groups would not make any money.

During the managed care era, with its emphasis on multispecialty medical groups that used primary care physicians to coordinate and control patient care, expectations were that a surplus of specialists would occur. These predictions proved inaccurate.

The emergence of new imaging and surgical technologies made it possible to provide outpatient imaging and surgical services. In addition, use of these new technologies was profitable, as they were reimbursed by Medicare and health plans at very favorable rates. Specialists have an incentive to move these services out of the hospital and into their own facilities. Physicians with specialties in cardiology and orthopedics have invested in freestanding specialty hospitals and ambulatory surgical centers that compete with their own community hospitals. Further, larger groups, particularly large single-specialty groups, have been able to secure private investment capital (Casalino, Pham, and Bazzoli 2004) for investing in costly imaging equipment, surgical services, and information technology, which are usually beyond the means of smaller groups. By investing in these facilities, specialists are able to receive the facility fees for such services (which would otherwise go to the hospital) and thereby increase their incomes.[1] Physicians have claimed that such "focused factories" are more convenient for patients and improve patient care.

The profit potential of performing services with a high markup over cost in their own outpatient facilities provided specialists with an incentive to form large single-specialty groups. Specialists are able to generate more profit than are primary care physicians. Specialty groups that own their own expensive imaging equipment, magnetic resonance imaging (MRI) equipment, and facilities, such as ambulatory surgery centers, are more profitable when paid on a fee-for-service basis than are primary care physicians providing cognitive services. Further, single-specialty groups do not have to share their revenues or governance with primary care physicians, as occurs in a multispecialty group.

An economic advantage of single-specialty groups is the increased leverage such groups have in bargaining with health plans and community hospitals. The consolidation of many specialists into a single group lessens competition among specialists, enabling them to increase their fees in negotiations with health plans. Health plans are reluctant to lose a large network of specialists. Physicians in solo practice and small groups are at a competitive disadvantage in dealing with health plans.

The Growth of Hospital-Employed Physicians

A second trend is hospital employment of physicians. In the 1990s period of tightly managed care, excess capacity existed among physicians, the demand for primary care physicians increased as they became gatekeepers and restricted access to specialists, and specialist fees decreased. To increase their referrals, hospitals bought medical practices. As managed care became less restrictive and hospitals found they were losing money on their medical groups, they divested them. Hospitals have again started to employ physicians, generally specialists (Casalino et al. 2009).

Hospitals have several reasons for again employing physicians: an important medical group may be considering moving its admissions to another hospital, the hospital may be trying to enter a new market, the hospital may lack specialists in some services, or the hospital may be trying to preempt competition from specialists who have started their own outpatient services. Also, employing specialists and primary care physicians is likely to increase the hospital's negotiating leverage over health plans; if the health plan does not increase the hospital's rates, it may lose both the hospital and its physicians. Further, as quality reporting and pay for performance become more important, the hospital is better able to monitor performance and align hospital and physician incentives.

Physicians have become more receptive to hospital employment, since it gives them regular work hours and eliminates the administrative responsibilities of dealing with insurers and the financial risk of having their own medical practice. Specialists are also concerned that the hospital may hire specialists to compete with them.

The Effect of Payment Changes on Medical Practices

Medicare payment changes are likely to have a major effect on the organization of physician and hospital services, decreasing the growth of single-specialty groups while increasing the number of multispecialty groups and the hospital employment of physicians.

The organization of medical services has been greatly affected by the payment system. Fee-for-service (FFS) encourages the provider to perform more services and shifts the open-ended financial risk of paying for all the services to the insurer or to Medicare and Medicaid. When each type of provider hospital, primary care physician, specialist, nursing home, home health agency, and so on is paid FFS, the delivery system is likely to be fragmented. Coordination of services and the alignment of each provider's incentives are less likely to occur than under a broader payment system.

Capitation payment shifts the financial risk to the provider; the provider receives a fixed payment and has to provide all the necessary medical services, so its incentive is to provide fewer services. Under a broader payment system, however, the incentive is greater to coordinate care by each of the participating providers so as to reduce the costs of providing that treatment.

Each type of payment system requires monitoring and quality reporting. Under FFS it becomes more difficult to monitor quality provided by many different unaffiliated providers; duplication of services is more likely to occur and costs are more difficult to control. Since the incentive under capitation is to provide fewer services, it is also necessary to monitor treatment outcomes, which is less difficult than measuring the care provided by each provider, as under FFS. Controlling rising medical costs is less difficult under capitation, as the organization bears the financial risk of exceeding the overall payment per enrollee.

Over time Medicare has recognized the difficulty in controlling utilization of services and costs under FFS payment and has tried to move to a broader payment system. One such example is the change from paying hospitals according to their costs to a fixed price per admission. The financial risk of the costs per admission was shifted from Medicare to hospitals. Hospitals responded by reducing lengths of stay and becoming more efficient. Medicare was better able to control rising hospital costs. However, hospitals have no incentive to be concerned with the costs of treating the patient either before or after being discharged from the hospital. Thus, a still broader hospital payment system is being considered. Medicare still relies on FFS for physician payment. Although physician fees are regulated, use of physician services is not; consequently, Medicare finds it difficult to limit rising physician expenditures. Medicare Advantage plans, which are like HMOs, are paid a risk-adjusted capitation amount for each Medicare enrollee, and the private plans compete against each other as well as with traditional Medicare FFS. In return for limiting their access to the plan's provider network, Medicare Advantage enrollees are provided with increased benefits and decreased cost sharing. The political parties differ on the use of private managed care plans, and as part of the Patient Protection and Affordable Care Act of 2010, payments to Medicare Advantage plans were reduced. This will likely decrease enrollment in such plans as they increase fees to their Medicare enrollees.

Medicare is considering moving toward broader payment systems, such as using episode-based payment and providing payment incentives for organizations to form accountable care organizations (ACOs), thereby shifting more of the financial risk of controlling costs to providers. Under episode-based payment, the insurer pays a single fee that includes all the services by all providers involved in providing treatment for certain procedures, such as heart surgery or hip replacements. Eventually, the goal is to use episode-based payment for more types of treatments. ACOs are meant to encourage hospitals and physicians to collaborate to manage care and limit rising costs.

These broader payment systems, if successful, are likely to transform the delivery of medical services. Multispecialty medical groups will increase to be able to undertake financial risk by becoming ACOs, and hospital employment of physicians will expand to enable the hospital to provide episode-based care in a less costly manner and to become an ACO. Under this scenario, single-specialty medical groups will be at a disadvantage (and would be expected to oppose the implementation of the payment system), as will physicians who own various surgery and imaging centers and those who are not affiliated with a hospital or a multispecialty group. With broader-based payment, the financial risk of rising costs is shifted to providers, and provider incentives for coordinating care and investing in electronic information systems will increase.

Should attempts by Medicare to institute broader-based payment systems be politically unsuccessful and FFS remain the predominant payment system, the current trend toward single-specialty medical groups and hospital-employed physicians will likely continue. The financial risk of controlling Medicare costs will remain with the government, and price controls will become more likely.

Summary

The organization of medical practices is changing. Large medical groups have advantages over physicians in solo or small group practices. In addition to being able to hire professional management, achieve economies of scale, and attain greater bargaining leverage with health plans and hospitals, large medical groups, particularly large single-specialty groups, are able to increase their revenues by taking more services that were previously provided in hospitals to their own outpatient settings.

As budget pressures from federal (Medicare) and state (Medicaid) governments limit physician fee increases, new sources of revenue will increase in importance for physicians. The trend by multispecialty and single-specialty medical groups to invest in technologically advanced services that can be provided in an outpatient setting will continue. Hospitals, to prevent the loss in revenues, will likely participate with medical groups in joint ventures and continue to employ more physicians.

Medical groups face challenges in coming years. Employers, insurers, and Medicare are increasing emphasis on monitoring patient outcomes and satisfaction. As payers become more sophisticated and quality is rewarded, medical groups should have an advantage, because quality and outcome measures are more accurate for medical groups than for individual physicians. Medical groups will also have to become more proficient in managing chronic illness for an increasingly aged population while demonstrating improved medical outcomes and patient satisfaction. Large medical groups will be better able than smaller medical groups to invest in the necessary information technology to evaluate practice patterns and patient outcomes.

As pay for performance among insurers and Medicare becomes a more important source of revenue for physicians, well-managed medical groups, using information technology, will be better able to compete for pay-for-performance bonuses.

Large medical groups have the potential to increase their role in the delivery of medical services. It is uncertain whether medical groups will achieve their promise in innovating new treatment methods that decrease medical costs while demonstrating improved patient outcomes. If medical groups are unable to do so, insurers will develop the information systems and databases to analyze physicians' practice patterns, disseminate practice guidelines to physicians, and monitor the quality of care provided by physicians.

Whether and how the Medicare payment system changes will affect medical practices. A broader payment system will provide incentives for hospitals and physicians to create larger, more integrated systems that consist of hospitals employing physicians and large multispecialty medical groups; this will occur at the expense of single-specialty groups. Conversely, continuing with the fee-for-service payment system with few restrictions on access to specialist services is likely to favor the formation of large single-specialty medical groups.

Discussion Questions

1. Why has the size of multispecialty medical groups increased?
2. Why do large medical groups have market power?
3. Why do medical groups occasionally break up?
4. Describe how an IPA functions.
5. What are the different types of capital partners available to medical groups? What do they expect in return for providing capital?

Additional Readings

Berenson, R., P. Ginsburg, and J. May. 2006. "Hospital–Physician Relations: Cooperation, Competition, or Separation?" *Health Affairs* Web Exclusive 5 December: w31–w43.

Goldsmith, J. 2010. "Analyzing Shifts in Economic Risks to Providers in Proposed Payment and Delivery System Reforms." *Health Affairs* 29 (7): 1299–1304.

Pham, H., and P. Ginsburg. 2007. "Unhealthy Trends: The Future of Physician Services." *Health Affairs* 26 (6): 1586–98.

Note

1. To forestall such competition from specialists, the American Hospital Association was successful in having Congress, as part of the Patient Protection and Affordable Care Act (PPACA) of 2010, prohibit the development of additional physician-owned single-specialty hospitals.

RECURRENT MALPRACTICE CRISES

Three malpractice "crises" have occurred in the last 35 years. The last one began in 2002. The median annual increase in malpractice premiums was between 15 and 30 percent in most states, and some states experienced rate increases as high as 73 percent. The first malpractice crisis occurred in the mid-1970s, when physicians' malpractice premiums rose more than 50 percent between 1974 and 1976; for some specialties, such as obstetrics/gynecology and surgery, the increases were even greater. During this first malpractice crisis, some insurers completely withdrew from the malpractice insurance market, while others increased their premiums by as much as 300 percent. Physicians threatened to strike if state legislatures did not intervene. To ensure access to malpractice insurance at the lowest possible rates, some medical societies formed their own, mutual, insurance companies.

By the late 1970s and early 1980s, malpractice premiums had stabilized somewhat, but they rose sharply again in the mid-1980s, precipitating a second malpractice crisis. Again, physicians demanded that state legislatures take action to alleviate the burden of high premiums. In the late 1980s, malpractice premiums and awards started to decline and then stabilized through the mid-1990s.

The annual percentage change in malpractice premiums appears to be cyclical. After years of falling malpractice premiums, in 2002 premiums again rose rapidly, and premiums for some medical specialties sharply increased. With the rapid rise in premiums, medical societies once again pressured federal and state legislatures for malpractice reform, that is, tort changes that would limit malpractice awards and claims filed.

In more recent years, malpractice premiums have been relatively stable. If history is any guide, it is likely that in several years another malpractice crisis will arise.

Explanations for the Rise in Malpractice Premiums

Insurers take several factors into account when setting malpractice premiums, such as recent payments, the anticipated cost of future payments, the expected rate of return on invested premium income, and administrative expenses. Further, because malpractice claims may take years to settle, insurers may find that previously they did not correctly predict malpractice payments and therefore have to either increase premiums to cover their losses or decrease premiums. This uncertainty in the market for medical malpractice insurance, together with changes in interest rates, contributes to the cyclical nature of this industry.

The components of malpractice premiums that receive the most attention are, first, economic costs, which include current and future medical expenses and lost wages. Second are the costs of pain and suffering, which usually cover the physical and emotional stress caused by an injury; this is the component that damage caps seek to limit. And third are factors affecting the malpractice insurer's profitability, including its operating loss ratio, investment returns, and legal defense costs. To understand the cyclical rise in malpractice premiums, it is important to understand how each of these components has been changing.

Insurers' malpractice payments per physician are based on economic costs and the costs of pain and suffering. These payments are based on two factors: the number of claims filed and the size of jury awards and out-of-court settlements per claim.

Claims Filed

Two reasons account for the general increase in malpractice cases over time. First, physicians are performing more procedures using complex new technologies, which carry greater risks of injury. Second, liberalized applications of tort law have created uncertainty among insurers concerning the size of awards for pain and suffering and who is liable; this has placed some defendants (those with "deep pockets," such as health insurers and hospitals) at greater financial risk, although their contributions to injuries may be minor. Larger jury awards and the ability to include more defendants increase the likelihood of a greater payoff to lawyers for bringing a malpractice case, hence increasing the number of such claims.

The number of claims per 100 physicians has risen at various times and then declined. Since 1990, the number has been declining. Claims against obstetricians, typically the group with the highest number of claims filed, have declined sharply since the early 1990s. The number of claims filed does not appear to explain the sharp increase in malpractice premiums in 2002, as the frequency of claims has continued to decline (CBO 2004).

Claims Payment

The second component of malpractice payments is the average payment per claim. Most claims—about 14,000 per year—are resolved by settlement with the insurer, whereas successful jury awards to the injured party number only about 400 per year.

EXHIBIT 13.1 Jury Awards for Medical Malpractice Cases, 1975–2007

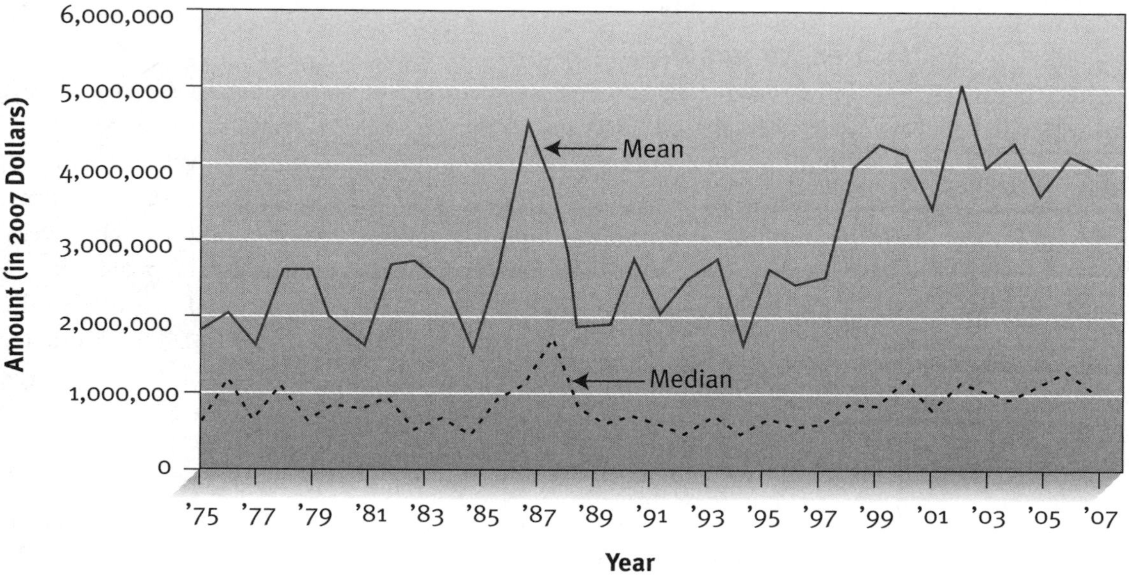

SOURCES: 1975–1990 data from American College of Surgeons, *Socioeconomic Factbook*, various editions, Chicago: American College of Surgeons; 1991–1992 data from *Trends in Health Care Provider Liability*; 1993–2007 data from *Current Award Trends in Personal Injury*, various editions. Jury Verdict Research, Horsham, PA: LRP Publications.

An interesting factor in the rising costs for malpractice insurance is the difference between the average (mean) jury award and the median jury award, which represents the midpoint of all of the awards (half the awards are above and half are below the median award). Although the median jury award has risen slightly over time, the average jury award has increased sharply since the late 1990s (see Exhibit 13.1). The average jury award in any year is generally three to five times greater than the median award (e.g., $4 million versus $1 million in 2007), meaning that juries make many small awards and a few large ones, although the latter receive the greatest publicity. Trial judgments, which account for only 4 percent of all malpractice payments, are, on average, about twice the size of settlements, which account for the remaining 96 percent (though the median settlement award also has increased, from $500,000 in 1997 to $1 million in 2007).

Large damage awards and financial settlements for patients, however, do not appear to be the driving force behind the explosive increase in physicians' malpractice insurance premiums in 2002. One study, based on data from the National Practitioner Data Bank, found that payments to patients between 1991 and 2003 increased by 4 percent annually, a figure that is consistent with increases in overall medical costs over that same period (Chandra,

Nundy, and Seabury 2005). Malpractice premiums, however, increased much more rapidly.

Insurer Profitability

The third possible explanation for recurrent malpractice crises is based on the changing financial condition and market structure of malpractice insurers. Profitability of insurers is determined by their loss ratio (jury awards, settlements, and defense costs as a percentage of premiums) and their investment returns, which are often used to offset high loss ratios. If the loss ratio is high, investment returns may offset those losses and the insurer may still be profitable.

As the frequency and size of physicians' malpractice claims rose in the early 1980s, several large insurers sharply increased their rates. The frequency and size of claims leveled off by the late 1980s, leaving insurers with large reserves that had been set aside for expected continued increases in malpractice payouts. During the early and mid-1990s, these insurers had substantial reserves against possible losses, so by releasing these reserves (changing them from expenses to income), insurers greatly increased their income. Also during this period, insurers' loss ratios were favorable, at about 92 percent, and investment returns were high; insurers were profitable and malpractice premiums were generally stable.

Seemingly unaware that insurers' high profitability was based on prior years' reserves (when insurance actuaries were predicting that previous claims trends would continue to increase) and believing large profits could be had in malpractice insurance, new insurers entered the business. To attract business, these new insurers offered lower premiums; existing insurers responded by cutting their premiums. Intense price competition among insurers led to premiums that were inadequate to cover malpractice payouts (Zimmerman and Oster 2002). As a result, the loss ratio began to greatly exceed premium income, reaching 112 percent by 2001 (see Exhibit 13.2). Reserves were consumed; furthermore, investment returns fell sharply as bond yields and equities declined.[1] To improve their loss ratios and compensate for their lower investment returns, insurers increased their premiums. Another malpractice crisis occurred.

Two additional factors reinforced insurers' rate increases. Reinsurers, who cover larger malpractice insurance payouts, began to increase their reserves, and consequently their rates to malpractice insurers, as the percentage of million-dollar jury awards increased. Second, the structure of the malpractice insurance industry changed. By 2001, many insurers were losing money, became insolvent, and either exited the business or withdrew from markets in which they had been losing money. These temporary disruptions in availability of coverage in several markets led to much higher rates.[2]

By increasing their premiums, insurers became profitable by 2003. Insurer loss ratios declined, and they started to build up their reserves. As loss ratios continued to decline relative to premiums, investment income increased,

EXHIBIT 13.2 Malpractice Insurers' Financial Ratios, 1997–2006

Year	Broad Combined Ratio[a] (%)	Loss Ratio[b] (%)	Investment Income Ratio[c] (%)	Net Income Ratio[c] (%)
1997	111	92	48	20
1998	114	92	48	16
1999	113	92	36	13
2000	120	98	35	6
2001	134	112	33	−7
2002	129	110	16	−10
2003	122	105	25	−2
2004	109	93	21	7
2005	98	82	17	12
2006	87	70	27	29

[a]Awards, settlements, and defense costs plus dividends, administrative costs, and corporate income taxes as a percentage of premium.

[b]Awards, settlements, and defense costs as a percentage of premium.

[c]As a percentage of premium.

SOURCE: Hurley, J. D. 2007. "Medical Malpractice—Financial Update." [Online information; retrieved 3/29/11.] http://www.willis.com/documents/publications/Industries/Healthcare/MedMal_Financial_Update707.pdf.

profitability continued to grow, and malpractice premium increases became stable and even declined. By 2006 the financial results of malpractice insurers indicated that profitability continued to increase. With rising profitability and low loss ratios, premium competition among insurers for market share is likely to increase and, as this occurs, loss ratios will similarly increase, leading to another malpractice crisis in several years. The cycle is likely to repeat itself.

Objectives of the Malpractice System

Tort law is the basis for medical malpractice. It entitles an injured person to compensation as a result of someone's negligence. Damages include economic losses (lost wages and medical bills) and noneconomic losses, referred to as pain and suffering. Thus, physicians have a financial incentive to provide good treatment and perform only those procedures for which they are competent.

The purposes of tort law are to compensate the victim for negligence and to deter future negligence. How well does the malpractice system fulfill these two objectives? Can legislative reforms achieve them at a lower cost than the current system? Physician advocates maintain that too many claims have little to do with negligence (so the insurer will settle to avoid legal expenses that would exceed the settlement cost) and that juries award large sums unrelated to actual damages. Furthermore, "defensive" medicine—additional tests prescribed by physicians to protect themselves against malpractice claims—adds billions of dollars to the nation's health expenditures.

Patient advocates counter those claims. They say physician negligence is more extensive than the number of claims filed reflects, large jury awards are infrequent, incompetent physicians must be discouraged from practicing because physicians do not adequately monitor themselves, and defensive medicine is caused by the fee-for-service insurance system, which rewards physicians for performing more services and eliminates patients' incentives to be concerned about the cost of care.

Compensation of Victims

Which arguments are correct? A 1990 Harvard University study found that too few of those injured by negligence are compensated under the malpractice system (Localio et al. 1991). The authors examined hospital records from 1984 in 51 New York hospitals and determined that almost 4 percent of all patients suffered an injury while in the hospital and that one-quarter of those injuries were the result of negligence. Thus, about 1 percent of all patients discharged from New York hospitals in 1984 experienced some type of negligence. Examples of injuries occurring in hospitals are errors in diagnosis, falls, hospital-caused infections, and surgical complications.

Surprisingly, fewer than 2 percent of the patients identified as victims of negligence filed malpractice claims. However, 6 percent of injured patients who had not been victims of negligence filed claims. (Even though there may have been no negligence on the part of the surgeon, not all surgical procedures are successful, and the patient could be left with a disability or even die.) According to the Harvard researchers, half the patients who file claims eventually receive some compensation. Many patients settle within two years without receiving any compensation, and the rest may wait years for compensation. Few victims of actual negligence ever receive compensation—only about 1 percent. Of those patients injured through negligence who do not file claims (98 percent of negligence victims), 20 percent have serious injuries—disabilities that last six months or more—and this figure includes fatalities (Localio et al. 1991).

A more recent study of different states (Colorado and Utah) also found a poor relationship between medical negligence and malpractice claims;

97 percent of those who suffered a medical negligence injury did not sue. Studdert and colleagues (2000) found that the elderly and the poor were least likely to sue for medical negligence. When physicians were sued, the claims were generally for injuries not caused by negligent care.

Several reasons account for the low percentage of negligence claims filed. A patient may not know that negligence caused an injury. Some claims may be difficult to prove. Recoverable damages may be less than the litigation costs, particularly in the case of minor injuries.

The cost of administering the compensation system is high, and only a small portion of malpractice premiums, 28 to 40 percent, is returned to those injured through negligence. Overhead, including legal fees, consumes the major portion of premiums. Health insurance, on the other hand, returns 85 to 90 percent of the premium for medical expenses.

If the sole purpose of malpractice insurance is to compensate those who are negligently injured, more efficient means at lower administrative costs exist. A different approach could compensate a greater number of victims and return a greater portion of premiums to those injured.

Deterrence of Negligence

Justification of the current malpractice system must depend, therefore, on how well it performs its second, more important role: preventing negligence. Compensation tries not only to make whole the injuries suffered by victims of negligence but also to force negligent healthcare providers to exercise greater caution in future caregiving situations. Concerns exist, however, that not enough injuries are prevented by the current system to justify the high costs of practicing defensive medicine, determining fault, and prosecuting malpractice claims.

The standard of care used in determining negligence is what one would expect from a reasonably competent person who is knowledgeable about advances in medicine and exercises care. Some cases of malpractice, such as amputating the wrong leg or leaving surgical supplies in a patient's abdomen, are easily established. With other forms of physician behavior, however, uncertainties exist in both diagnosis and outcome of medical treatment. Many medical procedures are inherently risky. Even with correct diagnosis and treatment, a patient may die because of poor health conditions, or a baby may be born with a birth defect through no fault of the obstetrician. Physicians do differ in the quality of care they provide and in their success rates, but it is difficult, hence costly, to determine whether a specific outcome is a result of physician negligence, poor communication of the risks involved, or the patient's underlying health condition.

The potential for malpractice suits increases the cost of negligent behavior to the physician. Physicians therefore would be expected to change their behavior and restrict their practices to forestall such costs, to stop performing procedures and tasks for which they lack competence. Prevention costs time and resources; therefore, physicians should invest their time, training, and medical testing in prevention up to the point at which the additional cost of prevention equals the additional value of injuries avoided (forgone malpractice costs). Too much prevention could occur if a great deal of time and resources (the additional costs) are used to prevent occasional minor injuries. A requirement that the injury rate be zero would be too costly for society and would discourage skilled specialists from performing procedures that involve an element of risk of injury but could benefit the patient.

How Well Does the Malpractice System Deter Negligence?

More precisely, is the value to patients of the negligence prevented greater than the costs (defensive medicine, determining liability, and litigation) of the malpractice system? Experts differ on this issue.

First, critics of the current system claim that physicians are not penalized for negligence, as only 2 to 3 percent of negligence victims file claims. Second, because less than half of malpractice insurance premiums—approximately $3.5 billion, or one-sixth of 1 percent of total healthcare spending—are returned to victims of negligence and the remainder is spent on overhead and legal fees, the malpractice system is too costly. Third, because most malpractice insurance does not experience rate physicians within their specialties, incompetent physicians are not penalized by higher premiums; their behavior merely increases premiums for all physicians in that specialty. Fourth, not all physicians who are sued are incompetent. Although incompetent physicians may be sued more often, competent physicians may also be sued because of occasional errors or because they are specialists who treat more difficult cases; for example, board-certified physicians are sued more often than other physicians. Fifth, a characteristic of the current system is the amount of money spent on tests and services that are not medically justified but that help protect physicians from malpractice claims. Physicians overuse tests because the costs of such defensive medicine are borne by patients and insurers, whereas an injury claim could result in physician liability. Thus, physicians are able to shift the costs of their greater caution to others.

In Defense of the Malpractice System

Defenders of the malpractice system claim that the incentive to avoid malpractice suits changes physicians' behavior and makes them act more carefully. Physicians have limited their scope of practice, they are more conscientious in documenting their records, and they take the time to discuss the risks involved in a procedure with their patients. Although physician premiums are not experience rated, lawsuits are a costly deterrent in terms of time spent defending against them and potential damage to the physician's reputation.

The Costs of Defensive Medicine

The costs of defensive medicine are probably overstated because, under a fee-for-service system, excessive testing would occur even if the threat of malpractice were eliminated. Physicians order too many tests because insured patients pay only a small portion of their price. Although the benefits of the tests are less than the costs of performing them, it is rational for patients to want those tests because the benefit to them may be greater than their share of the costs. Physicians reimbursed fee-for-service also benefit from prescribing extra tests. Physicians in HMOs have less of an incentive to perform excessive testing. Thus, physicians' use of excessive testing results in part from traditional insurance payment systems and a lack of policing of such tests by insurers, not necessarily from malpractice.

The costs imposed by defensive medicine are difficult to measure. Estimates of the extent of that practice often rely on conjectural surveys of providers, and what one provider may consider defensive medicine may be deemed prudent medicine by another. However, Mello and colleagues (2010) estimated the cost of defensive medicine in 2008 dollars to be $45.59 billion ($38.79 billion for hospital services and $6.8 billion for physician/clinical services), which is not an insignificant amount. A survey of physicians in Pennsylvania found that 93 percent said they sometimes or often practiced defensive medicine (Studdert et al. 2005). Diagnostic tests were ordered more than was medically necessary, as were referrals to other physicians.

Removing the threat of malpractice leaves few alternatives for monitoring and disciplining physicians. The emphasis on quality control in organized medicine has always been on the process of becoming a physician, that is, the number of years of education, graduation from an approved medical school, and passing national examinations. However, once a physician is licensed, she is never re-examined for re-licensure. State medical licensing boards do not adequately monitor physician quality or discipline incompetent physicians. Finally, patients have little or no access to information on physicians' procedure outcomes. Until recently the medical profession actively discouraged public access to such information. What recourse, other than filing a malpractice claim, would a patient have after being injured by an incompetent physician?

Few would disagree that victims of negligence are not adequately compensated. The controversial issues are whether malpractice actually deters negligence and whether alternatives are available for monitoring and disciplining incompetent physician behavior.

Proposed Changes to the Malpractice System

Many changes have been proposed to correct perceived inadequacies in the malpractice system. Generally, proposals seek to lower malpractice premiums by limiting the size of jury awards for pain and suffering (economic costs for medical expenses and lost wages are not subject to a cap) and reduce the number of claims filed. Both changes would reduce lawyers' incentives to accept malpractice cases.

Damage Caps

Proposals to limit the potential recovery of damages decrease the value of malpractice claims and thereby reduce the number of malpractice claims filed. One study found that malpractice premiums in states with damage caps are 17 percent lower than in states without damage caps (Thorpe 2004).[3] In 1975, California enacted a $250,000 damages cap on pain and suffering, which has not been updated for inflation. (If adjusted for inflation, the cap would be $1 million in 2009 dollars.) Caps such as California's reduce the amount of malpractice awards that can be used to pay legal fees, as the remainder of the award is for lost wages and medical expenses. California's malpractice premium increases also have been lower than those in states without such stringent caps.

Collateral Offset Rule

Under the collateral offset rule, an injured party will have the amount of his award or settlement reduced by amounts paid by other sources, such as health insurance and worker's compensation. Proponents of this rule believe payments from other sources, in addition to the jury award or insurer's settlement, provide an injured person with much more than he is entitled to. Opponents believe that unless the injured party collects the full amount of his award, even though he has already been paid by other sources, a negligent defendant benefits by having his liability reduced. Proposals to reduce awards by amounts already paid to the victim by other sources would have the same effect as reducing damage caps. Lawyers would have a reduced incentive to bring suits on behalf of patients.

Limits on Attorney's Fees

Fewer malpractice cases would be brought if a limit were placed on lawyers' contingency fees (currently these can be as high as one-third to one-half of the award). Lawyers accept malpractice cases based on the probability of winning and the size of the likely award. Lawyers have less financial incentive to invest their resources in cases whose awards would be smaller. Lawyers are in a competitive market and may represent either plaintiffs or defendants in malpractice cases. Lawyers for defendants are paid hourly rates. Fewer lawyers would choose to represent plaintiffs if contingency fees were reduced.

Joint and Several Liability

Joint and several liability occurs when an injured person sues multiple defendants and is able to collect the entire award from any of the defendants, regardless of the defendant's degree of fault. Even if a defendant is only 10 percent liable, she may end up paying most of the damages. This rule creates an incentive for the injured party to sue as many defendants as possible to make sure the damages can be paid. Some states have limited a defendant's liability to the individual degree of fault. Limiting a defendant's liability decreases the potential size of the award, which might lessen the defendant hospital's oversight of its staff physicians to avoid malpractice suits.

Special Health Courts

In a special health court, the jury is replaced with a specially trained judge (with both medical and legal training) who would be advised by neutral experts. Proponents of this approach claim that proceedings would be expedited (the case would be decided in a matter of months); costs would be dramatically lower than those of the current system, which consumes about 60 percent of the premium for legal fees and administrative costs and takes about five years to resolve a case; and it would provide a system of justice based on accepted medical standards, thereby reducing the need for defensive medicine.

As part of the proposal for special health courts, patient compensation for medical negligence would be decided not in the court but by a separate administrative agency, which would act as a neutral fact finder. In contrast, the current system is adversarial, and each side has its own experts.

If special health courts were adopted, filing a claim would be less costly, a greater number of patients would be able to file claims, and more injured patients would be compensated for medical negligence. It is likely that the amount of compensation for a patient negligently injured would be lowered since so many more patients would receive compensation. Although special courts have been used in other areas where special expertise is needed, such as in tax courts, bankruptcy courts, family courts, and so on, special health courts have not been used in the United States; their implementation is opposed by trial lawyers.

No-Fault Malpractice

A no-fault system would compensate an injured patient whether or not negligence was involved. In return, patients would forfeit their right to sue. A no-fault system has two main advantages. First, litigation costs would be lower because it would not be necessary to prove who was at fault for the injury, and these savings could be used to increase victim compensation. Second, all injured patients, most of whom could not win malpractice suits because either their claims were too small to attract a lawyer's interest or no one was at fault in causing their injuries, would receive some compensation. A no-fault system could have a payment schedule according to types of injuries to compensate the injured for loss of income and medical expenses. The schedule could include payment for pain and suffering in cases of severe injury.

A no-fault system, however, has two important problems. First, such a system has no deterrence mechanism to weed out incompetent providers or encourage physicians to exercise greater caution. Second, because all injuries would be subject to compensation, no clear line would be drawn between injuries that result from negligence; injuries that are not the result of negligence; unfavorable treatment outcomes because of the patient's health condition and lifestyle; and outcomes of risky procedures, such as transplants and delivery of low-birth-weight infants, which are never 100 percent favorable. Compensating patients for all injuries and unfavorable outcomes could be very expensive given the large number of injuries for which no claims are filed.[4] Who should bear these costs?

Studdert, Brennan, and Thomas (2000) estimated that a no-fault compensation system that would compensate patients who are injured from all events (negligent and non-negligent) would cost more than four times as much as the current tort system.

Enterprise Liability

Deterring physician negligence continues to be difficult. Regulatory approaches, such as state licensing boards for monitoring and disciplining physicians, have performed poorly. One approach that seeks to improve on the malpractice system for deterring negligence is enterprise liability. Changing the liability laws so that liability is shifted away from the physician to a larger entity of which the physician would be required to be a part, such as a hospital, medical group, or managed care plan, would place the incentive for monitoring and enforcing medical quality with that larger organization. These organizations would balance the increased costs of prevention and risk-reducing behavior against the potential for a malpractice claim.

The shift to enterprise liability is already occurring because of market trends and court rulings. The growth of managed care organizations and the fact that they are liable for physicians they employ or contract with have increased such organizations' monitoring of physician behavior. Furthermore, the concept of joint and several liability, wherein the physician is the primary defendant but the hospital or managed care plan is also named as a defendant with potentially 100 percent liability for damages (although it may have been only 10 percent at fault), provides hospitals and HMOs with an incentive to increase their quality assurance and risk management programs.

Many physicians, however, perform surgery only in outpatient settings or do not practice within a hospital. Others may have multiple hospital staff appointments, and still others do not belong to large health plans. These physicians would be most affected by such a shift in liability laws because they would lose some of their autonomy as they become subject to greater supervision by larger entities.

Placing liability for malpractice on a larger organization would enable insurers to experience rate the organization.[5] As more healthcare organizations become experience rated, they will devote more resources to monitoring their quality of care and disciplining physicians for poor performance. Many organizations, such as HMOs, PPOs, and large medical groups, have information systems in place to profile the practice patterns of their physicians. Competition among healthcare organizations on price and quality provides them with an incentive to develop quality-control mechanisms. These organizations, rather than regulatory bodies, have the incentives and the ability to evaluate and control physicians.

The Effects of Various Tort Reforms

Many proposals have been made to improve the current tort system, which does not adequately compensate patients injured by medical negligence or act as a deterrent to negligent physicians. Exhibit 13.3, adapted from Mello and Kachalia (2010), summarizes the likely impact of selected proposals on the following outcomes of malpractice reform: frequency of malpractice claims and costs, overhead costs of the medical liability system (including legal defense costs), healthcare providers' liability costs, defensive medicine, supply of medical services (including supply of physicians and patients' health insurance premiums), and quality of care. In addition to indicating the likely effects of these proposals, the exhibit also indicates the certainty of the evidence as to these effects. Unfortunately, for many of the proposals the level of certainty is low.

Summary

The current medical malpractice system has several important flaws. First, most patients injured by medical negligence (97 to 98 percent) do not sue and are not compensated for their injuries. Second, given the small percentage of such injured patients who sue, physicians' negligent behavior is rarely deterred. And third, the current malpractice system is inefficient. A large percent of the malpractice premium is not used for patient compensation but for legal costs and administrative expense. Further, physicians have an incentive under fee-for-service payment (and insurance that results in low patient co-payments) to engage in defensive medicine, prescribing care of doubtful value to decrease the probability of a malpractice lawsuit.

Experts do not agree on malpractice reform. Proposals that decrease the size of an award or make it more difficult to bring claims are addressing the wrong problem. These "remedies" are directed at decreasing the number

EXHIBIT 13.3 Evidence and Probable Effects of Malpractice Reform

	Claims Frequency and Costs	Overhead Costs	Liability Costs	Defensive Medicine	Supply	Quality of Care
Caps on noneconomic damages	o for frequency (M) ↓↓ for costs (M)	↑ (L)	↓ for premiums (M)	↓ (H)	↑ (M) for physician supply o (L) for health insurance premiums	o (L)
Attorney fee limits	o (H) for frequency and costs	↓ (L)	o (H)	o (L)	o (M)	o (L)
Joint-and-several liability reform	o (L) for frequency o (H) for costs	o (L)	o (M)	o (M)	o (M) for physician supply ↓ (L) for health insurance premiums	o (L)
Collateral-source rule reform	o (M) for frequency o (H) for costs	o (L)	o (M)	o (H)	o (M) for physician supply ↓ (L) for health insurance premiums	o (M)
Administrative compensation systems or health courts	Medical court model: o (L) for frequency o (L) for costs Administrative model: ↑↑ (M) for frequency o (L) for costs	Medical court model: ↓ (L) Administrative model: ↓↓ (H)	Medical court model: o (L) Administrative model: o (L)	Medical court model: o (L) Administrative model: ↓ (L)	Medical court model: o (L) Administrative model: o (L)	Medical court model: o (L) Administrative model: ↑ (M)
Enterprise liability	o (L) for frequency o (L) for costs	↓ (L)	↓ (L)	↓ (L)	o (L)	↑ (L)

NOTE: L = low, M = moderate, H = high. The double arrow represents a large increase or decrease, the single arrow a modest increase or decrease, and the zero (0) no change.
SOURCE: Adapted from Mello and Kachalia (2010, tables 3 and 4).

of claims, but the real problem appears to be that too few bona fide *negligence* claims are brought. Malpractice reforms should be evaluated in terms of whether they deter negligent behavior and improve victim compensation. Some proposals, such as special health courts and enterprise liability, have academic support. However, enacting malpractice reform is a difficult political problem. Proposals for change often reflect the interests of those who might benefit from the change. Medical societies are often pitted against the trial lawyers' associations (and their respective political parties). The battle for changes in the malpractice system is occurring in almost every state and, due to the opposition of trial lawyers, only demonstration projects were included in the Patient Protection and Affordable Care Act of 2010. All proposals for reform, by whatever interest group, should be judged by how well they achieve the two goals of the malpractice system: compensating victims injured by negligence and deterring future negligence.

Discussion Questions

1. How well does the malpractice system compensate victims of negligence?
2. How effective is the deterrence function of the malpractice system?
3. Discuss the advantages and disadvantages of no-fault insurance.
4. Do you think the costs of defensive medicine would be reduced under a no-fault system?
5. Evaluate the possible effects of the following on deterrence and victim compensation:
   a. Limiting lawyers' contingency fees
   b. Special health courts
   c. Limiting the size of malpractice awards
   d. Placing the liability for malpractice on the healthcare organization to which the physician belongs

Notes

1. A decline in investment returns of 1 percent is estimated to lead to a 2 to 4 percent increase in malpractice premiums (Thorpe 2004, W4-23).
2. Rising malpractice premiums are not the result of collusion among insurers. Collusion would be difficult given the large number of insurers, including physician-owned insurance companies (although there are fewer companies from whom these insurance companies purchase reinsurance), and the high level of competition among them.
3. Malpractice liability has affected physicians' participation in a market. Physicians claim that the financial burden of high malpractice premiums

has led some physicians to retire early, others to stop performing high-risk procedures, and still others to move to states with lower malpractice premiums—all of which affect patients' access to medical care. For example, states that capped noneconomic damages in malpractice cases experienced a relatively modest 3.3 percent increase in physician supply compared with states without such caps (Kessler, Sage, and Becker 2005). Rural counties in states with noneconomic damage caps had 3.2 percent more physicians per capita than rural counties in states without caps. Obstetricians and surgeons, who are considered more vulnerable to lawsuits, were most influenced by the presence or absence of caps (Encinosa and Hellinger 2005).

4. The Institute of Medicine and others have issued reports documenting high rates of medical error in causing serious harm or death in the United States. Not all of these injuries to patients, however, are believed to be the result of provider negligence. Instead, appropriate systems are lacking to prevent human error (Kohn, Corrigan, and Donaldson 1999).

5. The reason generally given for the lack of experience rating except by specialty is that malpractice suits and awards are unrelated to medical negligence, or the physician's history of negligence, and are more related to her manner in relating to the patient, that is, her bedside manner. Whether this is correct is debatable.

14

DO NONPROFIT HOSPITALS BEHAVE DIFFERENTLY THAN FOR-PROFIT HOSPITALS?

Hospitals initially cared for the poor, the mentally ill, and those with contagious diseases, such as tuberculosis. Many hospitals were started by religious organizations and local communities as charitable institutions. More affluent patients were treated in their own homes. Things began to change with the development of ether in the mid-1800s, which allowed operations to be conducted under anesthesia. By the late 1800s, antiseptic procedures began to increase the chances of surviving surgery. Then the introduction of the X-ray machine around the beginning of the twentieth century enabled surgeons to become more effective by improving their ability to determine the location for the surgery, and some exploratory surgery was eliminated.

As a result of these improvements, hospitals became the physician's workshop. Similarly, the type of patients the hospital served changed. Hospitals were no longer places to die or be incarcerated but rather places where paying patients could be treated and returned to society. The development of drugs and improved living conditions reduced the demand for mental and tuberculosis hospitals, and the demand for short-term general hospitals increased.

The control of private nonprofit hospitals also changed. As more of the hospital's income came from paying patients, reliance on trustees to raise philanthropic funds declined, and physicians, who admitted and treated patients, became more important to the hospital. As they were responsible for generating the hospital's revenue, their control over the hospital increased.

Most hospitals in the United States are nonprofit, either nongovernmental institutions or controlled by religious organizations. Together, these are referred to as *private nonprofit hospitals*. As Exhibit 14.1 shows, the ownership of a majority of hospitals (2,918 of the 5,023 hospitals in 2009) is voluntary, meaning private nonprofit. Next in ownership are state and local governmental (1,092) and federal hospitals (201). Investor-owned (for-profit) institutions account for 998 of the total hospitals. Together, private nonprofit and for-profit hospitals admit 82 percent of patients (69 percent and 13 percent, respectively).

Exhibit 14.1 Selected Hospital Data, 2009

Type of Hospital	Number of Hospitals	Percentage Change 75–'85	Percentage Change '85–'95	Percentage Change '95–'09	Beds	Admissions	Percentage Distribution of Admissions	Occupancy Rate[a]
Short-term							97.7	
General[b]	5,023	–3.3	–9.8	–3.8	807,447	35,603,469	95.0	65.5
State and local government	1,092	–10.4	–16.5	–19.2	127,116	4,857,113	13.0	65.0
Not-for-profit	2,918	0.3	–8.1	–5.6	556,406	25,783,321	68.8	67.4
Investor-owned	998	3.9	–6.6	32.7	122,071	4,886,943	13.0	57.7
Federal	201	–10.2	–12.8	–32.8	41,466	1,024,487	2.7	68.6
Long-term[c]	571	–6.3	4.0	–25.9	95,364	851,753	2.3	87.0

[a]Ratio of average daily census to every 100 beds.

[b]"Short-term general" includes community hospitals and hospital units of institutions. Community hospitals consist of state and local government, nongovernment not-for-profit, and investor-owned hospitals.

[c]Includes general, psychiatric, tuberculosis and other respiratory diseases, and all others.

SOURCE: American Hospital Association, *Hospital Statistics* (Chicago, IL: American Hospital Association), various editions: 1986 ed., text table 2, 1995–96 ed., table 3A, and 2011 ed., table 2.

The main legal distinctions between nonprofit and for-profit hospitals are that nonprofits cannot distribute profits to shareholders and their earnings and property are exempt from federal and state taxes; they also may receive donations.

Since the mid-1980s, when managed care competition started, debate has ensued concerning whether nonprofit hospitals are really different from for-profit hospitals. The issues surrounding this debate concern the following questions: Do nonprofits charge lower prices than for-profits? Do nonprofits provide a higher level of quality? Do nonprofits provide more charity care than for-profits? Or, as some critics of nonprofits maintain, does no difference exist between the two other than the tax-exempt status of nonprofits' surpluses?

If the latter position is correct, is continuing nonprofit hospitals' tax advantages and government subsidies justified? Alternatively, if nonprofits provide more charity care and a higher quality of service and charge lower prices, will eliminating for-profit hospitals enable nonprofits to better serve their communities?

Why Are Hospitals Predominantly Nonprofit?

Several hypotheses have been offered to explain the existence of nonprofit hospitals. The most obvious is that when hospitals were used predominantly as institutions to serve the poor, they were dependent on donations for their funds. However, the possibility of receiving donations does not explain why the majority of hospitals continue to be nonprofit. Donations account for a small percentage of hospital revenue. As public and private health insurance became the dominant sources of hospital revenue, the potential for profit increased, as did the number of for-profit hospitals.

Although both public and private insurance have increased, many people are still uninsured. Some believe that only nonprofit hospitals provide uncompensated care to those who are unable to pay. Nonprofit hospitals presumably are willing to use their surplus funds to subsidize both the poor and money-losing services.

Another related explanation is the issue of trust. A relationship based on trust is needed in markets in which information is lacking. Patients are not sure what services they need. They are dependent on the provider for their diagnoses and treatment recommendations, and they do not know the skill of the surgeon. The quality of medical and surgical treatments is difficult for patients to judge, and they cannot tell whether the hospital failed to provide care to save costs. In such situations patients are more likely to rely on nonprofit providers, believing that because they are not interested in profit, they will not take advantage of a patient who lacks information and is seriously ill.[1]

Another explanation for nonprofit status is that the hospital's managers and board of directors want to be part of a nonprofit hospital, where their activities would be subject to limited community oversight. The managers and board would have greater flexibility to pursue policies according to their own preferences, such as offering prestigious but money-losing services even if these services are provided by other hospitals in the community.

Still another explanation is that hospitals are nonprofit because it is in physicians' financial interest. Being associated with nonprofit organizations allows physicians to exercise greater control over the hospital's policies, services offered, and investments in facilities and equipment. In a for-profit hospital, physicians have less money available for facilities and equipment of their choosing because the surplus has to be divided with shareholders and the government through payment of dividends and taxes. The hospital's physicians also benefit from the hospital's ability to receive donations and from the trust the community has in a nonprofit hospital.

The importance of trust, the provision of community benefits, and the financial interests of physicians appear to be key reasons for the nonprofit status of hospitals.[2]

Performance of Nonprofit and For-Profit Hospitals

For-profit hospitals have a more precise organizational goal than nonprofit hospitals, namely profit. A concern of any organization is monitoring its managers' success in achieving the firm's goal. In a for-profit firm the objective is straightforward, and the shareholders have an incentive to monitor the performance of its managers and replace them if their performance is lacking.

A nonprofit firm has multiple objectives, making it more difficult to monitor its managers. The various stakeholders of the nonprofit hospital—medical staff, board members, managers, employees, and the community—have different and conflicting objectives as to how the hospital's surplus should be distributed. Should the profits be used to subsidize the poor, increase compensation for managers, increase wages for employees, establish prestige facilities, or provide benefits (e.g., low office rent and resources) to medical staff?

Less incentive exists to monitor a nonprofit hospital, as the board of directors generally has less financial interest in the hospital's performance and must depend on the managers for information on achieving the hospital's multiple goals. Furthermore, if the nonprofit hospital is not performing efficiently, it may be able to survive on community donations.

Given the differing goals and incentive-monitoring mechanisms between for-profit and nonprofit hospitals, it is important to examine how the behavior of nonprofit hospitals differs from that of for-profit hospitals.

Pricing

For-profit hospitals attempt to set prices to maximize their profits.[3] Do non-profit hospitals set lower prices than for-profit hospitals do? Three aspects of hospital pricing shed light on how nonprofit hospitals set prices. The first is the cost-shifting argument, namely that nonprofit hospitals price to earn sufficient revenues to cover their costs. The nonprofits set prices to private insurers below their profit-maximizing price, but increase those prices when the government reduces the price it pays for Medicare or Medicaid patients. For cost shifting to occur, a hospital must (1) have market power (i.e., be able to profitably raise its price) and (2) decide not to exploit that market power before the government reduces its price. The extent to which cost shifting occurs indicates that hospitals do not set profit-maximizing prices to private payers. (A more complete discussion of cost shifting is provided in Chapter 17.)

Evidence for cost shifting is based on data from before the mid-1980s, before managed care competition. With the start of intense price competition among hospitals, insurers became more sensitive to the prices charged by hospitals. Hospitals' market power declined because insurers were willing to shift their volume to hospitals offering lower prices. Any ability nonprofit hospitals may have had to cost shift disappeared with hospital competition for managed care contracts. Instead, as the government reduced the prices it paid for Medicare and Medicaid patients, hospitals experienced greater pressure to lower their prices to be included in an insurer's provider network.

Second, the pricing practices of nonprofit hospitals to uninsured patients have received a great deal of media publicity recently. Large purchasers of hospital services, such as health insurers, Medicare, and Medicaid, receive large discounts from a hospital's billed charges—often as high as 50 percent. Uninsured patients were asked to pay 100 percent of the hospital's billed charges. Newspaper stories have described the hardship faced by many of these patients who do not have the resources to pay their hospital bills. Several lawsuits have been filed on behalf of the uninsured against nonprofit hospitals because they charged those least able to pay the highest prices and hounded patients for unpaid debts. These lawsuits (several of which have been settled by hospitals) claimed that nonprofit hospitals violated their charitable mission by overcharging the uninsured and seek to have their tax-exempt status revoked. The pricing practices of nonprofit hospitals with regard to the uninsured appear to be no different from those of for-profit hospitals. (Under public and political pressure, both types of hospitals have modified their pricing practices to the uninsured.)

The third indication of whether nonprofit hospitals set lower prices than for-profits is whether they raise prices if they merge with other nonprofit hospitals. The number of hospital mergers has increased in recent years. Consolidation of for-profit firms or hospitals in a market raises concern that competition will be reduced, enabling the hospitals to increase their prices. Would a merger of nonprofit hospitals similarly result in higher hospital prices, or are nonprofit hospitals different?

In previous court cases in which the merger of nonprofit hospitals was contested by federal antitrust agencies, the presiding judge ruled that nonprofit hospital mergers are different from mergers of for-profits. The judges believed that merging nonprofit hospitals were unlikely to raise their prices, even if they acquired monopoly power, because the boards of directors are themselves local citizens and would not take advantage of their neighbors by raising prices.

Empirical studies, however (Melnick, Keeler, and Zwanziger 1999), contradict the judges' belief that nonprofit ownership limits price increases after a merger. Researchers found that nonprofit hospitals with greater market power charge significantly higher prices than nonprofits in more competitive markets. These results suggest that some nonprofit hospitals merge simply as a means to increase their market power and negotiate higher prices with managed care plans. This type of behavior is no different from what one would expect from for-profit hospitals.

In October 2005, the Federal Trade Commission (FTC) won an antitrust suit against nonprofit Northwestern Healthcare for a previously consummated hospital merger. The FTC claimed that a hospital merger that occurred in 2000 violated federal antitrust law because the newly created three-hospital system was able to sufficiently increase its market power to illegally control hospital prices in its market. The FTC claimed that, as a result of the merger, the nonprofit hospital system used its post-merger market power to impose huge price increases—of 40 percent to 60 percent, and in one case, 190 percent—on insurers and employers (FTC 2006). The FTC's decision was upheld on appeal and, rather than have Northwestern divest itself of one hospital as the initial decision recommended, the hospitals are to negotiate independently with insurers. Mergers of nonprofit hospitals are no longer likely to be viewed as different from mergers of for-profit hospitals (Morse et al. 2007).

Quality of Care

Sloan (2000) reviewed several large-scale empirical studies of quality of care received by Medicare beneficiaries in nonprofit and for-profit hospitals. The studies examined various measures of quality, such as the overall care process and the extent to which medical charts showed that specific diagnostic and therapeutic procedures were performed competently. They examined different hospital admissions, such as hip fracture, stroke, coronary heart disease, and congestive heart failure, and different outcome measures, such as survival, functional status, cognitive status, and probability of living in a nursing home. These studies found that although patients admitted to major teaching hospitals did better, no statistically significant differences were found between non-teaching private nonprofit hospitals and for-profit hospitals.

In an extensive study, McClellan and Staiger (2000) compared patient outcomes of all elderly Medicare beneficiaries hospitalized with heart disease (more than 350,000 per year) in for-profit and nonprofit hospitals between 1984 and 1994. They found that:

> On average, for-profit hospitals have higher mortality among elderly patients with heart disease, and...this difference has grown over the last decade. However, much of the difference appears to be associated with the location of for-profit hospitals. Within specific markets, for-profit ownership appears if anything to be associated with better quality care. Moreover, the small average difference in mortality between for-profit and not-for-profit hospitals masks an enormous amount of variation in mortality within each of these ownership types. Overall, these results suggest that factors other than for-profit status per se may be the main determinants of quality of care in hospitals. (McClellan and Staiger 2000, 4)

Charity Care

Nonprofit hospitals have a long tradition of caring for the medically indigent. They were given tax-exempt status and community donations in the belief that they would provide charity care. However, the advent of price competition in the mid-1980s has changed the ability of nonprofit hospitals to provide the level of charity care some believe is necessary to maintain their tax-exempt status.

The extent of charity care provided by nonprofit hospitals has been examined with respect to (1) hospital conversions (a nonprofit becomes a for-profit hospital) and (2) the effect of increased competitive pressures resulting from managed care.

Concern has arisen that once a hospital converts to for-profit status, its charity care will decline as the profit motive becomes dominant. Various studies, however, have found no difference in provision of uncompensated care once a hospital converts from nonprofit to for-profit status. Norton and Staiger (1994) found that for-profit hospitals are more often located in areas with a high degree of health insurance (Medicare, Medicaid, and private insurance). However, once differences in hospital location are accounted for, such as by examining nonprofit and for-profit hospitals in the same market, no difference was found in the volume of uninsured patients cared for by the two types of hospitals.

Price competition is expected to negatively affect a nonprofit hospital's ability to provide charity care by decreasing the "profits" or surplus available for such care. As competition reduces prices charged to privately insured patients, profits are reduced and less is available for charity care. Gruber (1994a) found that increased competition among hospitals in California during the period from 1984 to 1988 led to a decrease in their revenues from private payers, a decrease in their net income, and consequently a reduction in the hospitals' provision of uncompensated care.

The comptroller general, David Walker (2005), stated that in four of the five states studied in 2003, state and locally owned hospitals provided an average of twice as much uncompensated care as either not-for-profit or for-profit hospitals. In Florida, Georgia, Indiana, and Texas, not-for-profit hospitals provided more uncompensated care than for-profit hospitals. The difference, however, was small. In California, for-profit hospitals provided more uncompensated care than not-for-profit hospitals, according to the study. In another study of uncompensated care in five states, the US Congressional Budget Office (2006, 2) found that the cost of uncompensated care as a percentage of hospital operating expenses was much larger in government hospitals (13 percent) than in nonprofit hospitals (4.7 percent) or for-profit hospitals (4.2 percent). Individual nonprofit and for-profit hospitals, however, varied widely in the amount of uncompensated care provided.

Overall, competitive pressures result in less income available for charity care in nonprofit and for-profit hospitals, and public hospitals find themselves with increased uncompensated care costs.

The Question of Tax-Exempt Status

Nonprofit hospitals have received tax advantages that obligate them to serve the uninsured. Nonprofits, however, vary greatly in the amount of care they provide to the uninsured. In some cases, the value of the hospital's tax exemption exceeds the value of charity care it provides. Consequently, it has been proposed that in return for their tax-exempt status, nonprofit hospitals should be required to provide a minimum amount of charity care.

If the tax exemption is to be tied to the value of charity care/community benefits, the measure to be used and the amount of care the hospital should provide must be defined. The following are different possible measures that have been proposed.

- *Pure charity care:* care for which payment is not expected and patients are not billed
- *Bad debt:* value of care delivered and billed to patients believed to be able to pay but from whom the hospital is unable to collect
- *Uncompensated care:* the sum of bad debt and charity care
- *Medicaid and Medicare shortfalls:* the difference between hospital charges and the amount Medicare and Medicaid reimburse the hospital
- *Community benefits:* the previous items plus the amount of patient education, prevention programs, medical research, and provision of money-losing services, such as burn units and trauma centers

Deciding which definition should be used and what percentage of a nonprofit hospital's revenue should be devoted to that measure is an important public policy issue being debated by state and federal governments. For example, if the charity care definition is used, is the amount of free care provided measured using the hospital's full charges (which few payers actually pay) or the lower prices an HMO would pay? Furthermore, using the broadest definition, community benefits, may result in a hospital providing no charity care and relying instead on Medicare and Medicaid shortfalls and some community prevention programs, which may also be viewed as a marketing effort by the hospital. If such a broad definition were used, little difference would be found between many nonprofit and for-profit hospitals.

Many states have begun to engage in limited monitoring of the uncompensated care provided by nonprofit hospitals (see, e.g., Reece 2011; Allen and Bombardieri 2009; Day 2006; Pear 2006; Vesely 2005; McDermott Newsletters 2005; Countryman 2004). Congress has also held hearings on nonprofit hospitals' tax-exempt status. Explicit rules should be specified for a hospital to maintain its tax-exempt status.

Stringent requirements have not been imposed on hospitals to maintain their tax-exempt status. Included as part of the 2010 Patient Protection and Affordable Care Act (PPACA) is the requirement that nonprofit hospitals conduct and submit a community needs assessment, after which their progress toward meeting those needs will be measured every three years. Those nonprofit hospitals making little or no progress toward meeting those identified needs will risk losing their nonprofit status. Also, nonprofit hospitals are required to ensure that their patients are aware when free or discounted care is available. These conditions are less severe than requiring nonprofit hospitals to spend a given percentage of their surplus on charity or uncompensated care.

Summary

In examining whether the behavior of nonprofit hospitals is different from that of for-profit hospitals, one must keep in mind that wide variations in behavior exist within both types of hospitals. Although little difference is found between ownership type in pricing behavior, quality of care delivered, or even the amount of uncompensated care provided, these comparisons are based on averages.

As price competition among hospitals increases, ownership differences become less important in determining a hospital's behavior with regard to pricing, quality of care, and even charity care. In a price-competitive environment, both nonprofits and for-profits must have similar behavior to survive; nonprofits will have less of a surplus to pursue other goals.

Ideally, the poor and uninsured should not have to rely on nonprofit hospitals for charity care. Expanding health insurance to the uninsured, either through private insurance vouchers or Medicaid, will more directly solve the problem of providing care for the medically indigent. According to the PPACA, starting in 2014, 95 percent of the uninsured are to have insurance coverage, either through increased eligibility for Medicaid or tax credits. As more of the population have some form of coverage, the tax-exempt status of many nonprofit hospitals is likely to be questioned. Although certain nonprofits will continue to provide care to those who remain uninsured, the majority of nonprofit hospitals will have to justify their role in society.

Discussion Questions

1. Discuss the differences and similarities among theories for why many hospitals are nonprofit.
2. Do you agree with the ruling by a federal judge that mergers of nonprofit hospitals should not be subject to the same antitrust laws as mergers of for-profit hospitals?
3. How has price competition affected the ability of nonprofit hospitals to achieve their mission?
4. What conditions should be imposed on nonprofit hospitals for them to retain their tax-exempt status?
5. In what ways, if any, are nonprofit hospitals different from for-profit hospitals?

Notes

1. The trust relationship between the patient and provider, however, applies more strongly to the patient–physician relationship. The physician diagnoses the illness, recommends treatment, refers the patient to specialists, and monitors the care the patient receives from different providers. Yet physicians are for-profit.
2. An additional explanation that has been offered for the existence of nonprofit status is that the stochastic nature of the demand for medical services requires hospitals to maintain excess capacity for certain services. It can be very "costly" to patients if they cannot have access to hospital care when needed. For-profit hospitals, some believe, would be unwilling to bear the cost of idle hospital capacity. Furthermore, certain hospital services (e.g., emergency departments, trauma centers, NICUs, teaching, research, and care for certain groups such as AIDS patients and

drug addicts, all of which benefit the community) are generally money-losing services and would otherwise not be provided.

3. Lakdawalla and Philipson (2006) claim that the traditional for-profit analysis of a firm can be used to explain nonprofit hospitals but with a lower cost structure because of their nonprofit status. In addition to its pricing strategy, the type of services a hospital chooses to offer will also affect its profitability. Horwitz and Nichols (2009) examined the services offered by nonprofit hospitals and finds that nonprofit hospitals' services varies according to the relative market share of nonprofit, for-profit, and government hospitals in a market. Nonprofits in markets with high for-profit market share were more likely to offer relatively profitable services and less likely to offer unprofitable services compared to markets with low for-profit penetration.

COMPETITION AMONG HOSPITALS: DOES IT RAISE OR LOWER COSTS?

Current federal policy (the antitrust laws) encourages competition among hospitals. Hospitals proposing a merger are scrutinized by the Federal Trade Commission (FTC) to determine whether the merger will lessen hospital competition in that market, in which case the FTC will oppose the merger. Critics of this policy believe hospitals should be permitted, in fact encouraged, to consolidate and co-operate the facilities and services they provide. They claim that the result will be greater efficiency, less duplication of costly services, and higher quality of care. Who is correct, and what is appropriate public policy for hospitals—competition or cooperation?

Important to understanding hospital performance are (1) the methods used to pay hospitals (different payment methods provide hospitals with different incentives) and (2) the consequences of having different numbers of hospitals compete with one another.

Origins of Non-price Competition

After the introduction of Medicare and Medicaid in 1966, hospitals were paid their costs for the services they rendered to the aged and poor. Private insurance, which was widespread among the remainder of the population, also reimbursed hospitals generously according to either their costs or their charges. The extensive coverage of hospital services by private and public payers removed patients' incentives to be concerned with the costs of hospital care. Patients pay less out-of-pocket costs for hospital care (3 percent) than for any other medical service.

Third-party payers (government and private insurance) and patients had virtually no incentives to be concerned with hospital efficiency and duplication of facilities and services. Furthermore, most hospitals are organized as not-for-profit (nongovernment) organizations that are either affiliated with religious organizations or controlled by boards of trustees selected from the community. With the introduction of extensive public and private hospital insurance after the mid-1960s, the use of nonprofit hospitals increased. Lacking a profit motive and assured of survival by the generous payment methods, nonprofit hospitals also had no incentive to be concerned with efficiency. This caused the costs of caring for patients to rise rapidly.

Exhibit 15.1 illustrates the dramatic rise in hospital expenditures from the 1960s to the present. After Medicare and Medicaid were enacted in 1965, hospital expenditures increased by more than 16 percent per year. These large increases were primarily attributable to sharp increases in hospital prices, as shown in Exhibit 15.2. Hospital price increases moderated during the early 1970s, when wage and price controls were imposed, but then increased sharply once they were removed in mid-1974. Hospital expenditure increases were less rapid in the mid- to late 1980s as Medicare changed its hospital payment system and price competition increased.

The rate of increase in hospital expenditures and hospital prices continued to fall during the 1990s.[1] These decreases, discussed later, are indicative of the changes that have occurred in the market for hospital services.

In the late 1960s, the private sector also did not encourage efficiency. Although services such as diagnostic workups could be provided less expensively in an outpatient setting, BlueCross paid for such services only if they were provided as part of a hospital admission. Small hospitals attempted to emulate medical centers by having the latest in technology, although those services were infrequently used. It did not matter whether larger organizations had lower costs per unit and higher-quality outcomes than smaller facilities, because cost was of little concern to patients or purchasers of the service.

The greater the number of hospitals in a community, the more intense was the competition among the nonprofit hospitals to become the most prestigious hospital. Hospitals competed for physicians by offering them all the services available at other hospitals so that the physicians' productivity and convenience would be increased and they would not have to refer patients to another hospital. This wasteful form of non-price competition was characterized as a "medical arms race" and resulted in rapidly rising hospital expenditures.

As the costs of non-price competition increased, federal and state governments attempted to change hospitals' behavior. Regulations were enacted to control hospital capital expenditures; hospitals were required to have certificate-of-need (CON) approval from a state planning agency before they could undertake large investments. According to proponents of state planning, controlling hospital investment would eliminate unnecessary and duplicative investments. Unfortunately, no attempts were made to change hospital payment methods, which would have changed hospitals' incentives to undertake such investments.

Numerous studies concluded that CONs had no effect on limiting the growth in hospital investment. Instead, CONs were used in an anticompetitive manner to benefit existing hospitals in the community, which ended up controlling the CON approval process. Ambulatory surgery centers (unaffiliated with hospitals) did not receive CON approval for construction because

Exhibit 15.1 Trends in Hospital Expenditures, 1966–2009

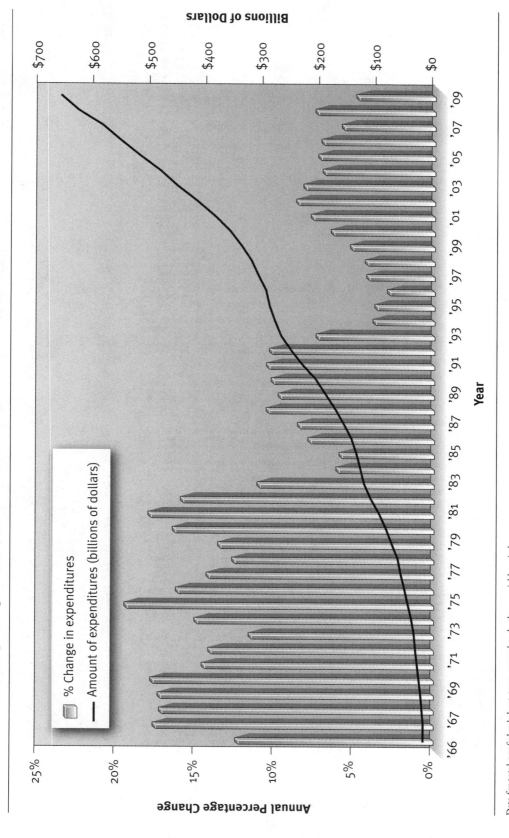

Data for total nonfederal short-term general and other special hospitals.

SOURCE: Data from American Hospital Association, *Hospital Statistics*, 2011 edition. Table 1. Chicago: Health Forum LLC, an affiliate of the AHA.

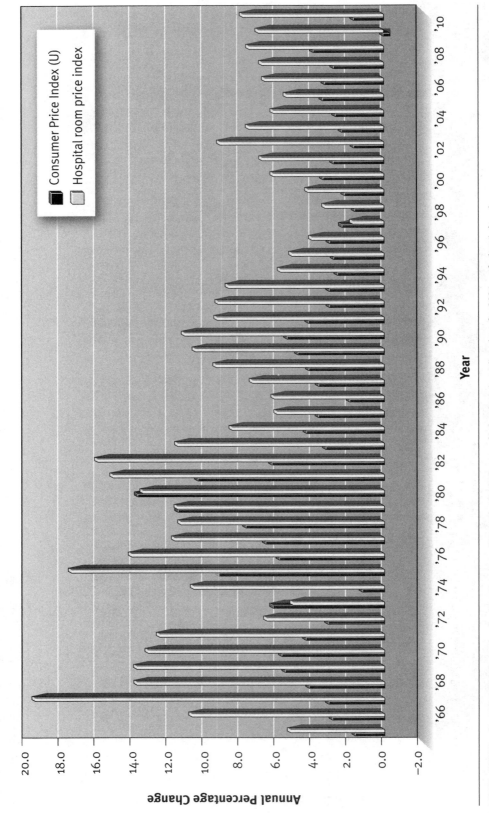

Exhibit 15.2 Annual Percentage Changes in the Consumer Price Index and the Hospital Room Price Index, 1965–2010

NOTE: CPI(U) = Consumer Price Index for all urban consumers. Due to changes in Bureau of Labor Statistics coding, data after 1996 are for hospital services.

SOURCE: US Department of Labor, Bureau of Labor Statistics, 2011. http://www.bls.gov.

they would take away hospital patients; HMOs such as Kaiser found entering a new market difficult because they could not receive CON approval to build a new hospital; and the courts found that the CON process was used in an "arbitrary and capricious manner" against for-profit hospitals attempting to enter the market of an existing nonprofit hospital (Feldstein 2011).

Transition to Price Competition

Until the 1980s, hospital competition was synonymous with non-price competition, and its effect was wasteful and rapidly rising expenditures.

During the 1980s, hospital and purchaser incentives changed. Medicare began to pay hospitals a fixed price per admission (which varied according to the type of admission). This new payment system, referred to as diagnosis-related groups (DRGs), was phased in over five years starting in 1983. Faced with a fixed price, hospitals now had an incentive to reduce their costs of caring for aged patients. In addition, hospitals reduced lengths of stay for aged patients, which caused declines in hospital occupancy rates. For the first time, hospitals became concerned with their physicians' practice behavior. If physicians ordered too many tests or kept patients in the hospital longer than necessary, the hospital lost money, given the fixed DRG price.

Pressure to reduce hospital costs also came from private insurers, primarily because employers became concerned about the rising costs of insuring employees. Insurers changed their insurance benefits to encourage patients to have diagnostic tests and minor surgical procedures performed in outpatient settings. Insurers instituted utilization review to monitor the appropriateness of inpatient admissions, which further reduced hospital admissions and lengths of stay. These changes in hospital and purchaser incentives reduced hospital occupancy rates from 76 percent in 1980 to 67 percent by 1990; as of 2009, the rate was about 66 percent. The decline in occupancy rates was much more severe for small hospitals, where they fell to below 50 percent (HHS n.d).

As hospital occupancy rates declined, hospitals became willing to negotiate price discounts with insurers and HMOs that were able to deliver a large number of patients to their hospitals. As a result, price competition had started among hospitals by the late 1980s.

Price competition does not imply that hospitals compete only on the basis of which hospital has the lowest price. Purchasers are also interested in other characteristics of a hospital, such as its reputation, its location in relation to its patients, which facilities and services are available, patient satisfaction, and treatment outcomes.

In more recent years, as hospitals have merged and price competition among hospitals lessened, hospital market power has increased relative to that of health insurers, and hospital prices, adjusted for inflation, have increased more rapidly, as shown in Exhibit 15.2.

Price Competition in Theory

How did hospitals respond to this new competitive environment in which purchasers demand lower prices? Let us examine two hypothetical situations. In the first situation, only one hospital exists in an area; it has no competitors, and no substitutes for inpatient services are available. The hospital is a monopolist in providing hospital services and has no incentive to respond to purchaser demands for lower prices, quality information, and patient satisfaction. The purchaser has no choice but to use the only hospital available. If the hospital is not efficient, it can pass on the resulting higher costs to the purchaser. If the patients are dissatisfied with the hospital's services or the hospital refuses to provide outcomes information, the purchaser and patients have no choice but to use the only hospital in town. (Obviously, at some point it becomes worthwhile for patients to incur large travel costs to go to distant hospitals.)

When only one hospital serves a market, that hospital is unlikely to achieve high performance. The hospital has little incentive to be efficient or respond to purchaser and patient demands.

The second hypothetical scenario consists of many hospitals, perhaps ten, serving a particular geographic area. Now assume a large employer in the area is interested in lowering its employees' hospital costs and is also interested in the quality of and satisfaction with the care received. Furthermore, for simplicity, assume each of the ten hospitals is equally accessible to the firm's employees (with regard to distance and staff appointments for the employees' physicians). How are hospitals likely to respond to this employer's demands?

At least several of the hospitals would be willing, in return for receiving a greater number of patients from that employer, to negotiate lower prices and accede to the employer's demands for information on quality and patient satisfaction. As long as the price the hospital receives from that employer is greater than the direct costs of caring for its patients, the hospital will make more money than it would if it did not accept those patients. Furthermore, unless each hospital is as efficient as its competitors, it cannot hope to win such contracts. A more efficient hospital is always able to charge less.

Similar to competition on price is the competition that would occur among hospitals regarding their willingness to provide information on treatment outcomes. As long as the hospitals have to rely on purchaser revenues to survive, they will be driven to respond to purchaser demands. If a given hospital is not responsive to purchaser demands, other hospitals will be, and the first hospital will soon find that it has too few patients to remain in business.

When hospitals compete on price, quality, and other purchaser require-ments, their performance is opposite that of a monopoly provider of hospital services. Hospitals have an incentive to be efficient and respond to purchaser demands in price-competitive markets.

What if, instead of competing with one another, the ten hospitals de-cide to agree among themselves not to compete on price or provide pur-chasers with any additional information? The outcome would be similar to a monopoly situation. Prices would be higher, and hospitals would have less incentive to be efficient. Patients would be worse off because they would pay more, and patient quality and patient satisfaction would be lower because employers and other purchasers would be unable to select hospitals based on patient quality and satisfaction information.

The benefits to consumers are greater the more competitive the mar-ket. For this reason, society seeks to achieve competitive markets through its antitrust laws. Although competitive hospitals might be harmed and driven out of business, *the evaluation of competitive markets is based on their effect on consumers rather than on any competitors in that market.*

The antitrust laws are designed to prevent hospitals from acting anti-competitively. Price-fixing agreements, such as those described previously, are illegal because they lessen competition among hospitals. Barriers that prevent competitors from entering a market are also anticompetitive. If two hospitals in a market are able to restrict entry into that market (perhaps through the use of regulations such as CON approval), they will have greater monopoly power and be less price competitive and less responsive to purchaser demands. Merg-ers may be similarly anticompetitive. For example, if the ten hospitals merged so that only two hospital organizations remained, the degree of competition would be less than when there were ten competitors. For this reason, the FTC examines hospital mergers to determine whether they will lessen competition in the market.

Price Competition in Practice

The previous discussion provides a theoretical basis for price competition. To move from price competition's theoretical benefits to reality, we must con-sider two questions. First, does any market have enough hospitals for price competition to occur? Second, is there any evidence about the actual effects of hospital price competition?

The number of competing hospitals in a market is determined by the cost–size relationship of hospitals (economies of scale) and the size of the market (the population served). A larger-sized hospital, for example, one with 200 beds, is likely to have lower average costs per patient than a hospital with the same set of services that has only 50 beds. In a larger hospital, some costs can be spread over a greater number of patients. For example, some costs will be the same whether there are 50 or 200 patients, such as those for an administrator, an X-ray technician, and X-ray equipment, which can be used more fully in a larger organization. These economies of scale, however, do not continue indefinitely; at some point the higher costs of coordination of services begin to exceed the gains that accrue from a larger size. Studies have generally indicated that hospitals in the size range of 200 to 400 beds have the lowest average costs.

If the population in an area consists of 100,000, just one hospital of 260 beds is likely to survive (assuming 800 patient days per year per 1,000 people and 80 percent occupancy). If more than one hospital is in the area, each will have higher average costs than one larger hospital; one of the hospitals may expand, achieve lower average costs, and be able to set its prices lower than the other hospital. An area with a population of 1 million is large enough to support three to six hospitals in the 200- to 400-bed range.

Hospital services, however, are not all the same. The economies of scale associated with an obstetrics facility are quite different from those associated with organ transplant services. Patients are also less willing to travel great distances for a normal delivery than for a heart transplant. The travel costs of going to another state for a transplant represent a smaller portion of the total cost of that service than the travel costs of going to another state for childbirth would represent (and the travel time is less crucial). Thus, the number of competitors in a market depends on the particular service. For some services, the relevant geographic market served may be relatively small, whereas for others the market may be the state or region.

As of 2009, approximately 82 percent of hospital beds were located in metropolitan statistical areas (MSAs). An MSA may not necessarily be indicative of the particular market in which a hospital competes. For some services, the travel time within an MSA may be too great, whereas for other services (organ transplants) the market may encompass multiple MSAs. However, the number of hospitals in an MSA provides a general indication of the number of competitors in a hospital's market. As shown in Exhibit 15.3, 191 MSAs (45 percent) have fewer than four hospitals, and 80 MSAs (19 percent) have four or five hospitals. The remaining MSAs (36 percent) have six or more hospitals; however, that 36 percent of MSAs contains 76 percent of the hospitals located in metropolitan areas. Therefore, the large majority of hospitals in MSAs (76 percent) are located in MSAs with six or more hospitals. Even in an MSA with few hospitals, substitutes are often available to the hospitals' services—for example, outpatient surgery—which decreases those hospitals' monopoly power.

When few providers of specialized facilities exist in a market (because of economies of scale and the size of the market), the relevant geographic

EXHIBIT 15.3 The Number of Hospitals in Metropolitan Statistical Areas, 2009

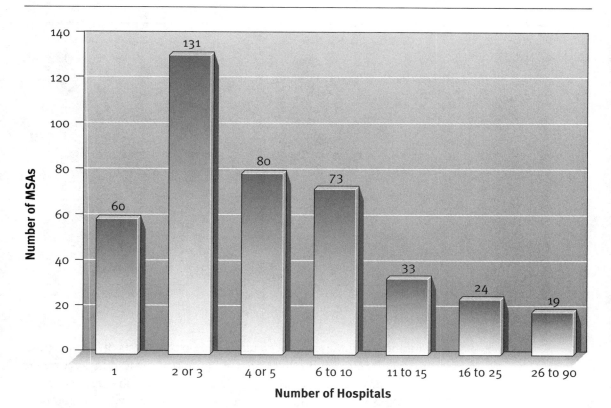

SOURCE: Data from American Hospital Association, *Hospital Statistics*, 2011 edition, Table 8. Chicago: Health Forum LLC, an affiliate of the AHA.

market is likely to be much larger because the highly specialized services are generally not of an emergency nature and patients are more willing to travel to access them. Insurers negotiate prices for transplants, for example, with several regional centers of excellence, hospitals that perform a high number of transplants and have good outcomes.

Thus, price competition among hospitals appears to be feasible. As insurers and large employers have become concerned over the costs of hospital care and are better informed on hospital prices and patient outcomes, hospitals are being forced to respond to purchaser demands and compete according to price, outcomes, and patient satisfaction. Data shown in Exhibits 15.1 and 15.2 show how competition lowered the rate of increase in hospital expenditures and prices. As hospitals had to compete to be included in provider panels of managed care plans, they had to become more efficient and discount their prices.

EXHIBIT 15.4 Hospital Cost Growth in the United States, by Level of Managed Care Penetration and Hospital Market Competitiveness, 1986–1993

Level of Managed Care Penetration	Level of Hospital Competition		% Difference
	Low	High	
Low	65	56	16 [a]
High	52	39	33 [a]
% Difference	25 [a]	44 [a]	67 [b]

[a] % Difference = [(high − low)/low]
[b] [Low/low (65)] − high/high (39)] / [high/high (39)]

A number of studies have been published on the effects of hospital price competition. This research provides further support for traditional economic expectations regarding competitive hospital markets. The change to hospital price competition was not uniform throughout the country. Price competition in California developed earlier and more rapidly than in other areas. Bamezai and colleagues (1999) classified hospitals within California according to whether they were in a high- or low-competition market and whether the managed care penetration was high or low. Hospitals in more competitive markets (controlling for other factors) were found to have a much lower rate of increase in the costs per discharge and per capita than were hospitals in less competitive markets.

The authors also found that an increase in managed care penetration reduced the rise in hospital costs (see Exhibit 15.4). The reduction in costs, however, was much greater for hospitals in more competitive markets. Also, regardless of the degree of managed care penetration, hospital competition was important in lowering hospital cost increases. These findings imply that hospital mergers that decrease competition are likely to result in higher hospital prices.

Other studies have found similar results using different methods and data on specific types of hospital treatment. For example, Kessler and McClellan (2000) analyzed Medicare claims data for Medicare patients admitted to the hospital with a primary diagnosis of a heart attack for the period from 1985 to 1994. They found that before 1990, hospital competition to have the latest technology led to higher costs and, in some cases, lower rates of adverse health outcomes. After 1990, hospital price competition led to substantially lower costs and to significantly lower rates of adverse outcomes. Patients had lower mortality rates in the most competitive markets.

After the consumer backlash against managed care in the late 1990s and early 2000s, health plans broadened their provider networks to give their enrollees more provider choices. As insurers included more hospitals in their networks, their bargaining power over hospitals decreased (Dranove et al. 2008). Reinforcing this shift in relative bargaining power was the decrease in the number of hospitals. Hospital closures and mergers resulted in fewer hospitals competing within a market.[2] The result was that hospital prices increased much more rapidly. Currently, insurers' reliance on broad provider networks and the decreased number of competing hospitals have enabled hospitals to maintain their relative bargaining power over insurers.

Summary

The controversy over whether hospital competition results in higher or lower costs is based on studies from two different periods. When hospitals were paid according to their costs, non-price competition occurred and resulted in rapidly rising hospital costs. Medicare's change to fixed-price hospital payment and managed care plans' change to negotiated prices changed hospitals' incentives. Hospitals had incentives to be efficient and compete on price to be included in managed care plans' provider panels. Consequently, hospital costs and prices rose less rapidly in more competitive hospital markets. Public policy, such as the antitrust laws, that encourages competitive hospital markets will be of greater benefit to purchasers and patients than policies that enable hospitals to increase their monopoly power.

As enrollment in managed care plans increased, the demand for hospital care decreased. Hospitals developed excess capacity and were willing to discount their prices to be included in insurers' limited provider networks. Hospital prices declined. With excess capacity, some hospitals closed and many merged with financially stronger hospitals. Under public pressure to expand their provider networks, insurers were less able to offer hospitals a greater volume of patients in return for heavily discounted prices. Currently, with fewer hospital competitors in a market and insurers' willingness to contract with a larger number of hospitals, the relative bargaining positions of hospitals and insurers changed. Hospital price increases have been higher than in the 1990s, when managed care limited provider networks and hospitals had excess capacity.

Discussion Questions

1. Why did hospital expenditures rise so rapidly after Medicare and Medicaid were introduced in 1966?
2. What changes did Medicare DRGs cause in hospital behavior?
3. What is the likely response of hospitals when there is only one hospital in a market compared with when ten hospitals are competing for a large employer's employees?
4. What determines the number of competitors in a market? Apply your answer to obstetrics and to transplant services.
5. What are some anticompetitive hospital actions that the antitrust laws seek to prevent?

Notes

1. Starting in the mid-1980s, hospital price increases, as calculated in the CPI, were greatly overstated because the CPI measured "list" prices rather than actual prices charged. The difference between the two became greater with the increase in hospital discounting (Dranove, Shanley, and White 1991). To correct this discrepancy, the Bureau of Labor Statistics, in constructing the CPI, began to use data on actual hospital prices in the early 1990s.
2. An example of the effect of fewer competing hospitals on hospital prices is the study by Wu (2008), who analyzed the effect of hospital closures between 1993 and 1998 and found that as the number of competitors decreased, competitors located near the closed hospitals improved their bargaining position over insurers. As these hospital markets became more concentrated, hospitals were able to raise their prices more than hospitals in less concentrated markets.

THE FUTURE ROLE OF HOSPITALS

Hospitals have traditionally been the center of the healthcare system. Before Medicare and Medicaid were implemented in 1965, hospital expenditures represented 40 percent of total health expenditures. During the late 1960s and the 1970s, the growth of Medicare, Medicaid, and private insurance stimulated the demand for hospital services. By 1975, 46 percent of health expenditures were for hospital services. Although hospital expenditures have continued to increase, hospitals' share of total health expenditures has declined, falling to 31 percent in 2009. Will the traditional role of the hospital continue to decline, or will hospitals expand their role beyond treating inpatients and become responsible for a greater portion of the spectrum of care?

From Medicare to the Present

During the post-Medicare period (from 1966 to the early 1980s), hospitals were reimbursed for their costs, they engaged in non-price competition to attract physicians, new technology was quickly adopted, facilities and services grew rapidly, and hospitals were the largest and fastest-increasing component of healthcare expenditures.

Starting in the mid-1980s, the financial outlook for hospitals changed. Medicare introduced diagnosis-related groups (DRGs), which changed Medicare payment from a cost basis to a fixed price per admission (by type of admission). Hospitals realized that reducing their costs and patients' lengths of stay increased their net income, because they could keep the difference between the DRG price and their cost of caring for Medicare patients. Under pressure from employers, insurers introduced managed care, with its cost-containment measures, such as utilization review, second surgical opinions, and lower-cost substitutes to inpatient care, including ambulatory surgery and outpatient diagnostic testing. To reduce treatment costs, managed care shifted services out of the most expensive setting, the hospital. Greater use occurred in outpatient facilities and step-down facilities, such as skilled nursing facilities, rehabilitation units, and home healthcare.

EXHIBIT 16.1 US Community Hospital Capacity and Utilization, 1975–2009

Year	Number of Hospitals	Number of Staffed Beds (Thousands)	Inpatient Admissions (Thousands)	Average Length of Inpatient Stay (Days)	Average Inpatient Occupancy Rate (%)	Outpatient Visits (Thousands)
1975	5,875	942	33,435	7.7	74.9	190,672
1980	5,830	988	36,143	7.6	75.6	202,310
1985	5,732	1,001	33,449	7.1	64.8	218,716
1990	5,384	927	31,181	7.2	66.8	301,329
1995	5,194	873	30,945	6.5	62.8	414,345
2000	4,915	824	33,089	5.8	63.8	521,404
2005	4,936	802	35,239	5.6	67.3	584,429
2009	5,008	806	35,527	5.4	65.5	641,953

SOURCE: Author's analysis based on data from American Hospital Association, *Hospital Statistics,* 2011 ed., Table 1 (Chicago: Health Forum LLC, an affiliate of the AHA, 2010).

Hospitals experienced excess capacity as they reduced Medicare patients' lengths of stay and private cost-containment measures reduced hospital use. With excess capacity, hospitals were willing to compete on price to be included in managed care preferred provider organizations (PPOs).

Managed care competition, hospitals' excess capacity, and the resultant pressures for hospitals to compete on price led to hospital bankruptcies, mergers, falling hospital profit margins, and, in general, a distressed hospital industry. The DRG Medicare payment system and managed care's utilization management methods left the industry with too much excess capacity. The financial survival of many hospitals was in doubt.

Exhibit 16.1 describes the changes that occurred in the hospital industry. The number of hospitals, beds, average length of stay, and occupancy rates all declined during the 1980s and 1990s. With the movement to less expensive settings, outpatient visits and surgeries sharply increased.

To increase their admissions, hospitals bought physicians' practices, thereby increasing physician referrals. However, employed physicians, with their changed incentives, became less productive, and hospitals abandoned the practice. Hospitals were not adept at managing physicians' practices, and physicians were suspicious of working too closely with hospitals. Hospital–physician relationships have been a continual concern to hospitals, especially as physician-owned outpatient surgery centers brought physicians into competition with hospitals.

Hospital profitability had gradually returned by the late 1990s. Financially troubled hospitals closed or merged with other hospitals. To survive and prosper, hospitals adopted strategies that emphasized monopolization of the market. Mergers among competing hospitals increased. Large multihospital systems developed. The number of hospital competitors in a market decreased. The Federal Trade Commission (FTC), concerned that mergers were creating monopoly power that enabled hospitals to raise their prices, brought several antitrust suits against hospital mergers. The FTC, however, lost every hospital merger case. The judges believed nonprofit hospitals were different from for-profit hospitals and would not exploit their market power by raising prices.

The managed care backlash, which occurred in the late 1990s, resulted in health plans expanding their provider networks, thereby providing enrollees with more choice. With broader networks, insurers were less able to guarantee hospitals increased patient volume in return for large price discounts. The weakening of managed care's cost-containment methods further increased hospitals' bargaining power over health insurers.

Population growth, an aging population, and medical advances led to an increase in hospital admissions. Those factors, combined with a reduction in the number of hospital beds, caused occupancy rates to increase from their 1995 low, despite the fact that lengths of stay continued to decline.

Hospital consolidation, the reduction in hospital bed capacity, and the demise of managed care's limited provider networks led to higher prices for hospital services and increased hospital profitability. As shown in Exhibit 16.2, hospital profit margins reached a high in 1996 and 1997. Profit margins then declined for several years as Medicare reduced hospital payments to postpone bankruptcy of the Medicare Trust Fund. Hospital profit margins increased throughout most of the decade leading up to 2008 (reaching a high in 2007). A deep recession, large numbers of uninsured, and bad debts reduced hospital profit margins after 2008.

Hospitals have gained greater market power as a result of mergers, decreased excess capacity, and insurers' reliance on broad provider networks. These actions enabled hospitals to increase their prices and profitability. Hospitals' market power has limited insurers' ability to reduce rising hospital expenditures, one of the fastest-increasing components of insurance premiums.

These changing trends, which have affected hospitals since the 1960s, are shown in Exhibit 16.3, which describes the annual rate of increase in hospital expenditures (adjusted for inflation). Medicare and Medicaid led to a large increase in spending growth rates in the late 1960s. Thereafter, annual

EXHIBIT 16.2 Aggregate Total Margins and Operating Margins for US Hospitals, 1980–2008

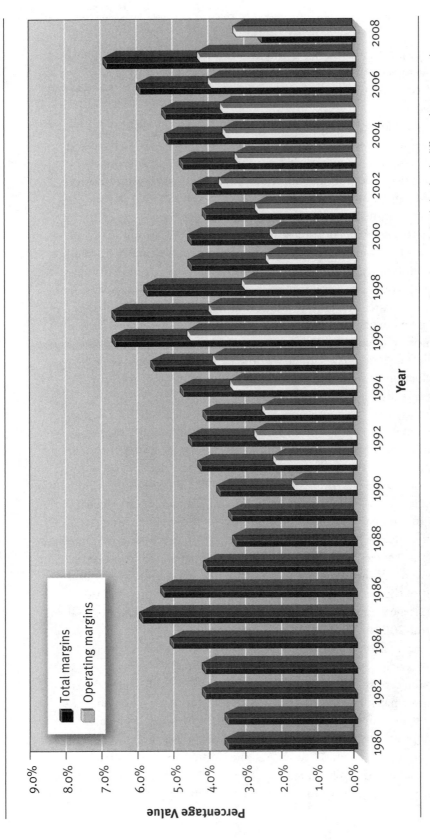

NOTE: Total hospital margin is calculated as the difference between total net revenue and total expenses divided by total net revenue. Operating margin is calculated as the difference between operating revenue and total expenses divided by operating revenue. Data on operating margin prior to 1990 not available.

SOURCES: 1990–2008 data from Lewin Group analysis of the AHA Annual Survey data presented in Lewin Group, *Trends Affecting Hospitals and Health Systems*, January 2010, table 4.1. http://www.aha. org/aha/trendwatch/2010/chartbook/2010/appendix4.pdf; 1980–1989 data are author's calculations based on data presented in *Hospital Statistics*, various editions (Chicago: American Hospital Association).

EXHIBIT 16.3 Annual Rate of Increase in Hospital Expenditures, Actual and Trend, GDP Price Deflated, 1961–2009

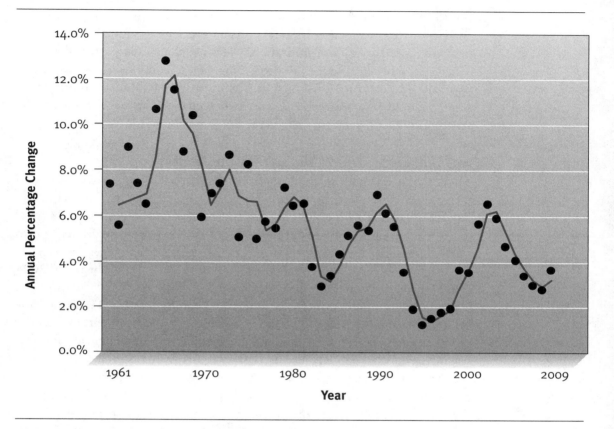

NOTE: Line represents two-year moving average.

SOURCES: Author's calculations based on data from Centers for Medicare & Medicaid Services, Office of the Actuary, National Health Statistics Group, 2011. http://www.cms.gov/NationalHealthExpendData/. GDP data from Executive Office of the President of the United States, *Budget of the United States Government: Historical Tables Fiscal Year 2011,* table 10.1. http://www.gpoaccess.gov/usbudget/fy11/pdf/hist.pdf.

growth rates have been on a generally downward trend. Although spending growth rates increased after the sharp declines during managed care, in recent years expenditure growth rates have continued to decline.

The future for hospitals is uncertain. The federal and state (Medicare and Medicaid) governments are major payers of hospital services, and both face severe financial deficits. The privately insured sector is declining, and new health legislation enacted in 2010, the Patient Protection and Affordable Care Act (PPACA), is likely to have significant effects on hospital revenues and their future role. Will hospitals be able to generate sufficient funds to replace aging buildings, upgrade their facilities, purchase the latest technology, and play an important role in the delivery of medical services?

The Hospital Outlook

Forecasting the industry outlook over the next five to ten years requires an analysis of trends affecting hospital costs and revenues (subdivided into hospital payment [price] and utilization). The hospital's margin (profit) is the difference between revenues and costs. Further, the actions of the two major payers of hospital care, government (Medicare and Medicaid) and private insurers, should be considered. Lastly, two scenarios can be envisioned: the status quo and hospital payment reform.

Hospital Costs: The Public and Private Sectors

The greatest certainty regarding hospitals is that their costs will continue to increase faster than inflation. Two drivers warrant discussion. First is increasing labor costs. Salaries and benefits are the largest component of hospital costs, making up 53 percent of hospitals' overall expenses. Registered nurses (RNs) represent 26 percent of hospital personnel, and RN wages are likely to rise more rapidly in coming years. Although the recession that began in 2008 caused many registered nurses who had left the workforce to return, this relief is probably temporary (Buerhaus, Auerbach, and Staiger 2009). As the baby boomers become eligible for Medicare and increase their demand for medical services and as the number of the old-old aged increases, the demand for RNs will increase. Although RNs are used predominantly in hospital settings, they are increasingly being used in lesser care settings, from outpatient facilities to home healthcare to hospices. The supply of and demand for RNs determine their wages. The RN workforce is aging, and unless a greater number of RNs are recruited from overseas or a greater number of men enter nursing, RN wages, relative to other occupations, will likely increase more rapidly, increasing hospital costs. If other states enact California's minimum RN staffing ratios, RN labor costs will rise even higher.

Economists name new technology, including equipment, technicians, and expensive drugs, as the most important reason for rising medical costs. In addition, hospitals will make large investments in information technology, such as electronic medical records, which capture patient information as patients visit their physicians, see specialists, take laboratory tests, fill prescriptions at pharmacies, and use hospitals and outpatient facilities in their communities. Hospitals will also make huge investments in clinical information technology to streamline clinical decision making, promote quality, and reduce medication errors. These investments, while likely to improve quality and reduce some costs, will require nonprofit hospitals to incur debt, which will add to their cost structure.

Caring for both public and private patients will continue to become more costly to the hospital. Whether hospitals will have the revenue to cover these costs, which will likely increase more rapidly than economy-wide inflation, depends on future utilization and hospital payments from the public and private sectors.

Hospital Revenues

Hospital revenues are determined simply by multiplying price by quantity, namely utilization. Several of the factors likely to affect trends in hospital utilization are considered in the following sections, followed by a discussion of likely changes in hospital payments.

Hospital Utilization

Demographically, the population is aging. In 2011, the baby boomers started becoming eligible for Medicare. Forty million people began shifting from private insurance to Medicare. While Medicare discharges per enrollee (a measure of hospital use) have been constant, outpatient services per enrollee have sharply increased as more surgical procedures are shifted to an outpatient setting. Both trends are likely to continue as more aged become Medicare eligible.

Utilization: The Public Sector

The PPACA, passed in 2010, expands coverage for an estimated 32 million currently uninsured persons starting in 2014. About half will become eligible for Medicaid, and the remainder will receive tax credits for private coverage. Further, eligibility levels for Medicaid will be increased. Previously, as eligibility for public insurance increased, demand for private coverage decreased. Many considered to be middle class have dropped their private insurance for these lower-priced government substitutes (this phenomenon is referred to as "crowd-out").

Advances in medicine and new technology have increased demands for medical services. They have also been a source of increased hospital utilization.

Each of these trends is likely to result in higher hospital use under public programs, through Medicare and Medicaid.

Hospital utilization by private, nongovernment patients is likely to decline as baby boomers become eligible for Medicare and, as a result of PPACA, more middle-income patients become eligible for Medicaid. As private insurance premiums increase, insurers will continue to examine approaches to decrease hospitalization, the most costly component of medical care. Hospitals will become more dependent on utilization from the increasing public sector.

Utilization: The Private Sector

Hospital Payment

How hospitals are paid, and how much, has a significant effect on hospital revenues. Individual hospitals cannot negotiate with the government over the

Exhibit 16.4 Sources of Hospital Revenues, by Payer, Selected Years, 1965–2009

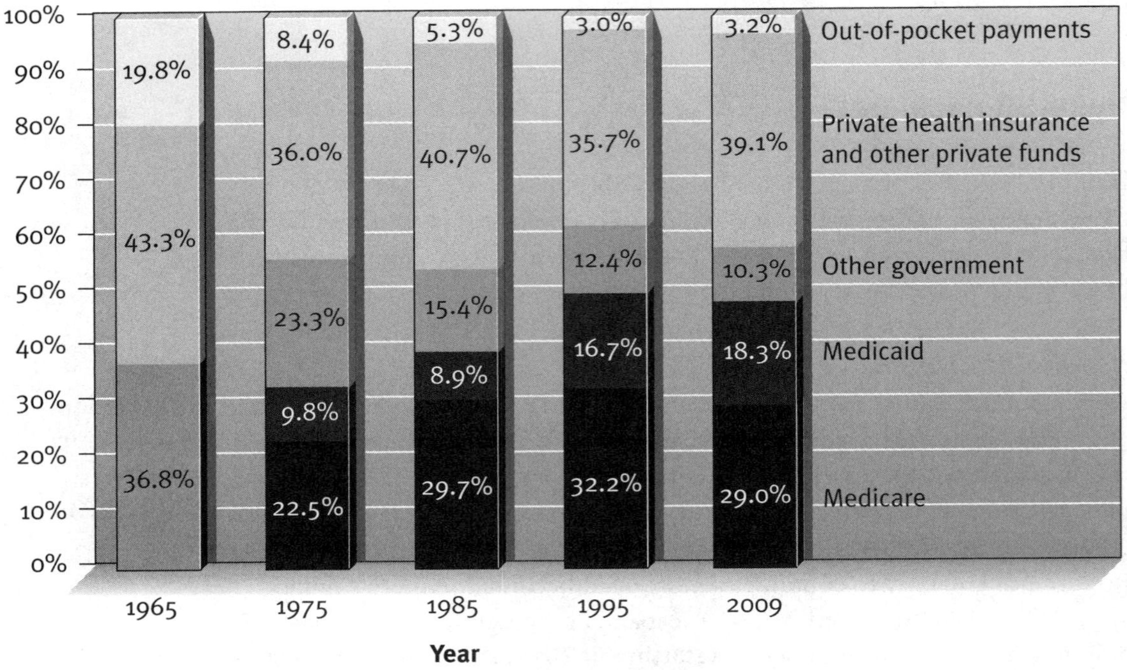

NOTE: Medicaid includes SCHIP and Medicaid SCHIP expansion. Other government includes workers' compensation, Department of Defense, maternal/child health, Veterans Administration, vocational rehabilitation, temporary disability, and state/local hospitals and school health.

SOURCE: Author's calculations based on data from Centers for Medicare & Medicaid Services, Office of the Actuary, National Health Statistics Group, 2011. http://www.cms.gov/NationalHealthExpendData/.

price Medicare pays for hospital services. Instead, hospital associations negotiate politically with legislators who determine Medicare's annual rate increases. Medicaid payment is determined at the state level. Hospital price negotiation with private insurers depends on their relative bargaining power. Thus, hospital prices are determined in a competitive and a political marketplace.

Prices: Public Payers

Hospital payment sources have changed over time. Government now accounts for about 57 percent of hospital revenue, and this is likely to sharply increase as the provisions of PPACA are instituted. (See Exhibit 16.4.) Hospitals receive about 89 percent of their average costs of treatment for Medicaid patients and 91 percent for Medicare patients. These percentages have varied over time and have a major effect on hospital profitability.

Medicaid will continue to be constrained in its payments to hospitals. States, which pay about half the costs of Medicaid, have difficulty financing rising Medicaid expenditures. The passage of PPACA increases Medicaid eligibility, thereby increasing the state's liability for this larger population. Medicaid payments will not keep up with hospital costs, considering rising medical costs and an increasingly large number of aged requiring long-term care.

Under the Medicare DRG system, Congress annually decides the percentage increase in the DRG price. This annual DRG update is supposed to be based on technical factors, such as hospital input price increases and productivity changes. However, Congress is also concerned with forestalling the projected bankruptcy of the Medicare Trust Fund, which pays for hospital services. The method Medicare uses to control hospital spending is to limit the rate of increase in the annual update of DRG prices.

Further, as part of PPACA, Medicare is required to reduce hospital spending by $500 billion over the next ten years. Thus, to save the Medicare Trust Fund and to reduce hospital spending per PPACA requirements, Medicare's DRG prices will likely fall further below hospital average costs. Congress can limit these reductions; however, such limits will increase the federal deficit, which is a political concern.

Rather than choose between increasing the deficit and reducing DRG payments, Medicare is considering reducing Medicare expenditure growth by changing how hospitals and physicians are paid.

Episode-Based Payment

Medicare is moving toward an episode-based (bundled) payment system, which means paying hospitals and physicians a single price for all the services included in a particular diagnosis (Mechanic and Altman 2009). The payment would be given to an organization, such as a hospital or medical group, which would then divide the payment among the participating providers. It is generally recognized that the fee-for-service (FFS) system does not necessarily promote coordination of care, high-quality outcomes, or efficiency in the use of services. Poor medical performance is not penalized; in fact, providers may receive additional revenues. Organizations that reduce unnecessary services and shift patients to lower-cost settings suffer decreased revenues. The financial risk and additional cost of complications and hospital readmissions under FFS is shifted from providers to insurers (and enrollees, in the form of higher insurance premiums). To reform the delivery system, it is necessary to reform the payment system.

Episode-based payment changes providers' incentives so that providers have incentives to innovate, reduce costs, and improve quality. Under this payment system, the financial risk is shifted from the payer to the providers.

Success under this payment system requires close integration of hospitals and physicians to reduce rising healthcare costs and improve quality. All participating hospitals would have to form physician–hospital relationships, and the bundled payment would consist of Medicare Parts A and B with a discount. Any savings would then be shared between the hospital and the physicians.

Geisinger Health System (Danville, Pennsylvania) uses a bundled payment model as follows: For cardiac procedures, bundled payment includes the costs of the physician visit at which surgery was determined to be necessary, all hospital costs for the surgery and related care for 90 days after surgery, and cardiac rehabilitation. Any associated complications and their treatment are also the provider's financial responsibility. As a result of this bundled payment model, since 2006 surgery complications have been reduced by 21 percent and readmissions have fallen by 44 percent. Average length of hospital stay has also been reduced by half a day (Paulus, Davis, and Steele 2008). This model has been expanded beyond cardiac procedures and now includes hip replacements, cataract surgery, obesity surgery, prenatal care, and cardiac catheterization.

Hospitals and physicians not participating in episode-based payment will have less access to Medicare dollars. Eventually, episode-based payment may move beyond acute care hospitalizations into post-acute care.

Expanding episode-based payment to many more diagnoses will be difficult. Patients are frequently treated for multiple chronic conditions, and bundled payment, which has a single-condition focus, may not be best for these patients.

Capitation Episode-based payment is a step toward capitation, which is a single payment per enrollee for all their medical services. HMOs and Kaiser are examples of organizations that are capitated. The broader the payment, the more incentive the organization has to be innovative in reducing medical costs, including the provision of preventive services. Under episode-based payment and capitation, hospitals and physicians have an incentive to form integrated organizations. Further, the measurement of quality and care outcomes becomes easier than under FFS. As hospital and physician Medicare payments are reduced over time, broader payment systems offer providers an opportunity to increase their revenues while reducing less effective medical services and providing care in a more efficient manner. However, moving the current FFS delivery system to capitation would be difficult. A bundled payment is a beginning in that direction.

As more hospital patients are covered by Medicare and Medicaid, a hospital's future will depend on payment rates relative to costs of caring for those patients and on whether hospitals and physicians are able to organize to deliver care under different payment systems.

Prices: Private Payers

Hospital prices are referred to as *charges*. However, few purchasers of hospital services pay full, or 100 percent of, charges.[1] Almost all payers receive discounts on charges. Hospitals may discount their charges by up to 50 percent. Insured patients are insensitive to the prices hospitals charge because they typically do not pay any out-of-pocket costs when they are admitted to the hospital.[2] (Only about 3 percent of hospital revenue is paid out of pocket by patients, which is lower than any other component of payment.) The insurer negotiates a prearranged price with the hospital, which has separate contracts with a large number of different health plans.

Insurers attempt to include in their network providers their enrollees prefer and providers willing to give larger price discounts in return for a greater volume of the insurer's enrollees. The insurer's ability to shift patients to competing hospitals determines its hospital discount. Insurers' ability to shift patients is limited by the degree of hospital competition in a market (the hospital market structure). In markets with only one hospital, the hospitals are monopolists and can exercise their market power by charging more than hospitals in markets where multiple similar hospitals exist. In competitive hospital markets, insurers will be able to shift their enrollees to lower-cost (but equal-quality) hospitals. The greater the number of hospitals competing on price, the lower will be the hospital's price markup and the greater the hospital discount (Ho 2009).

As a larger percentage of the population is included in Medicare and Medicaid, hospitals will try to serve more of the privately insured population, whose payment rates are higher. However, private insurers are also under pressure to reduce rising premiums. As Medicare moves toward episode-based payment systems, integrated hospital and physician organizations that are able to increase their incomes under this system will seek a similar payment system from private insurers. This will move the private sector in the same direction. Hospitals with little market power will face difficult price negotiations with insurers and will be pressured to move to episode-based payment, potentially causing conflict with their medical staff. Thus, in the private sector, hospitals integrated with their physicians are likely to fare better than those that continue to rely on FFS. Only those hospitals with strong market power will be able to receive high private FFS payments, though from a shrinking private sector.

Potential Hospital Threats

Physician Competition

Physician behavior can significantly affect hospital utilization, prices, and revenues. Many hospital services, such as diagnostic imaging and surgical procedures, are routinely performed in outpatient facilities. These procedures are substitutes for the same services performed in a hospital, and many of these facilities are owned by physicians who view such services as a means of increasing their incomes. (Physician convenience and patient satisfaction are additional reasons for the development of physician-owned outpatient facilities.)

When price markups are relatively high for certain hospital services, physician entrepreneurs enter the market by starting competing services, thereby reducing hospital use.

A more recent form of physician competition with community hospitals is the development of specialty hospitals (Schneider et al. 2008). Specialty hospitals primarily focus on profitable services, such as cardiology and orthopedic surgery.

Proponents of specialty hospitals claim that they offer patients greater choice and insurers lower prices, which forces hospitals to increase their efficiency, improve their quality, and be more responsive to patients. Critics claim that physicians on the hospital's staff refer less severely ill patients to the specialty hospital in which they have a financial interest and concentrate on providing only the most profitable procedures. Community hospitals are adversely affected when they lose high-margin services, which they say are used to underwrite charity care and money-losing services.

As part of the 2003 Medicare Modernization Act, hospital associations were successful in having a moratorium imposed on the development of new physician-owned specialty hospitals. Once that moratorium expired, new physician-owned specialty hospitals were built and competed with community hospitals. As part of PPACA, Congress again prohibited new or expanded physician-owned specialty hospitals.

Prohibiting specialty hospitals lessens competition. Relying on a competitive marketplace would determine whether specialty hospitals are better able to innovate in the delivery of medical services by concentrating on specific surgical procedures or specializing in particular diseases using coordinated treatment, as proponents claim.

Price distortions inherent in a regulated pricing system have served to accelerate the movement of care out of the traditional hospital setting. Advances in medical technology have enabled services previously provided in a general hospital to be provided in an outpatient facility and specialty hospitals. These technologic trends are likely to continue. A hospital's competitors are not just other hospitals. Unless prohibited by legislation, as occurred with physician-owned specialty hospitals, competition from physician-owned facilities is likely to limit the growth in hospital utilization and revenues.

Technologic Developments

Over time, technologic change is considered the most important determinant of rising health expenditures. Early advances in medicine increased the role of the hospital; anesthesia and control of surgical infections changed the hospital from an institution where little could be done for patients to a curative institution. Hospitals became the physician's workshop and central to the delivery of medical services. Additional advances in technology, such as cardiac surgery and organ transplants, further enhanced the role of the hospital.

Starting in the 1980s, the development of new technology enabled many services that previously had to be performed on an inpatient basis to be performed in outpatient facilities, such as diagnostic imaging services and less invasive surgeries. In contrast with previous technologic advances, these developments, which included new drugs and disease management techniques, decreased the demand for hospital inpatient care. Physicians shifted these diagnostic services and less invasive surgeries to outpatient centers, which they controlled, and thereby increased their incomes. To avoid losing the revenue from these new outpatient services, hospitals also developed their own ambulatory care facilities. Hospitals' service mix changed as a greater share of hospital revenue came from the provision of outpatient services (Goldsmith 2004).

Will emerging new technologies return hospitals to the central role in the delivery of medical services, or will new technologies continue to shift inpatient services to an outpatient setting, to be provided in physician-controlled facilities?

Goldsmith (2004) lists three emerging technologies that are likely to affect the role of the hospital. The first is "personalized" medicine, that is, the use of genetic profiling to better target drug treatments. Genetic testing will improve the clinical effectiveness of drug therapies by enabling practitioners to identify, for example, which types of cancer cells will be resistant to or more affected by different chemotherapy choices. Genetic testing will also identify those who will not benefit from some drugs and those who will suffer an adverse drug reaction (almost 2 million people each year).

The second emerging technology, "regenerative" medicine (i.e., culturing and grafting human cells to repair or replace damaged tissue), may someday allow practitioners to use stem cells to replace damaged tissue and repair spinal cord injuries. Patients with Alzheimer's disease and other irreversible conditions may become functional once again.

Monitoring systems, Goldsmith's third emerging technology, includes voice, visual images, and telemetry data. These systems enable specialists to monitor large numbers of patients in remote locations. Thus, patients who are not acutely ill but have some clinical risk can be discharged from the hospital and monitored in their homes or in other, less costly settings. Sensor monitoring will track a patient's physiologic condition, such as blood pressure and heart rate, and global positioning systems will track their physical movements, such as lying down and walking. Intelligent clinical information systems that integrate all these measures will enable a patient care team to monitor large numbers of patients and intervene when a patient's clinical measurement reaches a certain threshold.

These emerging technologies are likely to decrease hospital admissions, readmissions, lengths of stay, and emergency department visits, which are hospitals' traditional product lines. Does this mean hospitals will play a reduced role in patient care? The demand for these emerging technologies could be huge. The elderly are just one market segment; an aging population that is living longer will result in a great many frail, chronically ill patients. The cost of caring for the elderly using current medical practice would be very high. New remote monitoring technologies, however, will greatly reduce the need for labor.

Developing and implementing these technologies will require large sums of money. Skilled clinical teams will be needed to use the technologies, respond to patient needs, and serve a large population base over a wide geographic area. Will hospitals, multispecialty medical groups, or other providers be better able to capitalize on this evolving technology? As revenue from hospitals' traditional services declines and these and other new technologies generate huge new sources of revenue, those with entrepreneurial skills will be better able to anticipate and benefit from serving this potential market. It is too early to know whether there are any economies of scale or scope in restorative therapy that will provide hospitals with a competitive advantage over freestanding, specialized firms in providing such services.[3]

If hospitals are too slow to move from their traditional service lines or unable to develop the necessary physician relationships, large multispecialty medical groups and other entrepreneurial firms are likely to seize the opportunity presented by these new technologies. The managed care movement, HMOs, PPOs, and utilization management companies were not started by hospitals, practicing physicians, or traditional insurers but by entrepreneurs who were able to anticipate and capitalize on the employer demand for cost containment. A redistribution of revenues occurred, away from traditional providers and insurers to the new market entrants. Whether the same occurs with the new technologies will determine the future role of hospitals and their revenues.

Alternative Hospital Scenarios

Hospitals face several different future scenarios. The underlying assumption of each scenario is that Medicare hospital payments will be reduced. The Medicare Hospital Trust Fund is projected to be bankrupt in the not-too-distant future, and PPACA includes expected hospital cost savings of more than $500 billion over ten years.

Hospital Status Quo Scenario

As more of the population becomes eligible for Medicare and Medicaid, hospitals continue to receive Medicare DRG payments, but the annual updates are insufficient to cover rising hospital costs. As a consequence, hospital margins decline and hospitals cannot raise the capital to purchase the latest technology. Over time, hospitals no longer receive enough government funds to increase wages and have to reduce their staffing ratios. Eventually, access to care by publicly funded patients decreases, and quality of care slowly deteriorates.

Hospital consolidation and increased market power enable hospitals to raise their rates to private insurers. Insurance premiums increase. However, the federal government will have the authority to limit insurance premium increases as part of PPACA. Faced with rising hospital prices and limits on their rate increases, insurers are likely to limit their hospital and provider network, as they did during the 1990s, and to try and shift more hospital services to outpatient settings and physician groups.

Under the status quo scenario, hospitals with market power will perform better than those without such pricing power, but hospital expenditures will decline as a percentage of total medical expenditures.

Hospital Payment Reform Scenario

Medicare phases in an episode-based payment system, and hospitals and physicians form integrated organizations to deliver coordinated care. Private insurers, under government pressure to keep their premiums from rising rapidly, similarly offer bundled payment systems. As hospitals and physicians gain experience with bundled payment, they find it enables them to reduce treatment costs, improve treatment outcomes, and increase their incomes; they are able to increase their market share. The more aggressive of such integrated care organizations decide they can do even better, in terms of medical outcomes and their incomes, if they become capitated.

Hospitals and physicians reluctant to integrate and move toward episode-based payment find that other organizations, such as large medical groups or insurers partnering with physicians, are able to expand their market share at the expense of those unable to become integrated organizations. Hospitals will no longer be competing just against other hospitals but against medical groups and insurers who are also trying to expand their role in a reformed delivery system with new payment mechanisms.

Hospitals' future role will depend upon whether they expand to provide the complete cycle of medical care or remain in their more limited role.

Summary

Hospital fortunes have changed over time. Managed care and Medicare DRG payment greatly reduced hospital utilization, created excess capacity, and weakened hospitals' bargaining power with insurers. Over time, hospital capacity was reduced, mergers occurred, and managed care broadened its provider networks; hospitals used their increased bargaining power over insurers to increase their prices and profitability.

The future offers threats and opportunities. Technological developments have enabled a greater number of complex procedures to be performed in an outpatient setting. Physician entrepreneurs have been able to use these medical advances to establish physician-owned outpatient facilities, thereby increasing competition between physician-owned facilities and hospitals.

The growing reliance of hospitals on government payment, with the impending bankruptcy of the Medicare Trust Fund and government concern with reducing the huge federal deficit, is likely to result in a lower growth rate in hospital expenditures. As the number of publicly insured increases, shrinking the privately insured market, hospital competition will intensify for a diminishing pool of privately insured patients. Proposals to broaden the Medicare payment system to episode-based payment offer the potential for growth in revenues to those hospitals and physicians that are able to integrate their services. Hospitals unable to do so will rely upon FFS and a shrinking revenue base.

Not all hospitals are alike. Safety-net hospitals, which provide a significant amount of care to low-income and uninsured populations, and whose emergency departments attract patients who do not have regular physicians, are likely to experience greater financial pressures.

The greatest financial uncertainty for hospitals in coming years is political. How many people will be enrolled in public programs, and how much (and in what manner) will government pay hospitals?

Discussion Questions

1. What are several trends that are likely to increase hospital use?
2. What is the likely effect of physician-owned outpatient facilities and specialty hospitals on hospital expenditures?
3. How will emerging technologies likely affect hospital use?
4. Why do hospital mergers increase hospitals' bargaining power over insurers?
5. How will the projected insolvency of the Medicare Trust Fund affect DRG prices?

Notes

1. Although few payers pay full charges, hospitals will attempt to collect 100 percent of their charges from those who have not previously negotiated a discounted price. Those most likely to be billed full charges are those who are brought to the hospital by an ambulance as a result of

an auto accident. At that point, neither the accident victim nor his auto insurance company is in a position to negotiate a discounted rate from the hospital. Billing auto insurance companies full charges can be very profitable for hospitals.

2. Instead of price sensitivity, economists use the term *price elasticity of demand*, which is the percentage change in quantity demanded with a 1 percent change in price. When the percentage change in quantity demanded exceeds the percentage change in price, the good or service is considered to be price "elastic." For example, if the price decreases by 5 percent and the quantity demanded increases by 10 percent, the price elasticity equals –2. If the percentage change in price is greater than the percentage change in quantity, the service is price "inelastic" (price increases by 5 percent and quantity demanded decreases by 2 percent). Price elasticity is important in determining the effect of a change in price on revenue. When a service is price inelastic, increasing price will increase total revenue; decreasing price will decrease total revenue. Conversely, when the demand for a service is price elastic, increasing price decreases total revenue. Price elasticity is mainly determined by the closeness of substitutes. A hospital with good substitutes (i.e., comparable hospitals) will have a price-elastic demand curve; if it raises price its total revenue will decrease. By merging, hospitals decrease the number of substitutes the insurer can contract with, and their new demand curve will be less price elastic, enabling them to increase price and increase their total revenue.

3. Economies of scale occur when a firm's output increases by a greater proportion than the increase in its input cost; average total cost per unit therefore decreases as output increases. Larger firms will have lower unit costs than smaller firms. Economies of scope occur when it is less costly for a firm to produce certain services (or products) jointly than if separate firms produce each of the same services independently. An example is when the physician who undertakes stem cell research also provides stem cell therapy. In this case, it is less costly when the research and therapy are provided together than when each is provided separately by different firms. When economies of scope exist, multiproduct (service) firms will be more efficient than single-product (service) firms. Economies of scale are unrelated to economies of scope.

COST SHIFTING

Employers and insurers believe one reason for the rise in employees' health insurance premiums is *cost shifting*. When one purchaser, whether it is Medicare, Medicaid, or the uninsured patient, does not pay the full charges, many believe hospitals and physicians raise their prices to those who can afford to pay, namely those with private insurance. Cost shifting is considered unfair, and its elimination is an important reason large employers, whose employees have health insurance, favor mandating that all employers provide their employees with health insurance. "All-payer" systems, whereby each payer pays the same charges for hospital and medical services, are also favored by those who believe cost shifting increases their medical prices.

Evidence of cost shifting is based on the observation that different payers pay different prices for similar services (see Exhibit 17.1). Private payers have always had higher payment-to-cost ratios (higher price markups) than Medicare and Medicaid, and Medicare has generally paid more than Medicaid. The payment-to-cost ratios for all three payers have changed over time. Exhibit 17.1 suggests that when Medicare and Medicaid have low payment-to-cost ratios (which result in low profit margins for the providers), private payers have high price-to-cost ratios. Still to be discussed, however, is whether the relationships are causal, that is, whether low public payment–cost relationships lead to high private payment-to-cost ratios.

Although the logic of cost shifting may seem straightforward, it raises troubling questions. For example, can a hospital or physician merely increase prices to those who can pay to recover losses from those who do not pay? If the provider is able to shift costs, why do hospitals complain about the uncompensated care they are forced to provide? Furthermore, if providers are able to offset their losses by increasing prices to those with insurance, why have they not done so previously and thereby earned greater profits?

To better understand cost shifting, we must discuss (1) the provider's objective when it prices its services and (2) how different objectives result in different pricing strategies.

Exhibit 17.1 Aggregate Hospital Payment-to-Cost Ratios for Private Payers, Medicare, and Medicaid, 1980–2008

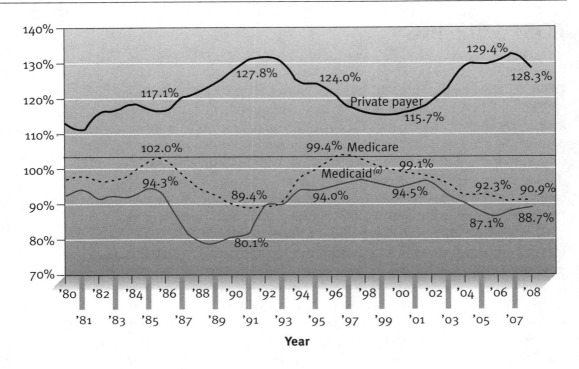

(a) Includes Medicaid disproportionate share payments

SOURCE: American Hospital Association/The Lewin Group, *Trends Affecting Hospitals and Health Systems,* January 2010. table 4.4. [Online information.] http://www.aha.org/aha/trendwatch/chartbook/2010/appendix4.pdf.

Setting Prices to Maximize Profits

Firms typically price their services to maximize profits, that is, to make as much money as possible. This is the simplest objective to start with in analyzing hospital and physician price setting. Assume that the hospital has two sets of patients, those who can pay and those who cannot pay for their services. Exhibit 17.2 illustrates how a profit-maximizing price is set for the insured group of patients. The relationship between price (P) and quantity (Q) is inverse, meaning the lower the price, the more units are likely to be purchased. Total revenue (TR) is price multiplied by quantity. As the price is reduced, more units will be sold and TR will increase; after some point, however, the increased number of units sold will not offset the lower price per unit, and TR will actually decline. The effect on TR when price is decreased and more units are sold is shown by the TR curve in Exhibit 17.3.

EXHIBIT 17.2 Determining the Profit-Maximizing Price

Price (P)	Quantity (Q)	Total Revenue (TR)	Total Cost (TC)	Profit	TC_2	$Profit_2$
11	1	11	9	2	11	0
10	2	20	13	7	17	3
9	3	27	17	10	23	4
8	4	32	21	11	29	3
7	5	35	25	10	35	0
6	6	36	29	7	41	−5
5	7	35	33	2	47	−12
4	8	32	37	−5	53	−21
3	9	27	41	−14	59	−32

EXHIBIT 17.3 Profit-Maximizing Price With and Without a Change in Variable Cost

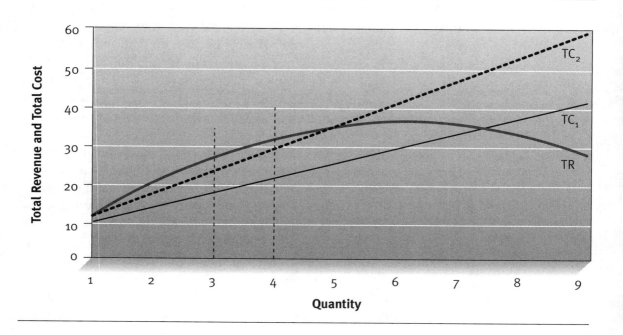

To determine the price and output that result in the largest profit, we must also know the costs for producing that output. Total cost (TC) consists of two parts: fixed costs, which do not vary as output changes (e.g., rent for an office or depreciation on a building), and variable costs, which do vary. For this example, fixed costs are assumed to be $5, and variable costs are constant at $4 per unit. The difference between TR and TC is profit. According to Exhibit 17.2, the largest amount of profit occurs when the price is $8 and output equals four units. At that price TR is $32, TC is $21 ($5 fixed cost plus $16 variable costs), and profit is $11. According to Exhibit 17.3, the greatest difference between the total cost line (TC) and TR (profit) occurs at four units of output.

Raising or lowering the price will only reduce profits. If the hospital lowers its price from $8 to $7, it will have to lower the price on all units sold. The hospital's volume will increase; TR will rise from $32 to $35, or by only $3. Because the variable cost of the extra unit sold is $4, the hospital will lose money on that last unit. The profit at a price of $7 will be $10. Similarly, if the hospital raises its price from $8 to $9, it will sell one less unit, reducing its variable cost by $4 but forgoing $5 worth of revenue (see Exhibit 17.4).[1] Changing the price once it is at the profit-maximizing price lowers the hospital's profit.

Exhibit 17.2 illustrates several important points. First, establishing a profit-maximizing price means the price is set so that the additional revenue received is equal to the additional cost of serving an additional patient. When the change in TR is equal to the change in TC, choosing any other price will result in less profit.

Second, if the hospital's fixed costs increase from $5 to $11, the hospital should not change its price; if it did, it would make even less profit. With an increase in fixed costs, profit would decline by $6 at every quantity sold. At a price of $8, the hospital would make a total profit of $5; TR is $32, while TC is now $27 ($11 plus $16). If the hospital raised its price to $9 to compensate for the rise in its fixed costs, TR would be $27, TC would be $23 ($11 plus $12), and total profit would fall to $4. Thus, changes in fixed costs should not affect the hospital's profit-maximizing price.

Third, if the hospital's variable costs changed, perhaps because nurses' wages or the cost of supplies increased, the hospital would find it profitable to change its price. For example, if variable costs increase by $2 and the price–quantity relationship is unchanged, the largest profit will occur at a price of $9 (TR $-$ TC_2 = $profit_2$ in Exhibit 17.2). The higher variable cost is shown in Exhibit 17.3 as TC_2. The distance between TR and TC_2, which is profit, is greatest at three units of output. If the price per unit remains $8 when variable costs increase to $6 per unit, the addition to TR from producing four rather than three units is only $5. The hospital will lose money on that last unit, the cost of which is $6. Thus, by raising price and producing fewer units,

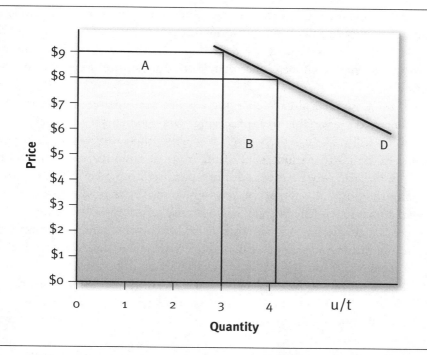

EXHIBIT 17.4
Effect on Total
Revenue of a
Change in Price

the increase in TR slightly exceeds the additional cost of producing that last unit. Hospitals therefore would be expected to raise their prices as their variable costs increased. Similarly, if variable costs decline, the hospital will realize more profit by lowering the price.

Fourth, hospitals would also be expected to change the price they charge if the relationship between price and quantity were to change. The price–quantity relationship is a measure of how price sensitive purchasers are to changes in the hospital's price. When the price is changed and quantity changes by a smaller percentage, purchasers are not very price sensitive; the demand for the hospital's service is *price inelastic*. Conversely, when quantity changes by a greater percentage than the change in price, purchasers are said to be more price sensitive; the demand is *price elastic*. As the demand for the hospital's services becomes more price sensitive (price elastic), a hospital would be expected to lower its price, even if there is no change in its costs.[2]

For example, if five hospitals exist in a market and each hospital is considered to be a relatively good substitute for the others in terms of location, services, reputation, medical staff, and so on, each hospital's demand is considered to be very price sensitive. In competing to be included in different HMO and insurer provider networks, each hospital will compete on price. If just one hospital lowers price, it will cause large increases in that hospital's patient volume. Similarly, raising its price when the other hospitals do not will cause that hospital to lose a large portion of its market share. Conversely, a hospital that is a sole community provider or that has the only trauma unit, for example, faces a less price-sensitive demand for its services or its trauma unit. That hospital's prices will be higher than if good substitutes were available for its services.

If the hospital is already charging a profit-maximizing price to its paying patients and the variable costs of serving paying patients have not changed, the hospital will make even less profit by further increasing prices to paying patients. Referring to Exhibit 17.2, if the hospital raises its price from $8 to $9 simply because other patients did not pay, the hospital will forgo profit. Assuming the hospital wants to make as much money as possible from those who can afford to pay, the hospital will not raise its price to those patients unless there is a change in variable costs or in their price–quantity relationship. Because neither factor changes when another group of patients pays less, it will not make sense for the hospital to charge its paying patients more.

Based on the above explanation of how a profit-maximizing price is set, changes in prices can be explained by changes in the variable costs of caring for patients or by a change in the price-sensitivity relationship facing a hospital (or a physician).

Contrary to what many people believe, when the government lowers the price it pays for Medicare or Medicaid patients, physicians will likely lower the prices they charge to higher-paying patients. For example, assume that a physician serves two types of patients, private patients and Medicaid patients. The government determines the price charged to Medicaid patients, whereas the physician sets the price for private patients. Traditionally, the price received by the physician for treating private patients is higher than that received for Medicaid patients. The physician presumably allocates his time so that revenues per unit of time are the same regardless of the types of patients served. To produce equal returns when the prices for Medicaid and private patients are different, the physician may spend less time on the Medicaid patient.

If the government further reduces the price it pays for Medicaid patients, the physician is likely to decide that she can earn more by shifting some time away from Medicaid patients and toward caring for more private patients. As more physicians reduce the time they spend with Medicaid patients and reallocate their time toward the private market, the supply of physician time in this market increases. With an increase in supply, physicians would be willing to reduce their prices to receive an increased number of private patients. Assuming limited demand creation by physicians, a lower price for Medicaid patients is likely to result in lower physician fees for private patients.

Assuming that the objective of hospitals and physicians is to make as much money as possible, these two examples suggest that prices for private patients will be either unchanged or reduced when another payer, government, pays the provider less.

Origins of Claims of Cost Shifting

Based on the previous discussion, why do private purchasers claim that they are being charged more to make up for the lower prices paid by government? The belief that cost shifting is occurring may simply be an artifact of trends over time in rising hospital prices and uncompensated care. Hospitals may appear to be raising prices to compensate for lower prices charged to other patients, but hospital prices to private payers have increased for two reasons: (1) variable costs have increased as expenses for wages and supplies have risen and (2) changes in the hospitals' payer mixes (an increase in the proportion of patients who are less price sensitive) may have enabled them to increase their markups on certain types of private patients. This association of rising prices and uncompensated care does not necessarily indicate a causal relationship.

There does exist, however, a logical explanation, unrelated to cost shifting, for why some purchasers pay more for the same service than other purchasers: Some purchasers might be more price sensitive than others. Previously, private patients had either indemnity insurance or BlueCross hospital coverage; because hospitals had a close relationship with BlueCross (hospitals started and controlled BlueCross), BlueCross was charged a lower price than indemnity insurers. The price–quantity relationship for those with indemnity insurance represented the average relationship for everyone in the indemnity plan. However, as employers began offering different types of health plans, such as HMOs, PPOs, and managed care, in addition to the traditional indemnity plan, and as employees had to pay different premiums and copayments under these different plans, the price–quantity relationships of these plans differed. Those with indemnity insurance could choose whatever hospital and physician they desired. Other plans, however, were more restrictive in deciding which providers their subscribers could use. HMOs and PPOs were likely to bargain with providers for lower prices in return for directing their subscribers to these approved providers.

Faced with different price–quantity relationships with different purchasers, hospitals began charging different prices to each type of payer. These prices take into consideration the price sensitivity of each of these different insurance plans. Patients remaining in the traditional indemnity plan are charged the highest prices because they are not restricted in their use of providers. Their insurers cannot promise to direct their subscribers to particular hospitals and are least able to negotiate lower hospital prices. It is the willingness of an insurer to shift its patients to another hospital that results in their greater price sensitivity.

Price Discrimination

Charging according to what the market will bear is not really cost shifting but rather simply charging a profit-maximizing price to each group; this is price discrimination. Services for which purchasers are willing to pay more have higher markups. Airlines charge higher prices for first-class seating and lower prices for 21-day advance purchases, for example. Movie theaters charge lower prices for matinees and to senior citizens. Each of these industries is pricing according to different groups' willingness to pay; each group has a different price–quantity relationship. Hospital pricing is no different. Hospitals placing a proportionately higher markup over costs on laboratory tests or drugs used by inpatients than on the room-and-board fee are engaging in price discrimination. Patients who have to pay part of the bill themselves can more easily compare hospital room-and-board rates before they enter the hospital; hospitals therefore have to be price competitive on their room rates. Once a patient is hospitalized, however, patients have little choice in what they pay for services rendered in the hospital. The price–quantity relationships for inpatient services are quite insensitive to prices charged. Hospitals do not face any competition for laboratory tests or other services provided to their inpatients. Thus, their markup for these services is much higher.

Price discrimination is an important reason some purchasers are able to pay lower hospital prices than others. A large employer or an HMO that is willing to direct its employees or enrollees to a particular hospital will receive a lower price for the same service than a single patient negotiating with the same hospital. The hospital's price–quantity relationship will be more price sensitive when the hospital negotiates with a large purchaser than when the hospital deals with a single insured patient. The single insured patient does not pay higher prices because the large purchaser pays a lower price. The hospital is less concerned with losing one patient's business than with losing 1,000 patients from a large purchaser.

Even if the government increased its payments to hospitals for treating Medicare patients, the price to the single insured patient would not be reduced because the price–quantity relationship for these patients, which is less price sensitive, would be unchanged. Only if the patient with indemnity insurance becomes part of a larger purchasing group, which is willing to offer a hospital a greater volume of patients in return for lower prices, can the indemnity patient receive a lower hospital price. Different prices to different purchasers are related to how price sensitive they are rather than to what other purchasers are paying. As the insurance market has become more segmented with HMOs, PPOs, self-insured employer groups, traditional indemnity-type insurance plans, and so on, hospitals have developed different pricing strategies for each group.

Empirical evidence supports the view that hospital prices are not raised to other purchasers when prices are reduced to large purchasers. Dranove and White (1998) found that hospitals that had a higher proportion of Medicaid patients (20 percent or more of their budgets) did not raise prices to other paying patients when Medicaid reduced its reimbursement; if anything, hospitals lowered their prices to private payers. Instead, the hospital reduced the service levels for Medicaid patients relative to those for privately insured patients. The amount of free or uncompensated care provided has also been found to be reduced, such as by reducing access to the emergency department, which serves a high proportion of uninsured patients.

Conditions Under Which Cost Shifting Can Occur

Under certain circumstances, however, cost shifting may occur. Some hospitals may have a different pricing objective—they do not price to maximize their profits. These hospitals may voluntarily forgo some profits to maintain good community relationships. When hospitals do not set profit-maximizing prices, increases in uncompensated care or fixed costs may cause the hospital to raise its prices to those groups who have a greater ability to pay. For example, average cost pricing occurs when a hospital sets its price by relating it to the average cost of caring for all of its patients. If one payer (e.g., the government) decides to pay the hospital less, the average price becomes higher for all other payers. For cost shifting to occur, the purchasers of hospital (or physician) services would also have to be relatively insensitive to the higher prices. If the purchasers switch to other providers or use fewer services as a result of the provider's cost shifting, the provider's revenues and profits will decline.

Is cost shifting an important reason private patients are paying higher medical prices today? Purchasers have become more price sensitive since the mid-1980s. Given the increased competitive market in which providers find themselves, it is unlikely that providers are willing to forgo profits by not setting profit-maximizing prices. Forgoing profits means the hospital has no better use for those funds. Two ways the hospital could use those higher profits would be to purchase new equipment or start new services to increase its revenues. The medical staff, an important constituency within the hospital, also desires new equipment and facilities. Paying higher wages makes it easier to attract needed nursing and technical personnel. Hospitals could enhance their community image and market themselves by providing screening and health awareness programs to their communities. Furthermore, additional funds could always be used to provide care to those in the community who are unable to afford it and who are not covered by public programs.

The benefits to the hospital of forgoing profit on some payer groups are unlikely to exceed the benefits to the hospital of using that forgone profit in other ways. By not setting profit-maximizing prices, the hospital's decision makers place a greater weight on benefiting some purchaser group than on using those funds for other constituencies.

One type of cost shifting occurs when the government pays hospitals a fixed price for Medicare patients' use of the hospital but reimburses outpatient services on a cost basis. If the hospital has $100 in indirect administrative costs to allocate between inpatient units (paid according to a fixed-price diagnosis-related group) and outpatient units (paid on a cost basis), the hospital will select a cost-allocation method that optimizes its payment from the government, namely the method that allocates a greater portion of the $100 to outpatient units.

Another type of cost shifting occurs when the government shifts its costs to employers, as when requirements that would otherwise cost the government money are imposed on employers. For example, if the government required all employers to buy health insurance for their employees, the government's Medicaid expenditures for low-income employees and their dependents would be reduced.

The Direction of Causality

Payment-to-cost ratios for all three payers—private, Medicare, and Medicaid—have fluctuated over time (see Exhibit 17.1). It would appear that the payment-to-cost ratios between public (Medicare and Medicaid) and private payers are inversely related; when public ratios decline (low or negative profit margins), private ratios increase (high profit margins). However, the causality likely goes in the opposite direction—when private payment-to-cost ratios increase, public payment-to-cost ratios decrease.

A recent study (Stensland, Gaumer, and Miller 2010) found that as hospitals gain market power, they have greater ability to increase their prices to private payers, hence increase their profits. Since nonprofit hospitals cannot distribute their profits to shareholders, the funds are used to expand services, invest in new technology, add staff, purchase physician practices, provide greater patient amenities, and so on. The expenditure of these "profits" increases hospital costs per discharge. The higher costs per discharge affect patients of all payer types, public as well as private payers. With higher hospital costs per discharge and fixed Medicare and Medicaid prices, the price-to-cost ratio of public payers declines; that is, the higher hospital costs and the same payment result in lower margins from public payers.

The authors found that more profitable hospitals had higher costs per discharge than less profitable hospitals and that more profitable hospitals also had lower Medicare payment-to-cost ratios. The opposite was also found: Hospitals under financial stress had lower costs per discharge and higher Medicare margins.

Over time, hospitals' market power has changed, leading to different private and public payment-to-cost ratios. During the early 1980s, the payment-to-cost ratios for private payers, Medicare, and Medicaid were relatively close, the economy-wide recession was ending, and Medicare was beginning to shift from cost-based payment to fixed prices per admission. The late 1980s and early 1990s was a period of economic growth, and hospital private payment-to-cost ratios increased. Managed care had its greatest effect in the mid- to late 1990s, hospitals developed excess capacity, intense price competition occurred among hospitals to be included in managed care's provider networks, hospitals reduced their costs to remain competitive, and managed care plans negotiated large price discounts from hospitals. Private payer payment-to-cost ratios declined. In the past decade hospital mergers have increased, hospital capacity has decreased, broadened managed care provider networks have resulted in lower insurer bargaining power, and hospitals have developed greater market power. Hospital price markups have increased rapidly, returning to the situation that existed before the managed care period.

Changes in hospital payment-to-cost ratios for each payer should be examined with regard to trends in hospitals' market power. Contrary to what many believe, namely that low Medicare and Medicaid payments lead to increases in hospital prices to private payers, the causality goes in a different direction: Hospitals' market power and their ability to increase prices to private payers result in a higher cost structure, which, with fixed public prices, leads to lower public payment-to-cost ratios.

Summary

Previously, when insurance premiums were paid almost entirely by the employer and managed care was not yet popular, hospitals were probably less interested in making as much money as possible. Many hospitals were reimbursed according to their costs, and they could achieve many of their goals without having to set profit-maximizing prices. However, as occupancy rates declined and left hospitals with excess capacity, price competition increased, HMOs and PPOs entered the market, and hospitals could no longer count on having their costs reimbursed, regardless of what those costs were. Hospital profitability declined. Those hospitals that did not price to make as much money as possible began to do so. Some cost shifting occurred during this transition period.

Differences in hospital prices for different payer groups today are more likely the result of price discrimination than cost shifting. The difference between these two explanations is significant. Cost-shifting proponents believe that unless government payments to hospitals and physicians are increased, private payers, such as insurers and employers, will have to pay higher prices for healthcare. Economists, however, predict that with lower government provider payments, medical prices to private payers will decrease, not increase. As the payment for one type of patient decreases and becomes less profitable, physicians can earn more money by shifting some time away from less profitable patients. The supply of physician time in the private market will increase, resulting in lower prices to private payers.

Further, as hospitals gain market power through mergers, they will be able to price discriminate and increase their prices to private payers. Because nonprofit hospitals cannot distribute their profits, they use them to increase the hospital's cost structure by adding new facilities and services. These higher costs per discharge affect all payers. Thus, while hospitals are able to increase their payment-to-cost ratios to private payers, higher costs per discharge and fixed government payments result in lower public payment-to-cost ratios.

Discussion Questions

1. Explain why an increase in a hospital's fixed costs or an increase in the number of uninsured cared for by the hospital will not change the hospital's profit-maximizing price.
2. Why would a change in a hospital's variable costs change the hospital's profit-maximizing price?
3. Why are hospitals able to charge different purchasers different prices for the same medical services?
4. Under what circumstances can cost shifting occur?
5. How does cost shifting differ from price discrimination?

Additional Readings

Morrisey, M. 2003. "Cost Shifting: New Myths, Old Confusions, and Enduring Reality." *Health Affairs* Web exclusive, October 8, w3-489–w3-491.
———. 1994. *Cost Shifting in Health Care: Separating Evidence from Rhetoric.* Washington, DC: American Enterprise Institute Press.
Changes in Health Care Financing & Organization. 2002. "When Public Payment Declines, Does Cost-Shifting Occur? Hospital and Physician Responses." [Online document; retrieved 4/8/11.] http://www.hcfo.org/events/when-public-payment-declines-does-cost-shifting-occur-hospital-and-physician-responses

Notes

1. Exhibit 17.4 is another way to illustrate how a change in price affects TR. Price is shown along the vertical axis, and quantity, or number of units sold each month or year, is shown along the horizontal axis. When the price is $9 per unit, three units are sold. When price is reduced to $8, four units will be sold. Reducing the price from $9 to $8 results in a decrease in TR of $1 for each of the three units that would have been sold at $9. This loss of $3 is shown by area A. However, lowering the price to $8 gains $8 for that additional unit sold, shown as area B. The difference between area A (loss of $3) and area B (gain of $8) is $5, which is the increase in TR from selling one additional unit. Increasing the price from $8 to $9 has the opposite effect, a loss of $5 in TR.

2. The effect of price sensitivity (economists use the term "price elasticity") on hospital prices and markups is based on the following formula:

$$\text{Markup} = \frac{MC}{1 - \dfrac{1}{\text{price elasticity}}}$$

MC is marginal cost of producing an additional unit and is assumed to be equal to average variable cost. For simplicity, assume MC = $1,000.

Thus, if a hospital believes the price sensitivity of a particular employee group is such that a 1 percent increase (decrease) in the hospital's price leads to a 2 percent decrease (increase) in admissions, the hospital's markup, applied to its average variable costs, would be 100 percent:

$$\frac{\$1,000}{1 - \dfrac{1}{2}} = \frac{\$1,000}{\dfrac{1}{2}} = \$1,000 \times \frac{2}{1} = \$2,000$$

If use of services were more price sensitive, such that a 1 percent price increase (decrease) leads to a 3 percent decrease (increase) in admissions, the markup would be 50 percent:

$$\frac{\$1,000}{1 - \dfrac{1}{3}} = \frac{\$1,000}{\dfrac{2}{3}} = \$1,000 \times \frac{3}{2} = \$1,000 \times 1.5 = \$1,500$$

If the hospital's variable costs of serving the patients were the same in both examples, the prices charged to each employee group could vary greatly depending on their price sensitivity. Even those hospitals that have few good substitutes and a less price-elastic demand for their services will always price in the elastic portion of their demand curve. For an explanation see Browning and Zupan (2009).

CAN PRICE CONTROLS LIMIT MEDICAL EXPENDITURE INCREASES?

In the debate over healthcare reform, proponents of regulation, such as those who favor a single-payer system, have proposed placing controls on the prices physicians and hospitals charge to limit the rise in medical expenditures. To prevent hospitals and physicians from circumventing such controls by simply performing more services, they would also impose an overall limit (a *global budget*) on total medical expenditures.

Price controls and global budgets may seem obvious approaches for limiting rising medical expenditures, but the potential consequences should be examined before placing one-sixth (17.6 percent) of the US economy (more than $2.4 trillion a year) under government control. The healthcare industry in the United States is larger than the economies of most countries. An announcement in any country that price controls would be imposed on the entire economy would seem incredible to all who have observed the previous communist economies of Eastern Europe and Russia. Widespread shortages occurred, many of the goods produced were of shoddy quality, and black markets developed. These countries have recognized the inherent failures of a controlled economy, and they have moved toward development of free markets.

Why should we think healthcare is so different that access to care, high quality, and innovation can be better achieved by price controls and regulation than by reliance on competitive markets? What consequences are likely if price controls are imposed on medical services?[1]

Effect of Price Controls in Theory

Imbalances Between Supply and Demand

Imbalances between demands for care and supply of services will occur. The demand for medical services and the cost of providing those services are constantly changing. Prices bring about an equilibrium between the demanders and suppliers in a market. Prices reflect changes in demand or in the costs of producing a service. When demand increases (perhaps because of an aging population or rising incomes), prices increase. Higher prices will cause some of the demand to decrease, but suppliers will respond to the higher prices by increasing the quantity of their services. Higher prices provide a signal (and an incentive) to suppliers that greater investment in personnel and equipment will be needed to meet the increased demand (Baumol 1988).

When regulators initially place controls on prices, they are assuming that the conditions that brought about the initial price, namely the demands for service and the costs of producing that service, will not change. However, these conditions do change for many reasons. Thus, the controlled price will no longer be an equilibrium price. The problem with price controls is that demand is constantly changing, as is the cost of providing services. Although regulators often allow some increases in prices each year to adjust for inflation, seldom if ever are these price increases sufficient to reflect the changes in demand or costs that are occurring. When prices are not flexible, an imbalance between demand and supply will occur.

Not only do the demand and costs of producing services change, but the product itself, that is, medical care, is also continually changing, which complicates the picture for regulators. For example, the population is aging, and older individuals consume more medical care. Relatively new diseases, such as AIDS, require extensive testing, treatment, and prolonged care. Technology continues to improve. Since the mid-1990s, transplants have become commonplace. Diagnostic equipment has reduced the need for many exploratory surgeries. Low-birth-weight infants can now survive. Such continuing advances increase the demand for medical services and require a greater use of skilled labor, expensive monitoring equipment, and new imaging machines. Unless regulators are aware of these changes in the medical product and technology, their controlled prices will be below the costs of providing these services. How will the demand be met? Imbalances will undoubtedly occur because regulators cannot anticipate all the changes in demand, costs, and technology.

Shortages

Shortages are the inevitable consequence of price controls. Demand for medical services is continually increasing, yet price controls limit increases in supply. To expand its services a hospital or a medical group must be able to attract additional employees by increasing wages to lure skilled and trained employees away from their current employers. Similarly, as wages increase, trained nurses who are not currently employed as nurses will find returning to nursing financially attractive, and more people will choose nursing careers as wages become comparable to those in other professions. However, if hospitals cannot raise wages because they cannot raise their prices, they will not be able to hire the nurses needed to expand their services.

Price controls not only limit increases in medical services, but they actually cause a reduction in such services, which exacerbates the shortage over time. As prices and wages continue to increase throughout the economy, price controls on the health sector make it difficult for hospitals and medical groups to pay competitive wages and rising supply costs. Hospitals must hire nurses and technicians, buy supplies, pay heating and electric bills, and replace or repair equipment. A hospital that cannot pay competitive wages will be unable to retain its employees. If the wages of hospital accountants are not similar to those of accountants working in non-hospital settings, fewer accountants will choose to work in hospitals (or those who do accept lower wages may not be as qualified). As medical costs increase faster than the permitted increases in prices, hospitals and medical groups will be unable to retain their existing labor forces and provide their current services.

As costs per patient rise faster than government-controlled prices, hospitals, outpatient facilities, and physician practices are faced with two choices: They can either care for fewer, more costly patients, or they can care for the same number of patients but devote fewer resources to each patient.

Eliminating all the waste in the current system would merely result in a one-time savings. If rising expenditures were caused by new technologies, aging of the population, and new diseases, and not by waste, medical costs would still rise faster than the rate at which hospitals and other providers would be reimbursed under price controls. Providers would then be faced with the same two choices: caring for fewer patients or devoting fewer resources to each patient and thus providing lower-quality service.

Price controls on medical services cause the demand for medical services to exceed the supply. The out-of-pocket price the patient pays for a physician visit, an MRI, an ultrasound, or laboratory tests will increase more slowly than it would if the price were not controlled. (The "real," or inflation-adjusted, price to the patient is likely to fall.) Consequently, although patient demand for such services increases, suppliers cannot increase their services if the cost of doing so exceeds the fixed price. In fact, over time the shortage will become even larger because the fixed price will cover the cost of fewer such services. We have seen this occur when rent controls are imposed on housing, such as in New York. The demand for rent-controlled housing continually exceeds its supply, and the supply of existing housing decreases as the costs of upkeep exceed the allowable increases in rent and cause landlords to abandon entire city areas.

Shift of Capital Away from Price-Controlled Services

Furthermore, as profitability is reduced on services subject to price control, capital investment will eventually shift to areas that are not subject to control and in which investors can earn higher returns. Less private capital will be available to develop new delivery systems, invest in computer technology for patient care management, and conduct research and development toward breakthrough drugs. Price controls on hospitals cause hospital investment to decline and capital to move into unregulated outpatient services and home healthcare services. Should all health services become subject to controls, capital would move to nonhealth industries and to geographic regions without controls.

Effect of Price Controls in Practice

Medicaid

Price controls have been tried extensively in the United States and other countries. Shortages and decreased access to care, which typify the Medicaid program, are caused by price controls. Once a patient is eligible for Medicaid, the price he has to pay for medical services is greatly reduced, increasing his demand for such services. Government Medicaid payments to physicians are fixed, however, and below what physicians could earn by serving non-Medicaid patients. Low provider payments have decreased the profitability of serving Medicaid patients and resulted in a shortage of Medicaid services. As the difference in prices for Medicaid and private patients increases, more of the physician's time is shifted toward serving private patients, thereby increasing the shortage of medical services faced by Medicaid patients.

Medicare

Hospitals are also subject to price controls on the payments they receive from Medicare. When fixed prices per diagnostic admission were introduced in 1984, hospitals began to "up-code" their Medicare patients' diagnoses to maximize their reimbursements. Medicare hospital payments increased sharply, and 75 percent of the increase was attributed to "code creep" (Sheingold 1989). Eventually, the government reduced Medicare payments so much that more than two-thirds of all hospitals lost money on their Medicare patients. After a few years of losses, payments were increased. Indications are that the Patient Protection and Affordable Care Act (PPACA) and Medicare reform to forestall bankruptcy of the Medicare Trust Fund will reduce hospital payments.

The failure of Medicare diagnosis-related group payments to accurately measure patient severity of illness has led some hospitals to "dump" on other hospitals those Medicare patients whose costs exceed their payments. Congress has enacted legislation to penalize hospitals that engage in dumping.

In the early 1970s, Medicare limited how rapidly physician fees could increase under Medicare. As the difference between Medicare and private fees became greater, physicians stopped participating in Medicare and billed their patients directly. To prevent this, Congress changed the rules in the 1990s. Physicians are no longer able to participate for some of their patients and not others (by billing them the balance between what Medicare paid and the physician's normal fee); instead, physicians must participate for all (or none) of their Medicare patients.

When price controls and fee reductions were imposed on Medicare physician fees in 1992, physicians whose fees were reduced the most showed the largest increases in volume of services (Nguyen 1996). For example, radiologists' fees declined by 12 percent, while their volume increased by 13 percent. Similarly, urologists' fees declined by 5 percent, while their volume increased by 12 percent. These specialists were apparently able to create demand among their Medicare fee-for-service patients.

When Medicare limited the rise in premiums for Medicare HMOs, a number of HMOs dropped out of the Medicare HMO market. Medicare Advantage plans were subsequently given significant premium incentives in 2003 to re-enter the Medicare market (their Medicare payments were about 14 percent higher than the cost of comparable risk-adjusted patients in traditional Medicare). As part of PPACA, these higher payments were removed, with the likely consequence in coming years that such plans will either again exit the Medicare market or charge their Medicare enrollees' higher premiums and copayments.

Rationing

Under price controls, as demand for medical services exceeds supplies, what criteria will be used to ration the supplies that are available? Undoubtedly, emergency cases would take precedence over elective services, but how would elective services be rationed? In some countries where age is a criterion, those above a certain age do not have access to hip replacements, kidney dialysis, heart surgery, and other services. Both quality of life and life expectancy are reduced.

Waiting Lists

Typically, waiting lists are used to ration elective procedures. In countries that rely on this approach, waiting times for surgical procedures, whether for cataracts or open-heart surgery, vary from six months to two years.[2] Delays are costly in terms of reduced quality of life and life expectancy. When resources are limited, acute care has a higher priority than preventive services. Women over the age of 50 years have a lower use rate of mammograms in Canada, where price controls and global budgets are used, than in the United States. (More than 60 percent of women aged 50 to 69 in the United States had a mammogram in the previous 12 months, compared with 48 percent in Canada [Sanmartin et al. 2004].)

Those who can afford to wait, that is, those with lower time costs, such as the retired, will be more likely to receive physician services than those with higher time costs. Access to nonemergency physician services will be determined by the value patients place on their time. Waiting is costly in that it uses productive resources (or enjoyable time). A large, but less visible, cost is associated with waiting. Suppose the out-of-pocket price of a physician's office visit is limited to $10, but the patient must take three hours off work to wait and see the physician. If the patient earns $20 an hour, the effective cost of that visit is $70.

The "lower" costs of a price-controlled system never explicitly recognize the lost productivity to society or the value of that time to the patient. Patients with high time costs would be willing to pay not to wait, but they do not have that option. They cannot buy medical services that are worth more than they are willing to pay.

The effects of price controls are often a greater burden on those with low incomes and those who do not know how to "work the system." Specialists frequently see those with "connections" more quickly, and those with higher incomes can travel elsewhere to receive care. For example, in 2010, the premier of Newfoundland went to the United States for heart surgery at his own expense (Wallace 2010).

Deterioration of Quality

As the costs of providing medical services increase faster than the controlled price, providers may reduce the resources used in treatment, resulting in a deterioration of quality. A physician may prefer a highly sophisticated diagnostic test such as an MRI, but to conserve resources she may order an X-ray instead. The value to the patient of a diagnostic test may exceed its cost, but an overall limit on costs will preclude performing many cost-beneficial tests or procedures. Experience with Medicaid confirms these concerns with quality of care. Large numbers of patients are seen for very short visits in Medicaid "mills." Such short visits are more likely to lead to incorrect diagnosis and treatment. Similarly, in Japan, where physicians' fees are controlled, physicians see many more patients per day than US physicians and spend 30 percent less time with each patient.[3]

When controlled prices do not reflect quality differences among hospitals or physicians, suppliers have less incentive to provide higher-quality services. If all physicians are paid the same fee, the incentive to invest the time to become board certified is reduced. In a price-controlled environment with excess demand, even low-quality providers can survive and prosper. Similarly, drug and equipment manufacturers have no incentive to invest in higher-quality products if such products could not be priced to reflect their higher value.

Gaming the System

Price controls provide incentives for providers to try to "game" the system to increase their revenues. For example, physicians paid on a fee-for-service basis are likely to decrease the time they devote to each visit, which enables them to see more patients and thus bill for more visits. Less physician time per patient represents a more hurried visit and presumably lower-quality care. Physicians are also likely to unbundle their services; by dividing a treatment or visit into its separate parts they can charge for each part separately. For example, separate visits may be scheduled for diagnostic tests, to receive the results of those tests, and to receive medications. Price controls also provide physicians and hospitals with an incentive to up-code the type of services they provide, that is, to bill a brief office visit as a comprehensive exam.

Gaming the system results in increased regulatory costs because a larger bureaucracy is needed to administer and monitor compliance with price controls. C. Jackson Grayson (1993), who was in charge of price controls imposed in the United States in 1971, stated, "We started Phase II [from 1971 to 1973] with 3½ pages of regulations and ended with 1,534."

Gaming is also costly to patients. Multiple visits to the physician, which enable the physician to bill for each visit separately, increase patient travel and waiting times, an inefficient use of the patient's time that may discourage patients from using needed services.

Global Budgets

To ensure that gaming does not increase total expenditures, an expenditure limit (global budget) is often superimposed on price controls. Included in a global budget are all medical expenditures for hospital and physician services, outpatient and inpatient care, health insurance and HMO premiums, and consumer out-of-pocket payments. Unless the global budget is comprehensive, expenditures and investments will shift to unregulated sectors. Additional controls will then be imposed to prevent expenditure growth in these areas, and monitoring compliance with the controls becomes even more costly.

What happens under global budgets when demand for certain providers or managed care organizations increases? The more efficient health plans cannot increase payments to attract a greater number of physicians and facilities to meet increased enrollment demands. Thus, the public is precluded from choosing the more efficient, more responsive health plans that are subject to overall budget limits. Limiting a physician's total revenue discourages the use of physician assistants and nurse practitioners who could increase the physician's productivity, because the physician would prefer to receive the limited revenue rather than share it. Once a physician has reached the overall revenue limit, what incentive does she have to continue serving patients? Why not work fewer hours and take longer vacations?

What incentives do hospitals or physicians have to develop innovative, less costly delivery systems, such as managed care, outpatient diagnostics and surgery, or home infusion programs, if the funds must be taken from existing programs and providers? Efficient providers are penalized if they cannot increase expenditures to expand, and patients lose the opportunity to be served by more efficient providers.

To remain within their overall budgets, hospitals will undertake actions that decrease efficiency and access to care. Hospitals adjust to stringent budget limits by keeping patients longer, as this requires fewer resources than does performing procedures on more patients. Strict budget limits will result in greater delays in admitting patients, and patients will have less access to beneficial but costly technology. Hospitals in the Netherlands under their previous global budget payment system (now changed to a more price-competitive system) typically reached the end of their budget in late fall and consequently sharply reduced accepting new admissions, causing long waiting times.

Global budgets are based on the assumption that the government knows exactly the right amount of medical expenditures for the nation. However, a correct percentage of GDP that should be spent on medical care has never been determined, and the fact that other countries spend less than the United States does not tell us which country we should emulate or what we should forgo. Medical expenditures increase for many reasons. No accurate information exists as to how much of the rise in expenditures is attributable to waste, new diseases, an aging population, and new technology. The quality of healthcare will deteriorate, and long waiting times for treatment will result if price controls and global budgets are set too low.

In 1997, Medicare's payment system to physicians was based on the premise that total Medicare physician expenditures should be tied to growth in the economy (adjusted for the number of Medicare beneficiaries), termed the sustainable growth rate (SGR). Even Congress admits that the SGR payment system is badly flawed and has consistently refused to implement the formula's payment reductions.

Whether politicians would permit a strict global budget to continue in the face of shortages and complaints about access to medical services is doubtful. More likely, politicians would respond to their constituents' complaints and relax the budget limit. This has in fact occurred in other countries when access to medical services became too limited because of price controls and global budgets. Great Britain, for example, permits "buyouts." A private medical market is allowed to develop, and those with higher incomes who can afford to buy private medical insurance jump the queue to receive medical services from private providers. To the extent that buyouts are permitted, medical expenditures will increase more rapidly, and a two-tier system will evolve. If a buyout is envisaged, the rationale for price controls and global budgets is questionable.

Summary

Price controls and global budgets provide the appearance of controlling rising prices and expenditures, but in reality, they lead to cheating and a reduction in quality, impose large costs on patients and providers, and do little to improve efficiency.

If the purpose of regulation is to improve efficiency, eliminate inappropriate services, and decrease the costly duplication of medical technology, government policies should provide incentives to achieve these goals. Such incentives are more likely to occur in a system in which purchasers make cost-conscious choices and providers must compete for those purchasers. Competitive systems provide both purchasers and providers with incentives to weigh the benefits and costs of new medical technology. When patients are willing to pay not to wait and to have access to new technology, medical expenditures will increase faster, but the rate of increase will be more appropriate.

Discussion Questions

1. Why do price controls cause shortages, and why do these shortages increase over time?
2. Why do price controls require hospitals to make a trade-off between quality of medical services and number of patients served?
3. What are the various ways in which a provider can game the system under price controls?
4. What "costs" do price controls impose on patients?
5. What are the advantages and disadvantages of permitting patients to "buy out" of the price-controlled medical system?

Notes

1. For a more complete discussion of this subject, see Haislmaier (1993).
2. The Fraser Institute (www.fraserinstitute.ca) collects data annually on waiting times in each of the Canadian provinces by procedure and on waiting time for a referral from a general practitioner to a specialist.
3. In 1991, Japanese physicians saw an average of 49 patients a day, and 13 percent saw 100 patients a day (Ikegami 1991). The US average was 22 patients per day in 1996. A more recent study (Ohtaki, Ohtaki, and Fetters 2003) analyzed the amount of time spent by Japanese and US physicians and found that Japanese physicians spent 30 percent less time with each patient.

THE EVOLUTION OF MANAGED CARE

An important policy debate concerns the organization and delivery of medical services—namely, should this country rely on regulation or on market competition to achieve efficiency in the provision of medical services? Market competition can take different forms; one was the emergence and rapid growth of managed care organizations during the 1980s and 1990s. What effect has managed care competition had? Has managed care improved efficiency and reduced the rate of increase in medical expenditures? What happened to patient satisfaction and quality of care? To discuss these issues, we must discuss what is meant by "managed care," why it came about, the evidence on how well it has performed, how it is evolving, and the recent development of consumer-driven healthcare (CDHC).

Why Managed Care Came About

Managed care was a market response to the wasteful excesses of the past, which resulted in rapidly rising medical costs in a system widely believed to be inefficient. Traditional indemnity health insurance, with its comprehensive coverage of hospitals and small patient copayments for medical services, lessened patient concerns with hospital and medical expenses. Physicians were paid on a fee-for-service basis and were not fiscally responsible for hospital use, which they prescribed. New medical technology was introduced rapidly because the insurer paid for its use and cost; insurers merely passed the higher cost on to employers.

The lack of incentives for insurers, patients, physicians, and hospitals to concern themselves with cost led to their rapid rise. Insured patients demanded "too many" services, physicians paid fee-for-service had an incentive to supply more services, and hospitals competed for physicians by making available to them the latest technology so their patients would not have to be referred to other hospitals and physicians. Advances in medical technology and the lack of cost incentives led to non-price competition among hospitals; technology was adopted no matter how small its medical benefits or how infrequently it would be used. This led not only to higher costs but also to lower quality, as studies demonstrated that hospitals that performed fewer complex procedures had worse outcomes than hospitals that performed more such procedures (Hughes, Hunt, and Luft 1987).

As large employers sought to reduce the rapid increases in health insurance premiums, physicians, hospitals, and traditional health insurers were not responsive to their cost concerns. Instead, entrepreneurs recognized the potential for reducing medical system inefficiencies and started HMOs, utilization review firms, and preferred provider organizations (PPOs). These innovators, who aggressively marketed their approaches to large employers, were richly rewarded for their efforts.

What Is Managed Care?

Managed care embodies a variety of techniques and types of organizations. Financial incentives, negotiation of large provider discounts, limited provider networks, physician gatekeepers, utilization management, and drug formularies are some of these techniques.

Managed care health plans were successful in interfering with the traditional physician–patient relationship because employees were willing to switch from traditional insurers in return for lower premiums. Managed care plans contracted with those physicians and hospitals willing to discount their prices, which was a precondition for joining the plan's limited provider network. Since physicians and hospitals had excess capacity in the 1980s and 1990s, they were willing to discount their prices in return for increased patient volume (Wu 2009). The patient's choice of physician was restricted to those in the plan's provider panel, as were the specialists to whom the patient could be referred and the hospitals in which the patient could stay. Decisions about whether to hospitalize a patient, length of stay, specialist referrals, and types of drugs prescribed—formerly made by the physician—were now influenced by the managed care plan.

Managed care techniques have changed over time. First-generation approaches were quite restrictive. Managed care plans relied on selective contracting, which limits the provider panel to those who are willing to discount their prices and are appropriate users of medical services, a gatekeeper model, and stringent utilization review. An enrollee in a managed care plan chose a primary care physician from among a panel of physicians who would manage that patient's care and control diagnostic and specialist referrals (this is the gatekeeper model). The primary care physician would often do some tasks previously performed by specialists. Utilization review includes prior authorization for hospital admission, concurrent review (i.e., the patient's length of stay is reviewed to make sure the stay does not exceed what is medically necessary), and retrospective review (to ensure that appropriate care was provided).

The initial sources of managed care savings were lower hospital use (the most expensive component of care) and deep provider price discounts. The HMOs were able to shift large numbers of their enrollees to those providers who competed to be included in the HMO's provider panel and were able to achieve cost savings relatively easily and without changing the practice of medicine.

To achieve further reductions in medical costs, managed care had to become more innovative and effective in managing patient care. So-called second-generation managed care approaches rely more on changing physicians' practice patterns, such as identifying high-risk enrollees early, decreasing the variation in physicians' utilization patterns, reducing inappropriate use of services, and substituting less costly in-home services for continued care in the hospital. They also are relying more on evidence-based medicine to achieve their savings. Access to large data sets on physicians' treatment patterns from around the country and information technology to analyze those data allow health plans to determine which treatment decisions have better outcomes. Integrated and coordinated care and disease management can decrease medical costs and improve patient outcomes.

Some managed care plans (particularly in California) have shifted more of the capitation payment, hence risk, to physicians and hospitals; providers are thereby given an incentive to innovate in the delivery of medical services. Furthermore, with the shifting of risk from employers to HMOs, large employers place greater emphasis on report cards. Because managed care plans and their providers have a financial incentive to provide fewer services under capitation, both the plans and their providers have to be continuously monitored for patient satisfaction and medical outcomes. Health plans and their providers are being held accountable for the health status of their enrolled populations.

Types of Managed Care Plans

Managed care health plans vary in the degree to which they use a select network of providers and limit access to specialists. Typically, the more restrictive the managed care plan, the lower its premium. The most restrictive type of managed care plan is an HMO, which offers the most comprehensive health benefits. An HMO relies on a restricted provider network, and the patient is responsible for the full costs of going to non-network providers. Cost control by an HMO is achieved through stringent utilization management, financial incentives to physicians, and limited access to providers.

Managed fee-for-service indemnity insurance plans include a PPO, which is a closed provider panel. Providers are paid fee-for-service, and enrollees have a financial incentive (lower copayment) to use the PPO providers versus going out of network. Costs are controlled through utilization management, patient copayments, and discounted fees from PPO providers.

Specialist referrals also vary. In an HMO, the primary care physician must recommend specialist referrals. In a PPO the patient may self-refer to a specialist, but the copayment is lower if the specialist is in the PPO.

Traditional HMOs began to offer a point-of-service option in the early 1990s to counter the growing popularity of PPOs. A point-of-service plan is an HMO that permits its enrollees to use nonparticipating providers if the enrollees are willing to pay a high copayment (e.g., 40 percent) each time they use such providers.

Exhibit 19.1 shows, for the working population, the market share of each type of managed care plan and how that share has changed over time. In the early 1980s, managed care was just beginning to grow. Traditional indemnity insurance, with free access to all providers ("unmanaged care"), was the dominant form (95 percent) of health insurance. Since that time, the distribution of different types of health plans has changed rapidly. By 2010, traditional insurance had virtually disappeared, and various types of managed care had become the predominant form of insurance.

The premium in a typical managed care plan is allocated as shown in Exhibit 19.2. In this example, the ABC Managed Care Health Plan retains 15 percent of the premium to cover expenses associated with marketing, administration, and profit. About 35 percent of the premium is allocated for hospital and other medical facility expenses, 40 percent is set aside for physician services, and 10 percent is allocated for pharmacy and ancillary services. Use of services by enrollees outside the plan's area and certain catastrophic expenses may also be included in the health plan's retained 15 percent.

Providers within each of these budgetary allocations may be paid in several ways. Some managed care plans (e.g., Kaiser Health Plan) place their physicians on a salary, others pay discounted fee-for-service, and still others capitate their physicians. (Capitation means to pay an annual amount to the physician group for each enrollee for whom they are responsible. Capitated medical groups are primarily found in California.) Within each of these payment arrangements, the organization that is at financial risk withholds a certain percentage of the budget allocated to the providers to ensure that sufficient funds are available to provide all the necessary services. Funds remaining at the end of the year are divided among the members of that provider group.

When medical groups and hospitals are capitated, a shared risk pool exists between them. Part of the hospital's capitated payment is set aside to be shared between the hospital and medical group to provide the medical group with an incentive to reduce use of the hospital.

Exhibit 19.1 The Trend Toward Managed Care

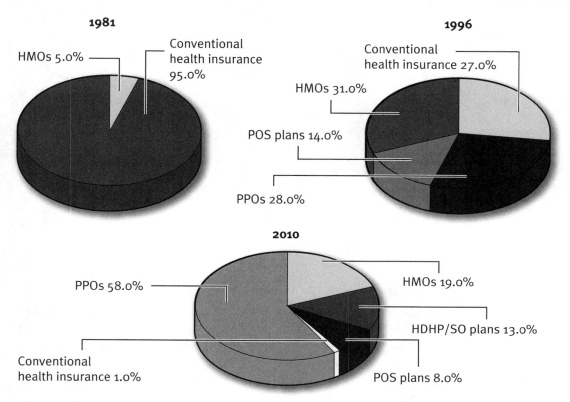

Health Maintenance Organization (HMO): An organization that provides comprehensive healthcare services to a voluntarily enrolled membership for a prepaid fee. HMOs control costs through stringent utilization management, payment incentives to its physicians, and restricted access to its providers.

Preferred Provider Organization (PPO): A third-party payer contracts with a group of medical providers that agrees to furnish services at negotiated fees in return for prompt payment and increased patient volume. PPOs control costs by keeping fees down and curbing excessive service through utilization management.

Point-of-Service (POS): An HMO that permits its enrollees access to nonparticipating providers if the enrollees are willing to pay a high copayment each time they use such providers.

Conventional Health Insurance: Patients are permitted to go to any provider and the provider is paid fee-for-service. The patient normally pays a small annual deductible plus 20 percent of the provider's charge, up to an annual out-of-pocket limit of $3,000.

High-Deductible Health Plan with Savings Option (HDHP/SO): A consumer-driven health plan that works like a PPO plan with in-network and out-of-network benefits for covered services. Patients can see a specialist without a referral. Selection of a primary care physician is not required. An HDHP plan has higher annual deductibles and out-of-pocket maximums but lower premiums. Patients with HDHP plans are able to set up a tax-deductible health savings account.

SOURCES: Kaiser Family Foundation and Health Research and Educational Trust, *Employer Health Benefits 2010 Annual Survey.* http://ehbs.kff.org/pdf/2010/8085.pdf; *KPMG Survey of Employer-Sponsored Health Benefits:* 1981, 1990.

Exhibit 19.2
How an HMO
Allocates the
Premium
Dollar

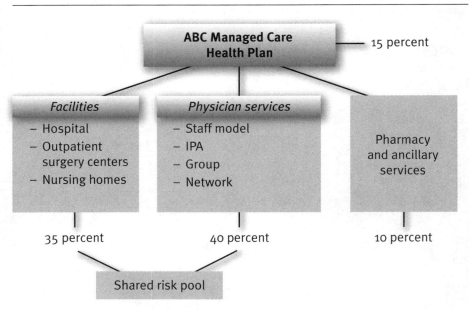

Types of HMOs

Staff model: An HMO that delivers health services through a physician group that is controlled by the HMO unit.

Independent practice association (IPA): An HMO that contracts directly with physicians in independent practices.

Group: An HMO that contracts with one independent group practice to provide health services.

Network: An HMO that contracts with two or more independent group practices.

How Has Managed Care Performed?

Managed care did not spread equally to all parts of the country or to all population groups. It moved more rapidly into those areas that had high healthcare costs, where the potential for cost reductions was greatest. Managed care plans were more likely to enter urban than rural areas. The West, particularly California, introduced managed care earlier and had a greater percentage of its population enrolled in managed care than did the East or Southeast. Those employed in large firms moved more rapidly into managed care than did those on Medicare and Medicaid, who had limited price incentives to enroll in managed care plans.

A significant portion of the population is still not subject to managed care. As of 2009, 24 percent of the 47 million aged were in managed care plans (referred to as Medicare Advantage plans) (Henry J. Kaiser Family Foundation and HRET 2010). In 2009, 48 million people were uninsured.

Only since the early 2000s has Medicaid managed care increased. By 2009, 72 percent of the 50.5 million on Medicaid were in managed care. Therefore, about 104 million, or 32 percent of the population, is not in managed care and instead relies on the unmanaged fee-for-service system.

To determine the performance of managed care competition, we must examine the population groups subject to managed care, namely the remaining 68 percent of the population. (For example, using total healthcare expenditures, which include Medicare and Medicaid, rather than employer-paid health insurance premiums, will not provide as accurate a description of the effect of managed care.)

The Issue of Biased Selection

Managed care plans initially attracted younger enrollees, persons new to an area, and fewer persons who were chronically ill—people who did not have long-standing physician relationships. If HMOs and managed care plans enrolled a healthier population group, a comparison of their performance relative to traditional health insurers would be biased. Better health outcomes and lower healthcare costs in an HMO would be more related to the population enrolled than to its performance. Thus, crucial to any study determining whether managed care plans are better at controlling growth in costs and improving treatment outcomes is the ability to control for lower-risk groups enrolled in managed care.

A large number and wide variety of studies have been conducted on the performance of HMOs, managed care plans, and traditional insurers (Glied 2000). Following is a brief summary of the results of these studies (which have controlled for biased selection).

Rise in Health Insurance Premiums

Managed care competition worked in the following manner. As managed care plans entered a market and enrolled a significant number of members, hospitals and physicians competed on price to be included in the managed care plan's provider network. Given their excess capacity and need for more patients, providers were also willing to accept utilization review, which decreases hospital use. These cost savings (discounted prices and lower hospital use rates) enabled the managed care plan to lower its premium relative to those of non–managed care health plans. When employees are required to pay the additional cost of more expensive health plans, studies show that premium differences as small as $5 to $10 a month will cause 25 percent of a health plan's employees to switch (Buchmueller and Feldstein 1996). Employees are very price sensitive. Health plans therefore have to be very price competitive.

To prevent further losses in their market share, indemnity, non–managed care insurers adopted managed care techniques, such as utilization review and PPOs, to limit the rise in their premiums. Managed care plans not only reduced their own medical costs but, by their competitive effect, forced other insurers to adopt managed care techniques to reduce their costs and remain price competitive.

Managed care competition dramatically slowed the rise in health insurance premiums. Exhibit 19.3 shows the national trend in employer-paid health insurance premiums and the annual percentage change in the Consumer Price Index (CPI). Also included are premium data from California, where managed care competition started earlier and was more extensive than in the rest of the country. Clearly, as managed care market share increased (see Exhibit 19.1), insurance premiums rose more slowly. (In California, the managed care effect was even more pronounced; it occurred earlier and included a greater percentage of the population. For several years, health insurance premiums in California actually declined.)

A major source of the early savings from managed care was reduced hospital use, which is shown in Exhibit 19.4. Hospital patient days per 1,000 population declined from 1,302 in 1977 to 628 by 2009. Also shown is the earlier and larger decline in hospital use rates in California; rates there declined from 996 to 476 per 1,000 population over that same period. New York, which had a hospital use rate higher than the national average, also saw a decline, although at 894 in 2009 it was still much higher than the national average and almost twice as high as in California.

Hospital admissions per 1,000 population have also fallen, although not as dramatically as patient days. Admission rates in 1978 were 162 nationally, 147 in New York, and 141 in California. By 2009, these rates had declined to 116, 130, and 93, respectively.

As a consequence of managed care, hospitals' share of total medical expenditures declined. The decline in hospital use rates that occurred in California indicates the reductions in hospital use that are still possible in other parts of the country.

One-Time Versus Continual Cost Savings

Managed care achieved the easiest cost reductions, such as decreased hospital days, substitution of less costly settings for costly inpatient stays, and lower provider prices. These reductions, however, are one-time cost savings, although they occur over a period of years and are instituted at different times in different parts of the country. An important policy question is whether managed care competition is only able to produce these one-time savings or whether it can achieve continual cost reductions.

The two most important factors that determine the rate at which medical expenditures will increase are demographics—an older population has

EXHIBIT 19.3 Annual Percentage Increase in Health Insurance Premiums for the United States, California, and the CPI, 1988–2010

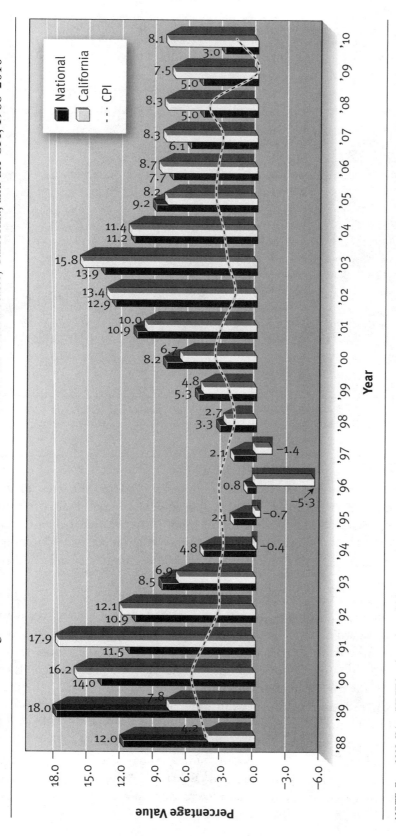

NOTE: From 2008, Kaiser/HRET has changed a method to report the US annual percent premium increase. Prior to 2008, percent increase was calculated as the average of percent changes in premium for a family of four in the largest plan of each plan type. From 2008, percent increase reflects the overall percent increase in premium for family coverage using the average of the premium dollar amounts for a family of four in the largest plan of each plan type and weighted by covered workers.

SOURCES: National data: 1988–2007, 2007 *Kaiser/HRET Employer Health Benefits Survey.* http://www.kff.org/insurance/7672/upload/7693.pdf; 2008–2010 data from *Kaiser/HRET Employer Health Benefits Survey, 2008, 2009, and 2010.* http://ehbs.kff.org/pdf/7790.pdf, http://ehbs.kff.org/pdf/2009/7936.pdf, and http://ehbs.kff.org/pdf/2010/8085.pdf; California data: CALPERS (California Public Employees Retirement System) and CHCF California Employer Health Benefits Survey: 2010. http://www.chcf.org/~/media/Files/PDF/E/PDF%20EmployerBenefitsSurvey10.pdf; CPI data: Bureau of Labor Statistics. 2011. http://www.bls.gov.

EXHIBIT 19.4 Trends in Hospital Utilization per 1,000 Population: United States, California, and New York, 1977–2009

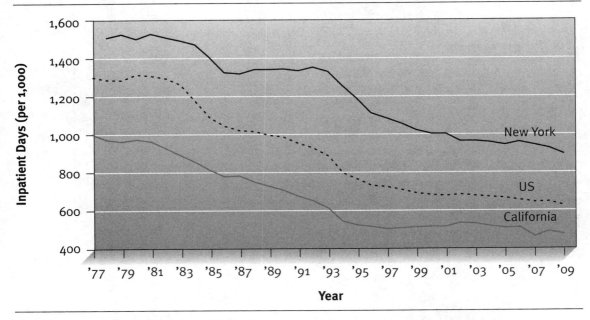

SOURCES: Population data from US Census Bureau, http://www.census.gov. Data as of July 1, except 1980, 1990, and 2000, as of April 1. Utilization figures from American Hospital Association. 2011. *Hospital Statistics*, various years. Chicago: Health Forum LLC, an affiliate of the AHA.

more costly care needs—and the development and adoption of new medical technology. Whether managed care is able to achieve continual cost reductions will depend on whether it is able to innovate in the management of care of the aged and the chronically ill and whether it can reduce the rate of new technology diffusion while encouraging the development of cost-reducing technology.

Under unmanaged fee-for-service indemnity insurance, new technology was adopted as long as it provided some additional benefit, no matter how small, regardless of its cost. There was little financial incentive to develop cost-reducing technology. For managed care to produce continual savings, new technology must be justified on its costs as well as its benefits. To the extent that investment in technology can be directed to reducing the use of more costly procedures, using less invasive procedures, enabling care to be provided in the home or an outpatient setting, and preventing the need for costly acute care, continual reductions in medical costs are possible.[1]

Based on a limited number of studies, managed care slowed the rate at which new technology was adopted (Baker and Wheeler 1998). Furthermore, as managed care penetration increased in an area, capacity use of the equipment increased; consequently, fewer facilities were needed than under the unmanaged fee-for-service system. Managed care appears to have been able to achieve continual reductions in the cost of medical care.

Managed care achieved one of the main goals it was meant to accomplish: It reduced the rise in healthcare expenditures. Without managed care, insurance premiums would have increased more rapidly. Higher insurance premiums make health insurance less affordable; consequently, the number of uninsured would have been greater because the demand for insurance is inversely related to its price. Furthermore, the lower rate of increase in insurance premiums resulted in a redistribution of income from hospitals and physicians (an important reason for their opposition to managed care) to employees. Lower health insurance premiums meant that employees had greater take-home pay. Lower premiums also meant, however, that less revenue was available for physicians, hospitals employed fewer people, and their wages increased more slowly.

Patient Satisfaction and Quality of Care

An evaluation of managed care performance should be broader than just examining whether it results in lower insurance premiums. Managed care competition (and any system for organizing the delivery of medical services) should also be evaluated on whether it promotes efficiency (the rate at which premiums increase), desired treatment outcomes, and patient satisfaction (Glied 2000).

Many studies have examined member satisfaction in managed care plans, such as HMOs and non-HMOs (Glied 2000). (These studies typically compare the most restrictive form of managed care, an HMO, to less restrictive forms or to non–managed care insurance plans.) Measures of member satisfaction typically include waiting times for an appointment, referrals to a specialist, and travel times to a panel provider. These results typically show a high degree of member satisfaction in HMOs. Such studies, however, have limited usefulness because most people do not have health problems and therefore do not make costly demands on the HMO.

More recent surveys attempt to measure patient satisfaction by those who are chronically ill and have serious health problems. Such studies have examined access to care by those with low incomes, those who are HIV positive, and those who are chronically ill. The results of these studies are mixed. Either there are no significant differences between the health plans, or in some HMOs patient satisfaction is better, whereas in others it is not. On one hand, in traditional unmanaged health plans, the patient has easier access to specialists and fewer restrictions on hospital use. In managed care plans, however, coordination of care is better for those with chronic illness; otherwise a chronically ill patient can be hospitalized multiple times, increasing the managed care plan's costs. Early managed care plans were not experienced in caring for those with chronic illness, and as a result of anecdotal stories of access problems, regulatory restrictions were placed on managed care plans; this has since changed in most managed care plans.

With regard to quality of care in managed care versus traditional insurance, the empirical literature suggests little difference between the two. Some studies indicate that traditional insurance may perform better for those who have serious health conditions, particularly those with low incomes. Given the large number of managed care plans and the different types of such plans, generalizations as to whether one type of health plan results in greater or worse patient satisfaction and treatment outcomes are difficult to make. How the providers are paid (fee-for-service, salary, or capitation), who is at financial risk, the type of decision-making structure, and the managed care culture of the medical group are likely to be more important determinants of patient satisfaction and outcomes than the type of health plan.

To the extent that risk-adjusted premiums are used to pay for high-risk patients and those who have serious illnesses, a higher capitation rate paid by the employer to the health plan for such groups provides managed care plans with an incentive to compete for such patients, improve their access to care, and innovate in devising new treatment methods. An example of these types of managed care plans are Medicare demonstration projects that pay such firms risk-adjusted premiums to care for special-needs populations, such as frail elderly. The HMO has an incentive to provide the necessary services, including preventive care, to keep their enrollees in the community rather than admitted to nursing homes.

The Change in Managed Care

Managed care underwent a change starting in the late 1990s. Several events occurred that resulted in a loosening of managed care's more restrictive cost-containment measures.

Economic Prosperity of the 1990s
In the late 1990s, the US economy was expanding, the stock market was reaching new highs, dot-com companies were the craze, and firms had difficulty attracting and retaining skilled employees. In that prosperous period, employees wanted health plans that were less restrictive on specialist referrals and that offered broader provider networks. Given the tight labor market, employers were more concerned with keeping their employees than with the costs of healthcare; employers were willing to pay higher insurance premiums for more generous health plans. Enrollment growth in HMOs, the most restrictive type of plan, began to decline, and PPO plans became more popular.

As health plans restructured themselves to accommodate employees' demands, the health plans had more difficulty controlling medical costs. Changing from limited to broad provider networks meant that health plans had less leverage over the provider to negotiate large price discounts. The removal of physician gatekeepers meant an increase in self-referrals to specialists and more procedures. Less utilization review by health plans also led to greater use of medical services. Greater use of specialists, more procedures, and reliance on fee-for-service payment over a broad provider network not only made coordinating and monitoring patient care more difficult but also increased the cost of care and, consequently, premiums.

Furthermore, to the extent that managed care plans have broader provider networks and providers participate in multiple health plans, holding the health plan accountable for the performance of its providers is difficult. Similarly, a single health plan has difficulty collecting data from providers, monitoring their performance, and changing their practice patterns. The broader the provider network and the fewer the restrictions on specialist referrals, the less control health plans have over providers.

Higher Prices for Hospitals, Physicians, and Prescription Drugs

The industry structure was also changing during the late 1990s. To improve their bargaining power with fewer but larger health plans, hospitals and physicians began merging and consolidating into fewer, larger organizations. Hospital mergers within a market meant fewer competitors among which the health plan could negotiate discounts. Also, excess capacity among hospitals was reduced as a result of hospital closures and mergers. Hospitals were therefore able to charge the health plans higher prices. Drug costs began to increase sharply as new, more effective drugs became available and pharmaceutical companies were successful in stimulating demand with direct-to-consumer advertising. Health plans had to increase their premiums to pay for these higher costs.

Regulation of Managed Care

By the end of the 1990s, a backlash by providers and patients forced many managed care plans to abandon the strict cost-containment methods, such as gatekeepers and specialist referral requirements, and adopt less-restrictive options. Increased government regulation of managed care occurred for several reasons:

- Widespread media attention was given to certain cases of denial of care by HMOs.
- The public wanted increased access to specialists (without paying more).
- The American Medical Association wanted to redress the balance of power between managed care plans and physicians; physicians' bargaining power would be increased if limited provider networks could be

opened to all physicians, thereby allowing patients greater choice of physician ("any willing provider" laws).

- Some were opposed to managed care because they wanted a single-payer system and regulation would eliminate managed care's success in reducing medical costs.

Legislators saw an opportunity to gain visibility by holding hearings on HMO practices and receive the public's support by enacting legislation making certain managed care practices (e.g., outpatient mastectomies and "drive-through deliveries") illegal.

Legislators did not discuss the trade-offs between legislating freer access to care and the increased premiums that would result. The public was led to believe increased access would come at no additional cost, and Congress and the states increased regulation. To the extent that government intervenes in the practice of medicine (establishing minimum lengths of stay and determining which procedures can be performed in an outpatient setting) and regulates how managed care plans structure their delivery systems, treatment innovation is inhibited and health insurance premiums will increase by more than they would otherwise.

In October 1999, a class-action lawsuit requesting billions of dollars in damages was filed against a managed care firm (Humana), alleging that by using cost-containment methods the firm reneged on its promise to pay for all medically necessary care. Although the lawsuit was dismissed three years later, along with similar suits against other managed care plans, managed care plans relaxed their cost-containment methods.

Recent Developments in Managed Care

As managed care's stringent cost-containment methods and limited provider networks were loosened, premiums began increasing rapidly in the late 1990s. Employers and their employees once again became concerned with rising premiums. Employers started shifting a greater portion of the insurance premium to their employees and pressured managed care firms to better control rising healthcare costs.

New Cost-Containment Approaches

Managed care's cost-control approaches have evolved from restricting access to developing innovative approaches for managing care and reducing medical costs. Approaches being used today include the early management of diseases such as diabetes, hypertension, and congestive heart failure, as these diseases can lead to catastrophic medical expenses (Villagra 2004). Managing chronic illness includes developing clinical guidelines or protocols, clinical integration and coordination of care, and early identification and treatment of high-risk patients. With the aging of the population, managed care firms are learning how to manage chronic care needs for which they are at financial risk.

Assisting in the development of innovative approaches are computer information systems and large databases, which can revolutionize treatment patterns (known as "evidence-based medicine"). Large data sets that track specific diseases over long periods will enable providers to determine which variations in treatment methods have the most desired patient outcomes; this information could be used to promote changes in physicians' practice patterns. Information technology and large amounts of data will also enable managers to increase efficiency by better understanding their enrollees' medical costs as well as improve clinical outcomes and quality of care. Provider performance will be evaluated in terms of patient outcomes, satisfaction, and cost of care.

In addition to these approaches, some managed care plans have re-instituted some previously used methods, such as pre-approval for certain surgical procedures and specialist referrals (Mays, Claxton, and White 2004). As a means of reducing their premiums some HMOs are also returning to the use of narrow provider panels (Hughes 2010).

Report Cards

Previously, consumers had little or no information by which to judge the quality of different providers or the quality of care they received. The development of managed care made it possible to evaluate patient satisfaction and treatment outcomes of enrolled population groups. By having limited provider panels of physicians and hospitals, together with a defined group of enrollees, a managed care plan is able to develop information on the practice patterns of and patient satisfaction with its providers and the care received by its enrollees.

Under pressure from employer coalitions for more information by which their employees can judge different managed care plans and their participating providers, managed care plans have provided data to independent organizations for developing report cards. These report cards include information on patient satisfaction, quality process measures, and outcomes data on health plans and their participating providers. When these report cards are made available to employees during open enrollment periods, the additional information influences their choice of health plan (Kolstad and Chernew 2009). Public information increases the pressure on health plans and their providers to compete on satisfaction and outcome measures as well as on premiums. Employees can then make a more informed trade-off between lower premiums and desirable plan characteristics.

Pay for Performance

Incentive-based provider payments, referred to as *pay for performance,* began around 2000. Insurers typically pay physicians and hospitals for providing services, and little if any attempt has been made to reward providers who provide higher-quality services or who reduce treatment costs. This is beginning to change. Although quality of medical care is difficult to measure, medical experts agree that certain standards should be met for preventive care and specified diagnoses (Rosenthal et al. 2005). Although the measures used for incentive payments are not standardized across different health plans, three types of measures are being used: (1) clinical quality, including childhood immunization rates, breast cancer and cervical cancer screening rates, and measures related to the management of chronic diseases, such as diabetes and asthma; (2) patient satisfaction measures; and (3) measures related to investment in information technology that enables clinical data integration.

The pay-for-performance experiments have been started by those managed care plans having a large market share (and therefore greater bargaining power over their providers). Incentive payments paid to providers represent 1 to 5 percent of a provider's total revenue. Pay for performance is still in its early stages. Medical societies have generally been opposed on grounds that the quality measures are not fully developed, and that there is an implication that providers are not providing high-quality care. Although these incentive payments have been widely adopted by health plans, studies examining their impact have found mixed results depending on the size of the incentive bonus, the competitiveness of the market, and the financial situation of participating providers (Werner et al. 2011). Pay-for-performance programs will continue to evolve; the size of the incentive payment will likely increase, standards for judging providers will become uniform across health plans, and medical groups will have to invest more in information technology to be able to provide the data by which they will be measured.

Consumer-Driven Healthcare

An approach gaining in popularity for lowering rising insurance premiums is CDHC. More of the financial risk and responsibility for controlling cost, such as seeking lower provider prices and using fewer services, is placed on the consumer. A CDHC plan relies on a large-deductible insurance policy, making the enrollee responsible for large out-of-pocket payments. The Medicare Modernization Act of 2003 provided tax advantages to employees who establish health savings accounts (HSAs). An HSA has two parts: the first is a high-deductible health insurance policy; the second is a tax-free savings account for the employee, to which her contribution can be as large as the size of her deductible. Each year, funds in the savings account that are not spent on medical services can be accumulated. When the employee retires, the accumulated funds and the earnings on those funds belong to the employee.

A number of websites provide information on hospital and physician quality rankings and prices for different treatments to help employees with high-deductible plans choose their providers.

About 10 million people have CDHC plans, and they are achieving greater acceptance among employees. Enrollment in managed care plans appears to have stabilized, and more managed care plans have begun marketing CDHC plans. Managed care plans are also partnering with financial institutions to manage the tax-free savings accounts. Evidence on CDHC plans indicate that they are associated with lower costs and lower cost increases; however, some studies suggest that CDHC plans may also attract healthier enrollees (Buntin et al. 2011; GAO 2010).

Accountable Care Organizations

As part of the 2010 Patient Protection and Affordable Care Act alternative methods of paying healthcare providers under Medicare were proposed. One such approach, to start in 2012, would encourage providers to organize as accountable care organizations (ACOs), which would provide primary care, specialty services, and inpatient care for a defined population of Medicare beneficiaries. An ACO and its physicians would be responsible for the overall care of their Medicare beneficiaries, have adequate participation of primary care physicians, provide coordinated care, promote evidence-based medicine, and report on their quality and costs of care. ACOs that meet their quality and cost thresholds would share in the cost savings they achieve for the Medicare program.

ACOs are an undeveloped concept. The regulations on the structure of ACOs, performance guidelines, payments, and cost-sharing arrangements with Medicare are in the process of being determined. There is also concern that combinations of multiple hospitals and physician groups, if they are permitted to form large ACOs, may lessen competition, thereby increasing prices to the private sector. The hope is that ACOs will transform not only the Medicare system but also the delivery of medical services to the private sector, improving the quality of care and reducing rising medical costs. ACOs are a new attempt at strengthening managed care by encouraging hospitals and physicians to join together, align hospital and physician incentives, and provide coordinated care. Whether the incentives for forming ACOs prove successful remains to be seen.

Summary

As a consequence of the economic prosperity that led to employee demands for less restrictive health plans in the 1990s, hospital mergers and physician consolidations that led to higher provider prices, increased drug prices, regulations imposed on managed care plans, and advances in medical technology, health insurance premiums once again began to increase sharply. Managed care plans have demonstrated less ability to control costs today than they had previously.

Employers and employees are searching for new approaches to limit their premium increases. Employers are shifting more of the insurance premium to their employees, and health plans are developing new cost-containment strategies, such as disease management and evidence-based medicine. Under pressure from employers, health plans are using report cards to enable employees to make more informed choices of health plans and participating providers. Health plans are also beginning to use incentive-based payment to encourage their participating providers to improve quality of care, patient satisfaction, and the use of information technology to integrate clinical data.

A recent trend affecting the growth of managed care plans is CDHC. These high-deductible plans, sold at lower premiums, shift more of the financial risk to consumers and require them to become more informed about their purchases of healthcare services and their choice of providers.

The market is responding to rising premiums by offering a variety of health plans, as consumers have different preferences and abilities to pay. Increased emphasis is being placed on consumer cost sharing to hold down costs and use of services.

Discussion Questions

1. What is managed care, and what are managed care techniques?
2. When managed care enrollment increases in a market, how does it affect other insurers and providers?
3. Why did managed care occur?
4. What are the different types of managed care plans?
5. What are report cards, and what effects are they expected to have on managed care competition?
6. How has the growth of managed care affected the performance of the medical sector?

Additional Reading

Dranove, D. 2000. *The Economic Evolution of American Health Care: From Marcus Welby to Managed Care.* Princeton, NJ: Princeton University Press.

Note

1. On balance, new technology has led to increased, not decreased, medical expenditures. However, increased medical expenditures resulting from new technology are not the same as inflation in medical costs. The medical treatment the patient receives is different and improved. Furthermore, as long as the public is willing to pay for those increased benefits, it is appropriate for medical costs to increase.

HAS COMPETITION BEEN TRIED—AND HAS IT FAILED—TO IMPROVE THE US HEALTHCARE SYSTEM?

Critics claim that market competition has been tried but it has failed to improve the US healthcare system. Once again, healthcare costs are rising rapidly, per capita healthcare spending is the highest in the world, and yet more than 15 percent of Americans—about 48 million people—are without health insurance. More of the middle class are finding that health insurance has become too expensive, life expectancy is lower than in other countries, and the US infant mortality rate is higher than in some countries with lower per capita healthcare expenditures. In other words, is it time to try something different? Specifically, is it time for more government regulation and control of the healthcare system?

"Some say that competition has failed, I say that competition has not yet been tried." Alain Enthoven (1993, 28) wrote that statement in 1993, and it continues to be correct today.

This chapter discusses how medical markets differ from competitive markets, why making medical markets more competitive is desirable, the changes needed to bring about greater competition, whether competitive markets are responsible for the growing numbers of uninsured, and the role of government in a competitive medical care environment.

Criteria for Judging Performance of a Country's Medical Sector

The health of a population, as measured by life expectancy or infant mortality rates, is not solely the consequence of the country's medical system. How people live and eat are more important determinants of life expectancy than whether they have good access to medical services once they become ill. Life expectancy is related to a number of factors, such as smoking, diet, marital status, exercise, drug use, and cultural values. Although universal access to health insurance is desirable, studies have shown that medical care has a smaller effect on health levels than personal health habits and lifestyle (see Chapter 3).

Therefore, it is inappropriate to compare the medical care system on measures that are more affected by lifestyle factors. After all, the financing and delivery of medical services has been based on treating people once they are ill, not on keeping them well. Several healthcare organizations in the United States have gone beyond treating people when they become ill and have tried to lower costs by preventing illnesses that are expensive to treat. Reducing hip fractures among the elderly and instituting monitoring mechanisms for diabetes patients, for example, have been shown to prevent more costly treatments later. The financial incentives of these organizations differ from the typical fee-for-service payment methods predominantly used in the United States and other countries.

Assuming the purpose of a medical care system is more narrowly defined, that is, treating those who become ill, what criteria should be used to evaluate how well that system performs? The criteria should be the same as those used to evaluate the performance of other markets, such as housing, food, automobiles, and electronics—markets that produce necessities and luxuries. The following are performance criteria of a medical care system.

1. *Information:* Do consumers have sufficient information to choose the quantity and type of services based on price, quality, and other characteristics of the services being supplied?
2. *Consumer incentives:* Do consumers have incentives to ensure that the value of the services used is not less than the cost of producing those services?
3. *Consumer choices:* Does the market respond to what consumers are willing to pay? If consumers demand more of some services, will the market provide more of those services? If consumers differ in how much they are willing to spend or want different types of services, will the market respond to those varied consumer demands?
4. *Supplier incentives:* Do the suppliers of the goods and services have an incentive to produce those services (for a given level of quality) at the lowest cost?
5. *Price markups:* Do the prices suppliers charge for their services reflect their costs of production? (This occurs when suppliers compete on price to supply their services.)
6. *Redistribution:* Do those who cannot afford to pay for their medical services receive medically necessary services?

To the extent that the medical sector approximates the first five criteria, the system will produce its output efficiently, and medical costs will rise at a rate that reflects the cost of producing those services.[1] The type of services available, as well as the new medical technology adopted, will be based on what consumers are willing to pay.

Competitive markets, compared with monopoly markets or markets with government controls on prices and investment, come closest to achieving the first five criteria. Competitive markets are the yardstick by which all markets are evaluated, and they underlie the antitrust laws. Proponents of competition believe the same benefits can be achieved by applying competitive principles to medical care.

Competitive markets, however, do not help those unable to afford the goods and services produced. It is government's role, not the market's, to subsidize those with low incomes so they can receive the necessary amounts of food, housing, and medical services. When subsidies are provided to those with low incomes through a competitive market in the form of vouchers for health insurance, the value of the subsidies will be greater; providers have incentives to produce those services efficiently, and patients have greater choice when using them.

Market forces are powerful in motivating purchasers and suppliers. The search for profits is an incentive for suppliers to invest a great deal of money to satisfy purchaser demands. Suppliers innovate to become more efficient, develop new services, and differentiate themselves from their competitors, thereby increasing their market share and becoming more profitable.

Incentives exist in both competitive and regulated markets. The incentives appropriate to a competitive market are those where both the purchaser and the supplier bear the cost and receive the benefits of their actions. When a purchaser's and a supplier's costs and benefits are not equal, the market becomes less competitive and its performance suffers.

How Medical Markets Differ from Competitive Markets

The Period Before Managed Care
Prior to the start of managed care in the 1980s, health insurance coverage was predominantly traditional indemnity insurance. Patients had little or no out-of-pocket cost when they used medical services, and hospitals and physicians were paid on a fee-for-service basis. Information on providers was nonexistent, as it was prohibited by medical and hospital associations, and accrediting agencies, such as The Joint Commission (formerly the Joint Commission on Accreditation of Healthcare Organizations), did not make their findings public. Insurance companies merely passed higher provider costs on to employers, who paid their employees' insurance premiums. Medicare and Medicaid greatly reduced their beneficiaries' concern with medical prices. Medicare paid hospitals according to their costs, and physicians were paid on a fee-for-service basis. Medicaid paid hospitals and physicians fee-for-service.

Regulatory policies at the state and federal levels, enacted at the behest of provider groups, led to greater market inefficiency. Restrictions were imposed on any form of advertising, on the tasks different health professionals were permitted to perform, on entry by new hospitals and freestanding outpatient surgery centers into hospital markets, on requiring HMOs to be not-for-profit, and on which healthcare providers would be eligible for payment under Medicare, Medicaid, and even BlueCross and BlueShield.

Neither patients nor physicians had any incentive to be concerned with the use or cost of services. Comprehensive health insurance results in a "moral hazard" problem; patients use more services because their insurance has greatly reduced the price they have to pay. The additional benefit of using more services is much lower than if the patient had to pay more of the cost. Exhibit 20.1 illustrates how payment for medical services has changed since 1960. Private insurance and government currently pay for most medical services; out-of-pocket payments by patients have declined from almost 50 percent of total medical expenditures to just 12 percent (as of 2009). Furthermore, physicians, because they are paid on a fee-for-service basis, have a financial incentive to provide more services. Given the lack of patient and provider incentives to be concerned with the cost and use of services, too many services are provided; wide variations in care occur because factors other than clinical value are used to decide whether the services should be provided; and rapid increases have occurred in the growth of medical spending.

To control rapidly rising medical costs from the late 1960s to the early 1980s, federal and state governments used regulatory approaches. The medical sector was placed under wage and price controls from 1971 to 1974, health-planning legislation placed controls on hospital investment, many states used hospital rate regulation, and Medicare instituted hospital utilization review and limited physicians' fee increases. Medicaid simply reduced payments to hospitals and physicians. These regulatory approaches failed to limit rising medical costs.

Managed Care

Managed care was the reaction of large employers against a medical care system that was out of control and had resulted in rapidly rising health insurance premiums. Under pressure from large employers and unions, health insurers and providers became adversaries. Health plans negotiated price discounts with providers and instituted cost-containment measures that reduced use of services (gatekeepers, prior authorization for specialist and hospital services, and covering care in less expensive settings than the hospital). These cost-reduction measures achieved large savings in insurance premiums, as shown in Exhibit 19.3.

EXHIBIT 20.1 Trends in Payment for Medical Services, 1960–2009

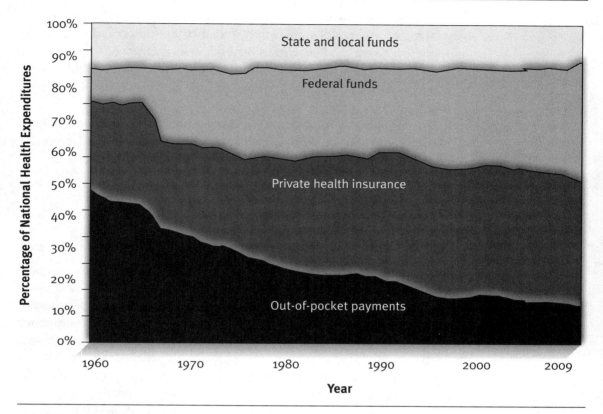

NOTE: Private health insurance category includes other private funds.

SOURCE: Centers for Medicare & Medicaid Services, Office of the Actuary, National Health Statistics Group, 2011. http://www.cms.gov/NationalHealthExpendData/downloads/tables.pdf.

When employees were offered a choice of health plans and given an opportunity to save on their monthly premiums, they switched plans. Price competition penalized higher-cost plans.

A backlash against managed care and its cost-containment methods occurred by the end of the 1990s. As more low-risk low users switched to HMOs for lower premiums, those remaining in traditional indemnity plans—patients with chronic illnesses and those with established physician and specialist relationships—faced high premiums. They joined HMOs to reduce their premiums and were dissatisfied with restrictions on access to providers. The backlash against managed care was likely driven by those forced to join HMOs.

Managed care was, at most, an example of partial market competition. Although managed care competition achieved large private-sector cost savings for a limited time, much of the previous regulatory and economic framework under which competition occurred was unchanged. Any framework includes a set of consumer and supplier incentives. Market performance responds to these incentives. When these incentives influence consumers and suppliers to consider the full costs and benefits of their decisions, market outcomes will be efficient. At times, however, the legal and economic framework within which consumers and producers make their choices distorts their costs and benefits, in which case markets perform inefficiently.

The following sections provide examples of how the medical care market's legal and economic framework has distorted consumer and producer incentives, hence their choices, leading to inefficient market outcomes.

Demand-Side Market Failures

Tax-Exempt Employer-Paid Health Insurance

When an employer purchases health insurance on behalf of employees, these contributions are not considered taxable income to the employee. Compared with other employee purchases paid for with after-tax income, the purchase of insurance is subsidized; employees do not pay the full price of their insurance as they would if they had to buy the same amount with after-tax income. When the price of a good or service is reduced, consumers will purchase an increased quantity of that service (this is known as the *law of demand*).[2] The price of insurance, when purchased by the employer, is not the same for all employees. Those in the highest income tax brackets receive the largest tax subsidies. On average, changes in the out-of-pocket price of health insurance result in an approximate proportional change in the quantity demanded of insurance.[3] (A 5 percent decrease in price leads to about a 5 percent increase in the quantity demanded of health insurance.)

The tax subsidy for health insurance results in employees purchasing more comprehensive health insurance coverage with fewer deductibles and lower cost sharing (and additional benefits, such as vision and dental care) than they would if they had to pay the entire premium themselves.

Consumer incentives have been distorted because consumers do not pay the full cost of health insurance or of their use of medical services. When consumers pay only a small fraction of the provider's price out of pocket, they are less aware of and concerned with the prices charged by medical providers.

Health Plan Choices

Health plan competition could have been stronger for several reasons. First, many employers limited their employees' choice to only one health plan.[4] For competition to occur among plans, employees must be offered a choice. Yet almost 80 percent of insured employees were offered only one health plan (Marquis and Long 1999). When employees are unable to choose among substitutes, the single plan being offered has less incentive to respond to employees' preferences or to lower prices.

Second, many employers that offer their employees a choice of health plans either contribute more to the more expensive health plan or contribute a fixed percentage of the premium to the plan the employee chooses. A fixed-percentage contribution provides a greater dollar subsidy to the more expensive plan, thereby decreasing the employee's incentive to choose the less costly health plan. (If the employer pays 80 percent, the employee choosing the more expensive plan pays only 20 percent of the price difference, not 100 percent.) The more efficient health plan is at a competitive disadvantage because the more expensive competitor is more heavily subsidized.

When employees have a choice of plans, and the employer pays a fixed-dollar contribution to the chosen plan, most employees will select a more restrictive plan, such as an HMO. "For example, 70–80 percent of active employees and dependents covered by the University of California, CalPERS, and Wells Fargo in California [each company makes a fixed-dollar contribution] choose HMOs" (Enthoven and Tollen 2005, w5-429).

Third, when competing managed care plans offer broad networks with overlapping providers, the plans are not sufficiently differentiated and do not offer employees real choices. Overlapping provider networks make it difficult for the plan to control costs (because it cannot exclude providers) and for employees to observe quality differences. The plans are not competing on their provider's ability to manage care, on the quality of their providers, or on patient satisfaction and have little incentive to invest resources to do so, as all plans with the same providers will benefit. Consumers should be able to choose among health plans that vary in their premiums, quality of care, access to providers, provider network, and so on.

Fourth, few employers pay insurers risk-adjusted premiums for their employees. Paying the same premium for an employee who is older and has more risk factors than a younger employee with less likelihood of incurring a large medical expense provides the insurer with an incentive to engage in risk selection by seeking out younger employees. Paying risk-adjusted premiums provides an insurer with an incentive to compete on price for higher-risk employees. Insurers would then also have to compete on how well they can manage the care of high-risk enrollees, rather than on how well they can entice lower-risk employees to join their plans.

Lack of Information

Historically, healthcare providers have been opposed to being compared with one another. The Federal Trade Commission's (FTC) antitrust suit against the

American Medical Association, affirmed by the US Supreme Court in 1982, concerned the association's prohibitions on advertising. A consumer seeking information on a provider's prices and quality was unable to find it. Lack of information on how good a substitute one competitor is for another enables each competitor to charge higher prices or produce lower quality of care than they could if consumers were informed on the prices and quality of both.

One of the tenets of a competitive market is that not only do consumers bear the cost of their choices, but they are also informed purchasers. If consumers do not have access to information on provider quality, providers have little incentive to invest in higher-quality care, as they receive the same fee as those who do not.

In more recent years, quality and patient satisfaction measures on providers have been collected and disseminated in report cards to employees when they choose their health plans. One recent study found that two years after the publication of a report card, "more than 20 percent of bottom-quartile surgeons stopped practicing CABG surgery in New York ... whereas only about 5 percent of surgeons in the top three quartiles did so" (Jha and Epstein 2006).

Tax subsidies for purchasing health insurance have led to a demand for more comprehensive insurance—with lower out-of-pocket payments and larger employer subsidies for more expensive health plans—and have lessened consumer incentives to choose more efficient health plans. Subsidies, combined with a lack of information on health plans and providers, have resulted in a medical care market where purchasers have insufficient incentives and limited opportunity to make informed choices.

Medicare and Medicaid

About half of all medical expenditures are made by federal and state governments. Incentives for those beneficiaries and Medicare and Medicaid's provider payment policies have an important effect on the market's performance, similar to the impact of tax subsidies. Most Medicare beneficiaries have supplementary health insurance to cover their Medicare cost-sharing requirements. Because low-income persons are covered by Medicaid, there is no cost sharing. Thus, neither Medicare nor Medicaid beneficiaries have any incentive to be concerned with provider prices or their use of medical services.

Although Medicare allows beneficiaries a choice of health plans, the aged have little financial incentive to choose lower-cost, restrictive Medicare Advantage plans. Only if Medicare were to provide a fixed-dollar contribution, with the aged paying the additional cost of a more expensive health plan, would beneficiaries have an incentive to switch from the more costly, traditional fee-for-service plan. Medicaid enrollees, on the other hand, are not provided with a choice of health plans. Instead, Medicaid may enroll some of its (young, low-cost) enrollees in a health plan, but most Medicaid expenditures on behalf of the aged and disabled are paid on a fee-for-service basis to hospitals, physicians, and nursing homes.

These market failures on the demand side have limited the expansion of more competitive managed care firms.

Supply-Side Market Failures

Provider Consolidation

The greater the number of healthcare providers in a market, the greater the competition among them to respond to purchaser demands. Conversely, when only one provider is available in a market, the patient has no choice but to go to that provider. Providers respond when the purchaser has a substitute provider to choose from. A monopolist provider has no incentive to innovate, improve quality, respond to patients' needs, or offer lower prices.

A great deal of provider consolidation has been occurring. Insurers have fewer hospitals to negotiate with when hospitals merge in a market. The antitrust laws are meant to prevent suppliers, such as hospitals and physicians, from gaining market power. Unfortunately, the FTC has been unsuccessful in preventing hospital mergers that decrease competition. Federal judges, ruling in the merged hospitals' favor, believed merged not-for-profit hospitals would not exercise their market power as for-profit hospitals would. Consolidated hospitals and single-specialty groups currently dominate certain markets (Berenson, Ginsburg, and Kemper 2010). Only recently has the FTC been successful in winning an antitrust suit against a nonprofit hospital merger that occurred years earlier.

As the number of competitors has declined, health plans have been forced to pay higher prices, which are passed on to consumers in the form of higher insurance premiums.

State Regulations

The states have enacted a number of anticompetitive regulations that limit price competition and result in higher health insurance premiums. These regulations address such areas as the training of health professionals and the tasks they are permitted to perform, entry into medical markets, pricing of health insurance policies, health insurance benefit coverage, and rules covering provider networks.

More than 2,100 state mandates have been enacted that specify the benefits, population groups, and healthcare providers that must be included in health insurance policies. Large business firms are legally exempt from these state mandates when they self-insure their employees, which most large firms do. The higher cost burden of these state mandates falls predominantly on smaller businesses and individuals, raising the cost of insurance and thereby making health insurance unaffordable to those who prefer less expensive health plans. Although some of these state mandates may be beneficial, many small businesses and individuals would prefer to have insurance they can afford than no insurance at all.

Many states regulate health insurance premiums charged to small businesses and individuals. *Community rating* includes all types of small businesses or individuals in a common risk pool, and all are charged the same premium. Firms whose employees are engaged in high-risk jobs are charged the same as those with employees who have low-risk jobs. Firms that provide incentives to employees to engage in healthy lifestyles are charged the same premium as those that do not. Community rating eliminates price competition among insurers. Instead, insurers have an incentive to engage in favorable risk selection. Community rating increases the price of insurance to low-risk individuals, thereby leading many to drop their insurance.

Certificate-of-need (CON) laws prohibit competitors from entering a market. A CON protects existing providers from competition, thereby providing the existing hospital, home health agency, hospice, and nursing home with monopoly power.

Training of health professionals emphasizes process measures of quality as a prerequisite for licensure. Re-examination for re-licensure is not used, and physicians are rarely evaluated on outcomes-based measures of quality. Innovative methods of training health professionals are inhibited when rigid professional rules specify training requirements. The tasks health professionals are permitted to perform are specified in state practice acts, based on political competition by different health associations over which profession is permitted to perform certain tasks. A greater supply of health manpower can be achieved and care can be produced in a less costly manner when performance is monitored and flexibility is permitted in the tasks health professionals are qualified to perform.

Any-willing-provider (AWP) laws limit price competition among physicians (and dentists). Health plans were able to negotiate large price discounts from physicians by offering them exclusivity over their enrollees. The AWP laws enable any physician to have access to a health plan's enrollees at the negotiated price. As a result of AWP laws, physicians have no incentive to compete on price for a health plan's enrollees because they cannot be assured of a greater volume of patients in return for a lower price.

Lack of Physician Information

Competitive markets assume that demand-side and supply-side participants are well informed. Physicians, who act as the patient's agent and as a supplier of a service, are considered to be knowledgeable regarding the patient's diagnosis and treatment. Furthermore, the physician is assumed to act in the patient's best interest. If these assumptions are incorrect, medical services are not being provided efficiently, quality of care is lower, and the cost of medical services is higher than it would otherwise be.

Wide variations exist in the medical services provided by physicians in the same specialty, to patients with the same diagnosis, and across different geographic regions (CBO 2008a). These variations in medical services are likely attributable to two factors. First, physicians are not equally proficient in their diagnostic ability or in their knowledge of the latest treatment methods. These wide variations have given rise to evidence-based medicine, whereby large insurers analyze large data sets to determine best practices and disseminate clinical guidelines to their network physicians.

Second, physicians have a financial interest in the quantity and type of care they provide. Most physicians are paid fee-for-service; thus, the more they do, the more they earn. *Supplier-induced demand* is the term economists use to explain physicians' financial incentive to increase their services. When combined with the lack of consumer incentives regarding prices and use of medical services and their lack of knowledge regarding physicians' practice methods, both the use and the cost of medical services are greatly increased.

Medicare, where most aged have supplementary insurance to cover their cost sharing, is a prime example of how lack of patient price sensitivity and medical information, together with some physicians' lack of knowledge and the incentives inherent in fee-for-service, have resulted in large variations in the cost and number of services provided.

Based on the preceding discussion, it is clear that market forces have been greatly weakened. Given the lack of effective market competition in medical markets, one cannot claim that competition has been tried and has failed.

How Can Medical Markets Be More Competitive?

Markets always exist, but, depending on government rules, they can be efficient or inefficient. To improve market efficiency in medical care, several changes are needed in government regulations and in the private sector.

Government tax policy that excludes employer-paid health insurance from an employee's taxable income should be changed. Employer contributions should be treated as regular income; however, it would be more politically feasible to limit the amount that is tax free. This change will affect how much insurance consumers buy, their choice of health plans, and how much medical care they use. Additional needed government reforms include removing restrictions on market entry and on laws promoting anticompetitive behavior, such as CON and AWP laws, overriding state mandates that increase health insurance costs, eliminating state insurance regulations requiring community rating, enforcing antitrust laws, and reforming Medicare and Medicaid so that beneficiaries pay the additional cost of more expensive health plans, thereby giving these beneficiaries incentives to choose health plans based on their costs and benefits.[5] These policies should stimulate greater competition in the private and public medical sectors.

With regard to the private sector, employers who subsidize their employees' health insurance should be encouraged to offer a choice of health plans, to give fixed-dollar contributions, and to use risk-adjusted premiums in making such payments. With more plan choices and employee incentives to be concerned with the cost as well as the benefits of a health plan, information will become more accessible to help employees make choices. When consumers can choose, information has a value, and private sources will develop to provide it, as occurs in other markets.

In competitive markets, not all purchasers have to be informed or switch in response to changes in prices and quality for suppliers to respond and for markets to perform efficiently.[6] In competitive medical markets, as in other markets, the more responsive purchasers and suppliers drive the market toward greater efficiency.

What Might Competitive Medical Markets Look Like?

If medical care markets were to become more like a competitive market, what might one observe? As consumers (and Medicare and Medicaid enrollees) have to pay the additional cost of more expensive health plans and become more cost conscious, the variety and number of plan choices will increase; plans will attempt to match purchasers' preferences and willingness to pay. Some people would prefer to choose among health plans, which is less costly than choosing and evaluating different providers.

Competitive markets might evolve in several ways. Integrated delivery systems, as articulated by Enthoven (2004), are organizations with their own provider networks that offer enrollees coordinated care. These integrated delivery systems might be built around large multispecialty medical groups with relationships to hospitals, as well as other care settings, and be paid a risk-adjusted annual capitation amount per enrollee. Health plans would compete for consumers on the basis of risk-adjusted premiums. These systems would select healthcare providers, be responsible for monitoring quality, examine large data sets to develop evidence-based medicine guidelines, reduce widespread variations in physicians' practice patterns, provide coordinated care for patients across different care settings (the physician's office, the hospital, ambulatory care facilities, and the patient's home), have incentives to innovate in caring for patients with chronic conditions, and minimize total treatment costs, not just minimize the costs of providing care in one setting while shifting costs to other settings. In addition, health plans would be responsible for evaluating new technologies and would in turn be evaluated by how well they perform in improving the health of their enrolled populations, their premiums, and patient satisfaction.

At the other end of the spectrum of financing and delivering medical services is consumer-directed healthcare. Under this model, consumers purchase a high-deductible (catastrophic) plan, which provides them with the incentive to be concerned with their use of medical services and the prices of different healthcare providers. The health savings account approach combines a high-deductible plan with a savings account; money saved in the HSA belongs to the individual and can be accumulated year after year.

Health plans preferred by consumers will expand their market share, while others will decline. Health plans and large multispecialty medical groups will have an incentive to innovate in ways that reduce costs, improve quality and treatment outcomes, and achieve greater patient satisfaction, as by doing so they will differentiate themselves from their competitors and achieve a competitive advantage. Other health plans will copy methods used by more successful competitors; the process of innovation and differentiation will then start over again. (Economist Joseph Schumpeter referred to this as the process of "creative destruction.")

Are the Poor Disadvantaged in a Competitive Market?

Opponents of competitive medical care markets claim that the poor will be unable to afford medical services. Competitive markets are meant to produce the most goods and services, with a given amount of resources, that consumers are willing to buy and sell at the lowest possible price. By doing so, goods and services will be more affordable to those with low incomes. However, competitive markets should not be evaluated on whether the poor receive all the medical services needed.

Achieving market efficiency has little to do with ensuring that everyone's needs are met or that everyone receives the same quantity of services. It is the role of government, based on voters' preferences, to subsidize the healthcare of the poor, just as is done with regard to food and housing. Providing the poor with subsidies (e.g., vouchers for a health plan) to be exercised in a competitive market is more likely than any other approach to ensure that they receive the greatest value for those subsidies.

Competitive medical markets may be considered unfair because those with higher incomes are able to buy more than those with lower incomes. Those who are wealthy always have been, and always will be, able to buy more than the poor. Even in the Canadian single-payer health system, those with more money are able to skip the waiting lines and travel to the United States for their diagnostics and surgery.

Summary

Markets are evaluated by how closely they approximate a competitive market. The closer the approximation, the more likely the market will produce products efficiently and be responsive to consumer demands. Medical markets are not inherently different from other markets in their ability to efficiently allocate resources. It is the regulatory framework of medical markets that leads to inefficient outcomes.

Medical markets differ from competitive markets in significant ways. The tax treatment of health insurance lessens consumer incentives to be concerned with the price and use of medical services. Consumers lack the necessary information to make economic and medical choices; often they are not offered choices. Competition among suppliers is limited by laws barring market entry, restricting tasks health professionals are permitted to perform, preventing price competition, and regulating market prices.

These market failures have resulted in inefficiency, inappropriate care, less-than-optimal medical outcomes, and rapidly rising medical costs. Increased government regulation has been shown to worsen rather than improve market performance. Several of the major inefficiencies in medical care markets are the result of government intervention. Regulation to limit rising medical prices was tried in the 1970s and failed. Medicare, which controls hospital and physician fees, fails to limit overuse of services and gaming of the system; up-coding and unbundling of services are common.[7] Under a system of government regulation of prices, budgets, and entry restrictions, interest groups, such as hospitals, physicians, unions, and large employers, are more effective in representing their economic interests than, and at the expense of, consumers. Organized interest groups are more effective than consumers in the political marketplace. Consumer interests are best served in competitive economic markets.

Government has an important role to play. Government sets the rules for competitive markets, such as eliminating practices that result in anticompetitive behavior, monitoring inaccurate information, and enforcing antitrust laws. It is also government's responsibility to raise the funds to subsidize those unable to afford medical care; those subsidies can be provided at lower cost and higher quality in a competitive market.

Market competition has not failed in medical care; it has not had a full opportunity to work. Consumer incentives must be changed so that consumers consider the costs as well as the benefits of their choices. Medicare enrollees should be offered a choice of health plans and given the option to pay the additional cost of a more expensive plan. And restrictions on providers' ability to compete on price should be removed. Without competition, providers have no incentive to be efficient, innovate, invest in new facilities and services, improve quality, develop best practices and clinical guidelines, or lower prices.

Discussion Questions

1. Why is it said that competition in medical care has failed?
2. What are the criteria for a competitive market?
3. How well does medical care meet the criteria of a competitive market?
4. Is it the responsibility of a competitive market to subsidize care for those with low incomes?
5. What changes are required for medical care to more closely approximate a competitive market?

Notes

1. Increases in demand may result in temporary increases in prices (high price markups over cost), which equilibrate demand and supply so shortages do not occur and signal suppliers to increase their production to meet the increased demand. Over time, as supply is increased, prices will again reflect the cost of providing those services.
2. Not every consumer necessarily purchases more when the price is reduced, but, on average, there will be an increase in the quantity demanded of that product.
3. The tax exclusion for employer-purchased health insurance is unfair because employees in a higher tax bracket receive a greater subsidy (see Exhibit 6.2). It is also unfair to individuals who are not part of an employer group; they do not qualify for the same tax exclusion. Individual coverage is more expensive, not only because of higher marketing costs and insurer concern with adverse selection, but also because it is paid for with after-tax dollars.
4. Many small and medium-sized businesses were unable to offer their employees a choice of health plans; the indemnity plan was concerned that it would receive a higher-risk group. Thus, small businesses were typically offered only one plan for all of their employees.
5. Recent unsuccessful legislative proposals seeking to lower insurance premiums in the individual and small-group markets included permitting association health plans, which allow organizations, such as nonemployer groups, ethnic organizations, and small business associations, to form and negotiate with insurers on behalf of their members; these associations

would have stable insurance pools and greater bargaining power with insurers. Furthermore, legislation permitting insurers to sell their products across state lines would enable them to bypass costly mandates in those states requiring them.

6. In some markets, such as rural areas, competition among health plans is unlikely to be strong enough to achieve the same efficiency as in large urban areas. Rural populations do not have the same choices with regard to other services, either.

7. Unbundling occurs when a provider charges separately for each of the services previously provided together as part of a treatment. Up-coding occurs when the provider bills for a higher-priced diagnosis or service than was provided.

COMPARATIVE EFFECTIVENESS RESEARCH

A s part of the $787 billion stimulus bill passed in 2010, $1.1 billion was allocated for comparative effectiveness research (CER). Included in the Patient Protection and Affordable Care Act (PPACA) of 2010 was an additional $3 billion for studies to compare the effectiveness of different treatments for the same illness. The different treatments to be analyzed include drugs, medical devices, surgery, and other ways of treating a specific illness.

CER and the Role of Government

What Is CER?

The scope of comparative effectiveness research includes conducting, supporting, and synthesizing research that compares the clinical outcomes, effectiveness, and appropriateness of services and procedures that are used to prevent, diagnose, and treat diseases and other health conditions.

Comparative effectiveness research involves three major areas: (1) comparison of new treatments for an illness to the best available alternatives for treating that illness, (2) use of the information from CER to improve joint physician and patient decision making, and (3) basing the data upon which these comparative studies are to be conducted on a sufficiently large population.

Physicians lack information on the effectiveness of alternative treatments for many different diseases. For some diseases, the relative effectiveness of alternative treatments has not been studied; for others, the results of effectiveness studies have not been disseminated to all physicians. The CER's federal coordinating council has developed a priority list of diseases and is awarding grants to study the comparative effectiveness of alternative treatments for diseases highest on the priority list. CER will be a continuing process as it is conducted on more diseases and as new treatments become available for diseases whose alternative treatments have since been studied (Federal Coordinating Council 2009).

Why Is the Government Supporting CER?

Many policy experts acknowledge that insufficient information exists on which treatments work best for different diseases. Given the soaring cost of healthcare and the belief that each year hundreds of billions of dollars are

EXHIBIT 21.1 Medicare Spending per Decedent During the Last Two Years of Life (Deaths Occurring 2001–05), Selected Academic Medical Centers

Academic Medical Center	Inpatient Reimbursements per Decedent	Hospital Days per Decedent	Reimbursements per Day
Hahnemann University Hospital	$84,827	34.8	$2,437
University of Maryland Medical Center	$66,840	28.0	$2,383
Johns Hopkins Hospital	$59,759	28.6	$2,093
UCLA Medical Center	$58,557	31.3	$1,871
Massachusetts General Hospital	$38,844	28.9	$1,344
Mayo Clinic (St. Mary's Hospital)	$31,816	21.3	$1,497
Cleveland Clinic Foundation	$31,252	23.9	$1,307
Buffalo General Hospital	$22,463	24.3	$926
Scott & White (Texas A&M)	$22,069	15.9	$1,384

SOURCE: Adapted from the Dartmouth Institute for Health Policy & Clinical Practice, Center for Health Policy Research 2008. *Tracking the Care of Patients with Severe Chronic Illness: The Dartmouth Atlas of Health Care 2008.* Table 3 [Online information.] http://www.dartmouthatlas.org/downloads/atlases/2008_Chronic_Care_Atlas.pdf

spent on care that is of no value, more accurate information on which treatments perform better will improve quality of care and reduce the wide variations that occur in treatment methods, thereby reducing rising medical expenditures. Few people are opposed to providing consumers, physicians, and insurers with additional information on which treatments are more effective.

As shown in Exhibit 21.1, several well-known academic medical centers were compared according to their total reimbursements per decedent, hospital days per decedent, and reimbursement per day for treating a patient during the last two years of his or her life. Wide variations exist among these medical centers in each of these measures. The study authors further show that wide variations also exist among the underlying resources, such as nurse staffing and physician hours, used in treating these patients in the different institutions.

The federal government can play a crucial role in aggregating information about the effectiveness of various medicines and treatments and disseminating that information to physicians and their patients.

Advocates of public funding for CER claim that such information has the characteristics of a public good, that is, everyone benefits from the information generated and that information cannot be denied to anyone once it becomes available. Because the information cannot be restricted to just those who pay for it, the private sector (health plans) will invest too little to develop such information. Many, therefore, want government to fund CER and assist in the dissemination of such information.

Concerns over How CER Will Be Used

Using CER for Reimbursement

Funding for comparative effectiveness research generated a great deal of controversy when it was enacted. Although the legislation stated that information based on CER is *not* to be used for mandating coverage, reimbursement, or treatment decisions for public and private payers, many are concerned that under the fiscal pressures of rising medical costs, use of results of the CER effort will eventually move closer to how European countries use their findings on comparative effectiveness.

Some of the opponents of government-funded CER believe that the government would ultimately use the findings from such research to establish medical practice guidelines, limit access to treatments, and refuse to pay for expensive new drugs. Reinforcing this concern was the book by Tom Daschle, who was nominated by President Obama to become secretary of the Department of Health and Human Services. (He subsequently withdrew his name amid a growing controversy over his failure to accurately report and pay income taxes.) Daschle had proposed a federal health board that would promote high-value medical care by recommending coverage of drugs and procedures based on the board's research (Daschle, Greenberger, and Lambrew 2008).

Differences in Patient Responses to the Same Treatment

CER is a "one size fits all" approach to medicine; however, widespread variation occurs in patient responses to different drugs. Patients who do not respond well to the recommended treatment will be disadvantaged. For example, for most patients a generic drug will be cheaper and will work as well as a brand name drug. However, for some patients the generic version may cause serious side effects or have little effect. Thus, although a branded and a generic drug may be equally effective on average, not paying for the newer, more expensive drug will lead to increased hospitalization costs and worse health outcomes for those patients who did not respond well to the cheaper drug (Basu and Philipson 2010).

Variations in Medical Practice

While most agree that wide variation occurs in medical practice, huge amounts of money are wasted on ineffective treatments and testing, and more information is obviously beneficial, there is opposition to moving from information generation and dissemination to basing payment on CER.

A recent study attempted to explain why wide variations in medical spending occur. Using data on Medicare beneficiaries, Zuckerman and colleagues (2010) found that unadjusted Medicare spending per beneficiary was 52 percent greater in the highest-spending compared to the lowest-spending geographic region. The authors then adjusted the regions based on demographics, baseline health characteristics, and changes in health status. After these adjustments, the difference between the highest and lowest regions decreased to 33 percent. Health status was found to explain an important part of this variation. Although inefficiency in spending per Medicare beneficiary exists, wide cost differences across geographic areas in Medicare spending are not due to inefficiency alone.

Policies to decrease spending differences per beneficiary between high- and low-cost areas by reimbursing physicians only for treatments that follow certain protocols or guidelines should not ignore the legitimate reasons for some of these variations.

Accuracy and Timeliness of Comparative Effectiveness Studies

One study generally does not provide a definitive answer; several studies will likely have to be undertaken. For example, bone marrow transplantation for breast cancer was widely accepted as beneficial, and patients won lawsuits because some health plans refused to cover it. Subsequently, it was found that this treatment was ineffective.

Comparative effectiveness studies may not adequately evaluate alternative treatments for patients with multiple chronic diseases or rare illnesses. Similarly, CER often does not include sufficient numbers of women, blacks, and Hispanics. Some drugs appear to be more effective in women than in men, while other medicines are more likely to cause serious complications in women. Comparative effectiveness research has to include larger numbers of patients in clinical trials so that gender and minority differences can be considered. As CER studies are expanded to account for such differences, the time and money needed to complete these clinical trials will increase.

Because it takes time to complete CER and for guidelines to be approved by the government, physicians and their patients may be willing to try untested therapies, as occurred for AIDS patients. Will they be permitted to do so? Will these therapies be reimbursed?

CER and Innovation

An additional concern is that CER might lead to slower adoption of new, more effective technologies. As new treatments and prescription drugs are developed, will reimbursement for them be delayed until their comparative effectiveness has been determined? Physicians might be willing to try new surgical techniques that offer improved patient outcomes; will they and the hospital have to forgo payment because these possibly innovative techniques have not undergone CER? Will the healthcare system become more rigid and less innovative because physicians fear repercussions if their treatments differ from the official guidelines? And will health plans refuse to reimburse for procedures and treatments that are not within the federal recommendations?

Medical device and pharmaceutical companies are also likely to face another layer of government approval that would increase their cost to bring a product to market, thereby decreasing their incentive for innovation.

Dissemination of CER Findings

CER results have to be disseminated. Will dissemination of information, which is often slow and may go against the financial interest of different physicians, be sufficient to have the CER adopted? Or will financial incentives and reporting requirements be necessary? A concern with providing information to physicians is that their adoption rate of new practices is very slow. If information is to change medical practice, lower costs, and improve quality, physician practice behavior will have to change more rapidly. However, without appropriate incentives, new information often takes years to change physician behavior.

Exhibit 21.2 provides several examples of the time it takes for treatment information to be disseminated to physicians. In 1988 the Food and Drug Administration (FDA) approved the use of aspirin for the treatment of heart attacks. Use of aspirin by physicians for the treatment of heart attacks increased from 20 to 62 percent. However, by the mid-1990s it had only increased to 75 percent. After studies were published indicating the potential harmful effects of calcium-channel blockers, their use declined but still remained above 30 percent ten years later.

Possible Stages in the Use of CER

Again, the legislation providing government funding for CER states that CER will not be used for reimbursement or coverage decisions. However, some people believe that government funding of CER is just the first stage of its evolution. These opponents foresee the following stages. First, CER provides information on the clinical effectiveness of different treatments and

Exhibit 21.2 Use of Acute Interventions (Pharmaceuticals) for Myocardial Infarction

Pharmaceuticals	Year of Innovation	Pharmaceutical Use[a]				
		1973–77	1978–82	1983–87	1988–92	1993–96
Beta-blockers	1962	20.6	41.5	47.5	47.3	49.8
Calcium-channel blockers[b]	1971	0	0	63.9	59.0	31.0
ACE inhibitors	1979	0	–	–	–	–
Aspirin	1988[c]	15.0	14.1	20.1	62.0	75.0

[a] In hospital or 30-day use.

[b] Calcium-channel blocker use increased rapidly in the early 1980s and then fell following the publication of studies documenting potentially harmful effects of their use in acute management.

[c] In 1988 the FDA proposed the use of aspirin for reducing the risk of recurrent myocardial infarction (MI) or heart attack and preventing first MI in patients with unstable angina. The FDA also approved the use of aspirin for the prevention of recurrent transient-ischemic attacks or mini-strokes in men and made aspirin standard therapy for previous strokes in men.

SOURCE: Adapted from David Cutler, Mark McClellan, and Joseph Newhouse, "The Costs and Benefits of Intensive Treatment for Cardiovascular Disease," in Jack Triplett, ed., *Measuring the Prices of Medical Treatments,* Washington, DC: The Brookings Institution, 1999, 34–71, tables 3 and 5.

drugs for a particular disease. Second, their cost effectiveness is compared. Third, given the rising costs of medical care and its increasing burden on the federal deficit, the federal government only pays for those drugs and treatments that are cost effective, even though the effects may differ among people or population groups. Fourth, instead of deciding which drug to pay for based on cost effectiveness, the government decides which drugs and treatments to pay for by comparing the cost of the drug with the value of an additional year of life, as occurs in Great Britain.

The following sections discuss cost effectiveness, how it might be used for reimbursement, and how it is used in Great Britain.

Cost-Effectiveness Analysis

Cost-effectiveness analysis compares the additional costs of alternative approaches to achieve a specific outcome designed to improve health. For example, an organization interested in reducing hip fractures would want to know the different programs that can reduce hip fractures, the cost of expanding each program, and how great a reduction in hip fractures each would achieve. Results from a cost-effectiveness analysis are typically presented in the form of a cost-effectiveness ratio, where the numerator of the ratio is the additional cost of the intervention and the denominator is some measure of the outcome of interest.

Alternative approaches for reducing hip fractures are likely to differ in costs and effectiveness. Thus they can be compared according to their cost-effectiveness ratio, which would be the additional cost per averted hip fracture. (For an example of cost-effectiveness analysis, see Exhibit 3.3.)

Calculating the cost-effectiveness ratio for each alternative method of achieving a given health outcome allows the trade-offs of choosing one alternative over another to be compared. Decision makers, whether they are administrators in government agencies such as Medicaid or HMO managers, can make better-informed choices about the relative costs and effectiveness of alternative interventions by using cost-effectiveness analysis. When choosing among alternative expenditures to improve health, alternative interventions can be ranked according to their cost-effectiveness ratios, such as cost per death averted, giving the intervention with the lowest ratio the highest priority. Choosing according to those with the lowest cost-effectiveness ratio will maximize the outcome for a given budget.

Many cost-effectiveness studies have been conducted on the relative effectiveness of a new drug compared with existing drugs for treating the same disease. The originators of such studies include health plans seeking to determine which drugs to include in their formularies and pharmaceutical firms hoping to use their results to demonstrate to large purchasers the greater effectiveness of their new drugs when compared with the drugs of competitors.

A concern with cost-effectiveness analysis if it were used for reimbursement by the government is that, as discussed earlier, patients may differ in their response to different drugs or treatments. Medical costs could be higher if patients respond poorly to certain drugs and have to be hospitalized. Further, the cost-effectiveness ratio to the government may be different from the patient's cost or evaluation of the treatment's effectiveness.

Quality-Adjusted Life Years

A specific type of cost-effectiveness analysis uses quality-adjusted life years (QALYs) as an outcome measure. QALYs are an outcome measure indicating the increased utility achieved as the result of an intervention, such as comparing a new drug to an existing one. The cost-effectiveness ratios are in terms of the cost per QALYs gained. The advantage of using QALYs rather than, for example, life expectancy is that a QALY incorporates multiple outcomes—increase in length of life and quality of life. Using QALYs as an outcome measure also enables comparisons to be made across different disease conditions.

A QALY is calculated as follows: Each additional year of perfect health for an individual is assigned a value of 1.0, which is the highest value—a complete QALY. The assigned value decreases as health decreases, with death equal to 0.0. If the patient has various limitations, such as a disability, physical pain, or the need for kidney dialysis, the extra life years are assigned a value between 1.0 and 0.0. Thus, if new intervention A enables a person to live an additional five years, but with a quality of life weight of 0.7, then the QALY score for that intervention is $5 \times 0.7 = 3.5$ QALYs. If intervention B extends life for four years with a quality of life weight of 0.6, the additional QALYs provided are $4 \times 0.6 = 2.4$. The net benefit of intervention A over intervention B is 3.5 QALYs – 2.4 QALYs = 1.1 QALYs.

When comparing alternative interventions according to their additional cost per QALY, those with a lower cost per QALY are preferred to those with a higher cost per QALY.

A common approach for developing QALYs involves the use of an activities of daily living (ADL) scale. Patients are asked to rate their ability to function independently, such as dressing, bathing, and walking. Patient responses range from unable to perform the function to able to perform the function without difficulty. These scores are summed up over all the ADL categories to arrive at a patient's overall functional status.

The calculation of QALYs is the same regardless of a person's income, wealth, or age, and QALYs that occur in later years may be valued less than QALYs that occur earlier in life.[1]

QALYs have several drawbacks. For example, the QALY does not include the effects of a patient's disability on the quality of life of others, such as family members. Assigning a quantitative value to a disability may not be accurate, since people differ in their perception of the severity of various limitations to their normal activity. Further, applying these utility measures across a large, diverse population having differing utility preferences is unlikely to reflect many individuals' utility preferences. And yet developing a QALY to be used for a large population is necessary if alternative medical treatments are to be compared.

Applications of QALYs

QALYs have been used in two types of policy analysis. First, QALYs are used as an outcome measure in cost-effectiveness analysis to compare alternative interventions in determining which intervention offers the lowest cost per QALY. Second, and more controversial, cost per QALY has been used to determine benefit coverage, for example, to decide whether a costly treatment such as an expensive new drug should be provided to a breast cancer patient.

The results of several cost-effectiveness studies examining different drug therapies potentially applicable for the Medicare population are shown

EXHIBIT 21.3
Selected Cost-
Effectiveness
Ratios for
Pharmaceuticals,
with a Focus on
the Medicare
Population

Intervention vs. Base Case in Target Population	Dollars per QALY Gained [a]
Captopril therapy versus no captopril in 80-year-old patients surviving myocardial infarction	$4,000
Treatment with mesalazine versus no treatment to maintain remission in Crohn's disease	$6,000
One-year course of isoniazid (INH) chemoprophylaxis versus no INH chemoprophylaxis in 55-year-old white male tuberculin reactors with no other risk factors	$18,000
Treatment to reduce the incidence of osteoporotic hip fracture versus no treatment in 62-year-old woman with established osteoporosis	$34,000
Ticlopidine versus aspirin in 65-year-old with high risk of stroke	$48,000
Chemotherapy versus no chemotherapy in 75-year-old with breast cancer	$58,000
Captopril versus propranolol in persons in the US population ages 35–64 without the diagnosis of coronary heart disease but with essential hypertension	$150,000
Antiemetic therapy with ondansetron versus antiemetic therapy with metoclopramide in 70-kg patient receiving cisplatin chemotherapy who had not been previously exposed to antineoplastic agents	$460,000

[a] QALY is quality-adjusted life year; 1998 dollars.

SOURCE: Adapted from Neumann, P. J., E. A. Sandberg, C. M. Bell, P. W. Stone, and R. H. Chapman. 2000. "Are Pharmaceuticals Cost-Effective? A Review of the Evidence." *Health Affairs* 19 (2): 98.

in Exhibit 21.3. Each of the studies describes an intervention compared to the alternative of no treatment. The results, in the form of cost per QALY gained, are ranked from lowest to highest cost per QALY. Those therapies whose cost per QALY is relatively low, such as $4,000, are very favorable. Therapies with a relatively high cost per QALY, such as $460,000, would be considered unfavorable and less likely to be adopted.

The National Institute for Health and Clinical Excellence

Great Britain established the National Health Service (NHS) in 1948 as a single-payer system, administered by the government, funded through taxation, and provided by public institutions. The British government has a long history of underfunding the NHS, resulting in long waiting lines and failure to provide certain types of treatments. To limit expenditures on expensive innovative medical technology and drugs and to attempt to rationalize its limited budget, in 1999 the government formed the National Institute for Health and Clinical Excellence (NICE), a private, independent organization in the Department of Health, to provide guidance on health technology, clinical medicine, and new prescription drugs, basing its decisions on clinical efficacy and cost effectiveness (NICE 2011).

NICE uses QALYs to determine which treatments to cover in its National Health Service. Given that budget constraints exist on the amount the government can spend for medical services, NICE undertakes cost-effectiveness analysis for new drugs and treatments in an attempt to provide patients, health professionals, and the public with scientifically based guidance on current best practices. A NICE committee consisting of medical and other professionals, such as health economists, statisticians, managers, patient advocates, and manufacturer representatives, assists in its decision making.

Before NICE was established, availability of costly treatments varied greatly throughout the country, as did the level of medical services. NICE has made the availability of drugs and treatments more uniform throughout the NHS. Decisions by NICE are transparent to all, and the information used by NICE for its decisions is also publicly available. Further, when NICE believes that a particular treatment or drug is cost-beneficial, it will attempt to ensure that the treatment or drug becomes widely available.

The main criticism of NICE is that it bases its recommendations more on cost effectiveness than on clinical effectiveness (Steinbrook 2008). The criticism of NICE for being "coldhearted" stems from the fact that it uses cost per quality-adjusted life year to determine cost effectiveness. One of NICE's most contentious criteria is how much should be paid per additional year of life that a drug is expected to provide. NICE's general threshold is $47,000. If a treatment has a cost per QALY above that, NICE will deny the treatment.

The following example illustrates how NICE uses its cost per QALY to determine approval for costly treatments. A *New York Times* (Harris 2008) article tells the story of patient Bruce Hardy, who was fighting kidney cancer that was spreading. His physician wanted to prescribe a new drug from Pfizer, Sutent, which delays cancer progression for six months at a cost of $54,000. NICE, however, decided that the drug was too costly to be offered free to all those who needed it. According to NICE, the cost of saving six months of life should be no more than $22,750; therefore Mr. Hardy could not receive the drug. When NICE rejected Sutent, some patients mortgaged their homes to pay for the drug on their own. (After much protest, NICE reversed its decision and approved the drug.) NICE has also limited the use of certain breast cancer drugs, such as Herceptin, and drugs for osteoporosis and multiple sclerosis.

Great Britain has been explicit in recognizing that resources are scarce and that choices must be made on how to allocate those scarce resources. At some point, with rising medical costs and a huge government deficit, will the United States become as explicit or, more likely, make such decisions implicitly by limiting healthcare provider reimbursement and thereby limit the resources available for new technology and expensive drugs?

Summary

Comparative effectiveness research should provide additional information to physicians and their patients regarding the effectiveness of alternative treatments. To the extent that wide variations in medical practice are the result of lack of information, CER should improve patient outcomes and reduce medical costs. However, if the findings from CER are used for reimbursement or coverage decisions, some patients may suffer adverse health consequences, medical costs could increase, and the medical system could become less innovative.

Some policy experts are concerned that federal funding for CER is but the first step toward limiting government payment for treatments considered less effective than others or for treatments that are too expensive for their return in extending life expectancy. Great Britain's NICE is often cited as an example where the government determines which medical treatments will be covered based on cost effectiveness. Although the PPACA states that CER shall not be used as a basis for payment, some are concerned that the United States may eventually use cost effectiveness in reimbursement of medical services.

Society cannot spend an infinite amount of money to extend each person's life; society must make choices. Economics requires trade-offs, since resources are scarce and can be spent on increasing a life in other ways. The opportunity cost of spending $100,000 on a new drug that would extend the life of a terminally ill patient by three months is that those same funds could have been spent to increase the life expectancy of very low–birth-weight infants.

Spending resources on additional medical services to extend one person's life involves having fewer resources to spend on extending the lives of others. States and the federal government, faced with increasing limits on their expenditures and increasing demands for costly medical services, will have to make difficult choices in coming years.

The proposal to have a separate federal health board to make difficult political decisions regarding which medical services and prescription drugs to fund insulates legislators from making these difficult choices, such as denying expensive but potentially life-extending services to a patient whose need for the treatment is discussed in the media.

Discussion Questions

1. What are the advantages of comparative effectiveness research?
2. What are disadvantages of using comparative effectiveness research for federal payment?
3. What are QALYs?
4. How are QALYs used in cost-effectiveness analysis?
5. How does NICE use QALYs in determining whether to approve a new drug?

Additional Readings

Congressional Budget Office. 2007. *Research on the Comparative Effectiveness of Medical Treatments: Issues and Options for an Expanded Federal Role.* Congressional Budget Office: Washington, DC.

Congressional Budget Office. 2008. *Geographic Variation in Health Care Spending.* Congressional Budget Office: Washington, DC.

Health Affairs 29 (10) (October 2010) has many excellent articles on comparative effectiveness research. http://content.healthaffairs.org/content/vol29/issue10/index.dtl?etoc

Note

1. When interventions produce QALYs over different time periods, discounting may be used to convert them into equivalently valued units at the present period, similar to discounting future income streams (as is done in a cost-benefit analysis). To determine the present value of future QALYs, the number of QALYs in each future year should be multiplied by $(1/1 + r^t)$, where r is the discount rate, such as 0.05, and t represents the number of years from the future to the present.

US COMPETITIVENESS AND RISING HEALTH COSTS

One of the oft-cited reasons for controlling the rise in healthcare costs has been that it makes American business less competitive internationally. Automobile executives, for example, have complained that their competitors in other countries have lower healthcare costs per employee, enabling them to sell their products at a lower price than US manufacturers.[1] After labor costs, healthcare is often the largest cost for many firms. GM estimated that its employees' healthcare expenses were increasing faster than any other single cost incurred in producing a vehicle (Storm n.d.). Unless healthcare costs can be controlled, the executives claim, US business will be priced out of international markets and foreign producers will increase their market share in the United States.

Do rising health costs really make US industries less competitive than their foreign counterparts? To understand this controversy we must ask who actually bears the burden of higher employee medical costs—the employee, the firm, or the consumer?

Who Pays for Higher Employee Medical Costs?

The market for labor is competitive. Firms compete for different types of labor, and employees compete for jobs. This competition results in similar prices for specific types of labor. For example, if a hospital pays its nurses less than other hospitals in the area, the nurses will move to the hospital that pays the highest wages. Not all nurses have to change jobs to bring about similar pay among hospitals. Some nurses will move, and the hospital will find it difficult to replace them. The hospital will soon realize that its pay levels are below what nurses are receiving elsewhere. In reality, not all firms have the same working conditions, nor are they located next to one another. Employees are willing to accept lower pay for more pleasant conditions and require higher pay to travel longer distances. The greater the similarity in how firms treat their employees, and the more closely they are located, the more quickly wage differences disappear.

When an employer hires an additional employee, the cost of that employee cannot exceed the value of that employee to the firm; otherwise, the firm will not profit from hiring the employee. The total cost to the firm of an employee consists of two parts: cash wages and noncash fringe benefits. The cost of hiring an additional worker is the total compensation—cash and noncash benefits—that the firm would have to pay to that employee. The employer does not care whether employees want 90 percent of their total compensation in cash and 10 percent in noncash fringe benefits or a cash–noncash ratio of 60 to 40. The employer is only interested in an employee's total cost.

Employees working in high-wage industries typically prefer a higher ratio of fringe benefits to cash wages because of the tax advantages of having benefits purchased with pretax income. Low-wage industries typically provide their employees with few benefits; most of their compensation is in cash income. The combination of cash and noncash income reflects the preferences of employees, not employers. If an employer compensates its low-wage employees with a high proportion of fringe benefits, the employees will seek the same total compensation at another firm that pays them a higher ratio of cash wages.

What happens when the fringe benefits portion of total compensation rises sharply, as occurs when health insurance premiums increase? For example, assume that employees in a particular industry are expected to receive a 5 percent increase in compensation next year, but health insurance premiums, which are paid by the employer and represent 10 percent of the employees' total compensation, are expected to rise by 20 percent. The employer is always concerned with the total cost of its employees; thus, cash wages in that industry would rise by only 3.3 percent. There is a trade-off between fringe benefits and cash wages.

If one firm in the industry paid its employees 5 percent higher wages plus the 20 percent increase in insurance premiums, that firm would have higher labor costs than all the other firms in the industry. What are the consequences to the firm? To incur above-market labor costs, the firm would either have to make less profit or increase the prices of the products it sells. If the firm were to make less profit, it would earn a lower return on invested capital. A lower return on invested capital will lead investors to move their capital to other firms in the industry, to other industries, or to other countries where they can earn a higher return. Capital knows no loyalties or geographic boundaries; it will move to receive the highest return (consistent with a given level of risk). Thus, higher labor costs cannot impose a permanently lower return to a firm; otherwise, the firm will shrink as it loses capital. The same would be true if labor costs among all firms in the industry increased and profits declined.

What if the firm or industry passes the higher labor costs on to consumers by raising its prices? As long as the firm's products have competitors, either from other firms in the industry or from manufacturers in other countries, and consumers are price sensitive to the firm's product, the firm will lose sales.[2] Good substitutes to any firm's (or industry's) product are generally available, either from other products or other manufacturers. Thus, large price differences for the same or similar products cannot be maintained. The failure to keep prices in line with a competitor's prices will reduce sales, with a consequent flight of capital from that firm or industry.

As long as competition from other firms or from foreign competitors (or both) is possible and capital can move to other industries and countries, rising medical costs will not result in lower profits or higher prices but will be borne by employees in the form of lower cash wages.

Short-Term Effects

Although rising medical costs are typically carried by the employee in the form of lower cash wages, an employer could experience a short-term effect on its profits. Shifting the cost of health insurance back to employees is difficult in the short run. For example, if an employer did not anticipate how rapidly medical costs would increase and, perhaps because of a long-term labor agreement, the firm is unable to lower its employees' wages to compensate for the higher-than-expected medical costs, profitability could decline.

Few firms, however, have been unaware of how rapidly medical costs have been increasing. Thus, rising costs are built into labor agreements. However, medical costs could also rise less rapidly than anticipated, increasing profitability. In any case, unanticipated cost increases will be reflected in future wage agreements and will not affect profitability over time.

An Example

The following example illustrates why labor bears the burden of higher insurance premiums. Automobiles can be produced in Michigan or in the southern part of the United States. Unless the prices of cars produced in Michigan and in the South are the same, consumers will purchase the least expensive cars, assuming their quality is similar. Unless labor costs and productivity were similar in both places, the automobile manufacturers would move their production facilities to the less costly location to produce the car. Yet we observe that within the automobile industry employees' medical costs and insurance premiums are higher in Detroit than in the South. How can cars produced in the North compete with cars produced in the South?

Medical costs per employee could be higher in the North as long as northern employees' cash wages are lower. Unless total compensation per employee is the same in both places, the cars produced in different locations could not be sold at the same price and manufacturers would shift their production to the lower-cost site.

Effect of Unions

What if an industry were strongly unionized and the firms in that industry were not permitted to hire nonunion labor? Could the union then shift its higher medical costs to the firm or consumers? The extent to which a union can increase labor costs is always limited by the potential loss of its members' jobs. If US manufacturers increase their prices relative to their competitors, foreign competition and price-sensitive consumers will cause them to suffer declines in sales and profits. Even when foreign competitors are prevented from competing with US manufacturers, consumers will demand fewer automobiles as prices rise, although the declines would be less than if greater competition were permitted. Firms facing decreased demands for their products would hire fewer employees. A powerful union that is willing to accept a certain loss of its members' jobs by forcing firms to raise its members' compensation would do so regardless of whether the increase was for medical benefits or wages. Thus, increased medical benefits to the union members still come at the expense of higher wages.

Exhibit 22.1 illustrates the effect of rising medical costs on employees' wages. After 1973, total employee compensation rose less rapidly than previously because of a slowdown in employee productivity. The difference between total compensation and wages increased as a greater portion of employees' total compensation went to pay for fringe benefits. Between 1973 and 1990, employers' contributions to their employees' health insurance premiums "absorbed more than half of workers' real (adjusted for inflation) gains in compensation, even though health insurance represented 5 percent or less of total compensation" (CBO 1992, 5).

Total employee compensation increased in the 1990s, reflecting increased productivity. However, wages and salaries remained relatively constant from the late 1980s until the mid-1990s, reflecting the increasing importance of health insurance and retirement plans in employee compensation. Until the mid-1990s, employees' wages rose very slowly because most of the increase in compensation went to pay for higher health and retirement benefits.

From the late 1990s to 2000, total employee compensation and wages greatly increased, again reflecting increased productivity. However, in contrast to the earlier period of the late 1980s to the mid-1990s, wages increased at a slightly faster rate than total compensation; cost-containment activities by managed care plans resulted in a slower growth in premiums and greater wage increases for employees (see Exhibit 19.3).

The late 1990s, however, saw a backlash against restrictive managed care plans, with the consequence that between 2001 and 2009, total compensation once again increased faster than wages.

Rising medical costs have had a large effect on employees' take-home pay; employees have had less to spend on other goods and services. For this

EXHIBIT 22.1 Inflation-Adjusted Compensation and Wages per Full-Time Employee, 1965–2009

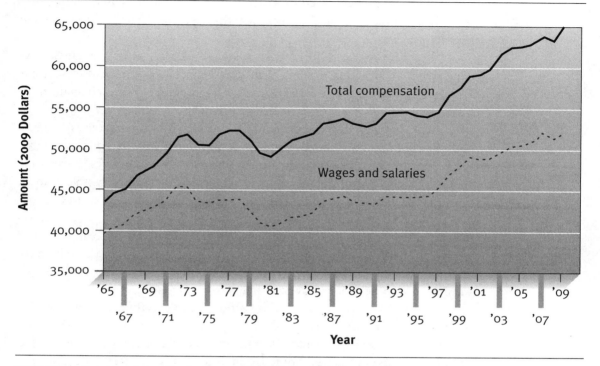

NOTE: Values adjusted for inflation using the Consumer Price Index for all urban consumers.

SOURCE: Adapted from Neumann, P. J., E. A. Sandberg, C. M. Bell, P. W. Stone, and R. H. Chapman. 2000. "Are Pharmaceuticals Cost-Effective? A Review of the Evidence." *Health Affairs* 19 (2): 98.

reason, unions have been strong advocates of using government controls to limit rising healthcare costs.

Who Pays for Retiree Medical Costs?

During labor negotiations in past years, many employers agreed to provide their employees with medical benefits when they retire, in return for wage concessions.[3] In 2010, 28 percent of large firms (firms with 200 or more workers) that offered health benefits to their employees offered retiree coverage (down from 66 percent in 1988 and 35 percent in 2000). Only about 3 percent of small firms (3 to 199 workers) offer retiree health benefits (Henry J. Kaiser Family Foundation and HRET 2010). At the time employers agreed to provide their employees with medical benefits, retiree medical costs were much lower than they are today, and employers undoubtedly underestimated how costly they could become. Instead of setting aside funds to pay these retiree obligations, as one would do with a pension obligation, firms paid their retirees' medical costs on a pay-as-you-go basis; that is, they paid their retirees' medical costs when they were incurred, out of current operating expenses.

Funding retiree medical costs changed as a result of a Financial Accounting Standards Board ruling that, starting in 1993, firms had to set aside funds for such benefits as they are earned. That is, retiree medical benefits must be treated similarly to pension benefits; as employees earn credit toward their retirement, the firm must set aside funds to pay for those employees' medical costs when they retire. Furthermore, the unfunded liability for current and future retirees must be accounted for on the firm's balance sheet. Firms were shocked by the size of their unfunded obligations. GM, for example, had an unfunded liability for its current and future retirees' medical costs of $77 billion (2005 data) (Latham and Watkins 2005). This liability had to be listed on its balance sheet, and an equivalent amount had to be deducted from the firm's net worth. GM's stockholders' equity was thereby decreased by $77 billion. In addition, GM had to expense part of that liability each year. For 2005, GM's earnings had to be reduced by $5.6 billion.

How did firms such as GM pay off these huge unfunded liabilities? Did they raise the prices of their products, harming US competitiveness? If they raised their prices, they would lose sales to competitors, both in the United States and overseas, that did not make such commitments to their employees. That evidently did not happen. Thus, US competitiveness is not harmed by firms having to list unfunded retiree medical benefits on their balance sheets. (In view of the auto industry's deteriorating financial condition, in 2008 GM, together with Ford and Chrysler, reached an agreement with the UAW to form a union-run retiree healthcare fund, Voluntary Employee Beneficiary Association [VEBA]. GM was released from UAW retiree healthcare claims incurred after 2009. The total value of the healthcare trust was about $60 billion, with GM providing around $33 billion, Ford roughly $15 billion, and Chrysler about $9 billion [Smerd 2008].)

Employers also cannot reduce the wages of current employees to pay for unfunded obligations to current retirees. If they were to do so, the firm would lose its employees. The labor market is competitive. If a firm decides to reduce its employees' wages, those employees will move to firms whose retirees have not been promised medical benefits. Instead, firms are likely to use current and future profits to pay off this liability, in which case the stockholders will be the losers.

Some firms have reneged on their promises to their retirees by either reducing benefits or requiring retirees to pay part of the cost; they have tried to shift these obligations from their stockholders back to their retirees. Retirees responded by bringing lawsuits against their former employers. Court rulings, however, have generally allowed employers to reduce or eliminate the benefits for salaried, nonunion retirees, even years after they have retired. When a firm declares bankruptcy and is reorganized, it is able to reduce its obligations to its unionized employees and retirees. If firms with large retiree liabilities declare bankruptcy, the stockholders, bondholders, employees, and retirees will all have to make some sacrifice for the firm to be viable again. Another option for lowering retiree medical costs is for the firm and its union to agree to such a reduction to prevent the firm from having to declare bankruptcy, in which case the retirees, the current employees, and the firm's stockholders would likely suffer greater losses. GM's renegotiation of retiree health benefits with its union to form a union-run fund is an example of this approach.

Rising medical costs will not directly affect US competitiveness by forcing firms to increase their prices. Instead, these higher costs will be borne by the employees themselves, who will receive lower cash wages. Similarly, the huge unfunded retiree medical liabilities will also not affect US competitiveness, because these liabilities will not be paid off by raising prices but will be shifted to the firm's stockholders in the form of reduced equity. Do rising medical costs have any adverse effects on the economy and US competitiveness?

Possible Adverse Effects of Rising Medical Costs on the US Economy

Rising medical costs could adversely affect the US balance of trade if they were to increase the federal deficit or decrease private savings.

Increase in the Federal Deficit

The argument on the deficit is as follows. Government expenditures for Medicare and Medicaid are the fastest-increasing portion of the federal deficit. In 1970, federal spending on these two programs represented 1 percent of GDP. By 2010, spending on these programs represented 5.5 percent of GDP. This figure is expected to reach 6.6 percent by 2020 (CBO 2010a). If left unchanged, these two programs will represent an increasing percentage of the federal government's nonhealth spending. To fund these additional expenditures, the government will have to increase its borrowing.

A higher level of government borrowing to finance a larger federal deficit will increase the value of the dollar relative to other currencies because interest rates in the United States will rise with the increased government demand for savings. In the process of moving their funds to the United States to take advantage of the higher interest rates, foreign investors will demand more dollars, which will increase their value. With a higher exchange value of the dollar, the prices of US-produced goods rise and foreign goods become less expensive. As the relative prices of US and foreign goods change, domestic manufacturers will sell less overseas, and imports into this country will increase as the price of foreign goods falls. American competitiveness and the trade balance will worsen.

However, the blame for the rising budget deficit need not be placed on rising medical costs. Many government programs contribute to the deficit, and many are of less value than Medicare and Medicaid. The deficit could be reduced by reducing expenditures on these other programs, such as farm subsidies and those military projects whose sole purpose is maintaining jobs in a community. Emphasizing medical spending as the cause of the rising federal deficit shifts attention from these other programs and reduces the government's incentives for eliminating wasteful programs that provide less benefit than medical expenditures. Reducing expenditures on Medicare and Medicaid could also merely result in shifting these savings into expanding other or creating new government programs.

Decrease in Private Savings

The second way increased medical spending could adversely affect the American economy is if private savings were reduced. To finance the federal deficit, the government has had to borrow, which has left less savings available for the private sector to invest in plant, equipment, and new ventures. Lower private investment eventually means lower productivity and lower real incomes. The US Congressional Budget Office (1992) estimated that if federal spending on Medicare and Medicaid had been limited to its 1991 share of GDP, real incomes would have been 2.4 percent higher by the year 2002.

Similar to the effects of government spending, rising medical costs cause the public to spend more on medical services, decreasing the amount it has available to save. Consequently, savings in the private sector decline, as do private investments. The argument blaming the lower rate of savings on rising medical expenditures is similar to blaming the federal deficit on Medicare and Medicaid. The government could reduce the deficit by eliminating and reducing other government programs. Medicare and Medicaid are not the sole cause of large federal deficits.

It is not clear that rising medical costs decrease or increase the private savings rate. Having health insurance may reduce the need for a person to save for his medical expenses. However, medical expenses increase with age, increased out-of-pocket payments may be required, and as people live longer they will have to save for their long-term-care needs if they do not want to rely on Medicaid (and have to spend down their assets to qualify). The expectation of higher medical costs and new technology may cause people to increase their savings. The effect of rising medical expenses on savings is uncertain.

The notion that the rise in medical expenditures should be limited because it increases consumption and reduces savings for investment is also a fallacy. Some medical expenditures are in fact investments that increase productivity, such as preventive measures and certain surgical procedures that enable a person to resume normal activity. More important, if increasing the savings rate by decreasing consumption is desired, many other consumer activities—some of which are harmful, such as alcohol and cigarette consumption—should probably be reduced before limits are placed on medical spending. Many people would place a higher value on medical services than on other goods and services.

Summary

It is not clear that increased medical spending has harmful effects on the economy, the budget deficit, or American competitiveness, as some have suggested. The fact that employees rather than employers bear the cost of rising healthcare benefits should not mean, however, that employers are absolved of the responsibility of ensuring that those funds are well spent. As Uwe Reinhardt (1989, 20) stated:

> Even if every increase in the cost of employer-paid healthcare benefits could immediately be financed by the firm with commensurate reductions in the cash compensation of its employees—so that "competitiveness" in the firm's product market is not impaired—it would leave employees worse off unless the added health spending is valued at least as highly as the cash wages they would forego [sic] to finance these benefits. Because it is the perceived value of a firm's compensation package that lures workers to the firm and away from competing opportunities, the typical business firm has every economic incentive to maximize this perceived value per dollar of healthcare expenditure debited to the firm's payroll expense account. Therein, and not in "competitiveness" on the product side, lies the most powerful rationale for vigorous healthcare cost containment on the part of the American business community.

Discussion Questions

1. What determines the ratio of cash to noncash (fringe benefits) compensation that an employer will pay to its employees?
2. What are the consequences if an employer raises its prices to pay for its employees' rising medical costs?
3. How can automobile employees in Michigan receive more costly health benefits than automobile employees in the South while automobiles produced in both locations sell for the same price?

4. Even if employees bear the entire cost (in terms of lower cash wages) of rising medical costs, why should employers still be concerned with cost containment?

5. Evaluate the following statement: Rising medical costs are harmful to the economy because greater consumption expenditures on medical services result in lower savings, hence reduced private investment.

6. Evaluate the following statement: Rising Medicare and Medicaid expenditures contribute to the growing federal deficit. To finance this larger deficit the government must borrow more, which in turn increases interest rates, raises the value of the dollar, and consequently makes US goods more expensive than foreign-produced goods.

Notes

1. At a meeting of the National Governors Association, former Ford Motor Company vice chairman Allan Gilmour stated that high healthcare costs could force Detroit automakers to invest overseas rather than in the United States to remain profitable. Ford spent $3.2 billion on healthcare in 2003 for 560,000 employees, retirees, and dependents. These costs added $1,000 to the price of every Ford vehicle built in the United States, up from $700 three years previously. Gilmour stated that their foreign competitors do not share these problems, and if healthcare costs are not controlled, investment will be driven overseas. He called on the states' governors to pass legislation to control healthcare costs (Mayne 2004).

2. The following is an example of how global competitiveness affects a firm's sales and its labor costs. Delphi, a US firm that sells automotive components, was forced into bankruptcy because of its high labor costs. To emerge from bankruptcy it had to reduce its US labor costs. The firm paid its US unionized employees $27 an hour, but when health and retirement benefits were included, its labor costs rose to $65 an hour. Delphi's Asian operations were highly profitable. In China, it paid its workers about $3 an hour, about a third of which was for medical and pension benefits (Sapsford and Areddy 2005).

3. Early retirees who are not eligible for Medicare are more costly than those who are. Early-retiree health benefits cost, on average, $14,988 in 2010, whereas Medicare-eligible retirees cost firms $7,848 on average. For retirees on Medicare, the firm usually pays for the portion of the retiree's medical expenses not covered by Medicare, such as deductibles and copayments (Towers Perrin 2009).

WHY IS GETTING INTO MEDICAL SCHOOL SO DIFFICULT?

I n 2009, only 19,332 of the 42,269 students who applied to 129 medical schools in the United States were accepted, for an applicant-to-acceptance ratio of 2.2:1. (The number of matriculants was 942 fewer because some applicants are accepted at more than one school.) The ratio, having reached a high of 2.8:1 in 1973, steadily declined to 1.58:1 in 1988, rose again in the mid-1990s, and, after declining again and reaching a low of 1.9:1 in 2002, has increased to 2.2:1. As shown in Exhibit 23.1, first-year medical school enrollments increased sharply in the early 1970s, mostly because federal legislation (the Health Manpower Training Act of 1964) gave medical schools strong financial incentives to increase their enrollments. When these federal subsidies phased out, enrollments leveled out. They have remained relatively steady since the early 1980s and have only recently started to increase. Since 2009 four new medical schools have started and several schools have increased their class size, which will lead to further increases in student enrollment. However, even with the increased school capacity, a large excess demand for a medical education will continue.

Many qualified students are rejected each year because of the limited number of medical school spaces. Some rejected students choose to enroll in medical schools in other countries, such as Mexico. Overseas medical schools often charge higher tuition and require longer training periods than US medical schools, which require four years of college before the four years of medical school. Residency training requires an additional three to seven years of graduate medical education. Unfortunately, academic excellence is not a sufficient qualification for admission to medical school. Other types of graduate-level professional education programs have experienced sharp increases in demand, but not the continual excess demands medical schools experience. Although every well-qualified student who wants to become a physicist, mathematician, economist, or lawyer cannot realistically expect to be admitted to her first choice in graduate schools, if such students have good academic qualifications, as do most medical students, she will likely be admitted to some US graduate school.[1]

Exhibit 23.1 Medical School Applicants and Enrollments, 1960–2009

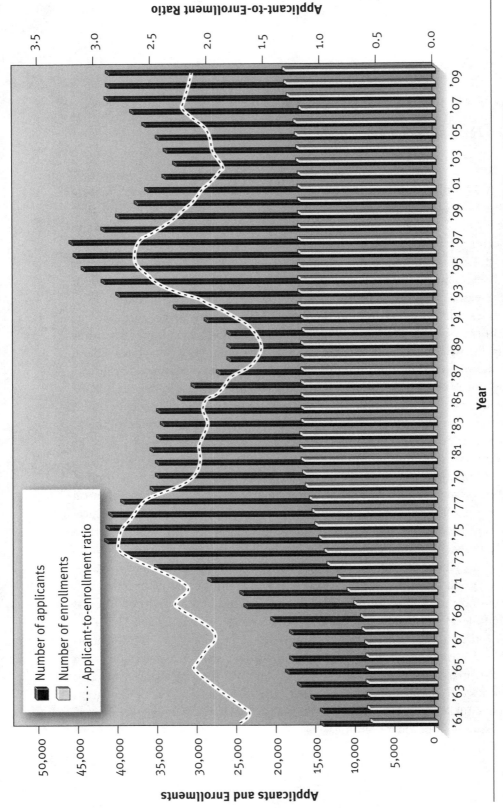

SOURCE: Data from American Association of Medical Colleges. 2010. *Medical School Admission Requirements, United States and Canada*, various editions. Washington, DC: AAMC.

The Market for Medical Education in Theory

When medicine is perceived as relatively more attractive than other careers, demand for medical schools will exceed the available number of spaces. If the market for medical education were like other markets, this shortage would only be temporary while more medical schools were built and existing schools recruited additional faculty and added physical facilities to meet the increased demand. Over time, the temporary shortage would be resolved as the supply of spaces increased. Crucial in eliminating a temporary shortage is a rise in price (tuition). Increased tuition would serve to ration student demand for the existing number of spaces and provide medical schools with a financial incentive (and the funds) to invest in facilities and faculty so they could accommodate larger enrollments. Subsidies and loan programs could be made available directly to low-income students faced with higher tuition rates.

The Market for Medical Education in Practice

The market for medical education, however, differs from other markets. The medical education industry produces its output inefficiently (at high cost and using too many years of a student's time), and the method used to finance medical education is inequitable (large subsidies go to students from high-income families). If medical education were similar to other industries, more efficient competitors would have driven out less efficient competitors and transformed the industry. How has this industry, with its record of such poor performance, been able to survive?

The producers of medical education have been insulated from the marketplace. Tuition, established at an arbitrarily low level, represents less than one-third of the costs of education and approximately 10 percent of medical school revenues. Medical schools can maintain low tuition because large state subsidies and research grants offset educational costs. Tuition, being such a small fraction of educational costs and not rising with increased demand, neither serves to ration excess demand among students nor provides an incentive to medical schools to expand their capacity. Medical schools, particularly public ones, do not depend on tuition revenue to even cover their operating expenses.

Lacking a financial incentive to expand, medical schools do nothing to alleviate the temporary shortage. Instead, the shortage becomes permanent, which is a far more serious situation.

For-profit businesses respond to increased consumer demands by raising prices and increasing supplies because they want to make greater profits. New firms enter industries in which they perceive they can earn more on their investments than they can earn elsewhere. When prices are prevented from rising or barriers exist to new firms entering an expanding market, temporary shortages can become permanent. Typically, barriers to entry are legal rather than economic and protect existing firms from competition. Protected firms are better able to maintain higher prices and receive above-normal profits than if new firms were permitted to enter the market.

Medical schools, being not-for-profit organizations, are motivated by more "noble" goals, such as the prestige associated with training tomorrow's medical educators. Most medical schools share the goal of having a renowned, research-oriented faculty who teach a few small classes of academically gifted students, who will be their successors as super-specialist researchers. Few, if any, medical schools seek acclaim for graduating large numbers of primary care physicians who practice in underserved areas.

Only by maintaining an excess demand for admissions can medical schools choose the type of student who will become the type of physician they prefer (who will meet their prestige goals). Both the type of student selected and the design of the educational curriculum are determined by the desires of the medical school faculty, not by what is needed to train quality physicians efficiently (in terms of student time and cost per student). As long as a permanent shortage of medical school spaces exists, medical schools will continue to "profit" by selecting the type of student the faculty desires, establishing educational requirements the faculty deems most appropriate, and producing graduates who mirror the faculty's preferences. The current system of medical education contains inadequate incentives for medical schools to respond cost effectively to changes in the demand for medical education.

How likely is it that an organization, perhaps a health plan, could start its own self-supporting medical school, one that would admit students after only two years of undergraduate training (as is done in Great Britain), with a revised curriculum and residency requirement that would combine the last two years of medical school with the first two years of graduate medical education (reducing the graduate medical education requirement by one year, as proposed by the former dean of the Harvard Medical School), and financed either by tuition or by graduates repaying their tuition by practicing for a number of years in the organization (Ebert and Ginzberg 1988)? Such schools could satisfy the excess demands for a medical education, reduce the educational process by at least three years, and at the same time teach students to be practitioners in a managed care environment.

Accreditation for Medical Schools

Not surprisingly, starting new and innovative medical schools is very difficult. The Liaison Committee on Medical Education (LCME) accredits programs leading to the MD degree and establishes the criteria to which a school must adhere to receive accreditation (Association of American Medical Colleges and American Medical Association 1991). For example, a minimum number of weeks of instruction and calendar years (four) for the instruction to occur are specified, and an undergraduate education, usually four years, is required for admission to a medical school. Innovations in curriculum and changes in the length of time for becoming a physician (and to prepare for admission to medical school) must be approved by the LCME. The LCME further states that the cost of a medical education should be supported from diverse sources: tuition, endowment, faculty earnings, government grants and appropriations, parent universities, and gifts. Through its concern that too great a reliance should not be placed on tuition, the LCME encourages schools to pursue revenue sources and goals unrelated to educational concerns.

To be accredited, medical schools must also be not-for-profit. The LCME's accreditation criteria in effect eliminate all incentives for health plans and similar organizations to invest in medical schools in hopes of earning a profit or having a steady supply of practitioners. Private organizations have no incentive to invest capital to start a new medical school.

The status quo of the current high-cost medical education system would be threatened if graduates of these new medical schools proved as qualified as those trained in more traditional schools (as evidenced by their licensure examination scores and performance in residencies offered to them) and could enter practice three years earlier.

Instead, to bring about medical education reforms, nine commissions have been set up since the 1960s to recommend changes. In a 1989 survey, medical school deans, department chairs, and faculty overwhelmingly endorsed the need for "fundamental changes" or "thorough reform" in medical student education. One examination of the lack of medical education reform indicated that faculty lack sufficient incentives to participate in reforming medical education programs because promotion and tenure are based primarily on research productivity and clinical practice expertise: "[There is] the relegation of students' education to a secondary position within the medical school....Faculty have tended to think of the goals of their own academic specialty and department rather than the educational goals of the school as a whole" (Enarson and Burg 1992, 1142).

Recommended Changes

Not surprisingly, without financial incentives the not-for-profit sector will fail to respond to increased student demands for a medical education and will not be concerned with the efficiency by which medical education is provided. Instead of relying on innumerable commissions whose proposed reforms go largely unimplemented, three changes in the current system of medical education and quality assurance should be considered: (1) ease the entry requirements for starting new medical schools, (2) reduce medical school subsidies, and (3) place more emphasis on monitoring physician practice patterns.

Ease the Entry Requirements for Starting New Medical Schools

The accreditation criteria of the LCME should be changed to permit other organizations, such as managed care organizations (MCOs)—including those that are for-profit—to start medical schools. A larger number of schools competing for students would pressure medical schools to be more innovative and efficient. With easier entry into the medical education market, the emphasis on quality would shift from the process of becoming a physician toward quality outcomes, namely toward examining physicians and monitoring their practice behavior. Directly monitoring physicians' practice behavior is the most effective way to protect the public against unethical and incompetent physicians.

As more physicians participate in managed care organizations and physicians and hospitals become more integrated, physician peer review would be enhanced. These organizations have a financial incentive to evaluate the quality and appropriateness of care given by physicians under their auspices, as these organizations compete with similar organizations according to their premiums, quality of care provided, and access to services. Report cards documenting physician quality of care and patient satisfaction are increasingly required by large employers and consumer groups. Quality assurance of physician services will increase as a result of competition among medical groups, integrated organizations, and health plans.

Reduce Medical School Subsidies

Reducing government subsidies would also cause medical schools to become more efficient by reducing the time required for a medical degree and the costs of providing it. Medical students should not be subsidized to a greater extent than students in other graduate or professional schools. A decrease in state subsidies to medical schools would force medical schools to re-examine and reduce their costs of education. Medical schools that merely raise their tuition to make up the lost revenues would find it difficult to attract a sufficient number of highly qualified applicants once more schools are competing for students. As tuition more accurately reflected the cost of education, applicants would comparison shop and evaluate schools with a range of tuition levels. To be competitive, schools with lesser reputations would have to have correspondingly lower tuition levels. The need to reduce student educational costs most likely would result in innovative curricula, new teaching methods, and better use of the medical student's time.

To ensure that every qualified student would have an equal opportunity to become a physician once subsidies were decreased, student loan and subsidy programs must be made available. Current low tuition rates in effect subsidize the medical education of all medical students, even those who come from high-income families; once these students graduate, they enter one of the highest-income professions. Providing subsidies directly to qualified students according to their family income levels would be more equitable.

Furthermore, instead of providing subsidies directly to medical schools, the subsidies should be given directly to students in the form of a voucher (to be used only in a medical school). Giving the state subsidies to students would be an incentive for them to select a medical school according to its reputation, total costs of education, and number of years of education required to graduate (college and medical school). Medical schools would be forced to compete for students based on these criteria.

Place More Emphasis on Monitoring Physician Practice Patterns

Currently, the process for ensuring physician quality relies wholly on graduating from an approved medical school and passing a licensing examination. Once a physician is licensed, no re-examination is required to maintain that license (although specialty boards may impose their own requirements for admission and maintenance of membership). State licensing boards are responsible for monitoring physicians' behavior and penalizing physicians whose performance is inadequate or whose conduct is unethical. Unfortunately, this approach for ensuring physician quality and competence is completely unreliable.

State licensing boards discipline very few physicians. In 1972 the disciplinary rate was only 0.74 per 1,000 physicians; a number of states did not undertake any disciplinary actions against their physicians. Between 1980 and 1982, the disciplinary rate rose to 1.3 per 1,000 physicians, or about one-tenth of 1 percent of all physicians. Although there have been some improvements in certain states in recent years, the number of disciplinary actions against physicians varies greatly among states. As of 2009, the number of disciplinary actions per 1,000 practicing physicians was 4.5 in California, 5.0 in New York, 7.6 in Ohio, 9.8 in Texas, and 12.4 in Colorado. Many states had much lower disciplinary rates. Three of the states with the lowest serious disciplinary action rates for 2009, Minnesota (2.3 actions per 1,000 physicians), South Carolina (1.45), and Montana (1.79), have been consistently among the bottom ten states for each of the last six three-year periods. In addition, Mississippi (3.07) has been among the bottom ten states for each of the last five three-year cycles (Federation of State Medical Boards of the United States, Inc. 2010).

It is unlikely that Colorado, which had 12.4 prejudicial acts per 1,000 physicians, has more unethical or incompetent physicians than other states, such as South Carolina, or more physicians requiring disciplinary action than Montana. Instead, the considerable variability among states represents the uneven efforts by the medical licensing boards of those states, which are mainly composed of physicians, to monitor and discipline physicians in their states. In fact, even when physicians lose their licenses in one state, they can move to another state and practice; some state medical boards encourage physicians to move to another state in exchange for dropping charges. Only five states permit their licensing boards to act based solely on another state's findings. The public is not as protected from incompetent and unethical medical practitioners as the medical profession has led it to believe.[2]

Monitoring the care provided by physicians through the use of claims and medical records data would more directly determine the quality and competence of a physician. And state licensing boards need to devote more resources to monitoring physician behavior. Requiring periodic re-examination and re-licensing of all physicians would make physicians update their skills and knowledge. Rather than requiring physicians to take a minimum number of hours of continuing education, re-examination would determine the appropriate amount of continuing education on an individual basis. (Continuing education by itself is a process measure for ensuring quality and does not ensure that physicians actually maintain and update their skills and knowledge bases.) Re-examination is a more useful and direct measure for assessing whether a physician has achieved the objectives of continuing education.

Periodic re-examination and re-licensure would determine what tasks an individual physician is proficient in performing. Currently, all licensed physicians are permitted to perform a wide range of tasks, although in some of these tasks they may have insufficient training. Physicians may designate themselves as specialists whether or not they are certified by a specialty board. At present, any physician can legally perform surgery, provide anesthesia services, and diagnose patients. Re-examination could result in a physician's practice being limited to those tasks for which she continues to demonstrate proficiency. Instead of all-or-nothing licenses, physicians would be granted specific-purpose licenses. Such a licensing process would acknowledge that licensing physicians to perform a wide range of medical tasks does not serve the best interests of the public because not all physicians are qualified to perform all tasks adequately.

Specific-purpose licensure would mean that not all physicians would need to take the same educational training; training in some specialties would take much less time, whereas training to become a super-specialist would of course take longer. Shorter educational requirements for family practitioners would lower the cost of their medical educations and enable them to graduate earlier and earn an income sooner. Even with higher tuition, family practitioners would incur a smaller debt and could begin paying it off at least three years earlier.[3] The number of family practitioners would increase because they would incur a much smaller investment (fewer years of schooling and lost income) in their medical education, which would more than compensate for not receiving as high an income as a specialist. When a physician wants an additional specific-purpose license, he can receive additional training and take the qualifying examination for that license. Training requirements for entering the medical profession would be determined not by the medical profession but by the demand for different types of physicians and the lowest-cost manner of producing them.

Summary

The competition among medical schools that would result from reducing their subsidies (or providing the subsidies directly to students) and permitting the opening of new schools would improve the performance of the market for medical education. Easing entry restrictions would make opening nontraditional schools (and innovating in existing schools) easier, allowing more qualified students to be admitted to a medical school. Qualified students would no longer have to incur the higher expense and longer training times of attending a foreign medical school. Emphasizing outcome measures and appropriateness of care would better protect the public from incompetent and unethical physicians. Reducing government subsidies to medical schools would force medical schools to be more efficient and innovative in structuring and producing a medical education. Further, distributing subsidies to students according to family income rather than to the medical school (which results in a subsidy to all students) would enhance equity among students receiving a medical education and force medical schools to compete for those students.

Discussion Questions

1. Evaluate the performance of the current market for medical education in terms of the number of qualified students admitted and the cost (both medical education and student forgone income) of becoming a physician.
2. The current approach for subsidizing medical schools results in all medical students being subsidized. Contrast this approach with one that awards the same amount of subsidy directly to students (according to their family incomes) for use in any medical school.

3. Medical schools are typically interested in prestige. How would medical school behavior change if schools had to survive in a competitive market (with free entry of new competitors) and without subsidies?

4. An important reason there are so few family practitioners is their much lower economic returns than specialists. How would a competitive market in medical education increase the relative profitability of becoming a family practitioner?

5. Currently, the public is protected from incompetent and unethical physicians by the requirement that physicians graduate from an approved medical school, pass a one-time licensing examination, and receive continuing education. What are alternative, lower-cost approaches for protecting the public's interest?

Additional Reading

Law, M., and Z. Hansen. 2010. "Medical Licensing Board Characteristics and Physician Discipline: An Empirical Analysis." *Journal of Health Politics, Policy and Law* 35 (1): 65–93.

Notes

1. Medical education also differs from other graduate programs in that once accepted to medical school, a student is virtually assured of graduating. The attrition rate is approximately 2 percent, compared with attrition rates of 50 percent in other graduate programs.

2. Improvements have been occurring slowly over time. All states now share formal action information with other states and report disciplinary actions to the National Practitioner Data Bank.

3. Jolly (2005) estimates that median debt levels for public medical school graduates from the class of 2007 would be $122,000. For class of 2007 graduates of private (nonprofit) medical schools the median debt level would be $158,000.

THE SHORTAGE OF NURSES

Since World War II, concerns over a national shortage of RNs have been recurrent. At times the shortage seems particularly acute; at other times it appears to be resolved, only to reassert itself several years later. Government and private commissions have attempted to quantify the magnitude of the shortage and have proposed remedies. Since 1964, the federal government has spent billions of dollars to alleviate the nursing shortage. Given the continuing concern over the shortage and the large federal subsidies that have supported nursing education, it is useful to examine why shortages of nurses recur and what, if anything, should be done about it.

Measuring Nursing Shortages

The measure commonly used to indicate a shortage of nurses is the nurse vacancy rate in hospitals, the percentage of unfilled nursing positions for which hospitals are recruiting. The vacancy rate attained a high of 23 percent in 1962, steadily declined throughout the 1960s, and reached single digits by the early 1970s. It rose in the late 1970s, reaching 14 percent in 1979, but by 1983 it had fallen to approximately 4.4 percent. By the mid-1980s, the vacancy rate was climbing again. It exceeded 12 percent by 1989, after which it declined to 4 percent in 1998 and then rose sharply to 13 percent in 2001. It then declined once again, to 4 percent in 2009 (see Exhibit 24.1).

Each of these periods of high or rising RN vacancy rates brought forth commissions to study the problem and make recommendations. The high vacancy rates in the early 1960s led to the start of federal support for nursing education, the Nurse Training Act of 1964, which has been renewed many times.

Nursing Shortages in Theory

What are the reasons for a shortage of RNs? The definition of a nurse shortage is hospitals' inability to hire all the nurses they want at the current wage. In other words, at the existing wage, the demand for nurses exceeds the number

EXHIBIT 24.1 RN Vacancy Rates, Annual Percentage Changes in Real RN Wages, and the National Unemployment Rate, 1979–2009

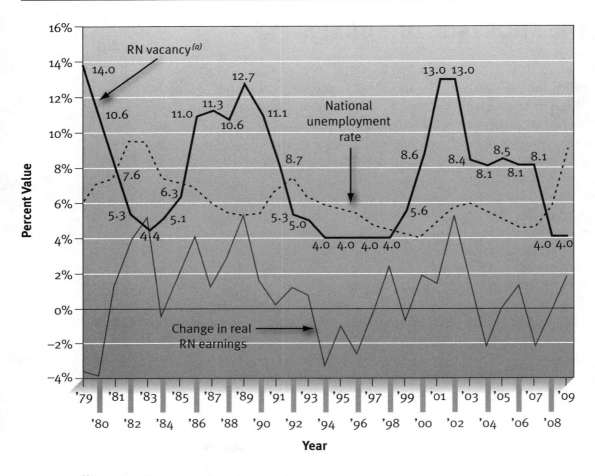

(a)Estimated data for 1997–98, 2006, and 2008.

SOURCES: 1979–2008 data on RN vacancy rates and the national unemployment rates compiled by Peter I. Buerhaus, Vanderbilt University School of Nursing; and Douglas O. Staiger, Dartmouth College and Research Associate, National Bureau of Economic Research, October 2009. 2009 data on RN vacancy rate from American Hospital Association, *The State of America's Hospitals—Taking the Pulse* (AHA, March/April 2010), http://www.aha.org/aha/content/2010/pdf/100524-thschartpk.pdf. Data on real RN earnings from Bureau of Labor Statistics. October 2010.

of nurses willing to work at that wage. However, economic theory claims that if the demand for nurses exceeds the supply of nurses, hospitals will compete for nurses and nurses' wages will increase. As nurses' wages rise, nurses who are not working will seek employment, and part-time nurses will be willing to increase the hours they work. Those hospitals willing to pay the new, higher wage will be able to hire all the nurses they want and will no longer have vacancies for nurses.[1]

Thus, economic theory predicts that once shortages begin, we observe rising wages for nurses followed by declining vacancy rates. Nurse employment will increase (more nurses will enter the labor force and others will work longer hours), and as nurses' wages increase, hospitals will not hire as many nurses at the higher wage as they initially wanted. Shortages could recur if the demand for nurses once again increases (more rapidly than supply). With an increase in demand, the process starts over: Hospitals find they cannot hire all the nurses they want at the current wage, and so on. Clearly, wages are not the only reason nurses work or increase their hours of work. The nurse's age, whether she has young children, and overall family income are also important considerations. A change in the nurse's wage, however, will affect the benefits of working versus not working and thereby affect the number of hours the nurse chooses to work.

Nursing Shortages in Practice

How well does economic theory that relies on increased demand for nurses explain the recurrent shortages of nurses? Nurse shortages must be separated into two periods: the period before the 1965 passage of Medicare and Medicaid and the period after.

Before the Passage of Medicare and Medicaid
Before Medicare, the vacancy rate kept rising, exceeding 20 percent by the early 1960s. Hospital demand for nurses continued to exceed the supply of nurses at a given wage. Surprisingly, however, nurses' wages did not rise as rapidly as wages in comparable occupations, which were not even subject to the same shortage pressures. Worsening shortages of nurses and limited increases in nurse wages over a period of years could only have resulted from interference with the process by which wages were determined.

Working on the hypothesis that nurse wages were being artificially held down, economist Donald Yett (1975) found that hospitals were colluding to prevent nurses' wages from rising. The hospitals believed competing for nurses would merely result in large nurse wage increases, hence a large increase in hospital costs, without a large increase in the number of employed nurses. This collusive behavior by hospitals on the setting of nurses' wages prevented the shortage from being resolved. (For additional references on the nursing shortage and a more complete discussion of the shortage over time, see Buerhaus, Staiger, and Auerbach [2009] and Feldstein [2011f].)

After the Passage of Medicare and Medicaid
Once Medicare and Medicaid were enacted, hospitals began to be reimbursed according to their costs for treating Medicare and Medicaid patients. Consequently, hospitals were more willing to increase nurses' wages, which they did

rapidly in the mid- to late 1960s. The vacancy rate declined from 23 percent in 1962 to approximately 9 percent by 1971. The increase in nurses' wages brought about a large increase in the number of employed nurses, contrary to hospitals' earlier expectations. Trained nurses who were not working decided to re-enter nursing. The percentage of all trained nurses who were working rose from 55 percent in 1960 to 65 percent in 1966 and 70 percent in 1972. Higher wages had an important effect on increasing nurse participation rates.

The artificial shortages created by hospitals before the mid-1960s are no longer possible. The antitrust laws make collusion by hospitals to hold down nurses' wages illegal. Therefore, the recurrent shortage of nurses since that time has been of a different type.

The lack of information in the market for nurses lengthens the time necessary to resolve shortages. For example, if a hospital experiences an increase in its admissions or a higher acuity level in its patients, it will try to hire more nurses. The hospital may, however, find that its personnel department cannot hire more nurses at the current wage. The hospital's vacancy rate increases. Other hospitals in the community may have the same experience. The hospital then has to decide whether and by how much to raise the wage to attract additional nurses. If the hospital decides to raise nurses' wages, it will have to pay the higher wage to its existing nurses as well. The hospital must then decide how many additional nurses it can afford to hire at the higher wage. The cost of a new nurse is not only the higher wage a hospital must pay that new nurse but also the cost of increasing wages to all of the other nurses.

The hospital may decide that other approaches for recruiting new nurses, such as providing child care and a more supportive environment, may be less costly than increasing wages. Thus, a lag exists between the decision to hire more nurses, the increase in wages, and the point at which the hospital is satisfied with the number of nurses it has.

A lag also exists before the supply of nurses responds to changed market conditions. Once nurses' wages are increased, it takes time for this information to become widely disseminated. Nurses who are not working may decide to return to nursing at the higher wage; this would be indicated by an increase in the nurse participation rate. Other nurses who are working part time may decide to increase the number of hours they work, and higher wages may make more high school graduates decide to undertake the educational requirements to become a nurse. The most rapid response to an increase in wages will come from those who work part time, followed by those who are already trained but not working as nurses. The long-run supply of nurses is determined by those who decide to enter nursing schools (and by the immigration of foreign-trained nurses). Short- and long-run supply responses to an increase in nurses' wages thus occur.

Let us now return to an examination of how well economic theory explains the recurrent shortage of nurses. Throughout the late 1960s and

EXHIBIT 24.2 Nursing School Enrollment, 1962–2008

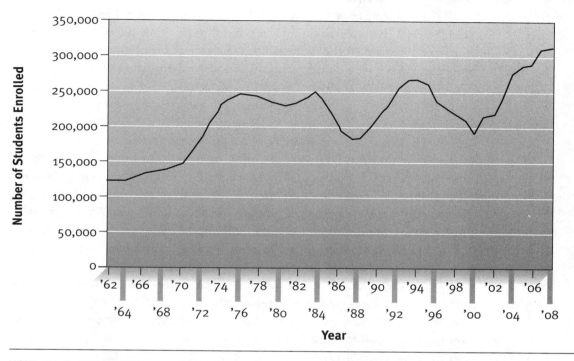

NOTE: Data for 1997 and 1998 are unavailable and are based on author's extrapolations.

SOURCES: American Nurses' Association. *Facts About Nursing,* various editions; National League for Nursing. *Enrollment in RN Programs.* 2009. [Online information.] http://www.nln.org/research/slides/pdf/AS0708_T03.pdf; US Census Bureau. *Statistical Abstract of the United States,* various editions; National Center for Health Statistics. *Health United States,* various editions.

early 1970s, nurses' wages increased more rapidly than wages in comparable professions, such as teaching, which resulted in declining vacancy rates and an increased nurse participation rate. Within several years, enrollments in nursing schools increased (a lag of several years always exists before the information on nurses' wages is transmitted to high school graduates and nursing school enrollments change) (see Exhibit 24.2).

By the late 1970s, concerns surfaced about a new shortage of nurses. The basis for this shortage began in 1971, when President Nixon imposed wage and price controls on the economy. Although these controls were removed from all other industries in 1972, they remained in effect for medical care until 1974. The wage controls, together with the increased supply of nurse graduates, began to have an effect by the late 1970s—well after the controls were lifted—because of the lag in transmission time mentioned above. Demand for nurses continued to increase throughout the 1970s, while the wage controls led to lower relative wages for nurses and, by the late 1970s, declining nursing school enrollments. By 1979, the vacancy rate reached 14 percent.

The shortage in 1979 and 1980, however, was short lived. As shown in Exhibit 24.1, nurses' wages rose sharply at the same time the economy entered a severe recession in the early 1980s. The rising unemployment rate caused more nurses to seek employment and increase their hours of work. Because 70 percent of RNs are married, the loss of a spouse's job or even the fear of it is likely to cause nurses to increase their labor force participation to maintain their family incomes (Buerhaus, Staiger, and Auerbach 2009, 201).

Higher wages and the rising unemployment rate increased nurse participation rates from 76 percent in 1980 to 79 percent by 1984. As a consequence, vacancy rates dropped to 4.4 percent by 1983. The nursing shortage had once again been resolved through a combination of rising wages, an increase in the nurse participation rate, and the national unemployment rate. RN wages remained stable (and actually declined in real dollars) between 1983 and 1985 and the vacancy rate dropped, and nursing school enrollments began a sharp decline through the late 1980s.

In the 1980s, the market for hospital services underwent drastic changes, which affected the market for nurses. Medicare changed hospital payment from cost-based to a fixed price per admission, and private insurers started utilization management. The trend by government and private insurers to reduce use of the hospital resulted in shorter hospital lengths of stay. Patients required more intensive treatment for the shorter time they were in the hospital. Hospitalized patients were more severely ill, a greater number of transplants were being performed, and the number of low-birth-weight babies increased. The recovery period, which requires less-intensive care, was occurring outside the hospital. As a result, hospitals began to use a greater number of RNs per patient. The greater demand by hospitals for RNs during this period is indicated by the fact that in 1975 there were 0.65 RNs per patient; this figure increased to 0.88 by 1980, to 1.31 by 1990, to 1.6 by 2000, and to 2.04 in 2008. The percentage increase in RNs per patient exceeded the decline in patient days.

The demand for nurses also increased in outpatient and nonhospital settings. As the use of the hospital declined, use of outpatient care, nursing homes, home care, and hospices for terminally ill Medicare patients increased. From 1980 to 2008, annual outpatient visits (ambulatory care visits to physicians' offices, hospital outpatient departments, and emergency departments) increased from 262 million to 1.19 billion (CDC 2010). Use of skilled nursing homes by Medicare patients increased from 8.6 million days in 1980 to 70.5 million days in 2008 (CMS 2010a). In addition to providing care in these alternative settings, cost-containment companies increased their demand for RNs to conduct utilization review and case management.

As the demand for nurses in these different settings increased faster than supply in the mid- to late 1980s, nurses' wages were slow to respond. Nursing school enrollments had been falling, and the national unemployment rate declined as the economy began to improve. Consequently, vacancy rates once again began to rise, from 5.1 percent in 1984 to 12.7 percent in 1989. By the late 1980s, concern again emerged over a shortage of nurses.

Hospitals again lobbied Congress for subsidies to increase nurse education programs and to ease immigration rules on foreign-trained nurses. The nursing shortage of the late 1980s resulted in Congress enacting the Nurse Shortage Reduction Act of 1988 and the Immigration Nurse Relief Act of 1989, which made it easier for foreign nurses to receive working visas.

Trends in the 1990s

Neither of these legislative acts was needed, however, as economic incentives again eliminated the shortage. As the economy weakened in the early 1990s and the unemployment rate began to rise, nurse participation rates increased to 82 percent by 1992. Nursing school enrollment had continued to increase in the early 1990s as a result of prior increases in nurses' wages. With the increase in supply of new nurses and the higher participation rate, vacancy rates declined to 4 percent by 1994. The nursing shortage ended.

One could have forecast that another shortage would occur by the end of the decade. As shown in Exhibit 24.1, nurses' real wages (adjusted for inflation) declined starting in 1994 and did not rise again until 1998. During this time, hospitals were trying to be more price competitive by reducing their costs so as to be included in managed care's provider networks. Only by 1998 did nurse wage increases finally begin to increase faster than inflation. The national unemployment rate also declined throughout the late 1990s, as the US economy was doing very well.

Nursing school enrollments typically decline several years after a decline in wages and vacancy rates. As shown in Exhibit 24.2, nursing school enrollments peaked at 270,000 in 1994 and then declined for the remainder of the 1990s. The reduction in nurse wages during the mid- to late 1990s led to a large reduction in nursing school enrollments and, consequently, in the number of nurse graduates.

In addition to declining enrollments, concern arose that the population of nurses is aging. In 1980, 25 percent of RNs were under the age of 30, compared with only 9.4 percent in 2008. The large 1950s cohort of RNs, who entered the workforce in the 1970s and 1980s, are approaching retirement age. The average age of a nurse was 37.9 in 1980 and 43.7 in 2006, and it is projected to increase to 44.6 by 2015 (Buerhaus, Staiger, and Auerbach 2009, 184). As the nurse population ages, participation rates decrease, as do the number of hours worked.

Current Supply and Demand for RNs

After years of declining (adjusted for inflation) nurse wages during the latter part of the 1990s, falling nursing school enrollments, and the aging of the nurse population, one would have expected to read newspaper articles about a new shortage of nurses and hospitals once again paying bonuses to attract nurses. After years of low vacancy rates, the vacancy rate started increasing in 1999 (from 4 percent in 1998 to 5.6 percent) and quickly rose to 13 percent by 2001.

As hospitals recognized the difficulty of attracting nurses in the beginning of the decade, nurses' real wages increased. With the increase in wages, RN supply started to increase faster. Nursing school enrollments increased, part-time RNs increased their hours of work, trained RNs rejoined the workforce, and immigration of RNs from other countries increased. Further stimulating the increase in supply of nurses in the beginning of the decade was the slowdown of the economy in 2001, leading to an increase in unemployment. Those states experiencing the greatest increases in unemployment saw the largest increases in married RNs re-entering the workforce (Buerhaus, Auerbach, and Steiger 2009). Almost all of the increase in RNs in 2002 (94 percent) occurred among married nurses. The nurse vacancy rate then declined, but it was still relatively high (at 8.1 percent) by the middle of the decade.

In the latter half of the decade the country slipped into a severe recession. A sharp increase occurred in the unemployment rate; the number of uninsured patients increased, as did hospital bad debts; and hospitals saw a decrease in the number of elective procedures. As occurred in previous periods of rising unemployment, the need to maintain their family incomes resulted in a large increase in nurse employment: Part-time RNs increased their hours of work and more trained RNs returned to the workforce. Hospitals (and other employers) did not need to increase RN wages to attract more RNs. Although RN wages did not keep up with inflation, a large decline occurred in the nurse vacancy rate, which fell to 4 percent. The shortage of RNs was once again resolved.

The Outlook for Registered Nurses

The increased demand for RNs in the United States has led to strong financial incentives for foreign-trained RNs to immigrate. In the United States, foreign-trained RNs have increased opportunities for much higher pay (allowing them to send funds home to assist their families), better working conditions, and greater prospects for learning and practice. In 2009, the median annual wage for RNs in the United States was $66,530, which is 20 to 30 times greater than what RNs earn in the Philippines (BLS 2009; Nursing Portal Philippines 2011). (These higher wages in the United States have even led physicians in the Philippines to train as RNs to be able to immigrate to the

United States.) In several countries, including the Philippines, RNs are trained for the purpose of being able to immigrate to the United States, as they provide a major source of remittances of hard currency to their countries of origin (Aiken et al. 2004, 72). To facilitate the immigration of foreign-trained nurses to the United States, for-profit firms have arisen to serve as brokers between US hospitals and foreign-trained RNs.[2]

The demand for hospital RNs, who represent 62 percent of RNs, is expected to continue to increase. The population is growing, and an increasing percentage of the population is becoming older; the baby boomers begin to retire in 2011. Medical advances will continue to stimulate the demand for expensive medical services provided by hospitals, increasing the demand for hospital nurses. Further, as more medical services are provided in outpatient settings and in patient's homes, the demand for RNs in these settings will continue to increase. Cost-containment efforts are further increasing use of less costly in-home and outpatient settings.

In addition, pressure by nursing organizations to have state-mandated minimum RN staffing ratios per hospital patient, such as exist in California, will increase hospitals' demand for RNs. (Hospital associations object to the minimum staff ratios, and one consequence of the conflict between nurse and hospital associations over increased RN staffing ratios has been research on whether the patient benefits of higher RN staffing ratios is worth the additional cost. [3])

With respect to the future supply of RNs to meet these expected increases in demand, several trends are emerging. The RN workforce is aging, and as these nurses retire, the supply of RNs will be reduced if efforts are not made to increase the number of younger nurses. Most of the increase in supply since 2000 came from older RNs re-entering the workforce and the immigration of foreign-born RNs. (The increase in unemployment rates was important in bringing older, married RNs back to nursing.) Increased immigration of foreign-trained nurses (and the return to work of older RNs) has offset the decline of younger people choosing a nursing career. Both have been responsive to higher RN wages. Unless the number of younger RNs increases, as older RNs start retiring after 2010, the United States will have to increasingly rely on foreign-born RNs.

Men could eventually be a major source of RN supply. Male RNs represent about 9 percent of the RN workforce. The stereotype of nursing as a female-dominated profession is an important reason men have not chosen to become nurses. Also underrepresented in the nursing profession are Hispanics, who account for 5 percent of RNs. Increases in the proportion of both these groups would lead to large increases in the supply of RNs (Buerhaus, Auerbach, and Staiger 2009, w666).

Expanding the supply of US-trained RNs is limited by the inadequate response by nursing schools to the increased demand for a nursing education.

In 2009, due to a lack of capacity and a shortage of faculty and resources, only 42 percent of student applicants were admitted to nursing programs. This represents a decrease from 45 percent in recent years (AACN 2010a, 2010b). The not-for-profit market for nursing education does not appear to be performing efficiently.

A concern regarding the long-run supply of nurses is President Obama's recently enacted healthcare legislation. Included in the legislation are reductions in hospital payment of $500 billion over the next ten years, which will limit hospitals' ability to increase nurse wages. It is uncertain whether these payment decreases will actually occur, since scheduled Medicare physician payment reductions, according to the sustainable growth rate formula, have been continually postponed for fear of reducing seniors' access to physicians. Should these reductions in hospital payments occur, however, hospitals will be unable to attract additional RNs by increasing wage rates. Registered nurse wages that fall behind wages in other careers available to potential nurses will result in a *permanent* shortage of nurses; the demand for nurses will exceed supply at the wage hospitals can afford to pay given their reduced budget.

Since the mid-1960s, the recurrent shortages of nurses have been caused by increased demands for nurses and the failure of hospitals to immediately recognize that, at the higher demand, nurses' wages must be increased. Once hospitals realize market conditions for nurses have changed, the process once again brings equilibrium to the market. Future nurse shortages, however, may take longer than usual to resolve because of the aging of the nurse population, higher state-mandated nurse-staffing ratios, capacity constraints among nursing schools, and reduced government payments to hospitals, limiting hospitals' ability to increase nurse wages.

Federal Subsidies to Nursing Schools and Students

Each time a new nursing shortage occurs, various bills are introduced in Congress to address different aspects of the shortage, such as increased funding for nurse scholarships, financial support for nurses seeking advanced degrees, and funding for increasing faculty in nursing schools. Proposals for federal funding to increase the supply of nurses have been made since the enactment of the 1964 Nurse Training Act. These recommendations ignore the important role played by higher wages in increasing the short- and long-run supply of nurses.

Federal subsidies to nursing schools and students cannot be directed only to those students who would otherwise have chosen a different career. Nurse education subsidies take years to affect the supply of nurses. More important, to the extent that federal programs are successful in increasing the number of nursing school graduates, nurses' wages rise more slowly. A larger supply of new graduates causes a lower rate of increase in nurses' wages, which in turn results in a smaller increase in the nurse participation rate. Nurses would be more reluctant to return to nursing or increase their hours of work if their wages did not increase.

Nursing programs complain that they cannot admit greater numbers of nursing students because of insufficient faculty. Colleges and universities attempting to expand their nursing faculties operate in a highly competitive market for RNs with graduate degrees who can receive much higher salaries from hospitals and health systems. A significant factor in the shortage of nurse faculty is salaries lower than the market wage. It is surprising that nursing schools are unable to resolve a problem of attracting new faculty, a problem that other academic programs must contend with and appear to have resolved. Given the high rate of return to students receiving their associate in arts degrees and their RN training in two-year colleges, such schools should be able to increase tuition levels to be able to attract the necessary resources to expand their capacity and admit a greater number of students.

Reliance on market mechanisms rather than federal subsidies is likely to bring about a quicker resolution of nurse shortages. For example, increased wages will bring about an increase in the number of hours part-time nurses work; about 25 percent of all employed nurses work part time. Higher wages also attract qualified RNs from other countries, such as the Philippines, which trains nurses for export to the United States and whose families depend upon their remittances. Higher wages for nurses will cause hospitals and other demanders of nurses to rethink how they use their nurses. As nurses become more expensive to employ, hospitals will use nurses in higher-skilled tasks and delegate certain housekeeping and other tasks currently performed by RNs to less-trained nursing personnel, such as licensed practical nurses. Higher wages and new roles for nurses would make nursing a more attractive profession, thereby increasing the demand for a nursing career. Finally, nursing is predominantly a female profession; there is no reason more men cannot be attracted to a nursing career. Higher wages and new nursing roles will increase the attractiveness of nursing to a larger segment of the population.

Summary

The nursing profession faces challenges and opportunities in coming years. The major reason for recurrent RN shortages is the cyclic pattern of nurse wages. As nurse wages stagnated, the rate of return on a nursing career fell and enrollments in nursing schools declined, as did numbers of graduates. With a reduced supply of nurses and an increased acuity level of patients, hospitals eventually found that they could not attract as many nurses as they wanted at the current nurse wage rate, and RN vacancy rates increased. Each of these shortages was resolved when nurse wages increased; nursing school enrollments increased, older RNs re-entered the workforce, and a greater number of foreign-trained RNs immigrated to the United States, all of which expanded the supply of nurses.

The aging of the nurse workforce is likely to result in a smaller supply of nurses over the next decade, unless there is increased immigration of foreign-trained RNs and expanded nursing school capacity.

To forestall future shortages and make the nurse market function more smoothly, better information must be provided to the demanders and suppliers of nursing services. Information will facilitate the market's adjustment process by eliminating the time lags in wage increases and enrollments that have caused these cyclical shortages. Hospitals and other demanders of nursing services must be made more aware of approaches that increase nurses' productivity and the wages and other working conditions necessary to attract more nurses. To realize the full potential of nursing as a profession and expand the supply of nurses, potential nursing students need to be provided with timely information that allows them to make informed career choices. Nurses, particularly those who are not employed or are working part time, have to be aware of opportunities in nursing, as well as wages and working conditions being offered. Efforts to increase information are more likely to eliminate shortages and lead to an increase in the supply of nurses than are policies that merely rely on large federal subsidies to nursing education.

Both public policy and private initiatives are directed at reducing the rising costs of medical care. If the outcome of public policy is to place arbitrary budget limits on hospitals and total medical expenditures, nurses' wages will not increase as rapidly as wages for comparably trained professions in the non-regulated health sector, and a permanent nurse shortage will occur. Innovation in the use of RNs and provision of new medical services will be stifled for lack of funds.

If, however, public policy reinforces what is occurring in the private sector, namely competition among managed care organizations on the basis of their premiums and quality of care, the demand for RNs will be determined by their productivity, the tasks they are permitted to perform, the improved patient outcomes they provide, and their wages relative to other types of nursing personnel. To the extent that RNs are able to perform more highly valued tasks, such as assuming responsibility for more primary care services, utilization management, and management of home healthcare, as is currently the case in many competitive organizations, they become more valuable to such organizations. In competitive markets, these organizations will be willing to increase their use of RNs and their wages to reflect the higher value of services rendered. The future roles, responsibilities, and incomes of RNs will be affected by the incentives created by a competitive healthcare system.

Discussion Questions

1. Why was the demand for RNs rising faster than supply during the 1980s?
2. How have the last several shortages of nurses been resolved?
3. How does an increase in nurses' wages affect hospitals' demand for nurses and the supply of nurses?
4. Why was the shortage of nurses that occurred before Medicare different from subsequent shortages?
5. Contrast the following two approaches for eliminating the shortage of nurses:
   a. Providing federal subsidies to nursing schools
   b. Increasing information on nurse demand and supply to prospective nursing students and demanders of nursing services, such as hospitals

Notes

1. Even when hospitals are able to hire all the nurses they want at the prevailing wage, a nurse vacancy rate will still exist because of normal turnover.
2. Foreign-trained RNs are limited in their entry to the United States by US immigration and licensure policies. "All U.S. nurses must pass the National Council Licensure Examination (NCLEX-RN) to practice as RNs. To take the exam, foreign applicants must demonstrate that their education meets U.S. standards—most notably, that their education was at the postsecondary level. Also, nurses trained in countries in which English is not the primary language must . . . pass an English proficiency test (the Test of English as a Foreign Language, or TOEFL). The U.S. Commission on Graduates of Foreign Nursing Schools (CGFNS) offers an exam in many countries that is an excellent predictor of passing the NCLEX-RN. The CGFNS exam reduces the number of foreign-trained nurses who travel to the United States expecting to work as RNs who cannot pass the licensing exam" (Aiken et al. 2004, 72).
3. Needleman and colleagues (2006) analyzed data from 800 hospitals in 11 states to determine whether, from the hospital's perspective, the cost-saving (or revenue-increasing) gains from expanding RN staffing ratios exceed the cost of implementing higher RN staffing ratios. The authors estimated the cost of increased RN staffing compared with the improvement in patient outcomes, such as avoided deaths, fewer adverse patient outcomes, and decreased hospital lengths of stay. The authors considered three options: The first was increasing the percentage of all nurses that are RNs (the 75th percentile) without changing the total number

of hours worked by all nurses; the second required increasing all nursing hours to the 75th percentile of all hospitals; and the third involved increasing both the percentage of RNs (option 1) and all nursing hours (option 2). The increased hospital costs for each of these options are, respectively, $811 million, $7.5 billion, and $8.5 billion. According to these results, option 1 produces a net saving of $242 million. Although options 2 and 3 are expected to produce large savings, these savings are less than the costs of the additional nurse staffing, resulting in net losses of $1.7 billion and $2.8 billion, respectively.

The authors conclude that implementing option 1 would save hospitals money, whereas options 2 and 3 might require government subsidies to make it worthwhile for hospitals to undertake the additional nurse staffing required. A study of this magnitude involves a number of assumptions regarding benefits and costs and the calculation of each; in addition, the benefits and costs are considered only from a hospital's perspective, not that of the patient or his family.

THE HIGH PRICE OF PRESCRIPTION DRUGS

Spending on prescription drugs has greatly increased since 1990, when drug expenditures were $40 billion. As of 2009, drug expenditures reached $250 billion (CMS 2011c). In the late 1990s and the early part of the past decade, drug expenditures increased more rapidly than other medical expenditures. After reaching a peak rate of increase of 18 percent in 1999, the annual rate of increase in drug expenditures has been declining and increased by only 5 percent in 2009, compared with the 5 percent and 4 percent increase in hospital and physician expenditures, respectively. The annual percentage increases in prescription drug expenditures and drug prices since 1980 are shown in Exhibit 25.1. Prescription drug expenditures also represent a smaller percentage of total health expenditures (10 percent) than hospital or physician services (31 percent and 21 percent, respectively).

Although prescription drug expenditures represent a smaller percentage of total medical expenditures and their annual rate of increase has slowed, drug expenditures are a cause for concern in the public and private sectors. Higher drug expenditures are a growing burden to state Medicaid programs, the federal deficit, and private insurance premiums. Furthermore, patients pay a higher percentage of drug expenditures out of pocket than they do for other major health expenditures. Not surprisingly, patients are more likely to complain about paying $50 for a prescription drug than about a $20,000 stay in the hospital, which is covered by insurance.

Reasons for the Increase in Pharmaceutical Expenditures

The major factors causing increased drug expenditures are an increase in the number of drug prescriptions (utilization), drug price increases, and changes in the types of drugs used.

Increases in the Number of Drug Prescriptions
Increased use of drugs is an important contributor to increased drug expenditures. As shown in Exhibit 25.2, the total number of prescriptions filled (including refills) increased from 1.9 billion in 1992 to 3.9 billion in 2009. On a per capita basis, the average number of retail prescriptions increased from 7.3 in 1992 to 10.4 in 2000 to 12.8 in 2009.

EXHIBIT 25.1 Annual Percentage Changes in the Prescription Drug Price Index and Prescription Drug Expenditures, 1980–2009

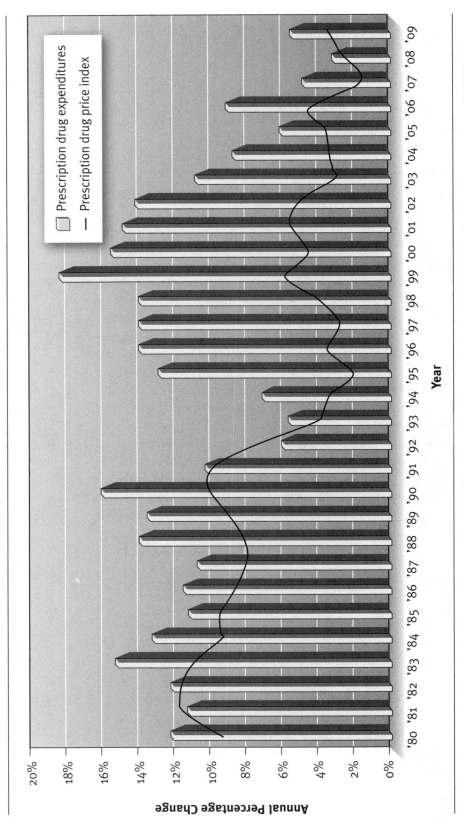

SOURCES: US Department of Labor, Bureau of Labor Statistics, 2011. http://www.bls.gov/cpi/home.htm; Centers for Medicare & Medicaid Services, Office of the Actuary, National Health Statistics Group, 2011. http://www.cms.gov/NationalHealthExpendData/downloads/tables.pdf

EXHIBIT 25.2 Total Prescriptions Dispensed and Prescriptions per Capita, 1992–2009

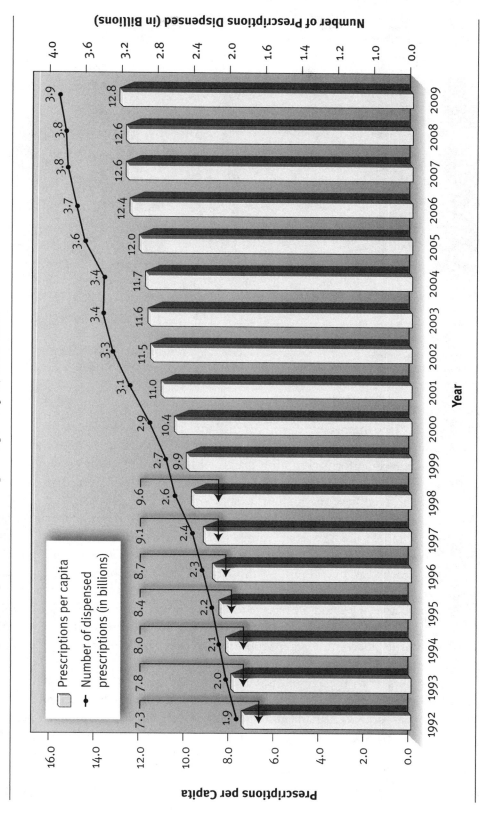

SOURCES: 1992–2001 data from the National Institute for Health Care Management, *Prescription Drug Expenditures in 2001: Another Year of Escalating Costs*, May 6, 2002, http://www.nihcm .org/spending2001.pdf; 2002–2009 data from IMS Health. 2010. *Top-Line Industry Data.* www.imshealth.com; US Census Bureau. *Statistical Abstract of the United States, 2010 ed.* http:// www.census.gov/compendia/statab/.

EXHIBIT 25.3 Average Number of Prescription Drug Purchases, by Age, 2006

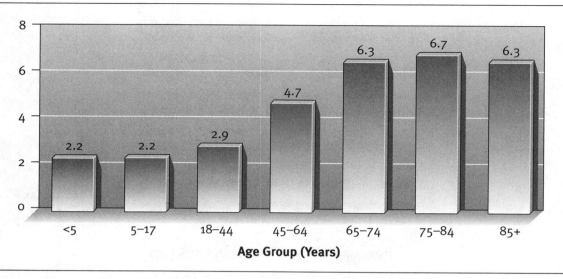

Age Group (Years)

NOTE: Average number of unique prescriptions.

SOURCE: Marie N. Stagnitti, *Average Number of Total (Including Refills) and Unique Prescriptions by Select Person Characteristics, 2006.* AHRQ Statistical Brief #245. May 2009. www.meps.ahrq.gov/mepsweb/data_files/publications/st245/stat245.pdf.

Two important reasons for the large increase in drug prescriptions over time have been the increase in the number of aged and the increased insurance coverage for prescription drugs. Although population growth is about 1 percent per year, the number of aged has been increasing more rapidly, and the aged have the highest use rate of prescription drugs. With regard to prescriptions purchased in an outpatient setting only, those between the ages of 18 and 44 use an average number of 2.9 prescriptions each per year, while those between the ages of 45 and 64 receive an average of about 4.7 prescriptions each year. In contrast, for those between the ages of 65 and 74, the average number of prescriptions increases to more than 6.3 per person, and those aged between 75 and 84 receive 6.7 prescriptions each (see Exhibit 25.3).

As the aged, who are the greatest users (and beneficiaries) of prescription drugs, become a larger proportion of the population, the volume of prescriptions should continue to increase. Starting in 2011, the first of the baby boomers reach the age of 65. Given the increase in the number of aged and the greater number of prescriptions per aged person, drug expenditures in general—and particularly among the aged—clearly will continue to increase.

The second reason for the increase in prescriptions per capita has been growth in private and public insurance coverage for prescription drugs. The percentage of the population with some form of third-party payment for prescription drugs has been increasing over time. Conversely,

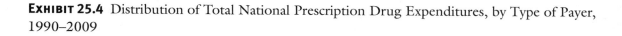

EXHIBIT 25.4 Distribution of Total National Prescription Drug Expenditures, by Type of Payer, 1990–2009

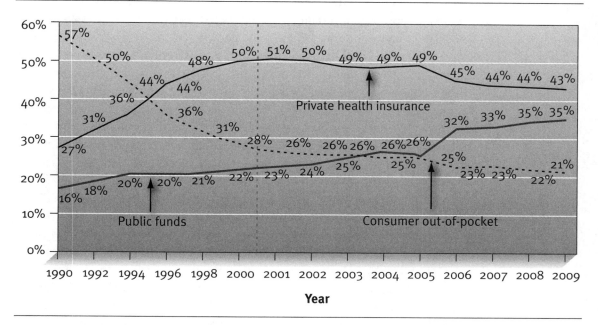

SOURCE: Centers for Medicare & Medicaid Services, Office of the Actuary, National Health Statistics Group, 2011. www.cms.gov/ NationalHealthExpendData/downloads/tables.pdf.

out-of-pocket expenditures for prescription drugs have been falling. As shown in Exhibit 25.4, in 1990, 57 percent of drug expenditures were out of pocket, 27 percent were covered by private insurance, and the remainder, 16 percent, were from public funds, primarily Medicaid. Currently (as of 2009), only 21 percent of drug expenditures are paid out of pocket by consumers, with the remainder paid by private insurance (43 percent) and by public funds, primarily Medicaid and Medicare (35 percent). Providing a drug benefit in which the patient's copayment is only $5 per prescription represents a large price decrease, and drug plans offered by health plans led to large increases in the use of prescription drugs.

The Medicare (Part D) prescription drug benefit, which became effective in 2006, stimulated greater use of prescription drugs among the elderly. (As shown in Exhibit 25.1, drug expenditures jumped in 2006.) With the new Medicare drug benefit, Medicare became the primary payer for many of the aged who were on Medicaid.

Medicare drug expenditures rose more slowly than expected because of the way the benefit was provided. Medicare beneficiaries had to choose between competing firms to receive their drug benefit. The competing firms that provided the drug benefit held down drug price increases through the use of several cost-containment approaches. One example was the use of formularies, which excluded certain drugs from coverage, requiring prior authorization for approval of certain drugs, and tiered cost sharing, such as 25 percent (or $10) copayment for generics, 30 percent (or $25) for branded drugs in the formulary, and 40 to 50 percent (or $50) for branded drugs not in the formulary (Kaiser Family Foundation 2010). The aged chose among the competing firms according to their premiums and whether their drugs were included in the firm's formulary. Without competition among firms providing the benefit and the ability of these firms to negotiate price discounts from pharmaceutical companies to include their drugs in their formularies, prices and expenditures would have increased more rapidly; the estimated federal cost of the drug benefit has been much less than anticipated.

As part of the 2010 Patient Protection and Affordable Care Act, Medicare beneficiaries will have reduced out-of-pocket payments for their prescription drugs under Medicare Part D. This change, which will be phased in over time, is likely to increase drug use and Medicare drug expenditures.

Exhibit 25.5 illustrates both the changing share of spending on prescription drugs and the growth in drug expenditures over time. The largest share of spending on drugs comes from private health insurance and health plans. After the new Medicare drug benefit became available, the share of total drug expenditures by private health plans declined, and those serving Medicare beneficiaries increased.

Drug Price Increases

Drug prices have been less of a contributing factor to expenditure increases than increased utilization. Drug prices, which had been increasing at double-digit rates during the 1980s, moderated to 4 to 5 percent annual increases during the 1990s. Recent annual price increases for prescription drugs have been less than price increases for hospital and physician services. Price increases (as measured by the Bureau of Labor Statistics) appear to be less of a contributing factor to the recent increases in drug expenditures than they were in the period before the mid-1990s.

An important reason for the slowdown in drug price increases is that patents for many top-selling drugs have expired and they have been subject to competition from less expensive generics, resulting in lower prices (and profits). Also, fewer high-priced new drugs have entered the market, resulting in a slowdown in overall drug price increases. In addition, health plans have tried to control the growth in drug expenditures by creating stronger incentives for their enrollees to choose generic or cheaper brand name drugs.

A number of studies have examined the relationship between the out-of-pocket drug price (copayments) and drug expenditures. These studies (e.g., Goodell and Swartz 2010) have found that higher cost sharing results in

EXHIBIT 25.5 Share of Prescription Drug Spending, by Source of Funds, Selected Years, 1960–2009

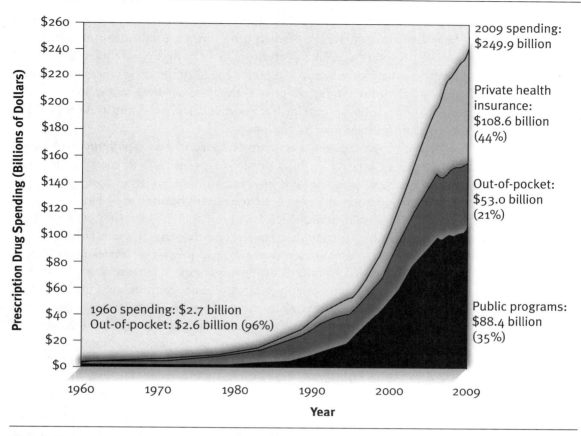

NOTE: Public programs cover federal, state, and local spending for prescription drugs, including Medicare, workers' compensation, temporary disability, public assistance (Medicaid and SCHIP), Department of Defense, maternal/child health, Veterans Administration, and Indian Health Services.

SOURCE: Centers for Medicare & Medicaid Services, Office of the Actuary, National Health Statistics Group, 2011. http://www.cms.gov/NationalHealthExpendData/downloads/tables.pdf.

more adverse health events, such as greater emergency room visits, and more inpatient admissions. Conversely, the use of newer drugs results in less inpatient care. Understanding the effect of price on use of drugs has important consequences on both drug and total medical expenditures. A substitution effect occurs between drug use and use of other medical services. Increasing the copayments of certain drugs not only decreases the demand for those drugs but is likely to result in greater use of more costly medical services, thereby increasing medical expenditures.[1] Health plans must consider these unintended consequences of imposing more stringent cost sharing on patients, particularly those with chronic conditions.

Changes in the Types of Drugs Prescribed

Over time, the composition of the types of drugs used changes, which in turn affects how fast drug expenditures increase. When a new, innovative drug enters the market, it will have a higher price than the drugs it replaces. When a "me-too" drug enters the market, it becomes a good substitute for the innovative drug and, as such, lowers the price of both drugs. Similarly, when the patent on a drug expires and a generic version of the drug enters the market, many switch from the higher-priced brand name drug to the lower priced generic. (About 80 percent of US Food and Drug Administration [FDA]–approved drugs have generic versions.)

Drug expenditures may increase more or less rapidly depending on the number of innovative, high-priced drugs brought to market, the entry of me-too drugs, whether (and how many) branded drugs lose their patent protection, and how rapidly generic substitutes become available.

The 1990s saw a large increase in the number of innovative new drugs with relatively high prices that have preventive and curative effects, which resulted in greater use. These drugs can treat previously untreatable illnesses and have substituted for more costly, invasive medical treatments, leading to lower overall treatment costs. New drugs reduce nonpharmaceutical medical costs, such as new antidepressants that have reduced costly psychotherapy as well as beta-blockers and blood pressure drugs that have reduced the costs of cardiovascular-related hospital admissions and surgeries. Lichtenberg (2007) concluded that the replacement of older drugs by newer drugs resulted in reductions in mortality, morbidity (as indicated by fewer days lost from work), and total treatment costs, particularly for inpatient care. The use of new drugs has resulted in large hospital savings because of reductions in lengths of stay and number of hospital admissions. The total reduction in nondrug medical expenses is about seven times the increase in the costs of drugs.

Some new drugs also have fewer adverse side effects. Many new lifestyle drugs, such as Viagra (treatment of male impotence), Claritin (relief from allergies), Prilosec (relief from stomach upsets), antidepressants, and pain relievers improve quality of life. However, they may be much more expensive than older drugs. For example, new pain relievers treat severe arthritis, but they cost $150 a month, nearly 20 times more than previous pain relievers. A new biotech drug that treats rheumatoid arthritis, Enbrel, can cost $1,500 a month. Whereas drugs such as penicillin would be prescribed for a brief period to cure an infection, some modern drugs, including lifestyle drugs, can be taken for decades. The prospect of better health and a higher quality of life has led to an increase in the number of prescriptions and the price of new drugs.

In the next five years, six of the ten largest-selling prescription brand name drugs are expected to go off their patent. As generic substitutes enter the market, prices for these drugs will decline, along with the rate of increase in drug expenditures. Unless new innovative drugs become available, drug

Exhibit 25.6 Prescription Sales by Outlet, US Market, 2009

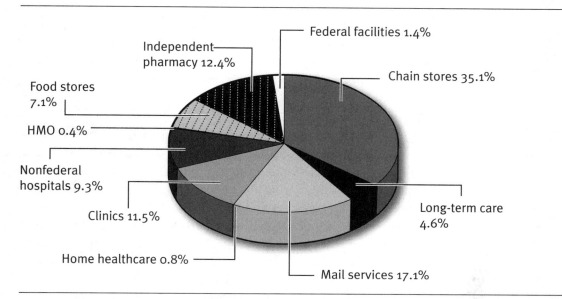

SOURCE: IMS Health. 2010. *Top-Line Industry Data*. http://www.imshealth.com/deployedfiles/imshealth/Global/Content/StaticFile/Top_Line_Data/Channel%20Distribution%20by%20U.S.Sales.pdf.

expenditures will be driven more by greater use than by increased prices for newer drugs.

Rising drug expenditures should be viewed with favor when innovative drugs become available to extend life, substitute for more costly treatments, and improve the quality of life. Further, a greater number of prescriptions per person, particularly for the aged, may indicate that chronic diseases can be better managed, the aged can live longer, and their quality of life can be improved.

Pricing Practices of US Pharmaceutical Companies

Drug manufacturers sell their drugs to different purchasers (intermediaries), who in turn sell them to patients. Retail (independent and chain) pharmacies sell about 47 percent of all prescription drugs; healthcare organizations such as HMOs, hospitals, long-term-care facilities, home health, federal facilities, and clinics sell 29 percent; mail-order pharmacies sell 17 percent; and food stores sell 7 percent (see Exhibit 25.6). (HMO and insurance company patients rely on mail-order and retail pharmacies that are in their insurers' networks for their drugs.)

Drug manufacturers sell the same prescription drug to different purchasers at different prices. An HMO pays less for its drugs than an independent retail pharmacy, although the latter sells a much greater volume of drugs. Similarly, patients without any prescription drug coverage (often the poor and sick) pay more for the same drug at a retail pharmacy than those who are part of a managed care plan.

Two aspects of the pricing practices of pharmaceutical companies have been criticized as unfair and have led to proposals for government intervention. First, different purchasers are charged different prices for the same drug, and second, prescription drugs have a high price markup.

Pricing According to Cost

A new prescription drug is priced many times higher than its actual costs of production. This high markup of price over cost has generated a great deal of criticism. If the drug were priced closer to its production cost, it would be less of a financial burden on those with low incomes, those without prescription drug coverage, and state Medicaid budgets.

Drug manufacturers often claim that their drug prices are determined by the high costs of developing those drugs. High research and development (R&D) costs, however, are not the reason for high or rising drug prices. Large fixed, or sunk, costs are costs that have already been incurred; hence, they are not relevant for setting a drug's price. Fixed costs must eventually be recovered, or the drug company will lose money; however, a new drug that is no different from drugs already on the market could not sell for more than these competitive drugs regardless of how much that drug cost to develop.

Pricing According to Demand

When price differences for the same drug cannot be entirely explained by cost differences, according to economic theory the reason for the differences must be related to differences in the purchaser's price sensitivity or willingness to pay. Purchasers who are not price sensitive will be charged higher prices than those who are. A purchaser who is willing to buy less or switch to other drugs when the price increases is more price sensitive than one who will not.

The higher price charged to one purchaser is not meant to make up for the lower price charged to another purchaser. Instead, the reason for different prices is that the seller can simply make more money by charging according to each purchaser's willingness to pay (Frank 2001).

The ability to shift market share rather than just the volume purchased drives discounts. Not all large-volume purchasers receive price discounts. Retail pharmacies in total sell a large volume of drugs, but they do not receive the same price discounts as do managed care plans. When an HMO negotiates with a drug company on one of several competing brand name drugs within a therapeutic class, the HMO's willingness to place the drug on its formulary while excluding a competitor's drugs can result in substantial discounts for the HMO.[2] Similarly, pharmacy benefit managers (PBMs), who manage health plans' drug benefits for drugs sold through retail pharmacies, can promote brand name substitution and thereby receive large discounts.[3]

Retail pharmacies pay the highest prices for their prescription drugs because they must carry all branded drugs. Furthermore, the pharmacy cannot promote substitution between branded drugs because the physician may be prescribing according to a health plan's formulary. Because pharmacies cannot shift volume, drug manufacturers see no need to give them a price discount.[4] (To receive price discounts, government entities have resorted to price regulation; see Chapter 28.) For a pharmacy to be included in a health plan or a PBM network it must charge lower dispensing fees, which also results in lower prices to the PBM and to health plan enrollees.

Price discrimination, whereby a seller charges different prices to different purchasers, occurs in many other areas of the economy. For example, seniors and students pay lower prices at the movies and other events. Prices may differ by time of day, such as early-bird dinner specials and drinks, and airlines charge business travelers more than vacationers because they book flights on short notice. Those who are less likely to switch are less price sensitive and are charged more for the same service.

Price discrimination actually promotes price competition between drug manufacturers for more price-sensitive purchasers, which results in lower prices for purchasers and consumers. To price discriminate a seller must prevent low-price buyers from reselling the product to those who are charged more. A 1987 federal law prevented resale of prescription drugs on the basis of preserving the safety and integrity of those drugs.

Pricing Innovative Drugs

Pharmaceutical manufacturers are strategic in how they mark up the price of their drugs (price-to-cost ratio) and negotiate price discounts. A drug's price markup is determined by demand. New drugs are priced according to their therapeutic value and the availability of good substitutes. When a new drug for which there is no close substitute comes on the market and is clearly therapeutically superior to existing drugs, it will have a higher price markup. Sometimes a drug is priced according to some concept of value, such as comparing it to the surgical procedure it replaces. Approving an existing drug for a new use also increases its value, as its therapeutic effects for that new use are greater than existing drugs; the drug company is thus able to increase its price.

The greater the price markup over costs, the more innovative the drug and the fewer the close substitutes to it. Innovative drugs command higher price markups than imitative drugs. Ultimately the price of a new drug is determined by a purchaser's willingness to pay for its greater therapeutic benefits. A new breakthrough drug is priced much higher than any other drug in its therapeutic class (typically more than three times the price) because no good substitutes are available. New drugs with modest therapeutic gains are priced about two times the average for available drug substitutes. New drugs with little or no gain over existing drugs are priced at about the same level as existing substitutes. Once the patent has expired on a branded drug, generic drugs are introduced and are typically priced at about 30 to 70 percent of the branded drug's price before the patent expired. As more generic versions become available, the prices of generic drugs fall.

New, higher-priced drugs will fail commercially if their therapeutic benefits are similar to those of existing drugs. As health plans evaluate drugs for inclusion in their formularies based on therapeutic benefits and price, differences in drug prices will reflect differences in therapeutic benefits. Knowledgeable purchasers evaluating a higher-priced new drug will pay a higher price only if its therapeutic benefits are greater than those of the older drug.

A new drug that is similar to an existing drug (a me-too drug) cannot be priced much higher than the existing drug because purchasers will switch to a good substitute (the existing drug) at a lower price. Although drug companies have been criticized for producing me-too drugs, their availability contributes to price competition. (Me-too drugs also provide value in that they may have fewer side effects than the existing drug.)

Once competitors enter the market originally served by an innovative drug, prices decline. Interestingly, when generic versions enter the market after the patent on a branded drug has expired, the branded drug loses market share to the generic drug but the price of the branded product actually increases; the price-sensitive customers switch to the generic drug, and those who do not switch are not price sensitive. Therefore, the seller of the branded drug is able to raise its price. Some physicians (and consumers) have strong preferences for the branded drug and do not want to substitute the generic version; they are willing to pay more for the security of the brand name drug.[5] Drug manufacturers have determined that serving a smaller market at a higher price is more profitable than reducing the price of the branded drug to compete with generic versions.[6]

Thus, the pricing strategy of pharmaceutical companies is based on two principles. The first is the price sensitivity of the purchaser. The greater the price sensitivity of the purchaser, such as an HMO that is willing to shift its drug purchases to a competitor's drug, the lower the price. Second, the more innovative the drug, the higher the price markup will be. These pricing strategies are designed to maximize drug firm profits.

Drug Companies' Marketing Response to Managed Care Plans

Purchaser decision making with respect to pharmaceuticals has changed. Previously, physicians chose a patient's prescription drug. As a result, drug manufacturers spent a great deal of money marketing directly to physicians. With the growth of managed care and its use of closed formularies, drug companies began to develop new marketing strategies. As the purchasing decision over prescription drugs shifted from the individual physician to the committee overseeing the organization's formulary, sending sales representatives to individual physicians caring for an HMO's patients was less useful than marketing to the HMO itself. Drug companies have had to demonstrate that their drugs are not only therapeutically superior to competitive drugs but that they are also cost effective, namely that the additional benefits of their drug are worth a higher price. Physicians continue to be important in prescribing drugs to their patients, but PBMs and health plans determine which brand name drugs the physician is able to prescribe and the prices paid for those drugs.

To counteract the closed formularies, drug manufacturers started direct-to-consumer television and newspaper advertising to generate consumer demand for certain drugs from their physicians. Direct-to-consumer advertising, the cost of which increased from about $600 million in 1997 (the first year it was permitted by the FDA) to $2.5 billion by 2000, to $11 billion by 2009, has proved effective in increasing sales of advertised prescription drugs (Henry J. Kaiser Family Foundation 2010b). Previously, physicians almost never wrote prescriptions for drugs requested by patients because most patients did not know enough to demand drugs by name or therapeutic class. As more medical information has become available to patients, they have begun demanding more input into the therapeutic decisions that affect their lives. Drug companies claim that ads are meant to inform the patient and stimulate a discussion between the patient and her physician. Critics claim that the ads do not inform patients about who is most likely to benefit from that drug, its possible side effects, or other treatment options.

Although drug costs have become an increasing expense for health plans, and health plans have introduced tiered copayments to provide their enrollees with an incentive to use less costly drugs, health plans have also reduced or eliminated copays for the use of certain drugs. Given the inverse relationship between price and use of drugs, health plans are using reduced drug copayments to encourage the use of drugs that reduce more costly medical episodes. If decreasing copayments, or even providing the drug for free, makes a patient more likely to follow the recommended drug therapy and thereby prevent recurrence of a heart attack or a stroke, the health plan is able to reduce its cost in addition to benefiting the patient.

Summary

Prescription drug expenditures will continue to increase because of increased use of drugs and the introduction of newer, higher-priced drugs. New drugs have a high markup in relation to their cost of production. To those without drug coverage and to large purchasers of drugs, such as health plans, Medicare, and state Medicaid agencies, these facts are a cause for concern.

However, the public should view rising drug expenditures and even high price markups favorably. Rising drug prices are often an indication that new drugs are more effective than existing drugs or alternative treatments. (When new drugs are of higher quality, that is, when they provide greater benefits than the drugs they replace, the "quality-adjusted" price of these drugs may well be lower than the price of older drugs. Thus, counting the higher prices of new drugs as mere price increases is misleading.) Furthermore, when new drugs replace older drugs, purchasers value the greater therapeutic benefits of the newer drugs more and are willing to pay higher prices for their increased value. Consumers are clearly better off. The replacement of older drugs by newer drugs is an important reason for the increase in drug expenditures. Also contributing to greater use of newer drugs is increased demand resulting from the increase in third-party payment for prescription drugs, population growth, and the aging of the population. All these factors will likely cause drug expenditures to continue to increase in the future.

Drug manufacturers charge different prices to different buyers for the same drug (price discrimination) so as to give price discounts to purchasers who are willing to switch their drug purchases and charge higher prices to those who are less price sensitive (unwilling to switch). The cost-containment strategies of health plans and PBMs have caused drug firms to compete on price to have their drugs included in the formularies of large purchasers and to emphasize the cost effectiveness of their drugs. Drug firms have also started direct-to-consumer advertising to develop consumer pressure to demand the drug from their physicians. To limit the effect of such tactics, health plans have instituted tiered copayment systems that give consumers incentives to use drugs on the health plan's formulary.

Discussion Questions

1. Which factors have contributed most to the increase in drug expenditures?
2. Are rising drug expenditures necessarily bad?
3. Is the high price of drugs determined by the high cost of developing a new drug?
4. Why do drug manufacturers charge different purchasers different prices for the same prescription drug?
5. What methods have managed care plans used to limit their enrollees' drug costs?

Notes

1. The relationship between the out-of-pocket price of drugs and drug expenditures has been estimated to be −1.13, that is, a 1 percent increase in price will result in a 1.13 percent decrease in drug expenditures over time (Gaynor, Li, and Vogt 2006).

2. As HMOs and health plans seek volume discounts from drug companies, they are willing to limit their subscribers' choice of drugs in return for lower drug prices. Drug formulary committees focus on drugs for which therapeutic substitutes exist and evaluate different drugs according to their therapeutic value and price; higher-priced drugs are used only when justified by greater therapeutic benefits. Restrictions are then placed on their physicians' prescribing behavior. These organizations are also using computer technology to conduct drug utilization review; each physician's prescription is instantly checked against the formulary, and data are gathered on the performance of each physician and the health plan's use of specific drugs.

3. PBMs are firms that provide administrative services and process outpatient prescription drug claims for health insurers' prescription drug plans. To control growth in prescription drug expenditures, PBMs will also contract with a network of pharmacies, negotiate pharmacy payments, negotiate with drug manufacturers for drug discounts and rebates, develop a drug formulary listing preferred drugs for treating an illness, encourage use of generic drugs instead of high-priced brand name drugs, operate a mail-order pharmacy, and analyze and monitor patient compliance programs. Some PBMs have been very aggressive in switching physicians' prescriptions; they may call a physician and tell him that a less expensive drug is available for the same medical condition and suggest that the physician switch drugs to one on which the PBM receives a large price discount or rebate.

4. In 1993, an antitrust suit was filed by 31,000 retail pharmacies against 24 pharmaceutical manufacturers, claiming that the drug companies conspired to charge HMOs, PBMs, and hospitals lower prices while denying price discounts to retail pharmacies. Most of the drug companies settled by paying a relatively small average amount per retail pharmacy and said they would give the same discounts to retail pharmacies if they could demonstrate that they were able to shift market share of their drugs. Five drug companies refused to settle. The retail pharmacies had to prove that price discrimination harmed competition and that the discounts were not a competitive response to another drug firm's lower prices. At the trial in 1998, the judge dismissed the lawsuit, which was upheld on appeal (Culyer and Newhouse 2000).

The drug companies claimed they did not offer a price discount to retail pharmacies because the discounts would not increase the drug company's market share. Retail pharmacies had to carry a wide selection of drugs because they merely filled orders of prescribing physicians. The greater the ability of the buyer to switch market share away from one drug manufacturer to a competitor's drug, the greater was the discount. The drug companies claimed that retail pharmacies were unable to switch volume from one drug company to another; therefore, there was no reason to give them a discount.

5. The Bureau of Labor Statistics drug price index overstates drug price increases when a generic equivalent of a branded drug comes on the market. The lower-priced generic drug rapidly expands its market share at the expense of the branded drug for which it is a substitute. As the branded drug loses market share to the generic drug, its price is increased to the remaining patients who are less price sensitive and more reluctant to use the generic version of the drug. The drug price index picks up the price increase of the branded drug but does not measure the price decline experienced by the large proportion of consumers who switch to the generic version. Thus, the drug price index fails to reflect the sharp price decline with the introduction of the generic drug.

6. When the patent on a branded drug expires, the first generic version of that drug has a six-month period of exclusivity over other generics; the first generic can capture up to 90 percent of the market from the branded drug. Typically, the branded drug manufacturer does not produce the generic version when its patent expires.

ENSURING SAFETY AND EFFICACY OF NEW DRUGS: TOO MUCH OF A GOOD THING?

Innovative new drugs have decreased mortality, increased life expectancy, and improved the quality of life for many millions of people. New drugs have also reduced the cost of medical care, substituting for more costly surgeries and long hospital stays. At the time of discovery, however, the effects of new drugs are not fully known. Powerful drugs that have the potential for curing cancer may also have harmful side effects. Some drugs may cause illness or even death for some people, while providing beneficial effects to others. New drugs offer a trade-off: improvements in the quality and length of life versus possible serious adverse consequences.

The FDA's approval is required before any new drug may be marketed in the United States. The FDA's objective should be to achieve a balance between the concerns of drug safety and the prospective benefits of pharmaceutical innovation. Ensuring that a new drug does not harm anyone delays the introduction of a beneficial drug that may save many lives. This delay may result in the deaths of thousands of people whose lives could have been saved had the new drug been approved earlier. On the other hand, introducing potential breakthrough drugs immediately may cause the deaths of many, as the full effects of the new drug are not completely understood.

How should this trade-off in lives be evaluated? Is each type of life—those potentially saved by early introduction of a new drug versus those who might die from early approval—valued equally? Regulatory delay increases the time and cost of bringing a new drug to market. Thus, excessive caution and excessive expediency both incur risks. Either may cause a loss of lives. This chapter discusses the FDA and its history and performance with regard to the drug-approval process.

History of Regulation of Prescription Drugs

The Pure Food and Drug Act of 1906 was the federal government's first major effort at regulating the pharmaceutical industry. The supporters of this act, however, were primarily concerned with the quality of food, not drugs. Pure food acts had been submitted to Congress for at least ten years before one was finally passed. Media publicity on the ingredients of food and drugs generated popular support for legislative action. A great deal of publicity was generated by newspapers, magazine articles, and Upton Sinclair's 1906 book *The Jungle*, with its graphic descriptions of what was being included in the foods the public was eating. The result was public outrage, to which Congress responded by passing the Pure Food and Drug Act.

The act required drug companies to provide accurate labeling information, including whether the drug was addictive. (A number of medicines contained alcohol, opium, heroin, and cocaine, which were legal at that time.) The government could verify the accuracy of the drug's contents. Subsequent court cases resolved that therapeutic claims made by the sellers of a drug would not be considered fraudulent if the sellers believed their therapeutic claims. Thus, the drug-related portion of the act was quite limited and was modeled by the public's concern with the contents of food.

In the 1930s, the modern drug era began with the development of sulfa drugs. As these drugs were introduced, a tragedy provided the impetus for new legislation. A company seeking to make a liquid form of elixir sulfanilamide for children dissolved it in diethylene glycol (antifreeze), unaware of the toxic effects. As a result, more than 100 children died before the drug was recalled. Responding to the public outcry, Congress passed the Food, Drug, and Cosmetic Act in 1938. This law, which created the FDA, was intended to protect the public from unsafe, potentially harmful drugs. A company had to seek approval from the FDA before it could market a new drug. Drug companies determined the necessary amount and type of pre-market testing to prove to the government that the drug was safe for its intended use.

A 1950 amendment to the 1938 act authorized the FDA to distinguish prescription from nonprescription drugs by stating that some types of drugs could only be sold by prescription, as they could be harmful to the individual if bought on their own.

In 1959, Senator Estes Kefauver (who was running for the Democratic nomination for president at that time) held hearings on the drug industry. Critics of the industry were concerned that drug prices were too high, that drug companies undertook unnecessary and wasteful advertising expenditures, and that the drug industry earned excessive profits.

In the late 1950s, a new drug was introduced in Europe to treat morning sickness for pregnant women. After the introduction of thalidomide in Europe, an FDA staff member expressed doubts about the safety of the drug because of reported side effects and delayed its approval. An American drug company, however, was able to introduce it into the United States on an experimental basis. (The 1938 FDA amendments permitted such limited distribution to qualified experts so long as the drug was labeled as being under investigation.) As soon as reports began to appear in Europe that deformed babies were born to mothers who had taken the drug during pregnancy, the American company withdrew the drug.

The resulting media attention given to thalidomide and its effects in Europe shifted Congress's concern about high drug prices, wasteful expenditures, and excessive profits to concern with public safety. Congress responded to the public's fears about drug safety and passed the 1962 amendments to the Food, Drug, and Cosmetic Act. (Richard Harris [1964] provides a history of the 1962 FDA amendments.)

The 1962 amendments resulted in a major change in the regulation of pharmaceuticals. Drug companies were now required to prove the safety of their new drugs and their efficacy (beyond a placebo effect) for the indications claimed for them in treating a particular disease or condition. (Effectiveness must be determined by a controlled study in which some patients are given the new drug and others are given a placebo, an inactive substance such as a salt or sugar pill.) Once the FDA approves a new drug for marketing, the drug is approved only for specific claims. If the drug company wants to broaden those claims, it must file a new application with the FDA and provide evidence to support the new uses of that drug. (Physicians may, however, prescribe a drug for a use for which the FDA has not approved it.)

The steps that a drug company must take to meet the FDA's safety and efficacy standards are costly and time consuming. The FDA specifies the type of pre-marketing tests that are required. Before undertaking clinical trials using humans, animal trials are used to determine whether the drug is sufficiently safe and promising to justify human trials. Based on this evidence the FDA will approve clinical trials using humans. Each of the three different stages of clinical trials uses a greater number of subjects so that more dangerous drugs are identified before they can affect larger numbers of patients. Stage one introduces the drug to a small number of healthy individuals, and stage two uses a small number of persons with the disease to be treated. The third stage uses a large number of patients, half of whom take a placebo, and is designed to demonstrate efficacy and provide additional evidence of safety. Clinical trials take, on average, six years to complete. Once completed, the drug firm must receive FDA approval, which can take an additional several years.[1] Once approved by the FDA, the new drug must be manufactured according to specified standards.

After the 1962 amendments were enacted, generic and patented drugs were treated in the same manner. Both had to meet the same stringent FDA requirements as a new drug seeking a patent. Manufacturers of generic drugs had to independently prove the safety and efficacy of their products to receive FDA approval. Because the research of generic drugs had to be undertaken in the same process as the patented drug, the cost and time for developing generic drugs increased. Once a new drug received its patent and was approved by the FDA, the drug had no competition for a longer period and the price could be kept high for a longer time. Consumers continued to face high prices for prescription drugs for which the patents had expired because of FDA requirements that delayed the entry of generic substitutes.

The 1984 Drug Price Competition and Patent Term Restoration (Hatch-Waxman) Act simplified and streamlined the process for FDA approval of generic drugs in exchange for granting patent extensions to innovative drugs. Generic drugs no longer had to replicate many of the clinical trials performed by the original manufacturer to prove safety and efficacy. Instead, the generic drug manufacturer was only required to demonstrate that the generic drug was "bioequivalent" to the already approved patented drug, which was much less costly than proving safety and efficacy. (Bioequivalence means the active ingredient is absorbed at the same rate and to the same extent for the generic drug as for the patented drug.) The effect of this act was to reduce the delay between patent expiration and generic entry from more than three years to less than three months. Generic substitutes for branded drugs with expired patents are now quickly available at much-reduced prices. Previously, only 35 percent of top-selling drugs whose patents expired had generic copies; currently, almost all do.[2]

Although the 1984 act made generic drug entry easier and less costly once a patent expired, it also extended the patent life of branded drugs to compensate for patent life lost during the long FDA approval process. (Effective patent life is measured from the time the FDA approves a new drug to the end of the patent.) The act permitted drugs that contain a new chemical entity to qualify for a patent life extension. These patent extensions postpone generic entry by an average of about 2.8 years. The 1984 act was a compromise between the generic drug manufacturers, who wanted easier entry, and the brand-name drug manufacturers, who wanted a longer patent life.[3]

State legislation in the 1970s and 1980s also enabled generic drugs to rapidly increase their market share. Through the early 1970s, pharmacists in many states could not legally dispense a generic drug when a prescription specified a brand name drug. By 1984, all states had enacted drug substitution legislation that permitted a pharmacist to substitute a generic drug even when a brand name drug was specified, as long as the physician had not indicated otherwise on the prescription.

During the 1980s and 1990s, AIDS activists were critical of the FDA's approval process. AIDS patients were dying from the disease and wanted promising new drugs to be immediately available. Approval would be too late for many if these drugs were delayed for years because of research protocols required by the FDA. To provide half of terminally ill AIDS patients with a placebo was believed to be immoral; they would be denied a possible life-saving drug. Many terminally ill AIDS patients were willing to bear the risk of taking drugs that might prove to be unsafe or have adverse side effects.

AIDS activists pressured Congress and the FDA for an accelerated approval process. As a result, new laws and regulations were enacted between

1987 and 1992 that enabled seriously ill patients to have access to experimental drugs. These types of drugs were provided with a "fast-track" approval process. For other serious or life-threatening diseases, drugs in the clinical trial stages that were shown to have meaningful therapeutic benefit compared with existing treatments were also given an expedited review. In return for early approval of these new drugs, the drug firm had to periodically notify the FDA about any adverse reactions to the drug that were not detected during the clinical trial periods.

In 1992, Congress enacted the Prescription Drug User Fee Act (renewable every five years), which authorized the FDA to collect fees from drug manufacturers seeking a drug approval. The revenues from these fees were to be used to increase the number of FDA staff reviewing drug approvals. As a result the approval process took less time and the number of new drugs approved increased compared with previous years.[4]

Both the fast-tracking approval process and the funds from user fees reduced the time for FDA approvals of new drugs. As shown in Exhibit 26.1, in the late 1980s the FDA took about 32 months to approve a new drug. By 1998, the average approval time was less than 12 months. Unfortunately, over the last decade the average FDA approval time has increased and has taken about a year and a half; in 2009 it was 16.6 months.

FDA's Stringent Guidelines for Safety and Efficacy

It is difficult to be opposed to increased drug safety. As a consequence of FDA regulatory requirements, physicians and the public are better informed about approved drug uses and possible side effects. However, FDA regulation has had some adverse consequences.

The US Drug Lag

One measure of the FDA's performance is how long it takes to approve a drug in the United States compared with other countries. After the 1962 drug amendments were enacted, a long lag developed between the time drugs were available for use in other countries and when they could be used in the United States. For example, drugs proven effective for treating heart disease and hypertension were used in Great Britain as early as 1965, but they were not fully approved for use in the United States until 1976. It has been estimated that between 7,500 and 15,000 people died in 1988 alone from gastric ulcers while waiting for the FDA to approve misoprostol, which was already available in 43 countries. Furthermore, about 20,000 people are estimated to have died between 1985 and 1987 while waiting for approval of streptokinase, the first drug that could be intravenously administered to reopen the blocked coronary arteries of heart attack victims (Gottlieb 2004).

Exhibit 26.1 Number of and Mean Approval Times for New Molecular Entities[a] in the United States, 1984–2009

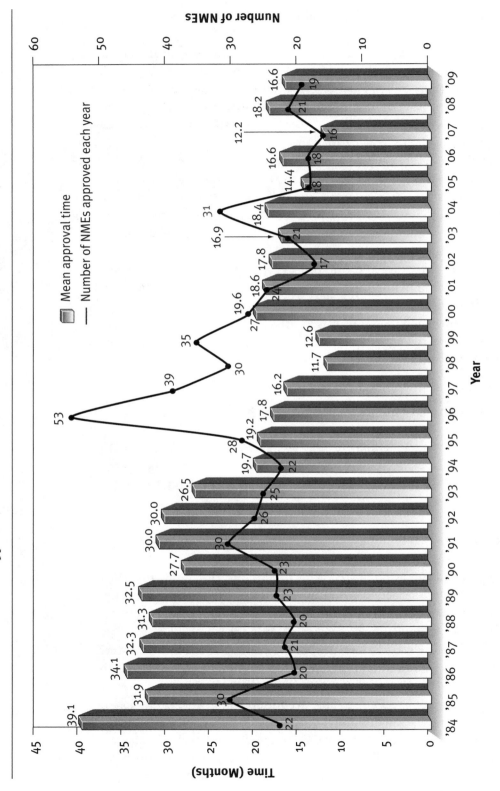

[a] New molecular entities (NMEs) are new medicines that have never been marketed before.

SOURCES: 1984–1999 data from US Food and Drug Administration, Center for Drug Evaluation and Research [Online information.] http://www.fda.gov/cder; 2000–2009 data from Tufts Center for the Study of Drug Development Approved New Molecular Entities Data Set.

The drug lag, the time it takes for a new drug to be approved in the United States after it has been approved in another country, has two effects. First, the longer the approval time, the greater the cost of producing a new drug and the fewer years remaining on the patent life of that drug, both of which reduce R&D profitability and decrease the number of new drugs likely to be developed. Second, and perhaps most important, the longer it takes to approve a new drug, the greater the harm to patients who would have benefited by having access to that drug sooner.[5]

Early studies looking at data through the 1970s concluded that a drug lag existed. Researchers compared drugs approved in the United Kingdom and the United States and concluded that drugs approved in the United States lagged behind those approved in the United Kingdom by about two years. However, in more recent years the US drug lag has decreased. As shown in Exhibit 26.1, the approval rate of new drugs by the FDA was 50 percent faster in the mid-1990s compared with the previous decade. Since then approval times have increased (between 2000 and 2009 the average approval time has varied from 12.2 to 19.6 months). Understanding changes in the FDA's drug approval rate requires an understanding of the FDA's decision process.

FDA's Incentives

The two main criticisms of FDA regulation are the long delays before new drugs are approved (currently about 16.6 months) and the increasing R&D cost imposed on drug companies for bringing a new drug to market. The FDA makes a choice when it decides how much emphasis to place on drug safety and efficacy versus approval delays and increased R&D cost. It is important to understand the political incentives that the FDA faces in making this trade-off.

Politically, a large difference exists between statistical (or invisible) persons who could have been saved and identifiable persons who died as a result of a new drug. When the FDA approves a drug that subsequently results in the deaths of a number of individuals, these deaths will be publicized in the media. Congress is likely to become involved as the publicity increases. The congressional committee that has oversight of the FDA will have hearings at which the relatives of the deceased patients testify. The FDA staff will have to explain why they approved an unsafe drug. As FDA Commissioner Schmidt stated in 1974 (76):

> In all of the FDA's history, I am unable to find a single instance where a Congressional Committee investigated the failure of the FDA to approve a new drug. But, the times when hearings have been held to criticize our approval of new drugs have been so frequent that we aren't able to count them.... The message to FDA staff could not be clearer. Whenever a controversy over a new drug is resolved by

its approval, the Agency and the individual involved likely will be investigated. Whenever such a drug is disapproved, no inquiry will be made.

Deaths caused by a drug are "visible" or "identifiable" deaths because the individuals affected can be readily identified. Minimizing identifiable deaths, however, delays the FDA approval process. Each day a life-saving drug is unavailable is a day someone may die for lack of that drug. Deaths of persons who may die because a life-saving drug is unavailable are referred to as statistical deaths.[6]

People who die because a life-saving drug has not yet received FDA approval, although it may be available in Europe, are difficult to identify and are not as visible. The media do not publicize all the nameless people who may have died because a new drug was too costly to be developed or was slow in receiving FDA approval. No media attention is given to the thousands of individuals in need of the drug and their families. Deaths that can be attributed to drug lag, particularly with the early beta-blockers to prevent heart attacks, number in the tens of thousands. The large number of these statistical deaths has greatly outweighed the number of victims of all drug tragedies before the 1962 amendments (including those deaths caused by elixir sulfanilamide in the 1930s).

Statistical lives and identifiable lives are not politically equal. The media and members of Congress place a great deal more pressure on the FDA when a loss of identifiable lives results from a prematurely approved drug than if a much greater loss of statistical lives occurs as a result of the FDA delaying approval of a new drug. The FDA's incentives are clearly to minimize the loss of identifiable lives at the expense of a greater loss of statistical lives. The FDA can make one of two types of errors, as shown in Exhibit 26.2. Type I error occurs when the FDA approves a drug that is found to have harmful effects; type II error occurs when the FDA either delays or does not approve a beneficial drug. These types of errors are not weighted equally by the FDA. The FDA places greater emphasis on preventing type I errors.

Although a human life is a human life, the decision maker's calculation of the costs and benefits of early versus delayed approval is on the side of delayed approval. The political pressure on FDA staff to justify their decisions will cause them to be overly cautious in approving new drugs until they can be sure no loss of life will occur.

However, the cost-benefit decision to the FDA of when to approve a drug has undergone a change in the last decade. Previously, the FDA bore little cost of delaying approval of a drug (from those who would have benefited from the drug), while it benefited by gathering more and more information as to the drug's safety; the FDA minimized the chances that Congress would criticize it for endangering the public's safety. Under these cost-benefit calculations, it was in the FDA's interest to delay approval until it was much

Exhibit 26.2

The FDA and
Type I and
Type II Errors

	Drug Is Beneficial	**Drug Is Harmful**
FDA Allows Drug	Correct decision	Type I error Allowing a harmful drug; victims are identifiable and FDA staff must explain to Congress
FDA Does Not Allow Drug	Type II error Disallowing a beneficial drug; victims are not identifiable	Correct decision

more certain as to the drug's safety. In recent years, the cost to the FDA of delaying approval has increased. Patient advocacy groups, at times allied with the drug company whose drug is being reviewed, have pressured the FDA for accelerated approval of drugs. Advocacy groups for AIDS patients were among the first such groups to publicize the cost of delays in drug approval. (Pharmaceutical firms supported these patient advocacy groups because they wanted to start earning revenues sooner.)

The effect of patient advocacy groups and media publicity on drug approval times is illustrated by data on approval times for different types of cancer drugs (Carpenter 2004). Although lung cancer has a higher mortality rate and is more costly to treat (requiring a greater number of hospitalizations and a longer length of hospital stay) than breast cancer, breast cancer has more advocacy groups who were able to generate greater media attention; consequently, breast cancer drugs were more quickly approved than drugs for lung cancer patients. The same relationship between media publicity and drug approval times exists for other drugs as well.

Patient advocacy groups that are able to generate a great deal of media attention have increased the visibility of the consequences of delay. In doing so, they have raised the political cost to the FDA of drug approval delays (type II errors). However, whenever an approved drug is shown to be less safe than originally believed, as occurred with the arthritis drug Vioxx, which was traced to a small but higher risk of heart attacks among patients who use it (type I error), the FDA staff will come under a great deal of criticism and revert toward excessive caution in approving new drugs.

Increased Cost of Drug Development

Stringent FDA guidelines and long approval times have greatly increased the cost of developing new drugs. After the 1962 drug amendments required more rigorous clinical testing, proof of efficacy, and safety criteria for FDA approval, the cost and time for bringing a new drug to market increased sharply. Before the 1962 amendments, the cost of a new drug, including the cost of failed drugs, was $7.3 million in 2009 dollars. The median time between starting clinical testing and receiving FDA approval has been increasing over time, from 4.7 years on average during the 1960s (after the 1962 drug amendments) to 6.7 years in the 1970s, to 8.5 years in the 1980s, and currently (2010) to 9 years. In the past decade it took, on average, between 10 and 15 years from a research idea until a drug was marketed.

The cost of developing a new drug has increased dramatically. In 1987, drug companies spent about $231 million to develop a new drug; if the costs had increased at the same rate as inflation, this would have been $436 million in 2009. However, a study conducted by DiMasi, Hansen, and Grabowski (2003) estimated that the cost has soared to $802 million. Using a different estimation technique, Vernon, Golec, and DiMasi (2010) calculate the costs to be $992 million. (Adams and Brantner [2006] estimate the cost to be from $500 million to more than $2 trillion.) An important reason for the rapidly increasing cost of drug development is the cost of human trials. The typical clinical trial currently involves 4,000 people, compared with 1,300 in the 1980s. Managed care companies are demanding that drug companies prove the value of their drugs in larger and longer clinical trials.

Included in the costs of drug development are actual expenditures as well as the opportunity cost of the interest forgone on these investment costs. For example, only $403 million of the estimated $802 million represents actual out-of-pocket costs. The rest is the estimated cost of capital, or the amount that investing the money at an 11 percent rate of return would have earned over time. This opportunity cost of capital is significant, as long time lags exist between investment expenditures and revenues generated by new drugs.

These investment costs include expenditures on many drugs that will never make it to market (failures). Of every 5,000 potential new drugs tested in animals, only five are likely to reach human clinical trials; of those five, only one will eventually be marketed.

Also important to a drug firm's profitability is the fact that the longer it takes to achieve the FDA's stringent research guidelines and receive FDA approval, the shorter the remaining patent life on the drug and the period in which to make profits. Profit is the principal motivating factor behind drug companies' willingness to assume risk and invest large amounts in R&D. The pharmaceutical manufacturers' profitability over time is determined by their investment in R&D. As shown in Exhibit 26.3, R&D expenditures as a

EXHIBIT 26.3 Domestic R&D Expenditures as a Percentage of US Domestic Sales, Pharmaceutical Companies, 1970–2009

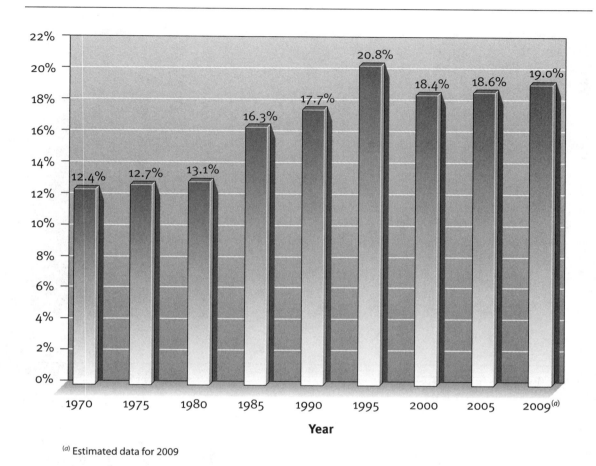

(a) Estimated data for 2009

SOURCE: Pharmaceutical Research and Manufacturers of America, *2010 Industry Profile,* 2010. [Online information.] http://www.phrma .org/files/attachments/Profile_2010_FINAL.pdf.

percentage of US sales are about 19 percent of revenue (as of 2009). This rate of investment is one of the highest of any industry.

Profitability over time (as a percentage of revenue) for pharmaceutical firms has also been higher than for any other industry. Although profits are high, so are the risks. The high rates of profit earned by drug manufacturers to finance R&D result from the few breakthrough drugs discovered. Even those that are marketed may not be financially successful; about three out of ten drugs marketed make a profit, and about 10 percent of all drugs marketed provide 52 percent of the industry's profits.

Exhibit 26.4 describes the percentage of drugs the profits of which exceed average R&D costs. As can be seen, the distribution of profits is skewed.

EXHIBIT 26.4 Decile Distribution of Present Values of Postlaunch Returns for the Sample of 1990–94 New Chemical Entities

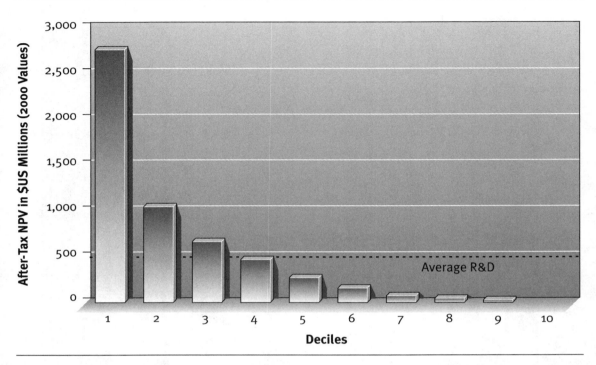

SOURCE: Grabowski, Henry G., et al. 2002. "Returns to Research and Development for 1990s New Drug Introductions." *Pharmacoeconomics* 20 (15, Supplement 3): 11–29, Figure 7.

Very few drugs offer a profitable return, but for the 10 percent of drugs considered "blockbuster" drugs the profits are substantial. Thus, a drug company needs a few "winners," especially blockbusters, to repay the costs on the majority of drugs that do not even repay their R&D investments.

Patent protection is essential for protecting a drug manufacturer's investments in R&D. Once a new drug is discovered, it can be reproduced relatively easily. Without the period of market exclusivity that patents provide, drug manufacturers could not recover their R&D investments. Patents provide a drug manufacturer with market power, the ability to price above costs of production. Breakthrough drugs have a great deal more market power than a "me-too" drug. Although a new breakthrough drug (the first drug to treat an illness) may initially have a great deal of market power, other companies can eventually patent drugs that use the same mechanism to treat the illness. Once patent protection expires, generic versions priced much below the branded drug quickly take a large part of the market. For example, in 1997, the patent on Zantac expired, and the generic version captured 90 percent of the market served by Zantac within two years (Berndt 2001). Currently, about 75 percent of all prescription drugs dispensed are off-patent generic drugs.

Public policy with respect to the drug industry must deal with the following trade-off. To increase R&D investments, drug manufacturers must earn high profits on innovative drugs that provide significant increases in therapeutic value. However, the cost of producing these drugs is but a small fraction of their selling price. If prices on these breakthrough drugs were made more affordable (closer to their production costs) to alleviate the large burden on those with low incomes, the high profits that provide the incentive to invest in R&D would disappear. Lower drug prices that benefit today's patients mean fewer innovative drugs in the future.

Orphan Drugs

As R&D costs and the time for drug approval have increased, long and costly clinical trials to develop "orphan" drugs, those that benefit only small population groups, became unprofitable. The potential revenue for a new orphan drug may be small, since they are designed to treat diseases that only affect a small number of people (or treat the small percentage of people who do not respond to standard treatments for more common illnesses). Congress enacted the Orphan Drug Act in 1984 to provide drug companies with a financial incentive (tax incentives or exclusive marketing rights) to develop drugs that provide therapeutic benefits for fewer than 200,000 patients.

Similar to the orphan drug issue is the concern that drug development is targeted toward people living in wealthy countries. Only 5 percent of global R&D is directed at health problems unique to developing nations, although 90 percent of the global disease burden is in the developing world. Private-sector R&D is determined by prospective demand conditions. For example, malaria is a parasitic disease that has a global incidence of 200 to 300 million cases annually. About 1 million deaths are caused by malaria each year, and the majority of these deaths are children under the age of five years living in sub-Saharan Africa (Bloom et al. 2006). Drug development aimed at health problems confronting people in poor countries will need to be subsidized from government sources.

Summary

The rationale for FDA regulation of drugs is presumably to provide a remedy for the lack of information that exists among physicians and consumers when buying drugs. Lack of information on a drug's safety could cause serious harm to patients. Given this serious information problem, what should the FDA's role be? Should the FDA continue to be the sole decision maker on the availability of new drugs? Or should the FDA play a more passive role by merely providing information on the safety and efficacy of new drugs and leave the decision about whether to use a new drug to the physician and the patient?

What is the optimum trade-off between statistical and identifiable deaths? Who should make that decision? Decreased identifiable deaths means increased testing, increased R&D costs, delays in FDA approval, and a consequent increase in statistical deaths. Clearly, for saving lives and treating serious illnesses the choice should be less concern with drug safety and efficacy and quicker approval to minimize the number of statistical deaths. The costs of delay vary depending on the seriousness of the illness. Even two patients with the same disease will differ on the types of risks they are willing to accept. Under the current system the FDA is determining the level of risk acceptable to society, while some patients would be willing to go above that level.

Proponents of strengthening the FDA's current role (rather than changing it to be merely a provider of information) are concerned that physicians and patients would still have incomplete information to make appropriate decisions on new drugs. Physicians may be too busy or unwilling to invest the time to fully understand the safety and efficacy information on new drugs and may even be influenced by drug company advertising. Changing the FDA's role from that of a decision maker to simply a provider of information does not appear to have much public support. Instead, public policy is more concerned with speeding up the FDA's approval process. Various proposals have been made to speed up the FDA's review process for drug approval, such as having the FDA also rely on evidence gathered from other countries that have high approval standards, dropping the proof-of-efficacy requirement, and requiring less evidence of a drug's safety for life-saving drugs that have no alternative therapy.

Speeding up the FDA's approval process will require greater postmarketing surveillance of drug interactions and safety. Evidence of the effects of a new drug may not be known for several years. The long pre-approval process continues to miss dangerous drugs. For example, Trovan, an antibiotic drug, had to be withdrawn because of unforeseen liver injuries. Only after a drug has been on the market and used by large numbers of people can its safety and efficacy be truly evaluated.

In addition to speeding up the FDA's approval process and expanding postmarket surveillance of new drugs, concerns exist about the time and cost required to bring a new drug to market. High R&D costs (such as longer times for approval that shorten patent life) decrease the profitability of an investment in new drugs. Decreased profitability leads to a lower investment and results in fewer new drugs being discovered. As the costs of drug discovery are increased, drug companies are less likely to develop drugs that have small market potential. An additional consequence of the high cost and long time requirements to introduce a new drug is that, with fewer new drugs being introduced, drug prices are higher because less competition exists than would if the process were easier.

High R&D costs also have a greater effect on small drug firms. Large drug firms have many new drugs in the discovery pipeline and on the market. Small firms invest their capital in the particular drug that is going through the R&D and approval process. The longer the delay in being able to market their drug, the greater is their capital requirement. To minimize its chance of running out of money, a small drug firm with a promising new drug will merge or partner with a larger firm that has greater capital resources and experience with the drug approval process.

Economics is concerned with trade-offs. Choosing one policy, namely increased drug safety and efficacy, has a "cost," namely fewer new drugs being developed. A greater number of statistical deaths will occur, the drug industry will become more consolidated, and drug prices will be higher because fewer new drugs will compete with existing drugs. Thus, merely favoring increased drug safety and efficacy is not a simple choice without consequences. The issue is how to strike an appropriate balance between these choices.

Discussion Questions

1. How have the 1962 drug amendments affected the profitability of new drugs?
2. What is the consequence of the FDA providing the public with greater assurance that a new drug is safe?
3. What is the difference between identifiable and statistical deaths?
4. What are orphan drugs, and why are drug firms less likely to develop such drugs today?
5. Why has the FDA's drug approval process sped up in recent years?
6. What are the advantages and disadvantages of greater reliance on pre-market testing versus postmarket surveillance?

Notes

1. Once the FDA approves a new drug as being safe and efficacious for its intended use, the new drug must also pass the health plan's review process to show that it is also cost effective. Unless the drug can pass this review, the new drug may not be added to the health plan's drug formulary.
2. The Federal Trade Commission has been investigating anticompetitive behavior in the drug industry. Drug companies that hold patents on brand-name drugs have been accused of making special deals with

generic drug manufacturers to keep the generic drugs off the market, thereby not competing with the branded drug, for longer than the 1984 Hatch-Waxman Act intended. Specifically, drug manufacturers have been alleged to have paid generic drug companies to delay introducing their products. Congress and the FDA are also examining whether changes to the 1984 act are required to close loopholes in the law. Industry critics claim that another tactic drug companies use to delay the entry of generic drugs is to sue the generic manufacturers, allowing the branded drugs months more of lucrative, exclusive sales.

3. Olson (1994) describes why, after several years of failure, the 1984 drug legislation was ultimately enacted. Her analysis includes the proposals of different interest groups, turnover in key Senate committees, and a change in the majority party.

4. In 1994, federal legislation (the Uruguay Round Agreements Act) changed the patent life of prescription drugs (and all types of inventions) from 17 years from the date a patent is granted to 20 years from the date the application is filed. Between two and three years elapse from the time an application is filed until a patent is granted. The average period for which a new drug can be marketed under patent protection has risen from about 9 years to about 13.5 years (Huang et al. 2009).

5. One analyst who examined the 1962 drug amendments concluded that they made the public worse off. Sam Peltzman (1974) attempted to quantify the benefits of the 1962 amendments by estimating the effect of the new regulations on keeping ineffective and dangerous drugs (of which there were very few before 1962) off the market compared with the lost benefits of having fewer new drugs, higher prices for existing drugs (because of less competition from new drugs), and reduced availability of drugs because of the time lag. The decline in the development of new drugs was the greatest disadvantage of the amendments; this factor alone, according to Peltzman, made the costs of the new amendments greatly exceed the potential benefits.

6. Statistical deaths are calculated as follows. Assume that a new drug is introduced in Europe and two years elapse before that same drug receives FDA approval to be marketed in the United States. Further assume that the new drug is more effective than the drug currently on the market to treat that same disease, such that it is able to decrease mortality from 5 percent to 1 percent. Suppose 100,000 persons each year are affected by that illness. The number of lives that would have been saved by earlier FDA approval is 8,000. The percentage difference in mortality rate ($0.05 - 0.01 = 0.04$), multiplied by the two-year lag when the drug could have been on the market ($0.04 \times 2 = 0.08$), multiplied by the number of people at risk each year ($0.08 \times 100,000$) equals 8,000 statistical deaths because of the two-year delay.

WHY ARE PRESCRIPTION DRUGS LESS EXPENSIVE OVERSEAS?

Anecdotes abound about people traveling to Canada or Mexico to buy a prescription drug at a much lower price than that offered by retail pharmacies in this country. In addition, studies by the US Government Accountability Office (GAO) (1992, 1994) have shown that branded prescription drugs are more expensive in the United States than in other countries. The studies concluded that US prices were 32 percent higher than prices in Canada and 60 percent higher than prices in the United Kingdom. Another study (US House of Representatives, Committee on Government Reform and Oversight 1998) found that senior citizens in Maine paid an average retail price of $116.01 for Prilosec, whereas consumers in Canada and Mexico paid $53.05 and $29.46, respectively (see Exhibit 27.1).

Cross-national comparison studies of branded (prescription) drug prices generally conclude that lower drug prices in other countries are a result of regulatory price controls, which implies that the United States can similarly lower drug prices by using price controls. The following sections discuss the accuracy of cross-national drug price studies, why higher prices for prescription drugs in the United States are not surprising, and the implications of requiring US drug manufacturers to charge a single uniform price overseas and in the United States.

Accuracy of Studies on International Variations in Drug Prices

The methodology used in the GAO studies and similar studies that concluded that prescription drug prices are higher in the United States than in other countries has been widely criticized. What these studies purport to analyze and the methods used should be subject to greater examination before their implications for the United States are accepted.

Retail Price Comparisons

Typically, cross-national studies compare the retail prices of selected prescription drugs that are bought by cash-paying patients in the United States to the retail prices of those same drugs in another country. (The GAO studies used

EXHIBIT 27.1
Prices for
Prilosec,
Selected
Countries,
2001

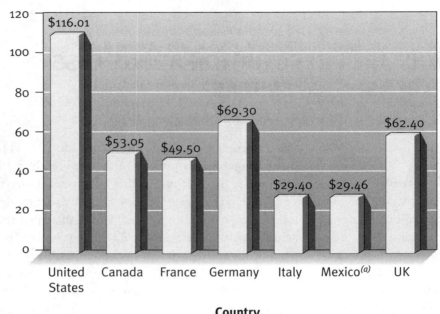

(a)1998 data

SOURCES: US House of Representatives, Committee on Government Reform, 2001. Minority Staff, Special
Investigation Division. Prepared for Rep. Tom Allen. *Rx Drugs More Expensive in Maine than in Canada, Europe,
and Japan* (June 15, 2001); US House of Representatives, Committee on Government Reform and Oversight,
1998. Minority Staff Report. Prepared for Rep. Thomas A. Allen. *Prescription Drug Pricing in the 1st
Congressional District in Maine: An International Price Comparison* (October 24, 1998).

listed wholesale prices in the United States, which were intended to approximate prices charged to retail pharmacies.) These comparisons greatly overstate US drug prices because they assume that all purchasers of the prescription
drug in the United States pay the same price. Using retail (or even wholesale)
prices as the prescription drug price in the United States does not account for
the large discounts and rebates received by large US purchasers such as managed care organizations (MCOs), pharmacy benefit managers (PBMs), mail-
order drug firms, and federal government programs, including Medicaid.
(Patients in these organizations merely pay a copayment that is a small fraction of the price the organizations pay for the drug.) Not only do these large
purchasers make up the majority of the US prescription drug market, but
large purchasers also represent a larger percentage of the purchasers in the
United States than in comparison countries.

These large purchasers pay substantially less for prescription drugs than
cash-paying US patients who do not have prescription drug insurance and
buy directly from a retail pharmacy. Cash-paying patients represent a small

segment of the prescription drug buyers in the United States, so comparisons using these patients greatly overstate prices.

Rather than assuming a single US retail price, comparing prices paid on average by all those purchasing drugs in the United States to the prices paid by overseas patients would be more appropriate.[1]

Cost of Drug Therapy

Given the public policy implications of cross-national studies, the purpose of these comparisons must be clarified so that an appropriate study design can be determined. One objective of such studies might be to estimate the cost of drug therapy (by disease) in different countries, not just the differences in prices for specific prescription products. To accurately examine differences in drug therapy costs across countries, such studies should adjust for the use of generic substitutes and weighting of the different drugs used in a country's drug price index.

Cross-national studies have excluded generic drugs, which are priced between 40 and 80 percent lower than branded drugs. Furthermore, US purchasers rely much more on generic drugs than do patients in other countries. (Generics accounted for 75 percent of prescriptions in the United States in 2009 [IMS Health 2010] whereas use of generics in countries with strict drug price regulation, such as France and Italy, is very low.) If generic drugs are more frequently substituted for expensive branded drugs in the United States than in other countries, a comparison based solely on branded drugs overstates the cost of a prescription for US patients.

Another important issue in cross-national comparisons is the mix or consumption pattern of drugs used in different countries. Comparisons of drug prices between countries rely on a simple average of the prices paid for several leading brand-name drugs. For example, the GAO study (1992) comparing branded drug prices in the United States and Canada merely compared US prices to Canadian prices for a number of branded drugs. (The Canadian prices were added up and compared to the sum of the US retail prices for those same drugs. Dividing the sum of the prices of one country by the sum of prices in the other country resulted in a ratio of prices between the two countries.) In doing so, the study gave an equal weight to each branded drug being compared. Whether some branded drugs were widely or infrequently used did not matter; each received an equal weight.

Because the United States and other countries have different drug consumption patterns, any price index should reflect these differences by weighting the volume of use of different branded drugs. Some branded drugs represent a greater percentage of purchased branded drugs than others; these percentages differ by country.

Cross-national comparisons should use a weighted average of the prices of branded drugs. The index should also include the use of generic drugs as well as the average prices paid for all drugs, including the discounted prices paid by MCOs and other large purchasers in the United States and the volume they purchase. This would result in a much lower weighted average price than simply observing the price of the branded drug (and its volume) sold to retail customers. Furthermore, for some branded drugs a great deal of substitution of the generic version, which is sold at a lower price, occurs. A weighted average price of that drug would include the branded and generic versions, which would result in a much lower price than simply using the branded version. Each drug should also be given a weight in the index according to its use in that country.

A Drug Price Index

Research conducted by Danzon and Chao (2000) determined that when a drug price index is constructed for each country using average prices paid by different purchasers, including generic drugs, and weighting drug prices by their frequency of use, the index may be no higher in the United States than in other countries. Although individual prescription drugs may be more expensive in the United States, the costs of drug therapy across countries (based on an accurately constructed drug price index) are not much different. (For a detailed discussion of cross-national comparisons, including additional limitations such as the unit of measurement and the availability of branded drugs, as well as appropriate methodologies and results, see Danzon and Furukawa [2003].)

Why Prescription Drugs Are Expected to Be Priced Lower Overseas

Numerous examples can be found of prescription drugs that are less expensive in other countries than in the United States. Why would a manufacturer of a patented prescription drug be willing to sell the same drug at greatly reduced prices overseas? This pricing behavior is based on two characteristics of the drug industry: its cost structure and differences in each country's bargaining power.

The costs of developing and bringing to market an innovative new drug are high (DiMasi, Hansen, and Grabowski 2003). The R&D costs for a prescription drug can go as high as $800 million. Experimental trials must be conducted, and the FDA's approval is required. It may take seven to ten years to develop a new drug and receive FDA approval. The R&D costs, including the interest that could have been earned on those funds and the costs involved in receiving FDA approval, are termed *fixed costs*. These development costs are the same regardless of how much of the patented new drug is produced and sold. The actual costs of producing the new drug, once its chemical entities have been determined through the R&D process and it has received FDA approval, are relatively small. Thus, patented drugs are characterized by large fixed costs and relatively small variable costs (the actual costs of producing the drug).

The drug manufacturer would like to receive the highest possible price for that new drug. For some purchasers, however, the manufacturer would be willing to accept any price that exceeds its variable costs. A price in excess of variable costs makes a contribution to covering those large fixed costs and to profit. The manufacturer is better off receiving $5 even if it costs $4 to produce that drug; the $1 revenue from some purchasers is better than nothing.

The drug industry is sophisticated in its pricing of the same medicine across different countries. A drug manufacturer would like to add new users (sell the drug in different countries) because the variable costs of producing the drug are so low, but it is not willing to add new users if it has to reduce the price and revenues it earns in higher-priced markets. The single largest market for new innovative drugs is the United States, which accounts for 37.5 percent of the world pharmaceutical market (North America, or the United States and Canada, represents 40 percent [Exhibit 27.2]). People in the United States are on average wealthier than those in other countries and want access to innovative drugs as soon as possible; they are therefore less price sensitive to high drug prices (about 80 percent of the US population in 2008 had insurance to pay for prescription drugs) (Henry J. Kaiser Family Foundation 2010c). Not surprisingly, drug manufacturers charge higher prices when consumers are less price sensitive.

In countries that regulate the price of drugs, the same manufacturer is willing to sell the same drug at a lower price as long as the regulated price exceeds the manufacturer's variable cost of producing that drug. The drug manufacturer would be concerned if purchasers in the lower-priced countries were to resell the drug in the higher-priced markets. If resale from the lower-priced countries to the higher-priced countries were possible, a differential pricing system could not persist.

As long as the manufacturer is able to prevent resale of the same drug from low- to high-priced markets, this system of differential pricing allows markets that would otherwise be neglected to be served. Differential pricing, whereby a drug manufacturer charges different prices to different countries for the same medicine, results in the greatest number of people gaining access to a drug. The manufacturer is willing to reduce its price to countries that regulate drugs and to poor countries that cannot afford to pay much for drugs, not because the manufacturer has a social conscience, but because any sales at a price that exceeds the drug's variable cost contribute to profits. By trying to increase profits, however, the drug manufacturer also provides the greatest number of people with access to its drug.

Canadian and European governments, which pay for most of their populations' health expenditures, keep drug prices down because they have

Exhibit 27.2
World
Pharmaceutical
Market, 2009

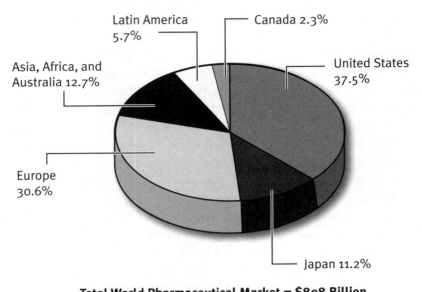

Latin America 5.7%

Canada 2.3%

Asia, Africa, and Australia 12.7%

United States 37.5%

Europe 30.6%

Japan 11.2%

Total World Pharmaceutical Market = $808 Billion

SOURCE: IMS Health. 2010. *Top-Line Industry Data.* [Online information.] http://www.imshealth.com.

limited budgets for healthcare. These tight budgets for drug expenditures have had unintended side effects. The introduction of cost-effective drugs has been delayed because the budget for drugs would be exceeded. Consequently, surgical and hospital expenditures have been greater than if costly new innovative drugs had been used, and delays have occurred in approving life-saving drugs for citizens of these countries.

For example, "Herceptin, which was considered to be a breakthrough drug for about a third of all breast cancer patients...was approved two years ago by regulators in the US, where it benefited from an accelerated review offered to novel cancer therapies. It is still awaiting regulatory approval in most of Europe" (Moore 2000). Furthermore,

> Many European countries also attempt to restrict demand after new medicines reach pharmacy shelves. European...countries with tight pharmaceutical budgets have made it difficult for cancer patients to have access to older cancer drugs (Taxol) that were top selling anti-cancer drugs. One study (industry funded) examining prescribing patterns between 1996 and 1998 finds the following: while 99.9% of patients with advanced breast cancer in the US received treatment with taxane, the comparable [rate] was 48% for the Netherlands and only 25% for Britain.

Another consequence of regulated lower drug prices overseas is that total drug expenditures represent a higher portion of total medical expenditures

EXHIBIT 27.3 Pharmaceutical Expenditures as a Percentage of Total Health Expenditures, Selected Countries, 2008

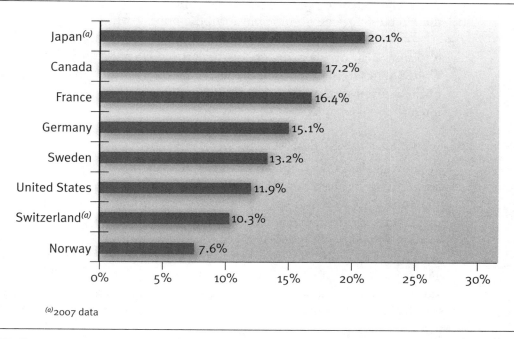

(a)2007 data

NOTE: Pharmaceuticals include prescription and nonprescription drugs.

SOURCE: Data from Organisation for Economic Co-operation and Development. 2010. *OECD Health Data 2010*. Paris: OECD.

in those countries than in the United States (see Exhibit 27.3) because the prices for drugs in those countries are quite low (generally for older molecules), and neither patients nor their physicians have any incentive to use fewer drugs. For example, to reduce drug expenditures, the German government in recent years imposed financial penalties on physicians to limit their prescriptions. The United States spends a smaller portion on drugs (11.9 percent of total health expenditures) than France (16.4 percent), Japan (20.1 percent), Canada (17.2 percent), or Germany (15.1 percent).

Public Policy Issues

Cross-national studies that have found that the United States has higher prescription drug prices imply that the United States should institute a price-control system similar to those of countries that have lower drug prices. By publicizing these study findings, along with examples of persons who cannot afford to pay high retail drug prices, advocates of price controls hope to build political support for imposing controls on US prescription drugs.

Two methods for equalizing US and overseas prices on prescription drugs are favored by proponents of a regulatory approach. The first is having the US government require that the retail price of prescription drugs sold in the United States be no different from the price at which those same drugs are sold in other countries, such as Canada and Mexico. The second approach is to allow pharmacists to import FDA-approved US prescription drugs to the United States from other countries where they sell for substantially less. Each of these proposals has short-term effects as well as indirect, or unintended, longer-term consequences.

A Single Price for Prescription Drugs Across Countries

What would happen to prescription drug prices in the United States and overseas if US drug manufacturers were required to price US-branded drugs at the same price at which they are sold to other countries? Proponents of a single price for the same medicine assume that the uniform price will be the lowest of the different prices charged for that same drug. Assume that a prescription drug, ABC, sells for $10 in the United States and $5 in Canada. Further assume that the United States enacts a law stating that the manufacturer of drug ABC must charge the same price regardless of the country in which the drug is sold. Would the price of drug ABC be reduced to $5 and US consumers receive a $5 benefit?

The answer is no.

The manufacturer of drug ABC would have to determine which single price would result in the greatest amount of profit. Because the United States is the largest single market for innovative branded drugs, and its consumers are less price sensitive, greatly reducing the drug's price in the US market would not result in a large increase in the number of users of that drug. Consequently, a large decrease in price (without a corresponding large increase in volume) would cause a large decrease in revenue.[2] Given the large profits earned in the United States (the price markup over variable cost in the United States multiplied by the large number of users), the uniform price of the drug would likely be closer to the US price than to the lower prices paid in other countries. The drug company would lose less money if it raised the prices in other countries by a greater amount than it lowered the US price.

Keeping the uniform price closer to the US price for a drug would mean the new uniform price of the drug would be increased in other countries. Raising the price in these countries would likely cause a decrease in use. These countries typically have limited government budgets for healthcare, and a large increase in the price of drugs would cause the government to restrict their use. Whether total revenue to the US manufacturer from sales of the drug in other countries increases or decreases depends on whether the percentage increase in price exceeds the percentage decrease in use in those countries.

In either case, requiring a uniform price for drug ABC in the United States and other countries means overseas patients who need the drug will be worse off. Whereas formerly they (or the government on their behalf) paid $5, they would now have to pay a higher price. Some patients would no longer have access to the drug. If close substitute drugs were available, patients would buy these other drugs (assuming the price of these other drugs had not also similarly increased). If close substitutes were not available for innovative drugs, patients/government would have to spend more of their income on the drug. If patients could not afford to buy the drug or their government restricted its use because of its higher price, adverse health consequences would occur. Thus, requiring a uniform pricing policy in the United States and other countries would likely lead to a small reduction in the US price of a drug and an increase in the drug's overseas price so that it would be equal to the new US price. This policy would inflict a loss on many patients in other countries, who would have to go without innovative drugs.

Reimportation

The second regulatory approach to reducing US retail prices for prescription drugs is to allow US pharmacists and drug wholesalers to buy lower-priced supplies of FDA-approved medicines in Canada and other nations for resale in the United States. Drugs reimported into the United States from Canada would likely be less expensive than the same drugs sold in the United States because of Canadian price controls on those drugs. The presumed effect of this policy would be to reduce the US retail price of drugs to prices comparable to those in the countries from which they are reimported.

A federal law permitting reimportation was enacted in October 2000. This law overturned a 1988 law that permitted only pharmaceutical manufacturers to reimport prescription drugs based on the concern that drugs were being improperly stored and repackaged overseas. Although reimportation was vigorously opposed by the pharmaceutical industry, senators and congressional candidates from both political parties running for reelection during fall 2000 voted for the bill, which was then signed into law by President Clinton. As both political parties could not agree on a Medicare prescription drug benefit, legislators running for reelection believed voting for reimportation would be viewed by the public as being in favor of helping the aged with their prescription drug costs.

In December 2000, Donna Shalala, secretary of the Department of Health and Human Services (HHS), refused to implement the new law, claiming that it was unworkable and would not lower drug costs (Kaufman 2000). (Since then no secretary of HHS under Republican or Democratic administrations has agreed to implement the law.) At the time of the debate, the FDA said it could oversee the drug reimportation system, but only at considerable cost. Unless funding was provided ($93 million a year), the safety of the reimported drugs could not be monitored; full funding was not included in the legislation. Furthermore, the administration believed the bill had several fatal flaws that would deter reimportation, namely that the drug companies would retaliate against reimporters and would not provide the reimporters with the necessary package labeling inserts.

A US manufacturer of a branded prescription drug would be unlikely to increase its sales to a country that resells that drug in the United States. Drug manufacturers could easily monitor drug sales to each country to determine whether sales of a particular drug had suddenly increased. (If the drug importer in a country resold the country's limited supply of that drug back to the United States, patients in that country would be harmed by not having access to that drug.)

Thus, to be able to reimport drugs into the United States, US pharmacists and wholesalers would have to buy those chemical entities from a foreign producer of those drugs. When a drug is manufactured in the United States, the manufacturer must adhere to strict FDA guidelines to ensure that the drug is produced with certain quality standards. If a drug is manufactured in another country without extensive monitoring of the reimported drug by the FDA, no guarantee can be given that the drug will meet the same quality standards. The concern over drug safety resulted in 11 former FDA commissioners opposing the reimportation bill (Dalzell 2000).

Thousands of illegal shipments of prescription drugs enter the United States each month through the postal service. This growth in overseas sales to US patients has dramatically increased because of the Internet. The sheer volume of these shipments has overwhelmed the ability of the FDA and customs officials to verify the safety of the imported drugs. Finally, on June 7, 2001, the FDA proposed stopping overseas drug products from being mailed to individuals unless they met certain strict conditions. The FDA claimed that these drug products could be counterfeit or even dangerous and that the volume is so large that it no longer has the ability to inspect them.

Reimportation is unlikely to be effective in reducing US prescription drug prices, first because US drug manufacturers would be unwilling to sell large quantities of their drugs at greatly reduced prices to other countries so that these countries could sell the same drugs back to US pharmacists at lower prices.[3] Second, if foreign drug manufacturers are permitted to produce a drug patented by a US manufacturer and sell that drug to customers in the United States, those foreign producers would be violating US patent laws and the imports would be prohibited. Third, if other countries were unable to receive sufficient supplies of US-produced drugs to sell back to the United States, counterfeit drugs would likely be produced and sold to US patients, resulting in significant safety issues, which would eventually halt mail-order drug sales from overseas.

The pressure to enact a stronger drug importation law that would permit reimportation without the consent of the secretary of HHS, as some in Congress have proposed, decreased once Medicare beneficiaries were provided with a prescription drug benefit as part of the Medicare Modernization Act, which lowered their out-of-pocket costs for prescription drugs.

Summary

Cross-national comparison studies that claim drug prices are lower in other countries have been seriously misleading. Although the retail prices of certain prescription drugs may be lower overseas than in the United States, the more relevant comparison is the cost of drug therapy in different countries. Only a small percentage of the US population pays retail prices for drugs. The majority of the US population has some form of third-party payment for drugs, and these large purchasers buy their drugs at discounted prices. Generic drugs are also much more widely used in the United States than in other countries. Absent from these cross-national comparisons is any discussion of the availability of innovative drugs overseas.

Public policy affecting prescription drugs should be evaluated on its effect on R&D expenditures. The incentive for drug manufacturers to invest large sums in R&D and develop breakthrough drugs is based on the prospect of earning large profits. Once a drug has been discovered and approved by the FDA for marketing, the actual cost of producing that drug is low. Not surprisingly, therefore, countries can regulate the price of drugs and still have access to US drugs. (Evidence exists that other countries' regulation of drug prices resulted in a decline in R&D by drug firms in those countries.) These countries can receive a "free ride" on the large R&D expenditures by US drug firms. However, if the United States were to regulate its drug prices as do other countries or permit reimportation by foreign drug producers, R&D investment would decline, as would the supply of innovative drugs. Without government enforcement of patent rights and pricing freedom, the drug industry would decrease its investment in R&D drugs that are easy to copy but expensive to develop. Consumers in the United States and other countries benefit from differential pricing policies. In other countries more consumers benefit by having access to lower-priced drugs, whereas in the United States the higher prices generate greater profits for the drug companies and provide them with an incentive to invest more in R&D.

If the objective of cross-national studies is to pressure legislators to lower the retail prices of drugs so that cash-paying seniors can buy them at lower prices, a better alternative than mandating uniform prices across all countries or permitting reimportation is available. Seniors were provided with a prescription drug benefit as part of the 2003 Medicare Modernization Act; they choose among competing drug plans based on the premiums charged and the plan's drug formulary. The competing plans negotiate lower drug prices from the drug manufacturer, substitute generic drugs when appropriate, and manage the drug benefit to reduce the total cost of drug therapy. The cost to the government of this Medicare drug benefit was lower than projected. Seniors now have better access to needed drugs, and competition has reduced their prescription drug prices as well as their monthly premium (CMS 2007).

Discussion Questions

1. What are some criticisms of cross-national studies of drug prices?
2. Although some prescription drugs are priced lower in other countries, is the cost of a drug treatment also lower in those countries?
3. Why would a drug manufacturer be willing to sell a drug that is priced high (in relation to its variable costs) in the United States at a low price overseas?
4. What would be the consequences, in terms of drug prices and drug users, if prices of prescription drugs sold in the United States had to equal the price at which those same drugs are sold in other countries?
5. Why would a policy of reimportation of prescription drugs be ineffective?

Additional Readings

Danzon, P., and M. Furukawa. 2008. "International Prices and Availability of Pharmaceuticals in 2005." *Health Affairs* 27 (1): 221–33.

US Congressional Budget Office. 2004. *Would Prescription Drug Importation Reduce US Drug Spending?* Economic and Budget Issue Brief, April 29. www.cbo.gov/showdoc.cfm?index=5406&sequence=0#F4.

Notes

1. A number of other issues are involved in examining retail drug prices, such as dosage form; strength; and pack size, for example, price per gram of active ingredient or price per dose (standard unit), which may be one tablet, one capsule, or 10 mL of a liquid. Differences in prescription drug prices also occur because of differences in dosage form, strength, and pack size used in the comparison countries.

2. When consumers are less price sensitive, changes in price cause smaller proportionate changes in volume. By increasing price, total revenue increases because the percentage change in price is greater than the percentage change in volume. Similarly, lowering price when consumers are not price sensitive will result in a decrease in total revenue. Conversely, when consumers are price sensitive, the percentage change in price is less than the percentage change in volume. With price-sensitive consumers, total revenue increases when prices are reduced, up to a certain point.

3. In an effort to eliminate drug shipments to Canadian Internet pharmacies that sell lower-cost US-produced drugs to US consumers, Pfizer notified all Canadian drug retailers of its policy to halt all sales of Pfizer drugs to them if they sell Pfizer drugs to US consumers. Pfizer receives information on all drug orders from individual drug stores from its distributors (Carlisle 2004).

THE PHARMACEUTICAL INDUSTRY: A PUBLIC POLICY DILEMMA

The pharmaceutical industry is subject to a great deal of criticism regarding the high prices charged for its drugs, its large (some would say "wasteful") marketing expenditures, and its emphasis on "lifestyle" and "me-too" drugs over drugs to cure infectious diseases and chronic conditions. Yet the industry has developed important drugs that have saved lives, reduced pain, and improved the lives of many. Public policy that attempts to respond to industry critics may at the same time change the industry's incentives for research and development (R&D) and thereby reduce the number of potential blockbuster drugs.

To evaluate the criticisms of this profitable industry and the consequences of public policy directed toward it, an understanding of the structure of this industry is needed.

The pharmaceutical industry is made up of two distinct types of drug manufacturers: pharmaceutical manufacturers, who engage in R&D and market brand-name drugs, and generic manufacturers. Pharmaceutical manufacturers invest large sums in R&D, whereas generic manufacturers do not. Consequently, the former group develops innovative branded drugs for new therapeutic uses, while generic firms sell copies of branded drugs (when their patents expire) at greatly reduced prices. These two industries differ in their economic performance and in the public policies directed toward them. Most public policy is directed at pharmaceutical manufacturers.

Understanding the distribution channel for prescription drugs is also essential in understanding the structure of the industry. Manufacturers produce the drugs and, for the most part, sell them to wholesalers, who then sell them to pharmacies, where they are purchased by patients. Pharmacies can be chain drug stores such as Rite-Aid, mass merchandisers such as Walmart, food store pharmacies such as Safeway, mail-order or retail pharmacies, or, more recently, Internet pharmacy websites. Over time, the number of independent retail pharmacies has declined. Wholesalers and retail pharmacies are each competitive industries.

Public Policy Dilemma

An important characteristic of the drug industry is the low cost of actually producing a drug once it has been discovered. Very large costs are incurred by the pharmaceutical manufacturer in the R&D phase and in marketing the new drug once it has been approved by the FDA. A new drug's price is not determined by its R&D costs, however, because these costs have already been incurred. Instead, the price is based on the demand for that drug, which is determined by its therapeutic value and whether it has close substitutes. Because the production costs of a drug (marginal costs) are low, a drug with great therapeutic value and few, if any, substitutes will command a high price. The resulting markup of price over production costs will therefore be high, leading to criticism of the drug company that the drug is priced too high for those who need it.

The public policy dilemma is that if the high price markups over cost are reduced so that more people can buy the drug, profits for R&D will also be reduced, thereby reducing future R&D investment and the discovery of new drugs with great therapeutic value.

Structure of the Pharmaceutical Industry

The structure of the pharmaceutical industry, together with regulatory restraints and government payment policies, affects drug prices and the rate of investment in new, innovative drugs. Industry performance is generally measured by the number of blockbuster drugs produced. High price markups for innovative, high-value drugs with no existing substitutes appear justified; high price markups on older drugs are simply an indication of lack of price competition, because the industry is unable (or lacks the incentive) to produce new, innovative drugs to take their place. Industry performance is also affected by regulations that increase the cost of developing new drugs, the time it takes for a new drug to receive FDA approval, and whether the government establishes the prices it will pay for new drugs; each of these government policies affects the profitability of new drugs, hence incentives for R&D investment.

The pharmaceutical industry has undergone major changes since the mid-1970s. Previously, most pharmaceutical firms were large, were able to take advantage of economies of scale, and were vertically integrated, that is, most activities were performed in-house, from drug discovery to clinical trials to regulatory approval processes to marketing. The firm's investments in R&D were financed by internally generated funds (Cockburn 2004).

Revolutionary discoveries in biologic sciences in the 1970s changed the structure of the industry. Thousands of new biotechnology firms were started. Venture capital funded many of these startups, which were not expected to be profitable for a number of years. Although the risk was high, the profit potential from new drug discoveries was believed to be so large that investors were willing to risk substantial sums on these new firms. The biotechnology industry became a major source of drug innovation (Cockburn, Stern, and Zausner 2010).

Large drug firms were concerned that they had fallen behind smaller biotechnology firms in their ability to develop innovative drugs. Small firms were more likely to take greater scientific risks and have a greater number of researchers devoted to a particular research idea, while larger firms became more bureaucratic in their scientific decision making. Large drug firms depended upon small biotech firms to fill their drug pipelines.

Most of the small, new biotechnology firms did not have the capabilities of large drug firms to bring a new product to market. At the same time, large drug firms recognized the profit potential of the drug research being undertaken by these small firms. Both types of firms realized that developing relationships would capitalize on each of their strengths. Large drug firms developed contractual relationships and bought smaller biotechnology companies. Thus far, few biotechnology firms have made a profit, although their products offer tremendous profit potential. These small firms face large risks and huge investment costs before their products can be marketed. The process of discovery, clinical trials, and drug approval is lengthy and costs hundreds of millions of dollars. Larger firms are able to bear these costs and have the expertise to navigate the drug-approval process. Greater risk pooling also occurs when many different drugs are in the discovery and development phase, as only a few of the many drugs developed will be successful. Only a large firm can afford to undertake these large research efforts. Small firms may not have the financial resources to complete the long drug-approval process or the expertise to perform all of the steps required (Golec and Vernon 2009; Lazonick and Tulum 2011).

Although the research innovation is being generated by smaller firms, large firms have an additional advantage when it comes to marketing and selling their drugs. Large pharmaceutical firms are able to offer health plans and pharmacy benefit managers (PBMs), who contract with large employers and medical plans, prescription drugs for almost all therapeutic categories at a package discount. Providing a full line of drugs for different therapeutic areas at a discount lowers the cost to the PBM, by removing the need to negotiate with multiple firms, while enabling the large pharmaceutical firm to include drugs in its package that the PBM might not otherwise select.

The Medicare Part D drug benefit reinforces these marketing advantages for the large drug firms; they are better able to provide the range of drugs used in the restricted formularies by the firms offering the Part D benefit to Medicare beneficiaries.

Thus, while smaller biotechnology firms have an advantage in research innovation, marketing advantages, the drug approval process, and regulatory expertise are pressuring firms to become larger.

Mergers and Acquisitions

Since the mid-1990s, a large number of mergers have occurred among pharmaceutical companies. These mergers have been of two types. The first were vertical mergers, whereby a firm diversifies into another product line. The growth of managed care and the growing importance of PBMs led several large drug manufacturers to spend many billions of dollars to buy PBMs in the early 1990s. (Merck, for example, paid $6.6 billion for the PBM Medco in 1993 [New York Times News Service 1993].) These drug firms believed that by buying PBMs they could gain greater control over the market for their drugs; the PBMs would presumably substitute their drugs for those of their competitors, increasing their market share and drug sales. PBMs, however, were unable to merely include their owners' drugs to the exclusion of others because their credibility in serving health plans would have been adversely affected. The drug firms' PBM strategy does not appear to have been worthwhile. Pharmaceutical companies that did not buy PBMs were also able to increase their drug sales, and some companies that bought PBMs sold them. The growth of managed care turned out to be a benefit rather than a threat to drug manufacturers. As more people enrolled in managed care, they received prescription drug coverage, use of prescription drugs increased, and sales at all drug firms sharply increased.

The second type of merger that has been occurring is horizontal, where one drug manufacturer purchases another. There are several reasons for horizontal mergers. First, by becoming larger, firms expect that economies of scale will increase efficiency and decrease costs. Merging two companies can decrease administrative costs and increase the efficiency of the two companies' sales forces, which is critical to the success of any drug firm. Consolidating research units can eliminate competing efforts.

For some large firms, mergers are a response to patent expirations and gaps in a firm's product pipeline (Danzon, Epstein, and Nicholson 2007). A wider array of prescription drugs diversifies the financial risk of a firm that has just a few best-selling drugs. For small pharmaceutical firms, mergers are primarily an exit strategy, an indication of financial trouble. Horizontal mergers can improve the combined drug firms' market power. However, few mergers have occurred between firms with drugs in the same therapeutic category.

Instead, the types of drugs offered by the combined drug firms are in different therapeutic categories, offering a broader range of prescription drugs across many therapeutic categories to large purchasers.

Industry Competitiveness

The pharmaceutical industry appears to be relatively competitive, as measured by the degree of market concentration. Concentration, which is measured by the combined market share of the top four firms, was only about 27 percent, based on data from IMS Health (2009). However, when therapeutic categories are used, the degree of market concentration is much higher, in some cases 100 percent, as a therapeutic category may include only one drug. Thus, the competitiveness of the pharmaceutical industry depends on the definition of the market.

Markets that are less concentrated (i.e., have more competitors) are typically more price competitive. The higher the degree of market concentration and the fewer the substitutes available for a particular drug, the greater the firm's market power, that is, the ability to raise price without losing sales. Thus, the manufacturer of the first breakthrough drug in a therapeutic category has a great deal of market power. As additional branded drugs are developed in that therapeutic category, substitutes become available and price competition increases. When the patents on those drugs expire and generic versions are introduced, a great deal of price competition occurs. At each of these stages purchasers are able to buy the prescription drug at a lower price.

Development of New Drugs by the US Pharmaceutical Industry

Several measures are used to indicate the productivity of the US pharmaceutical industry. One measure is designation as a "global new chemical entity" (NCE), which is a drug that is marketed to a majority of the world's leading purchasers of drugs; this designation is preferred over total NCEs as an indicator of a drug's commercial and therapeutic importance. "First in (a therapeutic) class" is another designation that reveals how innovative a drug is. In addition, the introduction of biotechnology and orphan drugs is examined, as both are major sources of industry growth and innovation.

Grabowski and Wang (2006) analyzed all NCEs introduced worldwide between 1982 and 2003. During that period, 919 NCEs were introduced: 42 percent were global NCEs, 13 percent were first-in-class NCEs, 10 percent were biotechnology drugs, and 8 percent were orphan drugs. Over this period, the total number of NCEs introduced each year showed a downward trend. However, the measures of the drugs' importance (global NCEs, first-in-class, biotechnology, and orphan drugs) have increased over the same time period. The authors conclude that although the trend in total NCEs declined, the relative quality of new drugs has been increasing, and most of the biotechnology and orphan drugs were introduced from 1993 to 2003. The number of NCEs considered global or first in class varied by therapeutic category, the highest number being oncology drugs, which is an emphasis of the biotech industry (the United States is the dominant source of biotech drugs).

When the introduction of drugs was analyzed by country, the United States was found to be a leader in the development of innovative drugs, particularly in the period from 1993 to 2003. US manufacturers accounted for 48 percent of first-in-class drugs, 52 percent of biotechnology products, and 55 percent of orphan drugs. (These data are shown in Exhibit 28.1.) Furthermore, when the countries in which important new drugs are first introduced (as opposed to developed) were examined, the United States was again a strong leader compared with the rest of the world in the most recent (1993 to 2003) period. Both foreign and domestic drug firms prefer to introduce their important new drugs first in the US market. US patients benefit from having earlier access to important new drugs (although there is also an associated risk with being the first users of such drugs).

The decline in the total number of NCEs appears to indicate that the productivity of the US drug industry has been declining. However, when measures of the importance of new drugs are used, productivity in the US drug industry has increased. Biotechnology drugs, in which the United States is a leader, have been a source of important new drugs and industry productivity growth.

The US market provides greater incentives to drug firms than markets in other countries for development of important new drugs and for the first introduction of innovative new drugs. Whether the US predominance in drug innovation and first choice of introduction will continue depends on government payment policies to reduce the costs of new drugs.

The Political Attractiveness of Price Controls on Prescription Drugs

For many years the high price of prescription drugs was a major concern of the elderly. When Medicare was enacted in 1965, prescription drugs were not included as a benefit. Many of the elderly, who are the highest users of prescription drugs, could not afford to buy needed prescription drugs; having a prescription drug benefit became their highest political priority. In 2003 the Medicare Modernization Act was enacted. It included a new Medicare Part D prescription drug benefit, which became effective in 2006 (see Chapter 8).

EXHIBIT 28.1 Country-Level Output of NCEs by Category and Time Period, 1982–92 and 1993–2003

Country	All NCEs		Global NCEs		First-in-Class NCEs		Biotech		Orphan NCEs	
	'82–'92	'93–'03	'82–'92	'93–'03	'82–'92	'93–'03	'82–'92	'93–'03	'82–'92	'93–'03
European Union total	230	183	99	112	23	27	6	23	9	20
France	35	18	9	11	2	3	0	3	0	4
Germany	53	42	21	27	5	5	2	6	2	5
Italy	29	14	4	1	1	0	0	0	0	0
Switzerland	42	41	26	30	8	11	3	8	1	8
UK	34	36	23	27	6	7	0	3	5	2
Others	38	33	17	16	2	2	1	3	1	2
Japan	125	88	12	12	5	3	5	9	1	0
US	120	152	66	81	24	30	9	37	10	27
Rest of the world	7	13	3	1	0	2	0	2	0	2
Total	482	437	179	206	53	62	19	71	20	49

SOURCE: Reprinted with permission as it appeared in Henry G. Grabowski and Y. Richard Wang, "The Quantity and Quality of Worldwide New Drug Introductions, 1982–2003," *Health Affairs*, 25(2), March/April 2006: 425–460, Exhibit 4 ©2006 Project HOPE–The People-to-People Health Foundation, Inc.

The new drug benefit increased the demand for prescription drugs by the aged, and pharmaceutical manufacturers benefited from increased revenues. However, increased revenues to the pharmaceutical companies meant higher federal expenditures for the aged's prescription drugs, 75 percent of which were being subsidized by the government. The Medicare drug benefit, similar to Medicare Part B, became another unfunded federal entitlement; no matter how much was spent on drugs by the aged, Medicare was committed to paying 75 percent of those expenditures. (As part of the 2010 Patient Protection and Affordable Care Act, the aged's cost sharing for prescription drugs will be reduced over time, leading to greater use of prescription drugs and higher drug expenditures.)

The Medicare Modernization Act prohibited the federal government from negotiating drug prices with pharmaceutical firms. The aged enroll in a private drug plan, which then negotiates drug prices with the drug manufacturer. As the cost of the drug benefit to the federal government continues to increase, the pharmaceutical companies are concerned that Congress will change the law and have the government regulate drug prices. (A number of legislators have already proposed changing the law to allow the government to negotiate directly with pharmaceutical companies.) The new drug benefit creates a huge unfunded federal liability at a time when the federal government's budget deficit is already very large. As long as the government is ultimately responsible for paying for the elderly's drug expenses, regardless of who administers the benefit, there is concern that drug expenditures will eventually be regulated, as the government currently regulates payment for each type of provider participating in Medicare.

Proponents of government regulation of drug prices claim that in addition to reducing federal expenditures, the aged would also benefit by lowering their out-of-pocket drug expenses and their premium for the Medicare drug benefit, which equals 25 percent of total Medicare drug expenditures. As evidence of the benefits of price controls, proponents claim that prices on branded drugs are as much as 30 percent higher in the United States than in Canada, which uses price controls.

Price controls on new breakthrough drugs are politically attractive. Politicians try to provide their constituents with short-term visible benefits, seemingly at no cost. In the short run, drug prices would be reduced and there would be no decrease in access to drugs currently on the market. Because the costs of R&D have already been incurred, the only cost of producing an existing drug is its relatively small variable costs. As long as the regulated drug price is greater than the drug's variable costs, the firm will continue selling the drug. Profits from that drug will be lower, but the drug firm will make more money by continuing to sell the drug, even at the regulated price, than by not selling it.

Consequences of Price Controls on Prescription Drugs

Price controls would not decrease access to innovative drugs currently on the market or even to those currently in the drug-approval process. Those who would benefit include patients who cannot afford expensive drugs, states with rapidly increasing Medicaid expenditures, and the federal government, which is responsible for bearing 75 percent of the cost of the prescription drug benefit. The aged, who have the highest voting-participation rate, state Medicaid programs, and legislators interested in decreasing federal drug expenditures are likely to favor legislation to reduce drug prices. The only apparent loser would be drug companies.

The real concern with price controls is their effects not on current drugs but on R&D for future drugs. Price controls reduce the profitability of new drugs. With lower expected profits, drug companies would be less willing to risk hundreds of millions of dollars on R&D. Most new drugs (about 70 percent to 80 percent) are not therapeutic breakthroughs and, although their price may exceed their variable costs, do not generate sufficient profit to cover their R&D investments. Thus, the drug company loses money on these drugs. (See Exhibit 26.4.) The small percentage that are considered to be blockbuster drugs have high price markups over their variable costs. The large profits generated by these blockbuster drugs generate the funding used for the drugs that lose money. Although there is a short-term visible benefit to price controls, they impose a long-term cost on patients. This long-term cost is not obvious because it occurs in the future, and the public would be unaware of breakthrough drugs that were never developed.

Blockbuster drugs, with their high price markups, would be targeted by price controls. With price controls, profit would be insufficient to provide R&D funding for new drugs. Fewer breakthrough drugs would mean treating a disease would be more costly; these drugs might make surgical intervention unnecessary or might even prevent the disease from occurring. Through R&D and the development of new drugs, the total cost of medical treatment is lowered. With price controls, R&D investments would decline. Drug companies would also reallocate their R&D efforts away from diseases affecting the elderly, where price controls limit profits, toward diseases affecting other population groups, where profits would not be limited.

Exhibits 28.2 and 28.3 illustrate the effects of imposing price controls on the product life cycle of a blockbuster drug (Helms 2004). During the beginning phases of R&D, including clinical trials, the company incurs a negative cash flow. Once the FDA approves the drug and the drug company markets the drug, the cash flow is positive, until other branded drugs (substitutes) enter the market, and eventually the patent expires and generics enter the market.

EXHIBIT 28.2 Life Cycle of a New Drug

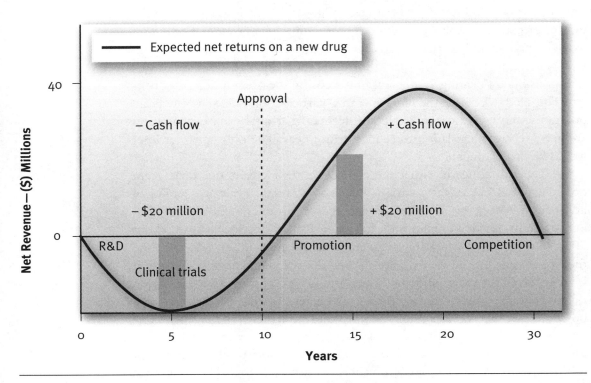

SOURCE: Helms (2004).

If price controls are imposed on a drug after it is approved by the FDA and marketed, the positive cash flow from the new drug is greatly diminished, as shown by the dashed line in Exhibit 28.3. To illustrate the financial effects of imposing price controls in the previous example, one would have to examine the present value of both the cash outlay and the positive cash return.

Money received in the future is worth less than the same amount of money received today. These money outflows (before the drug is being sold) and inflows occur at different times. The cost of developing a new drug includes all the costs of bringing it to market, such as research expenditures, the cost of clinical trials, the cost of having the drug approved by the FDA, and marketing costs once it is approved. A company would calculate what it could have earned on that investment if the funds were instead invested in a corporate bond and gained interest. For example, if $10 were invested today and earned 6 percent interest per year, in five years that initial investment would grow to $13.38. Thus, in calculating the cost of developing a new drug, the firm calculates both its cash outlay and what it could have earned on that

EXHIBIT 28.3 Effect of Price Controls on Drug Returns

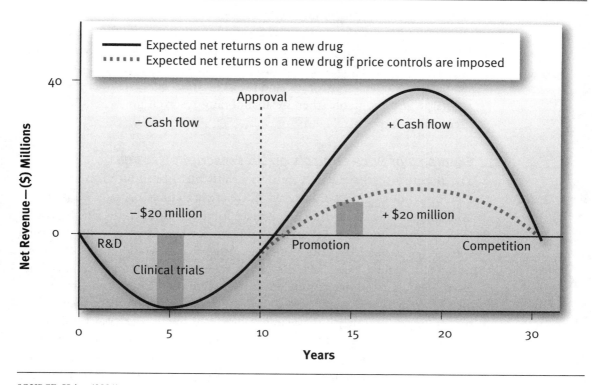

SOURCE: Helms (2004).

money (the opportunity cost). Similarly, in calculating the return received from that new drug, which generates a positive cash flow in the future, it is necessary to discount (using the same interest rate) the positive cash flow and determine what money received in the future is worth in today's dollars (the present value).

Using the example shown in Exhibits 28.2 and 28.3, if a firm invests $20 million in year five, the present value of that investment equals $14.95 million. (In other words, $14.95 million invested today would be worth $20 million in five years.) If, after 15 years, a new drug earns $20 million, the present value of that return is only $8.35 million. Clearly the $20 million spent and the $20 million earned are not equal. In this example, the drug firm would lose money on its investment—$6.6 million. Thus, the longer it takes to bring a drug to market, the longer the negative cash flow and the smaller the present value of the positive cash flow once the drug is marketed.

If price controls are imposed on a drug once it is marketed, as shown by the dashed line in Exhibit 28.3, both its positive cash flow and the present value of that reduced cash flow will be lower. Thus, if the firm earns only $10 million in year 15, the present value equals only $4.17 million. The present value of the cash outflow remains at $14.95 million (Helms 2004).

In the previous example of price controls reducing future returns, a drug firm would change its investment strategy: It would reduce its overall investment in R&D, invest in drugs with a quicker payoff, seek drugs with less-risky profitability outcomes, and invest in drugs whose market potential is very large and profitable, thereby abandoning research on drugs for diseases affecting fewer people.

Examples of Price Controls on US Prescription Drugs

The debate over President Clinton's health plan, introduced in the fall of 1993, provides an indication of the likely effect of price controls on prescription drugs. Included in the plan was an Advisory Council on Breakthrough Drugs, whose purpose was to review prices of new drugs. If the proposed council believed a new drug's price was excessive, it would try to have it reduced and, failing that, have the drug excluded from health insurance payment. The targeted drugs were those that were the most profitable and had high price markups, namely breakthrough drugs. The pharmaceutical industry was concerned that if the plan were enacted, price controls would be imposed on prescription drugs and the profitability of new drugs would be decreased. As a result, the annual rate of increase in R&D expenditures decreased sharply, falling from 18.2 percent in 1992 to 5.6 percent by 1994, the smallest annual rate of increase in 30 years (see Exhibit 28.4). Once it became clear that the Clinton health plan would be defeated and price controls would not be imposed on new drugs, the annual rate of increase in pharmaceutical R&D spending increased again.

The next threat to the drug companies occurred in 2002, when they believed Congress was going to legalize reimportation of drugs from Canada and Europe (without the approval of the secretary of Health and Human Services). As a result, in 2002 R&D expenditures increased by only 4.2 percent, after having increased by 14.4 percent in 2001. Once there was no longer a threat of a more stringent form of reimportation, R&D expenditures again increased, to 11.1 percent in 2003.

In 2008 and 2009 the annual change in R&D expenditures sharply decreased over concerns that the newly elected Democratic president and large Democratic majorities in Congress would adversely affect the industry by requiring reductions in Medicare and Medicaid prescription drug prices. In the fee-for-service part of Medicaid, drug firms pay a rebate to Medicaid for each drug the program purchases on behalf of its beneficiaries. President Obama's 2010 budget proposed to increase that rebate (ultimately lowering the price drug firms receive). Proposals were also made to require a rebate on drugs purchased by Medicare Part D beneficiaries. As the data indicate (CBO

EXHIBIT 28.4 Annual Percentage Change, US R&D, Pharmaceutical Companies, 1971–2009

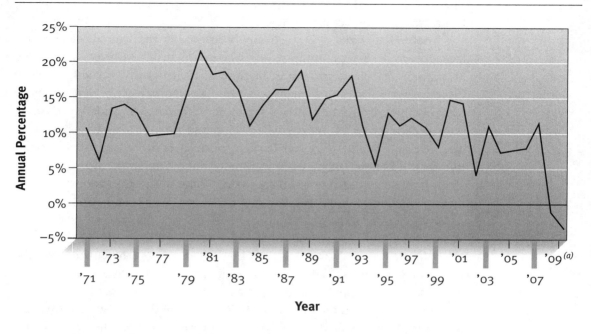

(a)Estimated data for 2009.

NOTE: Domestic US R&D includes expenditures within the United States by all PhRMA member companies. R&D abroad includes expenditures by US-owned PhRMA companies outside the United States and R&D conducted abroad by the US divisions of foreign-owned PhRMA member companies. R&D performed abroad by the foreign divisions of foreign-owned PhRMA member companies is excluded. Data for 1995 R&D affected by merger and acquisition activity.

SOURCE: Pharmaceutical Research and Manufacturers of America, *2010 Industry Profile*. [Online information.] http://www.phrma .org/sites/phrma.org/files/attachments/Profile_2010_FINAL.pdf.

2009), R&D expenditures are sensitive to possible legislative changes that would decrease drug firms' profits.

History does not offer much hope for drug manufacturers evading price controls. Governments in other countries have used various approaches to lower their drug expenditures. In a study of 19 Organisation for Economic Co-operation and Development countries, Sood and colleagues (2008) find various forms of regulation that decrease pharmaceutical revenues. The types of controls used by these countries include fixing the price of drugs; delaying approval for expensive new drugs for several years; restricting the use of a drug once it has been approved; establishing global (country) budget caps, annual physician prescribing budget limits, and profit controls; and setting the price of all drugs within a specific therapeutic category at the cost of the lowest-price drug. While a majority of the regulations decrease pharmaceutical revenues, direct price controls have the largest negative effect on revenues. If similar price controls were imposed in the United States, pharmaceutical revenues would fall as much as 20.3 percent. Further, the longer the regulations are in place, the greater their impact on revenues.

Several approaches have already been used in the United States to reduce government expenditures for prescription drugs (Vernon and Golec 2009). State Medicaid programs, because of their tight budgets, have more restrictive formularies than managed care plans. Newer drugs that are more expensive but also more effective are more likely to be excluded in favor of less-expensive generics. Furthermore, Medicaid programs delay inclusion of expensive new innovative drugs in their formularies for several years. Studies have shown that the effect of limiting access to preferred drugs results in a shift to more costly settings, higher nursing home admissions, and greater risk of hospitalization among Medicaid populations (Soumerai 2004). Further, the savings in drug costs were offset by increases in the costs of hospitalization and emergency department care (Hsu et al. 2006).

A price-control approach used by the federal government requires the drug manufacturer to sell the drug to the government at its "best" price. In the 1980s, as a result of price competition among drug companies to have HMOs and group purchasing organizations (GPOs) include their drugs in HMO and GPO drug formularies, drug manufacturers gave large price discounts to certain HMOs and GPOs. In 1990, the federal government, in an attempt to reduce Medicaid expenditures, enacted a law that required drug manufacturers to give state Medicaid programs the same discounts they gave their best customers. Consequently, the drug companies gave smaller discounts to HMOs and GPOs. A study by the Congressional Budget Office (1996) found that the best (largest) price discount given to HMOs and GPOs declined from 24 and 28 percent, respectively, in 1991 to 14 and 15 percent, respectively, the minimum amount required by the government, by 1994. The study concluded that drug companies were much less willing to give steep discounts to large purchasers when they had to give the same discounts to Medicaid. Drug prices and expenditures consequently increased for many private buyers.

Summary

Two important characteristics of the pharmaceutical industry are, first, the low costs of actually producing a drug pill and, second, the high cost of developing a new drug. The price at which a new drug is sold is determined not by its cost of production or the R&D investment in that drug, but instead by its value to purchasers and whether there are any close substitutes to that drug. Valuable drugs that have no close substitutes (blockbuster drugs) will be priced high relative to their costs of production. Lowering the price of these blockbuster drugs to make them more affordable will decrease pharmaceutical companies' incentive to invest hundreds of millions of dollars in drugs that may have great value to society. That is the public policy dilemma.

The pharmaceutical industry has been changing over time from large, vertically integrated organizations to an industry that still has large firms but also many small biotechnology firms, funded by venture capital, that are also engaged in developing new blockbuster drugs. A great deal of private money is invested in these highly risky ventures in the hope of developing a valuable (and profitable) new drug.

The United States, compared with the rest of the world, has been a leader in developing important new drugs and is the country of first choice for introducing innovative new drugs. Government payment policies to reduce drug expenditures threaten both the US industry's leadership and patients' access to innovative drugs.

A growing concern is that federal government, which has become a large indirect purchaser of prescription drugs as a result of including a prescription drug benefit in Medicare, will attempt to lower its drug expenses by controlling the price of prescription drugs. Direct government negotiations with drug companies over the price of their drugs will be tantamount to the government fixing the price of drugs.

Implementing price controls will not have any immediate effect on access to drugs by the aged. However, over time drug companies will invest less in R&D and redirect their R&D toward population groups and diseases where profitability is greater.

In coming years, enormous scientific progress is likely. The mapping of the human genome and advances in molecular biology are expected to lead to drug solutions for many diseases. Drug prices and expenditures will also likely be higher to reflect the increased willingness of people to pay for these new discoveries. It would be unfortunate if the desire to reduce the cost of drugs through price controls decreased the availability of breakthrough drugs.

Any public policy must deal with trade-offs: reducing the high price markup of breakthrough drugs versus maintaining incentives for investing in R&D. It is important to distinguish between the short- and long-term effects of public policy. Using price controls to lower drug prices results in a visible short-term benefit but comes at a less-visible longer-term cost of fewer breakthrough drugs. Future patients would be willing to pay for lifesaving breakthrough drugs that were not developed because the government removed the incentives to do so. Given the trade-off between instituting regulation to reduce the cost of drugs or having innovative drugs to cure disease, reduce mortality, and reduce the cost of medical treatment, society would likely choose the full benefits scientific discovery will offer.

Discussion Questions

1. How has the structure of the pharmaceutical industry changed over time?
2. What are alternative ways of judging whether the pharmaceutical industry is competitive?
3. Why are price controls on prescription drugs politically attractive?
4. Why would price controls not limit access to blockbuster drugs that are either currently on the market or have almost completed the FDA approval process?
5. What are the expected long-term consequences of price controls on R&D investments, quality of life, mortality rates, and the cost of medical care?

Additional Readings

Schweitzer, S. O. 2007. *Pharmaceutical Economics and Policy.* New York: Oxford University Press.

Vogel, R. 2007. *Pharmaceutical Economics and Public Policy.* Binghamton, NY: Haworth Press.

SHOULD KIDNEYS AND OTHER ORGANS BE BOUGHT AND SOLD?

Between 1995 and 2010, 104,923 people on waiting lists for an organ died. During this period, the number of people waiting for a transplant rose 173 percent, from 43,937 to 119,776, while the number of organs donated increased by just 50 percent, from 23,254 in 1995 to 35,020 in 2010 (see Exhibit 29.1). More than 75 percent of those waiting for organ transplants are waiting for kidneys; the remainder are waiting for a heart, liver, lung, or pancreas. The number of people who die each year while waiting for an organ transplant is increasing: In 2010, the number was 6,706, up from 6,439 in 2005.

Although the total number of transplants is increasing each year (see Exhibit 29.2), the gap between those waiting for organ transplants and the supply of organs has also been growing rapidly as more patients are recommended for such transplants. The discovery of immunosuppressive drugs to reduce the risk of rejection has greatly increased the success rate of organ transplants; success rates for kidney transplants have increased from approximately 60 percent in the late 1950s to 96 percent as of 2010. Unfortunately, the number of organs is insufficient to keep up with the growing demand. Consequently, many of those waiting for a transplant die before an organ becomes available.

Patients waiting for a kidney transplant must rely on kidney dialysis, which is costly. Kidney transplantation is a lower-cost form of treatment than dialysis. If all of the patients on dialysis who are waiting for a transplant could be given a kidney, the federal government, which pays for kidney dialysis and kidney transplants under Medicare, could save approximately $17 billion over a five-year period.[1] In addition to being higher cost, dialysis takes time, up to seven hours per day for several days a week. Kidney dialysis patients have a reduced quality of life as well as lower productivity.

Sources of Organs for Transplant

Two sources of supply for organ transplants exist: living donors, such as family members who donate one of their kidneys, and cadavers. Approximately 62 percent of kidneys, as well as other organs used for transplants (96 percent

EXHIBIT 29.1 Demand for Organs and Total Number of Organs Donated, 1995–2010

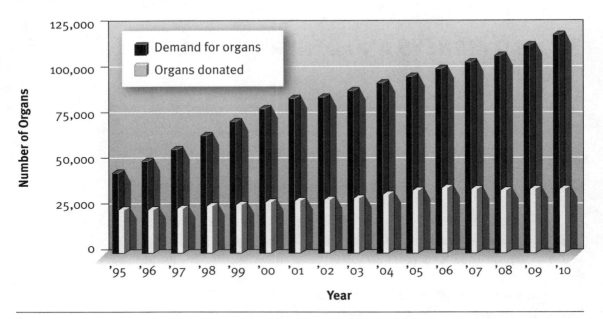

SOURCES: Data on the number of organs donated are based on Organ Procurement and Transplantation Network (OPTN) Waiting List on the last day of each year. Data for the number of organs demanded are based on OPTN data as of March 4, 2011. http://optn.transplant .hrsa.gov.

of livers, 99 percent of lungs, and 100 percent of pancreases and hearts), come from victims who have just been killed in an accident. A total of 77 percent of all organs come from accident victims (OPTN 2011).

The motivating force on which transplant patients have long depended is altruism. According to the National Organ Transplant Act of 1984, purchase or sale of human organs is illegal. Current efforts to increase the supply of organs rely on approaches to stimulate voluntary organ donations by the family members of those who die in accidents.

Currently, shortly after they have been notified of the death of a family member, medical personnel ask the family of the deceased to donate their loved one's body organs. Physicians are often reluctant to make such a request to a grieving family, and the grieving family is reluctant to agree while still shocked by the death of a loved one. For some families, the sorrow might be somewhat offset by the belief that another person's life might be saved. However, only about 15 to 20 percent of families are willing to give permission for their deceased family member's organs to be used for transplant patients (Spital 1991). For psychological reasons, such as the thought of dismemberment of a loved one, and religious reasons, families of the deceased

Exhibit 29.2 Number of Organ Transplants, Selected Years, 1981–2010

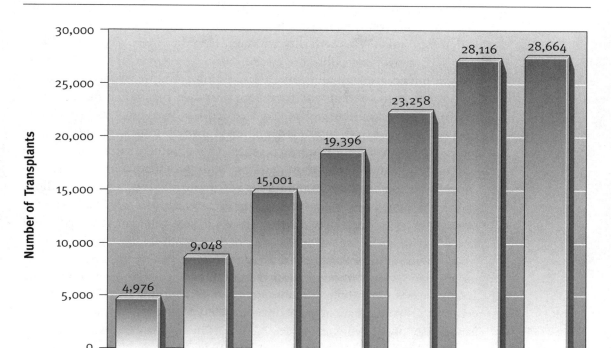

SOURCE: Based on Organ Procurement and Transplantation Network (OPTN) data as of March 4, 2011. http://optn.transplant.hrsa.gov.

are often reluctant to donate the deceased's organs. The period in which such a request can be made is short (tissues may be recovered from donors up to 24 hours after the cessation of heartbeat); the organ will quickly deteriorate. The family must be located, permission must be received, a recipient must be located through the national organ network, and a tissue match must be made between the recipient and the deceased.

Various approaches have been proposed to increase voluntary organ donations. One is to use improved "marketing" techniques on how to approach (and who should talk to) grieving families, whose sorrow, as already mentioned, may be lessened by the knowledge that they have saved another person's life by donating the deceased's organs. Another approach is to provide greater publicity and education to the public on the use of signed donor cards, which make a person's organs available to potential recipients.

Although education and publicity are likely to increase the number of signed donor cards, hence potential organs, the organ transplant community still seeks permission from the donor's family before harvesting organs. In some states, such as Texas, medical authorities have been legally granted permission to harvest organs from bodies if the family has not been identified within four hours. This authority, however, has rarely been used. Fear of lawsuits and unfavorable publicity and the desire to maintain the public's trust prevent physicians from immediately harvesting a deceased donor's organs.

Presumed consent laws have been proposed that would make the deceased's organs available unless the deceased or their family had previously opposed it. These laws, which are in force in many European countries, have increased organ donation rates about 25 to 30 percent over those in the United States, although in most countries with presumed consent laws, such as Spain, medical authorities do not authorize the removal of organs without an explicit family approval. Thus, while presumed consent would alleviate the organ shortage in the United States, it would not eliminate it (Abadie and Gay 2006).

Waiting for permission from the deceased's family often results in the organs being lost. Although about 20,000 people who die each year in the United States have organs suitable for harvesting, again, only 15 to 20 percent of those organs are actually donated. Under the current system of altruism, the supply of living and deceased donors has increased very slowly, from 5,909 in 1988 to 9,220 in 1996 and 14,503 in 2010.

Donor Compensation Proposals

The growing imbalance between supply and demand for organs has led some persons to advocate compensating donors to increase the supply of donated organs. Compensating donors (or their families) is highly controversial and would require a change in current legislation prohibiting the purchase or sale of body organs. Organ payment proposals cover the spectrum from mild—paying family members for organs of their deceased kin—to strong—paying a living donor for his second kidney. The following discussion covers three such proposals.

Compensating Families After the Death of the Donor

One approach proposes that the burial costs of the deceased be paid if the family permits harvesting of the deceased's organs. Similarly, the family of the deceased could be paid an amount varying between $1,000 and $5,000. A potential problem with these proposals is that negotiating a financial transaction with a family traumatized by the death of a loved one may be awkward. Another possible problem is that organ purchases of the deceased, which would presumably be directed toward those with low incomes, might offend low-income minority families, who may feel that they are being exploited to benefit wealthy white people.

Compensating Donors Before Death

Allowing people to sell their organs in advance of their death has the advantage that family members would not be subject to the psychological and social pressure to make a quick decision at the time they suffer the loss of a loved one. Thus, a second approach is to allow people to sell the rights to their organs in return for reducing their health or auto insurance premiums. Health or automobile insurance companies might offer annually a choice of lower premiums to those who are willing to donate their organs if they die during the coming year. The insurance company would then have the right to harvest the deceased's organs during the period of the insurance contract. Each of the potential donors would be listed in a central computer registry, which a hospital would check when a patient died. Transplant recipients would also be listed in a national registry, and their health insurer or the government would reimburse the insurer a previously stated price for the organ.

For example, if the value of all of a deceased's organs is $100,000 at time of death and the probability of dying during the year is 10,000:1 (the current average chance of dying during a year), the annual premium reduction would be $10. If the value of all of the organs is greater than $100,000 or the probability of death is lower than 10,000:1, the premium reduction would be greater. Young drivers and motorcyclists, who are more likely to die in accidents, would presumably be offered larger automobile insurance reductions.

The price of organs could either be established competitively or by the government, for example, $10,000 for a kidney. These prices would be used by insurance companies, together with the probability that a subscriber would die during the next year, to establish the annual premium reduction for a potential donor. If too few insurance subscribers were willing to accept the premium reduction, the price of the organ (if established by the government) could be increased until the likely supply is large enough to satisfy the estimated demand for transplants. The greater the shortage of organs, the larger would be the reductions in insurance premiums for organ donors.

Paying Living Kidney Donors

The most controversial approach for increasing the supply of organs is to pay living donors a sufficiently high price for them to part with one of their kidneys. Paying a market price to bring forth an increase in supply is already occurring in other highly sensitive areas of human behavior, such as with the use of sperm banks and surrogate mothers, who are willing to be impregnated with another couple's fertilized egg in return for a fee.

Market transactions consist of a voluntary exchange of assets between two parties. People engage in voluntary exchange because they differ in their valuation of the asset and both parties expect to benefit from the transaction. If sales of kidneys were permitted, the person selling the kidney would receive a fee that she believes would compensate her for the loss of a kidney. The purchaser believes the kidney is worth at least what he is willing to pay for it. The purchaser is likely to be the government rather than an individual, as kidney transplants are covered under Medicare; in this case, paying for the kidney would be similar to paying the surgeon for the operation. No one is made worse off by voluntary trade. Thus, the first major advantage of legalizing the sale of kidneys is that both parties are likely better off with the voluntary exchange than when it is prohibited.

Permitting a commercial market for kidneys has other important advantages. Organs that would save the lives of all those waiting for a kidney could be purchased. No longer would they have to endure the suffering that occurs while waiting for a kidney donation, possibly dying before one becomes available. Furthermore, the government would save a great deal of money by substituting kidney transplants for kidney dialysis, as a transplant is a lower-cost method of treatment than dialysis. Lastly, the quality of donated kidneys would increase, increasing the success rate of transplants. Currently, donated kidneys that do not have good tissue matches are used because of the severe shortage of kidneys. Paying living donors for their kidneys would result in greater choice of donors, enabling tissue matches between recipient and donor to be made in advance.

Opposition to Financial Incentives to Organ Donation

Opposition to using financial incentives to increase the supply of organs is based on several factors. First, some believe using financial incentives would discourage voluntary donations of organs, resulting in a smaller supply of organs. Evidence that may indicate the likely consequences to the overall supply of organs when financial incentives are offered is what happened when financial incentives were used to increase the supply of blood (Dunham 2008). Voluntary donations of blood declined, but the decline was more than offset by an increase in the supply of paid donations.

Second, some claim that paying living donors for their organs would exploit the poor to benefit the wealthy; the poor are likely to be the sellers of organs, whereas those with higher incomes would be the beneficiaries. The poor, it is claimed, would be forced to sell their organs to provide for their families. However, if the poor have inadequate funds, it is because society is unwilling to provide them with sufficient subsidies to increase their incomes or provide them with education that would increase their productivity and incomes. Prohibiting the poor from selling one of their assets would leave them worse off, and they would be prevented from doing something they believe will improve their situation.

Although little risk is involved in selling one's kidney, a donor would be accepting a slightly higher risk of dying in return for increased financial rewards. Many people seek additional compensation by choosing to work in higher-risk occupations. Working in a coal mine, on a skyscraper, or on an offshore drilling platform carries occupational risks, yet society does not interfere with these voluntary transactions. Someone willing to make the trade-off between greater compensation and the loss of a kidney is not "forced" to sell her organs.

Third, some are concerned that those selling their kidneys might be subject to fraud and then regret selling their kidneys. Various protections could be included in legislation legalizing the sale of kidneys. A waiting period, such as six months, could be used in case the person decides to change his mind. The donor could be required to be of a minimum age. The donor could also be approved by a panel that includes a psychiatrist or social worker to assess her ability to make rational choices.

When demand exceeds supply in a market, prices rise. When prices are not permitted to rise or sales are illegal, the potential for a black market exists. Although the sale of kidneys in the United States is illegal, a wealthy patient has access to an international black market, particularly from donors from less-developed countries, such as India and China. Demand for organs is lower when the activity is illegal than it would be if sales were legal. Finding an organ donor on the black market incurs higher search costs, purchasers are less certain of the organ's quality, no legal remedies are available if fraud occurs, and the purchaser would have to pay the hospital's and surgeon's costs out of pocket. However, again, this option is available to the wealthy. Therefore, prohibiting the sale of organs discriminates against the poor, who do not have access to the international black market in kidneys.

If a legal market in organs were permitted, would only the wealthy be able to afford kidney transplants once the price of a kidney is included in the already-high price of a transplant? The answer is no. Kidney transplants are currently paid for by the federal government; the higher cost would not be a deterrent to any recipient needing a transplant. Most of the costs for a transplant are for hospital and physician services; including the price of the organ would not be a large addition to those costs. Currently, everyone associated with the transplant benefits—the recipient receives a new kidney, and the physician and hospital are paid for the transplantation surgery. Why should the donor not also benefit?

What if a low-income person desperate for money sells his kidney and subsequently suffers from kidney disease? Because the government currently pays for all kidney transplants as part of Medicare, that donor would become eligible for a free transplant. A new donor would be paid for a kidney to be used for the previous donor's transplant.

Would the opponents of a compensation system who are concerned with its effects on the poor be more positively inclined to using financial incentives if the poor (defined, for example, as those with incomes below the federal poverty level) were prohibited from selling their organs? Would the poor be better off if they were denied the right to sell one of their assets? A belief that society helps the poor when those with higher incomes limit their choices is paternalistic.

Additional Considerations

The poor and minority groups are placed at a disadvantage by the present altruistic system for securing and allocating organs. Many of those waiting for transplants have low incomes. Furthermore, although African Americans are statistically more likely to suffer from kidney disease than whites, they are less likely to receive an organ transplant. In fact, while African Americans make up 12.6 percent of the population, they make up 34 percent of the waiting list for kidney transplants. The relatively higher proportion of African Americans on the waiting list is due to three factors: They need proportionately more kidneys than whites, their tissue match rate with whites is low, and they are not as likely to get donations from African American families as from white families (the refusal rate for organ donations among African American families is 60 percent, compared with 29 percent for white families) (GAO 1997).

As Epstein (2006) wrote, "Only a bioethicist would prefer a world in which we have 1,000 altruists per annum and over 6,500 excess deaths over one in which we have no altruists and no excess deaths." Markets and altruism are differing approaches for increasing the number of organ donations; they should be evaluated on the basis of which produces less loss of life.

Summary

As the feasibility of transplants increases and more hospitals and physicians find status and profit in performing transplants, the demand for transplantation will continue to grow. However, without any incentives on the part of donors, the shortage of organs will become more severe. As Cohen (2005) says, "If the benefits of an organs market are so clear, then why do we still ... condemn people to death and suffering while the organs that could restore them to health are instead fed to worms?"

Perhaps the strongest objection to compensating donors for their organs is some people's ideological and moral beliefs. Financial incentives governed by greed would substitute for altruism as the motivating force for donating one's organs, an idea that is deeply offensive to many persons. However, a trade-off must be considered. Although the thought of having people sell their organs is offensive, thousands of people die each year for lack of a kidney donor, and this number will increase. Which choice is more offensive—violating the strongly held beliefs of some persons regarding the repugnance of a market for human organs or the suffering and loss of life of thousands of people needing an organ transplant?

Discussion Questions

1. Why have voluntary methods for increasing the supply of body organs been unsuccessful?
2. Evaluate the following proposal: People would be permitted to sell the rights to their organs (in the form of reduced health or auto insurance premiums) if they die in an accident in the coming year.
3. Would government expenditures for kidney disease (currently covered as part of Medicare for all persons) be higher or lower under a free-market system for kidneys?
4. Would the poor be disadvantaged to the benefit of the wealthy under a free-market system for selling kidneys?
5. Would it be more equitable to prohibit the poor from selling their kidneys in a free market that otherwise permitted the sale of kidneys?

Additional Readings

Becker, G., and J. Elias. 2007. "Introducing Incentives in the Market for Live and Cadaveric Organ Donations." *Journal of Economic Perspectives* 21(3): 3–24.
Howard, D. 2007. "Producing Organ Donors." *Journal of Economic Perspectives* 21(3): 25–36.

Note

1. The following is a rough calculation of Medicare's five-year savings: $70,000 is the annual cost of kidney dialysis, and $100,000 is the one-time cost of a kidney transplant, plus $12,000 a year for the cost of immunosuppressive drugs after a transplant. According to the United

Network for Organ Sharing, 90,000 patients are currently waiting for kidney transplants. Assuming that these patients receive a kidney transplant this year, Medicare costs over a five-year period will equal $(90,000 \times \$100,000 + 90,000 \times 5 \times \$12,000) = \$14,400,000,000$ (or $14.4 billion). However, if these patients use dialysis for the next five years, Medicare would spend $90,000 \times \$70,000 \times 5 = \$31,500,000,000$ (or $31.5 billion). Therefore, if all of the patients on dialysis who are waiting for a transplant could receive a kidney, the federal government would save $31.5 billion minus $14.4 billion = $17.1 billion over a five-year period. Satel (2007) and Martin (2009) contain estimates of the cost of kidney dialysis and kidney transplants.

THE ROLE OF GOVERNMENT IN MEDICAL CARE

Government intervention in the financing and delivery of medical services is pervasive. On the financing side, newly enacted health legislation will provide subsidies and tax credits to individuals, small businesses, and low-income employees, and employers will be required to provide health insurance benefits to their employees; hospital and physician services for the aged are subsidized (Medicare), and a separate payroll tax pays for those subsidies; Medicaid, a federal/state matching program, pays for medical services for the poor and near-poor; a large network of state and county hospitals is in place; health professional schools are subsidized; loan programs for students in the health professions are guaranteed by the government; employer-paid health insurance is excluded from taxable income; veterans have access to a separate medical program; the Civilian Health and Medical Program of the Uniformed Services (CHAMPUS) finances health benefits for military dependents; and medical research is subsidized. These programs and others make government a greater than 50 percent partner in total health expenditures.

In addition to these financing programs, extensive government regulations influence the financing and delivery of medical services. For example, state licensing boards determine the criteria for entry into the different professions, and practice regulations determine which tasks can be performed by various professional groups. In some states hospital investment is subject to state review, hospital and physician prices under Medicare are regulated, health insurance companies are regulated by the states, and each state mandates what benefits (e.g., hair transplants in Minnesota) and which providers (e.g., naturopaths in California) should be included in health insurance sold in that state (Bunce and Wieske 2009).

The role of government in the financing and delivery of medical services, and through federal and state regulation, is extensive. To understand the reasons for these different types of government intervention and at times seemingly contradictory policies, it is necessary to have a view of what the government is attempting to achieve.

Public-Interest View of Government

The traditional, or public-interest, role of government can be classified according to its policy objectives and the policy instruments used to achieve those objectives. The policy objectives of government in the health field are twofold: (1) to redistribute medical resources to those least able to purchase medical services and (2) to improve the economic efficiency by which medical services are purchased and delivered. These traditional objectives of government, redistribution and efficiency, can be achieved by using one or more of the following policy instruments: expenditures, taxation, and regulation. (Government provision of services, such as Veterans Administration hospitals, is rarely proposed as a policy instrument in the United States.)

These policy instruments—expenditures, taxation, and regulation—can be applied to either the purchaser (demand) side or the supplier (provider) side of the market. For example, expenditure policies on the demand side are Medicare and Medicaid; on the supply side are subsidies for hospital construction and health manpower training programs. A taxation policy on the demand side is tax-exempt employer-paid health insurance; on the supply side are tax-exempt bonds for nonprofit hospitals. A regulatory policy on the demand side is an individual mandate to buy health insurance; on the supply side are licensing requirements, restrictions on the tasks different health professionals can perform, entry barriers to building a hospital or a new hospice in a region, and regulated provider prices for hospitals and physicians under Medicare. These policy objectives and instruments, which can be used to classify each type of government health policy according to policy objectives, the type of policy instrument used, and whether the policy instrument is directed toward the demand or supply side of the market, are shown in Exhibit 30.1.

Redistribution

Redistribution causes a change in wealth. According to the public-interest view of government, society makes a value judgment that medical services should be provided to those with low incomes and financed by taxing those with higher incomes. Redistributive programs typically lower the cost of services to a particular group by enabling members of that group to purchase those services at below-market prices. These benefits are financed by imposing a cost on some other group. Two large redistributive programs are Medicare for the aged and Medicaid for the medically indigent. The benefits and costs of a redistributive medical program, such as Medicaid, are shown in Exhibit 30.2.

EXHIBIT 30.1 Health Policy Objectives and Interventions

Government Policy Instruments		Government Objectives	
		Redistribution	*Improve Efficiency*
Expenditures	{ Demand side Supply side		
Taxation (+/−)	{ Demand side Supply side		
Regulation	{ Demand side Supply side		

EXHIBIT 30.2 Determining the Redistributive Effects of Government Programs

	Low Income	High Income
Benefits	X	
Costs		X

Efficiency

The second traditional objective of government is to improve the efficiency with which society allocates resources. Inefficiency in resource allocation can occur, for example, when firms in a market have monopoly power or when externalities exist. A firm has monopoly power when it is able to charge a price that exceeds its cost by more than a normal profit. Monopoly is inefficient because it produces too small a level of service (output). The additional benefit to purchasers from consuming a service (as indicated by its price) is greater than the cost of producing that benefit; therefore, more resources should flow into that industry until the additional benefit of consuming that service equals the additional cost of producing it.

The bases of monopoly power are several: There may be only one firm in a market, as with a natural monopoly such as an electric company; there may be barriers to entry in a market; firms may collude on raising their prices; or a lack of information may mean consumers are unable to judge price, quality, and service differences among different suppliers. In each of these situations, the prices charged will exceed the costs of producing the product (which includes a normal profit). The appropriate government remedy for decreasing monopoly power is to eliminate barriers to entry into a market, prevent price collusion, and improve information among consumers.

The second situation in which the allocation of resources can be improved is when externalities occur, that is, when someone undertakes an action and in so doing affects others who are not part of that transaction. The effects on others could be positive or negative. For example, a utility using high-sulfur coal to produce electricity also produces air pollution. As a result of the air pollution, residents in surrounding communities may have a higher incidence of respiratory illness. Resources are misallocated because the cost of producing electricity excludes the costs imposed on others. As a result, too much electricity is being produced. If the costs of producing electricity also included the costs imposed on others, the price of electricity would be higher and its demand lower. The allocation of resources would be improved if the utility's cost included production costs and external costs.

The appropriate role of government in such a situation is to determine the costs imposed on others and to tax the utility an equivalent amount. (This subject is discussed more completely in Chapter 31.)

Economic Theory of Regulation

Dissatisfaction with the public-interest theory occurred for several reasons. Instead of simply regulating natural monopolies, government has also regulated competitive industries, such as airlines, trucks, and taxicabs, as well as various professions. Furthermore, unregulated firms always want to enter regulated markets. To prevent entry into regulated industries, the government establishes entry barriers. If the government supposedly reduces prices in regulated markets, hence the firm's profitability, why should firms seek to enter a regulated industry?

To reconcile these apparent contradictions with the public-interest view of government, an alternative theory of government behavior, the economic theory of regulation, was developed (Stigler 1971). (For a more complete discussion of this theory and its applicability to the health field see

Feldstein [2006c].) The basic assumption underlying the economic theory is that political markets are no different from economic markets; individuals and firms seek to further their self-interest. Firms undertake investments in private markets to achieve a high rate of return. Why would the same firms not invest in legislation if it also offered a high rate of return? Organized groups are willing to pay a price for legislative benefits. This price is political support, which brings together the demanders and suppliers of legislative benefits.

The Suppliers: Legislators

The suppliers of legislative benefits are legislators, and their goal is assumed to be to maximize their chances for reelection. As the late Senator Everett Dirksen said, "The first law of politics is to get elected; the second law is to be reelected." To be reelected requires political support, which consists of campaign contributions, votes, and volunteer time. Legislators are assumed to be rational, that is, to make cost-benefit calculations when faced with demands for legislation. However, the legislator's cost-benefit calculations are not the costs and benefits to society of enacting particular legislation. Instead, the benefits are the additional political support the legislator would receive from supporting the legislation, and the costs are the lost political support she would incur as a result of her actions. When the benefits to the legislators exceed their costs, they will support the legislation.

The Demanders: Those with a Concentrated Interest

Those who have a concentrated interest—that is, those on whose profitability the legislation will have a large effect by affecting their revenues or costs—are more likely to be successful in the legislative marketplace. It becomes worthwhile for the group to incur the costs to organize, represent its interests before legislators, and raise political support to achieve the profits favorable legislation can provide. For this reason, only those with a concentrated interest will demand legislative benefits.

Diffuse Costs

When legislative benefits are provided to one group, others must bear those costs. When only one group has a concentrated interest in the legislation, that group is more likely to be successful if the costs to finance those benefits are not obvious and can be spread over a large number of people. When this occurs, the costs are said to be diffuse. For example, assume there are ten firms in an industry, and if they can have legislation enacted that limits imports that compete with their products, they will be able to raise their prices and thereby receive $300 million in legislative benefits. These firms have a concentrated interest ($300 million) in trying to enact such legislation. The costs of these legislative benefits are financed by a small increase in the price of the product amounting to $1 per person.

Often the fact that legislation increases their costs is not obvious to consumers. Furthermore, even if consumers were aware of the legislation's effect, it would not be worthwhile for them to organize and represent their interests to forestall a price increase that will decrease their incomes by $1 a year. The costs of trying to prevent the cost increase would exceed their potential savings.

It is easier (less costly) for providers than for consumers to organize, provide political support, and impose a diffuse cost on others. For this reason, much legislation has affected entry into the health professions, which tasks are reserved to certain professions, how (and which) providers are paid under public medical programs, why subsidies for medical education are given to schools and not students (otherwise schools would have to compete for students), and so on. Most health issues have been relatively technical, such as the training of health professionals, certification of their quality, methods of payment, controls on hospital capital investment, and so on. The higher medical prices resulting from regulations that benefit providers have been diffuse and not visible to consumers.

Entry Barriers to Regulated Markets

The economic theory of legislation provides an explanation for these dissatisfactions with the public-interest theory. Firms in competitive markets seek regulation to earn higher profits than are available without regulation. Prices in regulated markets, such as interstate air travel, were always higher than in unregulated markets, such as intrastate air travel, enabling regulated firms to earn greater profits. These higher prices provided unregulated firms with an incentive to try to enter regulated markets. Government, on behalf of the regulated industry, imposes entry barriers to keep out low-priced competitors. Otherwise, the regulated firms could not earn more than a competitive rate of return. Through legislation, firms try to receive the monopoly profits they are unable to achieve through market competition.

Opposing Concentrated Interests

When only one group has a concentrated interest in the outcome of legislation and the costs are diffuse, legislators will respond to the political support the group is willing to pay to have favorable legislation enacted. When there are opposing groups, each with a concentrated interest in the outcome, legislators are likely to reach a compromise between the competing demanders of legislative benefits. Rather than balancing the gain in political support from one group against the loss from the other, legislators prefer to receive political support from both groups and impose diffuse costs on those offering little political support.

Visible Redistributive Effects

When the beneficiaries are specific population groups, such as the aged, the redistributive effects of legislation are meant to be very visible. An example of this is Medicare. By making clear which population groups will benefit, legislators hope to receive their political support. The costs (taxes) of financing such visible redistributive programs, however, are still designed to be diffuse so as not to generate political opposition from others. A small, diffuse tax imposed on many people, such as a sales or a payroll tax, is the only way large sums of money to finance visible redistributive programs can be raised with little opposition. These taxes are regressive—the tax represents a greater portion of income from low-income employees and consumers. Economists have determined that payroll taxes, even when imposed on the employer, are borne mostly by the employee. (The employer is only interested in the total cost of an employee; thus, the employee eventually receives a lower wage than if those costs were not imposed.) By imposing part of the tax on the employer, however, employees appear to be paying a smaller portion of it than they really are. The remainder of the tax is shifted forward to consumers in the form of higher prices for the goods and services they purchase, which is also regressive.

Medicare: A Case Study of the Success of Concentrated Interests

The concentrated interests of medical providers and the subsequent diffuse (small) costs imposed on consumers explain much of the legislative history of the financing and delivery of medical services until the early 1960s. The enactment and design of Medicare illustrates the real purpose of visible redistribution policy: to redistribute wealth, that is, increase benefits to politically powerful groups without their paying the full costs of those benefits by shifting the costs to the less politically powerful.

Throughout the 1950s and early 1960s, the American Federation of Labor–Congress of Industrial Organizations unions had a concentrated interest in their retirees' medical costs that placed them in opposition to the American Medical Association (AMA). Employers had not prefunded union retirees' medical costs but instead paid them as part of current labor expenses. If union retirees' medical expenses could be shifted away from the employer, those funds would be available to be paid as higher wages to union employees.

To ensure that their union retirees would be eligible for Medicare, the unions insisted that eligibility be based on those who had paid into the Social Security system while they were working and that the new Medicare program (hospital services) be financed by a separate Medicare payroll tax to be included as part of the Social Security tax. Although the current retirees had not contributed to the proposed Medicare program, they were to become immediately eligible because they had paid Social Security taxes. The use of the Social Security system to determine eligibility became the central issue in the debate over Medicare (Feldstein 2006).

The AMA was willing to have government assistance go to those unable to afford medical services, which would have increased the demand for physicians. Thus, the association favored a means-tested program funded by general tax revenues, because it was concerned that including the non-poor in the new program would merely substitute government payment for private payment. The AMA believed such a program would cost too much, leading to controls on hospital and physician fees.

With the landslide victory of President Johnson in 1964, the unions achieved their objective. Once Social Security financing was used to determine eligibility for Medicare, Medicare Part B (physician services) was added, financed by general tax revenues.

Although the unions won on the financing mechanism, Congress acceded to the demands of the medical and hospital associations on all other aspects of the legislation. The system of payment to hospitals and physicians promoted inefficiency (cost-plus payments to hospitals), and restrictions limiting competition were placed on alternative delivery systems.

This historic conflict between opposing concentrated interests in medical care left both sides victorious and illustrates how the power of government can be used to benefit politically important groups. As a result of Medicare, a massive redistribution of wealth occurred in society. The beneficiaries were the aged, union members, and medical providers, and the benefits were financed by a diffuse, regressive tax (the Medicare payroll tax) on a large group, the working population, who also paid higher prices for their medical services and more income taxes to finance Medicare Part B. Medicare was designed to be both inefficient and inequitable simply because it was in the economic interests of those with concentrated interests.

Medicaid and Medicare

Differences in the sources of political support are important for understanding the two main redistributive programs in the United States. Medicaid is a means-tested program for the poor funded from general tax revenues. Because the poor (who have low voting-participation rates) are unable to provide legislators with political support, the support for Medicaid comes from the middle class, who must agree to higher taxes to provide the poor with medical benefits. The inadequacy of Medicaid in every state, the conditions necessary for achieving Medicaid eligibility, the low levels of eligibility, and beneficiaries' lack of access to medical providers are related to the generosity (or lack thereof) of the middle class. The beneficiaries of Medicare, on the other hand, are the aged, who generally have the highest voting-participation rate of any age group. The aged (together with their adult children) provide the political support for the program. As the cost of Medicare has risen, government has raised the Medicare payroll tax and reduced payments to providers rather than reducing benefits or beneficiaries from this politically powerful group.[1]

The political necessity of keeping costs diffuse explains why Medicare and producer regulation are financed using regressive taxes, either payroll taxes or higher prices for medical services. Spreading the costs over large populations keeps those costs diffuse, with the net effect that low-income persons pay the costs and higher-income persons, such as physicians or high-income aged, receive the benefits. Those receiving the benefits and those bearing the costs, according to the economic theory, are not based on income (see Exhibit 30.2), but instead according to which groups are able to offer political support (the beneficiaries) and which groups are unable to do so (they bear the costs). Regressive taxes are typically used to finance producer regulation and to provide benefits to specific population groups.

Changes in Health Policies

Health policies change over time because groups who previously bore a diffuse cost develop a concentrated interest. Until the 1960s, medical societies were the main group with a concentrated interest in the financing and delivery of medical services. Thus, the delivery system was structured to benefit physicians. The physician-to-population ratio remained constant for 15 years (until the mid-1960s) at 141 per 100,000, state restrictions were imposed on HMOs to limit their development, advertising was prohibited, and restrictions were placed on other health professionals to limit their ability to compete with physicians. Financing mechanisms also benefited physicians; until the 1980s, capitation payment for HMOs was prohibited under Medicare and Medicaid, and competitors to physicians were excluded from reimbursement under public and private insurance systems.

As the costs of medical care continued to increase rapidly to government and employers, their previously diffuse costs became concentrated. Under Medicare the government was faced with the choice of raising taxes or reducing benefits to the aged, both of which would have cost the administration political support. Successive administrations developed a concentrated interest in lowering the rate of increase in medical expenditures. Similarly, large employers were concerned that rising medical costs were making them less competitive internationally. The pressures for cost containment increased as the costs of an inefficient delivery and payment system grew larger. Rising medical expenditures are no longer a diffuse cost to large purchasers of medical services.

Other professional organizations, such as those for psychologists, chiropractors, and podiatrists, saw the potentially greater revenues their members could receive if they were better able to compete with physicians. These groups developed a concentrated interest in securing payment for their members under public and private insurance systems and expanding their scope of practice. The increase in opposing concentrated interests weakened the political influence of organized medicine.

Summary

The public-interest and economic theories of government provide opposing predictions of the redistributive and efficiency effects of government legislation, as shown in Exhibit 30.3. To determine which of these contrasting theories is a more accurate description of government, we must match the actual outcomes of legislation to each theory's predictions. Do the benefits of redistributive programs go to those with low incomes, and are they financed by taxes that impose a larger burden on those with higher incomes? Does the government try to improve the allocation of resources by reducing barriers to entry and, in markets where information is limited, by monitoring the quality of physicians and other medical services and making this information available?

The economic theory of regulation provides greater understanding of why health policies are enacted and why they have changed over time than other theories do. The difficulty of placing demand- and supply-side policies for each of the three policy instruments—expenditures, taxation, and regulation—described in Exhibit 30.1 into a redistributive or efficiency objective according to the criteria used in the public-interest theory is an indication of the inadequacy of the public-interest theory. The economic theory predicts that government is not concerned with efficiency issues. Redistribution is the main objective of government, but that objective is to redistribute wealth to those who are able to offer political support from those who are unable to do so. Thus, medical licensing boards are inadequately staffed, have never required re-examination for re-licensure, and have failed to monitor practicing physicians because organized medicine has been opposed to any approaches for increasing quality that would adversely affect physicians' incomes. Regressive taxes are used to finance programs such as Medicare not because legislators are unaware of their regressive nature, but because the taxes benefit economically those who have a concentrated interest.

The structure and financing of medical services is rational; the participants act according to their calculations of costs and benefits. Viewed in its entirety, however, health policy is uncoordinated and seemingly contradictory. Health policies are inequitable and inefficient; low-income persons end

Exhibit 30.3
Health Policy
Objectives
Under Differ-
ent Theories of
Government

Theories of Government	Objective of Government	
	Redistribution	*Improve Efficiency*
Public interest theory	Assist those with low incomes	Remove (and prevent) monopoly abuses and protect environment (externalities)
Economic theory of regulation	Provide benefits to those able to deliver political support and finance from those having little political support	Efficiency objective unimportant More likely to protect industries so as to provide them with redistributive benefits

up subsidizing those with higher incomes. These results, however, are the consequences of a rational system. The outcomes were the result of policies intended by the legislators.

Discussion Questions

1. What were the dissatisfactions with the public-interest view of government?
2. Contrast the benefit-cost calculations of legislators under the public-interest and economic theories of government.
3. Why are concentrated interests and diffuse costs important in predicting legislative outcomes?
4. Contrast the predictions of the public-interest and economic theories of government with regard to redistributive policies.
5. Evaluate the following policies according to the two differing theories of government:
   a. Medicare and Medicaid beneficiaries, taxation, and generosity of benefits
   b. The performance of state licensing boards in monitoring physician quality

Note

1. The political support offered by providers, such as hospitals and physicians, is important in determining how such redistributive legislation is designed. Providers benefit because such programs increase demand by those with low incomes. However, medical societies have opposed government coverage of entire population groups, such as the aged, regardless of income level, because government payment would merely substitute for private payment for those who are not poor. Physicians were concerned that if government covered everyone or all of the aged, regardless of income, the cost of such programs would increase, and the government would eventually control their fees. This was the American Medical Association's basic reason for opposing Medicare. To gain the political support of physicians, Congress acceded to physicians' preferences when Medicare was established by permitting physicians to decide whether or not to accept the government payment for treating Medicare patients. Medicaid was not controversial because it covered those with low incomes, and hospitals and physicians were paid according to their preferences. As the federal and state governments experienced large expenditure increases under each of these programs, government developed a concentrated interest in controlling hospital and medical expenditures.

MEDICAL RESEARCH, MEDICAL EDUCATION, ALCOHOL CONSUMPTION, AND POLLUTION: WHO SHOULD PAY?

An important role of government is to improve the way markets allocate resources. When markets perform poorly, fewer goods and services are produced, and incomes are lower than they would be otherwise. The usual policy prescription for improving the performance of markets is for the government to eliminate barriers to entry and increase information. Competitive markets, in which no entry barriers are in place and purchasers and producers are fully informed, are likely to produce the correct (or optimal) rate of output. The correct rate occurs if individuals benefiting from the service pay the full cost of producing that service.

Resources are optimally allocated when the additional benefits from consuming the last unit equal the cost of producing that last unit. When still more units are consumed, the costs of those additional units exceed the benefits provided, and the resources would be better used to produce other goods and services whose benefits exceed their costs. As shown in Exhibit 31.1, when the costs are C_1 and benefits are B_1, the correct rate of output is Q_1. The benefit curve is declining because the more one has of a good, the lower the value of an additional unit will be.

Under certain circumstances, however, even a competitive market may not allocate resources correctly. The optimal rate of output in a market occurs when all costs and benefits are included. Private decision makers consider only their own costs and benefits and exclude the costs or benefits imposed on others, if any. The effect may be that some services are underproduced, while others are overproduced.

The quantity of medical and health services may not be optimal because costs and benefits may be imposed on persons other than those who purchase and provide the service. What happens when costs or benefits are imposed on someone who is not a voluntary participant in that private transaction? Such external costs and benefits must be included; otherwise, either too much or too little of the service is produced and purchased. For example, when external costs are imposed on others, as shown by C_2 in Exhibit 31.1, the correct rate of output declines from Q_1 to Q_2, where both private (C_1)

Exhibit 31.1
Optimal Rate
of Output

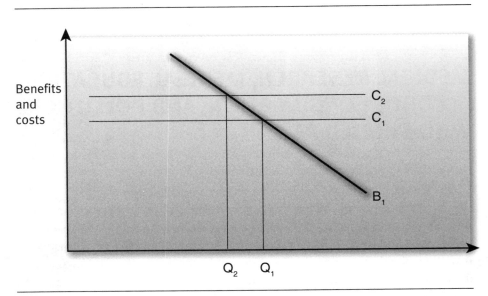

and external (C_2) costs equal the benefits (B_1) from consuming that good or service.

When such external costs or benefits exist, government should calculate their magnitude and use subsidies and taxes to achieve the "right" rate of output in the affected industry. Subsidies or taxes on the producers in that industry will change the costs of producing a service so producers will adjust their levels of output. The difference between C_1 and C_2, the external cost, is also the size of the tax to be imposed on each unit of the product.

External Costs and Benefits

Pollution

One reason externalities, such as pollution, occur is that no one owns the resource being exploited. When a resource such as air or water is scarce and no one owns it, a firm may use it as though it were free; it does not become a cost of production as it would if the firm were charged a fee for its use. The lack of property rights over scarce resources is the basis for government intervention. For example, when a firm pollutes a stream in the process of producing its product, those who use the stream for recreational purposes are adversely affected; they bear a cost not included in the firm's calculation of its costs of producing the product. Because the firm has not had to include the external costs of production, it sells the product at a lower price, and the user pays less for that product than the product actually costs society. Because of its lower price, a greater quantity of the product is purchased and produced.

When no property rights over a scarce resource exist and that resource is used by large numbers of people and firms, negotiations among the parties over the use of that resource are likely to be difficult and costly. Government intervention is needed to calculate the external costs and, in the case of pollution, to impose a tax based on the proportional amount of pollution caused on each unit of the product sold. The product's higher price would include both the cost of production and the unit tax; therefore, less of the product would be sold. If all costs and benefits, both private and external, are part of the private decision-making process, the industry will produce the right rate of output.

A pollution tax could not be expected to eliminate all pollution, but it would reduce it to the correct level; the tax revenues received by the government would go toward cleaning up the pollution or compensating those who were adversely affected. If the government attempted to eliminate all of the pollution, it would have to stop production of that product completely. Eliminating all pollution could adversely affect a great many people if the total benefits derived from that product outweigh its costs, including the costs of pollution. Consider, for example, the effect of eliminating all air pollution originating from automobiles or electricity production. Clearly, people prefer some quantity of these products to zero air pollution.

Imposing a tax on pollution has another important consequence. The producer of the product will attempt to lower the tax by devising methods to reduce pollution.[1] The firm may move to an area where the costs of pollution (hence the tax) are lower, or the firm may innovate in its production process to reduce pollution. The tax creates incentives for producers to lower their production costs, which include the tax.

Imposing a tax directly on pollution is preferable to such indirect methods of controlling pollution as allowing existing firms to continue polluting but not permitting others to enter the market or mandating that all firms use a particular production process to reduce pollution. Such indirect approaches eliminate incentives for producers to search for cheaper ways to reduce pollution.

Based on the example of the external costs of pollution, the role of government seems straightforward: When widespread external costs exist, the government should calculate the size of those costs and assess a tax on each unit of output produced. The purchasers and producers of that product will base their decisions about how much to purchase on all of the costs and benefits (external as well as private) of that product.

Medical Research

The analysis is similar when applied to external benefits. If a university medical researcher develops a new method of performing open-heart surgery that reduces the mortality rate of that procedure, other surgeons will copy the technique to benefit their own patients. An individual researcher/surgeon cannot declare ownership over all possible uses of that technique. However, if the university medical researcher were not compensated for all those who would eventually benefit, she would not find it feasible or worthwhile to invest time and resources to develop new medical techniques.

Similarly, if medical researchers were not properly compensated in some fashion, they would underproduce the discovery of basic scientific knowledge, since they presumably would not be able to charge all those who would eventually benefit from their research. Although it would be difficult, the government should attempt to calculate the potential benefits and subsidize medical research. Unless the external benefits are assessed and the costs shared by potential beneficiaries, the costs of producing medical research will exceed the private benefits.

An alternative to offering a subsidy to private firms is to give them property rights or ownership over their discoveries in the form of patent protection. Drug companies need incentives to compensate them for the risks and investments made in R&D. Patent protection, however, is not possible for all basic research or for new surgical techniques. Unpatented medical research or new drug discoveries can be copied by others who then benefit from the discoveries.

Immunization

Another example of external benefits involves protection from contagious diseases. Individuals who decide to be immunized against contagious diseases primarily base their decisions on the costs and benefits to themselves of immunization. However, those who are not immunized also benefit by receiving a "free ride"; their chances of catching that disease are lowered. If immunization were solely a private decision, not enough individuals would be immunized. The costs incurred by those who choose to be immunized should be subsidized by imposing a small tax on those who are not immunized but who also benefit. In this manner, the "right" numbers of people become immunized. The immunization decision thus encompasses private benefits, external benefits, and the costs of immunization.

When transaction costs are high, that is, the administrative costs of monitoring, collecting taxes, and subsidizing individuals are substantial, it may be less costly to simply require everyone to be immunized against certain diseases.

Subsidies to the Medically Indigent

Externalities are also the rationale for providing subsidies to the medically indigent. If the only way the poor received medical care were through voluntary contributions, many people who did not make such contributions would benefit by knowing that the poor were cared for through the contributions of others. Too little would be provided to the medically indigent because those who did not contribute receive a free ride; they would benefit without having to pay for that benefit. Government intervention would be appropriate to tax those who benefit by knowing the poor receive medical care.

Government Policies When Externalities Exist

In the examples described, the subsidies and taxes are related to the size of the external benefits and costs. Furthermore, the taxes imposed on products that pollute are to be spent for the benefit of those adversely affected. When external benefits exist, the subsidies are financed by taxes on those who receive the external benefit. Patents are an attempt to recover the external benefits of research. In each case, taxes and subsidies are matched according to external costs and benefits.

Recognizing how externalities affect the correct rate of output in an industry is useful for understanding which government policies would be appropriate in a number of additional areas. For example, when a motorcyclist has an accident and suffers a head injury as a result of not wearing a helmet, government (society) pays the medical expenses if the cyclist does not have insurance or sufficient personal funds. Fines for not wearing helmets are an attempt to make motorcyclists bear the responsibility for external costs that they would otherwise impose on others. At times, imposing requirements (e.g., helmet use, immunizations, grade school education) may be the least costly approach for achieving the correct output.

The same analogy can be used to describe those who can afford to buy health insurance but refuse to do so. When they incur catastrophic medical expenses they cannot pay for, they become a burden on society. Requiring everyone who can afford it to have catastrophic medical coverage is a way of preventing individuals from imposing external costs on others.

Similarly, drunk drivers frequently impose costs on innocent victims. Penalties, such as jail terms, forfeiture of driver's licenses, fines, and higher alcohol taxes, have been used as attempts to shift the responsibility for these external costs back to those who drink and drive. One study concluded that federal and state alcohol taxes should be increased (from an average of 11 cents to 24 cents a drink) to compensate for the external costs imposed on others by excessive drinkers (Manning et al. 1989).

We should be aware, however, that some people might misapply the externalities argument to justify intervention by the government in all markets. For example, if you admire someone's garden, should you be taxed to subsidize the gardener? Should the student who asks a particularly clever question in class be subsidized by a tax on other students? These examples, although simple, illustrate several important points about externalities. First, when only a few individuals are involved, the parties concerned should be able to reach an accommodation among themselves without resorting to government intervention. Second, even when ownership to the property is clear, high transaction costs may make it too costly to charge for external benefits or costs. The owner of the garden can decide whether it is worthwhile to erect a fence and charge a viewing fee. Chances are the cost of doing so will exceed the amount others are willing to pay. Many may thus receive external benefits simply because excluding them or collecting from them is too costly. Only when the external benefits (or costs) become sufficiently large relative to their transaction costs does it pay for the provider of external benefits to either exclude others or charge them for their benefits.

A third point these examples illustrate concerns the relative size of private benefits compared with external benefits. Would the output of the gardener be too small if neighbors did not contribute? Although many goods and services provide external benefits to others, excluding these external benefits does not result in too small a rate of output. In markets in which the external benefits are sufficiently small relative to the total private benefits, excluding external benefits does not affect the optimal rate of output. This type of externality, referred to as an *infra-marginal* externality, occurs within the market. Thus, gardeners may receive so much pleasure from their gardens that they put forth the same level of effort with or without their neighbors' financial contribution.

The concept of infra-marginal benefit is important to understanding the issue of financing education for health professionals. We all benefit from knowing that we have access to physicians, dentists, and nurses if we become ill. However, if their educations were not subsidized, would too few physicians be available? The education of physicians is heavily subsidized. The average four-year subsidy for a medical education exceeds $500,000. One reason this cost is so high is that medical schools have little incentive for reducing those costs. Given the continual excess demand for a medical education, large subsidies that go to the school rather than directly to prospective medical students, and entry barriers established by the accrediting commission, non-profit medical schools have little incentive to be efficient or innovative. This would change if medical schools had to compete for students who bore more of the cost themselves. For example, some medical educators claim that medical students could be admitted to medical school after two years of college, medical education could be reduced by at least one year, the residency period could be shortened, and innovations in teaching methods and curricula could reduce the cost still more.

Even if physicians had to pay their entire educational costs themselves, however, the economic return on the costs of becoming a physician has been estimated to be sufficiently attractive that we would have had no less than the current number of physicians. Over time, these economic returns on a medical (or dental) education have changed and varied according to specialty status; returns were higher in the 1950s to 1970s than they are currently. Thus, the concept of external benefits in the number of physicians is more likely a case of infra-marginal benefits; sufficient private benefits to individuals from becoming a physician would ensure a sufficient supply of physicians even if no subsidies were provided.

A separate issue is whether low-income individuals could afford a medical education if subsidies were removed. Yet making medical and dental education affordable to all qualified individuals could be accomplished more efficiently by targeting subsidies and loan programs to those who need them than by equally subsidizing everyone who attends medical school regardless of income level. The rationale for large educational subsidies for a health professional education should be re-examined.

Divergence Between Theoretical and Actual Government Policy

Correcting for external costs and benefits creates winners and losers. Taxes and subsidies have redistributive effects; taxpayers have lowered incomes, whereas subsidy recipients have increased incomes. Every group affected by external costs and benefits desires favorable treatment and has incentives to influence government policy. For example, an industry that pollutes the air and water has a concentrated interest in forestalling government policy that would increase its production costs. All who benefit from environmental protection must organize and provide legislators with political support if anything more than symbolic legislation is to be directed at imposing external costs on those who pollute. The growth of the environmental movement was an attempt to offset the imbalance between those with concentrated interests (polluters) and those bearing the diffuse costs (the public).

The Clean Air Act (1977 amendments) illustrates the divergence between the theoretical approach for resolving external costs and the real-world phenomenon of concentrated and diffuse interests. A greater amount of air pollution is caused when electric utilities burn high-sulfur coal rather than low-sulfur coal. Imposing a tax on the amount of sulfur dioxides (air pollution) emitted would shift the external costs of air pollution to the electric utilities, which would then have an incentive to search for ways to reduce this tax and consequently the amount of air pollution. One alternative would be for the utilities to switch to low-sulfur coal.

Low-sulfur coal, however, is produced only in the West; furthermore, it is less expensive to mine low-sulfur coal than high-sulfur coal. Low-sulfur coal is therefore a competitive threat to the Eastern coal interests that produce high-sulfur coal. Faced with taxes based on the amount of air pollution emitted, Midwestern and Eastern utilities would find it less expensive to pay added transportation costs to have low-sulfur coal shipped from the West. However, the concentrated interests of the Eastern coal mines, their heavily unionized employees, and the senate majority leader at that time (who was from West Virginia, which would have been adversely affected) were able to have legislation enacted that was directed toward the *process* of reducing pollution rather than the *amount* of pollution emitted. Requiring utilities to merely use specified technology for reducing pollution eliminated the utilities' incentives to use low-sulfur coal. When specific technology is mandated, the utility loses its incentive to maintain that technology in good operating condition and to search for more efficient approaches to reducing pollution. Western utilities that used low-sulfur coal bore the higher costs of using mandated technology although they could have achieved the desired outcomes by less expensive means (Feldstein 2006).

Summary

Even if medical care markets were competitive, the right quantity of output might not occur because of external costs and benefits. With regard to personal medical services, externalities are likely to exist related to medical services for the poor and for those who can afford catastrophic medical insurance but refuse to buy it. Why should medical and dental education be so heavily subsidized? Any external benefits are likely to be infra-marginal, thereby not affecting the optimal number of health professionals. Imposing taxes on personal behaviors (or products), such as excessive alcohol consumption, that may result in external costs, will also serve as an incentive to reduce these external costs. Most externalities in healthcare in the United States derive from medical research, medical services for the poor, lack of catastrophic insurance for those who can afford it, alcohol consumption, and pollution.

Implicit in discussions of externalities is the assumption that government regulation can correct these failures of competitive markets. Politicians, however, may at times be even less responsive to correcting external costs and benefits than producers and consumers. When externalities occur, a theoretical framework for determining appropriate government policy provides a basis for evaluating alternative policies. The divergence between theoretical and actual policies can often be explained by a comparison of the amounts of political support offered by those with concentrated and diffuse interests.

Discussion Questions

1. What is the economist's definition of the correct, or optimal, rate of output?
2. Why do externalities, such as air and water pollution, occur?
3. Why do economists believe there can be an optimal amount of pollution? What would occur if all pollution were eliminated?
4. Explain the rationale for requiring everyone who can afford it to purchase catastrophic health insurance.
5. The number of medical school spaces in this country is limited. Would fewer people become physicians if government subsidies for medical education were reduced?

Additional Reading

Joskow, P., R. Schmalensee, and E. Bailey. 1998. "The Market for Sulfur Dioxide Emissions." *American Economic Review* 88 (4): 669–85.

Note

1. Another approach to reducing pollution that also provides incentives for polluters to search for the most efficient method of reducing pollution is to establish a market for pollution rights. The 1990 Clean Air Act Amendments established the first large-scale use of the tradable permit approach to pollution control. A market for transferable sulfur dioxide emission allowances among electric utilities was established. Along with a cap on annual emissions, electric utilities had an opportunity to trade rights to emit sulfur dioxide. Firms facing high abatement costs had an opportunity to purchase the right to emit pollution from firms with lower costs.

THE CANADIAN HEALTHCARE SYSTEM

The Canadian healthcare system, a single-payer system, has been suggested as a model for the United States. Starting in the late 1960s, the Canadian government established the basic guidelines for the system, and each province was provided with federal funds contingent on its adherence to them. Under these guidelines everyone has access to hospital and medical services, and no one has to pay any deductibles or copayments. Patients have free choice of physician and hospital. Unlike the single-payer system in Great Britain, it is not possible to buy out of the system; private health insurance is not permitted for these basic hospital and medical services.

The basic cost-control mechanism used in Canada is expenditure limits on health providers. Each province sets its own overall health budget and negotiates a total budget, which it cannot exceed, with each hospital. The province also negotiates with the medical association to establish uniform fees for all physicians, who are paid on a fee-for-service basis and must accept the province's fee as payment in full for their services. In some provinces, physicians' incomes are also subject to controls; once physicians' revenues exceed a certain level, further billings are paid at 25 percent of their fee schedule.

These cost-containment measures have limited the increase in Canadian health expenditures, although providers complain about their budgets and occasionally physicians go on strike. Because each province finances its services through an income tax, receives federal funds, and pays all medical bills, the need for insurance companies is eliminated. The province controls the adoption and financing of high-technology equipment.

According to its proponents, the Canadian system offers higher life expectancy, universal coverage, comprehensive hospital and medical benefits, no out-of-pocket expenses, and lower administrative costs, while devoting a smaller percentage of the GDP to healthcare and spending less per capita than the United States. Would the United States be better off if it adopted the Canadian single-payer health system?

Higher Life Expectancy and Lower Infant Mortality Rate

Proponents of the Canadian system claim that for less money they can achieve better health outcomes than the US healthcare system. Life expectancy at birth for Canadians is about two years higher than for US whites and about one year higher at age 65. Canada has a lower infant mortality rate per 1,000 live births (5.3 versus 5.7 for US whites) (Preston and Ho 2009).

Life expectancy and infant mortality rates, however, are inappropriate measures of the output of each country's medical care system. Many factors other than medical services affect these measures, such as lifestyles, including diet, exercise, smoking, homicides, and so on. For example, the obesity rate among males and females is much greater in the United States than in Canada; the difference in mortality rates among those younger than 40 years old due to accidents and homicides is also much higher in the United States than in Canada, as is the mortality rate for heart disease among those older than 45 years of age (O'Neill and O'Neill 2007).

Treatment Outcomes and Prevention

More relevant to a comparison of each country's medical system are the treatments and outcomes once people are ill. The United States has a greater percentage of total births that are low-birth-weight infants (under 1,500 grams) than does Canada (likely related to lifestyle factors); however, the United States has a lower mortality rate for those infants than does Canada (which is an effect of the medical system). Examining the percentage of those with a specific medical condition, such as high blood pressure or heart disease, who receive treatment shows that whites in the United States are more likely to be treated for their disease than are white Canadians. Similarly, rates of preventive screening for various types of cancer, such as mammograms for breast cancer, Pap smears for cervical cancer, PSA tests for prostate cancer, and colonoscopies for colorectal cancers, are much higher in the United States than in Canada (O'Neill and O'Neill 2007).

Another important indication of the performance of a country's medical system is the survival rate for those with cancer. The CONCORD study, the first worldwide analysis of cancer survival, examined five-year relative survival rates for different types of cancers (Verdecchia et al. 2007). (Relative survival is the ratio of survival noted in patients with cancer to patients subjected to normal mortality.) As shown in Exhibit 32.1, overall cancer survival rates are higher in the United States than in Canada. In addition, US cancer survival rates are among the highest in the world. Although cancer survival rates vary among regions in the United States, the variation in survival rates is much greater in Europe and among Canadian provinces.

The above discussion is not meant to imply that the current US medical system does not need important reform changes to make it more equitable and efficient, just that, contrary to the beliefs of single-payer proponents, the Canadian system does not have better medical outcomes than the United States.

EXHIBIT 32.1 Five-Year Relative Survival Rates for Cancer in the United States and Canada, 1999

	Breast Both	Colon Male	Colon Female	Rectum Male	Rectum Female	Colorectum Male	Colorectum Female	Prostate Both
Canadian registries	82.5	56.1	58.7	53.1	58.7	55.3	58.9	85.1
US registries	83.9	60.1	60.1	56.9	59.8	59.1	60.2	91.9

SOURCE: Michael Coleman, et al. "Cancer Survival in Five Continents: A Worldwide Population-Based Study (CONCORD)," *Lancet Oncology,* August 2008, Vol. 9, pp. 730–56.

Universal Coverage

According to its proponents, the Canadian system has two major advantages. The first is universal coverage. However, as adoption of the Canadian system is but one proposal for reform, it should be compared not to the current US system but to other healthcare reform proposals to achieve universal coverage (see Chapter 34). Thus, adopting the Canadian system solely to achieve universal coverage is not necessary. To many the real attractiveness of the Canadian system is based on its presumed ability to control the rising costs of healthcare.

Controlling Healthcare Costs in Canada

Proponents of a Canadian system point to two cost savings. The first is lower administrative costs; the second is a lower rate of increase in healthcare costs. Each is discussed in the sections that follow.

Administrative Costs

Advocates of the Canadian system claim that if the United States adopted the Canadian system, it could greatly reduce its administrative costs, as health insurance companies would no longer be necessary; therefore universal access could be financed at no additional cost (Woolhandler and Himmelstein 1991). Many agree that administrative costs in the United States could be somewhat lowered with standardization of claims processing and billing.

Simple comparisons of administrative expenses between the two countries, however, are misleading.[1] Administrative and marketing costs could be reduced if the United States eliminated choice of health plans and agreed to a standardized set of health benefits. The United States has a wide variety of health plans, such as HMOs, point-of-service plans, and PPOs, that offer different benefits, cost-sharing levels, and access to providers. Competition among health plans offers consumers greater choice at different premiums.

Choice is costly. However, without choice, less innovation would occur in benefit design, patient satisfaction, and competition on health plan premiums. The diversity of insurance plans reflects differences in enrollees' preferences and how much they are willing to pay for those preferences.

Lower administrative costs are not synonymous with greater system efficiency. One can imagine very low administrative costs in a system in which physicians and hospitals send their bills to the government and the government simply pays them. These lower administrative costs cause higher healthcare expenditures because they do not detect or deter inappropriate use or overuse of services. A trade-off occurs between lower administrative costs and higher health expenditures caused by insufficient monitoring of physician and hospital behavior. If higher administrative cost resulting from utilization management did not pay for itself by reducing medical expenses and overutilization, managed care plans would not use these measures.

For example, the US Medicare system, which has a similar design to the Canadian system, has much lower administrative costs than private managed care plans. However, the Government Accountability Office has criticized Medicare for having administrative costs that are "too low"; billions of dollars could be saved "by adopting the healthcare management approach of private payers to Medicare's public payer role" (US GAO 1995). Studies have shown that cost-containment approaches, such as preauthorization for hospital admissions, utilization review for hospitalized patients, catastrophic case management, and physician profiling for appropriateness of care, save money (e.g., Kane et al. 1996).

Due to its lack of controls and oversight, Medicare fraud and waste is widespread. The Office of Inspector General (2009) reported that Medicare had an error rate of 31.5 percent in overpayment for improper or fake claims for medical equipment. Medicare's lack of scrutiny (it automatically pays 95 percent of all claims) results in lower overhead costs but makes the program highly vulnerable to fraud.

The health insurance industry in the United States is very competitive and would only increase administrative costs if the benefits from doing so exceeded their costs. Any savings in administrative costs by eliminating cost-containment techniques and patient cost sharing would be more than offset by the increased utilization that would occur. The Canadian system is forgoing substantial savings by not increasing its administrative costs, investing more in cost-containment programs, and developing monitoring mechanisms of physicians' practice patterns.

Rising Healthcare Costs

An oft-cited measure of the cost-containment success of the Canadian system is the smaller percentage of Canada's GDP that is devoted to healthcare. Although correct, this information can be misleading. At different times, GDP may increase faster in one country than in another, distorting any conclusion as to which country's healthcare costs are rising faster.

A more accurate indication of which country's health costs have risen more slowly is a comparison of the rise in per capita health expenditures. Again, one must be careful in making such comparisons, as almost 50 percent of US medical expenditures are by the government for Medicare and Medicaid, which have limited cost controls. Some regions of the United States also have greater managed care penetration than others. This country's medical system has evolved from one that, until the 1980s, provided limited if any incentives for efficiency to one in which the private sector—in some states more than others—emphasizes managed care delivery systems. Thus, the 1990s performance of the US system, particularly in states with a greater portion of the population in managed care, would be more relevant to compare with the Canadian system.

As shown in Exhibit 32.2, since the 1980s, per capita health expenditures (adjusted for inflation) have increased at a lower rate in Canada than in the United States. However, during some periods Canada's rate of increase has been higher to compensate for the serious lack of funding in previous years. The effect of managed care can be seen by the lower rate of increase in the United States during the mid-1990s than in prior years. (As a result of the backlash against managed care in the late 1990s, managed care's cost-containment methods were loosened and premiums increased more rapidly.) In the last ten years, and particularly since 2004, Canada has had higher annual rates of increase in per capita health expenditures than the United States.

Does the Canadian healthcare system achieve lower per capita health costs and a lower percentage of its GDP devoted to healthcare because of greater efficiency?

Differences in Hospital Length of Stay

What were the reasons for the lower rate of increase in per capita healthcare spending in Canada than in the United States? Is Canada more efficient in the way it produces medical services? Although efficiency studies would have to control for many differences between the two countries, such as populations served, distribution of illnesses, outcomes of care, staffing patterns, wage rates, and so on, one simple, although partial, measure of efficiency is differences in lengths of hospital stay.

EXHIBIT 32.2 Annual Percentage Growth in Real per Capita Health Expenditures in Canada and the United States, 1980–2008

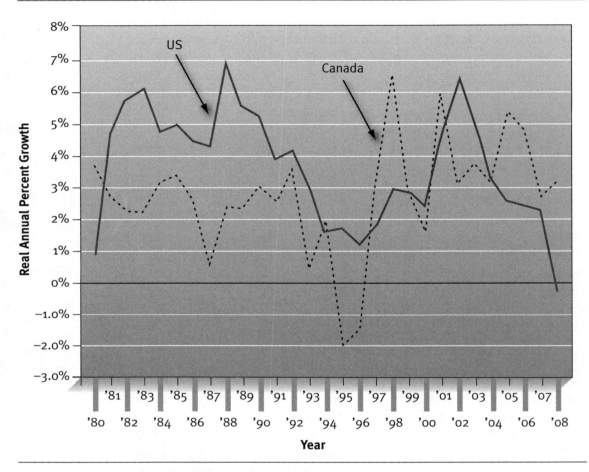

NOTE: Values adjusted for inflation using the Consumer Price Index for each country.

SOURCES: Health expenditures per capita data from Organisation for Economic Co-operation and Development. *2010 OECD Health Data*. Paris: OECD. Consumer Price Index data from Bureau of Labor Statistics. 2010. [Online information.] http://www.bls.gov and Statistics Canada. 2010. [Online information.] http://www.statcan.gc.ca.

Managed care systems in the United States have a financial incentive to use the least costly combination of medical services. Hospitals are the most expensive setting for providing care. Use of the hospital is subject to review; outpatient diagnostics and surgery are used whenever possible, and catastrophic case management may involve renovating a patient's home to make it a lower-cost and more convenient setting in which to care for the patient.

The efficiency gains from managed care are evident in a comparison of utilization data between the United States and Canada. As shown in

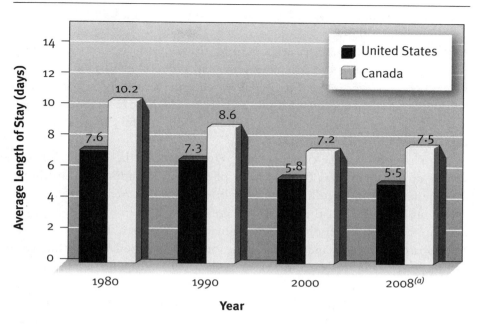

EXHIBIT 32.3
Average Length
of Hospital
Stay in Canada
and the
United States,
1980–2008

(a)2007 data for Canada

SOURCE: Data from Organisation for Economic Co-operation and Development, *2010 OECD Health Data.* Paris, France: OECD.

Exhibit 32.3, Canadian hospitals have a higher average length of stay than hospitals in the United States, but the difference is becoming smaller. In 1980, the length of stay in Canada was 10.2 days, compared with 7.6 days in the United States. In 2007 in Canada and in 2008 in the United States (the most recent data available) the rate was 7.5 days and 5.5 days, respectively. In California, a state with high managed care penetration, it was 4.9 days. The average length of stay for those aged 65 years and older is very high in Canada because few alternative arrangements are available. Canadian hospitals are used inappropriately; many services could be provided in an outpatient setting, the physician's office, or the patient's home.

Annual hospital budgets in Canada also provide administrators with an incentive to fill a portion of their beds with elderly patients who stay many days. If more surgical patients were admitted, hospitals would not receive additional funds to purchase the necessary supplies and nursing personnel to serve them. Thus, as inflation diminishes the real value of Canadian hospitals' budgets with which to purchase resources, they admit fewer acutely ill patients and prolong their stays.

If the lower rate of increase in Canada's health expenditures is not a result of greater efficiency, to what is it attributable?

Consequences of Strict Limits on Per Capita Costs

In the late 1980s, Canada was experiencing rising healthcare costs and a deep recession. As a result, the federal government reduced its financial commitment to the provinces from its initial 50 percent of each province's health spending to a 2010 average of about 20 percent. As these federal cash and tax transfers fell, the rising cost of the Canadian health system placed an increasing financial burden on each province.

The consequence of these rising costs for both the federal and provincial governments has been periods of reduced spending on healthcare and then increased spending to compensate for the lack of access to care. As shown in Exhibit 32.2, the annual percentage increase in inflation-adjusted per capita health expenditures fell dramatically between 1990 and 1996. In contrast to the managed care revolution in the United States, this steep decline in Canada was attributable to reduced government funding rather than new cost-containment approaches. In the past when such large declines occurred, such as in the early and late 1970s, they were followed by sharp increases in following years. Consequently, over the period 2004–08 Canada had a more rapid rate of increase in its per capita health expenditures to make up for the low and negative budgetary allocations in previous years. This pattern—years of low rates of increase in per capita health expenditures followed by a few years of high expenditures to make up for the resulting severe reductions in access to care—repeats itself.

Government expenditure limits are the inevitable consequence of an unlimited demand for medical services. No government can fund all of the medical care that is demanded at zero price. Because expenditure limits result in less care being provided than is demanded at zero price, choices must be made as to how scarce healthcare resources are to be allocated. Many trade-offs must be made, for example, among preventive care, acute care, access to new technology, and decreasing patient waiting times to receive treatment. With limited dollars, providing more of one choice means less money is available to fulfill other choices.

The inevitable consequences of tight per capita expenditure limits, as have occurred in Canada, are increasing shortages of medical services and decreased access to new technology. Furthermore, since the beneficial effects of preventive care occur in the future, resources are allocated to acute services for patients whose needs are more immediate.

Access to Technology

One of the distinguishing features of the US medical system is the rapid diffusion of technologic innovation. Major advances in diagnostic and treatment procedures have occurred. Imaging equipment has improved diagnostic accuracy and reduced the need for exploratory surgery. New technology has resulted in less invasive procedures, quicker recovery times, and improved treatment outcomes. Technologic advances have increased the survival rate of low-birth-weight babies and permitted an increasing number and type of organ transplants. Any comparison of the Canadian and US health systems should consider the rate at which new technology is diffused and made available to patients.

Managed care, which is characteristic of the US healthcare system, uses different criteria for adopting and diffusing new technology than does the Canadian system. Two types of technologic advances occur. The first, and simplest to evaluate under managed care, is when new technology reduces costs and increases patient satisfaction. A competitive managed care system will invest the necessary capital to bring about these technologic savings.

The more difficult decision on adopting new technology concerns technology that improves medical outcomes but is much more costly than existing technology. Particularly troublesome is new technology that may have only a low probability of success, for example, 10 to 20 percent. In such cases, the patient would like access to the expensive treatment, while the insurer may believe it is not worth the expenditure given the low success rate.

Technology that is clearly believed to be beneficial is highly likely to be adopted. If one health plan decided not to adopt the technology when its competitors did, it would lose enrollees. Competition among health plans forces the adoption of highly beneficial technology. The costs of such technology are eventually passed on to enrollees in the form of higher premiums.

New technology that offers small beneficial effects (e.g., a new method of conducting Pap smears that increases cancer detection by 5 percent or experimental breast cancer treatments for late-stage cancer patients) has caused problems for managed care firms. Several health plans that have denied such treatments have suffered penalties of up to $100 million as a result of lawsuits. To reduce their liability, an increasing number of health plans have delegated such decisions to outside firms made up of ethicists and physicians who have no financial stake in the decision.

In Canada the availability of capital to invest in cost-saving and benefit-increasing technology is determined by the government, not the hospital. Given their budget constraints and reluctance to raise taxes, governments are less likely to provide capital for new technology and for as many units as when firms compete for enrollees. Outpatient diagnostic and surgical services are less available in Canada, denying patients the benefits (and society the cost savings) of such technologic improvements. Costly benefit-increasing technology, such as transplants and experimental treatments, is also less available to Canadians.

A competitive managed care system may adopt technology too soon and have excess technologic capacity. Excess capacity, however, means faster access and lower patient risks. Enrollees may be willing to pay higher premiums to have that excess capacity available. If so, excess technologic capacity is appropriate; the benefits to enrollees of that excess capacity are at least equal to their willingness to pay for it. The adoption of new technology under managed care competition is different from what a government (or quasigovernmental agency) would use, as the government would be concerned with losing political support if it had to raise taxes or incur large budget deficits to increase access to new technology.

Examples of differences in availability of technology between Canada and the United States are shown in Exhibit 32.4. There are six times more lithotriptors available per person in the United States than in Canada, four times as many MRI units, and almost three times as many CT scanners per person. Clearly, the likelihood of a patient in the United States receiving any of the services shown in Exhibit 32.4 is much greater than that of a similar patient with equal needs who lives in Canada. (How successful would an HMO be in this country if it used access criteria similar to those used in Canada?)

The Technological Change in Health Care (TECH) Research Network is an international group of researchers who examine differences in technologic change across countries in the treatment, resource costs, and health outcomes for common health problems (TECH 2001; Bech et al. 2009). Because knowledge of heart attack treatment has greatly changed in recent years and data from various studies have shown that improvements in outcomes may be the result of differences in medical practices, differences in the adoption of technology are likely to occur between countries in inpatient care for heart attacks.

The researchers found different patterns of technologic change between countries in adopting more intensive cardiac procedures. The United States adopted an "early start and fast growth" pattern, which resulted in relatively high treatment rates in the overall population as well as in the elderly population. Conversely, in Canada the adoption of new technology starts later, its diffusion is slower (as well as lower than in the United States), and both the elderly and general populations have lower treatment rates.

The TECH (2001) researchers attribute these differences in the adoption and diffusion of beneficial technology for care of heart attack patients to differences in funding and decision making, "such as global budgets for hospitals and central planning of the availability of intensive services" in Canada (37). The researchers further state that "It is clear that if high-quality care requires rapid innovation and diffusion of valuable high-cost as well as low-cost treatments, quality of care may differ greatly around the world, and national health policy may influence quality in important ways" (38).

EXHIBIT 32.4 Indicators of Medical Technology per Million People, 2004, 2006, and 2007

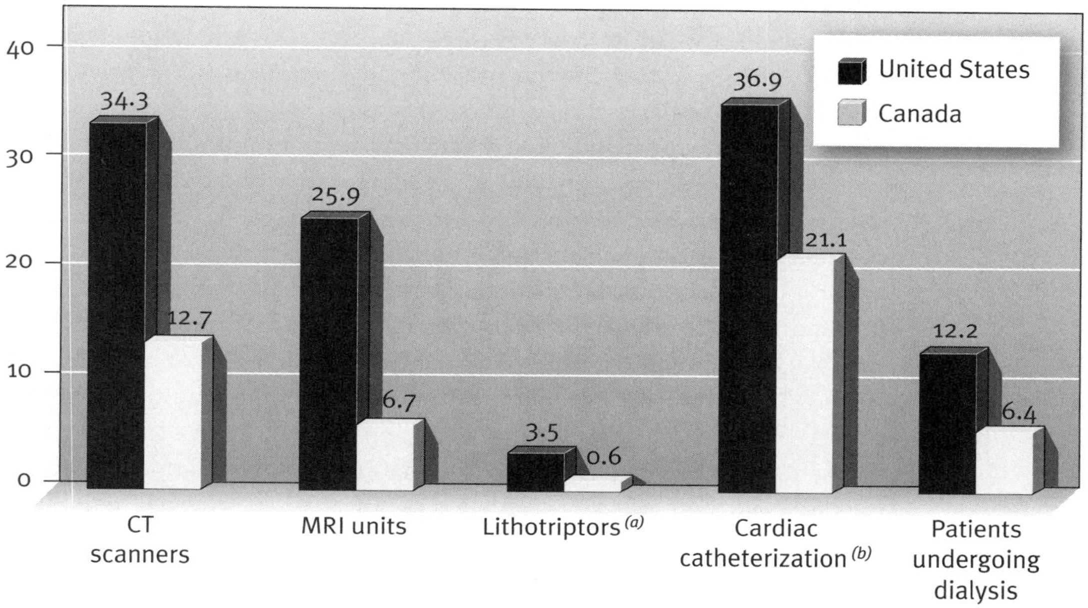

$^{(a)}$2004 data for US

$^{(b)}$2006 data for US

SOURCES: Organisation for Economic Co-operation and Development. 2010. *OECD Health Data, 2006* and *OECD Health Data, 2010*. Paris, France: OECD.

Patient Waiting Times

As demand for services exceeds available supply, waiting time is used to ration nonemergency care. For some types of care, the quantity demanded increases because patients have no copayments. Facing a zero price, patients will demand a high volume of physician visits. Consequently, to see more patients, physicians must spend less time per visit. The physician has the patient return for multiple short visits rather than providing the services previously provided in one visit. Patient time costs are therefore higher under a "free" system with tight fee controls because each visit requires the same patient travel and waiting time regardless of the length of the visit.[2]

Expenditure limits invariably result in high time costs being imposed on patients. However, not all care rationed by waiting time is of low value to the patient. According to a Fraser Institute (Esmail 2009) report on the Canadian healthcare system, in 2009 Canadian patients had to wait, on average,

9 weeks for an MRI (the range was 6 to 15.5 weeks, depending on the province), 4.6 weeks for a CT scan (the range was 4 to 8 weeks), and almost 5 weeks for an ultrasound (the range was 2 to 15 weeks). The long waits for first-time mammograms, which can vary from several weeks to a year within the same province, virtually eliminate this screening mechanism as a preventive method (CBC News 2009).

Acknowledging these long waits and their adverse effects on patients, several Canadian provinces pay for heart surgery and radiation oncology treatment in the United States, which is Canada's safety valve. Ontario has contracted with hospitals in Buffalo and Detroit for MRI services. Quebec has sent hundreds of cancer patients to the United States for treatment, since they waited more than eight weeks for radiation or chemotherapy (more than four weeks' waiting time is considered medically risky) (Anstett 2009).

The Fraser Institute performs annual surveys on waiting times from referral by the general practitioner to an appointment with a specialist and on the waiting time from appointment with a specialist to treatment. These surveys are done by medical specialty for each Canadian province. Exhibit 32.5 describes the waiting time for treatment by specialty. For example, for orthopedic surgery (e.g., hips and knees) a person would have to wait, on average, 34 weeks to receive treatment; in some provinces, however, the wait to have the surgery performed may be as short as 24 weeks or as long as 85 weeks. (In 1991, aged patients in some provinces had to wait up to four years for a hip or knee replacement.) Ophthalmology (e.g., cataract removal) requires an average wait of 19 weeks, but this can vary by province from 13 to 34 weeks. For neurosurgery, the average waiting time is 33 weeks, but it varies by province between 8 and 58 weeks.

The Fraser Institute also asks specialists how long a patient *should* wait before he receives the recommended treatment. For example, the actual waiting time for urgent cardiovascular surgery in New Brunswick after a patient had seen a specialist was six weeks, whereas specialists believe the reasonable waiting time should not exceed one week; for elective cardiovascular surgery, the actual waiting time is of course much greater. There have been reports of patients who have died waiting for heart surgery. Clearly, access to care depends on the province in which one lives. Furthermore, the waiting time is not the same for all procedures in a province.

Canada does not have an egalitarian system. Access to care depends not only on the province in which one lives but also on whether a person can afford to pay for her care in the United States. The failure to consider the higher patient time costs in the Canadian system *understates* health expenditures in Canada. As demand for services exceeds the available supply, many people would be willing to pay more rather than incur the cost of multiple trips, waiting, or doing without. Unfortunately, the Canadian system prohibits the purchase of private health insurance for hospital and medical services. Thus,

Exhibit 32.5 Canadian Hospital Waiting Lists: Total Expected Waiting Time from Referral by General Practitioner to Treatment, by Specialty, 2009

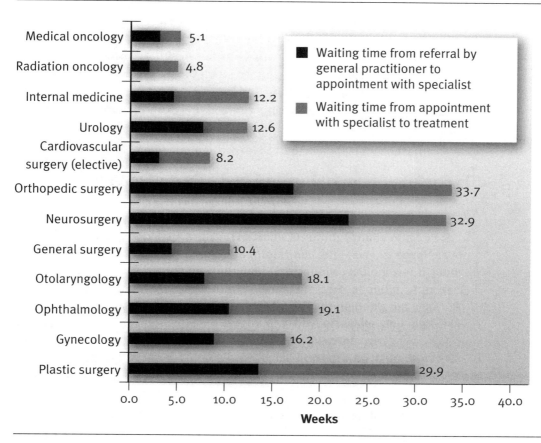

SOURCE: Esmail, N. 2009. *Waiting Your Turn: Hospital Waiting Lists in Canada, 2009 Report,* 19th ed., The Fraser Institute. October. [Online information.] http://www.fraserinstitute.org/commerce.web/product_files/WaitingYourTurn_2009.pdf.

people are legally prohibited from insuring themselves against the risks of not receiving timely care when they require it.

An important consequence of these long waits for medical service is that patients (GAO 1991, 59)

> experience pain and discomfort, and some may develop psychological problems.... The condition of some patients may worsen, making surgery more risky....because of the long queue for lithotripsy treatment, many doctors perform surgery to remove kidney stones (also resulting in higher costs), putting the patient at higher risk than with a lithotripsy procedure.... Often patients experience a financial setback, such as decreased income or loss of a job (while waiting in queues).... Patients are unable to work because they are physically immobile while they wait for a hip or other joint replacement.

Those who are wealthy can afford to skip the queues and purchase medical services in the United States, as did the premier of Newfoundland. When he learned that he needed heart surgery in 2010, instead of waiting his turn, at his own expense he went to the United States for his operation (CBC News 2010). Similarly, the politically powerful are able to jump to the head of the queue, as occurred with Canada's health minister, who was able to have his surgery after being diagnosed with prostate cancer in 2001. Other prostate cancer patients were angered by his quick surgery after they had to wait much longer, some as long as a year between diagnosis and surgery (Rupert 2001).

Is Canada Abandoning Its Single-Payer System?

A Quebec patient, forced to wait a year for a hip replacement and prohibited from paying privately for his operation, brought a lawsuit against the Quebec government to the Canadian Supreme Court. In a surprise ruling, the Supreme Court in 2005 concluded that the wait for medical services had become so long that the health system and its ban on private practice violated patients' "life and personal security, inviolability and freedom," which are part of Quebec's Charter of Rights and Freedoms. Furthermore, "The evidence in this case shows that delays in the public healthcare system are widespread, and that, in some serious cases, patients die as a result of waiting lists for public healthcare…. In sum, the prohibition on obtaining private health insurance is not constitutional where the public system fails to deliver reasonable services." Although the ruling applied to Quebec, it is widely believed the court's ruling will affect all of Canada's provinces (Krauss 2005).

As a consequence of the court's ruling, private diagnostic and special surgery clinics have opened in Quebec. The federal government, opposed to the introduction of private medicine, is under great pressure to increase healthcare spending to reduce waiting times for medical services. To provide quicker access to medical services, Quebec is paying private clinics to serve orthopedic and cataract patients. Supporters of the single-payer system are opposed to a two-tier medical system, believing the private sector will draw physicians and nurses away from the public system, where a severe physician shortage already exists, making waiting times even longer.

The dam may have already broken. In anticipation of these changes, private clinics are opening all over Canada; as of 2011, 130 for-profit clinics are in operation across that country, offering surgeries, MRIs, and access to physician services (CUPE 2011). Patients must pay with cash, with the trade-off being that the wait time is short. Private insurance companies will soon follow;[3] it will be difficult to stop the trend toward privatization and a two-tier medical system that already exists in all other countries.

Should the United States Adopt the Canadian System?

Canada has been the only Westernized country with a single-payer system. Other countries that started with a single-payer system, such as Great Britain, moved to a two-tier system that permitted private medical markets. Canada appears to be moving in the same direction. Governments find that it eventually becomes too expensive to fund all the new technology and medical services its population demands when they do not have to pay any out-of-pocket costs. Inequities develop in a single-payer system; the wealthy can reduce their waiting by traveling to another country, and the politically powerful are able to jump the queue. A two-tier medical system recognizes that there are those who are willing to spend more of their money in return for quicker access to medical services and the latest medical technology.

Alternative approaches exist to achieve the objectives claimed for a single-payer system. With regard to the equity criterion, namely how to provide for the uninsured, the Canadian system should be compared not to the current US system but to one in which the goal is universal coverage. This goal can be achieved in alternative ways, such as by providing income-related subsidies to those with low incomes (see Chapter 34). A single-payer system, as evidenced by the Canadian system, does not provide everyone with equal access to medical care. It should be acknowledged that every health system has multiple tiers; those who can afford it will be able to purchase more medical services or have quicker access to care. Unequal access to care exists in Canada depending on the province in which people live or whether they can afford to pay for their care in the United States.

Arbitrarily limiting the growth in medical expenditures, the cost-containment method used in single-payer systems, will not increase efficiency. Efficiency incentives on the part of patients or medical providers are not used in the Canadian system. Efficiency incentives are important because they affect the cost of any national health insurance plan and the willingness of the public to provide subsidies to those less fortunate than themselves. To whom are government decision makers accountable? What information do they have to make decisions? In a competitive market, people can leave a health plan when they are dissatisfied with that plan; in a monopolized system (single payer), they have no similar way in which to express their dissatisfaction with the system. In a single-payer system information is either unavailable or dated (providers have no incentive to increase supply, and thus no incentive to collect data on wait times and other supply/demand factors), making it difficult for decision makers to make adjustments based on changes in demand or supply conditions. Also important to which national health insurance plan is adopted are the criteria used for access to and investment in new medical technology. Efficiency, innovation, and capital investment are determined by incentives; a government bureaucracy is highly unlikely to outperform competitive markets in this regard.

Political versus private decision making will result in differences in access to care, technology adoption, efficiency, equity, and even health outcomes. Before the United States places its healthcare system, which accounts for almost one-sixth of its economy, under complete government control, single-payer advocates should provide evidence—more than just opinion—showing why a US single-payer system will not suffer the same fate experienced by other countries that have tried and subsequently abandoned their own single-payer systems.

Summary

Proposals for healthcare reform, such as a single-payer system, should not be evaluated against the current US health system but against other national health insurance proposals to achieve universal coverage and methods to limit rising healthcare expenditures. Furthermore, single-payer advocates should not dismiss the flaws of the Canadian system by claiming that the United States would be able to devote more money to a US single-payer system. Given rising medical costs, advancements in medical technology, and no limits on patients' access to care, evidence suggests, based on every country that has tried a single-payer system, that a US single-payer system would eventually suffer the same fate as the Canadian system.

Before the United States selects another country's medical system to emulate, it should be clear as to the accuracy of the statements made about the performance of that country's medical system and the criteria by which a system should be evaluated. Controlling the percentage of GDP devoted to medical care or the rise in per capita expenditures should not be the overriding objectives of a medical system; if they were, the United States could use the British National Health Service, which performs better on these criteria but is clearly unacceptable on other grounds.

The appropriate rate of growth in medical expenditures should be based on how much people are willing to pay (directly and through taxes). There are legitimate reasons for increased medical expenditures, such as an aging population, more chronic illness, new technology that saves lives and improves the quality of life, new diseases, shortages of personnel (thereby requiring wage increases), and so on. Arbitrary expenditure limits would result in reduced access to medical services and technology.

Discussion Questions

1. Describe the Canadian healthcare system and the methods used to control costs.

2. What are the consequences of making medical services free to everyone?
3. Why is the size of administrative expenses (as a percentage of total medical expenditures) a poor indication of a healthcare system's efficiency?
4. What are the costs (negative effects) of expenditure limits?
5. Contrast the criteria used in Canada and in competitive managed care systems for deciding whether an investment should be made in new technology.

Additional Reading

Goodman, J. 2005. *Health Care in a Free Society: Rebutting the Myths of National Health Insurance.* Policy Analysis No. 532, 1–26. Washington, DC: Cato Institute.

Notes

1. The administrative savings of moving to a Canadian system are believed to be grossly overstated. For example, in calculating administrative savings, the expense of administering self-insured employer plans was included in the expense ratio of insurers. However, the claims payments made on behalf of self-insured employers were not included as part of the insurers' premiums, falsely inflating the expense ratio. Furthermore, included as part of insurers' overhead are premium taxes (a transfer payment to state governments), investment income (essentially a return to employers for advance payment of premiums), and a return on capital (which would also have to be calculated for a public insurer). (See Danzon [1992].)
2. The value to the patient of additional physician visits when there are no out-of-pocket payments is low. Generally, the approaches used to limit use of services whose value is worth less than their costs of production are cost-containment techniques and requiring patients to wait longer. Cost containment is included as an explicit administrative expense, whereas implicit patient waiting cost is not.
3. One physician who is opening private medical clinics said, "This is a country in which dogs can get a hip replacement in under a week and in which humans can wait two to three years" (Krauss 2006). Dogs have also had preferential treatment with regard to diagnostic tests. The government provides funding for hospitals to operate its MRIs only eight hours a day. In 1998, a Canadian hospital offered MRIs to pets in the middle of the night in an effort to make money. After an outcry from angry humans, who at that time were waiting up to a year for nonurgent scans, the hospital was forced to stop this practice (Walkom 2002).

EMPLOYER-MANDATED NATIONAL HEALTH INSURANCE

A n employer mandate for health insurance has had a great deal of political support. President Nixon proposed it, as did President Clinton; Hawaii and Massachusetts instituted it; and it was included as part of President Obama's reform legislation that was enacted into law in 2010. Starting in 2014, employers are required to provide health insurance to their employees and dependents or pay a tax per employee.

In 2009, approximately 55 million people under the age of 65 years were uninsured. About two-thirds of the uninsured were either employed (full or part time) or in a family with an employed member. Therefore, mandating employers to provide their employees with health insurance will cover a large percentage of the uninsured at small cost to the government. If employers choose not to provide health insurance to their employees, they will have to pay a new payroll tax, $2,000 per employee, into a pool for the uninsured, hence the name "play-or-pay" national health insurance.

Several variations on the basic approach have previously been proposed. Mandated employer proposals have generally required the employer to pay 80 percent and the employee 20 percent of the cost of the insurance. And instead of a fixed tax per employee, President Clinton proposed requiring employers to spend a fixed percentage of wages for health insurance. Employees working part time are also eligible for the employer's health insurance. Play-or-pay proposals generally mandate that all employers with more than 50 employees participate; firms with fewer employees are to be provided with a tax credit to offset the higher costs, which might ease the transition.

Before analyzing the economic consequences of mandating employers to provide health insurance to the working uninsured, it is useful to examine who the uninsured are and why they do not have insurance.

The Uninsured

Of the 263 million persons who were under the age of 65 in 2009 (Medicare eligibility begins at age 65), 21 percent, or 55 million, were without health insurance (AHRQ 2010).[1] Medicaid covers about 16 percent, or 30 million, low-income nonelderly (18 to 64 years of age). About 12.5 percent of those

EXHIBIT 33.1 Uninsured Workers, by Age Group, 2008

Age in Years	Working Population in Thousands[a]	% Distribution of Workers	% Uninsured Within Each Age Group	% Distribution of All Uninsured
16–18	4,954	3.1	12.5	2.3
19–24	18,873	11.9	26.4	18.2
25–34	35,676	22.5	20.8	27.2
35–44	36,882	23.3	25.6	21.1
45–64	62,000	39.2	13.7	31.2

[a]Excludes persons with unknown self-employment status, hours of work, hourly wages, and size of establishment.

SOURCE: Agency for Healthcare Research and Quality, Center for Cost and Financing Studies, Medical Expenditure Panel Survey Household Component, personal correspondence with Jeffrey Rhoades, March 30, 2011.

below the age of 18 years who work are uninsured (see Exhibit 33.1). The age group with the highest percentage of uninsured employees is 19- to 24-year-olds; 26.4 percent of them do not have insurance. These people are generally single adults who are no longer eligible for their parents' health insurance. The percentage of uninsured workers declines with each higher age group.

When uninsured workers in each age group are examined as a percentage of all uninsured workers, those aged 45 to 64 years represent the greatest portion of all uninsured workers, 31.2 percent. The second highest are those aged 25 to 34 years, at 27.2 percent. The distribution of uninsured workers in the remaining age groups, 19 to 24 and 35 to 44 years of age, are both about 20 percent of the total number of uninsured workers. (As part of the recently enacted health legislation, young adults can join or remain on a parent's health insurance policy until they reach age 26, as long as they are not eligible for coverage under their own employer's policy. It is uncertain how much this change will reduce the number of uninsured in the lower age groups; it will increase premiums for those families adding children to their policies.)

A closer examination of the percentage distribution of the total uninsured population reveals that about 11.7 percent of the uninsured are children. This number has decreased since the 1997 enactment of the Children's Health Insurance Program, which covers low-income children.

EXHIBIT 33.2 Uninsured Workers, by Size of Firm, 2008

Characteristic	Working Population in Thousands[a]	% Distribution of Workers	% Uninsured Within Each Age Group	% Distribution of All Uninsured
Self-employed	16,991	11.7	31.6	22.1
Fewer than 10 workers	25,744	17.7	27.5	29.0
10–24 workers	20,739	14.3	20.6	17.6
25–49 workers	16,195	11.2	17.0	11.3
50–99 workers	16,253	11.2	11.7	7.8
100–499 workers	27,491	18.9	7.3	8.2
500 or more workers	21,748	15.0	4.5	4.0

[a]Excludes persons with unknown self-employment status, hours of work, hourly wages, and size of establishment.

SOURCE: Agency for Healthcare Research and Quality, Center for Cost and Financing Studies, Medical Expenditure Panel Survey Household Component, personal correspondence with Jeffrey Rhoades, March 30, 2011.

Whites represent 51 percent of the total number of uninsured, although only 14 percent of all whites are uninsured. Twenty-one percent of all African Americans are uninsured, and Hispanics have the highest uninsured percentage at 34 percent. Regionally, most of the uninsured (42 percent) are in the South. The West is second with 26 percent; the Midwest has 19 percent, and the Northeast has the fewest (13 percent) (AHRQ 2010).

An important characteristic of the employed uninsured is the size of the firm in which they work. The smaller the number of employees, the greater is the likelihood that the employer does not provide health insurance. Twenty-nine percent of employees in small firms (defined as those with fewer than ten employees) are uninsured, compared with only 4 percent in large firms (those with more than 500 employees). Of all the employed uninsured (including self-employed workers), 69 percent are in firms with fewer than 25 employees, and 19 percent are in firms with 25 to 99 employees. Thus, 88 percent of the total employed uninsured are in firms with fewer than 100 employees (see Exhibit 33.2). If self-employed workers are excluded,

EXHIBIT 33.3 Percentage Distribution of Uninsured Workers, by Wage Rate and Hours Worked, 2008

Characteristic	Working Population in Thousands[a]	% Distribution of Workers	% Uninsured Within Each Age Group	% Distribution of All Uninsured
Hours of Work				
Fewer than 20	11,351	7.4	19.3	8.5
20–34	23,507	15.3	24.8	22.6
35 or more	118,951	77.3	15.0	68.9
Hourly Wage				
Less than $5.00	2,479	1.8	36.1	4.2
$5.00–$9.99	31,126	22.4	30.5	45.0
$10.00–$14.99	34,302	24.7	18.8	30.6
$15.00–$19.99	22,706	16.4	9.0	9.7
$20.00 or more	48,197	34.7	4.6	10.4

[a]Excludes persons with unknown self-employment status, hours of work, hourly wages, and size of establishment.

SOURCE: Agency for Healthcare Research and Quality, Center for Cost and Financing Studies, Medical Expenditure Panel Survey Household Component, personal correspondence with Jeffrey Rhoades, March 30, 2011.

47 percent of uninsured workers are in firms with fewer than 25 employees, and 19 percent are in firms with 25 to 99 employees.

A second important work-related characteristic of the employed uninsured is their low wages. As shown in Exhibit 33.3, as of 2008, 49 percent of the employed uninsured earned less than $10 an hour, and another 31 percent earned between $10 and $15 per hour. Thus, 80 percent earned less than $15 per hour. With respect to part-time work, 31 percent of uninsured workers work fewer than 35 hours per week.

The picture of the uninsured that emerges is of generally young people who work in small firms and earn low wages.

Why the Uninsured Do Not Have Health Insurance

The employed uninsured do not have health insurance for two important reasons. First, the price of insurance is higher (consequently the demand is lower) for those who are employed in small firms. Smaller firms are unable to take advantage of economies in administering and marketing health insurance, which results in higher insurance costs per employee. Insurance companies also charge small firms higher premiums to make allowance for adverse selection, believing many employees will join just to take advantage of health benefits. For example, an owner might hire a sick relative so her medical costs can be paid. In larger firms with lower turnover rates, employment is less likely primarily for the purpose of receiving health benefits. Finally, many states have mandated various benefits, such as in vitro fertilization and hair transplants, that must be included in any health insurance plan sold in their state. Once included in the insurance policy, employees use these services, increasing the insurance premium. Larger firms, however, are able to self-insure, making them exempt from the costs of these additional mandates. Smaller firms are too small to self-insure and therefore have to pay the higher premium, which lessens their demand for health insurance.

The second reason for the lower demand for health insurance in small firms is the low incomes of their employees. Because 80 percent of the employed uninsured earn less than $15 per hour, health insurance premiums would result in a major reduction in their funds available for other necessities. For example, most uninsured workers earn $10 an hour or less, or roughly $20,000 a year. Requiring them to purchase health insurance would reduce their incomes by 24 percent (insurance cost an average of $5,049 per person per year and $13,770 per year for a family of four in 2010) (Kaiser Family Foundation and Health Research and Educational Trust 2010). Instead, when these low-wage employees or their families become ill, they are likely to become eligible for Medicaid, which does not cost them anything. For low-wage workers and their families, Medicaid is their health insurance plan.

Consequences of Employer-Mandated Health Insurance

Failure to Achieve Universal Coverage

Employer-mandated health insurance by itself cannot achieve universal coverage. Even if all working uninsured were covered by an employer mandate, those employed part time and those not employed, together with their dependents, would still not have insurance coverage. This would leave approximately one-third of the uninsured without coverage. To achieve universal coverage an employer mandate must be combined with an individual mandate, together with insurance subsidies for these other population groups. Unless everyone is required to have health insurance (with subsidies for those unable to afford insurance), universal coverage will not occur.

Inequitable Method of Financing

Advocates of an employer mandate have proposed that small firms be given tax credits or subsidies to induce them to offer health insurance to their employees. This approach, however, will likely be inequitable. Although many low-wage employees work in small firms, not everyone employed by small firms earns a low income; consider those who work for small legal firms or physician groups. The subsidy could be limited to those small firms with low average incomes. However, some low-wage employees in large firms would not receive subsidies. To eliminate these inequities, tax subsidies should be targeted to those in need (i.e., they should be income related) regardless of the size of the employer.

Who Pays for Employer Mandates?

Some proposals for an employer mandate require the employer to pay 80 percent and the employee 20 percent of the cost of health insurance.[2] Thus, most of the cost would appear to be borne by the firm. However, whether the employer or the employee actually bears the burden of the tax does not depend on whom the tax is imposed. In competitive industries, firms do not make excess profits; otherwise, other firms (including foreign firms) would enter that industry until excess profits ceased to exist. When employers are earning a competitive rate of return, they are unable to bear the burden of an additional tax themselves—or they eventually go out of business. Instead, faced with a new employee tax, within a short period employers shift the cost of that tax to others by increasing their prices, decreasing the cash wages paid to their employees, or both.

Imposing a per employee tax on the employer is likely to result in one of three possible outcomes (Blumberg 1999). Exactly which combination occurs depends on the particular labor and product markets in which the firm competes, because the nature of these markets determines how much of the higher labor cost is shifted back onto the employee and how much is shifted forward in the form of higher consumer prices. First, to the extent that employees are flexible about the relative portions of their total compensation that go to cash wages and fringe benefits (including health insurance), the cost of labor to the employer is unchanged. An increased employer tax to pay for employees' insurance would result in lower wages, consequently not increasing the cost of labor to the firm. Although employees receive more health insurance, they clearly value the health insurance less than the cash wages it takes to purchase it, because they could have purchased the insurance previously but chose not to. Thus, the first effect of a per employee tax is to make uninsured low-wage employees worse off by forcing a change in how they spend their limited incomes.

The employee tax, however, is unlikely to be shifted entirely back to the employee in the form of lower cash wages. Many employees are at or near the minimum wage; minimum-wage laws prevent the transfer of the health insurance costs to the employee because employees cannot receive cash wages that place them below the minimum wage.

Furthermore, the mix between wages and health insurance is not perfectly flexible, particularly right away; therefore, the cost of labor to the firm will be increased. With higher labor costs, the firm will have to increase the prices of its goods and services. These increased prices in turn will lead consumers to purchase fewer goods and services. With a smaller demand for its output, the firm will need fewer employees. The firm will also decrease its use of part-time employees (if they must be covered by an employer insurance mandate) and increase the overtime work of full-time employees, because it would cost less to insure one person working overtime than one person working normal hours and a second person working part time. Thus, a second effect of a health insurance tax per employee is that fewer of them are employed.

To the extent that labor costs are increased, part of the employee tax is shifted forward in the form of higher consumer prices. This third effect of the tax results in a regressive form of consumer taxation because all consumers, regardless of their income, pay higher prices. Those higher prices represent a greater portion of the incomes of low-income consumers than of high-income consumers. Such a tax is an inequitable method of financing universal health insurance.

Cost to Government

The employer mandate is attractive to government because it shifts the cost of low-wage labor off Medicaid onto the employees and their employers. However, an employer mandate is more costly to the government than it appears. First, because employer-paid health insurance is not considered to be taxable income, the change in compensation from cash wages to health insurance would decrease Social Security taxes as well as state and federal income taxes. Second, government welfare expenditures would be higher as a result of the increase in unemployment that would result from layoffs of those near the minimum wage. Third, additional subsidies and taxes would be necessary to finance care for approximately one-third of the uninsured who are not employed or dependents of an employee if this approach is to achieve universal coverage.

Under play-or-pay proposals many employers would conclude that paying an employee tax is less costly than providing their employees with health insurance. The average annual health insurance premium per employee for a family of four was $13,770 per year in 2010. (Workers contributed, on average, about 30 percent of that amount. The average annual premium for insured workers, single coverage, was $5,049.) If an employer has to purchase health insurance for its employees or pay $2,000 per employee into a government pool (as specified in the 2010 legislation), it would cost less to pay the $2,000 tax for most of its employees (particularly those with families). As medical costs continue to increase, more employers are likely to opt for the "pay" rather than the "play" option. One study estimated (at a time when insurance premiums were much lower than today) that 35 percent of employers providing their employees with health insurance would find it cheaper to drop that coverage and pay the proposed tax, which was assumed to be 7 percent of payroll. Zedlewski, Acs, and Winterbottom (1992) estimate that as many as 40 million employees and their dependents would lose their coverage and be forced into the government pool.

If employers have an option to pay or play, setting the tax too low would make it less costly for employers to pay an employee tax than to provide health insurance. The government would discover that it cannot fund the same set of benefits on the $2,000 tax revenue; estimates place the amount needed to fund the minimum benefits much higher. The employer's incentive is to pay the tax rather than provide the more costly insurance, which will shift more employees into the subsidized exchanges. Revenues would be insufficient to finance the expanded public pool, hence the federal deficit will increase.

Just as the cost of other health programs, such as Medicare Parts A and B, increased beyond initial expectations, the necessary tax to finance an employer mandate would have to rise beyond $2,000 or become a progressive percentage tax on payroll. As the number of employees (particularly low-wage employees) in the government pool increased, the government would be faced with the choice of raising taxes or limiting payments to hospitals and physicians. The likely result would be a large Medicaid program for the increasing number of employees shifted to the government pool.

Under the Clinton administration's proposed employer mandate, no employer would have had to pay more than 8 percent of payroll for its employees' insurance coverage. The automobile companies and their unions would have benefited greatly under this proposal. Health expenses for auto employees exceed 15 percent of payroll; thus, these companies and their employees would presumably receive the same benefits for less and be able to have higher cash wages. Who would have been paying the higher taxes to make this possible?

Financing national health insurance through an employer mandate relies on a hidden and inequitable method of financing health insurance for the uninsured. Imposing the tax on the employer would make it appear as though the employer bears the cost of the tax. The tax, however, would be shifted to both consumers and employees. In both cases, the tax would be regressive. If the tax were borne by labor in the form of lower cash wages, low-wage employees would have to pay a higher percentage of their incomes for health insurance than high-wage employees would.

One of the major concerns with an employer mandate is its effect on firms' demand for labor. As the cost of labor increases, the demand for labor decreases. The job loss will be particularly high among those employees near the minimum wage whose wages cannot be reduced to offset the employer tax. The Congressional Budget Office (2011) estimates that the PPACA employer mandate will result in a decrease in employment of approximately one-half of 1 percent. This is equivalent to about 700,000 people losing their jobs. Those at the greatest risk of job loss are low-income workers.

This hidden tax on consumers and employees also understates its budgetary effects on the government. Federal and state governments lose tax revenues.

Given the inequities and inefficiencies associated with an employer mandate, why has it received so much political support?

Political Consequences of Employer-Mandated Health Insurance

Advantages

The political advantages received by various interest groups outweigh the inequities and inefficiencies that an employer mandate imposes on others. Congress would not have to raise a large amount of tax revenues for an employer-mandated national health insurance plan; such a plan could even reduce Medicaid expenditures. Thus, national health insurance offers the illusion that federal expenditures are little affected. States, whose Medicaid expenditures are increasing faster than any other expenditure, are reluctant to raise taxes. If the states are able to shift the medical costs of low-wage employees and their dependents from Medicaid onto the employees and their employers, the states' own fiscal problems would be alleviated.

Hospital and physician organizations favor an employer mandate because it would provide insurance to those previously without it, increasing the demand for hospital and physician services. Payment levels to health providers would be higher than Medicaid payment levels are. Health insurance companies would similarly benefit because the demand for their services would increase. (Health insurers favored the employer mandate as part of the 2010 health legislation but opposed the final bill when the penalty for not buying insurance under the individual mandate was weakened. With the requirement of the elimination of the pre-existing condition exclusion and a very small penalty for not having insurance, insurers were concerned about adverse selection.)

Large employers and their unions, who would be unaffected because they already provide health benefits in excess of the mandated minimum, believe they will benefit competitively from employer-mandated insurance because the labor costs of their low-wage competitors would increase, making them less price competitive. Over two decades ago, Robert Crandall, the chairman of American Airlines, stated that as a result of the difference between the medical costs of American employees and Continental Airlines employees, "Continental's unit cost advantage vs. American's is enormous— and worse yet, is growing! ... which is why we're supporting ... legislation mandating minimum [health] benefit levels for all employees" (*Wall Street Journal* 1987).

Opposition

The major political opposition to an employer mandate has been by small business. They are aware of the consequences of an employee tax on the prices they would have to charge, demand for their goods and services, and their demand for labor. Opposition by small business was an important reason for the failure of the Clinton administration's legislation. In an attempt to buy off the political opposition of the powerful small business lobby, the Obama administration treated small businesses (those with 50 or fewer employees) differently; they would be provided with subsidies to offset their higher costs. These promised subsidies did not overcome the skepticism of small businesses.

Summary

An employer-mandated national health insurance plan has numerous political advantages. Although an employer mandate statutorily imposes most of the cost on employers, in reality a large portion of the cost is shifted to the employee in the form of lower wages (or other fringe benefits). An employer mandate would not be equitable, because it would disproportionately affect less-skilled employees. It would increase the cost to employers of low-wage labor and impose a financial burden on those least able to afford it. An important reason for low-wage employees' lack of insurance is that they have more pressing needs for their limited incomes, and Medicaid is available to them as a substitute to buying private health insurance. An employer mandate does not achieve universal coverage, because not all of the uninsured are employed. (Thus an individual mandate has to be added to an employer mandate to achieve universal coverage.) Furthermore, an important unintended consequence of an employer mandate is the displacement of many low-wage employees. Alternative approaches for achieving national health insurance need to be examined.

Discussion Questions

1. What are the characteristics of the uninsured?
2. Would it be equitable to provide all employees in small firms with a subsidy to purchase health insurance?
3. What is the likely effect of employer-mandated health insurance on the employer's demand for labor?
4. Does an employer-mandated health insurance tax have a regressive, proportional, or progressive effect on the incomes of employees and consumers?
5. Which groups favor and which groups oppose an employer mandate for achieving national health insurance? Why?

Additional Reading

Krueger, A., and U. Reinhardt. 1994. "Economics of Employer Versus Individual Mandates." *Health Affairs* 13 (2, Part II): 34–53.

Notes

1. The Medical Expenditure Panel Survey–Household Component produces estimates of the uninsured for three different periods within a year: at any time during the year, throughout the first half of the year, and the entire year. In 2007, the latest year for which all three measures are available, 26.9 percent of the population aged younger than 65 years (nonelderly) were uninsured at some point during the year, 20.6 percent were uninsured throughout the first half of the year, and 15.2 percent were uninsured the entire year (Chu and Rhoades 2009).
2. According to the 2010 legislation, effective 2014, employers with 50 or more employees that have at least one employee who receives a premium tax credit will have to pay $2,000 for *each* employee in the firm, excluding the first 30 employees.

NATIONAL HEALTH INSURANCE: WHICH APPROACH AND WHY?

Ntional health insurance is an idea whose time has often come and then gone. However, in 2010 President Obama and a predominately Democrat Congress enacted health legislation (over the opposition of Republicans) intended to eventually cover an additional 32 million and provide medical coverage for 95 percent of the population. The legislation is complex; it expands coverage by increasing eligibility for Medicaid, by providing credits for private insurance, and by requiring everyone to have insurance (an individual mandate). Also included are financial penalties if people are not insured, a series of different types of taxes, and reductions in Medicare to pay for the program. Regulations were imposed on the insurance industry, and state-based insurance exchanges are to be established. Most of the legislation's benefits are to be phased in starting in 2014 and ending in 2019. (See the appendix for a brief description of different elements of the legislation and the year each is to become effective.)

The new legislation is not the end of the quest for national health insurance; instead, it is a beginning. It is likely that many aspects will be revised as regulations are written regarding its implementation; cost-containment features, which have been excluded (because it was politically difficult to include them), are developed; and the financial bases for the plan are improved so that it does not contribute to an already enormous federal deficit.[1] Thus many of the plan's features will change, evolve over time, and return to the political agenda.

To have a basis by which the new legislation can be evaluated, different proposals for national health insurance are examined. The current system is a mixture of private and public financing, together with elements of market competition and regulation; the new legislation continues this mix of public and private aspects. In contrast, general national health insurance proposals rely more on one approach to financing and delivery.

A variety of national health insurance plans have been proposed, from replicating the Canadian (single-payer) system to expanding existing public programs for the poor, mandating employers to provide coverage for their employees, and providing tax credits for the purchase of health insurance or health savings accounts (HSAs). The proponents of each approach claim different virtues for their plans—one plan is more likely to limit the rise in medical expenditures, another will require a smaller tax increase to implement, one will allow individuals greater choice, and still another may be more politically acceptable. Unless some commonly accepted criteria as to what national health insurance should accomplish are established, evaluating and choosing among these plans will be difficult.

Criteria for National Health Insurance

Production Efficiency

Economists are concerned with two issues: efficiency and equity. (When national health insurance proposals are evaluated, the equity criterion is concerned with equitable redistribution.) Efficiency has two parts. The first is *production efficiency*, which determines whether the services (for a given level of quality) are produced at the lowest cost. Efficiency in production not only includes whether the hospital portion of a treatment is produced at lowest cost but also whether the treatment itself is produced at minimum cost. Unless the treatment is provided in the lowest cost mix of settings, such as hospitals, outpatient care, and home care, the overall cost of providing the treatment will not be as low as possible.

Ensuring that each component of the treatment (such as hospital services), as well as the entire medical treatment, is produced efficiently requires appropriate financial incentives. These incentives are usually placed on the providers of medical services; however, they could also be placed on consumers, as would occur under an HSA approach. On whom to place the incentives is a controversial issue, but whether the plan includes appropriate incentives for efficiency in production is not.

Efficiency in Consumption

The second aspect of efficiency, referred to as *efficiency in consumption*, is controversial. In other sectors of the economy consumers make choices regarding the amount of income to allocate to different goods and services. Consumers have incentives to consider the costs and benefits of their choices. Spending their funds on one good or service means forgoing the benefits of another good or service. When consumers allocate their funds in this manner, resources are directed to their highest-valued uses as perceived by consumers.

Some are opposed to having consumers decide how much should be spent on medical services. They would prefer to have the government decide how much is allocated to medical care, as in the Canadian system. Yet Canadians are unable to purchase additional private health insurance to forgo waits for open-heart surgery, hip replacements, or treatment of other illnesses. Inherent in the concept of efficiency in consumption is that the purpose of national health insurance is to benefit the consumer and that the consumer will be free to purchase more medical services than the minimum level offered in any health insurance plan.

Even if one accepts the concept of consumer decision making, concern has arisen that the costs of consumers' choices may be distorted. If the cost of one choice is subsidized and other choices are not, consumers will demand more of the subsidized choice than if they had to pay its full costs, resulting in inefficiency in consumption. For example, the government does not consider employer-purchased health insurance to be taxable income to the employee. Consumers purchase more health insurance because health insurance is paid with before-tax dollars, whereas other choices, such as education and housing, must be paid for with after-tax dollars. The tax-free status of employer-paid health insurance, therefore, is a cause of inefficiency.

Thus, a second criterion for national health insurance plans is whether consumers are able to decide how much of their income they want to spend on medical services and whether any subsidies distort the costs of their choices.

When production and consumption efficiency are achieved through the use of appropriate incentives, the rate of increase in medical expenditures is considered to be appropriate. Having a national health insurance objective of limiting the rate of increase in medical expenditures to, for example, percent increase in GDP per capita, would be inappropriate if achieving this objective meant sacrificing the goals of consumption and production efficiency.

Equitable Redistribution

Presumably, an important (some would say the only) objective of national health insurance is to provide additional medical services to the poor. When national health insurance plans are evaluated on how those with low incomes are to be subsidized, one must examine which population groups benefit (are subsidized) and which population groups bear the costs (pay higher taxes). For equitable redistribution to occur, those with higher incomes are expected to incur net costs (their taxes are in excess of their benefits), whereas those with low incomes should receive net benefits (benefits in excess of costs). When an individual's costs are not equal to the benefits he receives, redistribution occurs. Thus, high-income groups should subsidize the care of those with lower incomes; whether equitable redistribution occurs is the third criterion for evaluating alternative national health insurance plans.

Crucial for determining whether redistribution goes from high- to low-income groups is the definition of beneficiaries and how the plan is financed. Ideally, those with the lowest incomes should receive the largest subsidy (which would decline as income rises), and the subsidy should be financed by a tax that is either proportional or progressive to income. If the tax is proportional to income (e.g., a flat tax of 5 percent regardless of income), those with the lowest incomes will receive a net benefit because the subsidy they receive (sufficient to purchase a minimum benefit package) will exceed the taxes they pay. When a progressive tax, such as an income tax (with a rate that increases as income level increases), is used to finance benefits to those with low incomes, the redistribution from those with high incomes to those with low incomes is even greater.

A regressive payroll tax (a percentage of earned income up to a maximum income level), such as Social Security or a sales tax, takes a higher portion of income from those who have low incomes than from those with high incomes (because those with high incomes have a greater portion of their income above the threshold for taxation). Therefore, such taxes are a less desirable method of financing redistributive programs.

In fact, when a regressive tax is used, the tax paid by many low-income persons may exceed the value of the benefits they receive. For example, if everyone is eligible to receive the same set of benefits but those with higher incomes use more medical services, perhaps because they are located closer to medical providers or their attitudes toward seeking care are different from those with less education (who also have low income), the taxes paid by those with low incomes may exceed the benefits they receive. Perversely, those with low incomes may end up subsidizing the care received by those with higher incomes. (This also occurs when low-income workers subsidize the health benefits of high-income aged.)

An examination of the size of the benefits received by income level in relation to the amount of tax paid is important. Income tax financing is the preferred way to achieve redistribution because it results in greater net benefits to those with low incomes.

Based on the above discussion of efficiency and equitable redistribution, a national health insurance plan should provide incentives for efficiency in production, enable consumers to decide how much of their income they want to spend on medical care, and be redistributive—those with lower incomes should receive net benefits, whereas those with higher incomes should bear costs in excess of their benefits. All national health insurance proposals should be judged by how well they fulfill these criteria.

An important reason national health insurance plans fail to meet these efficiency and equitable redistribution criteria is that national health insurance proposals have objectives other than improving efficiency or equitable redistribution. These other objectives become obvious when the explicit efficiency and redistributive criteria are used.

National Health Insurance Proposals

Many different types of national health insurance plans have been proposed. Some proposals are incremental in that they build on the current system and do not propose changes in the delivery of medical services. Others are more radical, and dramatic changes are proposed in the financing and delivery of medical services. In general, however, the types of national health insurance plans proposed can be classified into three broad categories: a single-payer (Canadian) system, employer-mandated health insurance, and an individual mandate with refundable tax credits. Although separate chapters are devoted to the Canadian approach and an employer mandate, a brief description of each, together with an evaluation of how well they achieve the three criteria, is briefly presented.

Single-Payer National Health Insurance

Under a single-payer system the entire population is covered, benefits are uniform for all, no out-of-pocket expenses are incurred for basic medical services, and, most important, private insurance for hospital and medical services is not permitted (one cannot opt out of the single-payer system). The method of financing may be a combination of income taxes and other sources of funds, such as payroll taxes on the employer and employee, Medicare and Medicaid payments, sin taxes (on alcohol and tobacco), or even a sales tax.

The major advantage of a single-payer system is its apparent simplicity in achieving universal coverage. Access to care by those with low incomes and the uninsured is likely to be improved. Single-payer proponents also claim that less would be spent per capita on medical services (and they would account for a smaller percentage of GDP).

The major disadvantages of a single-payer approach concern consumption and production efficiency (see Chapter 32). Global budget caps are used to limit total medical expenditures. Fixed budgets are imposed on hospitals, their capital outlays are controlled by a central authority, and annual limits are placed on the amount each physician can earn. These arbitrarily determined budget levels limit the amount consumers can spend on medical services, forcing them to wait for services or do without. The result is consumer inefficiency. Furthermore, incentives to achieve production efficiency are lacking in a single-payer system, as are incentives for prevention and innovation.

Expansion of Public Programs

Somewhat similar to a single-payer system is the proposal to expand existing public programs, such as Medicaid, by increasing the income limits to allow greater numbers of those with low incomes and the uninsured to become eligible.[2] Medicaid is funded by general income taxes, and its beneficiaries are those with low incomes; thus, the equitable redistribution goal would be appropriate. Advocates of expanding public programs claim that no major changes in the financing or delivery system are required; only changes in the eligibility criteria are needed. Similarly, more uninsured children could be covered by SCHIP simply by expanding its eligibility levels, which was done in the 2010 renewal of SCHIP.

Some have also proposed that uninsured adults aged 55 to 65 years be allowed to buy into Medicare. Expanding Medicare to include those younger than age 65 and increasing Medicaid and SCHIP eligibility to include those with higher incomes would eventually bring greater numbers of the population into a single-payer-type system. Although differences between Medicare and Medicaid exist, both programs have the same characteristics as a single-payer system. Beneficiaries of these programs pay little if anything for use of medical services (when the Medicare patient has Medigap supplementary coverage) and have free choice of provider (except for those enrolled in a Medicaid HMO), providers are paid fee-for-service, and the government controls expenditures by limiting provider fees. These programs have none of the cost-containment programs, such as utilization management, used by the private sector, nor do they have any incentives for provider efficiency.[3]

Some advocates of expanding public programs view this as an approach to achieve a single-payer system for the United States. Over time, privately insured employees would also prefer to buy into Medicare as their private health insurance premiums and out-of-pocket expenses increase.

The problem with expanding public programs to care for all of the uninsured is that many states cannot afford their share of the matching funds required to include more of the uninsured. Particularly in times of recession, states lack the funds and are reluctant to increase taxes to expand eligibility limits. In fact, many states have been reducing enrollment in SCHIP as their tax revenues have fallen and they face budget deficits. Medicaid and SCHIP do not have a stable source of funding, and states are reluctant to commit themselves to expanding these programs. Allowing the uninsured to buy into Medicare would result in *adverse selection*; sicker individuals (those without employment-based health insurance) would pay a premium that is below their expected costs. Expanding Medicare to include those younger than 65 would merely worsen Medicare's already precarious financial outlook.

Employer-Mandated National Health Insurance

An employer mandate requires employers to either purchase health insurance for their employees or pay a specified amount per employee into a government pool. Although the financial burden for purchasing health insurance is placed on the employer, studies have found that the burden is shifted back to the employee in the form of lower wages. In effect, a tax is imposed on low-wage workers (who are typically without health insurance), requiring them to buy health insurance. The amount of health insurance employees would be required to purchase is more than most low-wage workers are willing or able to pay. (Congress is likely to establish a comprehensive minimum benefit package, as was proposed under President Clinton's health plan. Thus, consumption efficiency would be difficult to achieve. Another option would be to establish a catastrophic plan as the minimum benefit level and allow employees to purchase more insurance.) To assist low-wage workers, it has been proposed that small firms receive tax credits.

Production efficiency can be achieved by having health plans compete for employees.

The inability to achieve equitable redistribution is the biggest disadvantage of this approach. Furthermore, unless subsidies are provided to those who are not in the workforce or who work part time (about 40 percent of the uninsured), an employer mandate would not achieve universal coverage.

Refundable Tax Credits: An Income-Related Proposal

Various income-related tax credit approaches have been proposed over the years. The following proposal attempts to achieve universal coverage in an equitable manner while providing incentives for efficiency in the use and delivery of medical services.

An Individual Mandate

To achieve universal coverage the government must ensure that the two groups without insurance—those who can afford insurance but refuse to purchase it and those who cannot afford insurance—have a minimum level of health insurance. To do so the federal government should first require everyone to have a minimum level of health insurance (an individual mandate), which could be a catastrophic policy for higher-income persons. Many uninsured are financially able to purchase a high-deductible health insurance plan but choose not to do so. If someone who can afford insurance does not have catastrophic coverage and suffers a large medical expense that has to be subsidized by the community, the person is shifting the risk, hence the cost of catastrophic coverage, to the rest of the community.[4]

Proof of insurance would be attached to the person's federal income tax form. Lack of such evidence would result in the government collecting the appropriate premium as it would if the individual paid insufficient income taxes.[5] The government would then assign the person to a health plan in her area, which the person could change. Thus, those who could afford health insurance would not become a burden to others if they suffered a serious illness or accident.

Refundable Tax Credit

The second important role of government in ensuring universal coverage is to provide a refundable tax credit (subsidy) to those with low incomes so they can purchase health insurance. Taxpayers would be allowed to subtract the tax credit to purchase health insurance from their income taxes. Individuals whose tax credit exceeded their tax liabilities would receive a refund for the difference. Thus, if a person's income is too low to pay taxes, the full amount of the credit would be used to provide him with a voucher. As a person's income increased to the point where he had an income tax liability, the tax credit would offset part of the liability, leaving him with part of the tax credit to be used toward purchasing a health insurance voucher. The tax credit would have to be refundable, or the benefits would go only to those who pay taxes, excluding those with low incomes.

The full tax credit subsidy would be equal to the premium of a managed care plan. (These refundable tax credits would be essentially vouchers for a health plan for persons with little or no tax liability.) The tax credit could be an equal dollar amount for all families, such as $6,000, or it could decline with higher incomes. Under a refundable tax credit that declines with higher incomes, the subsidy would go to those with the lowest incomes. However, providing a tax credit of an absolute dollar amount would be more politically acceptable in that those with middle and higher incomes would also receive some benefit.

The value of the voucher could be determined in several ways. One would be for the government to take bids from managed care plans. Alternatively, the voucher could equal the premium of the lowest-cost managed care plan in the market. (This approach is used by an increasing number of employers.) In this manner the preferences of the nonpoor for what they want to purchase from a managed care plan would determine the benefits to be offered to those with low incomes. (Those receiving a full or partial voucher could choose a more expensive health plan by paying the additional cost themselves.)

Consumption efficiency would be achieved by permitting individuals to purchase greater coverage or policies with fewer restrictions on access to providers by paying the additional premium for such plans. Production efficiency would presumably occur as health plans compete for enrollees based on price, quality of services, and access to care. By providing a refundable tax credit, financed from general income taxes, redistributive equity would be achieved.

Health Savings Accounts

A proposal that places greater responsibility for medical expenses on the individual is the use of HSAs in conjunction with a high-deductible, catastrophic health insurance policy. HSAs could be an option under the individual-mandate proposal as well as an alternative to be included in Medicare reform proposals.

The basic idea behind an HSA is to combine an inexpensive high-deductible insurance policy with a tax-free savings account. An HSA plan works as follows: A person (or her employer acting on her behalf) purchases a high-deductible health plan and then annually contributes a specified tax-free amount into the HSA. (A high-deductible catastrophic policy has a much lower premium than a comprehensive health insurance policy.) The maximum that can be contributed each year to the HSA account is $2,700 for an individual and $5,450 for a family—or the amount of the deductible of the high-deductible health plan, whichever is lower. (People aged 55 years and older can make additional "catch-up" contributions of $700 each year until they enroll in Medicare.) The maximum out-of-pocket expenses for which the person is liable can be as high as $5,250 a year for an individual or $10,500 for a family. The person would be at risk for the difference between the out-of-pocket maximum ($5,250) and his annual contribution to his HSA ($2,700), which is $2,550.[6]

HSA proponents claim that an HSA reduces the monthly insurance premium and provides individuals with a financial incentive to be concerned with the prices they pay for medical services and think carefully about which services they really need. (Most high-deductible health plans also include several preventive visits.) Proponents believe that if consumers have a greater financial incentive, medical expenditures will increase at a lower rate. The funds in the HSA account can be invested, grow tax free, and be used later for long-term care expenses (or any other uses, since the funds belong to the individual).

Opponents of HSAs claim that any savings would be relatively small because once the out-of-pocket maximum is reached, the patient has no incentive to spend less. Critics also claim that the adoption and availability of new technology, which is typically used in an inpatient setting, determine expenditure increases, not spending for outpatient services. HSA critics further claim that HSAs would split the insurance risk pools; healthier, lower-risk persons would choose HSAs (thereby gaining financially), and higher-risk persons would remain in more comprehensive plans. HSA proponents disagree, arguing that higher-risk persons would also benefit from and choose HSAs because their total medical out-of-pocket expenses, including prescription drugs, would be subject to a limit. Under Medicare, for example, out-of-pocket expenses are not limited.

HSAs include financial incentives for consumption efficiency to occur. (If consumers are to become informed purchasers, however, more information on provider performance and prices is needed.) Presumably, production efficiency would result as providers compete on price and managed care plans became responsible for providing catastrophic services. Government subsidies would be needed to enable those with low incomes to establish HSAs.

Eliminating the Tax Exclusion for Employer-Purchased Health Insurance

As part of the proposal for an individual mandate, the current exclusion of employer-purchased health insurance from an employee's taxable income would be removed as the tax credit is substituted in its place. The lost revenues from this open-ended subsidy (in 2010 dollars this will amount to $297 billion in lost federal, state, and Social Security taxes each year) would be an important revenue source to offset the new tax credit to those with low incomes (Sheils 2009). (For political reasons the entire tax subsidy for employer-purchased health insurance may not be eliminated; it could be phased out over time, or amounts above a certain limit could be subject to income taxes. As part of the 2010 health legislation a 40 percent tax will be imposed on health coverage that exceeds $10,200 for individuals and $27,500 for families, thereafter indexed for inflation, starting in 2018.)

Replacing Medicare and Medicaid

The refundable tax credit could replace Medicare and Medicaid, using their expenditures to partially offset the cost of the credit. Because the tax credit declines with increased incomes, a sharp cutoff of Medicaid benefits (the "notch" effect) and the previous disincentive to work would no longer exist.

Over time, the Medicare system, which is financially unsustainable, could also become part of this new national health insurance plan. It would be politically difficult to institute an income-related system for those currently on Medicare. Thus, all current Medicare beneficiaries (and those close to the Medicare eligibility age) would receive a fully subsidized voucher in a managed care plan. Those who are perhaps between the ages of 45 and 60 years could receive a partially subsidized voucher related to their Medicare contributions, and the Medicare system could be phased out for those aged younger than 45 years.

Health Insurance Exchanges

Together with an individual mandate and a refundable tax credit, the health insurance would belong to the individual. If the individual changed jobs, she would not have to worry about what type of coverage the new employer offered or whether she would have a waiting period for a pre-existing medical condition. Further, employers, particularly small employers, would not have to be concerned with administering or bearing any health insurance costs if they hire low-wage employees; health insurance would no longer be connected to the workplace. Previously, employers purchased the employees' health insurance because employer-paid health insurance was tax-exempt. In place of the employer, state health insurance exchanges would be established. Everyone would be able to choose among competing insurers offering different benefit coverage. (State health insurance exchanges were included in the new health legislation.) State health insurance exchanges, which currently exist in a number of states, including Massachusetts and Utah, would make for a more competitive health insurance market.

With an individual mandate and no exclusions for pre-existing conditions, insurers would be less concerned with adverse selection.[7] People buying insurance on the exchange would be classified into risk categories by age and family status.

Eliminating State Mandates

State health mandates require private health insurance to cover specific health providers, such as chiropractors, acupuncturists, marriage therapists, and athletic trainers; specific insurance benefits, such as hair transplants, in vitro fertilization, and massage therapy; and specific populations, such as noncustodial children and terminated workers. There are 2,156 state mandates across the 50 states (as of 2010). Many states also have regulations requiring Any Willing Provider laws, which restrict a health plan's ability to exclude hospitals and physicians from its provider networks. Some states have enacted community rating laws, which require insurance premiums to be the same regardless of an individual's (or a group's) risk level or claims experience. Furthermore, several states have adopted legislation that requires health insurers to accept anyone who applies, regardless of health status ("guaranteed issue").

These state mandates increase the cost of health insurance, making it too expensive for those with low incomes. Depending on where one lives, mandates can increase the cost of a policy by between 20 and 45 percent (Bunce and Wieske 2010). The high cost of state mandates (as high as several thousand dollars in insurance premiums per person per year) directly affects the number of insured (and uninsured) in a state.

These state regulations would not be needed under this proposal, and eliminating them would reduce the cost of health insurance. If individuals wished to purchase these services—such as hair transplants and fertility treatments—on their own with after-tax dollars, they would be free to do so.

Advantages of Income-Related Refundable Tax Credits

The income-related voucher meets the efficiency and equitable redistribution criteria in the following ways. Everyone is obligated to have a minimum set of health insurance benefits. Those with the lowest incomes would be ensured adequate health insurance and would receive the largest net benefits under the proposed plan. The size of the subsidy would decline as income increases. Employer-purchased health insurance (above a certain dollar amount) would become part of the employee's taxable income. The resulting increased tax revenues, together with funds from the income tax system and Medicaid, would provide the funding for the income-related subsidies. Thus, the financing source is based on progressive taxation. Requiring universal coverage through an individual mandate means that cost shifting by those who do not purchase insurance to those who do would no longer occur.

The mandate to have insurance is on the *individual*, not on the employer; thus, the individual would be able to change jobs without fear of losing insurance or being denied coverage because of a pre-existing condition. Because everyone would be required to have insurance, an employer should be willing to hire someone who is older, is less healthy, or has a pre-existing condition because no additional health insurance cost would be incurred by the employer or other employees.

Employees would have incentives to make cost-conscious choices, and a competitive health insurance market would help achieve efficiency and quality. The greater out-of-pocket liability for employees purchasing more expensive health plans would increase their price sensitivity to different managed care plans. Price (premium) sensitivity by employees (and employers acting on their behalf) would provide price incentives for managed care plans and providers, such as hospitals and physicians, to be as efficient as possible. Unless health plans were responsive to consumers at a premium the consumer was willing to pay, the health plans would not be able to compete in a price-competitive market.

Summary

National health insurance proposals should be judged according to their efficiency in production, efficiency in consumption, and equitable redistribution (whether those with low incomes receive a net benefit). Market-based systems, in contrast to single-payer systems, have demonstrated their ability to achieve the goals of production and consumption efficiency. Subsidies to those with low incomes, as through a refundable tax credit, are a direct method of improving equity and can provide increased choice and result in production efficiency when provided through a market-based system.

A brief description and comparison of the three national health insurance proposals is presented in Exhibit 34.1.

An important role of government under national health insurance would be to monitor quality and access to care received by those with low incomes. Government has not performed this function well for Medicaid patients. However, Medicaid can be eliminated by providing everyone with a refundable tax credit. Allowing those with low incomes to enroll in managed care plans that also serve other population groups and establishing state insurance exchanges would provide consumers with more choice of health plans and achieve greater competition among insurers. Information on health plans, their prices, and the quality and access they provide would be important in achieving a competitive market. In addition to states providing information on each plan's performance, it is likely that other organizations and websites would develop and provide information to assist consumers in making informed choices. These reporting and monitoring activities would benefit all enrollees, including those subsidized by government.

EXHIBIT 34.1 A Comparison of Three National Health Insurance Proposals

Feature	An Employer Mandate	Single-Payer System	Individual Mandate with Refundable Tax Credit
How does it work?	Requires all employers to buy health insurance for their employees or pay into a pool.	Provides comprehensive coverage with no out-of-pocket payments. Private insurance not permitted.	Everyone is required to purchase at least a high-deductible plan, and subsidies are provided to those with low incomes.
Does it provide universal coverage?	Excludes those who work part-time and those who are not working.	Achieves universal coverage.	Achieves universal coverage.
Is there consumption efficiency?	Partially. Minimum mandated benefits are greater than low-income workers prefer, and employer may not provide choice of health plans.	No. Persons are not permitted to buy medical services or private insurance for services covered by the basic health plan.	Yes. Participants can purchase additional medical services and insurance above minimum required insurance.
Is there production efficiency?	The plan relies on market-based competition to achieve production efficiency.	No consumer or provider incentives are included to encourage efficiency, to minimize the cost of a treatment, or to provide preventive care.	The plan includes consumer and provider incentives for efficiency. It relies on market-based competition to achieve production efficiency.
Is it equitably financed?	Regressive. The plan retains tax-exempt employer coverage and a tax is imposed on employers and employees, including low-income employees without insurance.	Partially regressive. There is pooling of funds from employers, Medicare, Medicaid, and increased payroll taxes.	Progressive. Income-related subsidies are provided, and there is a limit/phaseout of tax-exempt employer-paid insurance.
What are the administrative costs?	High, because of multiple health plans, monitoring, and enforcement of mandate.	Costs are too low to detect fraud and abuse or to institute disease management and other types of programs.	High, because of multiple health plans, monitoring, and enforcement of mandate.
How are healthcare costs controlled?	The plan relies on the market to achieve appropriate rate of increase in costs.	The plan relies on arbitrary budget caps and regulated fees.	The plan relies on market to achieve appropriate rate of increase in costs.

Under a market-based national health insurance system, the rate of increase in medical expenditures would be based on what consumers, balancing cost and use of services, decide is appropriate. The government would not need to set arbitrary limits on total medical expenditures. Instead, the rate of increase in medical expenditures would be the "correct" rate because consumers, through their choices, would make the trade-off between access to care and premiums to pay for that level of access.

Discussion Questions

1. Discuss the criteria that should be used for evaluating alternative national health insurance proposals.
2. Evaluate the desirability of the following types of taxes for financing national health insurance: payroll, sales, and income tax.
3. What is the justification for requiring everyone (all those who can afford it) to purchase a minimum level of health insurance?
4. Outline (and justify) a proposal for national health insurance. As part of your proposal, discuss the benefit package, beneficiaries, method of financing, delivery of services, and role of government. How well does your proposal meet the criteria discussed in the chapter?
5. What are alternative ways for treating Medicare under national health insurance?

Additional Readings

Fuchs, V. 2009. "The Proposed Government Health Insurance Company: No Substitute for Real Reform." *New England Journal of Medicine* 360 (22): 2273–75.

Fuchs, V., and E. Emanuel. 2005. "Health Care Reform: Why? What? When?" *Health Affairs* 24 (6): 1399–1414.

Furman, J. 2008. "Health Reform Through Tax Reform: A Primer." *Health Affairs* 27 (3): 622–32.

Hall, M., and C. Havighurst. 2005. "Reviving Managed Care with Health Savings Accounts." *Health Affairs* 24 (6): 1490–1500.

Notes

1. One stated objective of the administration in designing the new legislation was that it would not contribute to the federal deficit over a ten-year period. To achieve this goal, the new taxes and the reductions in

Medicare expenditures used to finance the new benefits start at the beginning of the ten-year period while the benefits (expenditures) become effective in only the last six of the ten years.

2. The Obama administration's 2010 healthcare legislation, which it claims will reduce the uninsured by 32 million, expands Medicaid eligibility to cover 16 million of the uninsured.

3. Production efficiency could be achieved in Medicaid if the state were to offer Medicaid recipients a choice of competing health plans. Proposals for Medicare reform have similarly proposed providing all the aged with a subsidy to cover the cost of a basic health plan and allowing the aged to choose among different competing health plans, paying a higher out-of-pocket premium if they decide to choose a more expensive health plan, such as traditional Medicare. Such Medicare reform proposals would achieve consumption and production efficiency.

4. The recently enacted health legislation includes an individual mandate, but only those younger than age 30 are permitted to buy a catastrophic health plan.

5. Two serious problems with the individual mandate as enacted in the 2010 legislation are that the penalty for not buying insurance is very low and that, effective in 2014, all insurers must accept anyone who wants to buy insurance, even if they have a preexisting medical condition. Thus it is expected that many will pay the annual penalty and then, when they become ill, buy health insurance. Once they are better, they will drop their insurance. This form of adverse selection, unless changed, can destroy the health insurance market.

6. Additional information on HSAs may be found at www.treas.gov/offices/public-affairs/hsa.

7. Until the individual mandate becomes effective for all, people who are uninsured and have serious health problems will be unable to purchase insurance. These individuals would have to be included in subsidized high-risk pools, as occurs in many states. Over time, high-risk pools would become unnecessary as everyone would be required to have insurance and would be included in a health plan before they became ill.

CHAPTER

35

FINANCING LONG-TERM CARE

Spending for long-term care services is expected to increase sharply over the next several decades and will be placing great pressure on federal and state budgets, as well as on the elderly and their families (GAO 2005). The population is aging; as shown in Exhibit 35.1, the number of aged is expected to increase from 40.3 million in 2010 (13 percent of the population) to 72.2 million in 2030 (19.3 percent of the population), to 88.5 million in 2050 (20.2 percent of the population). An aging population that is living longer increases the number at risk for requiring long-term care services. The fastest-increasing portion of the aged is those aged 85 years and older. This older group is expected to increase from 14 percent of all aged in 2010 to 21.5 percent in 2050. As the impaired aged increase their demand for services to assist them in those activities necessary for daily living, the cost of providing those services is rising at a faster rate than general inflation.

How long-term care services should be financed, and by whom, is an important public policy dilemma.

The Nature of Long-Term Care

Long-term care consists of a range of services for those who are unable to function independently, including services that can be provided in the person's home, such as shopping, preparing meals, and housekeeping; in community-based facilities, such as adult day care; and in nursing homes for those who are unable to perform most of the activities necessary for daily living, such as bathing, toileting, dressing, and so on. A nursing home is but the end of a spectrum for those with the most physical and mental impairments.

The need for long-term care increases with age. As shown in Exhibit 35.2, the greatest needs for long-term care are of those aged 85 years and older, 50 percent of whom require long-term care services. The need for nursing home care also increases with age. At any point in time (as of 2004), approximately 3.8 percent of the aged (about 1.3 million) are in a nursing home. An estimated 1 percent of those aged 65 to 74 years are in nursing homes, compared with 3.7 percent of those aged 75 to 84 years and 18.9 percent of those aged 85 years old and older (CDC 2009). The main reasons for nursing home use are severe functional deficiencies, mental disabilities (such as Alzheimer's disease), and lack of a family to provide services in the person's own home.

Exhibit 35.1 Percentage of US Population Aged 65 Years and Older, 1980–2050

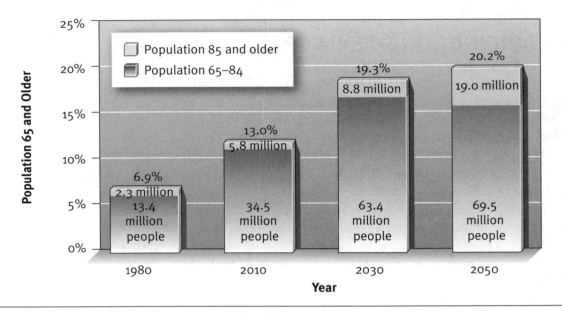

SOURCE: US Bureau of the Census, US Population Projections. 2010. [Online information.] www.census.gov/population/www/projections/summarytables.html.

Exhibit 35.2

Percentage of People Aged 65 Years and Older, by Age and Disability Level, 2004/2005

Age Group	Nondisabled	One or Two ADLs	Three to Six ADLs	Institution
65–74	91.1	3.1	3.1	0.9
75–84	78.1	6.7	8.5	4.1
85 and over	50.3	12.1	17.8	15.6

NOTE: ADLs = activities of daily living.

SOURCE: Manton, K. G., Gu, X., and Lamb, V. L. (2006). "Change in Chronic Disability from 1982 to 2004/2005 as Measured by Long-Term Changes in Function and Health in the U.S. Elderly Population." *PNAS* 103 (48): 18374–9.

Most long-term care occurs in the home rather than in an institutional setting. Informal caregivers are predominantly family members or close relatives. Older men with a disability requiring long-term care are more likely to have a surviving spouse to provide them with that care than are older women. As those requiring long-term care services age, it becomes increasingly difficult for a spouse to provide the services needed by the disabled spouse. In 2004, wives provided 19.3 percent of husbands' long-term care needs; husbands (because there were fewer husbands) provided 14.7 percent of wives' long-term care needs. Daughters provided 43.2 percent, and sons provided 22.8 percent (Houser, Gibson, and Redfoot 2010).

Children are bearing an increasing portion of the informal care needs of their parents. Women more often than men provide the uncompensated care. When the impaired aged is a woman, typically a widow, children and relatives are the most frequent caregivers. These services by family members, while uncompensated, are costly to the caregivers in terms of added strain and reduced hours at work.

Current State of Long-Term Care Financing

Long-term care is expensive and represents a significant financial risk to the elderly. The national average annual cost for a private room in a nursing home was $83,585 in 2010, and this figure is expected to almost triple by 2025 (MetLife Mature Market Institute 2010). A person turning 65 in 2000 had a 44 percent chance of entering a nursing home at some point in his life. Most of the aged who enter a nursing home will do so for a short period, but 19 percent will stay longer than five years and incur 89 percent of all nursing home costs. Because women have a longer life expectancy, a 65-year-old woman has a 51 percent chance of entering a nursing home during her lifetime and, upon entering, has an expected average stay of two years. In-home care is also expensive; the average cost for a home health aide is $21 an hour (MetLife Mature Market Institute 2010). Thus, long-term care services in a nursing home or an aide to provide care in the home are too costly for most of the aged on fixed incomes with limited assets.

Many aged mistakenly believe Medicare will pay for their long-term care needs; in fact, it only pays for certain, limited long-term care expenses. Included as part of Medicare are home health services for those aged who need part-time skilled nursing care or therapy services and are under the care of a physician. A limited number of post-acute care days (100) in a skilled nursing home are covered for those discharged from a hospital. Medicare spending on these services accounted for about 28.2 percent of total long-term care spending in 2009 (about $57.8 billion). Medicare does not cover the services needed when an aged person has decreased ability to care for herself because of chronic illness, a disability, or normal aging.

In 2009, spending from all public and private sources for long-term care (for all ages) was $205.3 billion, which represented about 8.3 percent of total healthcare expenditures. The largest component of long-term care services is for nursing homes, which represents 67 percent of such expenditures; home care represents 33 percent (Exhibit 35.3). The major sources of long-term care financing are public programs, primarily Medicaid and Medicare, at 63.3 percent. Individuals provide about 26.1 percent of the costs out of pocket, and the remainder, about 7.6 percent, is covered by private long-term care insurance. These percentages differ according to whether the long-term care is provided in a nursing home or in the patient's home. Long-term care insurance covers 7.7 percent of nursing home costs and 7.3 percent of home healthcare. Private long-term care insurance is beginning to increase, but very few of the aged have such insurance.

On average, 34 percent of all nursing home care costs, a significant financial burden for many, is out of pocket. Although the aged and their families pay about 10 percent of home health costs, these costs do not include the substantial nonfinancial burden imposed on families and relatives who are unpaid caregivers. Houser and Gibson (2008) estimate that the economic value of family caregiving in 2007 was $375 billion.

Medicaid

Medicaid is a joint federal–state financing program for those with low incomes. Total Medicaid expenditures were $368 billion in 2009, of which 32.5 percent was for payment of long-term care services; the remainder was for acute care services (CMS 2011c). States vary greatly in their per capita (per person within the state) annual expenditures for long-term care, from $1,107 in New York to $145 in Nevada.

Medicaid is the major payer for nursing home care (32.8 percent) and pays for a limited amount of in-home coverage (35.6 percent). Medicaid is the payer of last resort, covering long-term care expenses only after the impaired aged have exhausted their own financial resources. To qualify for Medicaid, an individual must first spend down his assets and is allowed to keep only $2,000. Current law permits a spouse to retain half of the couple's financial assets, up to a maximum of $109,560 (inflation adjusted) in addition to a private home of any value if it is the principal residence (CMS 2010f).

To limit their Medicaid expenditures, states have restricted the availability of nursing home beds, paid nursing homes low rates, and provided limited in-home services to those eligible for Medicaid. The consequence of these policies has been a continual excess demand for nursing home beds by the impaired aged. Because demand exceeds supply and states set low payment rates, the quality of services provided is often poor. Few states pay

Exhibit 35.3 Estimated Spending on Long-Term Care Services, by Type of Service and Payment Source, 2009

Payment Source	Nursing Home Care	Home Healthcare	Total
	Billions of Dollars		
Total	$137.0	$68.3	$205.3
Medicare	28.0	29.8	57.8
Medicaid	45.0	24.3	69.3
Other federal	4.0	0.6	4.6
Other state and local	2.9	1.5	4.4
Private insurance	10.6	5.0	15.6
Out-of-pocket and other sources	46.6	7.0	53.6
	% of Total		
Total	100.0	100.0	100.0
Medicare	20.4	43.6	28.2
Medicaid	32.8	35.6	33.8
Other federal	2.9	0.9	2.2
Other state and local	2.1	2.2	2.1
Private insurance	7.7	7.3	7.6
Out-of-pocket and other sources	34.0	10.2	26.1

SOURCE: Data from Centers for Medicare & Medicaid Services, Office of the Actuary, National Health Statistics Group, 2011. http://www.cms.gov/NationalHealthExpend Data/.

nursing homes according to the level of care needed by the patient; thus, nursing homes have an incentive to admit Medicaid patients who have lower care needs and are less costly to care for. When a private-pay patient seeks nursing home care, she will be admitted before the Medicaid patient because her payment exceeds Medicaid reimbursement. As nursing home demand by private patients increases, the excess demand by Medicaid patients will become greater in those states that continue to limit the number of nursing home beds.

The risk of a person entering a nursing home as a private patient and having to spend down his assets was only 6.3 percent in 1985. (The probabilities vary by race and gender.) Most of the aged (59.2 percent) entering a nursing home were private patients; the remainder were those already eligible for Medicaid (17.3 percent) and Medicare or other payers (23.5 percent). Of those private-pay patients who used fewer than three months of nursing home care, 2.7 percent had to spend down their assets to qualify for Medicaid eligibility. For a stay up to six months, a total of 10.5 percent of the aged had to spend down. As the stay increased up to two years, 18.2 percent had to spend down (Spillman and Kemper 1995).

The probability of entering a nursing home for 65-year-old men is 27 percent and for 65-year-old women is 44 percent. Of those who do, 12 percent of men and 22 percent of women will spend more than five years there (Brown and Finkelstein 2008). Nursing homes cost nearly $80,000 per year. Although the lifetime risk of a person entering a nursing home and having to spend down her assets is relatively low, the fear of incurring this financial burden is the basis of the demand for long-term care insurance and government subsidies.

Home care expenditures have become a growing share of Medicaid long-term care expenditures. From 2000 to 2008, Medicaid spending on home care increased from $6.8 billion to $22.4 billion, an average annual rate of 29 percent, compared with 4 percent on nursing homes (CMS 2011c). States have also attempted to reduce their nursing home spending by substituting less costly in-home and community-based long-term care services.[1]

Private Long-Term Care Insurance

When many people are at risk for a large unexpected expense but only a few will incur such catastrophic costs, private insurance is a solution for those who can afford it. A private insurance market enables people to reduce their financial risk in exchange for a premium. Given the growing number of aged at risk for financially catastrophic nursing home (and in-home) costs, the potential market for long-term care insurance is huge. Dependence on Medicaid and the need for government long-term care subsidies would diminish if more of the aged purchased private long-term care insurance. Yet fewer than 10 percent of the elderly have private long-term care insurance.

Why Do So Few Aged Buy Long-Term Care Insurance?

Why has private long-term care insurance not grown more rapidly? How feasible is it to expect private long-term care insurance to alleviate the middle-class aged's concerns that their long-term care needs will be met without burdening their family caregivers or having to spend down their estates?

Characteristics of Long-Term Care Insurance Policies

Most long-term care insurance (about 80 percent) is sold to individuals, in contrast to medical insurance, which is mainly sold to groups. Most long-term care policies cover all forms of long-term care needs, including nursing homes, home care, and assisted-living facilities. Case management services, medical equipment in the home, and training of caregivers may also be included. Most long-term care plans also have a deductible in the form of days of care the individual must pay (30 to 100 days) before the policy is effective. These deductible provisions ensure that the long-term care policy is for a chronic condition and does not cover acute medical or rehabilitative services, which is the responsibility of Medicare or private medical insurance.

Long-term care plans also contain benefit maximums. Policies may limit lifetime benefits to five years in a nursing home. In addition, most policies contain a maximum daily payment for care in a nursing home or for reimbursement for care in the home. These maximum daily benefits are either fixed over time or (for an additional premium) increased by an annual percentage amount. Furthermore, to qualify for long-term care benefits, the individual must meet certain criteria, such as requiring substantial assistance to perform several specified activities of daily living for an extended period, such as 90 days.

Long-term care insurance premiums reflect the cost of providing the services and the risk that the person will need the services as she ages. In 2010, the average annual premium for long-term care insurance (with 5 percent inflation protection) was $2,853 at age 65; if purchased at age 75 it was $4,715; and at age 85, the average premium was $9,150. If a policy was purchased at age 30, the premium would be only $770 per year, reflecting both the lower risk that a young person would require long-term care services and that younger people would be paying the premium over a greater number of years than someone who purchased coverage when he was older (FLTCIP 2011).

The type of benefits included in a long-term care policy will greatly affect premiums charged. For example, a policy sold in 2010 for a 70-year-old person will vary from a low of about $1,377 to a high of $4,892 per year depending on the benefits included.

Long-term care insurance premiums are also higher if the purchaser wishes to protect himself against inflation in long-term care costs. Because most long-term care policies provide specified cash benefits in the event that the purchaser requires long-term care, a long-term care policy that pays $100 per day for care in a nursing home would not be sufficient if nursing home costs increase at their previous annual growth rate of 6.7 percent; over 20 years, the cost per day will be $366. Protection against these additional financial risks increases the premium.

Long-term care policies are guaranteed renewable, and premiums vary by age and risk class, of which there are usually three: preferred, standard, and extra risk. Once a person has purchased a long-term care plan, she is not charged an additional amount as her age or health condition changes (RMM n.d.).

Factors Limiting Demand for Long-Term Care Insurance

Possible explanations why only 10 percent of the elderly have long-term care insurance can be classified, first, according to the factors that limit the demand for private long-term care insurance and, second, according to imperfections on the supply side of the long-term care insurance market.

The aged's income and ability to pay for long-term care insurance are quite variable. The oldest old, those most in need of long-term care, generally have lower incomes than the younger aged and are in a higher-risk group, which makes their insurance premiums much higher.

A great deal of misinformation exists among the aged—many believe Medicare and Medigap insurance (private insurance that pays Medicare's deductibles and copayments) also cover long-term care (they do not). Also, the elderly may be unaware of their potential long-term care risks and the financial consequences of those risks. Furthermore, the number of policies, with their differing copayments and benefits, may be confusing to some of the elderly.

An important reason the elderly may not have long-term care insurance is the availability of Medicaid. To the extent that the elderly view Medicaid as a low-cost substitute to private long-term care insurance, they will be less likely to purchase private long-term care insurance. If the older aged need to enter a nursing home, they have to rely on Medicaid, which is their low-cost long-term care insurance. To those elderly, however, who wish to bequeath their assets to their children, Medicaid is a poor substitute to privately purchased insurance, because the elderly need to spend most of their assets before Medicaid kicks in.

Expectations of the elderly that their family will provide financial and nonfinancial support if they require long-term care also affect their demand for insurance. Publicly funded or family-provided long-term care decreases the demand for privately funded insurance.

Possible Market Imperfections in the Supply of Long-Term Care Insurance

Supply-side concerns relate to whether long-term care plans are priced significantly above their actuarial fair value (their pure premium), in which case the premiums would greatly exceed the policy's expected benefits. The greater the difference between the premium and expected benefits (referred to as the loading charge), the lower the demand for such insurance.

Premiums for long-term care plans may be much higher than the expected benefits for several reasons. When long-term care insurance is sold to individuals, the marketing and administrative costs are much higher than if such insurance were sold to large employer groups. (Individually sold medical insurance contains loading charges as high as 50 percent, compared with loading charges of 10 percent to 15 percent when sold to groups.)

Also increasing the loading charge is insurers' concern about adverse selection.[2] Long-term care insurance is sold to individuals on a voluntary basis, whereas employer-paid health insurance includes everyone in the group, which eliminates the chance that only sick employees will buy the insurance. Because insurance premiums are based on the average expected claims experience (use rate multiplied by the price of the service) of a particular age group, insurers are concerned that a higher proportion of the impaired aged will buy long-term care insurance. If the premium is based on a higher expected risk group than exists among the general population of elderly desiring to buy insurance, those elderly of an average risk level will find the premium greatly in excess of their expected benefits. ("Delay of benefits" provisions, indemnity coverage with a large deductible, and copayments are usually included to discourage adverse selection.)

Insurers are also concerned that as insurance becomes available to pay for in-home services, the demand for such services will sharply increase beyond the amount believed necessary. To the extent that such moral hazard occurs and is not controlled by the insurer, the premium will reflect these higher use rates and greatly exceed the expected benefits for those aged who would not similarly increase their use of services once their insurance started paying for those services.[3]

Conclusions Regarding the Small Market for Private Long-Term Care Insurance

The size of the loading charge does not seem to be the determining factor causing the small demand for long-term care insurance.[4] Such policies charge the same premiums for men and women of the same age. Brown and Finkelstein (2007) estimate the loading charge for a 65-year-old man to be 44 percent; he would expect to receive $56 worth of benefits in return for paying a $100 premium. However, because premiums are the same regardless of sex, the loading charge for a 65-year-old woman was estimated to be negative, that is, her expected benefits are greater than the premium paid: $104 in expected benefits in return for a $100 premium. Despite the favorable pricing of long-term care policies for women, still only about 10 percent of elderly women purchase such policies, which is no different from the percentage of men purchasing such policies. These findings suggest that market-supply imperfections, reflected by the loading charge, are insufficient for understanding the limited demand for long-term care insurance.

Demand factors are therefore more likely explanations for the limited demand for private long-term care policies. In a second study, the authors conclude that the availability of Medicaid is critical in explaining the limited demand for long-term care insurance; Medicaid crowds out the private demand for insurance (Brown and Finkelstein 2008). For an elderly person with median wealth, most of the premiums for a private long-term care policy pay for the same benefits that would be covered by Medicaid. Furthermore, women are more likely than men to end up on Medicaid, regardless of whether they have private long-term care insurance, because of their much greater expected lifetime utilization of long-term care services. Thus, women, even though they might be able to buy private long-term care insurance with a zero loading charge, would still not buy long-term care insurance because of the availability of Medicaid.

As long as Medicaid exists in its present form, it will be difficult to increase the demand for private long-term care insurance.

Approaches to Financing Long-Term Care

The long-term care needs of the older aged, the aged's fear of having to spend down their assets, and the high cost of private long-term care insurance form the basis of the aged's demand for government long-term care subsidies. Providing the aged with a range of long-term care services, from in-home services to nursing home care, without financially burdening the aged or their children, would require huge government subsidies. Given the rapid increase in the number and proportion of aged, federal and state subsidies for long-term care would be a very large financial burden on the nonaged.

Federal spending on programs benefiting the aged—Medicare, Medicaid, and Social Security—consumed 10.3 percent of GDP as of 2009. By 2035, inflation-adjusted expenditures on these programs will increase to 15.9 percent of GDP (CBO 2010c). Federal spending on the elderly will absorb a larger and ultimately unsustainable share of the federal budget and economic resources. Thanks in part to medical advances, people are living longer and spending more time in retirement, which places greater demands on these three federal programs. The aged are an increasing portion of the total population, and as the baby boomers start retiring in 2011, the number of workers per aged to finance the growing costs of Medicaid, Medicare, and Social Security will decline. These demographic, technologic, and economic pressures have profound implications for our economy and the continued funding of these entitlement programs.

Medicaid is also the fastest-growing and second-largest program in state spending. About 67 percent of Medicaid spending is on behalf of the aged and those with disabilities. The growing number of aged will place a greater burden on state budgets in coming years. Expanding public subsidies for long-term care would not only exacerbate federal and state fiscal pressures but also serve as a disincentive to the purchase of private long-term care insurance.

Given these trends in both the number and percentage of aged and the likely inability of government to continue financing these benefits, subsidies for financing the long-term care needs of the aged are likely to be curtailed rather than expanded. The public policy dilemma concerns the role of government in financing long-term care for the aged.

Stimulating the Demand for Private Long-Term Care Insurance

Increasing the demand for private long-term care insurance would, over time, decrease the demand for Medicaid subsidies for long-term care services. However, recent government legislation has created a new role for government as the insurer for long-term care. As an insurer, the government, rather than private insurers, bears the liability if premiums fall short of the program's outlays.

As part of the recently enacted (2010) Patient Protection and Affordable Care Act (PPACA), a new voluntary federal insurance program for long-term care was established, beginning in 2011, the Community Living Assistance Services and Supports (CLASS) Act (Iglehart 2010). Those who contribute to the program must wait a minimum of five years before they become eligible to collect benefits. Once eligible, if a person has two or more functional limitations, that is, being unable to perform certain activities of daily living, such as eating or bathing, and they are certified by a healthcare practitioner that these limitations would continue for more than 90 days, they will receive a cash benefit of not less than $75 per day (adjusted for inflation) for the rest of their lives, assuming they continue to have the limitations. These funds may be used to purchase nonmedical services and supports necessary to maintain a community residence, such as hiring an aide (or a family member) to bathe them or prepare meals at home.

Proponents of the CLASS Act claim that the new program, which is to be entirely privately financed by premiums, will reduce Medicaid expenditures, since care in the home is less costly than being institutionalized in a nursing home. Further, those needing long-term care services prefer to remain in their home over being in a nursing home.

Critics claim the CLASS Act will become another unfunded federal entitlement that will contribute to the already huge federal deficit. PPACA included the CLASS Act premiums in justifying its budget neutrality: that the revenues and expenditures of PPACA would not add to the federal deficit. Thus CLASS Act premiums will be spent on general government programs that are part of PPACA, and the Treasury will issue IOUs that will eventually be used to pay CLASS Act benefits. When the IOUs have to be converted into cash to pay benefits, the government will either have to raise taxes or increase the deficit to generate those funds. CLASS Act premiums do not go into a trust fund, as would occur in a private insurance program, where they would be invested and earn a return to be used to pay future benefits.

The Congressional Budget Office (CBO) estimates that CLASS Act premiums during the first ten years of the program will exceed benefit payouts by $70 billion; in later years payouts will exceed premiums and the federal unfunded liability will increase.

Another concern with the voluntary aspect of the CLASS Act is the problem of adverse selection. A voluntary program is more likely to attract those who expect to benefit from the program, particularly since the premiums are adjusted for age but not for health status. As more high-risk people enroll, the premium will increase and those who are low risks will either not enroll or will drop out. As proportionately more high risks enroll, benefit payouts will exceed premiums earlier than CBO's estimates.

To decrease adverse selection and enroll healthier risk groups, employers are to automatically enroll all their employees; the employee can disenroll if he so chooses. It is expected that fewer employees would bother to opt out than would tell their employers they wish to join the program.

As the unfunded deficit for this program increases over time, premiums will likely have to be increased and, possibly, everyone will be required to enroll to increase the size of the risk pool (to include more healthy enrollees).

The Government as a Safety Net

Given the fiscal pressures on the federal and state governments, government policy is likely to be, first, a safety net for low-income aged and, second, a method to increase the effectiveness of how those subsidies are spent. When government acts as a safety net, primary responsibility for paying long-term care expenses is placed on the individual and the family. The government fills the gap between the needs of the elderly and what their families and financial resources can provide. Availability of government assistance, such as Medicaid, is based on the elderly person's income and assets and is financed from general taxes; those with higher incomes bear the financial burden of subsidizing low-income aged. Because states differ in their generosity and financial capacity, the availability of long-term care services—access to nursing homes and in-home services—varies greatly among state Medicaid programs.

Most states now have provisions that prevent people from qualifying for Medicaid within three years of voluntarily impoverishing themselves through bequests of their assets to family members. (States are going after middle- and high-income persons who have adopted estate-planning strategies that permit them to qualify for Medicaid by transferring their assets just before they need nursing home care.) Furthermore, because some assets are excluded for purposes of determining Medicaid eligibility—such as having a house, spending assets on home improvements, having an automobile, and placing assets in certain types of trusts—tightening Medicaid requirements would further reduce eligibility and increase public subsidies for those most in need.

Lengthening the period for asset transfers from three to five years (which is opposed by the AARP), limiting excludable assets, and enforcing these requirements would reduce Medicaid expenditures, make Medicaid a less desirable substitute to private long-term care insurance for middle- and high-income persons, and, consequently, increase the demand for private long-term care insurance.

Improving the Effectiveness of Government Long-Term Care Programs

Several states have developed innovative long-term care programs in the expectation that Medicaid's long-term care expenditures will be reduced. These states also hope to improve patient satisfaction with the care they receive. Several states use consumer-directed "cash and counseling" programs, for example. Under this approach, Medicaid beneficiaries living in the community are provided with funds to purchase long-term care services rather than rely on Medicaid-provided services. Beneficiaries are given more choice in the type and providers of long-term care services. Medicaid beneficiaries currently have no financial incentive to use long-term care efficiently. Cash and counseling programs give beneficiaries an incentive to shop for lower-priced services and get more care for their budgets. Preliminary evidence from these demonstration projects indicates that participants are more satisfied with the care received and have fewer unmet needs than beneficiaries in traditional Medicaid (Doty, Mahoney, and Sciegaj 2010).

Other innovative programs integrate acute and long-term care. Social HMOs (S/HMOs) receive a monthly premium in return for providing acute and long-term care services to their enrollees. The S/HMO is at financial risk for the cost of all the medical and long-term care services its enrollees require. Both healthy and impaired aged are able to enroll in the S/HMO, which has an incentive to improve the efficiency of the care received by its enrollees by coordinating care and reducing unnecessary services.

The Program for All-Inclusive Care for the Elderly (PACE) model is directed toward Medicare- and Medicaid-eligible beneficiaries who are eligible for nursing home care but want to continue living at home. PACE organizations receive a monthly capitation payment; use a multidisciplinary team of providers, such as physicians, nurses, and case managers; and provide services to enrollees in adult day care centers. Preliminary evaluations indicate less nursing home and hospital use by PACE enrollees. These results may be biased, however, by favorable selection; PACE enrollees may be less impaired than nursing home patients, which is their comparison group.

Public long-term care subsidies affect the demand for private long-term care insurance. The lower the aged's responsibility for their long-term care expenses, the lower is their likelihood of buying private long-term care insurance. Appropriate public policy should do two things: encourage those who can afford it to purchase private long-term care insurance and stipulate that limited public funds be used for those unable to afford private insurance.

Summary

Fewer than 40 percent of the aged will likely be able to afford private long-term care insurance. Although this percentage indicates that the private insurance market can greatly increase, it also indicates that a sizable number, mainly the older aged, will be unable to purchase insurance or other long-term care services.

A fundamental issue concerns the extent to which the government should provide long-term care subsidies to the aged.

Long-term care policy requires choices to be made. The aged have greater needs for care, do not wish to be a burden on family members, do not want to spend down their hard-earned assets, and would like to be assured of a high-quality nursing home, should they require one. Yet given the projected number of aged, government long-term care subsidies would be very costly. Such subsidies would require large tax increases at a time when Medicare taxes will also be increased to keep it from going bankrupt. These tax increases would represent a huge financial burden on workers because the number of workers per aged person is declining.

Subsidies also reduce the incentive for many aged to rely on their children or to purchase private long-term care insurance. To reduce the cost of long-term care subsidies, subsidies should be targeted to those with the lowest incomes. Estate-planning strategies that enable middle- and high-income aged to transfer their assets shortly before qualifying for Medicaid are inequitable in that they shift their costs to others. To the extent that Medicaid rules are enforced and it becomes a less desirable substitute to private long-term care insurance, the demand for private long-term care insurance will increase. Greater growth in the demand for long-term care insurance will reduce Medicaid long-term care expenditures. Educating both workers and the aged about the need to protect themselves against catastrophic long-term care costs is also important.

The new CLASS Act, assuming large numbers of employees participate, will reduce Medicaid subsidies for those employees when they require long-term care services. However, since participation is voluntary, adverse selection is likely to occur. Although the premiums will exceed payouts in the next decade, the funds will be used for general government programs and be unavailable when payouts are required. The new CLASS Act merely postpones the time when greater government deficits for long-term care will occur.

Discussion Questions

1. Describe the demographic and economic trends affecting the outlook for long-term care.
2. What should be the objectives of a long-term care policy? How do these objectives differ from the long-term care goals of the middle class?
3. Why has the market for long-term care insurance grown so slowly?
4. How can Medicaid be changed so it is not a low-cost substitute for private long-term care insurance for middle-income aged?
5. Why does private long-term care insurance, when sold to the aged, have such a high loading charge relative to the pure premium?

Notes

1. States cover nonmedical and social support services to allow people to remain in the community. These services include personal care, homemaker assistance, adult day care, chore assistance, and other services shown to be cost effective and necessary to avoid institutionalization. To control costs, however, states limit eligibility and the scope of services covered.
2. Since the late 1980s, insurers have marketed long-term care insurance to large employee groups. Group policies have lower loading charges because of their lower administrative and marketing costs. Adverse selection is also less of a concern when everyone in a group participates, particularly when they are at low risk for long-term care. Furthermore, because employees would not be at risk for many years, group long-term care policies could be sold at very low premiums. Employer-sponsored long-term care policies are a more useful financing source for future than for current aged.
3. To lower the cost of providing long-term care, insurers provide comprehensive services, both in-home assistance and nursing home care. In-home services are less expensive (and are preferred by the impaired aged) when they reduce use of the more expensive nursing home. Case managers would ideally be used to evaluate the elderly's needs and

determine the mix of services to be provided. In-home services could be substituted for nursing home care, and the discretionary use of in-home assistance could be minimized. Controlling adverse selection and discretionary use of services is essential to keeping private long-term care insurance premiums low. Currently, greater reliance is placed on financial incentives (deductibles and copayments) than on the use of case managers to control costs.

4. The importance of price on the demand for long-term care insurance has been estimated to be between –0.23 and –0.87; that is, if the price of long-term care insurance were to decrease by 1 percent, demand would increase by less than 1 percent (Stevenson, Frank, and Tau 2009).

THE POLITICS OF HEALTHCARE REFORM

In 2010 the Patient Protection and Affordable Care Act (PPACA) was enacted. The legislation was several thousand pages long. Many legislators never read or fully understood the legislation. Its provisions were controversial, and it was passed with only Democratic support. Not one Republican senator or representative voted for the final bill. The bill's major provisions do not become effective until 2014—some as late as 2018 and 2020. (See the appendix for a brief summary of the legislation.)

Although there is dissatisfaction with this country's health system, the PPACA proved relatively unpopular. The Obama administration believed that Democrats would receive political support from the public for enacting the PPACA, which included extending health coverage to an additional 30 million people, enacting insurance regulations that would eliminate the fear of losing their health insurance in case of illness, and limiting premium increases. When campaigning during the congressional midterm (2010) elections, however, many legislators who voted for PPACA were reluctant to publicize their vote in TV ads.

To understand the difficulties of enacting healthcare reform and the relative unpopularity of PPACA, one must examine the goals of different political constituencies, how the Obama administration attempted to satisfy these constituencies, and what the Obama administration's own objectives were in designing PPACA. In doing so, it becomes obvious that healthcare reform and national health insurance mean different things to different groups. Further, the process and outcome of the legislation were a cause for dissatisfaction among many of the middle class, including the aged.

Differing Goals of Healthcare Reform

National Health Insurance: Benefiting the Poor?

Many assume that the main purpose of healthcare reform and national health insurance is to increase the availability of medical services to those with low incomes. Certainly many individuals support increased services to the poor, but this is not and has never been the driving force behind national health insurance. Medicaid is national health insurance for the poor. To use the power of government to achieve one's objectives requires political power. The inadequate structure and funding of Medicaid is indicative of the limited political power of the poor and their advocates. These inadequacies are not attributable to the actions of a few miserly bureaucrats or legislators but instead are reflective of the resources that society—mainly the middle class—is willing to devote to the poor. States vary in their generosity and in the criteria used for determining Medicaid eligibility. Few states provide Medicaid eligibility for all those at the federal poverty level, and some states provide benefits only to people whose income is 17 percent of the federal poverty level (Henry J. Kaiser Family Foundation 2011). How much the non-poor are willing to tax themselves for charity depends on how much the non-poor themselves have, how culturally similar the poor are to the non-poor, and how much it costs to provide for the poor.

Because the non-poor have the political power to determine the allocation of resources to the poor, one must assume that the inadequacies of Medicaid are reflections of insufficient interest among the non-poor in improving Medicaid and increasing funding for the poor. If society is unwilling to improve Medicaid, why would it tax itself to enact national health insurance for the poor?

National Health Insurance: Benefiting Politically Powerful Groups

If national health insurance is not primarily for the poor, its broader purpose must be to use the power of government to benefit politically powerful groups. Important groups must receive benefits in excess of their costs, if visible redistributive legislation affecting everyone's health coverage is to be enacted. These groups are the middle class and the aged, who determine the outcome of elections, as well as healthcare providers, business, and labor groups, who have a concentrated interest in the legislation's provisions and are able to provide legislators with financial support. Healthcare providers and other interest groups are relatively easy to accommodate in the short run. The problem with enacting healthcare reform or national health insurance has always been the middle class. If the middle class is to receive net benefits, which group will have to bear the costs of financing those benefits? Whichever group has to pay more will oppose legislators who vote to raise their taxes. The major difficulty in healthcare reform has been finding groups that can be taxed to provide net benefits to politically powerful constituencies.

In the past, politically important groups received visible redistributive benefits that less politically powerful groups were taxed to provide. Regressive taxation was typically used to finance universal redistributive legislation, such as Social Security and Medicare Part A.[1] Over time these regressive taxes became more progressive as the cost of the programs exceeded projections. Second, to lessen the opposition of those being taxed, the tax was hidden. Splitting the Social Security tax and the Medicare payroll tax between the employer and the employee makes it appear that the employee bears only half of the tax. In reality, economists believe that most of the employer share is shifted back to the employee in the form of lower wages, while the rest is shifted forward to consumers in the form of higher prices for goods and services.

Politically influential groups have a concentrated interest in a particular issue and are able to organize themselves to provide political support to legislators by means of campaign contributions, votes, and volunteer time. A group is said to have a concentrated interest if specific regulation or legislation will have a sufficiently large effect to make it worthwhile for the group to invest its resources either to forestall or to promote that effect. The potential legislative benefits must exceed the group's costs of organizing and providing political support.

This discussion of concentrated interests assumes that legislators will respond to political support because their objective is to be reelected. Legislators are assumed to be similar to other participants in the policy process and to rationally undertake cost-benefit calculations of their actions. However, they weigh the political support gained and lost by their legislative actions and not by the legislation's effect on society.

Initially, physicians and hospitals were the major groups with a concentrated interest in health legislation. Physician and hospital associations represented (successfully) their concentrated interests before both state and federal legislatures and in so doing were able to affect the financing and delivery of medical services. These legislative actions by physician and hospital associations were neither very obvious nor initially very costly to the consumers of medical services. Medical prices rose faster than they would have otherwise; and alternatives to the fee-for-service system, such as managed care, were delayed for many years. These costs to consumers were not sufficiently large to make it worthwhile for them to organize, to represent their interests before legislatures, and to offer political support to legislators who were favorable to their interests.

Over time, increasing medical costs resulted in the rise of other groups, such as unions and employers, with a concentrated interest in limiting medical cost increases. Groups with opposing concentrated interests, such as physicians and hospitals, who wanted increased medical spending, while other groups, such as unions and employers and their insurers, who wanted to limit medical spending, made political compromise more difficult. Healthcare reform had to attempt to receive support from such opposing groups.

The Need for Visible Benefits to the Middle Class and Aged

In 2009, the first year of the Obama administration, the country was in a severe recession, unemployment and the number of uninsured were increasing, and, since insurance was tied to their jobs, the middle class were concerned with losing their health insurance. The administration believed that with the country's economic stress the public would be amenable to government programs that provided greater healthcare security. Given the growing public concern with the increasing federal deficit, the administration realized that a new healthcare reform program had to be financed without visibly further expanding the huge federal deficit. In addition, while expanding health coverage to an additional 32 million people, the administration had to gain the political support of the middle class and the aged.

The middle class and the aged are two important voting constituencies who determine the outcome of elections. The middle class (those in the middle income group) has a disproportionate amount of political power because they are the median voters. It is difficult to form a majority of voters without those in the middle. The aged have the highest voting rate of any age group (see Exhibit 36.1). The near-aged have the next highest voting participation rate. Those aged 18 to 24 have the lowest voting participation rates, and future generations who do not currently vote offer the least amount of political support to legislators. Thus, the cost of providing current benefits is shifted to those who are less important politically. To enact highly visible redistributive legislation, such as healthcare reform, legislators attempt to provide the middle class and the aged with benefits at no additional cost so as to gain their political support for reelection.

The Middle Class

As medical costs and insurance premiums continue their rapid increase, middle-class dissatisfaction with the current system has increased. They are paying more out of pocket as employers begin shifting a greater portion of their health costs back to employees by asking them to pay a greater portion of their health insurance premiums and pay higher copayments and deductibles. The middle class are also concerned that if they lose their jobs or change jobs, they will lose their health insurance. The middle class would like unrestricted access to specialists (traditional fee-for-service insurance), low out-of-pocket copayments, limited monthly health insurance premiums, and the security of having health insurance.

The problem with coming to grips with serious reform is not with special-interest groups but with the middle class. They are unwilling to have the government increase their taxes to pay for health insurance for the uninsured. Furthermore, the middle class are unwilling to recognize that they must make a trade-off between the higher cost of unlimited access to medical services and the amount they are willing to pay.

The difficulty in enacting healthcare reform is that legislators are unable to provide the middle class with benefits at no additional cost. Which population group can be made to bear the cost of subsidizing the middle class?

To receive the political support of the middle class, the Obama administration emphasized "health insurance" reform rather than "healthcare"

EXHIBIT 36.1 Voting Participation Rates in Presidential Elections, by Age, 1984–2008

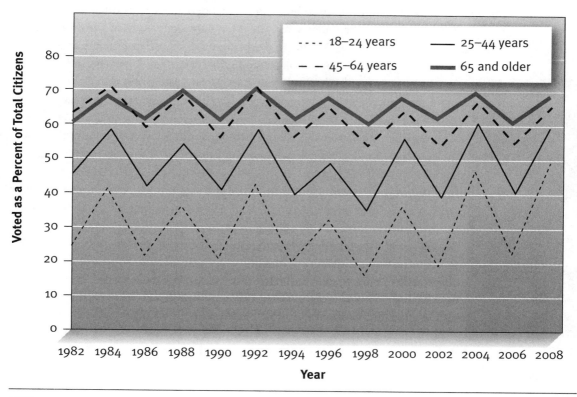

SOURCE: US Census Bureau. 2010. *Current Population Reports. Population Characteristics, P20 Series:* various editions. [Online information.] http://www.census.gov/prod/www/abs/p20.html#vote.

reform. Since the middle class has health insurance, they do not want to lose it or pay more in premiums. Thus President Obama promised the following: "if you like your insurance you can keep it," insurance premiums will *decrease* because the legislation will "bend the cost curve down," the legislation will not "add a dime to the deficit," and "it will be fully paid for." Further, the middle class will not have to pay higher taxes; only those whose family income is greater than $250,000 will pay increased taxes. To increase coverage to the uninsured, the administration had to assure the middle class that health reform would not cost them anything, that, in fact, they would also receive benefits. It was to be a "free lunch."

The Aged

The second politically powerful group is the aged (and near-aged). The aged have their national health insurance, Medicare. The near-aged want to ensure that Medicare is available for them when they retire. The children of the aged and near-aged also want to ensure that Medicare is maintained, since they do not want the financial responsibility of caring for their parents' health needs. In addition to maintaining Medicare, the aged want to reduce their out-of-pocket expenses, particularly for the Medicare drug benefit, and limit their premium increases for Medicare Parts B and D. Both political parties compete for the political support of the aged; in December 2003 this led to a new prescription drug benefit, Medicare Part D (Feldstein 2006). To reduce the cost of the drug benefit, Congress created a "doughnut hole" (a large deductible), which became a large financial burden for seniors with high drug costs.

As part of the new legislation, the doughnut hole is to be phased out. Further, because this benefit will not be immediately visible to the aged, to secure their political support for the PPACA before the 2010 midterm elections, the administration sent $250 checks to millions of middle-class seniors who fell into the doughnut hole. (Seniors with low incomes and high drug costs were already on Medicaid.)

The premiums of the near-aged, those aged younger than 65 years, who will be buying insurance through the new health insurance exchanges, will be reduced by requiring health insurers to only allow age-related premiums to vary by a difference of 3:1, rather than a 6:1 ratio, which reflects the much higher medical costs of older compared to younger adults. The effect of lowering premiums for older adults by the narrowing of age-related premiums is to increase premiums for young adults, who happen to have lower voting participation rates.

Groups with a Concentrated Interest in Healthcare Reform

Many groups have a concentrated interest in health legislation. To understand the conflicting forces that affected the design of PPACA, one has to examine the objectives of several of the more important groups.

At the time the PPACA was being drafted, President Obama had a high approval rating and the Democrats controlled a large majority in the House of Representatives as well as a filibuster-proof margin (60) in the Senate. (Senator Arlen Specter switched from the Republicans to the Democrats, and a contested Minnesota Senate election was decided in favor of the Democrats, giving them the 60 votes needed for cloture.) It appeared that healthcare reform was inevitable, so provider organizations thought they had to negotiate the best possible deal with the administration, which promised them a better deal than if their fate was left to Congress, which was anxious to impose severe payment reductions. The saying was "you're either at the table or on the menu." Consequently, the Obama administration was able to induce almost all of the major groups with a concentrated interest in health reform—the American Medical Association (AMA), the American Hospital Association (AHA), pharmaceutical firms, AARP, and unions—into supporting PPACA. Industry groups were also promised an increased pool of millions of additional patients, funded in full or in part by the government.

PhRMA

Pharmaceutical firms have an interest in expanding their market of paying patients and retaining their ability to price their drugs according to what the market will bear. Yet the trade association for the pharmaceutical industry (PhRMA) agreed to reduce drug prices by $80 billion over ten years (the time frame for calculating the revenues and costs of PPACA). The administration used this reduction estimate in its budget calculations to reduce the overall cost of PPACA. In addition, PhRMA agreed to spend $100 million in TV advertising to endorse the legislation. In return, PhRMA received the administration's protection when representatives and senators wanted PhRMA to reduce drug costs by a greater amount, $100 to $160 billion. The drug firms also received protection for their high-tech biological medicines against early competition from low-cost generics.

The American Medical Association

The AMA has had a long history of opposing federal intervention in healthcare, opposing President Truman's proposed national health insurance bill in 1946, Medicare in 1965, and President Clinton's healthcare proposal in 1993. The AMA's endorsement of PPACA was important to the administration since it did not want physicians claiming that not enough physicians are available to care for an additional 30 million people; if that were to happen, the middle class and aged would become concerned about their decreased access to care.

It is difficult to know the AMA's rationale for endorsing the bill without being fully assured that they would achieve their objectives. However, three reasons seem possible, all of which concern money. The first, and most likely, reason was to influence the government to change Medicare's physician payment system that relies upon the sustainable growth rate (SGR) for determining annual fee updates. According to the SGR formula, physicians were scheduled for a 21 percent decrease in Medicare fees. However, each year Congress overrules the proposed decrease. To achieve a permanent fix would require an increase in the federal deficit of $280 billion over the next ten years. The AMA's support for PPACA, surprisingly, was not contingent on a permanent payment fix, and the Democratic Congress did not include a permanent fix as part of PPACA.

A second legislative priority of the AMA has long been tort reform. While PPACA includes a section establishing an incentive program for states to adopt and implement alternatives to medical liability litigation, tort reform is essentially negated by another provision in PPACA that states that a state is not eligible for the incentive payments if that state enacts a law that limits attorney fees or imposes caps on damages. Limits on attorney fees and damage caps were two tort reform priorities of the AMA. Given the significant financial support provided by trial lawyers to Democrats, the trial lawyers were protected from any harm to their incomes.

Third, the AMA has a trademark monopoly, created by the federal government, on the medical coding system known as Current Procedural Terminology (CPT) (Geiger 2009). Each medical and surgical procedure and diagnostic service used by hospitals and healthcare professionals is assigned a CPT code, and insurers pay the AMA a fee when using the CPT codes to reimburse healthcare providers. Annual income generated by this monopoly provides the AMA with about $70 million a year, more than they receive from membership dues. Perhaps the administration threatened the AMA that it would lose its CPT monopoly (and revenues). These revenues are extremely important to the AMA, since its membership has declined from 75 percent of all physicians in the 1970s to 25 percent currently.

If the AMA's support was based on increasing the association's revenues (maintaining CPT revenues), the association was not acting in its members' economic interests. (Several state associations and many members denounced the AMA's PPACA endorsement.) If the AMA's support was based on having PPACA include a permanent fix to the SGR system or meaningful tort reform, it would be expected that its support would be contingent on having both included in the final legislation, which they were not. In any case it appears the AMA either acted in the association's own economic interest (maintaining or increasing CPT revenues) or based its support on the expectation that the SGR system or tort legislation would be changed, but without an assurance of that.

American Hospital Association

A significant portion of hospital revenues are derived from Medicare and Medicaid, which places hospitals in direct conflict with state and federal efforts to reduce public expenditures. The AHA's objective in health reform has been to achieve increased hospital reimbursement.

Given the political environment, the AHA agreed, on behalf of hospitals, to accept $155 billion in payment reductions from the federal government over ten years to help pay for healthcare reform. In return, under the new law hospitals will receive a large increase in the number of funded patients. Previously, hospitals treated a great many uninsured patients and incurred a large amount of bad debts. The additional revenues hospitals stand to gain from the increase in patients, funded either by the federal government or government-subsidized private insurance, is expected to more than offset their agreed-upon payment reductions. In addition, in exchange for agreeing to these payment reductions, hospitals are exempt for ten years from additional payment cuts that may be recommended by PPACA's newly established Independent Payment Advisory Board.

Another benefit of agreeing to the administration's proposed cuts in hospital payment was that hospitals forestalled threatened changes in non-profit hospitals' tax-exempt status and were able to eliminate competition from physician-owned specialty hospitals by making the development of new physician-owned facilities illegal.

Unions

Unions were among the strongest supporters of healthcare reform and spent a great deal of money in support of it. The unions publicly argued that the healthcare system performs poorly, and they strongly favored the government-run public option, which they believed would lead to a single-payer system. The unions had several self-interest motives for favoring a government-run health plan. The economic interests of the major unions, such as the United Auto Workers (UAW), have not changed since the enactment of Medicare. At that time, they were successful in shifting part of their retirees' medical costs onto the general working population. Since then, the unions' legislative objective has been to maintain their benefits without having to pay the required cost.

Large private-sector unions, such as the UAW, have generous medical benefits, which are among the most expensive of any employee benefits. As the cost of medical care has risen, these unions have had to accept smaller wage increases to maintain their comprehensive medical benefits. These private-sector unions prefer a single-payer system so that their members' healthcare costs can be shifted to the taxpayer. Since employers are only interested in the total cost of labor, not how the compensation is divided between wages and benefits, the unions could increase their members' wages by the cost of health benefits shifted to the taxpayer.

A second reason for union support of the public option plan was to expand the number of unionized employees. Unions have been more successful in organizing public-sector employees than those in the private sector. The percentage of unionized private-sector employees is declining and was only 6.9 percent in 2010. In contrast, 36.2 percent of government employees are unionized. The Canadian single-payer system has a much higher rate of unionization than exists in the US healthcare system. Unions in the United States believe that under a government health system they could increase their membership by millions of employees, who would then pay billions of dollars in union dues.

Unions have far more power in a single-payer system to increase their wages and benefits. A powerful public-sector union bargaining with a public-sector health monopoly will do better than if it were bargaining against competing private-sector providers. Examples of union success in bargaining with public entities are the higher wages, pensions, and health benefits of union members who work for cities, counties, and states compared to workers in the private sector.

Unions benefited from PPACA in additional ways. The legislation included $5 billion to pay for medical costs for millions of unionized autoworkers, steelworkers, schoolteachers, and other early retirees in underfunded retiree health benefit plans. Company, municipal, and union-sponsored plans that meet certain eligibility criteria will be reimbursed up to 80 percent for early retirees' (ages 55 to 64) medical costs.

To help fund the legislation, Senator Max Baucus (D-MT), chairman of the Senate finance committee, proposed taxing health insurance plans, a proposal favored by many economists to provide enrollees with an incentive to choose less costly health plans. Unions strongly opposed this tax on "Cadillac" health plans. Many unionized state employees, such as teacher unions, receive generous health benefits for which they would have been taxed. To assuage the unions, the premium threshold for the tax was increased and the implementation date delayed until 2018.

AARP

AARP is supposed to represent the economic interests of the aged, particularly those on Medicare. Although the legislation includes almost $600 billion in cuts to the Medicare program over ten years plus about a $150 billion reduction in payments to Medicare Advantage plans, which enroll about 25 percent of Medicare beneficiaries, and the bill did not forestall the scheduled 21 percent reductions in Medicare physician fees scheduled to occur (thereby reducing seniors' access to physicians), AARP strongly endorsed PPACA. Is it possible that AARP's interests and those of the seniors it purports to represent are not aligned?

AARP claimed that it did not oppose the almost $600 billion in Medicare cuts because reducing fraud and waste will make Medicare stronger over time. An alternative hypothesis is that AARP has a conflict of interest between representing seniors and increasing its own revenues. AARP receives hundreds of millions of dollars each year from health insurers and others who use AARP's endorsement in selling their products. The largest share of these royalty revenues comes from insurers that sell Medigap policies (supplemental insurance to cover Medicare's deductibles and copayments). If more such Medigap policies are sold, AARP makes more money.

Medicare Advantage plans are strong competitors to Medigap plans. Medicare Advantage plans receive about 12 to 14 percent more funding per enrollee than traditional Medicare and are able to provide additional benefits to their enrollees. Reducing payments to Medicare Advantage plans by about $150 billion forces these plans to reduce benefits while increasing copayments and premiums; consequently, many of these plan's enrollees will switch and buy Medigap plans, thereby increasing AARP's royalties.[2]

Employers

Many employers believe they bear part of the cost of their employees' health insurance premiums, and when premiums increase employers believe this causes them to increase their prices. Consequently, employers favor reform that lowers rising healthcare costs or enables those costs to be shifted to others. The business community was divided on the employer mandate, which requires employers either to provide their employees with health insurance that meets federal standards or to pay a tax. The highest percentage of uninsured employees work for small businesses. The National Federation of Independent Business (NFIB), the trade association for small business, opposed PPACA because it would increase their labor costs, thereby forcing them to raise their prices and hire fewer workers. The NFIB also opposed the income tax increase imposed on those with high incomes to help fund the legislation, because it would affect many small business owners. Several large businesses, such as Walmart (the nation's largest private employer), favored the bill because they currently provide health insurance to their employees and wanted to increase the cost to competitors who do not. Walmart also felt that if the employer provision were enacted, more onerous provisions affecting lower-wage employers would be less likely to be enacted.

Health Insurers

Insurers have a concentrated interest in healthcare reform, namely, to have access to a greater number of potential enrollees and not be displaced by a government plan. Health insurers were initially in favor of healthcare reform because they believed that since the employer market was decreasing, the only way for them to increase enrollment was through government subsidies to the uninsured. They were strongly opposed, however, to the government-run public option, which they saw as a subsidized competitor, crowding out private insurance by forcing hospitals and physicians to accept low rates (as is done in Medicare) and, together with unlimited federal subsidies, undercut the premiums charged by private insurers. With lower premiums in the government plan, private enrollees would shift to the public plan.

The public option was viewed by insurers (and others) as a forerunner to a single-payer system. In 2003 President Obama stated, "I happen to be a proponent of a single-payer universal healthcare program...But as all of you know, we may not get there immediately." Further, Barney Frank (D-MA), commenting on why the Democrats were not backing a single-payer system, said, "We don't have the votes for it. I wish we did. I think if we had a good public option it would lead to single-payer" (*Wall Street Journal* 2009).

Once the Senate removed the public option, insurers thought that competition from a government plan was eliminated and the individual mandate requiring everyone to buy insurance would provide them with more enrollees. The small penalty included in the individual mandate for not buying insurance, however, concerned insurers that they would be subject to adverse selection; people would wait until they were sick to buy insurance. Insurers were also opposed to many aspects of insurance reform included in the bill, such as mandated minimum medical loss ratios, government-standardized generous benefit coverage, limits on out-of-pocket spending, and review of their premium increases, all of which would adversely affect their business. Insurers claimed that various insurance requirements, such as elimination of caps on lifetime benefits and adding children up to age 26 on family policies, would result in higher costs, hence higher premiums, which would then subject them to rate review. The insurance industry was criticized as villains by the administration.

The Legislative Process

The Obama approach to healthcare reform appeared to follow what Tom Daschle (who was nominated to become secretary of Health and Human Services but withdrew over income tax problems) wrote in his book outlining his proposal for healthcare reform (Daschle, Greenberger, and Lambrew 2008). Daschle, formerly Democratic Senate majority leader, advised the administration to move fast before there could be public debate and to write as vague a bill as possible. The bill would delegate to the secretary of Health and Human Services the authority to write many regulations governing the financing and delivery of medical services. President Obama accepted the advice and wanted the bill to be quickly enacted before the summer 2009 legislative recess.

The 2008 elections gave Democrats an overwhelming majority in the House of Representatives and a filibuster-proof majority (60) in the Senate. Liberal House Democrats enacted their version of healthcare reform since they saw little reason to negotiate a compromise healthcare reform bill with House Republicans given their large Democrat majority.

The Ideological Divide

Ideological differences on healthcare reform between the two parties, which also represented differing economic interests, such as unions and trial lawyers versus health insurers, healthcare providers, and pharmaceutical firms, had previously been an impediment to healthcare reform. In the latter half of the 1990s, huge federal budget surpluses were projected far into the future. The middle class would not have been required to tax themselves to provide for the uninsured. It was an opportune time to cover the uninsured without seeming to impose a financial burden on anyone. And yet the ideological divisions between the political parties made it impossible for Congress to enact universal healthcare.

Since the 1990s Congress had not been able to agree on how the uninsured should be assisted. Republicans favored providing the uninsured with refundable tax credits to buy insurance.[3] Their objective was to strengthen the private health insurance system and to allow the insured to have greater choice of health plans. They also favored placing greater fiscal responsibility on the insured for their healthcare choices and relying on health plan competition to reduce rising medical costs.

Conversely, the Democrats supported making the uninsured eligible for existing public programs, such as Medicaid. President Clinton proposed expanding Medicare by allowing those between the ages of 55 and 65 to buy into Medicare. The Democrats also favored expanding Medicaid eligibility of children (up to age 18) and childless adults. Expanding the number of people in public programs (Medicare and Medicaid) makes it easier to convert these programs into a single-payer system like the Canadian healthcare system. The next step would have been to include in the single-payer system employer health insurance premiums on behalf of their employees. Accumulating all these funds would not necessitate a huge tax increase.

Proponents of a single-payer system oppose proposals such as refundable tax credits and competitive health plans, including Medicare Advantage plans, in which plans compete to enroll seniors. Providing incentives for the aged and others to choose less costly health plans would strengthen a competitive private healthcare system. Democrats prefer the traditional Medicare approach, which resembles a single-payer system. Proposals allowing greater choice of health plans move the medical care system away from the direction single-payer proponents favor. Instead, single-payer proponents favor increasing the cost of private health insurers, such as imposing additional regulations, to increase their premiums, which will cause the public to demand an alternative system, namely a publicly financed system, such as "Medicare for All." This ideological dispute between proponents of strengthening the private system and those favoring an expanded public (eventually single-payer) system limited opportunities for reaching a compromise on healthcare reform.

The Public Option

Democrats in the House of Representatives included in their version of PPACA a public option. The initial design of the public option would have had the government establish a single national health plan, set provider payment equal to Medicare rates, and allow anyone to join the public option plan. Proponents of the public option claimed insufficient competition existed among health insurers. A public option plan, it was claimed, would provide more choice and compete against the private health insurance industry, driving down premiums and reducing healthcare costs, since the government plan's bargaining power would be able to negotiate lower prices directly with healthcare providers.[4]

In markets with few competitors, the dominant insurer is typically a nonprofit BlueCross plan. Nonprofit insurers, such as BlueCross and BlueShield plans, currently compete in the health insurance market, and it is not obvious how the objectives and performance of a public option would differ from these nonprofit plans. It is not clear that a public plan would have lower costs, and thereby the ability to charge a lower price than health insurers, unless it was subsidized and subject to a different set of rules. Its administrative costs would be higher than Medicare's since it would have to incur marketing costs to compete for enrollees, profile physicians and other providers as it forms provider networks in different markets, offer different benefit plans, perform utilization management to reduce fraud and waste, and bill and collect premiums from enrollees. None of these tasks is currently performed by Medicare (Conover and Miller 2010).

It is likely that the real purpose of a public plan is quite different than its stated purpose. If a subsidized government insurer competes with private insurers, private insurers are likely to suffer large declines in their market shares, leading to the government becoming the dominant health insurer.[5]

If too few insurers are available because they have monopolized the market—no evidence of which was presented—the appropriate remedy would be to use the antitrust laws, as is done in every other industry. If barriers to entry exist in health insurance, those barriers should be eliminated. Concern over monopoly behavior with Microsoft, among hospitals, or in other industries has not led to proposals for the federal government to go into the software business to compete with Microsoft or have the government build its own hospitals.

Growing Opposition by the Middle Class and Aged to Healthcare Reform

The House and Senate missed the administration's summer deadline for passing healthcare reform. The delay in passing the bill provided the opposition with the opportunity to disparage the bill and weaken political support for it.

When legislators returned home for the summer recess and held town hall meetings, they were met with a great deal of public anger. The unexpected anger was driven by both accurate and inaccurate media discussions of various provisions being considered as part of the healthcare legislation, such as paying doctors to provide end-of-life counseling to Medicare patients; talk of government-run "death panels" frightened the aged. Included in the legislation were funds for comparative effectiveness research, which opponents claimed would go beyond simply providing information on the effectiveness of different treatments and eventually be used by the government for deciding which treatments would be reimbursed.

Distrust of the proposed bill grew. Coverage was to be expanded to an additional 32 million people, Medicare expenditures were to be reduced by almost $600 billion over ten years, payments to Medicare Advantage plans would be decreased, access to care would be less for seniors if they had to compete with more newly insured amidst a growing shortage of primary care physicians, out-of-pocket payments and premiums would be increased, and there was growing doubt that the legislation would "bend the cost curve down." Instead, more people became concerned that the plan would increase the deficit, contrary to the administration's and the Congressional Budget Office's projections. (To be fully paid for over ten years, the legislation delayed the start of the costly benefit increases for four years but the taxes, excise fees, and provider payment reductions were to start at the beginning of the ten-year period.)

The administration failed to convince the middle class or Medicare seniors that they would benefit from reform.

The administration and Congress were surprised by this intense opposition to PPACA. The protests were not from the healthcare industry, which came out in favor of healthcare reform, but from grassroots segments of the public, some of whom were members of the newly formed but loosely organized Tea Party. Initially these angry protests and the Tea Party were derided by most of the media, but they proved to be an early indication of the public's dissatisfaction with the proposed healthcare bill and, increasingly, with the growing role of government.

The public also became concerned about the increasing federal deficit and the government's involvement into different sectors of the economy, such as with the bailouts of the auto companies and the banks, the large amount spent on the stimulus bill, and the government "takeover" of the health sector. The public also feared that the new reform bill would not be completely paid for. There was a great deal of confusion concerning various provisions and what they meant. And many legislators admitted to not having read the complex 2,600-page draft of the legislation.

During this period, congressional Republicans and other opponents of the legislation proposed going slower on health reform, doing more to reduce rising healthcare costs before greatly expanding public and private coverage, and working to reduce the growing federal deficit. Since the bill was being crafted without Republican support, it was in their political interest to criticize the bill as the public turned against it.

Enactment of the Patient Protection and Affordable Care Act of 2010

As polls showed the legislation was losing public support, the administration believed that Democrats had more to lose politically by abandoning the health bill than by pushing it through. It was argued that in 1994 as a result of failing to pass the Clinton healthcare bill, the Democrats lost control of Congress. The administration believed that by the 2010 midterm election the public would favor the bill.

The House of Representatives finally enacted their reform bill in November 2009, but with a surprisingly close vote, 220 to 215; Democratic legislators had become fearful of their reelection prospects after the public's anger during the summer. The next step was the Senate. Attempts by the Senate finance committee chairman to devise a compromise bill delayed the Senate's vote until the end of 2009. Liberal senators were reluctant to make many concessions to achieve a broad bipartisan bill since the Democrats had a filibuster-proof majority.

To secure the 60 votes needed to withstand a Republican filibuster, it was necessary that all Senate Democrats vote in favor of the legislation. Consequently, each Democratic senator had market power; many Democratic senators were able to negotiate special deals for their constituents, several of which became publicized and derided. For example, a senator from Nebraska engineered the "Cornhusker Kickback," which stipulates that the federal government will pay 100 percent of Nebraska's Medicaid expansions in perpetuity.[6] Media publicity on some of these special deals angered the public. The Senate passed its bill in late December 2009.

The outcome of the bill, which received 60 Senate votes, had more to do with special deals than good public policy: $100 million for a particular but unnamed hospital in Connecticut, ethanol subsidies, exemption from a new insurance tax for Blue Cross Blue Shield in Michigan, increased payments for hospitals in Nevada, and so on. (All the hundreds of special deals and exemptions from taxes negotiated on behalf of groups with a concentrated interest illustrate how budget and allocation decisions are made when the government enacts a broad redistributive program and how such future decisions are likely to be influenced.)

Since the Senate bill differed in substantial ways from the House bill, the normal process would have been for the two bills to be reconciled in a House and Senate conference committee and then for the Senate and House to vote on the new compromise bill. An unexpected event derailed the normal process of using the conference committee. In a major upset, a Republican won the January special Senate election to fill the late Senator Edward Kennedy's (D-MA) seat. Senator Scott Brown (R-MA) vowed to vote against the healthcare bill. A conference committee bill could not be sent back to the Senate, where the Republicans gained their forty-first seat, sufficient to filibuster the bill. Thus the previously passed Senate bill became the basis for the legislation. To make some changes in the Senate bill desired by House leaders, a budget reconciliation bill was agreed upon between the House and Senate, which only required a simple Senate majority to pass. PPACA was enacted in March 2010.

The administration believed it could enact near universal coverage by convincing the middle class and the aged that not only would it not cost them anything but that they would benefit from the legislation—a necessary condition for a far-reaching, expensive, visible redistributive program. By the time Congress voted on the legislation, many of the middle class and aged concluded they would be better off without it.

The Administration's Objective for Healthcare Reform: A Hypothesis

The healthcare reform legislation had conflicting objectives.

- Insurance coverage was to be expanded (through increased Medicaid eligibility and tax subsidies) to an additional 32 million—yet the administration claimed it would also reduce the federal deficit.
- Insurance benefits were to be increased, although the administration said premiums would be reduced.
- The president stated that "if you are happy with your insurance, you can keep it." However, if the employer makes changes to employees' health benefits, their plan is no longer grandfathered, and they can't keep their plan. Also, payments to Medicare Advantage plans would be decreased, causing seniors to pay increased premiums or receive fewer benefits.
- Healthcare reform, it was claimed, was going to increase health plan choices, yet insurance regulations, such as minimum loss ratios, would force many plans to exit the individual market.
- Over the next ten years the rate of increase in Medicare expenditures would be reduced by almost $600 billion, but the administration stated that access and quality of care would not be affected.
- Lastly, healthcare reform was going to "bend the cost curve." Yet no consumer or provider incentives were changed that would reduce healthcare spending.

To drastically change the healthcare system, it is necessary to have political support from the middle class and the aged. Thus the administration had to promise them that they would benefit from the change.

These conflicting objectives and statements, however, do not clarify the administration's goal in proposing such a vast undertaking. If the administration just wanted to cover the uninsured, it could have done so with less change to the entire system and without a complicated bill that few legislators who voted for it even read.

One can only hypothesize what the administration's underlying objective was for healthcare reform. Coverage is to be expanded to an additional 32 million people and insurance benefits for the middle class and the aged are to be increased—at no additional cost, which should result in a great increase in demand for medical services. During this period of increased demand, the supply of medical services, such as physicians and other medical personnel, will not be similarly increased. Medical prices and expenditures would be expected to sharply increase.[7] However, the administration claimed that broad tax increases will not be needed to pay for the increased coverage or benefits, nor will the federal deficit be increased. Since the legislation does not change consumer and provider incentives to spend less money, the only way this conflicting scenario can be achieved is by imposing stringent government controls over medical prices and expenditures.[8]

Medicare expenditures have been increasing at an unsustainable rate and are an unfunded liability for the federal government. These expenditures are an increasing portion of the federal budget, leaving less money available for other federal programs, and are projected to greatly explode the federal deficit. Estimates are that Medicare benefits for current and future participants, discounted to their present value, will add $38.2 trillion to the deficit (Part A $13.8 trillion, Part B $17.2 trillion, and Part D $7.2 trillion) (Peter G. Peterson Foundation 2010). In addition, the federal government is responsible for its share of Medicaid expenditures, which were $251 billion in 2009 and are projected to increase to $542 billion in 2020, or a total of $4.426 trillion over the period from 2009 to 2020. The federal government will be unable to fund these programs without decreasing access to care and increasing taxes.

If Medicare expenditures were to be reduced by paying physicians and other providers less, providers would reallocate their time to where they can make more money; they would serve fewer Medicare patients and care for more privately insured patients, as occurs with Medicaid. Reduced access by Medicare patients would become a significant political problem. The government would have to reduce providers' incentives to serve fewer Medicare patients. To do so, providers would have to receive the same fees for serving Medicare and private patients.

Thus a proposed solution to Medicare and Medicaid's unsustainable increases in the federal deficit while preventing providers from reducing access to Medicare patients is a Canadian-type single-payer system. Everyone would have the same benefits and would be in the same system. The government would establish provider payments and control total expenditures. The aged would continue to have the same benefits (as would everyone) and no less access than anyone else.

The government-run public-option plan was meant to evolve into a single-payer system. A heavily subsidized government plan available to everyone, together with stringent regulations on private insurers, would eventually drive most insurers out of the market. Medicare, Medicaid, and the public option plan would then encompass most of the population. Remaining employer health plans would eventually be included in the single-payer system at no visible cost to the employee; the government would collect the funds from the employer.

Orzag and Emanuel (2010), two administration architects of PPACA, explain how regulation would be used to control rising medical costs.

> The most important institutional change in the ACA, however, is likely to be the establishment of the Independent Payment Advisory Board (IPAB), an independent panel of medical experts tasked with devising changes to Medicare's payment system. Beginning in January 2014, each year that Medicare's per capita costs exceed a certain threshold, the IPAB will develop and propose policies for reducing this inflation. The secretary of HHS must institute the policies unless Congress enacts alternative policies leading to equivalent savings. The threshold is a bit complex; initially, it is a combination of general and medical inflation, but in 2018 and thereafter, the cap is set at general inflation plus 1%.

The PPACA, however, prohibited the IPAB from proposing to control expenditure growth rates by changing Medicare benefits or eligibility, or increasing beneficiary cost sharing or premium percentage. The only alternative cost control measure left to the IPAB is to cut provider payments.

Limiting cost growth to a level below medical inflation is difficult to achieve. The fact that legislators regularly ignore Medicare physician payment reductions indicated by the SGR is cited by some as proof that Congress cannot cut Medicare costs. The reason for the establishment of the IPAB and why it was made so difficult for Congress to simply override its recommendations is that legislators would be unable, politically, to reduce benefits or provider payments.

If the IPAB is able to reduce Medicare's payment rates but not private payers' rates, the gap between Medicare rates and private rates will increase and providers will be less likely to serve Medicare patients. To prevent physicians from abandoning Medicare patients, prices in the private market would have to be similarly controlled through the adoption of a single-payer system.

The Years Ahead

The purpose of visible redistributive legislation is to be able to provide politically powerful groups with benefits in excess of their costs. The only way this can be achieved is if the government legislates it. The Obama administration was able to receive the political support for its healthcare reform legislation from most groups with a concentrated interest, such as the AHA, the AMA, the pharmaceutical industry, and the unions. However, the administration failed to convince two crucially important constituencies, the middle class and the aged, that they would benefit without incurring any additional cost. Healthcare reform has to impose increased cost, such as higher taxes, fewer benefits, or reduced access, on some population groups if increased benefits are to be provided to others, such as the uninsured and those with low incomes. The administration tried to convince the middle class and aged that they can keep what they have at no additional cost.

The middle class and the aged feared they would be worse off than before. For broad visible redistribution to occur, general agreement is needed from the middle class and the aged; if not, it will eventually be changed. This is what occurred with the Medicare Catastrophic Act of 1988, which was repealed the following year.

PPACA expands coverage but, except for the tax on Cadillac plans (which is set high and will not take effect till 2018), the bill does little to change the fundamental incentives that drive healthcare cost increases. Expanding access to an additional 32 million and increasing benefits to others, without changing consumer or provider incentives, while claiming costs will be lower, is irreconcilable.

It is difficult to predict how the healthcare reform legislation will change over time. Many parts of the bill do not become effective for a number of years, and many regulations have yet to be written. Whether the government exercises greater control over the financing and delivery of medical services as enacted in the bill or whether the bill is drastically changed to include patient and provider incentives in a more competitive medical marketplace remains to be seen. Unless the legislation is significantly changed, the probability of moving toward a single-payer system will be greatly increased.

Many employers may decide it is less costly to pay a tax per employee than provide more comprehensive benefits mandated by the law, thereby expanding the number of employees buying insurance from a health plan on the insurance exchanges. Although opposition in the Senate to the public option resulted in its exclusion from the final bill, regulations imposed on the health insurance industry may result in the same outcome. Stringent minimum medical loss ratios will cause greater consolidation of the insurance industry, as small insurers are unable to meet those minimums. Elimination of preexisting condition exclusions and minor penalties for not buying insurance will increase adverse selection and insurer losses. Stringent government reviews of insurers' premium increases and the possible exclusion of insurers from participating in the insurance exchanges for "unjustified" premium increases are likely to lead to more insurers exiting the market.

Having too few private insurers, as a result of government regulation, is likely to renew administration calls for a public plan to increase choice and competition. The bill states that at least one nonprofit plan must be made available on the insurance exchanges; these nonprofit plans, which are likely to be no different from a public plan, will require subsidies to start, as well as ongoing subsidies, given the stringent insurance regulations. Remaining private insurers are unlikely to be able to compete against these subsidized plans; they will either exit the market or become similar to regulated public utilities.

The above scenario is just one of many that may occur. Only time will tell.

Discussion Questions

1. What are alternative hypotheses regarding what national health insurance should achieve?
2. Why are groups that have a concentrated interest in particular legislation likely to be more influential in the policy process than groups that have a diffuse interest in the legislation's outcome?
3. What are the conflicting objectives of healthcare reform?
4. How did President Obama try to convince the middle class that they would benefit from healthcare reform at no additional cost?
5. What benefits did the health reform legislation provide for the aged?
6. Why were many aged opposed to the healthcare reform plan?
7. What aspects of the public option plan concerned health insurers?
8. Why are health insurers concerned that even without the public option being explicitly included in the legislation, a government-run health plan may still occur?

Notes

1. Regressive taxation occurs when the tax represents a greater percent of income for lower-income groups than for higher-income groups. A payroll tax of a flat dollar amount or a percentage of income up to a certain level of income will result in higher-income groups paying a smaller percent of their income than those with lower incomes.
2. Another example of AARP's possible conflict of interest was the Medicare Catastrophic Act of 1988, which provided seniors with a prescription drug

benefit and financed it by increasing taxes on higher-income aged. The AARP's endorsement convinced legislators that seniors would be pleased by their efforts. The AARP offered drug plans and stood to make a great deal of money from the increase in demand for such plans. Many seniors, however, were so upset with the financing provisions that Congress repealed the law the following year.

3. Persons whose tax credit exceeds their tax liabilities would receive a refund for the difference. For those with little or no tax liability the tax credit is essentially a voucher for a health plan.

4. While claiming that the public option would create needed competition to insurers, various provisions in the bill were expected to *reduce* the number of competing insurers and reduce choice of coverage, suggesting that its advocates were really opposed to increasing competitive forces in healthcare. The successful competition among private firms to deliver the Medicare Part D drug benefit, which reduced premiums, was to be limited by requiring competing firms to only offer one, rather than multiple, drug plans. Regulations imposed on insurers, such as specifying minimum loss ratios, standard benefit plans, and review of premium increases, all belie the notion that increased competition was truly desired by the bill's proponents.

5. One study estimated that about 140 million would switch to the public option. As the public option was unacceptable to various senators, compromises were made with respect to payment rates (Medicare rates plus 5 percent), having state-level plans rather than a national plan, and restricting eligibility to join the plan, permitting only those not eligible for public or employer insurance (Halpin and Harbage 2010).

6. When Republicans complained about special deals being included in the bill, Harry Reid, the Senate majority leader, replied, "There's a hundred senators here, and I don't know if there is a senator that doesn't have something in this bill that was important to them. If they don't have something in it important to them, then it doesn't speak well of them. That's what this legislation is all about. It's the art of compromise" (Pear 2010).

7. A recent study by the Office of the Actuary claims that medical expenditures will be greater, not less, under healthcare reform (Sisko et al. 2010).

8. Included in the new law are various approaches to control medical costs, such as eliminating fraud and waste (which has been proposed by various administrations), greater use of electronic medical records, and new pilot programs, such as developing accountable care organizations, bundled payment, and comparative effectiveness research. Although these programs may have promise, it has not been shown that they can control costs.

A BRIEF SUMMARY OF THE PATIENT PROTECTION AND AFFORDABLE CARE ACT (PPACA) OF 2010

I n 2010 President Obama and large Democratic majorities in the House and Senate, without any support from House or Senate Republicans, were able to enact healthcare legislation that has been described as the most far-reaching health legislation since Medicare and Medicaid were enacted in 1965. This law, the Patient Protection and Affordable Care Act (PPACA), which will affect everyone in one way or another, is very complex.[1] Many legislative aspects of the law have yet to be specified in greater detail, and over the next year regulations will have to be written to define how various programs will be implemented, such as the insurance exchanges.

The following describes the basic elements of the law, much of which will not take effect until 2014 and not be completely phased in until 2019.[2]

Coverage

Medicaid Expansions

States are required to expand their Medicaid programs by covering individuals and families up to 133 percent of the federal poverty level (FPL), effective 2014. The federal government will pay 100 percent of the cost of Medicaid expansion in 2014–2016; thereafter the federal share will decline to 90 percent in 2020 and beyond. (For individuals 133 percent of the federal poverty level is $14,404, and for a family it is $29,326.)

The federal government will pay the states to increase fees to those physicians providing primary care services to at least 100 percent of the Medicare payment rate for the years 2013 and 2014.

An Individual (and an Employer) Mandate

Individuals must obtain minimum essential coverage for themselves and their families, effective 2014. Failure to do so will result in a tax of $95 in 2014, increasing to $695 by 2016 and beyond (indexed for inflation). The tax might alternatively be a percentage of income, 0.1 percent in 2014 up to 2.5 percent of taxable income in 2016. (The maximum tax will be $2,085 in 2016). Individuals who qualify on hardship grounds are exempt from the tax.

Employers with *more than 50 employees* must offer qualified coverage to their employees. If an employer does not offer qualified coverage and has at least one employee receiving a premium tax credit, the employer is fined $2,000 multiplied by the number of employees (excluding the first 30 employees).

A qualified health plan limits cost sharing to the high-deductible plan limit, limits the annual deductible for small group market plans to $2,000 (individual) and $4,000 (family), and does not require cost sharing for preventive services or immunizations.

Individual Tax Credits

Individuals and families with incomes between 133 percent and 400 percent of the federal poverty level who want to purchase their own insurance on an insurance exchange will receive premium credits and cost-sharing reductions on a sliding scale and as a percent of income. (Four hundred percent of the federal poverty level is $43,320 for individuals and $88,200 for a family of four). For example, a family with income at 400 percent of the FPL would pay 9.5 percent of its income, or $8,379.

Small Business Tax Credits

Small firms can receive tax credits equal to 50 percent of the amount paid for their employees' health coverage if they have 25 or fewer employees with average annual wages below $50,000, effective 2010.

Medicare Prescription Drug Benefit (Part D)

The Medicare "doughnut hole," which refers to the point in coverage where seniors pay 100 percent of the costs of drugs, was reduced by 50 percent in 2011, and by 2020 that gap will be eliminated. Seniors who reach the doughnut hole in 2010 will receive a $250 rebate.

Medicare Preventive Services

The legislation waives cost sharing for preventive services, such as prostate, colon, and breast cancer screenings, and provides seniors access to a comprehensive health risk assessment.

Public Health and Workforce Issues

The federal government will finance various grant, loan, and funding programs for healthcare professionals. Also included is funding for community health centers ($11 billion).

Health Insurance Changes

Dependent Coverage

Insurers that offer dependent coverage must allow uninsured children to remain on or join their parent's coverage until age 26, regardless of whether the child has a pre-existing condition, effective 2010. Insurers can increase the premium for adding the dependent child.

Also, people in their 20s will have the option of buying a catastrophic plan ($6,000 out-of-pocket expenses before coverage begins) that has lower premiums, starting in 2014.

Preventive Services

Insurers must offer preventive services and immunizations, without cost sharing, effective 2010.

Guaranteed Issue

Insurers will be barred from rejecting applicants based on health status, medical condition or history, or genetic information once the exchanges become effective in 2014. (This is the elimination of the pre-existing conditions exclusion).

High-Risk Pools

Until the health insurance exchanges become available in 2014, a temporary high-risk insurance pool will be available for uninsured people who have been denied coverage by insurers because of a pre-existing medical condition, effective 2010.

Medical Loss Ratio (MLR)

Group plans must have a medical loss ratio not less than 85 percent and individual plans not less than 80 percent, effective 2011.

Insurance Rating (Pricing)

Differential prices cannot be based on health or gender, effective 2014. Insurance prices can only vary according to family composition and geography, tobacco use (limited to a ratio of 1.5:1), and age (limited to a ratio of 3:1).

Insurer Rate Review

Insurers will be required to submit justifications for premium increases, effective 2011. Plans with "excessive" rate increases will be prohibited from participating in the insurance exchanges, effective 2014.

Health Insurance Exchanges

States are required to set up an insurance exchange by 2014 that will facilitate the purchase of "qualified" health plans. The exchange can only be a government agency or a nonprofit organization.

Health insurance plans in the individual and small group market must provide the "essential" benefits package beginning in 2014. Four benefit categories of plans will be offered on the exchange. All plans offered on the exchange must include basic medical services and will be one of four types—bronze, silver, gold, or platinum—based on their coverage. The bronze plan would cover 60 percent of the benefit costs, silver would cover 70 percent, gold 80 percent, and platinum 90 percent.

A catastrophic plan will be available on the exchange for those under age 30. The catastrophic plan includes a deductible equal to the high-deductible health plan limit; three primary care visits and preventive care are to be included in the plan with no cost sharing.

Small employers (100 or fewer employees) are eligible to use the exchange and, with state permission, so are employers with more than 100 employees. Qualified individuals are also eligible to use the exchange.

Long-Term Care

A new voluntary long-term care program is established for the purpose of purchasing community living assistance services and supports (CLASS Act). After a five-year vesting period the program will provide individuals with functional limitations a cash benefit of not less than $50 per day to purchase non-medical services and supports necessary to maintain a community residence. All working adults will be automatically enrolled in the program unless they choose to opt out, effective 2011.

How the Health Benefits and Coverage Are Financed

The increased government expenditures called for in the legislation were estimated to be paid for by increased taxes on individuals and different segments of the health industry and $500 billion in Medicare payment reductions to different providers. Newly established institutes were established in the expectation that they would eventually be able to reduce rising healthcare costs, but no specific estimate of potential savings was included.

Individual Income Taxes

The Medicare payroll tax is increased to 2.35 percent, up from the current 1.45 percent, on individuals earning more than $200,000 and families earning over $250,000, effective for the 2013 tax year. The income amounts are not adjusted for inflation.

In addition, a 3.8 percent Medicare tax is imposed on all unearned income, such as investment income, dividends, royalties, capital gains, etc., for individuals earning more than $200,000 and families earning over $250,000, effective for the 2013 tax year. The income amounts are not adjusted for inflation.

Reduced Medicare Healthcare Provider Payments

All Medicare providers will have their annual provider payment updates reduced, either as a result of changes in their market basket updates or by an assumed productivity increase, which would reduce annual update payments, effective 2011. Physicians are provided with a financial incentive to participate in a quality reporting system and are penalized if they do not participate by 2015.

Medicare Advantage Plans

Medicare Advantage plans had been receiving payments in excess of the costs of treating comparable (risk-adjusted) Medicare beneficiaries in traditional (fee-for-service) Medicare; these additional payments will be reduced effective 2012.

Excise Tax on High-Cost Health Plans ("Cadillac" Plans)

A 40 percent tax will be imposed on health coverage that exceeds $10,200 for individuals and $27,500 for families (thereafter indexed for inflation), effective 2018. Stand-alone dental and vision plans are not subject to the tax.

Health Insurance Industry User Fee

An annual fee will be imposed on the health insurance industry of $8 billion in 2014 rising to $14.3 billion in 2018 and increasing by the rate of growth in premiums thereafter.

Medical Device Industry Excise Tax

A 2.3 percent excise tax is imposed on all medical devices sold in the United States, effective in the 2013 tax year.

Prescription Drug Industry User Fee

An annual fee is imposed on manufacturers of brand name prescription drugs of $2.5 billion in 2011, increasing to $4.1 billion in 2018, then $2.8 billion in 2019 and beyond.

Medical Expense Deduction
The medical expense deduction threshold for claiming the itemized deduction for medical expenses is increased from 7.5 percent to 10 percent, effective 2013.

Employer Tax Deduction for Medicare Part D Expenses
The tax deduction for employers who receive Medicare Part D drug subsidy payments will be eliminated effective 2013.

Health Savings Accounts (HSAs)
A 20 percent tax is imposed on funds from those accounts that are not used for medical expenses, effective 2011.

Flexible Spending Accounts (FSAs)
FSA contributions are limited to $2,500 per year adjusted for inflation, effective 2013.

Medicare Fraud and Abuse
Compliance programs are required of all Medicare providers, and funds will be allocated to combat fraud and abuse.

Cost-Containment Approaches
The legislation does not list any specific cost-containment approaches.

Independent Payment Advisory Board (IPAB)
An IPAB is established to develop and submit proposals to Congress aimed at extending the solvency of Medicare, slowing growth in costs, improving quality of care, and reducing national health expenditures. Congress constrained the board's options in that the board cannot include recommendations to ration healthcare, raise revenues by increasing premiums, increase beneficiary cost sharing, or restrict benefits. Options available to the board to reduce Medicare expenditures may include reductions in provider payments, changing the age of eligibility, or changing the benefits offered.

The IPAB's proposals will be automatically implemented unless Congress opposes them. Proposals to modify Medicare payments will be effective starting in 2015 (2020 for hospitals).

Comparative Effectiveness Research
The Patient-Centered Outcomes Research Institute is established to identify national priorities for comparative clinical effectiveness research. The institute is prohibited from mandating coverage or reimbursement policies based on its research.

Other Legislative Initiatives

Accountable Care Organizations (ACOs)

Medicare will establish a shared savings program to promote accountability and coordination of Medicare Parts A and B. Groups of providers who meet certain criteria will be recognized as ACOs and become eligible to share in the cost savings achieved by Medicare.

Medicare Payment Innovations

In 2011 Medicare established the Center for Medicare and Medicaid Innovation to test, evaluate, and expand different payment structures and methodologies.

The government will develop a national, voluntary, bundled-payment pilot program to provide incentives for providers to coordinate care, effective 2013.

The IPAB will test medical home models.

Specialty Hospitals

New or expanded physician-owned specialty hospitals are prohibited as of 2010; existing physician-owned specialty hospitals are grandfathered in.

Medicare Quality and Transparency Initiatives

Several approaches are proposed to increase quality reporting and transparency.

Notes

1. The Kaiser Family Foundation website has a detailed summary of the Patient Protection and Affordable Care Act. http://www.kff.org/healthreform/upload/8061.pdf.
2. A contentious issue in the healthcare debate was that the cost of the bill should not add to the federal deficit over a ten-year period. Thus various taxes used to finance the bill start at the beginning of the ten-year period, while much of the cost is postponed until 2014.

GLOSSARY

actual versus list price—Actual prices are the fees collected or paid for a particular good or service. The difference between actual and list prices are provider discounts, which vary by type of payer.

actuarially fair insurance—Insurance in which expected payments (benefits) are equivalent to premiums paid by beneficiaries (plus a competitive loading charge).

adverse selection—Occurs when high-risk individuals have more information on their health status than the insurer and are thus able to buy insurance at a premium based on a lower-risk group.

all-payer system—A system in which each payer pays the same charges for hospital and medical services.

American Medical Association (AMA)—A national organization established in 1897 to represent the collective interests of physicians.

antitrust laws—A body of legislation that promotes competition in the US economy.

any-willing-provider (AWP) laws—Laws that lessen price competition in that they permit any physician to have access to a health plan's enrollees at the negotiated price. Because physicians cannot be assured of having a greater number of enrollees in return for discounting their prices, physicians have no incentive to compete on price to be included in the health plan's network.

assignment/participation—An agreement whereby a provider accepts an approved fee from a third-party payer and is not permitted to charge the patient more, except for the appropriate copayment fees.

balance billing—When the physician collects from the patient the difference between the third-party payer's approved fee and the physician's fee.

barriers to entry—Obstacles, which may be legal (e.g., licensing laws and patents) or economic (e.g., economies of scale), that limit entry into an industry.

benefit–premium ratio—The percentage of the total premium paid out in benefits to each insured group divided by the price of insurance. (Also referred to as the medical loss ratio.)

breakthrough (or innovator) drug—The first brand-name drug to use a particular therapeutic mechanism, that is, to use a particular method of treating a given disease.

budget neutral—When total payments to providers under a new payment system are set equal to what was spent under the previous payment system.

Canadian-type health system—A form of national health insurance in which medical services are free to everyone and providers are paid by the government. Expenditure limits are used to restrict the growth in medical use and costs.

capitation incentive—When a provider is capitated, he becomes concerned with the coordination of all medical services, providing care in the least-costly manner, monitoring the cost of enrollees' hospital use, increasing physician productivity, prescribing less-costly drugs, and being innovative in the delivery of medical services. A more negative aspect of capitation is that the provider has an incentive to reduce use of services and decrease patient access.

capitation payment—A risk-sharing arrangement in which a provider group receives a predetermined fixed payment per member per month in return for providing all of the contracted services.

case-mix index—A measure of the relative complexity of a patient mix treated in a given medical care setting.

certificate-of-need (CON) laws—State laws requiring healthcare providers to receive prior approval from a state agency for capital expenditures exceeding certain predetermined levels. CON laws are an entry barrier.

coinsurance—A fixed percentage of a medical provider's fee paid by the insurance beneficiary at the point of service.

copayment—A specific dollar amount paid by the patient at the point of service.

community rating—A rating that sets an insurance premium at the same level to all of the insured, regardless of their claims experience or risk group.

competitive market—The interaction between a large number of buyers and suppliers, where no single seller or buyer can influence the market price.

concentrated interest—When some regulation or legislation has a sufficiently large effect on a group to make it worthwhile for that group to invest resources to either forestall or promote that effect.

consumer-driven healthcare (CDHC)—When consumers purchase high-deductible health insurance and bear greater responsibility for their use of medical services and the prices they pay healthcare providers.

consumer sovereignty—When consumers, rather than health professionals or the government, choose the goods and services they can purchase with their incomes.

cost-containment program—A program that reduces healthcare costs, such as through utilization review and patient cost sharing.

cost shifting—The belief that providers charge a higher price to privately insured patients because some payers, such as Medicaid or the uninsured, do not pay their full costs.

declining marginal productivity of health inputs—The situation that exists when additional contribution to output of a health input declines as more of that input is used.

deductible—The flat dollar amount consumers pay for medical services before their insurance picks up all or part of the remainder of the price of that service.

diagnosis-related group (DRG)—A method of reimbursement established under Medicare to pay hospitals based on a fixed price per admission according to the diagnosis for which the patient is admitted.

diffuse cost—When the burden of a tax or program is spread over a large population and is relatively small per person, so that the per person cost of opposing such a burden exceeds the actual size of the burden on the person.

economic theory of government—A theory of legislative and regulatory outcomes that assumes political markets are no different from economic markets in that organized groups seek to further their self-interests.

economies of scale—The relationship between cost per unit and size of firm. As firm size increases, cost per unit falls, reaches a minimum, and eventually rises. In a competitive market each firm operates at the size that has the lowest per unit costs. For a given size market, the larger the firm size required to achieve the minimum costs of production, the fewer the number of firms that will be able to compete.

economies of scope—When it is less costly for a firm to produce certain services (or products) jointly than if separate firms produced each of the same services independently.

employer-mandated health insurance—Under this health reform plan, all employers are required to purchase medical insurance for their employees or pay a specified amount per employee into a state fund.

experience rating—When insurance premiums are based on the claims experience or risk level, such as age, of each insured group.

externality—When an action undertaken by an individual (or firm) has secondary effects on others, and these effects are not taken into account by the normal operations of the price system.

fee-for-service payment—A method of payment for medical care services in which payment is made for each unit of service provided.

free choice of provider—This was included in the original Medicare and Medicaid legislation and specified that all beneficiaries had to have access to all providers. This precluded closed provider panels and capitated HMOs. Economists consider the provision to be anticompetitive in that it limits competition; beneficiaries could not choose a closed provider panel in return for lower prices or increased benefits.

gatekeeper—In many HMOs the primary care physician, or "gatekeeper," is responsible for the administration of the patient's treatment and must coordinate and authorize all medical services, laboratory studies, specialty referrals, and hospitalizations.

generic drug—A copy of a breakthrough drug that the FDA judges to be comparable in terms of such factors as strength, quality, and therapeutic effectiveness. Generic drugs are sold after the patent on a brand-name drug has expired and generally under their chemical names.

geographic market definition—Used in antitrust analysis; determines the relevant market in which a healthcare provider competes. The broader the geographic market, the greater the number of substitutes available to the purchaser, and hence the smaller the market share of merging firms.

guaranteed issue—A requirement that insurers offer health insurance to anyone willing to purchase it.

guaranteed renewal—The requirement that health insurers renew all health insurance policies within standard rate bands, thereby precluding insurers from dropping individuals or groups who incur high medical costs.

health maintenance organization (HMO)—A type of managed care plan that offers prepaid comprehensive healthcare coverage for hospital and physician services. The HMO relies on its medical providers to minimize the cost of providing medical services. HMOs contract with or directly employ participating healthcare providers. Enrollees must pay the full cost of receiving services from nonnetwork providers.

health savings account (HSA)—Enacted as part of the Medicare Modernization Act, health savings accounts allow users to accumulate money tax free to be used toward healthcare expenses. The unused portion of the savings account can accumulate over time.

horizontal merger—When two or more firms from the same market merge to form one firm.

income elasticity—The percentage change in quantity that occurs with a given percentage change in income. When the percentage change in quantity exceeds the percentage change in income, the service is income "elastic."

indemnity insurance—Medical insurance that pays the provider or the patient a predetermined amount for the medical service provided.

independent practice association (IPA)—A physician-owned and physician-controlled contracting organization comprising solo and small groups of physicians (on a nonexclusive basis) that enables physicians to contract with payers on a unified basis.

individual mandate—A proposed national health insurance plan under which individuals are required to buy a specified minimum level of health insurance (catastrophic insurance). Refundable tax credits are provided to those who have incomes below a certain level.

insurance premium—The amount of money an insured pays to the insurance company. The premium consists of two parts: the expected medical expense of the insured group and the loading charge, which includes administrative expenses and profit.

integrated delivery system (IDS)—A healthcare delivery system that includes or contracts with all of the relevant healthcare providers to provide coordinated medical services to a patient. An IDS also views itself as being responsible for the health status of its enrolled population.

law of demand—A decrease in price will result in an increase in quantity demanded, other factors affecting demand held constant.

managed care organization (MCO)—An organization that controls medical care costs and quality through provider price discounts, utilization management, drug formularies, and the profiling of participating providers according to their appropriate use of medical services.

mandated benefits—Specific medical services, providers, or population groups that must be included in health insurance policies according to state insurance laws.

marginal benefit—The change in total benefits from purchasing one additional unit of a healthcare service or good.

marginal contribution of medical care to health—The increase in health status resulting from an additional increment of medical services.

marginal cost—The change in total costs from producing one additional unit.

Medicaid—A health insurance program financed by federal and state governments and administered by the states for qualifying segments of the low-income population.

Medicaid risk contract—A Medicaid managed care program in which an HMO contracts to provide medical services in return for a capitation premium.

medical care price index—A measure of the rate of inflation in medical care prices; calculated by the Bureau of Labor Statistics and included as part of the Consumer Price Index.

medical group—A group of physicians who coordinate their activities in one or more facilities and share common overhead expenses; medical records; and professional, technical, and administrative staffs.

medical loss ratio—See *benefit–premium ratio*.

Medicare—A federally sponsored and supervised health insurance plan for the elderly. *Part A* provides hospital insurance for inpatient care, home health agency visits, hospice, and skilled nursing facilities. The aged are responsible for a deductible but do not have to pay an annual premium. *Part B* provides payments for physician services, physician-ordered supplies and services, and outpatient hospital services. Part B is voluntary, and the aged pay an annual premium that is 25 percent of the cost of the program in addition to a deductible and copayment. *Part C* permits private health plans to compete for serving the aged. *Part D* is a new prescription drug benefit that includes deductibles and copayments and requires a monthly premium.

Medicare Advantage plans—Enacted as part of the Medicare Modernization Act, private health plans that receive a monthly capitation payment from Medicare and accept full financial risk for the cost of all medical benefits (Part A, Part B, and Part D services) to which their enrollees are entitled. Enrollees using nonparticipating providers are responsible for the full charges of such providers. Previously referred to as Medicare+Choice plans.

Medicare risk contract—See *Medicare Advantage plans.*

Medigap insurance policy—Insurance policy privately purchased by the elderly to supplement Medicare coverage by covering deductibles and copayments.

"me-too" drug—A brand-name drug that uses the same therapeutic mechanism as a breakthrough drug and thus directly competes with it.

monopoly—A market structure in which there is a single seller of a product that has no close substitutes.

moral hazard—Occurs when an individual changes his behavior toward a risk when he is insured against that risk, as when a patient is less careful with his health because he knows his health insurance will pay for his care if he becomes ill.

multihospital system—A system in which a corporation owns, leases, or manages two or more acute care hospitals.

multipayer system—A system in which reimbursement for medical services is made by multiple third-party payers.

multiple-source drug—A drug available in both brand-name and generic versions from a variety of manufacturers.

network HMO—A type of HMO that signs contracts with a number of group practices to provide medical services.

nonprice hospital competition—When hospitals compete on the basis of their facilities and services and the latest technology rather than on price.

not-for-profit—An institution that cannot distribute profits to shareholders and is tax exempt.

nurse participation rate—The percentage of trained nurses who are employed.

opportunity costs—Relevant costs for economic decision making; they include explicit and implicit costs. For example, the opportunity costs of a medical education include the forgone income the student could have earned had she not gone to medical school.

out-of-pocket price—The amount a beneficiary must pay after all other payments have been considered by his health plan.

over-the-counter drug—A drug that is available for public purchase and self-directed use without a prescription.

patient dumping—A situation in which high-cost patients are not admitted to or are discharged early from a hospital because the patient has no insurance or the amount reimbursed by the third-party payer will be less than the cost of caring for that patient.

pay for performance—A system in which higher payments are made to those healthcare providers who demonstrate that they provide higher-quality services.

per diem payment—A method of payment to institutional providers that is based on a fixed daily amount and does not differ according to the level of service provided.

pharmacy benefit manager (PBM)—Firm that provides administrative services and processes outpatient prescription drug claims for health insurers' prescription drug plans.

physician agency relationship—The relationship between a physician and a patient characterized by the fact that the physician acts on behalf of the patient. Agency relationships may be perfect or imperfect, and the method of physician payment—fee-for-service or capitation—produces different behavioral responses among imperfect physician agents.

physician hospital organization (PHO)—An organization in which hospitals and their medical staffs develop group practice arrangements that allow the hospitals to seek contracts from HMOs and other carriers on behalf of the physicians and hospitals together.

play or pay—Under this form of national health insurance (also referred to as an employer mandate), employers are required to provide some basic level of medical insurance to their employees ("play") or pay a certain amount per employee into a government pool that would provide the employees with insurance.

point-of-service plan—A plan that allows the beneficiary to select from participating providers (the health plan) or use nonparticipating providers and pay a high copayment.

portability—A characteristic of health insurance that enables the insured to change jobs without losing his insurance or being liable for another preexisting exclusion period. Portability was mandated as part of heath reform.

preexisting exclusion—An insurance clause that excludes treatment for any or specified illnesses that have been diagnosed within the previous (usually) 12 months. Insurers use such clauses to protect themselves against adverse selection by new enrollees.

preferred provider organization (PPO)—An arrangement between a panel of healthcare providers and purchasers of healthcare services in which a closed panel of providers agrees to supply services to a defined group of patients on a discounted fee-for-service basis. This type of plan offers its members a limited number of physicians and hospitals, negotiated fee schedules, utilization review, and incentives to use PPO-participating providers.

preferred risk selection—Attempts by insurers to attract only group plan enrollees with lower risks, whose expected medical costs would be less than the group's average premium. This occurs when insurers receive the same premium for everyone in an insured group.

prescription drug—A drug that can be obtained only with a physician's order.

price discrimination—The practice of charging different purchasers different prices according to the purchaser's elasticity of demand (willingness to pay) for the same or a similar service. An ability to price discriminate indicates monopoly power by a provider.

price elasticity—The percentage change in quantity divided by the percentage change in price. When the percentage change in quantity exceeds the percentage change in price, the service is price "elastic."

primary care physician—A physician who coordinates all of the routine medical care needs of an individual. Typically, this type of physician specializes in family practice, internal medicine, pediatrics, or obstetrics/gynecology.

process measures of quality—A type of quality assessment that evaluates process of care by measuring the specific way in which care is provided or, with respect to health manpower, the educational requirements.

product market definition—A description of a product's or service's market. Used in antitrust cases to determine whether the product or service in question has close substitutes, which depends on the willingness of purchasers to use other services if the relative prices change. The closer the substitutes, the smaller the market share of the product being examined.

prospective payment system (PPS)—A method of payment for medical services in which providers are paid a predetermined rate for the services rendered regardless of the actual costs of care incurred. Medicare uses a PPS for hospital care based on a fixed price per hospital admission (by diagnosis).

public-interest theory of government—A theory that assumes that legislation is enacted to serve the public interest. According to this theory the two basic objectives of government are to improve market efficiency and, based on a societal value judgment, redistribute income.

pure premium—The expected claims experience for an insured group, exclusive of the loading charge. The pure premium for an individual is calculated by multiplying the size of the loss by the probability the loss will occur.

redistribution—When, as a result of public policy, the benefits and costs to a person are not equal. For example, based on a societal value judgment that those with higher incomes should be taxed to provide for those with lower incomes, the benefits and costs are not equal for either of the groups affected.

refundable tax credit—A proposal for national health insurance under which individuals would be given a tax credit to purchase health insurance. The tax credit may be income related (i.e., declining at higher levels of income). Persons whose tax credit exceeds their tax liabilities would receive a refund for the difference. For those with little or no tax liability the tax credit would essentially be a voucher for a health plan.

regressive tax—A tax that costs those with lower incomes a higher portion of their income than it costs those with higher incomes.

report card—Standardized data representing process and outcome measures of quality that are collected by independent organizations to enable purchasers to make more informed choices of health plans and their participating providers.

resource-based relative value scale (RBRVS)—The current Medicare fee-for-service payment system for physicians, initiated in 1992, under which each physician service is assigned a relative value based on the presumed resource costs of performing that service. The relative value for each service is then multiplied by a conversion factor (in dollars) to arrive at the physician's fee.

risk-adjusted premium—An insurance premium adjusted by an employer to reflect the risk levels of the employees.

risk pool—A population group defined by its expected claim experience.

risk selection—What occurs when insurers attempt to attract a more favorable risk group than the average risk group, which was the basis for the group's premium (preferred risk selection). Similarly, enrollees may seek to join a health plan at a premium that reflects a lower level of risk than their own (adverse selection).

rule of reason—A doctrine in antitrust cases that only activities (such as mergers) that unreasonably restrain trade should be prohibited.

second opinion—A utilization-review approach in which decisions to initiate a medical intervention are reviewed by two physicians.

self-funding self-insurance—A healthcare program in which employers fund benefit plans from their own resources without purchasing insurance. Self-funded plans may be self-administered, or the employer may contract with an outside administrator for an administrative-service-only arrangement. Employers who self-fund can limit their liability via stop-loss insurance.

single payer—A form of national health insurance in which a single third-party payer, usually the government, pays healthcare providers and the entire population has free choice of all providers at zero (or little) out-of-pocket expense.

single-source drug—A brand name drug that is still under patent and thus is usually available from only one manufacturer.

skilled nursing facility—A long-term-care facility that provides inpatient skilled nursing care and rehabilitation services.

specialty PPO—A type of PPO that offers one or more limited healthcare services or benefits, such as anesthesia, vision, or dental services.

staff-model HMO—A type of HMO that hires salaried physicians to provide healthcare services on an exclusive basis to the HMO's enrollees.

stop-loss insurance—Insurance coverage providing protection from losses resulting from claims greater than a specific dollar amount (equivalent to a large deductible).

supplier-induced demand—When physicians modify their diagnosis and treatment to favorably affect their own economic well-being.

sustainable growth rate (SGR)—The rate at which Medicare expenditures on physician payments may increase. The formula consists of four elements: the percentage increase in real GDP per capita, the inflation rate of physician fees, the annual percentage increase in Part B enrollees, and the percentage change in spending for physicians' services resulting from changes in laws and regulations (e.g., expanded Medicare coverage for preventive services).

target income hypothesis—A model of supplier-induced demand that assumes physicians will induce demand only to the extent they will achieve a target income, which is determined by the local income distribution, particularly with respect to the relative incomes of other physicians and professionals in the area.

tax-exempt employer-paid health insurance—Health insurance purchased by the employer on behalf of its employees that is not considered to be taxable income to the employee. By not taxing health insurance benefits, the government essentially lowers the price of insurance, thus increasing the quantity demanded (and increasing its comprehensiveness). The major beneficiaries are those in higher income-tax brackets.

tertiary care—Care that includes the most complex services, such as transplantation, open-heart surgery, and burn treatment, provided in inpatient hospital settings.

third-party administrator (TPA)—An independent entity that provides administrative services, such as claims processing, to a company that self-insures. A third-party administrator does not underwrite the risk.

third-party payer—An organization, such as an HMO, insurance company, or government agency, that pays for all or part of an insured's medical services.

triple-option health plan—A type of health plan in which employees may choose from an HMO, a PPO, or an indemnity plan depending on how much they are willing to contribute.

unbundling—When a provider charges separately for each of the services previously provided together as part of a treatment.

uncompensated care—Services rendered by a provider without reimbursement, as in the case of charity care and bad debts.

universal coverage—When the entire population is eligible for medical services or health insurance.

up-coding—When a provider bills for a higher-priced diagnosis or service than the service actually provided.

usual, customary, and reasonable fee—A method of reimbursement in which the fee is "usual" in that physician's office, "customary" in that community, and "reasonable" in terms of the distribution of all physician charges for that service in the community.

vacancy rate—The percentage of a hospital's budgeted RN positions that are unfilled.

vertical integration—The organization of a delivery system that provides an entire range of services, including inpatient care, ambulatory care clinics, outpatient surgery, and home care.

vertical merger—A merger between two firms that have a supplier–buyer relationship.

virtual integration—The organization of a delivery system that relies on contractual relationships rather than complete ownership to provide all medical services required by the patient.

voluntary performance standard—An expenditure target adopted by the Medicare program in 1992 to limit the rate of increase in its expenditures for physicians' services. This was replaced by the SGR formula as part of the Balanced Budget Act of 1997.

REFERENCES

Abadie, A., and S. Gay. 2006. "The Impact of Presumed Consent Legislation on Cadaveric Organ Donation: A Cross-Country Study." *Journal of Health Economics* 25 (4): 599–620.

Adams, C., and V. Brantner. 2006. "Estimating the Cost of New Drug Development: Is It Really $802 Million?" *Health Affairs* 25 (2): 420–28.

Agency for Healthcare Research and Quality (AHRQ). 2010. *Health Insurance Coverage of the Civilian Noninstitutionalized Population: Percent by Type of Coverage and Selected Population Characteristics, United States, First Half of 2009*, table 1. [Online information; retrieved 4/19/11.] www.meps.ahrq.gov/mepsweb/data_stats/ summ_tables/hc/hlth_insr/2009/t1_a09.pdf

Aiken, L., J. Buchan, J. Sochalski, B. Nichols, and M. Powell. 2004. "Trends in International Nurse Migration." *Health Affairs* 23 (3): 69–77.

Allen, K. G. 2005. "Medicaid: States' Efforts to Maximize Federal Reimbursements Highlight Need for Improved Federal Oversight." Testimony Before the Committee on Finance, US Senate. GAO-05-836T. June 28, 1–27.

Allen, S., and M. Bombardieri. 2009. "Much Is Given by Hospitals, More Is Asked." [Online article; retrieved 4/6/11.] www.boston.com/news/local/massachusetts/ articles/2009/05/31/much_is_given_by_hospitals_more_is_asked/

American Association of Colleges of Nursing (AACN). 2010a. "Amid Calls for More Highly Educated Nurses, New AACN Data Show Impressive Growth in Doctoral Nursing Programs." [Online article; retrieved 3/20/11.] www.aacn.nche .edu/media/newsreleases/2010/enrollchanges.html

———. 2010b. "New AACN Data Show That Enrollment in Baccalaureate Nursing Programs Expands for the 10th Consecutive Year." [Online article; retrieved 3/20/11.] www.aacn.nche.edu/Media/pdf/TurnedAway.pdf

American Hospital Association (AHA). 2011. *Hospital Statistics*. Chicago: AHA.

———. 2010. *Hospital Statistics*. Chicago: AHA.

American Medical Association (AMA), Division of Survey and Data Resources. 2010. *Physician Characteristics and Distribution in the United States*. Chicago: AMA.

———. 1991. *Physician Characteristics and Distribution in the United States*. Chicago: AMA.

Anstett, P. 2009. "Canadians Visit US to Get Health Care." [Online article; retrieved 3/28/11.] www.freep.com/article/20090820/BUSINESS06/908200420/ Canadians-visit-US-to-get-health-care

Association of American Medical Colleges and American Medical Association. 1991. *Liaison Committee on Medical Education: Functions and Structure of a Medical School*. Washington, DC: AAMC and AMA.

Baker, L., and S. Wheeler. 1998. "Managed Care and Technology Diffusion: The Case of MRI." *Health Affairs* 17(5): 195–207.

Bamezai, A., J. Zwanziger, G. Melnick, and J. Mann. 1999. "Price Competition and Hospital Cost Growth in the United States: 1989–1994." *Health Economics* 8 (3): 233–43.

Barua, B., M. Rovere, and B. Skinner. 2010. *Wait Times for Health Care in Canada, 2010.* [Online report; retrieved 3/17/11.] www.fraserinstitute.org/uploadedFiles/fraser-ca/Content/research-news/research/publications/waiting-your-turn-2010.pdf

Basu, A., and T. Philipson. 2010. "The Impact of Comparative Effectiveness Research on Health and Health Care Spending." NBER Working Paper 15633. [Online document; retrieved 3/14/11.] www.nber.org/papers/w15633

Baumol, W. 1988. "Containing Medical Costs: Why Price Controls Won't Work." *Public Interest* 93 (Fall): 37–53.

Bech, M., T. Christiansen, K. Dunham, J. Lauridsen, C. H. Lyttkens, K. McDonald, A. McGuire, and TECH Investigators. 2009. "The Influence of Economic Incentives and Regulatory Factors on the Adoption of Treatment Technologies: A Case Study of Technologies Used to Treat Heart Attacks." *Health Economics* 18 (10): 1114–32.

Berenson, R., P. Ginsburg, and N. Kemper. 2010. "Unchecked Provider Clout in California Foreshadows Challenges to Health Reform." *Health Affairs* 29 (4): 699–705.

Berndt, E. R. 2001. "The US Pharmaceutical Industry: Why Major Growth in Times of Cost Containment." [Online article; retrieved 4/14/11.] http://content.healthaffairs.org/content/20/2/100.full

Bloom, B. R., C. M. Michaud, J. R. La Montagne, and L. Simonsen. 2006. "Priorities for Global Research and Development of Interventions." [Online information; retrieved 4/14/11.] www.ncbi.nlm.nih.gov/books/NBK11751/

Blumberg, L. 1999. "Who Pays for Employer-Sponsored Health Insurance?" *Health Affairs* 18 (6): 58–61.

Brittain, J. A. 1971. "The Incidence of Social Security Payroll Taxes." *American Economic Review* 61 (1): 110–25.

Brown, J., and A. Finkelstein. 2008. "The Interaction of Public and Private Insurance: Medicaid and the Long Term Insurance Market." *American Economic Review* 98 (3): 1083–1102.

———. 2007. "Why Is the Market for Long-Term Care Insurance So Small?" *Journal of Public Economics* 91 (10): 1967–91.

Browning, E., and M. Zupan. 2009. *Microeconomics: Theory and Applications*, 10th ed., 319. New York: John Wiley & Sons.

Buchmueller, T., and P. Feldstein. 1996. "Consumers' Sensitivity to Health Plan Premiums: Evidence from a Natural Experiment in California." *Health Affairs* 15 (1): 143–51.

Buerhaus, P., D. Auerbach, and D. Staiger. 2009. "The Recent Surge in Nurse Employment: Causes and Implications." *Health Affairs* (June 12): w657–w668.

Buerhaus, P., D. Staiger, and D. Auerbach. 2009. *The Future of the Nursing Workforce in the United States: Data Trends, and Implications.* Boston: Jones and Bartlett.

Bunce, V. C., and J. P. Wieske. 2010. *Health Insurance Mandates in the States 2010.* [Online report; retrieved 4/27/11.] www.cahi.org/cahi_contents/resources/pdf/MandatesintheStates2010.pdf

———. 2009. *Health Insurance Mandates in the States 2009.* Alexandria, VA: Council for Affordable Health Insurance.

Buntin, M., A. Haviland, R. McDevitt, and N. Sood. 2011. "Healthcare Spending and Preventive Care in High-Deductible and Consumer-Directed Health Plans." *American Journal of Managed Care* 17 (3): 222–30.

Bureau of Labor Statistics (BLS). 2011. "Consumer Price Index History Table." [Online information; retrieved 4/27/11.] www.bls.gov/cpi/#tables

———. 2009. "Registered Nurses." [Online information; retrieved 3/20/11.] www.bls
   .gov/oes/current/oes291111.htm

Burt, C., and J. Sisk. 2005. "Which Physicians and Which Practices Are Using Electronic
   Medical Records?" *Health Affairs* 24 (5): 1334–43.

Canadian Union of Public Employees (CUPE). 2011. "Report: Private Clinics Threaten
   Public Health Care." [Online information; retrieved 4/20/11.] http://nb.cupe
   .ca/research/report-private-clinics-threaten-public-health-care

Carlisle, T. 2004. "Pfizer Pressures Canadian Sellers of Drugs to US." *Wall Street Journal,* January 14, A6.

Carpenter, D. 2004. "The Political Economy of FDA Drug Review: Processing, Politics,
   and Lessons for Policy." *Health Affairs* 23 (1): 52–63.

Casalino, L., E. November, R. Berenson, and H. Pham. 2009. "Hospital-Physician
   Relations: Two Tracks and the Decline of the Voluntary Medical Staff Model."
   Health Affairs 27 (5): 1305–14.

Casalino, L., H. Pham, and G. Bazzoli. 2004. "Growth of Single-Specialty Medical
   Groups." *Health Affairs* 23 (2): 82–90.

CBC News. 2010. "Heart Surgery to Sideline N.P. Premier for Weeks." [Online
   article; retrieved 3/28/11.] www.cbc.ca/canada/newfoundland-labrador/
   story/2010/02/02/nl-williams-heart-010310.html

———. 2009. "Digital Mammography Cuts Wait Times in Moncton." [Online article;
   retrieved 3/28/11.] www.cbc.ca/canada/new-brunswick/story/2009/09/29/
   nb-moncton-mammography-wait-times-533.html

Centers for Disease Control and Prevention (CDC). 2010. *Preliminary Data for
   the 2008 NAMCS and NHAMCS,* table 1. [Online information; retrieved
   3/20/11.] www.cdc.gov/nchs/data/ahcd/preliminary2008/table01.pdf

———. 2009. *Health, United States, 2009,* table 105. [Online information; retrieved
   3/30/11.] www.cdc.gov/nchs/data/hus/hus09.pdf#105

Centers for Medicare & Medicaid Services (CMS). 2011a. *Data Compendium, 2010 Edition.*
   [Online information; retrieved 4/27/11.] https://www.cms.gov/DataCompen-
   dium/ 14_2010_Data_Compendium.asp#TopOfPage

———. 2011b. "Table 12.6: Percent Distribution of Disabled and Aged Beneficiaries
   in Medicare Advantage Plans and Fee-for-Service: December 2009." *Medicare
   & Medicaid Statistical Supplement, 2010 Edition.* [Online information; retrieved
   4/27/11.] cms.gov/MedicareMedicaidStatSupp/09_2010.asp#TopOfPage

———. 2011c. "National Health Expenditure Data." [Online information; retrieved
   3/18/11.] https://www.cms.gov/NationalHealthExpendData/01_Overview
   .asp#TopOfPage

———. 2010a. *Data Compendium, 2009 Edition.* [Online document; retrieved
   3/20/11.] www.cms.gov/DataCompendium/15_2009_Data_Compendium
   .asp#TopOfPage

———. 2010b. "National Health Expenditures 2009 Highlights." [Online information;
   retrieved 4/27/11.] cms.gov/NationalHealthExpendData/downloads/highlights
   .pdf

———. 2010c. "Table 1: National Health Expenditures Aggregate, Per Capita Amounts,
   Percent Distribution, and Average Annual Percent Growth, by Source of Funds:
   Selected Calendar Years 1960–2009." [Online information; retrieved 4/27/11.]
   cms.gov/nationalhealthexpenddata/downloads/tables.pdf

———. 2010d. "Table 2: National Health Expenditures Aggregate Amounts and
   Average Annual Percent Change, by Type of Expenditure: Selected Calendar

Years 1960–2009." [Online information; retrieved 4/27/11.] cms.gov/nationalhealthexpenddata/downloads/tables.pdf

———. 2010e. "2010 SSI and Spousal Impoverishment Standards." [Online information; retrieved 4/26/11.] https://www.cms.gov/MedicaidEligibility/downloads/1998-2010SSIFBR122909.pdf

———. 2007. "Strong Competition and Beneficiary Choices Contribute to Medicare Drug Coverage with Lower Costs than Predicted." [Online information; retrieved 3/21/11.] www.cms.gov/apps/media/press/factsheet.asp?Counter=2402&intNumPerPage=10&checkDate=&checkKey=2&srchType=2&numDays=0&srchOpt=0&srchData=drug+coverage&keywordType=All&chkNewsType=6&intPage=&showAll=1&pYear=&year=0&desc=&cboOrder=date

———. 2000. *Medicare 2000: 35 Years of Improving Americans' Health and Security.* Baltimore, MD: CMS.

Chandra, A., S. Nundy, and S. Seabury. 2005. "The Growth of Physician Medical Malpractice Payments: Evidence from the National Practitioner Data Bank." *Health Affairs* (May 31): w5-240–w5-249.

Chu, M. C., and J. A. Rhoades. 2009. "The Uninsured in America, 1996–2008: Estimates for the US Civilian Noninstitutionalized Population under Age 65." [Online information; retrieved 4/19/11.] http://meps.ahrq.gov/mepsweb/data_files/publications/st259/stat259.shtml

Cockburn, I. 2004. "The Changing Structure of the Pharmaceutical Industry." *Health Affairs* 23 (1): 10–22.

Cockburn, I. M., S. Stern, and J. Zausner. 2010. "Finding the Endless Frontier: Lessons from the Life Sciences Innovation System for Technology R&D." [Online article; retrieved 4/13/11.] www.nber.org/chapters/c11749.pdf

Cohen, I. 2005. "Directions for the Disposition of My (and Your) Vital Organs." *Regulation* 28 (3): 32–38.

Congressional Budget Office (CBO). 2011. "Economic Effects of the March Health Legislation." Director's Blog. [Online information; retrieved 4/17/2011.] http://cboblog.cbo.gov/?p=1478

———. 2010a. *The Budget and Economic Outlook: Fiscal Years 2010 to 2020.* [Online report; retrieved 4/12/11.] www.cbo.gov/ftpdocs/108xx/doc10871/01-26-Outlook.pdf

———. 2010b. *CBO's August 2010 Baseline: Medicare.* [Online information; retrieved 4/8/11.] www.cbo.gov/budget/factsheets/2010d/MedicareAugust2010FactSheet.pdf

———. 2010c. *Historical Budget Data.* [Online document; retrieved 3/4/11.] www.cbo.gov/budget/budget.cfm

———. 2010d. *The Long-Term Budget Outlook.* [Online information; retrieved 3/30/11.] www.cbo.gov/ftpdocs/115xx/doc11579/06-30-LTBO.pdf

———. 2009. "Pharmaceutical R&D and the Evolving Market for Prescription Drugs." [Online document; retrieved 3/23/11.] www.cbo.gov/ftpdocs/106xx/doc10681/10-26-DrugR&D.pdf

———. 2008a. *Geographic Variation in Health Care Spending.* [Online information; retrieved 3/17/11.] www.cbo.gov/ftpdocs/89xx/doc8972/02-15-GeogHealth.pdf

———. 2008b. *Technological Change and the Growth of Health Care Spending.* [Online report; retrieved 3/17/11.] http://www.cbo.gov/ftpdocs/89xx/doc8947/MainText.3.1.shtml

———. 2006. "Nonprofit Hospitals and the Provision of Community Benefit." [Online information; retrieved 3/10/11.] www.cbo.gov/ftpdocs/76xx/doc7695/ 12-06-Nonprofit.pdf

———. 2004. "Limiting Tort Liability for Medical Malpractice." [Online information; retrieved 4/8/11.] www.cbo.gov/doc.cfm?index=4968&type=0

———. 1996. *How the Medicaid Rebate or Prescription Drugs Affects Pricing in the Pharmaceutical Industry.* [Online information; retrieved 6/3/11.] www.cbo .gov/ftpdocs/47xx/doc4750/1996Doc20.pdf

———. 1995. "Managed Care and the Medicare Program." [Online information; retrieved 4/27/11.] cbo.gov/ftpdocs/105xx/doc10593/1995_04_26_managed.pdf

———. 1992. *Economic Implications of Rising Health Care Costs.* Washington, DC: US Congressional Budget Office.

Conover, C., and T. Miller. 2010. "Why a Public Option Is Unnecessary to Stimulate Competition." Washington, DC: American Enterprise Institute for Public Policy Research.

Corman, H., and M. Grossman. 1985. "Determinants of Neonatal Mortality Rates in the US: A Reduced Form Model." *Journal of Health Economics* 4 (3): 213–36.

Council on Graduate Medical Education (COGME). 2005. *Physician Workforce Policy Guidelines for the United States, 2000–2020.* Sixteenth Report. [Online document; retrieved 3/7/11.] www.cogme.gov/report16.htm

———. 1992. *Improving Access to Health Care Through Physician Workforce Reform: Directions for the 21st Century.* Third Report. [Online document; retrieved 3/7/11.] www.cogme.gov/rpt3.htm

Countryman, C. J. 2004. "Number of Non-Profit Hospitals Sued in Charity Care Class Actions Continues to Grow." [Online article; retrieved 4/6/11.] www .louisianalawblog.com/class-action-number-of-nonprofit-hospitals-sued-in-charity-care-class-actions-continues-to-grow.html

Culyer, A. J., and J. P. Newhouse. 2000. *Handbook of Health Economics*, vol. 1B. New York: North-Holland.

Coughlin, T., S. Long, T. Triplett, S. Artiga, B. Lyons, R. Duncan, and A. Hall. 2008. "Florida's Medicaid Reform: Informed Consumer Choice?" *Health Affairs* 27(6): w523–w532.

Cutler, D. M., and S. Kadiyala. 2003. "The Return to Biomedical Research: Treatment and Behavioral Effects." In *Measuring the Gains from Medical Research: An Economic Approach,* edited by K. M. Murphy and R. H. Topel, 110–62. Chicago: University of Chicago Press.

Cutler, D., and S. Reber. 1998. "Paying for Health Insurance: The Trade-Off Between Competition and Adverse Selection." *Quarterly Journal of Economics* 113 (2): 433–66.

Cutler, D. M., and E. Richardson. 1999. "Your Money and Your Life: The Value of Health and What Affects It." In *Frontiers in Health Policy Research*, vol. 2, edited by A. Garber, 99–132. Cambridge, MA: MIT Press.

Dalzell, M. 2000. "Prescription Drug Reimportation: Panacea or Problem?" [Online article; retrieved 4/13/11.] www.managedcaremag.com/archives/0012/0012 .reimport.html

Danzon, P. M. 1992. "Hidden Overhead Costs: Is Canada's System Really Less Expensive?" *Health Affairs* 11 (1): 21–43.

Danzon, P. M., and L. W. Chao. 2000. "Cross-National Price Differences for Pharmaceuticals: How Large, and Why?" *Journal of Health Economics* 19 (2): 159–95.

Danzon, P., A. Epstein, and S. Nicholson. 2007. "Mergers and Acquisitions in the Pharmaceutical and Biotech Industries." *Managerial and Decision Economics* 28: 307–28.

Danzon, P., and M. Furukawa. 2003. "Prices and Availability of Pharmaceuticals: Evidence from Nine Countries." *Health Affairs* (October 29): W3-521–W3-536.

Dartmouth Atlas Project. 2006. *The Care of Patients with Severe Chronic Illness.* [Online document; retrieved 3/6/11.] www.dartmouthatlas.org/downloads/atlases/2006_Chronic_Care_Atlas.pdf

Daschle, T., S. Greenberger, and J. Lambrew. 2008. *Critical: What We Can Do About the Health-Care Crisis.* New York: Thomas Dunne.

Day, K. 2006. "Hospital Charity Care Is Probed." [Online article; retrieved 4/6/11.] www.washingtonpost.com/wp-dyn/content/article/2006/09/12/AR2006091201409.html

Decker, S. 2009. "Changes in Medicaid Physician Fees and Patterns of Ambulatory Care." *Inquiry* 46 (3): 291–304.

DiMasi, J., R. Hansen, and H. Grabowski. 2003. "The Price of Innovation: New Estimates of Drug Development Cost." *Journal of Health Economics* 22 (2): 151–85.

Doty, P., K. Mahoney, and M. Sciegaj. 2010. "New State Strategies to Meet Long-Term Care Needs." *Health Affairs* 29 (1): 49–56.

Dranove, D., R. Lindrooth, W. White, and J. Zwanziger. 2008. "Is the Impact of Managed Care on Hospital Prices Decreasing?" *Journal of Health Economics* 27 (2): 362–76.

Dranove, D., M. Shanley, and W. White. 1991. "How Fast Are Hospital Prices Really Rising?" *Medical Care* 29 (8): 690–96.

Dranove, D., and W. White. 1998. "Medicaid-Dependent Hospitals and Their Patients: How Have They Fared?" *Health Services Research* 33 (2, Part I): 163–85.

Dunham, C. C., IV. 2008. "'Body Property': Challenging the Ethical Barriers in Organ Transplantation to Protect Individual Autonomy." *Annals of Health Law* 17: 64.

Ebert, R. H., and E. Ginzberg. 1988. "The Reform of Medical Education." *Health Affairs* 7 (2, suppl.): 5–38.

Enarson, C., and F. Burg. 1992. "An Overview of Reform Initiatives in Medical Education: 1906 Through 1992." *Journal of the American Medical Association* 268 (9): 1141–43.

Encinosa, W., and F. Hellinger. 2005. "Have State Caps on Malpractice Awards Increased the Supply of Physicians?" *Health Affairs* (May 31): W5-250–W5-258.

Enthoven, A. 2004. "Market Forces and Efficient Health Care Systems." *Health Affairs* 23 (2): 25–27.

———. 1993. "Why Managed Care Has Failed to Contain Health Costs." *Health Affairs* 12 (3): 27–43.

Enthoven, A., and L. Tollen. 2005. "Competition in Health Care: It Takes Systems to Pursue Quality and Efficiency." *Health Affairs* (September 7): w5-420–w5-433.

Epstein, R. 2006. "Kidney Beancounters." *Wall Street Journal*, May 15, A15.

Esmail, N. 2009. *Waiting Your Turn: Hospital Waiting Lists in Canada*, 2009 Report, 19th ed. [Online document; retrieved 4/20/11.] www.fraserinstitute.org/research-news/display.aspx?id=13589

Federal Coordinating Council for Comparative Effectiveness Research, US Department of Health and Human Services. 2009. *Report to the President and the Congress.* [Online report; retrieved 4/11/11.] www.hhs.gov/recovery/programs/cer/cerannualrpt.pdf

Federal Long Term Care Insurance Program (FLTCIP). 2011. "FTLCIP 2.0 Monthly Premium Rates." [Online information; retrieved 3/30/11.] www.ltcfeds.com/programdetails/monthlyrateschart.html

Federal Trade Commission (FTC). 2006. "In the Matter of Evanston Northwestern Healthcare Corporation." [Online information; retrieved 4/6/11.] www.ftc.gov/os/adjpro/d9315/070806opinion.pdf

Federation of State Medical Boards of the United States, Inc. 2010. *Summary of 2009 Board Actions.* [Online information; retrieved 3/17/11.] www.fsmb.org/pdf/2009-summary-board-actions.pdf

Feldstein, P. 2011. *Health Care Economics,* 7th ed. Albany, NY: Delmar.

———. 2006. *The Politics of Health Legislation: An Economic Perspective,* 3rd ed. Chicago: Health Administration Press.

Frank, R. G. 2001. "Prescription Drug Prices: Why Do Some Pay More than Others Do?" *Health Affairs* 20 (2): 115–28.

Fuchs, V. R. 2009. "Eliminating Waste in Health Care." *Journal of the American Medical Association* 302 (22): 2481–82.

———. 1993. "No Pain, No Gain—Perspectives on Cost Containment." *Journal of the American Medical Association* 269 (5): 631–33.

———. 1992. "The Best Health Care System in the World?" *Journal of the American Medical Association* 268 (19): 916–17.

———. 1974. *Who Shall Live? Health, Economics, and Social Choice,* 30–55. New York: Basic.

———. 1968. "The Growing Demand for Medical Care." *New England Journal of Medicine* 279 (4): 190–95.

Gaynor, M., J. Li, and W. Vogt. 2006. "Is Drug Coverage a Free Lunch? Cross-Price Elasticities and the Design of Prescription Drug Benefits." NBER working paper 12758. Cambridge, MA: National Bureau of Economic Research.

Galston, W. A. 2010. "Reviewing the Federal Budget." [Online article; retrieved 3/23/11.] www.brookings.edu/opinions/2010/0201_halls_budget.aspx

Geiger, K. 2009. "Medical Billing Code Monopoly Explains American Medical Association's Support for Health Plan, Critics Say." [Online article; retrieved 3/30/11.] www.chicagotribune.com/health/chi-sun-health-ama-1227dec27,0,4125322.story

Gillies, R., S. Shortell, L. Casalino, J. Robinson, and T. Rundall. 2003. "How Different Is California? A Comparison of US Physician Organizations." *Health Affairs* (October 15): W3-492–W3-502.

Glied, S. 2000. "Managed Care." In *The Handbook of Health Economics,* edited by J. P. Newhouse and A. J. Culyer, 707–53. New York: North-Holland Press.

Goldsmith, J. 2004. "Technology and the Boundaries of the Hospital: Three Emerging Technologies." *Health Affairs* 23 (6): 149–56.

Golec, J., and J. A. Vernon. 2009. "Financial Risk of the Biotech Industry Versus the Pharmaceutical Industry." *Applied Health Economics and Health Policy* 7 (3): 155–65.

Goodell, S., and K. Swartz. 2010. "Cost-Sharing: Effects on Spending and Outcomes." [Online information; retrieved 4/27/11.] www.rwjf.org/files/research/121710.policysynthesis.costsharing.brief.pdf

Gottlieb, S. 2004. "The Price of Too Much Caution." [Online article; retrieved 4/27/11.] www.aei.org/news/newsID.21746, filter./news_detail.asp

Grabowski, H., and Y. Wang. 2006. "The Quantity and Quality of Worldwide New Drug Introductions, 1982–2003." *Health Affairs* 25 (2): 452–60.

Grayson, C. J. 1993. "Experience Talks: Shun Price Controls." *Wall Street Journal,* March 29, A14.

Gruber, J. 1994a. "The Effect of Competitive Pressure on Charity: Hospital Responses to Price Shopping in California." *Journal of Health Economics* 13 (2): 183–212.

———. 1994b. "The Incidence of Mandated Maternity Benefits." *American Economic Review* 84 (3): 622–41.

Gruber, J., and K. Simon. 2008. "Crowd-Out Ten Years Later: Have Recent Expansions of Public Insurance Crowded Out Private Health Insurance?" *Journal of Health Economics* 27 (2): 201–17.

Hadley, J., J. Reschovsky, C. Corey, and S. Zuckerman. 2009. "Medicare Fees and Volume of Physician Services." *Inquiry* 46 (4): 372–90.

Haislmaier, E. F. 1993. *Why Global Budgets and Price Controls Will Not Curb Health Costs.* Washington, DC: Heritage Foundation.

Hall, M. J., C. J. DeFrances, S. N. Williams, A. Golosinskiy, and A. Schwartzman. 2010. "National Hospital Discharge Survey: 2007 Summary." [Online information; retrieved 4/27/11.] http://cdc.gov/nchs/data/nhsr/nhsr029.pdf

Halpin, H., and P. Harbage. 2010. "The Origins and Demise of the Public Option." *Health Affairs* 29 (6): 1117–23.

Harris, G. 2008. "British Balance Benefit Versus Cost of New Drugs." *New York Times,* December 3.

Harris, R. 1964. *The Real Voice.* New York: MacMillan.

Health Policy Center, Urban Institute. 2010. "Private Health Insurance." [Online information; retrieved 3/18/11.] www.urban.org/health_policy/private_insurance/

Helms, R. 2004. "The Economics of Price Regulation and Innovation." *Supplement to Managed Care* 13 (6): 10–12.

Henry J. Kaiser Family Foundation. 2011. "Medicare Spending and Financing: A Primer." [Online information; retrieved 3/23/11.] www.kff.org/medicare/upload/7731-03.pdf

———. 2010a. *Financing New Medicaid Coverage Under Health Reform.* [Online document; retrieved 3/6/11.] www.kff.org/healthreform/upload/7952-03.pdf

———. 2010b. *Medicare Chartbook.* [Online information; retrieved 4/8/11.] www.kff.org/medicare/upload/8103.pdf

Henry J. Kaiser Family Foundation and the Health Research and Educational Trust (HRET). 2010. *Employer Health Benefits, 2010 Annual Survey.* [Online information; retrieved 4/19/11.] http://ehbs.kff.org/pdf/2010/8085.pdf

Ho, K. 2009. "Insurer-Provider Networks in the Medical Care Market." *American Economic Review* 99 (1): 393–430.

Holahan, J. 2011. "The 2007–2009 Recession and Health Insurance Coverage." *Health Affairs* 30 (1): 145–52.

Horwitz, J., and A. Nichols. 2009. "Hospital Ownership and Medical Services: Market Mix, Spillover Effects, and Nonprofit Objectives." *Journal of Health Economics* 28 (5): 924–37.

Houser, A., and M. Gibson. 2008. "Valuing the Invaluable: The Economic Value of Family Caregiving, 2008 Update." Washington, DC: AARP Public Policy Institute.

Houser, A., M. Gibson, and D. Redfoot. 2010. "Trends in Family Caregiving and Paid Home Care for Older People with Disabilities in the Community: Data from the National Long-Term Care Survey." Washington, DC: AARP Public Policy Institute.

Hsiao, W. C., P. Braun, D. Yntema, and E. R. Becker. 1988. "Estimating Physicians' Work for a Resource-Based Relative Value Scale." *New England Journal of Medicine* 319 (13): 835–41.

Hsu, J., M. Price, J. Huang, R. Brand, V. Fung, R. Hui, B. Fireman, J. Newhouse, and J. Selby. 2006. "Unintended Consequences of Caps on Medicare Drug Benefits." *New England Journal of Medicine* 354 (22): 2349–59.

Huang, T., Z. Liu, E. Howard, and D. Fishman. 2009. "Biosimilar Legislation and Its Impact on IP Protection." [Online article; retrieved 4/14/11.] www.tbiweb .org/tbi/file_dir/TBI2009/Tracy%20Huang.pdf

Hughes, P. 2010. "The Limited Network Era." [Online article; retrieved 4/11/11.] www.bizjournals.com/boston/stories/2010/10/04/editorial2.html

Hughes, R., S. Hunt, and H. Luft. 1987. "Effects of Surgeon Volume and Hospital Volume on Quality of Care in Hospitals." *Medical Care* 25 (6): 489–503.

Iglehart, J. 2010. "Long-Term Care Legislation at Long Last?" *Health Affairs* 29 (1): 8–9.

———. 1992. "The American Health Care System—Introduction." *New England Journal of Medicine* 326 (14): 962–67.

Ikegami, N. 1991. "Japanese Health Care: Low Cost Through Regulated Fees." *Health Affairs* 10 (3): 87–109.

IMS Health. 2010. "IMS Health Reports US Prescription Sales Grew 5.1 Percent in 2009, to $300.3 Billion." [Online article; retrieved 4/12/11.] www.imshealth.com/ portal/site/imshealth/menuitem.a46c6d4df3db4b3d88f611019418c22a/ ?vgnextoid=d690a27e9d5b7210VgnVCM100000ed152ca2RCRD

———. 2009. "Top Corporations by US Sales." [Online information; retrieved 4/13/11.] www.imshealth.com/deployedfiles/imshealth/Global/Content/ StaticFile/Top_Line_Data/Top%20Corps%20by%20U.S.Sales.pdf

Jha, A., and A. Epstein. 2006. "The Predictive Accuracy of the New York State Coronary Artery Bypass Surgery Report-Card System." *Health Affairs* 25 (3): 844–55.

Joint Committee on Taxation, US Congress. 2008. *Tax Expenditures for Health Care*. JCX-66-08.

Jolly, P. 2005. "Medical School Tuition and Young Physicians' Indebtedness." *Health Affairs* 24 (2): 527–35.

Joyce, T., H. Corman, and M. Grossman. 1988. "A Cost-Effectiveness Analysis of Strategies to Reduce Infant Mortality." *Medical Care* 26 (4): 348–60.

Kaiser Commission on Key Facts. 2011. "Medicaid and the Uninsured." [Online information; retrieved 3/23/11.] www.kff.org/medicaid/upload/8139.pdf

Kane, R., R. Kane, N. Kaye, R. Mollica, T. Riley, P. Saucier, K. Irvin Snow, and L. Starr. 1996. "The Basics of Managed Care." [Online information; retrieved 4/20/11.] http://aspe.hhs.gov/Progsys/Forum/basics.htm

Kaufman, M. 2000. "Shalala Halts Bid to Lower Drug Costs." *Washington Post*, December 27, A1.

Kessler, D., and M. McClellan. 2000. "Is Hospital Competition Socially Wasteful?" *Quarterly Journal of Economics* 115 (2): 577–615.

Kessler, D., W. Sage, and D. Becker. 2005. "Impact of Malpractice Reforms on the Supply of Physicians." *Journal of the American Medical Association* 293 (21): 2618–25.

Kohn, L., J. Corrigan, and M. Donaldson, eds. 1999. *To Err Is Human: Building a Safer Health System*. Washington, DC: National Academies Press.

Kolstad, J. T., and M. E. Chernew. 2009. "Quality and Consumer Decision Making in the Market for Health Insurance and Health Care Services." *Medical Care Research and Review* 66 (1, Suppl.): 28S–52S.

Krauss, C. 2006. "Canada's Private Clinics Surge as Public System Falters." *New York Times*, February 28, A3.

———. 2005. "In Blow to Canada's Health System, Quebec Law Is Voided." *New York Times,* June 10, A3.

Lakdawalla, D., and T. Philipson. 2006. "The Nonprofit Sector and Industry Performance." *Journal of Public Economics* 90 (8): 1681–98.

Latham & Watkins LLP. 2005. "Pension and OPEB Obligations in US Bankruptcies—Answers to the Most Frequently Asked Questions." [Online information; retrieved 4/12/11.] www.lw.com/Resources.aspx?page=FirmPublicationDetail&attno=01754&publication=1309

Lazonick, W., and Ö. Tulum. 2011. "US Biopharmaceutical Finance and the Sustainability of the Biotech Business Model." [Online article; retrieved 4/13/11.] www.theairnet.org/files/research/lazonick/Lazonick-TulumUSBPFinance20110120.pdf

Lichtenberg, F. R. 2007. "The Benefits and Costs of Newer Drugs: An Update." *Managerial and Decision Economics* 28: 485–90.

Localio, A. R., A. Lawthers, T. Brennan, N. Laird, L. Hebert, L. Peterson, J. Newhouse, P. Weiler, and H. Hiatt. 1991. "Relation Between Malpractice Claims and Adverse Events Due to Negligence." *New England Journal of Medicine* 325 (4): 245–51.

Manning, W., E. Keeler, J. Newhouse, E. Sloss, and J. Wasserman. 1989. "The Taxes of Sin: Do Smokers and Drinkers Pay Their Way?" *Journal of the American Medical Association* 261 (11): 1604–9.

Marquis, S., and S. Long. 1999. "Trends in Managed Care and Managed Competition, 1993–1997." *Health Affairs* 18 (6): 75–88.

Martin, A. 2009. "Living with Dialysis." [Online article; retrieved 3/23/11.] www.marketwatch.com/story/the-growing-human-and-economic-toll-of-dialysis

Mayne, E. 2004. "Ford: Health Costs Could Drive Investment Overseas." *Detroit News,* July 20.

Mays, G., G. Claxton, and J. White. 2004. "Managed Care Rebound? Recent Changes in Health Plans' Cost Containment Strategies." *Health Affairs* (August 11): W4-427–W4-436.

McCarthy, T. 1985. "The Competitive Nature of the Primary Care Physician Services Market." *Journal of Health Economics* 4 (2): 93–117.

McClellan, M., and D. Staiger. 2000. "Comparing Hospital Quality at For-Profit and Not-for-Profit Hospitals." In *The Changing Hospital Industry: Comparing Not-for-Profit and For-Profit Institutions*, edited by D. Cutler, 93–112. Chicago: University of Chicago Press.

McDermott Newsletters. 2005. "New Congressional Scrutiny of Hospital Tax-Exempt Status." [Online article; retrieved 4/6/11.] www.mwe.com/index.cfm/fuseaction/publications.nldetail/object_id/79dc6db8-02f9-43af-b847-eb883f3d4d20.cfm

McGuire, T. G. 2000. "Physician Agency." In *Handbook of Health Economics*, edited by A. J. Culyer and J. P. Newhouse, 461–536. New York: North-Holland Press.

Mechanic, R., and S. Altman. 2009. "Payment Reform Options: Episode Payment Is a Good Place to Start." *Health Affairs* (January 27): w262–w270.

Medicare Payment Advisory Commission (MedPAC). 2010. "Appendix A. Report to the Congress: Aligning Incentives in Medicare." [Online document; retrieved 3/7/11.] http://medpac.gov/documents/Jun10_EntireReport.pdf

Mello, M., and A. Kachalia. 2010. *Evaluation of Options for Medical Malpractice System Reform.* Washington, DC: Medicare Payment Advisory Commission.

Mello, M., A. Chandra, A. A. Gawande, and D. M. Studdert. 2010. "National Costs of the Medical Liability System." *Health Affairs* 29 (9): 1569–77.

Melnick, G., E. Keeler, and J. Zwanziger. 1999. "Market Power and Hospital Pricing: Are Nonprofits Different?" *Health Affairs* 18 (3): 167–73.

MetLife Mature Market Institute. 2010. *The 2010 MetLife Market Survey of Nursing Home, Assisted Living, Adult Day Services, and Home Care Costs.* [Online information; retrieved 3/30/11.] www.metlife.com/assets/cao/mmi/publications/studies/2010/mmi-2010-market-survey-long-term-care-costs.pdf

Moore, S. D. 2000. "In Drug-Cost Debate Europe Offers US a Telling Side Effect." *Wall Street Journal,* July 21, 1.

Monheit, A., J. Cantor, M. Koller, and K. Fox. 2004. "Community Rating and Sustainable Individual Health Insurance Markets in New Jersey." *Health Affairs* 23 (4): 167–75.

Morrisey, M. 2005. *Price Sensitivity in Health Care: Implications for Health Care Policy.* Washington, DC: National Federation of Independent Business.

Morse, M. H., B. C. Kevin, R. W. McCann, and L. E. Bryant Jr. 2007. "Federal Trade Commission Finds Evanston Northwestern Healthcare Merger Unlawful but Orders 'Separate and Independent Negotiating Teams' Rather than Divestiture." [Online memo; retrieved 4/6/11.] www.drinkerbiddle.com/files/Publication/2be7d509-61f4-4745-9bd6-28ec6366c168/Presentation/PublicationAttachment/d68f52b8-6ac2-437d-bdef-01281b45dc61/Federal_Trade.pdf

National Bipartisan Commission on the Future of Medicare. n.d. "Medicare from the Start to Today." [Online information; retrieved 3/23/11.] http://thomas.loc.gov/medicare/history.htm

National Center for Health Statistics. 2010. "Deaths: Preliminary Data for 2008." [Online article; retrieved 4/27/11.] www.cdc.gov/nchs/data/nvsr/nvsr59/nvsr59_02.pdf

National Institute for Health and Clinical Excellence (NICE). 2011. "About NICE." [Online information; retrieved 3/17/11.] www.nice.org.uk/aboutnice

Needleman, J., P. I. Buerhaus, M. Stewart, K. Zelevinsky, and S. Mattke. 2006. "Nurse Staffing in Hospitals: Is There a Business Case for Quality?" *Health Affairs* 25 (1): 204–11.

New York Times News Service. 1993. "Merck & Co. Completes Medco Purchase." [Online article; retrieved 4/14/11.] http://articles.baltimoresun.com/1993-11-19/business/1993323090_1_medco-merck-wygod

Nguyen, X. N. 1996. "Physician Volume Response to Price Controls." *Health Policy* 35 (2): 189–204.

Norton, E., and D. Staiger. 1994. "How Hospital Ownership Affects Access to Care for the Uninsured." *RAND Journal of Economics* 25 (1): 171–85.

Nursing Portal Philippines. 2011. "Pinoy RN, Why Rush to Go Abroad?" [Online article; retrieved 3/20/11.] www.nursing.ph/pinoy-rn-why-rush-to-go-abroad.html

Office of Inspector General. 2009. *Semiannual Report to Congress, Oct. 1–March 31.* [Online document; retrieved 3/28/11.] http://oig.hhs.gov/publications/docs/semiannual/2009/semiannual_spring2009.pdf

Office of Management and Budget. 2011. *Budget of the US Government, Fiscal Year 2011.* [Online report; retrieved 3/21/11.] www.gpoaccess.gov/usbudget/fy11/pdf/budget.pdf

———. 2010. *Fiscal Year 2012: Historical Tables. Budget of the US Government.* [Online report; retrieved 4/27/11.] www.gpoaccess.gov/usbudget/fy12/pdf/BUDGET-2012-TAB.pdf

Ohtaki, S., T. Ohtaki, and M. Fetters. 2003. "Doctor-Patient Communication: A Comparison of the USA and Japan." *Family Practice* 20 (3): 276–82.

Olson, M. K. 1994. "Political Influence and Regulatory Policy: The 1984 Drug Legislation." *Economic Inquiry* 32 (3): 363–82.

O'Neill, J., and D. O'Neill. 2007. "Health Status, Health Care and Inequality: Canada vs. the US." *Frontiers in Health Policy Research* 10 (1).

Organ Procurement and Transplantation Network (OPTN). 2011. "Data Reports." [Online information; retrieved 4/19/11.] http://optn.transplant.hrsa.gov/data/default.asp

Orzag, P., and E. Emanuel. 2010. "Health Care Reform and Cost Control." [Online article; retrieved 3/30/11.] http://healthpolicyandreform.nejm.org/?p=3564

Paulus, R. A., K. Davis, and G. D. Steele. 2008. "Continuous Innovation in Health Care: Implications of the Geisinger Experience." *Health Affairs* 27 (5): 1235–45.

Pear, R. 2010. "In Health Bill for Everyone, Provisions for a Few." *New York Times,* January 4.

———. 2006. "Nonprofit Hospitals Face Scrutiny over Practices." [Online article; retrieved 4/6/11.] www.nytimes.com/2006/03/19/politics/19health.html?_r=1

Peltzman, S. 1974. *Regulation of Pharmaceutical Innovation.* Washington, DC: American Enterprise Institute.

Peter G. Peterson Foundation. 2010. *State of the Union's Finances: A Citizen's Guide.* [Online document; retrieved 3/30/11.] www.pgpf.org/~/media/PGPF/Media/PDF/2010/05/PGPF_CitizensGuide_2010.ashx?pid={4F7D605D-BE87-4B20-A867-EA24ACB761C8

Pham, H., K. Devers, J. May, and R. Berenson. 2004. "Financial Pressures Spur Physician Entrepreneurialism." *Health Affairs* 23 (2): 70–81.

Preston, S. H., and J. Y. Ho. 2009. "Low Life Expectancy in the United States: Is the Health Care System at Fault?" [Online article; retrieved 4/27/11.] www.nber.org/papers/w15213

Reece, M. 2011. "Bill Scrutinizes Nonprofit Property Tax Structure." [Online article; retrieved 4/6/11.] www.flatheadbeacon.com/articles/article/bill_scrutinizes_nonprofit_property_tax_structure/21719/

Reinhardt, U. E. 1989. "Health Care Spending and American Competitiveness." *Health Affairs* 8 (4): 5–21.

Rice, T., S. C. Stearns, D. E. Pathman, S. DesHarnais, M. Brasure, and M. Tai-Seale. 1999. "A Tale of Two Bounties: The Impact of Competing Fees on Physician Behavior." *Journal of Health Politics, Policy and Law* 24 (6): 1307–30.

RMM Inc. n.d. "What Senior Citizens Need to Know About Private Long Term Care Insurance." [Online information; retrieved 4/26/11.] www.rmminc.net/articles-ltc_ins/need_to_know.shtml#Premium%20Increases

Robinson, J. C. 1997. "Use and Abuse of the Medical Loss Ratio to Measure Health Plan Performance." *Health Affairs* 16 (4): 164–87.

Rosenthal, M., R. Frank, Z. Li, and A. Epstein. 2005. "Early Experience with Pay-for-Performance." *Journal of the American Medical Association* 294 (14): 1788–93.

Rupert, J. 2001. "Man Protests Rock's Speedy Surgery." *Ottawa Citizen,* February 17, D3.

Sanmartin, C., E. Ng, D. Blackwell, J. Gentleman, M. Martinez, and C. Simile. 2004. *Joint Canada/United States Survey of Health, 2002–03.* [Online document; retrieved 3/12/11.] www.cdc.gov/nchs/data/nhis/jcush_analyticalreport.pdf

Sapsford, J., and J. Areddy. 2005. "Why Delphi's Asia Operations Are Booming." *Wall Street Journal,* October 17, B1.

Satel, S. 2007. "Supply, Demand, and Kidney Transplants." [Online article; retrieved 3/23/11.] www.hoover.org/publications/policy-review/article/6060

Schmidt, A. 1974. "The FDA Today: Critics, Congress, and Consumerism." Speech given at the National Press Club, Washington, DC, October 29. Quoted in Grabowski, H. 1976. *Drug Regulation and Innovation.* Washington, DC: AEI Press.

Schneider, J., T. Miller, R. Ohsfeldt, M. Morrisey, B. Zelner, and P. Li. 2008. "The Economics of Specialty Hospitals." *Medical Care Research and Review* 65 (5): 531–53.

Sheils, J. 2009. "Ideas for Financing Health Reform: Revenue Measures That Also Reduce Health Spending: Statement for the Senate Committee on Finance." [Online information; retrieved 4/27/11.] http://finance.senate.gov/imo/media/doc/John%20Sheils.pdf

Sheingold, S. H. 1989. "The First Three Years of PPS: Impact on Medicare Costs." *Health Affairs* 8 (3): 191–204.

Sisko, A., C. Truffer, S. Keehan, J. Poisal, M. K. Clemens, and A. Madison. 2010. "National Health Spending Projections: The Estimated Impact of Reform Through 2019." *Health Affairs* 29 (10): 1–9.

Skinner, J., D. Staiger, and E. Fisher. 2006. "Is Technological Change in Medicine Always Worth It? The Case of Acute Myocardial Infarction." *Health Affairs* (February 7): W-34–W-47.

Sloan, F. 2000. "Not-for-Profit Ownership and Hospital Behavior." In *Handbook of Health Economics,* vol. 1B, edited by A. J. Culyer and J. P. Newhouse, 1141–73. New York: North-Holland Press.

Smerd, J. 2008. "UAW's VEBA Board: Autoworkers' Health Care Benefits in Peril." [Online article; retrieved 4/12/11.] www.crainbenefits.com/news/uaw's-veba-board:-autoworkers'-health-care-benefits-in-peril_print.php

Sood, N., H. deVries, I. Gutierrez, D. Lakdawalla, and D. Goldman. 2008. "The Effect of Regulation on Pharmaceutical Revenues: Experience in Nineteen Countries." *Health Affairs* (December 16): w125–w137.

Soumerai, S. 2004. "Benefits and Risks of Increasing Restrictions on Access to Costly Drugs in Medicaid." *Health Affairs* 23(1): 135–46.

Spillman, B., and P. Kemper. 1995. "Lifetime Patterns of Payment for Nursing Home Care." *Medical Care* 33 (3): 288–96.

Spital, A. 1991. "The Shortage of Organs for Transplantation—Where Do We Go from Here?" *New England Journal of Medicine* 325: 1243–46.

Steinbrook, R. 2008. "Saying No Isn't NICE: The Travails of Britain's National Institute of Health and Clinical Effectiveness." *New England Journal of Medicine* 359 (19): 1977–81.

Stensland, J., Z. Gaumer, and M. Miller. 2010. "Private-Payer Profits Can Induce Negative Medicare Margins." *Health Affairs* 29 (5): 1–7.

Stevenson, D., R. Frank, and J. Tau. 2009. "Private Long-Term Care Insurance and State Tax Incentives." *Inquiry* 46 (3): 305–21.

Stigler, G. J. 1971. "The Theory of Economic Regulation." *Bell Journal of Economics* 2 (1): 3–21.

Storm, P. n.d. "VEBA Accounts and Health Insurance." [Online PowerPoint presentation; retrieved 4/12/11.] www.gvsu.edu/cms3/assets/A710F777-E74C-F8BD-F645CFB2BE41D80C/Bargaining/VEBA%2520Accounts%2520and%2520Health %2520Insurance%2520-update.ppt

Strombom, B. A., T. C. Buchmueller, and P. J. Feldstein. 2002. "Switching Costs, Price Sensitivity, and Health Plan Choice." *Journal of Health Economics* 21 (1): 89–116.

Studdert, D., T. Brennan, and E. Thomas. 2000. "Beyond Dead Reckoning: Measures of Medical Injury Burden, Malpractice Litigation, and Alternative Compensation Models from Utah and Colorado." *Indiana Law Review* 33: 1643–86.

Studdert, D., M. M. Mello, W. M. Sage, C. M. DesRoches, J. Peugh, K. Zapert, and T. A. Brennan. 2005. "Defensive Medicine Among High-Risk Specialist Physicians in a Volatile Malpractice Environment." *Journal of the American Medical Association* 293 (21): 2609–17.

Studdert, D., E. Thomas, H. Burstin, B. Zbar, E. Orav, T. Brennan, and A. Troyen. 2000. "Negligent Care and Malpractice Claiming Behavior in Utah and Colorado." *Medical Care* 38 (3): 250–60.

Technological Change in Health Care (TECH) Research Network. 2001. "Technological Change Around the World: Evidence from Heart Attack Care." *Health Affairs* 20 (3): 25–42.

Thorpe, K. 2004. "The Medical Malpractice 'Crisis': Recent Trends and the Impact of State Tort Reforms." *Health Affairs* (January 21): W4-20–W4-30.

Towers Perrin. 2009. *2010 Retiree Health Care Cost Survey Shows Continuing Affordability and Access Concers.* [Online information; retrieved 3/17/11.] www.towersperrin.com/tp/showdctmdoc.jsp?url=Master_Brand_2/USA/Press_Releases/2009/20091118/2009_11_18.htm&country=global

US Census Bureau. 2011a. *Current Population Survey, Annual Social and Economic Supplement, 2007 Through 2010.* [Online information; retrieved 3/6/11.] www.census.gov/hhes/www/poverty/microdata.html

———. 2011b. *Statistical Abstract of the United States.* Washington, DC: US Census Bureau.

———. 2009a. "Table 108." *Statistical Abstract of the United States.* [Online information; retrieved 4/27/11.] www2.census.gov/prod2/statcomp/documents/1985-01.pdf

———. 2009b. "Table 112 Infant, Neonatal, and Maternal Mortality Rates by Race: 1980 to 2005." *Statistical Abstract of the United States* [Online information; retrieved 4/27/11.] www.census.gov/compendia/statab/2010/tables/10s0112.pdf

US Department of Health and Human Services (HHS). n.d. "HHS Gateway to Data and Statistics." [Online reports; retrieved 5/6/11.] www.hhs-stat.net/scripts/result.cfm?id=AHAASH&lk=6

US Government Accountability Office (GAO). 2010. *Consumer-Directed Health Plans.* GAO-10-616. [Online information; retrieved 4/8/11.] www.gao.gov/new.items/d10616.pdf

———. 2005. "Long-Term Care Financing: Growing Demand and Cost of Services Are Straining Federal and State Budgets." Testimony before the Subcommittee on Health, Committee on Energy and Commerce, US House of Representatives, April.

———. 1997. *Organ Procurement Organizations*, 8. GAO/HEHS-98-26. Washington, DC: US Government Printing Office.

———. 1995. *Medicare: Rapid Spending Growth Calls for More Prudent Purchasing.* GAO/T-HEHS-95-193. Washington, DC: US Government Printing Office.

———. 1994. *Prescription Drugs: Companies Typically Charge More in the United States than in the United Kingdom.* GAO/HEHS 94–29. Washington, DC: US Government Printing Office.

———. 1992. *Prescription Drugs: Companies Typically Charge More in the United States than in Canada.* GAO/HRD 92–110. Washington, DC: US Government Printing Office.

———. 1991. *Canadian Health Insurance.* GAO/HRD-91-90. Washington, DC: US Government Printing Office.

US House of Representatives, Committee on Government Reform and Oversight. 1998. *Prescription Drug Pricing in the 1st Congressional District in Maine: An International Price Comparison.* Minority Staff Report Prepared for Rep. Thomas A. Allen. Washington, DC: US Government Printing Office.

US Social Security Administration. 2011. "Medicare Premiums: Rules for Higher-Income Beneficiaries." [Online information; retrieved 3/23/11.] http://ssa.gov/pubs/10536.html

———. 2010. "Contribution and Benefit Base." [Online information; retrieved 3/18/11.] www.ssa.gov/oact/cola/cbb.html

Vaughn, B., S. DeVrieze, S. Reed, and K. Schulman. 2010. "Can We Close the Income and Wealth Gap Between Specialists and Primary Care Physicians?" *Health Affairs* 29 (5): 933–40.

Verdecchia, A., S. Francisci, H. Brenner, G. Gatta, A. Micheli, L. Mangone, I. Kunkler, and EUROCARE-4 Working Group. 2007. "Recent Cancer Survival in Europe: A 2000–02 Period Analysis of EUROCARE-4 Data." *Lancet Oncology* 8 (9): 784–96.

Vernon, J., and J. Golec. 2009. *Pharmaceutical Price Regulation: Public Perceptions, Economic Realities, and Empirical Evidence.* Washington, DC: American Enterprise Institute Press.

Vernon, J., J. Golec, and J. DiMasi. 2010. "Drug Development Costs When Financial Risk Is Measured Using the Fama-French Three Factor Model." *Health Economics* 19 (8): 1002–5.

Vesely, R. 2005. "Hearing Examines Hospital Chains' Nonprofit Status." [Online article; retrieved 4/6/11.] www.redorbit.com/news/health/326578/hearing_examines_hospital_chains_nonprofit_status/index.html

Villagra, V. 2004. "Integrating Disease Management into the Outpatient Delivery System During and After Managed Care." *Health Affairs* (May 19): w4-281–w4-283.

Vogel, R. J. 1988. "An Analysis of the Welfare Component and Intergenerational Transfers Under the Medicare Program." In *Lessons from the First Twenty Years of Medicare: Research Implications for Public and Private Sector Policy,* edited by M. V. Pauly and W. L. Kissick, 73–114. Philadelphia: University of Pennsylvania Press.

Walker, D. M. 2005. "Nonprofit, For-Profit and Government Hospital Uncompensated Care and Other Community Benefits." Testimony before the Committee on Ways and Means, House of Representatives. GAO-05-743T. [Online document; retrieved 3/10/11.] www.gao.gov/new.items/d05743t.pdf

Walkom, T. 2002. "No Pets Ahead of People." *Toronto Star,* January 11, A6.

Wall Street Journal. 2009. "The Public Option Goes Over." *Wall Street Journal,* August 18, A16.

———. 1987. "Notable and Quotable." *Wall Street Journal,* August 8, 16.

Wallace, K. 2010. "N.L. Premier Williams Set to Have Heart Surgery in US." *National Post,* February 2.

Weaver, C. 2010. "Closing Medicare Drug Gap Helps Democrats Sell Reform." [Online article; retrieved 3/23/11.] www.kaiserhealthnews.org/Stories/2010/March/29/health-reform-doughnut-hole.aspx

Weeks, W., D. Gottlieb, D. Nyweide, J. Sutherland, J. Bynum, L. Casalino, R. Gillies, S. Shortell, and E. Fisher. 2010. "Higher Health Care Quality and Bigger Savings Found at Large Multispecialty Medical Groups." *Health Affairs* 29 (5): 991–97.

Weeks, W., and A. Wallace. 2002. "The More Things Change: Revisiting a Comparison of Educational Costs and Incomes of Physicians and Other Professionals." *Academic Medicine* 77 (4): 312–19.

Werner, R., J. Kolstad, E. Stuart, and D. Polsky. 2011. "The Effect of Pay for Performance in Hospitals: Lessons for Quality Improvement." *Health Affairs* 11 (4): 690–96.

Woolhandler, S., and D. Himmelstein. 1991. "The Deteriorating Administrative Efficiency of the US Health Care System." *New England Journal of Medicine* 324 (18): 1253–58.

Wu, V. 2009. "Managed Care's Price Bargaining with Hospitals." *Journal of Health Economics* 28 (2): 350–60.

———. 2008. "The Price Effect of Hospital Closures." *Inquiry* 45 (3): 280–92.

Yett, D. 1975. *An Economic Analysis of the Nurse Shortage.* Lexington, MA: D.C. Heath.

Yu, W. 2010. Agency for Health Care Quality and Research, personal correspondence. August 3.

Zedlewski, S., G. Acs, and C. Winterbottom. 1992. "Play-or-Pay Employer Mandates: Potential Effects." *Health Affairs* 11 (1): 62–83.

Zimmerman, R., and C. Oster. 2002. "Assigning Liability: Insurers' Missteps Helped Provoke Malpractice 'Crisis.'" *Wall Street Journal,* June 24, A1, A8.

Zuckerman, S., T. Waldman, R. Berenson, and J. Hadley. 2010. "Clarifying Sources of Geographic Differences in Medicare Spending." *New England Journal of Medicine* 363 (1): 54–62.

Zuckerman, S., A. Williams, and K. Stockley. 2009. "Trends In Medicaid Physician Fees, 2003–2008." *Health Affairs* 28 (3): w510–w519.

INDEX

AAMC. *See* Association of American Medical Colleges

AARP, 496–97, 507–8

Accountable care organization (ACO), 163, 265

Activities of daily living (ADL) scale, 292

Actual premium, 61

Actuarial expertise, 158

ADL. *See* Activities of daily living

Adverse selection, 75–78, 82, 479

Advisory Council on Breakthrough Drugs, 388

Aging population, 4, 472

All-payer system, 225

AMA. *See* American Medical Association

Ambulatory care facilities, 219

American Hospital Association, 494–95

American Medical Association (AMA)
  advertising policy, 276
  healthcare reform support, 493–94
  managed care–physician balance of power, 261–62
  Medicare opposition, 414
  retiree benefits, 409–10

Anticompetitive regulations, 277–78

Antitrust laws, 10, 201

Any willing provider laws, 262, 278

Association of American Medical Colleges (AAMC), 147

Bad debt, 190

Balance billing
  limits, 128
  nonparticipating physician, 121, 122
  price controls and, 243

Balanced Budget Act of 1997
  annual update, 126
  purpose, 84
  SCHIP provisions, 107

Baucus, Max, 496

Biased selection issues, 255

Blockbuster drug, 385–86

Bundled payment system. *See* Episode-based payment system

Canadian healthcare system
  administrative costs, 428–29, 441
  cost-control mechanism, 425
  drug prices, 363
  expenditure limits, 432
  flaws in, 440
  infant mortality rate, 425–26
  life expectancy, 425–26
  per capita expenditures, 429, 430
  prevention rates, 426
  rationing, 50
  single-payer issues, 438
  technology, 433–35
  treatment outcomes, 426
  utilization data, 430–31
  wait times, 435–38, 441

Cancer survival rate, 426–27

Capital expenditures, 196

Capitation
  definition, 140, 252
  effect on medical practices, 162
  explanation, 216
  full-risk arrangements, 114

Case management, 10, 17

Catastrophic expense, 60, 61

CDHC. *See* Consumer-driven health-care

CER. *See* Comparative effectiveness research

Certificate of need (CON), 196, 199, 278

CHAMPUS. *See* Civilian Health and Medical Program of the Uniformed Services

Children's Health Insurance Program (CHIP), 107–8, 111, 444, 459

Chronic illness
 management of, 164, 263
 Medicare and, 103
 patient satisfaction, 259–60

Civilian Health and Medical Program of the Uniformed Services (CHAMPUS), 403

Claims experience, 71–73

Clean Air Act, 421, 423

Clinical information technology, 212, 219

Code creep, 129, 242

COGME. *See* Council on Graduate Medical Education

Coinsurance, 60

Collateral offset rule, 176

Community Living Assistance Services and Support Act, 481–82

Community rating, 80–81, 278

Comparative effectiveness research (CER)
 alternative treatments, 285
 areas, 285
 benefits, 295
 funding, 285, 289
 government support for, 285–87
 innovation and, 289
 reimbursement uses, 287
 scope of, 285
 stages, 289–90

study accuracy, 288–89
 use issues, 287–88

Competitive market
 consumer sovereignty, 16
 evolution, 280–81
 failures, 422
 fairness in, 281–82
 government role, 282
 incentives, 271
 medical market versus, 271–74, 282
 resource allocation, 415

CON. *See* Certificate of need

Concentrated interests
 case study, 409–10
 environmental movement, 421–22
 legislative benefits, 407
 opposing, 408

Consumer
 choice, 270
 incentives, 270, 274, 282
 information availability, 275–76
 sovereignty, 15–17, 24–25

Consumer-driven healthcare (CDHC)
 cost containment, 11–12
 explanation, 264–65, 281

Consumer Price Index (CPI)
 annual change in, 141–42
 hospital price increases, 206
 insurance premiums, 256, 257

Consumption efficiency, 456–57, 462

Conventional health insurance, 253

Conversion factor, 126

Cost–benefit relationship, 52–53

Cost containment, 11

Cost-effectiveness analysis, 290–94

Costs per discharge, 234–35

Cost per life saved, 30

Cost sharing, 60

Cost shifting
 claims of, 231–32
 conditions, 233–34
 evidence, 187, 225

questions, 225
types of, 234
Council on Graduate Medical Education (COGME), 135
CPI. *See* Consumer Price Index
Cranhill, Robert, 452

Damages, medical malpractice monetary, 171–72
Dartmouth Atlas Project, 103
Daschle, Tom, 287, 498
Deductible, 59–60, 67
Defensive medicine, 172, 174–75
Defined-benefit plan, 101
Defined-contribution plan, 101, 116–17
Delay of benefits clause, 76, 77, 479
Demand of healthcare services
demanders, 407
factors influencing, 6
inducement, 41–42, 43–44
price elasticity of, 222
Diagnosis-related group (DRG)
annual update, 215
definition, 9
hospital incentives with, 199
Medicare, 17, 93
Differential pricing, 367–69
Diffuse costs, 407–8, 411
Direct-to-consumer advertising, 343
Dirksen, Everett, 407
Discounted rate of return, 138
Disease management programs, 12
Disproportionate share, 117
Donor compensation proposals, 396–98
DRG. *See* Diagnosis-related group
Drug formulary committee, 345
Drug lag, 351, 353
Drug price index, 346, 366
Drug Price Competition and Patent Term Restoration Act, 350, 362

Drug therapy, 365–66

Economic theory, 406–12
Economies of scale
explanation, 222
group practice, 156
hospital services, 202
informational, 156
restorative therapy, 220
Economies of scope, 222
Efficiency
Economic, 15
government objective, 405–6
incentives, 93–95, 439, 456
Employee
cost of, 298–99
insurance cost shifting to, 299
medical costs, 299
Employer, 497
Employer-mandated health insurance
consequences, 447–51
government costs of, 449–51
inequities, 448
options, 460–61
political consequences, 451–52
responsibility for, 448–49
Employer-paid health insurance
administrative costs, 64
advantages, 62–64
changes, 9–10
consequences, 64–65
decline in, 71
growth of, 64
information availability, 275–76
market failure, 274
plan choices, 274–75
premium, 65, 275
subsidy, 5–6
tax exclusion, 66, 283, 463–64
tax-free status limitations, 66–68
use inefficiencies, 18–19
Enterprise liability, 178–79
Enthoven, Alain, 269, 280

Entry barriers, 408
Environmental movement, 421
Episode-based payment system, 163, 215, 221
Equilibrium price, 240
Equitable redistribution, 457–58
Evidence-based medicine, 11, 263
Experience rating
    malpractice and, 179, 182
    premium, 71, 81
Experimental drug access, 350–51
External costs/benefits, 416–19
Externalities
    effect on output, 419
    government intervention, 416–19
    illustrative points, 420–21
    infra-marginal, 420, 422
    resource allocation, 406

FDA. *See* Food and Drug Administration
Federal deficit, 303–4
Federal Employee Health Benefit Plan, 101
Federal Trade Commission (FTC)
    anticompetitive behavior, 361
    antitrust suits, 275–76
    hospital mergers, 188, 195, 209, 277
Financial Accounting Standards Board, retiree medical benefits, 21, 302
First-in-class, 381–82
Fixed costs, 228
Flat-of-curve medicine, 55
Food and Drug Administration (FDA)
    approval process, 352, 360
    cost-benefit decision, 354
    creation of, 348
    fast-track approval process, 351
    generic drug approval, 350
    information dissemination, 289
    purpose of, 348

safety and efficacy guidelines, 349, 351–59
    type I/type II errors, 355
Food, Drug, and Cosmetic Act, 348, 349
Formularies, 10
For-profit hospitals. *See* Investor-owned institutions
Frazier Institute, 435, 436
Free choice of provider rule, 7, 8
FTC. *See* Federal Trade Commission
Fuchs, Victor, 40

Gaming the system, 244–45
GAO. *See* Government Accountability Office
Geisinger Health Services (Pennsylvania), 216
Generic drugs, 350
Genetic profiling, 219
Genetic testing, 219
Global budget, 239, 243, 245–46, 459
Government
    cost/benefit interpretation, 16
    economic theory, 406–12
    expenditure concerns, 19–24
    medical services role, 403
    policy, 404, 419–21
    programs, 405
    public-interest theory, 404–6
    rationing, 49–50, 56
    response to rising costs, 7–12
    role of, 1–4
Government Accountability Office (GAO), 363
Graduate Medical Education Advisory Committee, 136
Grayson, C. Jason, 245
Great Britain
    cost-effectiveness analysis, 294–95
    rationing, 50

Hatch-Waxman Act, 350, 362
Health
    definition, 28
    measures, 28
    medical care relationship, 34, 35
    medical expenditure effects on, 29
    plan choices, 274–75
Healthcare reform
    aged opposition to, 500–502
    aged support for, 491–92
    concentrated interest groups,
        492–98
    goals, 487–89
    ideological differences, 499
    legislative process, 498–503
    middle-class opposition to, 500–
        502
    middle-class support for, 490–91
    Obama administration's objective
        for, 503–5
    public option, 500
    visible benefits, 489–92
Health insurance
    administrative costs, 64
    administrative functions, 74
    adverse selection, 75–78, 82
    community rating, 80–81, 278
    conventional, 253
    cost–benefit analysis, 74
    cost sharing, 60
    deductible, 59–60, 61
    delay of benefits clause, 76, 77
    dental/vision coverage, 67
    employer mandate, 13, 443
    employer-paid. See Employer-paid
        health insurance
    exchanges, 13, 81
    experience rating, 81
    high-deductible plans, 60, 76, 253,
        463
    individual mandate, 13, 77, 461
    legislative changes, 80–82
    markets, 75–79

    medical expenditure role, 35–36
    moral hazard issues, 272
    pre-existing conditions, 76
    preferred-risk selection, 78–79, 82
    prior to managed care, 271–72
    private non-group, 5–6, 71
    purchase decision making, 61–62
    pure premium, 60–61, 478
    purpose of, 59
    service benefit policy, 59
    sports medicine program, 79
    state mandates, 77
    stop loss, 60
    subsidies, 25, 75–76, 274
    waiting period, 76
    wellness emphasis, 79
Health insurance premium, 65
    costs, 21
    determinant, 72
    exchange, 81
    increases, 255–56
    limits, 22, 81
    regulation, 278
    risk-adjusted, 83
Health legislation, 4
Health maintenance organization
        (HMO), 11
    access restrictions, 273
    capitation payments, 155
    CON approval, 199
    cost control, 251
    definition, 253
    excessive testing, 175
    full risk capitation, 114
    group model, 254
    Medicare beneficiaries, 79
    moral hazard controls, 55–56
    performance, 255
    physician monitoring, 45–46
    physician rewards, 44
    point-of-service plan, 252
    premium allocation, 254
    prescription drug negotiation, 340

price control effects, 243
price–quantity relationship, 231
rationing care, 56
reputation, 45
risk shifting, 155
specialist referrals, 252
staff model, 254
types of, 254
underservice issues, 44–45
HMO Act of 1974, 8
Health policy
changes in, 411–12
goal, 28
objectives/interventions, 405, 413
Health production function, 28,
36–37
Health savings account (HSA),
264–65, 281, 462–63
Health status
improvement, 28, 30–33
lifestyle changes and, 33–34
medical expenditure relationship,
29
Heart disease, 32
High-deductible health plans, 60, 76,
253, 463
HMO. *See* Health maintenance organization
Home healthcare, Medicare changes
regarding, 94
Hospital
admissions, 9–10
bargaining position, 205, 206
as capital partner, 159
capacity/utilization, 208
charity care, 189–90
costs, 204, 212–13
costs per discharge, 234–35
cost–size relationship, 201–2
DRG effect on, 207
efficiency incentives, 6–7, 195–96
excess capacity, 205, 208

expenditures, 196–97, 207, 211,
221
insurance coverage, 40
length of stay, 429–31, 432
managed care effect on, 207–8
margin, 212
market power, 187, 188, 199–200,
209, 235
mergers, 11, 187–88, 209
monopoly power, 209
non-price competition, 205
occupancy rates, 9, 10, 199, 209,
235
outlook, 212–15
ownership, 183
patient dumping, 242
payment, 213–14, 221
physician competition, 217–18
physician employment, 163
physician owned, 165
physician relationships, 208–9, 215
potential threats to, 217–20
price discrimination, 236
price increases, 198
price–quantity relationship, 232
pricing, 187–88
profitability, 209, 210
quality of care, 188–89
revenues, 213–17
selected data, 184
status quo scenario, 220–21
utilization, 213, 258
Hospitalization rates, 17
HSA. *See* Health savings account
Hsiao, William, 25

Immigration Nurse Relief Act, 323
Immunization, 418
Indemnity insurance
definition, 59
80/20 plans, 60
cost-containment approaches,
43–44

fee-for-service environment, 43–44
physician reimbursement, 39–40
price–quantity relationship, 231
stop loss, 55
Independent Payment Advisory Board (IPAB), 505
Independent practice association (IPA), 151–52, 254
Infant mortality rate, 425–26
Information, health and healthcare
availability, 275–76
performance criteria, 270
technology, 212
Informed purchasers, 45–46
Innovative drugs, 341–42
Institute of Medicine, medical errors report, 182
Insurance exchanges, 13, 464–65
Integrated delivery systems, 280
Internal rate of return, 150
Investor-owned institutions, 183
charity care, 189–90
performance, 186–90
pricing, 187–88
quality of care, 188–89
services, 193
IPA. *See* Independent practice association
IPAB. *See* Independent Payment Advisory Board

Job lock, 77
Joint and several liability, 176–77, 178

Kefauver, Estes, 348
Kennedy, Edward, 503

Labor costs, 212, 298
Legislators, 407
Liaison Committee on Medical Education (LCME), 310–11
Life expectancy, 104

Canadian healthcare system and, 425–26
factors influencing, 269
increase in, 28
Lifestyle changes, 32, 37
Lifestyle drugs, 338
Loading charge, 61, 62, 71, 73, 478
group size and, 73
Long-term care
annual cost, 473
effectiveness improvement, 483–84
explanation, 471
financing, 473–76, 480–84
government subsidies, 484
home-care expenditures, 476
informal care providers, 473
need for, 471
nursing home costs, 476
safety net, 482–83
spending, 474, 475
Long-term care insurance
adverse selection, 479
characteristics of, 477–78
deductible provisions, 477
delay of benefits, 479
demand for, 479–80
demand-limiting factors, 478
employer-sponsored policies, 485
premiums, 477–78
private insurance, 476
stimulating demand, 481–82
supply-side issues, 478–79

Malpractice
change proposals, 175–78
claims filed, 168
financial settlements, 169–70
forgone malpractice costs, 174
insurer profitability, 170–71
jury awards, 168–69
loss ratios, 170
negligence–claims relationship, 172–73

payment per claim, 168–70
premium increases, 167–71,
    181–82
recurrent crises, 167
reform, 179–81
system flaws, 179
system objectives, 171–75
tort reforms, 179
victim compensation, 172–73
Managed care, 11
biased selection issues, 255
change, 260–62
competition, 255–56
cost-containment methods,
    262–63, 273
developments in, 262–64
dissatisfaction with, 4
drug companies' marketing re-
    sponse, 342–43
effect on physician, 153–54
efficiency gains, 430–31
evolution of, 249–66
explanation of, 272–74
growth of, 4, 10
insurance prior to, 271–72
market penetration–cost relation-
    ship, 204
Medicaid plans, 114–15, 255
Medicare plans, 88
member satisfaction, 259
methods, 55
performance, 254–56
physician monitoring, 178
plan types, 251–54
premium allocation, 252
price competition, 153
price–quantity relationship, 231
purpose, 249–50
quality of care, 260
regulation, 261–62
risk shifting, 251
saving sources, 251, 256
specialist access, 154

techniques, 250–51
technologic advances, 433
trends, 253
Marginal benefit, 30
Marginal benefit curve, 52–54
Marginal cost, 237
Market competition, 249
Market failure, 274–79, 282
Market forces, 271
Market power, 155–56
Medicaid, 8–12
administration of, 105
asset transfers, 119
beneficiary group distribution,
    108, 109
coverage, 1
defined contribution plan, 116–17
drug rebates, 388
eligibility, 12, 106–7, 108 118,
    213
expenditures, 19, 21, 105, 108–11
financial assets, 106
financing of, 1, 13, 91, 105, 112
formularies, 390
free choice of provider rule, 7
government controls, 7–8
government spending on, 65
HMO enrollment, 8
home-care expenditures, 476
home equity exclusion, 119
hospital payments, 214–15
income-related approach, 116
long-term care, 474–76
managed care, 114–15, 255
mandated population groups,
    105–6
payment determination, 214
payment-to-cost ratio, 235
physician reimbursement, 113
plan choice, 276–77
policy issues, 112–14
political support, 410
PPACA provisions, 111–12

price control effects, 242
production efficiency, 469
provider participation, 7–8
purpose of, 18
rationing, 50
reform, 115–17
replacement of, 464
savings, 8
service distribution, 109, 111
shortfalls, 190
spousal financial protections,
    106–7
state financing schemes, 118–19
supplementary payment, 118–19
uninsured children, 107–8
Medical costs
adverse effects of, 303–5
cost shifting to employee, 299
retiree, 21, 301–3, 306
union effect, 300–301
Medical education/medical school
accreditation, 310–11
applicants/enrollment, 308
application-to-acceptance ratio,
    139, 146–47, 307
attrition rate, 316
competition, 315
economic value, 145–46
graduate debt levels, 316
market for medical education,
    309–10
rate of return, 137, 139–40,
    145–46
recommended changes, 311–15
state licensing boards, 313–14
subsidies, 8, 312–13, 315, 420–21
Medical Expenditure Panel Survey–
    Household Component, 452
Medical expenditures
aging population and, 4
annual percentage change, 23
before-tax dollars, 19

components/selected calendar
    years, 3
concern over, 19–22
consumer sovereignty and, 15–17
consumption versus investment, 36
cost-containment methods, 24
distribution, 5, 79
drug expenditure percentage of,
    368–69
federal deficit and, 303–4
financial crisis effect on, 4
by funding source, 2
health insurance role, 35–36
health legislation effect on, 4
health status relationship, 29
hospital services percentage, 207
income relationship, 50–51
limits, 16, 22–24
medical technology effect on, 78
out of pocket, 2
per capita, 2, 429, 430
percent of Canadian GDP, 429
percent of GDP, 1, 2, 15
physician practice patterns and, 17
private savings and, 304–5
supply and demand, 4–5
Medical group
challenges, 164
chronic illness management, 157,
    164
compensation issues, 158
as competitive response, 152–55
economies of scale, 156
imaging equipment, 160–61
leverage, 155
management expertise, 158–59
market environment, 157–58
market power, 155–56
outlook, 159–63
payment change effect on, 162–63
quality of care and, 156–57
risk-sharing pool, 156
risk shifting, 155

size change, 152–57
types of, 151–52
Medical innovations, 13
Medical individual retirement account,
    102
Medical licensing boards, 412
Medical loss ratio, 61, 71, 73–75, 83
Medical market
    competition issues, 279–80
    competitive market versus, 271–
        74, 282
Medical practice, 288
Medical research, 417–18
Medical sector, performance criteria,
    269–71
Medical services
    ability to pay, 50
    consumer decision making, 51–52
    cost–benefit relationship, 52–53
    cost increases, 12
    delivery restrictions, 7
    demand for, 6–7, 12
    economic efficiency, 17–19
    federal spending on, 20, 21
    government rationing, 49–50
    government role in, 403
    health versus, 27–28
    marginal benefit curve, 52–54
    moral hazard behavior, 54–56
    payment trends, 273
    price sensitivity, 54
    private market for, 138–40
    provision inefficiencies, 17–18
    public market for, 140–41
    public policy issues, 27–28
    utilization inefficiencies, 18–19
    utilization rates, 6
Medical technology, 64, 78
Medically indigent, 13–14, 418–19
Medically needy group, 105
Medicare, 8–12
    administrative cost, 84, 428
    balance billing, 128

beneficiaries, 86
challenges facing, 95–99
chronic illness management, 103
concentrated interests, 409–10
concerns, 90–95
cost-sharing requirements, 276
discharges per enrollee, 213
drug expenditures, 335–36
efficiency incentives, 93–95
eligibility, 100, 108, 409–10
employee base, 96
expenditures, 20–21, 87, 94, 95,
    125–29, 133
fraud, 428
free choice of provider rule, 7
government controls, 7–8
HMO, 79
out-of-pocket expenses, 90
participating physicians, 121–22
payment determination, 214
payment-to-cost ratio, 235
payroll tax, 65, 86, 95, 98, 100
physician fee increases, 94, 95
physician payment system, 121
physician preferences, 414
political support, 98–99, 102,
    410–11
population pyramid, 97–98
preventive services coverage, 95
price controls, 84, 242–43
provider participation, 7–8
provider payment, 100
purpose of, 18
redistributive aspects, 90–93
reform proposals, 99–102
reimbursement under, 9
replacement of, 464
selected cost-effectiveness ratios,
    293
shortfalls, 190
spending, 286, 288
tax, 63
voucher proposal, 101

Medicare Advantage plans, 8, 88, 163, 243, 254
Medicare Catastrophic Act, 104, 506
Medicare Economic Index, 122, 123
Medicare Hospital Trust Fund, 86, 96, 99, 220
Medicare Modernization Act. *See* Medicare Prescription Drug, Improvement, and Moderniza-tion Act of 2003
Medicare Part A
    coverage, 1, 85–86
    expenditures, 93, 96, 104
    financing of, 1, 20, 86
    modeled after, 93
Medicare Part B
    coverage, 1, 87
    enrollment penalty, 78
    expenditures, 94, 96, 104, 122
    financing, 1, 20, 89
    modeled after, 93
    premium, 87–88, 100–101
    subsidies, 88, 91
Medicare Part C, 1, 88
Medicare Part D
    cost estimates, 95
    deductible, 89
    drug rebates, 388
    enrollment penalty, 78
    expenditures, 96, 104, 384
    financing of, 1, 20, 89
    pharmaceutical industry marketing advantage, 380
    premium, 100–101
    prescription drug use, 335–36
    subsidies, 91
Medicare Payment Advisory Commis-sion (MedPAC), 131–32
Medicare Prescription Drug, Improve-ment, and Modernization Act of 2003 (Medicare Moderniza-tion Act)
    health savings account, 264–65

income-related premiums, 100
outpatient prescription drug ben-efit, 88–89, 95, 373, 374, 382, 384
specialty hospitals under, 218
Medicare Supplementary Medical Insurance Trust Fund, 96
Medigap Supplementary Insurance, 90
Metropolitan statistical area (MSA), 202–3
Monitoring systems, as emerging tech-nology, 219
Monopoly power, 209, 405–6
Moral hazard, 54–56, 272
Mortality rate
    by age group, 33, 34
    factors affecting, 28, 34
    heart disease, 32
    neonatal, 31–32, 33
MSA. *See* Metropolitan statistical area
Multispecialty medical group, 151, 157, 163

National Council Licensing Examina-tion (NCLEX-RN), 329
National Federation of Independent Business (NFIB), 497
National health insurance
    for benefit of politically powerful, 488–89
    for benefit of poor, 487–88
    criteria, 456–58
    employer-mandated. *See* Employ-er-mandated health insurance
    government role, 466
    individual mandate, 469
    market-based systems, 466, 468
    plans, 455–56
    proposals, 458–61, 467
    public program expansion, 459–60
    refundable tax credits, 461–66
    single-payer system, 459

National Health Service (NHS)
(United Kingdom), 294, 440
National Institute for Health and
Clinical Excellence (NICE),
294–95
National Organ Transplant Act, 394
NCE. *See* New chemical entity
NCLEX-RN. *See* National Council
Licensing Examination
Negligence
deterrence of, 173–75
malpractice claims relationship,
172–73
standard of care, 173
Neonatal mortality rate, 31–32, 33
New chemical entity (NCE), 381–82,
383
NFIB. *See* National Federation of
Independent Business
NHS. *See* National Health Service
NICE. *See* National Institute for
Health and Clinical Excellence
No-fault malpractice, 177–78
Non-price competition, 195–96, 199
Nonprofit hospitals. *See* Private non-
profit hospitals
Notch effect, 113
Nurse
aging workforce, 323, 328
supply and demand, 322–23, 324
vacancy rate, 317, 318, 329
wage increases, 319–20
Nurse Shortage Reduction Act, 323
Nurse Training Act, 317, 326
Nursing home, 119
Nursing school
enrollment, 321, 323
subsidies, 323, 326–27
trends, 323

Opportunity cost, 137, 138, 356
Opposing concentrated interest, 408
Organ transplant

donor compensation proposals,
396–98
financial incentive opposition,
398–400
kidney transplantation, 393
number of, in selected years, 395
organ sources, 393–96
presumed consent laws, 396
success rates, 393
Orphan Drug Act, 359
Orphan drugs, 359
Out-of-pocket costs
for excluded services, 90–91
hospital care, 195
Medicare, 90
prescription drugs, 335, 345
stop loss, 55
trends, 2
Output rate, 415–16

PACE. *See* Program for All-Inclusive
Care for the Elderly
Patent life, 362
Patient advocacy groups, 355
Patient dumping, 242
Patient Protection and Affordable
Care Act (PPACA)
ACO, 265
CER funding, 285
community needs assessment, 191
community rating requirement, 81
effects of, 82
enactment of, 502–3
high-risk pool, 78
hospital cost savings, 220
hospital revenues, 211
individual mandate, 77
insurance exchange, 81
insurance mandate, 148, 192
insurance premiums, 221
long-term care provisions, 481–82
malpractice, 181
Medicaid, 111–12, 219

medical loss ratio limits, 74–75
Medicare Advantage plans, 163
Medicare Part D, 89
Medicare payroll tax, 65
Medicare provisions, 215
out-of-pocket prescription drug
    costs, 336
penalties, 77–78
physician-owned hospital, 165
premium limits, 81
specialty hospitals under, 218
uninsured coverage, 213
Patient
    response to treatment, 287–88
    satisfaction, 259–60
    physician relationship, 192
Pay for performance (P4P)
    competition, 164
    explanation, 12
    managed care, 115, 264
    revenue increases, 157–58
Payment systems
    capitation, 162
    episode-based, 163
    fee-for-service, 162
    risk-adjusted capitation, 163
Payment-to-cost ratio, 225
    private payer, 226
    private/public payers, 234–35
PBM. *See* Pharmacy benefit manager
Performance criteria, 270
Personalized medicine, 219
Pharmaceutical industry
    competitiveness, 381
    distribution channels, 377
    mergers/acquisitions, 380–81
    new drug development, 381–82
    public policy issues, 378
    structure, 377, 378–81
Pharmaceutical market, 368
Pharmacy benefit manager (PBM),
    340, 345, 380
PhRMA, 493

Physician
    as agent, 39–42
    balance billing, 121, 122
    competition, 217–18
    demand, 131, 137, 147–49
    fees, 126, 132–33, 141–42
    HMO rewards, 44–45
    hospital-employed, 161–62
    hospital relationship, 208–9, 215
    income trends, 143–45, 150
    inducement, 41–42
    information advantage, 43, 46
    information availability, 278–79
    long-term outlook, 147–49
    managed care's effects on, 153–54
    Medicare fee increases, 94, 95
    monitoring, 313–15, 456
    practice arrangements, 152
    practice patterns, 17
    procedure outcomes, 175
    profiling, 46, 179
    projected payment updates, 127
    reimbursement, 113
    requirements ratio, 136
    resource control, 39
    revenue sources, 164
    role of, 39
    shortage, 135, 138–39, 140
    specific-purpose licensure, 314–15
    supply, 8, 12, 40–42, 43
    surplus scenario, 138–39, 140–41
    target income theory, 42
    test overuse, 174–75
    training goals, 27
Physician practice management
    (PPM), 159
Physician-owned outpatient facilities,
    217–18, 221
Physician-to-population ratio
    components, 136
    health policy and, 411
    increases in, 135
    shortcomings, 137

supplier-induced demand model, 40–41

supply ratio, 136

Play-or-pay proposals, 450

Point-of-service (POS) plans, 252, 253

Pollution, 416–17, 422, 423

Population pyramid, 97–98

POS. *See* Point-of-service plans

PPACA. *See* Patient Protection and Affordable Care Act

PPM. *See* Physician practice management

PPO. *See* Preferred provider organization

Practice regulations, 403

Pre-existing conditions, 76–77

Preferred provider organization (PPO)
 cost controls, 251–52
 definition, 253
 formation of, 10
 physician selection, 43
 price–quantity relationship, 231
 specialist referrals, 252

Preferred-risk selection, 78–79, 82

Prescription drug
 average purchases, 333
 cash-paying patient, 364–65
 changes in types prescribed, 338–39
 clinical trials, 349
 cost pricing, 340
 cost-benefit decision, 354
 cost-sharing, 336–37
 cross-national studies, 365–66, 373
 demand pricing, 340–41
 development costs, 356–59
 differential pricing, 367–69
 distribution channels, 377
 effective patent life, 350
 entry of new innovative, 338
 expenditures, 331

first-in-class, 381–82
 generic, 338
 industry structure, 377, 378–81
 labeling, 348
 lag time, 351, 353
 large purchase discounts, 364
 lifestyle drugs, 338
 off-patent, 338
 other countries, 363
 out-of-pocket expenditures, 335
 patent life, 362
 price controls, 363, 382–90
 price increases, 336–37
 price index, 332
 price regulation, 368–69
 pricing practices, 339–43
 public policy issues, 369–73
 regulation, 347–51
 reimportation, 371–73
 research and development costs, 360–61, 366
 retail prescriptions per capita, 331, 333–34
 retail price comparisons, 363–64
 sales by outlet, 339
 spending by funding source, 337
 substitution legislation, 350
 total dispensed, 332
 uniform pricing policy, 370–71
 utilization, 331, 334–36

Prescription Drug User Fee Act, 351

Presumed consent laws, 396

Prevention, 29–30, 426

Price competition
 any willing provider laws effect on, 278
 effect on charity care, 189–90
 hospital behavior, 191
 increases in, 17
 in practice, 201–5
 precondition, 10
 in theory, 200–201
 transition to, 199–200

Price controls, 84
   capital shift, 241–42
   consequence of, 240–41, 385–88
   effect of, 239–45
   examples of, 388–90
   political attractiveness, 382–84
Price
   discrimination, 232–33, 236, 341, 344–46
   elasticity, 222, 229, 249
   markup, 270, 341
   private payers, 216–17
   profit maximizing, 226–27, 230, 236–37
   public payers, 214–16
   quantity relationship, 226, 229–32
Price sensitivity
   effect on hospital proceeds, 237
   outcomes, 67
   rationing and, 57
   utilization and, 54–56
Price-to-cost ratio, 341
Primary care case management, 114
Primary care physician
   concierge fee, 131
   RBRVS and, 130
Prior authorization, 9, 43, 55
Private health insurance
   expense ratios, 84
   growth of, 5–6
   payment-to-cost ratio, 226, 235
Private nonprofit hospitals, 183
   charity care, 189–90
   community needs assessment, 191
   oversight issues, 186
   performance issues, 186–90
   physician's financial interest, 186
   pricing, 187–88
   quality of care, 188–89
   services, 193
   tax-exempt status, 190–91
   trust issues, 185
Private savings, 304–5

Procedure-oriented specialists, 128–29
Production efficiency, 456, 469
Productivity changes, 137
Productivity incentives, 158
Profit-maximizing price, 226–27, 230
Program for All-Inclusive Care for the Elderly (PACE), 483–84
Provider
   consolidation, 277
   expenditure limits, 425
   efficiency incentives, 6–7
   Medicare/Medicaid participation, 7–8
   response to demand, 6
Public-interest theory, 404–6
Public program expansions, 459–60
Pure charity, 190
Pure Food and Drug Act, 347–48
Pure premium, 60–61, 478

QALY. *See* Quality-adjusted life years
Quality of care
   deterioration of, 244
   medical groups and, 156–57
   patient satisfaction and, 259–60
Quality-adjusted life years (QALY), 291–92, 294, 296

Rate of return, 137–38, 145–46
Rationing, 243
RBRVS. *See* Resource-based relative value scale
Redistribution
   definition, 90
   equitable, 457–58
   government role, 404–5
   performance criteria, 270
   program benefits, 412
   visible effects, 409
Regenerative medicine, 219
Registered nurse (RN)
   foreign-trained, 329

labor costs, 212
minimum staffing ratios, 325
outlooks for, 324–26
staffing ratios, 329
Regressive tax
definition of, 92, 409, 507
redistributive program financing,
458
Regulation
economic theory of, 406–12
of markets, 408
purpose of, 247
Reimportation, 371–73
Reinhardt, Uwe, 305
Relative value unit (RVU), 124
Report cards, 12, 263
Resource allocation, 405–6, 415
Resource-based relative value scale
(RBRVS), 9
effect on expenditures, 130
fee schedule, 123–25
geographic location adjustment, 124
payment rate calculations, 124
premise, 123
resource components, 123–24
Retail pharmacy, 345
Risk-adjusted capitation, 163
Risk-adjusted payments, 115
Risk-adjusted premium, 116, 275
Risk class, 61
Risky behavior, 80
RN. See Registered nurse
RVU. See Relative value unit

Safety-net providers, 117, 221
Schumpeter, Joseph, 281
Second opinion, 43, 55
Self-insure, 61
Sensor monitoring, 219
Service benefit policy, 59
SGR. See Sustainable growth rate
Shalala, Donna, 371
Shared risk pool, 252

Shortages, 240–41
Single-payer system, 438, 459
Single-speciality group, 160–61
Social HMO, 483
Social Security tax, 63
Special health courts, 177
Specialist
access to, 154
Medicare reimbursement, 129
procedure-oriented, 128–29
Specialty hospitals, 218
State Children's Health Insurance Pro-
gram (SCHIP). See Children's
Health Insurance Program
State licensing boards, 403
State mandates, 465
Statistical deaths, 362
Stop loss, 55, 60
Substitution effect, 337
Sulfa drugs, 348
Supplemental Security Income, 105
Supplier
incentives, 270
induced demand, 40–42, 279
of legislative benefits, 407
Supply and demand
effect on medical expenditures, 4–5
equilibrium, 283
imbalance, 138–41, 239–40
nurses, 324
trends, 141–47
Sustainable growth rate (SGR)
consequences, 94
economic growth, 246
elements, 126
GDP per capita, 26
increase in, 133
physician fee updates, 126, 127

Take-up rate, 113
TANF. See Temporary Assistance to
Needy Families
Target income theory, 42

Tax credits, 461–66

TECH. *See* Technological Change in Health Care Research Network

Technologic advances, 6, 216–20, 433

Technologic imperative, 40

Technologic innovation, 432–35

Technological Change in Health Care (TECH) Research Network, 434

Technological developments, 222

Temporary Assistance to Needy Families (TANF), 106

Thalidomide, 348–49

Tort law, 171–72

Total cost, 228

Total revenue, 226–29, 237

Transaction costs, 418

Treatment outcomes, 426

Two-tier medical system, 439–40

Unbundling, 284

Uncompensated care, 189–90

Uniform pricing policy, 371

Uninsured
    children, 107–8
    population, 187
    workers, 444, 445, 446

Unions, 409, 495–96

United Kingdom, drug prices, 363

Universal coverage, 427, 447–48

Up-code, 242, 245, 284

Uruguay Round Agreements, 362

Utilization
    inefficiencies, 18–19
    managed care techniques, 250
    patient cost relationship, 52–54
    price and, 18, 54–56
    private sector, 213
    public sector, 213
    purpose of, 199

Variable costs, 228, 237

Volume, 126

Volume expenditure limits, 9

Voucher system, 116

Wage growth, 103–4

Waiting costs, 53

Waiting lists, 243–44

Waiting times, 76, 247, 435–36

Walker, David, 190

Waste, economic, 17, 241

Yert, Donald, 319